Linda Alvarez is also the editor of the anthologies *Dyke the Halls*: *Lesbian Erotic Christmas Tales* (Circlet Press), which was a selection of both the InsightOut and Venus Erotic Book Clubs, and *Best Date Ever: True Stories that Celebrate Lesbian Relationships* (Alyson). Her short fiction has appeared in anthologies such as *Island Girls* (Alyson). She lives in New York City.

T0349105

THE MAMMOTH BOOK OF

Threesomes and Moresomes

Edited and with an Introduction
by Linda Alvarez

ROBINSON

ROBINSON

First published in Great Britain in 2010 by Robinson,
an imprint of Constable & Robinson Ltd

Reprinted in 2020 by Robinson

3 5 7 9 10 8 6 4

A CIP catalogue record for this book
is available from the British Library.

ISBN 978-1-84901-019-1

Printed and bound in Great Britain by Clays Ltd, Elcograf S.p.A.

Papers used by Robinson are from well-managed forests
and other responsible sources

Robinson
An imprint of
Little, Brown Book Group
Carmelite House
50 Victoria Embankment
London EC4Y 0DZ

An Hachette UK Company
www.hachette.co.uk

www.littlebrown.co.uk

Contents

Acknowledgments

"Forgiveness" © 2010 by Lacey Savage. Reprinted by permission of the Author.

"What If?" © 2008 by Cheyenne Blue. First published in *Best Women's Erotica 2009*, edited by Violet Blue, Cleis Press. Reprinted by permission of the Author.

"Lucky Pierre" © 2001 by Carol Queen. First published in *Best Bisexual Erotica Vol. 2*, edited by Bill Brent and Carol Queen, Black Books/Circlet Press. Reprinted by permission of the Author.

"The Magnificent Threesome" © 2007 by Elspeth Potter. First published in *Cowboy Lover: Erotic Stories of the Wild West*, edited by Cecilia Tan and Lori Perkins, Thunder's Mouth Press. Reprinted by permission of the Author.

"Blackberries" © 2005 by Nalo Hopkinson. First published in *Wanderlust: Erotic Travel Tales*, edited by Carol Taylor, Plume. Reprinted by permission of the Author.

"Karen Leaves her Husband for the First Time" © 2006 by Catherine Lundoff. First published in *Naughty Spanking Stories from A to Z, Volume 2*, edited by Rachel Kramer Bussel, Pretty Things Press. Reprinted by permission of the Author.

"Our Friend in Alaska" © 2010 by Olivia London. Reprinted by permission of the Author.

"In the Name Of . . ." © 2010 by Isabelle Gray. Reprinted by permission of the Author.

Introduction

Whether or not we've ever actually had sex with more than
one person at a time, I'd be very surprised if it's not something
just about everyone has fantasized about at some point. For
many of us, I have no doubt that it's a fantasy to which we
return, in one variation or another, again and again.

For me, the thrill lies in being the focus of so much attention
– sexual attention – and, in the realm of make-believe at least,
the more the merrier. Three is decidedly not a crowd, and nor
is more.

Unfortunately, the reality of these encounters seldom lives up
to the fantasy. I think this is mostly because a sexual relationship
between just two people is already sufficiently complicated,
without the exponentially increasing complications brought by
each additional lover. The chances of being with two or more
other people and everyone being sexually attracted to each
other, *and* in the mood for sex, are – let's face it – generally
very slim indeed.

This book makes no claim to being a guide to how to "open
up" your relationship, or otherwise engage in group sex.
However, many of these stories may very well inspire you to
try something similar – with your partner, if you have one (or
partners, if you have two or more), or by finding a couple (or
group) if you're solo.

These stories explore different variations of the ménage à
trois and group sex in erotic fantasies from diverse writers
– some male, some female – who conjure for us from their
intimate imaginations almost every possible permutation of

sex between more than two people. More than simply who is taking part, however, and what they are doing to each other, these writers explore, most importantly, *why* their characters are having sex.

This anthology contains a greater number of longer stories than any other collection I have edited. Partly this is due to the sheer size of a Mammoth book, which allows for much greater scope than a standard collection printed with fewer pages to keep costs down. A Mammoth undoubtedly provides a much broader canvas on which longer stories, and more of them, can be told. More importantly, though, the dynamics in a relationship between three or more people are complex and demand space to be set out and fully explored.

While I have chosen a few stories that are straightforward raunchy fantasies – sometimes we just need to get off, there and then – I have also selected some highly literary explorations of ménages à trois or group sex, which are emotionally insightful, beautiful and – sometimes – heartlessly cruel.

Sometimes, in these tales, an additional partner is included in the context of a "traditional" relationship between two people – either as a one-off to act out a certain fantasy or celebrate a special moment, or as a more permanent arrangement.

Sometimes the sex is spontaneous, a welcome surprise for those involved, who embrace the pleasure that's offered to them; at other times it is premeditated, a gift offered by one or more people, or something planned and longed for.

The stories come from a number of different sources: some were solicited from writers with whom I've worked before, or whose erotic writing I have read and admired; some were stories that I'd previously read and couldn't forget; finally, some of the writers I'd invited to contribute recommended their own favourite stories, or writers. Even with quite so many pages to fill, there was no shortage of excellent material.

Finally, I made a public call for submissions to fill the last few slots, hoping to be pleasantly surprised, both in terms of subject matter and fresh, new writers. And I was delighted by the material I received, even if I did have to sift through a lot of chaff to get at the few golden kernels that lurked in the pile – a metaphor, in a way, for the search for additional sex partners and the intense thrill of unanticipated pleasure which success can bring.

These stories are fantasies. Sometimes, the fictional characters engage in behaviour that is unsafe in terms of sexually transmissible diseases. While I hope these stories turn you on, if you feel inspired to act out your own fantasies involving sex with multiple partners, I urge you to practise safer sex.

For now, though, follow these writers along their many winding paths of erotic adventures with multiple partners, and allow your imagination to be beguiled.

Linda Alvarez

Forgiveness

Lacey Savage

"You want to fuck another man, don't you?"

My husband isn't a great communicator. But whatever his faults – and he has many – I've never been able to accuse him of being anything less than direct.

That night, he might as well have asked whether I remembered to drop off his dry-cleaning, or if I'd paid the gas bill before the date came due. His face remained smooth, unperturbed, marked only by the fine lines that had just recently started to appear at the corners of his eyes. He waited for my response with the kind of fathomless patience he'd exhibited when attempting to housebreak our puppy, Sam. Alas, Sam never took to peeing anywhere but in people's shoes, so we gave him away less than a month after rescuing him from the shelter. Richard had expected an eager, panting creature desperate to please. What he got was a stubborn animal.

Unfortunately for Sam, Richard already had one of those. And I was already housebroken.

"Don't be ridiculous." I took a bite of my dry salad. In the booth behind me, a woman moaned after every bite of her fragrant lobster bisque.

I swallowed the mouthful of tasteless lettuce and cursed the stupid diet I'd decided to follow a week earlier. Seven days of eating like a gazelle, and I was no closer to fitting into my never-worn little black size four dress than I'd been when I could happily devour chocolate sundaes with whipped cream.

My mouth watered. Just then, I couldn't think of anything I wanted more than a dollop of rich whipped cream. Except maybe for my husband to stop talking. We'd always done better together when we didn't speak.

"Don't lie to me, Dana."

I sighed and set my fork down. "You really want to talk about this, Richard? Now?" I indicated the restaurant around us with a sweep of my hand. From the sparkling chandelier that scattered fragmented golden light over my bland salad, to the affluent clientele dressed in tailored suits and skintight gowns adorned with glittering jewels, Antoine's wasn't the kind of place where a scene would go unnoticed.

As always, Richard had picked the restaurant. He read a stellar review in last weekend's *Times* and decided it would be the perfect spot for us to celebrate our tenth wedding anniversary. I agreed, already fantasizing about showing up in a black, backless little number that barely came down to mid-thigh. I pictured myself two sizes thinner, fabric draped around my curves like a second skin. I wanted to be the hottest woman here. A goddess, a sex kitten. The object of every man's fantasy.

All right, so my dreams have never been rooted in reality. If I'd realized that happily-ever-after endings were as unlikely as fat-free chocolate cake, I never would have walked down the aisle.

Besides, it was either go to the fancy restaurant, or tell Richard I'd rather stay home in my pyjamas with a carton of ice cream and the vibrator I hid in the refrigerator crisper.

"Why not?" He dabbed the corner of his mouth with the white linen napkin before setting it back on his lap. "You won't discuss sex at home."

"You never ask about it at home."

"You never talk to me at home."

I pursed my lips, instantly on the defensive. So what if I couldn't remember the last time we'd had a civil conversation? I also couldn't pinpoint exactly when we'd started leading separate lives, only that I liked it.

No. That wasn't quite right. I'd grown used to it. I told myself that it was well past time I put my childish ideas about love and marriage behind me and came to terms with the fact that married couples ignored each other, slept on their side of the bed careful not to touch, and bickered when someone failed to replace the toilet paper roll.

"What if I let you?"

I paused with a forkful of salad halfway to my mouth. The mini tomato I'd speared fell off and rolled on to the floor. My heartbeat kicked up a notch. "What if you let me do what?"

Richard leaned forward, elbows on the table, dark eyes spearing mine. "Don't play coy with me, Dana. I'm smarter than you think."

"I—"

"Save it. I saw the way you eyed the waiter when he walked over here. You stared at his crotch like he'd hidden an ice-cream cone down his pants. It's shameful, really. He must be half your age."

"Asshole," I said pleasantly, reaching for my glass of champagne. "If you're considering a mid-life crisis, leave me out of your kinky fantasies. I give you my blessing to buy a fast car and look up your secretary's skirt."

My voice hitched on that last bit, and Richard scowled. Just like that, I'd turned back the clock six years. Only it hadn't been his secretary then; it had been his personal trainer. And he didn't just look up her skirt. He'd burned a few extra calories fucking her on the fitness circuit after hours.

He stared at me, eyes black and hollow. "That was a long time ago. And you're not going to believe a word I tell you anyway, so I don't know why I bother."

I shrugged, saying nothing.

Richard hesitated, cleared his throat. "Look, Dana ... I don't want to look up Amy's skirt. I want to look up yours." He reached across the table for my hand, and the touch of his warm fingers on my wrist made me jump. "Only you won't let me."

For a tenuous moment, my breath caught in my throat and I had no reply. I'd grown so used to avoiding Richard's advances that I'd become an expert at it. Four years ago, I bought my first set of flannel pyjamas. I now owned twelve in different colours, all sporting playful kitten designs. They were the kind with thick elastic bands, and I wore granny panties beneath them. I stuck curlers in my hair and smeared green goo on my face before heading to bed. I'd done everything except tattoo "No Entry" on my crotch.

It wasn't that I didn't like sex. I thought of it constantly, wished for it incessantly. Nor was Richard's appearance the problem. I'd thought him irresistible once. His thick hair had been black then and hung down to his shoulders; now he wore it cut short, and grey showed at his temples. His suit jacket hugged broad shoulders, and although he didn't spend all his time at the gym like he once had, he still rose early to swim laps around the pool.

I waited for the urge to pull back my hand. For so long, the only reaction I had to my husband's touch was stark, pulsing anger. Sometimes, the spark of fury ignited my imagination and I'd picture him fucking his whore. That's when the slow burn of maddening rage would combine with sullen waves of revulsion to form the kind of temper that landed people in jail.

None of those turbulent responses came this time. Instead, the sultry warmth Richard's fingers had kindled in my wrist shot up my arm. My nipples tightened, fuelled by the intensity in his gaze.

Left momentarily speechless, I licked my lips. He focused on them, parted his as though he wanted to say something but couldn't find the words.

When he finally spoke, his tone took on a sharp edge. "How long will you hold my mistake against me?" His grip tightened on my wrist. Pain flowered in a savage burst that chased the lingering flash of awareness from my skin. "Another year? Two? Twenty? I need to know." He sucked in a breath. "I need to know, because if you won't put the past behind us, I'll—"

"You'll what?" I yanked my hand away and slammed my open palm on to the table. The silverware clattered. A few heads turned in our direction and I could hear curious murmurs from the diners around us. "Leave me? Fine, then. Leave me."

He furrowed his brows and slanted a glance at our neighbours. "Why not?" His voice was a low, violent whisper that hit me with the force of a slap. "You left me long ago."

Abruptly, Richard leaned back in his chair and signalled the waiter. "You want to punish me, Dana? You'll do it tonight. You're going to get it out of your system, teach me a lesson, show me the error of my ways. And in the morning, you'll let me prove to you that I've spent the last six years regretting what I've done."

The waiter hurried over, and I had to bite my tongue while he cleared our plates. Knowing Richard watched me, I looked the boy over again. He was young, maybe twenty-three, maybe slightly older. Dark stubble cast a shadow over his lean cheeks and square jaw. He'd slicked back his hair, allowing a light brown strand to escape and curl over his forehead for that 1950s movie star allure. He probably thought it made him look cool. I thought it only made him look younger.

I homed in on his behind as he walked away, admiring the smooth flex of the cheeks beneath the bulky fabric of his uniform pants. A sigh flew from my lips as I contemplated the myriad wicked things I could do to that ass if I only had a dollop of that whipped cream I'd been craving.

He disappeared behind the swinging kitchen doors, and I turned back. The Saturday night crowd was surprisingly loud for such a posh place, only Richard and I sat in silence, the weight of our stillness a marked contrast to the laughter and buzzing energy around us. I waited for him to say something first, to chastise my lecherous behaviour or let me in on his plan, but he simply watched me. The impulse to squirm in my seat made every muscle in my body coil with tension, but I didn't move an inch.

Whatever happened, I was suddenly glad I hadn't stayed home tonight. This evening would decide the fate of our marriage once and for all, and I was relieved to know the end was near. We couldn't go on like this.

I couldn't go on like this.

"Will there be anything else, sir?"

I glanced up, startled. I hadn't noticed the waiter approach.

"Yes. Hold up a minute." Richard pulled out his wallet and opened it to reveal a fat stack of hundred-dollar bills.

I watched the waiter's eyes widen. "I'll bring your check."

Richard smiled. It was a nasty, predatory smile that sent a shiver crawling down my spine and a rush of wanton anxiety pooling between my legs.

"This isn't for the restaurant. It's for you."

The waiter's throat worked as he swallowed hard. His gaze flicked from Richard to me.

I shrugged. I wanted to tell him that this was all for my benefit, that he was no more than a pawn in a game that would end badly for all of us. I didn't, though. I took another sip of champagne and let the bubbles take the edge off my nerves.

He turned back to my husband. "I don't understand."

"What's your name, son?" Richard asked, pocketing his wallet.

"Brent."

Richard crooked his finger, beckoning Brent closer. The boy dropped to a crouch and leaned forwards, eyebrows raised in interest.

"Do you like women, Brent?"

The waiter's smile faltered a little. Suspicion replaced the delight that had lit his eyes just moments earlier. "Yes, sir."

"I'll get right to the point, then. How much do you make working here? Eight bucks an hour?"

"Nine fifty, sir."

"Nine fifty . . . That's not bad, Brent, not bad."

Richard paused and looked over at me. My stomach tightened. Without tearing his gaze from mine, he said, in that same bland voice I was beginning to hate, "I'll give you ten thousand dollars to sleep with my wife."

Looking back, I can't help but think it should have taken more convincing. More theatrics, maybe. I'd expected Brent to be shocked, and he was, but the surprise wore off quickly, the lure of cash dislodging any misgivings he might have had.

We didn't even have to wait until Brent's shift ended. He faked some sort of fast-acting illness and followed us out to the car, while the restaurant manager scowled and shouted orders to the other waiters to pick up the slack.

The drive home is a blur, fragmented by flashes of memory: Richard's big hands cradling the smooth leather of the steering wheel; the minty scent of Brent's breath from the back seat; New York's city lights bouncing off the tinted windows of our BMW as we zoomed through Manhattan towards our loft. And my silk covered legs, crossing of their own accord, pressing down on the throbbing pressure building at the apex of my thighs.

The security guard in the lobby, a big black man whose uniform jacket was at least two sizes too small for his substantial muscles, nodded at Richard as the three of us whirled through the revolving doors. His gaze flicked over Brent, but he was too well trained to let his curiosity show.

While we stood in front of the bank of elevators waiting for the one that would take us to the penthouse, I leaned into Richard and whispered, "All right, you've made your point. Send the boy home."

The only answer he gave me was a narrow, cryptic tilt of the lips and, as the elevator doors split open with a ding, a chill crept through my veins. He'd given me no reason to think he was bluffing, but I *knew* him. Richard coloured within the lines. He followed a set of rules that would make the morality police proud. Even when he cheated on me, I'm sure he did it missionary style and used a condom. Good Catholic boys everywhere would have been proud.

But *this* . . . this was different. For both of us.

Brent stepped into the elevator after Richard. When I hesitated, Richard grabbed me by the shoulder and yanked me inside just before the doors closed in my face. His rough handling knocked me off balance, and I stumbled on my high heels, pitching forwards. I fell against Brent, who steadied me with a gentle hand.

"Whoa, careful, ma'am."

I cringed and backed away until there was nowhere else to go. "Call me Dana, please."

My spine pressed against the mirrored surface of one wall. Twin images of Richard and Brent stared back from the two mirrors in front and to the right of me.

"Be a good girl, Dana, and hike up your skirt," Richard said. "Show us that pretty pussy you hide so well."

My mouth went dry. If I wanted out of this game, now was the time to do it. I could refuse. If Richard insisted, I could hurl myself at the row of elevator buttons and slam my hand against the big red alarm. The burly security guard would come running to my rescue.

Truth be told, I considered it . . . for about two seconds. But the growing thrill of this indecent act filled me with a sense of anticipation. I caught the sides of my floor-length silk skirt and fisted my palms into the fabric before tugging it up . . . and up . . . and up.

The men's gazes followed the line of flesh I revealed. A jolt of awareness flashed through me. I was in charge here. This night, this game, would go nowhere if I chose to end it. I set the pace. I had full control.

I breathed in sharply and my lungs filled with a heady rush of power. I could smell my own arousal, a musky aroma that seeped through the wetness that plastered my panties to my skin. I pulled my skirt up to my waist and revealed my underwear – a plain black cotton number that covered more of me than it displayed.

A spark of disappointment flashed in Brent's eyes, but Richard's gaze darkened. The bulge tenting his black suit pants made my pulse speed. I found it difficult to believe that he still wanted me despite the lack of a killer black dress, despite the middle-aged body shaped more by chocolate sundaes than by hours at the gym, despite these horrid panties that hadn't belonged to my grandmother, but could have.

Still, I'd be a fool to ignore the growing evidence. Was it Brent's presence that turned him on? Or could it really have been the sight of me, the knowledge that only that strip of fabric kept him from feasting his eyes upon my cunt?

I hooked my fingertips into the waistband of my panties and yanked them down around my upper thighs. I bared my mound of dark curls, my pink, protruding labia, the pool of moisture slicking the crotch of my underwear. They could see it all.

Emboldened, I used my index and middle fingers to part the folds of my sex. I exposed everything I had, held myself open, and trembled while I waited for one of them to do something.

Before either man moved, the elevator dinged, announcing its arrival at the penthouse floor. Richard punched in the key code, and the doors slid open into our living room.

Brent stepped out first. I made to follow him, but Richard held out his arm, stopping me. "Take off your underwear. That's right . . . good girl. All the way off."

I obeyed, still hoisting my skirt around my waist. I wobbled on my heels as I lifted one leg, then the other, and soon had the panties down.

"Leave them," Richard said when I moved to pick them up. "Leave them right there. I want the world to know what a filthy, horny wife I have."

I stared at the fabric that so clearly betrayed my wantonness. The panties had bunched on one side, but the crotch area lay uncreased, and the slick smear of my cream glistened shamelessly from the cotton strip.

The old Dana, the one who'd spent years waiting for one last excuse to leave, would have picked up the underwear and thrown them at Richard's head before packing her bags and calling her lawyer. Or calling her lawyer and having *him* pack her bags.

I, however, did none of those things. Something had changed in that elevator. I wasn't yet certain it was a positive change, only that I wasn't willing to walk away until we'd played this game through to its conclusion.

Confusion made my head swim. Anxiety blended with arousal to form a miasma of uncertainty and apprehension. Yet despite the chaotic turmoil of emotions stirring inside me, I understood that no matter what happened tonight, my marriage would never be the same. And that frightened me more than anything.

More than being at the mercy of two men. More than fucking a stranger while my husband watched. More than letting down my guard and trusting them – trusting Richard – to bring me back to reality unharmed.

"Well?" Richard asked when I showed no sign of stepping over the threshold. "Are you coming in?"

I stepped inside and the metal doors whooshed closed behind me, sealing me inside a softly lit room as familiar to me as those panties I'd left behind. My heels made a tapping sound on the hardwood floor that echoed off the rose-coloured walls. I'd painted them a light fluorescent pink in an act of sheer rebellion. To my frustration, Richard claimed to like the colour. I hated it.

The energy in the room was palpable. It thrummed against my skin, causing goosebumps to rise along my arms. Tension filled my veins and welled up in my throat before exploding in the last sound I'd expected to ever hear reverberating through this house.

A giggle. *My* giggle.

Richard looked as startled as I felt. I slammed my palm over my mouth, but it was too late. He'd heard it, and he wasn't about to let me get away with it.

With a snap of his fingers, Richard had Brent's attention as closely as he had mine. He made a small inclination with his head, which must have meant something to Brent because before I could comprehend what had just happened, the younger man strolled across the hardwood floor, dropped to his knees, and tore my skirt.

The sound of the fabric tearing sent a frisson of raw delight scraping across my nerves. He'd ripped the skirt before realizing it tied at the side. I helped with that, just as I helped him remove my blouse and bra. In less than a minute, I stood in nothing but my heels, shivering in the wake of the air-conditioned breeze blowing over my skin.

My knees quivered. Brent used his hands to part my thighs, and I reached out to clench my fingers in his hair.

"That's right," Richard murmured, walking around us both. His voice traced a path along my naked body, dominating me with nothing more than words. "He's going to lick you, and you're going to let him. You get me, Dana? You're not going to push him away, or squirm out of his reach, or pretend you don't like it as you've done to me. He's going to tongue fuck you into oblivion if that's what I want him to do."

He didn't need an answer, and I didn't give him one. I spread my legs and pressed Brent's face into my sex. He kissed me deeply there, probing my lips, splitting me open with his tongue. His hands cupped my ass and brought me closer to him as he consumed me. I didn't resist. My hips moved in time with his mouth, seeking deeper contact, urging him on.

I ground my cunt in his face and he took it, letting me use him as roughly as I wanted while he worked me over. "Yes." I made a noise, something akin to a groan, hiss and moan all rolled up in a breathless sound of erotic torment.

Richard stood behind Brent. He leaned in, his face so close to mine I could smell the sweet scent of champagne on his breath. "Say it," he whispered. "Say it, you little slut."

Brent's lips fused to my clit. He tugged and I cried out as a shudder ran through me and coiled in my stomach. I shook my head. "What?"

"That you want to get fucked. I've been waiting for those words to fly from your mouth for six damn long years."

I sucked in a breath and flattened my lips together. Brent added a finger to his ministrations, first sliding it through my folds then thrusting it inside my quivering cunt. I squatted, needing to give him access, wanting more. So much more.

"Stop!" Richard's command was a slap; a warning. "Get off her."

Brent scrambled backwards and ran the back of his hand over his mouth, smearing my juices along one side of his jaw. I'd messed up his perfectly styled hair and it now stood on end, a dishevelled, endearing mess that made me want to grab his head again and hold it between my legs until he either suffocated, or I died first.

Richard grabbed my arm and shoved me towards the back of the couch. I lost my balance and fell forwards. We'd set the leather monstrosity in the middle of the room because it faced the TV, but now I realized it served another purpose. My ass thrust high in the air as my stomach flattened against the leather.

"You don't want this, huh?" Richard's fingers probed my cunt. I knew it was him and not Brent in an instant. I'd have recognized his hands anywhere.

"I—"

He thrust two fingers inside me in a savage motion made effortless by Brent's masterful tongue-lashing. With his thumb, he pressed down on my back entrance, testing me. I drew my lower lip between my teeth and bit down hard. And then I pushed back against him, once, twice, taking his fingers deeper inside me with each glide of my skin against the smooth leather of the couch.

Another snap of his fingers. Another unspoken man-to-man order.

This time Brent came to stand before me on the other side of the couch. He kneeled on the leather cushion and unzipped his pants. I watched him pull out his cock through the slit in his boxer shorts and admired the thick, meaty length of it. The depth of the perversity and depravity of our actions hit me then with an unexpected force that made my muscles clench. My cunt clenched around Richard's fingers and I shuddered in wanton surrender. The sweet rush of release tossed me around on a wave of pure physical pleasure, and I closed my eyes, losing myself in it.

I could have ridden that wave for hours. Hell, I might still be there now. But Brent brought me back to earth much too soon by shoving his cock in my face.

Not that I minded. I should have; I know that. But I didn't.

I opened wide, took him in like the good, horny wife Richard wanted. I drenched him with my tongue, laved at the veins snaking up the underside of his shaft, and sucked hard enough for my cheeks to hollow. All the while, Richard's fingers never stopped moving. He taunted me with his rough glides. His thrusts crossed the line from pleasure to pain, then jumped back again, eliciting the kind of ecstasy that made my head reel.

I closed my eyes and concentrated on the cock in my mouth. I buried my nose in Brent's thatch of neatly trimmed pubic hair and sucked like I hadn't known I could. I varied the pressure, caressed him with my tongue, slid my lips up and down his shaft while I listened to the sounds of his satisfied moaning. When it came, that soft grunt of inevitability I'd been waiting for, it fuelled my desire to work harder. He was close now, and, oh, how I wanted to taste him, to have him shoot his load down my throat.

And then I wanted to kiss my husband. Badly.

More than I could remember wanting to kiss him in my life.

Brent gripped my head and held it in place as his cock twitched and pressed against the roof of my mouth. My motions grew fevered. The anticipation of his salty come hitting the back of my throat was almost more delicious than the real thing.

He let out a low, guttural cry as his hips jerked in time with the spurting of his seed. I didn't have the patience to swallow it all, so I pulled away partway through his shuddering orgasm. Some of his come splattered on my chin and chest, but I didn't care. I swallowed most of what was in my mouth, then jerked myself away from Richard's hand and twisted on the couch so my ass perched on the backrest.

My arms came up around Richard's neck. My legs followed suit, wrapping around his waist, and I pulled him to me before either one of us could think too long about the implications of my actions. My lips parted. His did, too, and he sucked in a breath as I shared the remnants of Brent's come. Our tongues twined and twisted and I pressed my crotch against the thick length of his erection.

I humped him while we kissed, like a teenager whose parents had left her home alone for the first time. And like that teenager, a tumultuous flurry of emotions danced within me. Eager, unheeded lust jumbled with guilt and regret, making me woozy.

I closed my eyes to fight the dizziness, but Richard stopped me. "No. Look at me," he whispered after breaking the kiss. "I want you to see me. This is who I am. This is the man you married."

He picked me up by the waist and, without warning, threw me over the back of the couch. I landed on the cushions with an oomph that fled my lungs on a startled cry.

"Fuck her," Richard shouted at Brent. Gone was the cold indifference in his voice. I had the distinct feeling that he couldn't keep the fury at bay if he tried. "Fuck her now! Show my wife what it's like to be unfaithful. To think with your crotch rather than your head."

He wheeled around the couch and shot towards Brent so quickly that my breath leaped into my throat. For a terrified heartbeat, I wasn't sure if he was planning on forcing the other man on me, or if he was one fraction of a second away from beating him within an inch of his life.

Brent must have seen the savage uncertainty in Richard's movements too, because he didn't wait to be asked again. He climbed on to me, straddled my waist, and guided his semi-soft cock so the tip pressed against my folds.

It was too soon after the last orgasm for him to take me like the wild stallion my husband wanted him to be. Brent gripped his prick and stroked it with long, hard jerks. The delicate skin of his shaft turned an angry shade of red, but his dick obeyed, growing long and hard on demand.

With a satisfied smirk, he positioned himself right where he needed to be and gave a brief thrust. My labia parted and he filled me in one smooth glide. The fullness of his cock shocked me into realizing how easily I'd given in and how good it felt to spread my legs for someone other than the man I'd married.

"No!" I lashed out, slapped Brent's chest and shoved at those firm muscles with all the strength I didn't know I possessed. I was like a wild beast, fighting the man on top of me, despite the fact that his cock felt like heaven, despite knowing this was just what I wanted. What I needed.

Brent drew back, startled, but didn't pull out of me.

"Don't listen to her," Richard urged, his imposing presence no less menacing than it had been earlier. "Give it to her good. Harder. Faster . . . Yes, like that. Do it!"

Brent pinned me down. His hands locked around my wrists and he held me immobile while his cock pushed in and out of me. My climax built with each thrust, coiling in my cunt like a ball of fiery bliss waiting to explode.

I looked past Brent and met my husband's eyes. His gaze filled with lust, and so much torment I marvelled that he could hold it all in. His lower lip trembled and his eyes, those beautiful brown eyes I'd fallen in love with all those years ago, filled with tears.

"No!" I screamed, a long, piercing howl that drowned out the sound of my pummelling heartbeat. I struggled beneath Brent, but every writhing motion brought me closer and closer to release.

"N-not him," I managed to grind out. "Y-y-you. Always . . . you. Only . . . you."

We stopped then, all three of us, as though suspended in time and space, caught in a web shaped by every lousy choice we'd ever made. Whatever our faults – lust, frigidness, greed – they'd brought us here, to this moment.

Brent's cock slipped out of me. My pussy ached with frustration and my clit begged to be touched, but I couldn't move.

"You're a lucky man," Brent said. I realized with a start that those were the first words he'd spoken to either of us since the elevator.

I wasn't sure Richard would come to me then. That he wanted me, I had no doubt. But all the history standing between us might as well be a wall of barbed wire waiting to claw at his skin.

Through a film of tears, I saw him move. It was only a fraction of a step towards the couch, but he'd taken it, and the relief that filled my body nearly made me sob. I rose, too, and met him halfway.

He fell on top of me with a grunt, and soon we were both fumbling with his clothes. I'm not sure whether I managed to get his cock out of his pants or he did it himself, but I recall the exact moment he claimed my body as his own.

And for as long as I live, I'll remember the triumphant scream that broke loose from his throat as he came inside me.

Richard buried his head in my shoulder. His tears ran down my skin and pooled in the valley between my breasts. I held him, not saying a word, while my own tears fell silently and ruined the leather beneath my head.

By the time we got up an eternity later, Brent's clothes were gone. So was he.

Curiosity gnawed at me, so I called up the elevator. It opened with its customary ding. My panties had disappeared.

I have no way of knowing who took them, of course, but I like to think Brent wanted a souvenir. He never did get his ten grand.

For the last two years, Richard and I have worked at loving one another. Some days are more of a struggle than others. Trust takes time to rebuild when it's been shattered so completely, but we've kept at it.

The endless nights spent in each other's arms make the occasional shouting match worthwhile. At least we're talking, and that's a hell of an improvement.

All this time, I've been certain that one day Brent would turn up in our elevator, demanding his money. Every morning, I rifle through the mail looking for a letter from him. There hasn't been an email or a call, either. It's as though Brent never existed.

Richard went looking for him once, a couple of months after our threesome, convinced he had to hold up his end of the bargain. The manager of Antoine's told him Brent never returned to work after leaving with us that night. A thousand dollars later, Richard had Brent's last known address scribbled on the inside of a matchbook.

He found the place quickly enough. It was a one-room apartment in a rundown brownstone on the edge of Brooklyn Heights. A for rent sign hung in the window.

The landlord said Brent came by one morning and cleared out his stuff. He'd left the cash he owed for last month's rent, along with a note ... something about tracking down the teenage girl he'd knocked up before fleeing the middle of nowhere, Arkansas, to seek fame and fortune in the big city.

I thought about hiring a private investigator to track Brent down. It shouldn't be difficult, since we know his full name and his home state. Even if he doesn't want the ten grand, I'm willing to bet the mother of his child feels differently.

I assured Richard I wouldn't tell her how Brent earned the cash, but he refused. I think perhaps he's worried I have more devious things in mind than repaying an old debt.

He couldn't be more wrong. I don't want to fuck the man. I want to thank him.

What If?

Cheyenne Blue

"What if I wanted to visit Paris?" Peta began. "Would you come with me?"

Our favourite game. I rolled over and rested my head on my folded arms. Peta was also on her stomach, chewing on a grass stalk, the sunlight gilding her hair to a soft gold.

"Depends," I said. "Would we fly or sail?"

"Sail," she replied without hesitation. "On an ocean-going yacht, just you and me, and a discreet crew to actually make the thing go. Champagne and sunsets at sea—"

"Motion sickness and stinky pump toilets—"

"Waves lapping on the hull, dolphins leaping at the prow."

"I don't think there are dolphins in the Atlantic," I said, "but OK so far. Where would we stay when we got to Paris?"

"In a garret in the artists' quarter. Up seven flights of creaky wooden stairs. We'd have baguettes with unsalted butter and cherry jam for breakfast, and strong, thick coffee, and we'd wander the boulevards hand in hand buying cheese."

"Would this garret have hot water?"

"Sometimes. Other times it would be clanking pipes and a tepid dribble."

"Not so keen on that," I said. "So who would do the cooking?"

"*Moi*!" Peta showed one of her few French words.

I rolled on to my side and let my hand trace her sinewy arm. She looked damn hot in the white singlet, her tanned biceps displayed to perfection, and a hint of brown nipple through the clinging white top. "You win," I said. "I'll come with you."

She grinned and rolled on to her back, her arm over her eyes to keep out the sun. "So I get another go?"

"Yup. That's the game."

"What if . . ." And she hesitated.

"Can't think of anything?" I teased.

"What if I wanted to sleep with Suzie? Would you let me?"

My fingers stilled on her biceps. The muscle was taut – too tight – underneath my hand. The moment was frozen in time. Distantly, I registered traffic noise out on I-25, the way the sun skidded off the peaks of the Rockies turning the white snowcaps to amber, the bug that marched purposefully over Peta's hip. The tickle of the short grass of Washington Park, already turning brown even though it was only May.

She was watching me. Her eyes intent on my face, the time measured in the slow deep breaths that separated one plane of my life from the next.

Normal. Act normal.

"Just one time, or for a long time?"

"Just one time. Suzie's straight. Once would be enough."

Self-proclaimed straight, but 100 per cent bi-curious. She came into the Pink Light on Colfax most weekends, sitting up at the bar all quivering eagerness, shooting pool haphazardly, flirting with the butches, but always pulling away at the last moment, when it was time to leave, time to go home, time to go fuck.

"Would you take her to a motel, or go back to her place?"

"I'd take her to our apartment," Peta said.

Our apartment. Our Washington Park den, all polished floors and wide windows that let the setting sunlight stream through over the tops of the Rockies, over our collection of houseplants, over Moggie, our cat, as she lay sunning herself on the sill. Over our lives. Into our lives.

I glanced at Peta; she was still watching me and the slight quiver of her hard brown abs below the crop top told me how deadly serious she was.

Continue the game, continue the pretence.

"What would you do with her?"

"I'd kiss her in the shadows between the pools of light on Colfax, and she'd sigh into my mouth in acceptance. She's wanted this; she's wanted someone to seduce her slowly. It's all too hard and fast for her in the Pink Light. Then I'd take her hand and we'd go home."

"How would you get home?"

"Taxi. You and I never take the car when we go to the Pink Light as we always drink too much to drive. And Suzie would have had a couple too many, deliberately for Dutch courage. She wants to go through with this, she's just afraid of the unknown."

"Us? Where am I then?"

"You're following me and Suzie down Colfax, a few paces behind, and you're watching. Watching how our hands intertwine, watching the slant of her hips towards me, watching how she skips and prances like a little girl being led home by Daddy. And then you're in the front seat of the taxi, trying hard not to look at what we're doing in the back."

"What are you doing in the back?"

"Gentling her. Soothing her skittishness, like a filly that needs breaking. Calming her nerves, as now she knows there's no going back. So I'm holding her curved against my side, and I'm stroking that wispy blonde hair back from her face. Telling her how pretty she is, how desirable. Maybe I'm kissing her cheek, soft little kisses, sliding around to the edge of her lips."

"Why our apartment?"

Peta sat up in one smooth movement and her hand came out to touch me. The first time, I noted absently, that she'd touched *me* since this game began. Only it wasn't a game any more. Her fingers walked down my arm and laced themselves with mine.

"If it's in our apartment I'm not excluding you. You're a part of it, Ria. How could it happen otherwise?"

It need not happen at all, I wanted to shout. She could forget this crazy idea, this macho strutting to take Suzie's lesbian virginity. Was it something to boast about in the Pink Light? I wasn't sure I could handle that, if it was; sitting there, stony-faced staring into my beer, pretending not to care as Peta told and retold the story of her conquest.

And what of Suzie herself? Would she fade into the woodwork after this, curiosity assuaged? Or would she hang around, wanting more? *Would she want Peta for her own?*

I stared down at our intertwined fingers, at Peta's hard blunt paws, at my plump white manicured fingers. I didn't know what to say.

A thump in the small of my back toppled me forwards, my head coming to rest on Peta's knee. She settled me carefully, stroking the hair from my eyes with one hand, while the other scooted the football, which had hit me, back to its owner, reassuring them that there was no damage, no apology necessary.

Her expectant face peered down at me. "You OK?"

Somehow, I thought she meant more than simply the blow from the football. "I think so."

She nodded, and a finger traced the outline of my lips. I kissed it as it went by.

"So what happens when we arrive at our apartment?" I asked.

"Despite my consideration in not jumping her in the cab, Suzie's still nervous, so she asks if she can have a drink. I'm putting on some music – something mellow, like k.d. lang – so you go and get a bottle of red. You can't find the corkscrew – no doubt I've put it away in the wrong drawer again – so when you return, Suzie and I are dancing. I'm holding her close, and my hips are pressed into hers. My hand's on her butt, moulding her close to me."

"Are you packing?"

Her hand shifted to my arm, and her thumb stroked the side of my breast. I turned to rub my cheek against her thigh. She wasn't packing now.

"Yes, so Suzie can feel the outline of my rigid cock. She sighs a little and slides her arms around my waist. That's the sign I've been waiting for. Now I can move into a higher gear, so I kiss her properly. Harder, deeper. Really tasting her. She kisses me back, her tongue tangling with mine.

"You can see we don't need the wine now, so you put it down, and sit on the couch."

"Does Suzie mind that I'm there?"

"She never speaks to you, as if she did, she'd have to acknowledge that you were there, watching. She's pretending that it's just me and her."

"And what about you?"

"I'm happy you're there. I wouldn't be doing it unless you were. I want you to get off on this as much as me, so I'm putting on a show for you. Suzie's wearing a skirt of some soft cotton. And, slowly, inch by inch, I'm gathering it up at her butt. Now you can see the backs of her thighs. Now, the edge of her panties. What do they look like, Ria?"

"Peach," I said, without hesitation. "A real girly-soft peach. And lacy. She's worn her sexiest underwear deliberately. It looks good against her pale skin."

Peta's thumb stroked soft circles, inching ever closer to my nipple with each pass. I sighed gently – as Suzie would do – in acceptance of the spell her words were weaving.

"And her legs," prompted Peta. "What do they look like?"

"Pale. She keeps her skin out of the sun. Only a hint of sunbloom. Soft legs. She's not the sporty type. She stays slim by picking at her food, not by exercise."

"When I get her skirt up to her waist," Peta continued, "I slide my hand down the top of her panties. Her butt is smooth and warm, and I can feel her shiver. I curve my hand down until I'm tickling the crease between ass and thigh; nearly, not quite touching the fine hairs of her cunt. We're still moving slowly to k.d. lang, and I turn us around so that you have a full view of her ass—"

"And that's when you slip your fingers lower, further around, and move one up into her pussy. She gives a little gasp of surprise – she didn't expect you to move so quickly – but now it's too late, and you've got one, now two, fingers pistoning in and out of her cunt. She's wet; I can hear the squishy sound your fingers make—"

"She's not doing anything to me; she's simply holding on to my waist and riding my fingers. I want to add more, but the angle's all wrong. She hasn't touched *me* at all; my nipples are hard and tender against my shirt, and I want to adjust my cock so that the base of it gives me friction, but I don't want to let go of her. But, it's enough; because you're watching me, watching us, and your eyes are avid and intent, and now you're undoing the button on your jeans. You're shy; you don't want Suzie to see you, but *I* can see everything. You're wearing—"

"Simple black cotton panties. Unlike Suzie, I didn't dress for the occasion. They're old, and the waistband is a little loose, so I can work my fingers down to my pussy without pushing my jeans down further. My thighs are straining the denim apart, but it's enough. I've got a finger on my clit. You can't see my pussy, but you know what I'm doing, you know how I like to touch myself."

My eyes were closed to the rhythm of our words. Peta's thighs were hot underneath my cheek, and her own musky scent filled my nose, blending with the tang of grass clippings. I knew – I hadn't forgotten – that we were in one of Denver's busiest parks, but it was mattering less and less. I wanted to turn my face into her pussy, pull down her shorts, spread her thighs and push my nose into her thatch, my tongue into the folds and crevices of her cunt and suck and slurp and drown in her juices. But, even in the words she was weaving, Peta knew me well; public sex just wasn't my thing. So, I pressed my thighs tightly together, so that the pressure grew, and continued. "I know you want to fuck her, but there's no way to move into the bedroom without breaking the spell. So—"

"I decide to take her there, on the floor, on the only rug in the whole apartment, in front of the wide window that overlooks downtown. So, slowly, I withdraw my fingers from her cunt. She mews a little in disappointment, but she's looking at me with wide eyes, waiting to see what happens next. Her cheeks are flushed, the pinkness creeps down the front of her T-shirt. She still hasn't touched me, she won't touch me, that's too much for her right now. But it doesn't matter. I'll get my own pleasure, and your eyes watching me all the way will bring me there.

"I step back from her, and yank my T-shirt over my head, kick off my sandals, and push my shorts and jocks down, so that I'm naked in front of her. She may not want to touch me yet, but I want there to be no mistake as to whom she is fucking. My cock springs free, hard and needy. Her hands rise, and her fingers flutter in front of my breasts. She's wanting to touch, but hasn't the confidence. It's irking me a little; she's all take and no give, this woman. So I curve a hand behind her head and press it to my breast. Her nose bumps my nipple, she gasps, and hesitates, but now my nipple is at her lips, and she opens her mouth, sucks me in, tongues me, then suckles harder.

"Your eyes meet mine, over her head, and I wonder what you're thinking, seeing another woman touch me, suckle me, the first in our five years together."

"Part of me wants to scream and drag her off you, kick her perfect little pink bi-curious butt out of our apartment, but most of me wants to see you fuck her, make her scream and shudder around your cock. And now, I'm touching my own nipple under my top, flicking it in time to her suckling. But she's still dressed. I want to see more than her panties. Get her naked. Now!"

"Yes, ma'am! I push her away from me, and shuck the skirt off her like the husk of an ear of corn. She stands passively, raising her arms to let me pull her shirt over her head. Her bra matches her panties – she definitely dressed with this in mind. But I don't stop to admire then, I hook my fingers in the waistband and pull hard.

"She gives a little strangled cry; the panties must be digging into her sensitive pussy before the material gives way, but I don't stop, and there's a loud rip. I toss her ruined panties to one side, and she's naked, looking up at me with pleading eyes. I hesitate; I know she wants me to kiss her, but it's you I'm thinking of. A kiss at this moment is such an intimate act, I don't know if you want me to kiss her."

"Kiss her," I order. My eyes are still closed, but Washington Park has faded to a distant background buzz. It's just me, Peta and the ethereal Suzie, in the living room of our apartment.

"So I kiss her and she responds with gratitude. She wants the romance as well as the sex. She tastes of bourbon, so different from you. But kisses aren't enough—"

"Fuck her. Take her now."

"I direct her hand to my cock. She's now so far gone that she grasps it eagerly then strokes up and down the shaft. I push my hand on her shoulder, and she sinks to the floor underneath my touch. I kneel over her, part her soft white thighs with one hand. She's wet; I can see her pussy lips shining. Her pussy hair is so blonde and fine that at first I think she's shaved herself. She has sparse, soft hair, like a young girl."

"Do you go down on her?"

"I think about it, but I can see you, and your fingers working away underneath your panties. Your face is red, and your breath is hitching in your throat. I know you're about to come, and I want to see that. So no, I don't. I kneel between her thighs—"

"Which way are you facing? Can she see me?"

"I'm looking directly at you, over her head. If she turned her head to one side she could see you, but she doesn't. Her gaze is fixed on me, looming over her, cock in hand."

"And then—"

"I fuck her."

Oh God. Washington Park was gone, gone, gone, and my entire being was focused on our apartment and what we were doing – would do? may do? – there.

"I enter her with one sure thrust," continued Peta, "and she clutches my shoulder and pants into my face. Her other hand reaches around, underneath her thigh, to feel my cock and how it fits inside her. I start to move, and every thrust rubs my cock on my clit. It won't take much until I come.

"I rise up and reach between our bodies, find her clit and rub. And she comes. Just like that, clenching down on my cock, shuddering underneath me, her pretty white teeth biting her bottom lip. Her body goes limp; she lies as flaccid as a wet towel. She's not a giving lover, but I don't care. My eyes meet yours over her head—"

"You thrust harder, faster, until her whole body is shaking with the force of it. It must be uncomfortable for her – your cock is thick and long – and the force of your pounding must be hurting her, but you don't stop. Because you're about to come—"

"And your fingers are working frantically, and your face is flushed and your hair is wet with sweat. Any moment now—"

"I come. It's a long, hard, shuddering climax, my body jackknifes double, and my thighs are rigid. And I scream, uncaring of Suzie, great gulps of air, forcibly exhaled—"

"I'm coming with you. My final thrusts are almost savage, but I'm coming hard, deep into Suzie. She whimpers underneath me. I stroke her hair gently from her brow, soothing her with incoherent murmurs, but my eyes are still locked on you, and how beautiful you look in the low light, your sweaty hair over your face. And now it's over, doubt sets in. My eyes plead with you for reassurance—"

"I smile. It's OK. Suzie lies forgotten underneath you, and you and I communicate with our eyes. I love you."

"I love you too."

I opened my eyes, back in the real world, Washington Park swimming back into focus. Peta loomed above me, her hand knotted in the fabric of my T-shirt, taut with the spell of our words. She kissed me, her tongue running in demand around my mouth. I could smell her excitement in the cradle of her thighs, the waves of musk that permeated her shorts.

"So," she said, when she lifted her head. "Shall we do it?"

My cunt throbbed. "Do what?"

"Paris. You said you'd come with me. We might need to fly instead of taking the yacht, but we could still rent a garret and make love to the sound of the Parisian traffic."

Right then, I'd have followed her anywhere. "Let's do it!"

Lucky Pierre

Carol Queen

"You know," said Boyfriend, humping swivel-hipped, with the kind of satisfied tone he got when imparting the Great Wisdoms, "Lucky Pierre is the one in the middle."

The one in the middle this time was named Mark, however, not Pierre. I had found Mark myself – a rare circumstance. Boyfriend typically used his male sexual socialization to full advantage, plus his uncanny gaydar infallibly told him which fellow in the room might be most open to frank, affable erotic suggestion. Boyfriend was charmingly friendly and direct, asking, "Do you want to fuck?" as easily as most guys would say, "Hey, how about we grab a beer?" Of us two, he was invariably the more comfortable cruiser, and usually the most successful at bringing boys home. This did not always mean gay men; in fact, though Boyfriend was quite open to fucking gay men, being more or less a gay man himself, he was just as interested in bi men and even straight men.

I believe the proper term for Mark would be "bi-curious", and Boyfriend liked those, too. In fact, I never saw a reasonably cute man Boyfriend *didn't* like, though admittedly it helped if he had a foreskin. (Mark was not endowed with one of these, but he had many other charms.) Lucky me, it made for many erotic adventures of the kind I'd always dreamed of but had yet to achieve, my past boyfriends always too straight, my girlfriends too lesbian. Just coming off ten years of dykeitude, already a few months of bisexual adventures with Boyfriend had me well fucked and newly intrigued by the permutations available to bisexual boys and girls.

So I had gone out and found Mark, hoping to score as well as we did with some of Boyfriend's acquisitions. Well, actually, *I* didn't find him; Janice did, but she owed me one after the night I'd fucked one of the other guys she brought to our party. She showed up with this guy, having obviously hinted that he'd get sex – then she pretty much vanished. Well, I wasn't going to let him just sit there looking uncomfortable – how unhostesslike is that? – but the guy could have been a lot more fun. If Janice was going to show up now with a hot young stud and then bitch about me snagging him, words would be said about her conduct on the previous evening. But she didn't bitch at all. I can't imagine anyone feeling bitchy around Mark. He had an angelic demeanour, a gorgeous cock and, what's more, he shared the wealth.

See, we were taking a class about making movies, so we decided to get together on the weekend and make one for practice. Six women, all from the class, and Mark, who tagged along with Janice because he thought it sounded like a good time. God knows where she met this long, tall, twenty-something drink of water, with his sweet face – and did I mention his cock was perfect? – but Janice prowled many streets. Unlike some of her finds, Mark was a keeper. He wound up fucking each of us in turn, never coming, giving each woman his complete focus, a tall, young, adorable sex toy of a man.

Now, I've pulled a couple of trains in my time – nothing that set any records, but hot just the same. There's something about taking on all comers (so to speak) – maybe because it's the classic slut fantasy, the one so many women are ashamed to have, or maybe it's because when you fuck four or five or ten people, if you warm up at all, you get *really* warm. And I was raised to be a nice and compassionate person – it's sad to see someone moping on the sidelines, like the only little kid in the class not invited to the popular kid's birthday party. I've always figured that if you exercise some judgment in choosing people to socialize with, there should be no great problem with fucking them later in the evening, if it comes to that.

Still, there's something special about a guy who can fuck one after the other, never flagging, never letting one woman feel he liked the last one better or he's looking forward to the next. This man was not just thinking about baseball. He was truly sweet, truly present with each, which I knew because I was saving myself for last, magnanimously saying, "Oh, no, you go ahead," when it was time to switch. I knew this might leave me with leftovers – an exhausted boy who only wanted to cuddle – but it seemed as though he knew how to pace himself. So for most of the afternoon I sat at the head of the bed watching, studying Mark with each of them. I saw the sweat and the eye contact, the murmured getting-to-know-you that's so inexorable and intimate when it happens when you're already fucking. Don't get me wrong, I know plenty of fucks fly by with hardly any intimacy at all, but if you've never experienced the kind where you've barely said six words before your bodies meet, yet when you're done you feel like you know the person deeply – well, you'll just have to take my word for it.

I know what you're wondering: If this is a bisexual story, why didn't all the women get into a big pile? Maybe we weren't very attracted to each other. More likely, we were all a little mesmerized by this force of nature. Boys like this don't come down the pike every day.

When it was my turn, sure enough, Mark wrapped me up in a cloud of sweet, slow fuck. Jeez, he must have been studying tantra. Say all you want about casual sex, but I can tell you, it's completely possible to have a no-name fuck and get the message that you are precious, absolutely precious. Mark and I beamed that to each other as our hips escalated their speed. It was the only message to send, each of us a young seeker of exotic knowledge and true nirvana in the wild jungles of sex.

Of course my first thought (well, OK, my third or fourth thought) was that I wanted to take him home to Boyfriend.

The night Boyfriend said, "Lucky Pierrre is the one in the middle," Mark was in me just as deep as he'd been that first day, a slow pump that put me in such a fuck-haze that Boyfriend's presence was almost irrelevant. This is why people are scared to have threesomes: if two of them feel like this, what will the leftover person do? In real life, of course, a scene like this could turn into a jealous fit, even escalate into a divorce. But life with Boyfriend was like real life, only better: if his girlfriend was busy falling in love with the trick, no problem! He'd find something to keep himself amused. When you're fucking – especially when you're fucking more than one person at a time – there are always plenty of things to do. He had already slid his fingers into my cunt, massaging my wet velvet walls and Mark's cock simultaneously – this made everyone happy, including Boyfriend, because Mark really had the cock of an angel, big but not too, shaped like cocks were meant to be. And Boyfriend had had his hands on a lot of cocks – several thousand at least – which meant that he had hands that could probably have touched any cock in the world and made it happy, hence his remarkable rate of success with straight men. When your cock is in such hands, why fuck it up by getting all homophobic?

Boyfriend was, however, ready to up the ante. In fact, I think Boyfriend's middle name was "Up the Ante", or maybe just "Up the Ass", because that's where he liked to go, and that's where he usually wound up, even with men who had never before thought that they might *have* an asshole. As Mark fucked me, he made a moving target, but to an old pro like Boyfriend that didn't matter. I heard condom noises from miles away. I had already come several million times, it seemed, and neither Mark nor I focused much away from the slow dance that engaged our cunt and cock.

Until I felt a steady increase in the weight on me, heard Mark moan – a good moan, not a bad one, a deep *Ohhh* of a let-your-breath-out-and-the-cock-come-in moan – as Boyfriend's cock met Mark's back thrust and rode forwards along with us, burrowing into Mark's asshole just as slowly as Mark's cock sank into me. A perfectly timed, come-along-for-the-ride kind of move, Boyfriend's hips pumping exactly in time with Mark's, and the energy changed just as perfectly: all of a sudden I was fucking them both. Pierre may be the guy in the middle, the one who gets the most sensation and attention, but each of us could feel the other two, Boyfriend's cock gradually nudging Mark's cock into Boyfriend's own rhythm, driving us both like a team of horses. This made it feel as though there were two cocks in me, not filling me up like two cocks really would (yeah, of course we tried that later) but energetically, one fucking the other fucking me, as Boyfriend's cockhead rubbed the base of Mark's cock over and over.

Maybe this is the true basis of male homophobia. Guys, when fucking, know their ass is sticking up for anyone to plug. It might as well be painted on in neon letters: "Fuck me! I'm an ass-phobic straight guy!" Some big fag like Boyfriend is going to come along and become the ultimate topman, pin Mr Missionary Position like a bug on a corkboard. I'm sure the charm of this situation was not lost on Boyfriend, though he had the decency not to brag about it when he was fucking straight-boy butt: a fey boy, fag since youth, able, with the help of a glop of lube, to subvert a heterosexual coupling, turn it perverse, bend it from two to three, from straight to queer, from vanilla to kinky.

And if you do it right in the first place, he'll bend over any time you like. The arrow will never really straighten out again.

This was one of the bases for Boyfriend's and my arrangement; in a way, I helped get the boys in, held them down while he worked his ass magic, gave them just enough of the familiar – hot hungry pussy, legs wrapped around their backs – to allow them to assimilate his cock without freaking out. Together, we were a walk on the wild side.

Maybe some of the men we fucked went home and cried, got drunk, went into therapy. But Mark fucked back, ass opening easily to new knowledge, greedy for pleasure from both ends. He was as open to sensation as he was to love. If fucking me was like saying a mantra, getting fucked was like *being* the prayer. Filled with cock, his cock in me, he became a fulcrum, sex and sensation perfectly balanced, and I felt the song of his come build up in him as he climbed higher and higher. Surfing pure fuck, anyone's come was everyone's come – any one of us could have been Lucky Pierre, the one in the middle.

When you fuck someone over and over, you learn them and you create a new entity, the fuck of your relationship, your ongoing connection. Your sexual energy weaves together, making a new thing that is of you but beyond you. You can't create it again with anyone else, not exactly. This is true when you fuck one person, and it's just as true when you fuck more.

When you fuck someone only once you enter into chance, ride a wave of fate, then sweep up on the shore. Many waves, one ocean: most of us go out and ride the waves again, but not *that* wave.

Mark died shortly after I brought him home to Boyfriend, doubtless just after making someone else happy, for that seemed to be his brief and shining path. His motorcycle slid on a rainy curve; his last threesome was with it and a speeding car.

When you fuck someone only once, someone you'll never be able to fuck again, it's as evanescent as the spun sugar crown on top of the fancy dessert, and just as delicious. I imagine the three of us, on each other, and I circle around and around the image, stopping and starting us like we were wind-up toys, or computer animation. In a place where time stops, just like it did for Mark, we are fucking right now, will fuck perpetually – I visit that place in glimpses and always will. He will always be Lucky Pierre, and I – oh, I'm just lucky.

In memory of Mark.

The Magnificent Threesome

Elspeth Potter

The One-Eyed Man saloon was not providing the entertainment DeVille was waiting for. His companion, Harcourt, was hunched over a small bound notebook, turning his stub of pencil over and over between his big, blunt fingers. DeVille doubted the numbers would change tonight. The next town along was hosting a fandango after a performance of the travelling Grand Ethiopian Minstrel Choir, and the streets had emptied by noon. Not a soul had entered who was interested in playing cards or hiring guns; the patrons, all two of them, came in, drank, gave him and Harcourt a suspicious glance, and left. He'd seen pitched battles that were friendlier.

He fluttered his deck of cards between his hands in a never-ending stream while he pondered how best to irritate Harcourt, and thus distract him from his obsessive accounting. It wasn't getting them to San Francisco any sooner.

"It's closing time," the saloon's owner Miss Kitty said, leaning over their table. A tuft of dark hair poked out of her red dress' low-cut bosom, and she needed a shave. DeVille had been surprised, when they'd first arrived two days ago, how few of the customers seemed to mind Miss Kitty's eccentricities. Then again, it was the only saloon in town.

"I know you must get your beauty sleep every night," DeVille commented. He gathered the cards into one hand and smiled up at her.

Miss Kitty laughed like mountains crumbling and tapped the back of his head. He grabbed for his hat. She said, "You are a caution, Mr DeVille. Are you sure you don't want to spend the night?"

"I am so sorry, ma'am, but me and the captain here have other plans," DeVille said. "Right, Harcourt?"

Harcourt put away his notebook. He looked up long enough to say, "Yes." He pushed his chair back and stood.

DeVille knew what the locals thought: Harcourt looked dangerous. A coloured man with deep-set eyes and lean cheeks, he wore black from hat down to scarred cavalry boots. The grips of his two low-slung Colt revolvers gleamed with use, and he didn't hide the Bowie knife sheathed at his back. His voice was deep and rough as his appearance.

DeVille, a round-faced white man with a tidy moustache, knew he looked as if he'd come from another country entirely, though both men hailed from Holmestown, New Jersey. He made an effort to look less dangerous and more prosperous than Harcourt. Today he wore snug fawn pantaloons and a brocade frock coat the colour of good red wine. His embroidered gold waistcoat glowed over a minutely pleated cream linen shirt with a string tie. He reached into his breast pocket, but Miss Kitty laid a giant hand on his arm.

"I'll run you a tab," she purred.

"Why, thank you, Miss Kitty," DeVille said. "And I've been thinking – why don't you call me Virgil? It doesn't seem fair, me using your Christian name and you not knowing mine."

Miss Kitty giggled. This sound was more like rocks tumbling down a mineshaft. "Oh, you sweet thing," she said. "Don't you forget to have a drink with me next time."

"I most surely would never forget!" DeVille said. He bowed and kissed the back of her hand. Harcourt rolled his eyes.

As they exited, a slender young cowboy entered, battered hat in hand, his longish blond hair tied back into a stubby queue. He wore a long sourdough coat, stained dark with waterproofing. DeVille gave him a second glance, and then a longer, more appreciative one as he hurried into the saloon, graceful in his high-heeled boots. Harcourt elbowed him. He sighed and let himself be drawn out of the swinging doors.

They'd gone barely ten steps when Miss Kitty bellowed after them. "Virgil! Captain Harcourt!"

DeVille looked at Harcourt, who lifted his eyebrows. They retraced their steps. The cowboy sat at their vacated table. Seeing his face clearly for the first time, DeVille was startled by the softness of his features, though he was clearly no longer a young boy. Without beard or moustache, his lips had a plush curve, just waiting for someone to press with their thumb.

Miss Kitty poured the cowboy a glass of whiskey and placed it in front of him, but he didn't drink it. Miss Kitty said, her expression fierce, "Some rowdies attacked the Widow Larimer's spread, just outside of town. Austin here's her wrangler, and he thinks they'll be back."

The Widow Larimer was a coloured lady. DeVille imagined she hadn't been interested in the Grand Ethiopian Minstrel Choir, either. Before Harcourt could say they'd risk their lives for free, he named their rates.

Austin looked up at that. He was beardless, but no fool, that was clear. "She told me to hire Captain Harcourt."

"Where he goes, I follow," DeVille said. "Ever since we were boys. But I'm only half his price, since he's the better shot."

After a little haggling, DeVille stowed away their advance money. Austin would ride ahead; they had to retrieve their horses from the livery. As they headed for the Widow Larimer's ranch, Harcourt said, "You only follow me because it suits you. You've been getting me into trouble ever since we were boys."

"He paid up, didn't he?"

A few moments later, Harcourt said, "You keep your hands off the widow."

"What if she's pretty?"

"She's respectable, Virgil. God knows, you could inveigle a snake into bed with you, much less a defenceless coloured woman. I don't trust you farther than I could throw you."

"What if I inveigled for the both of us?"

"Virgil."

"Is it because she's coloured? Are you afraid I'll—"

"We were hired to protect her, not seduce her."

"That tart back in Boise stick your sabre up your ass?"

"Virgil."

"Jesus. You didn't do her at all, did you? You wasted my money and didn't do a damned thing."

"She appreciated your *money*, not me," Harcourt said, wryly.

"I paid her triple," DeVille said. "She claimed she would make you so happy you'd be singing for a week. She had this thing she did with her——"

"I didn't ask you for your help in getting a woman."

DeVille muttered, "If you're not careful, your cock's going to dry up and fall off."

Harcourt remarked, "Yours will wear out first. And remember, hands off the widow."

The Widow Larimer did not look as if she needed protection. It was clear she would repel seduction attempts with the shotgun she cradled competently and lovingly against her incredible bosom. A second shotgun leaned against the porch railing beside her. She was a veritable goddess. DeVille moaned softly.

She called out, "I don't need that fool gambler. I don't care how cheap he is."

"Boudicca!" DeVille rhapsodized. "Penthesilea! Mrs Bridger the Sunday school teacher back home!"

"Quiet," Harcourt growled out of the corner of his mouth. To the widow, he said, "An extra gun can never hurt, ma'am."

Austin stepped into view, cradling a rifle. "With all respect, ma'am, you sent me for some extra hands, what with everybody gone over to Destiny for the dancing."

The widow snorted audibly. "You keep them out of trouble, boy. And they're sleeping in the barn."

DeVille murmured to Harcourt, "*He's* got a pretty face. Can't be more than twenty-five. Wonder if he needs someone to teach him the wonderful ways of the world?"

Harcourt eyed him sourly. "Hands off the wrangler, too."

Austin didn't hear their exchange, too busy wondering if the two men were going to be more trouble than they were worth. At least they had guns. And the coloured man was right, more guns were better; though he looked like, alone, he could whip his weight in wildcats. Austin would have bet a month's pay he'd been in the war. What Harcourt was doing with a dandy like DeVille, Austin couldn't fathom. Perhaps he was DeVille's bodyguard. If DeVille was anything like Austin's daddy had been, he would have a lot of reasons to need one, but it wouldn't help him in the end.

Austin watched the visitors quickly care for their horses. The horses liked them, and they didn't stint on the work. Even knowing some men cared more for their horses than for other people, Austin relaxed a little.

DeVille glanced over as he gave his gelding's nose a final stroke. "How'd you come to work for Miz Larimer?"

He probably had his eye on the widow, or at least on her ranch. Since a gambler didn't seem likely to have money, maybe he was hoping his nice teeth would recommend him. Austin said, "How'd you come to be a dandified flatterer?"

DeVille said, without seeming to notice the insult, "Some are born to glory. I, however, am the son of the worst ruffian in Holmestown, New Jersey, saved from disgrace only by the good offices of Captain Harcourt." He plopped down on a hay bale.

"The archangel Michael couldn't save *you* from disgrace," Harcourt said.

His tone was familiar and absentminded, as if this sort of remark was common to him. They were friends, then, and not employer and employee? A strange pair. Austin said, "Don't let Miz Larimer hear you blaspheming. If she's your goal, that is."

Harcourt said, shortly, "I have no interest in the lady."

"She's rich," Austin said, testing.

"*Is* she?" DeVille asked. "Rich *and* a warrior queen. I think my heart just might leap out of my chest."

Harcourt thumped him on the back of the arm. "Later," he said.

A pistol slid into each of DeVille's hands. "Yessir," he drawled. "I'll take the cookhouse, sir, and cover the back. Austin, you coming with?" He smiled and winked. Austin startled; the smile charmed, and the wink had looked almost seductive. Some men would go after anything that moved, true, but surely not if it moved in pantaloons.

"I'll take the well," Harcourt said.

Outside, Austin settled with one hip braced against a water barrel while DeVille paced endlessly up and down the side yard between house and cookhouse, talking endlessly as well, his voice clearly audible across the yard.

"Speak up, I don't think they can hear you in town yet," Austin said.

Cheerfully, DeVille replied, "The widow seems to have an itchy trigger finger. I can't enjoy my money if she accidentally blows my head off."

"And Harcourt?" Austin asked. The other man was only just visible as a dark bump on the well house, if one knew where to look. It was too bad he wasn't over here, chatting. Austin had never seen anyone like him before. "Why's he hiding, then?"

"He's in reserve in case things get difficult," DeVille said. "So, Austin, you like poetry?"

"No!"

"Well, how about this one? You might like this one, it's better than you think." And, without letting Austin interrupt, DeVille charged into a recitation and then another and another.

Just after midnight, the attackers ran into the yard, whooping and firing pistols. Austin had never heard more than a single gun firing at once. The noise was bone-shaking.

DeVille appeared unaffected, apart from dropping Alexander Pope in the middle of a rhyme and plastering himself against a corner of the house. "How kind," he said. "They brought friends. At least they're not on horseback."

"Miz Larimer," Austin said, from behind the water barrel.

"Hush," DeVille said. "Stay hidden."

"I thought hired guns were supposed to be brave."

"Only an idiot nominates himself to get shot."

The widow's voice rang out. "Get off my property or I'll pump you full of buckshot."

A foul reply from the yard was followed by her shotgun blast. Shouts and pistol cracks, and more shotgun blasts, covered any more dialogue. Austin followed DeVille's slow creep around the corner and was nearly knocked down by a reeling, brawny figure wielding a flaming branch in one hand and a pistol in the other. The intruder swung the pistol at the side window; Austin leaped at him, wrestling for the torch before he could shove it through the hole in the glass and set the house afire. The torch went flying into the yard, but the big man still had his pistol. He shoved Austin backwards and aimed.

"Down!" DeVille yelled, and leaped. Both landed on the ground. Austin struggled free and sat up. The attacker fled, along with two others Austin hadn't seen, in a confusing melee overflowing with drunken curses.

"Cowards!" the widow yelled.

Harcourt stepped into view, rifle to shoulder. A hat flew into the air as if jerked on a string; its owner kept running.

"Great shot!" Austin said, feeling strangely euphoric.

"I was *aiming* for his—Virgil, you all right?"

In the sudden silence, DeVille's voice trembled. He still lay on the ground. "I can't believe, after all I've been through, some brainless lickfinger son of a bitch—"

Harcourt shoved Austin to the side and yanked open DeVille's coat. "No blood," he said.

"Jesus Christ, something sure hurts. Right here."

The Widow Larimer loomed over the men with a lantern. "Do *not* take the Lord's name in vain, for if you died right now, you would surely go to the fiery pits of hell."

DeVille squinted up at her. "I don't think I like you any more."

Events came together in Austin's mind. "Miz Larimer, I think he saved my life."

Harcourt produced a dented silver case from DeVille's coat. "And this saved his. Virgil, you don't smoke!"

Austin took the case and examined the bullet mashed into its tooled surface. The case would barely prise open. It held, not rolling papers at all, but pornographic playing cards. "Captain Harcourt, do you think they'll be back?"

The widow said, "If they do, I've got a whole case of shells right next to my coffee and my thunder mug. You men can leave my property to me, now. Go on, get."

There was no arguing with her. Austin carried Harcourt's rifle and the silver case, then lit and hung a lantern while Harcourt assisted DeVille back into the barn.

Once inside, DeVille snapped, "Get your damned hands off me!" and shoved Harcourt away. He spun his hat on to the pile of saddlebags, followed it with his gloves, ripped his necktie loose, then sat down, hard, on the same bale as before, wrapping his arms around his chest. He'd seemed perfectly collected while bullets whizzed by, but after his outburst, Austin could see him shaking.

Austin said, "I think we could all do with a drink."

"In my saddlebag," Harcourt said.

Austin had not imagined spending the night sitting around the barn on hay bales, passing a flask from hand to hand with two men who had been, at suppertime, complete strangers. DeVille didn't speak for a long time, only took two gulps of the smooth whiskey for Harcourt's every one. The two men sat shoulder to shoulder and wore still, tight expressions that made them seem oddly alike. Austin took the flask from Harcourt's hand and sipped, just enough for flavour and a touch of heat, and to try to ease an unexpected trembling.

At last, DeVille said, "That damned harpy is paying me double. You can tell her."

Sympathy evaporating in a flash of steam, Austin snapped, "Don't talk about her like that!"

DeVille snatched the flask, gulped, then upended it, looking disgusted when nothing dripped out. "She was awfully mean to me. You only like her because you think females have to stick together."

Austin's breathing stuttered. "What?"

"I've landed on more than a few women in my time," DeVille said, still vainly shaking the flask. "Also, you smell better than a cowboy. Doesn't the widow know?"

Austin glanced at Harcourt. He looked mildly curious. Austin took a deep breath and said, "The widow don't hold with women wearing men's clothes."

DeVille shrugged. "Lot of people don't hold with me being friends with Harcourt."

"The reverse is also true," Harcourt drawled. "What point are you making, Virgil?"

DeVille smiled, though Austin noted the smile wasn't as brilliant as before the fight. He said, "If nobody knows about Miss Austin, here, I thought it might be a relief to her to let her hair down for an evening. So to speak."

Before Austin could reply, Harcourt had thumped DeVille on the arm. "I told you, hands off the wrangler!"

"*She's* not paying us," DeVille pointed out. "What d'you think, Miss Austin? Care to be entertained by two fine and discriminating gentlemen?" DeVille appeared to be completely serious.

Harcourt said, "Now wait just a minute, I never said—"

DeVille held up a hand to stop his words, in a graceful gesture like an actor on stage. "We can't leave you out—"

"This woman is not a—"

"Don't say it. You have some cussed strange ideas about women—"

"I respect women!"

"So do I!"

"You respect them right into bed with you!"

"Jealous? That's not my fault. I sure as hell invited you along enough times!"

The two men glared straight into each other's eyes as they argued. DeVille wore a strange half-smile, which appeared to enrage Harcourt more every second. They were sitting so close they could, Austin thought dizzily, lean forwards and kiss each other with no effort at all. Such a thing had never occurred to her before. She hadn't even known she wanted to see it, until now.

She sprang to her feet. "It'll be both, or none!"

DeVille snorted and shoved at Harcourt's shoulder, then grinned. "I was right. They always like you best."

Harcourt glared at him, then stood and took off his hat. "Miss Austin, don't let that silver-tongued rascal talk you into something you might regret. Please understand, we'll keep your secret, there's no need to worry about that."

Rough as it was, he did have a lovely deep voice. She could've listened to him all night. Now she'd have the chance. "That's mighty kind of you," she said, looking him up and down. His shoulders were broad and strong; his torso narrowed down to a waist more slender than hers. His thighs looked hard beneath his worn denim pants, and when she looked at the bulge his cock made beneath the fabric, her mouth watered. "But it's you who don't understand. I was married once. Earning my living the way I do, though, I haven't been able to think about the pleasures of the flesh in a long time, because for sure, somebody would talk; and nobody's going to put a woman, a fallen woman, in charge of their remuda. You two don't have anything to do with that, do you? And I might as well make up for lost time." She looked at DeVille and smiled.

He said to Harcourt, "You can't complain about this one's intentions, can you?"

Austin took a step closer to the men and tipped her hat back on her head. "You ain't scared, Captain Harcourt?"

He glanced at DeVille, then back at her. His fingers tightened on his hat brim. "You two might want to speak in private. Perhaps I should take my leave."

"Don't," Austin said. "Please?"

DeVille reached out and slapped Harcourt's leg. "Come on, Harcourt. For the lady."

Austin stepped forwards quickly, tugged Harcourt's hat from his hand, and pressed her lips to his, interrupting whatever he had been about to say in protest. Her hat fell off. His lips were far softer than she'd expected, and he tasted like whiskey with all the burn gone.

She dropped his hat in the straw and ran her gloved hand up his chest. That was nice and firm. She scrubbed her palm across a nipple, but she could barely feel it beneath his clothing. His fingers closed over her wrist and lifted it. "Are you sure about this?" he said. Flickers of lantern light reflected in his eyes and glistened off the new dampness on his lips.

"As sure as shooting," Austin said. "Get over here, DeVille."

"That'd be Virgil to you."

"Then I'm Sarah. Sarah Jane Austin." Her free hand, ignoring the pleasantries, shaped Harcourt's narrow waist and rubbed next to the knife sheath at the small of his back.

Harcourt's eyes closed for a moment, then he grinned down at her, a quick flash. "Virgil, this lady is compromising me."

"I'll protect you," he said, solemnly.

Preparations took little time. Harcourt opened out the men's bedrolls atop their canvas tarps, with enough straw beneath for cushioning, while DeVille skimmed off Austin's coat, knelt, and unbuckled her chaps. His fingers danced along her hip bones, then slid down the outsides of her thighs and cupped her knees above her boots. He tipped his head back to look up at her and said, "It's a nice change from petticoats and corsetry. Downright inspirational, in fact."

Austin swallowed and said, "You've got considerable clothes yourself. Harcourt, you going to help me with this?"

"Give me his coat, and I'll hang it up."

That wasn't what she'd meant. She stripped off her gloves and, before laying her hands on DeVille's coat, cupped his face instead. Stubble rasped her palms; he turned his head to press a damp, whiskery kiss into her palm before she reached his mouth. He was more skilled and intent than she'd been prepared for, and when she finally tugged away from him and shoved his coat off, her vest was off, her shirt had been unbuttoned to the waist, and pulled mostly out of her pants. She didn't linger over DeVille's waistcoat buttons as she'd intended, fearing she'd find herself ravished and sated before she'd even extracted his watch from its pocket. That would hardly be fair to Captain Harcourt.

DeVille helped her with the shoulder holsters he wore, laying his guns carefully away on a big silk handkerchief. Austin then glanced at Harcourt, whose hands went to the buckle of his gun belt, letting it slither down his hips until she caught the worn leather and laid the weapons aside.

She said to Harcourt, "You take his shirt off."

A pause. DeVille said, "Lady's choice, Aaron." Their gaze met and held in silent conversation. Austin tried imagining using Harcourt's Christian name herself, and couldn't quite conceive of it.

Harcourt took a moment, visibly collecting himself, then

went to work in businesslike fashion on DeVille's cuffs and collar. He hesitated again. "You sure about this?"

DeVille shrugged. "I don't think our Sarah's that delicate, are you, honey?" He licked his lips, though, and looked away while Harcourt's hands, suddenly gentle, worked the linen over DeVille's shoulders and down his arms, and pulled off even his undershirt.

Austin understood, then. The bruise from earlier wasn't showing except as a red mark, but DeVille was scarred all over his ribs and belly, as if he'd been peppered with a giant shotgun. She forced herself to look away from the damage and saw he had a good pair of shoulders on him. He said, "It's from canister shot, down in Virginia. You got anything to say?"

"You look fine to me," she said. She elbowed Harcourt aside and set to DeVille's pants buttons. He didn't seem to mind her fumbling there, so she fondled his cock and balls through the fall of his pants before dipping her hands inside and drawing him out. His rosy cock had a pretty arch to it, and she imagined, with suddenly dry mouth, how it might feel inside her cunny.

Harcourt moved behind her and unknotted the thong binding her hair, then spreading her hair over her shoulders. He burrowed his calloused fingers down to her scalp and massaged, a pleasure that brought tears to her eyes. By the time she had DeVille fully naked, her own shirt had disappeared and Harcourt had his arms around her waist from behind, nuzzling her ear while neatly flicking open the buttons on her pants.

Harcourt lifted his head long enough to say to DeVille, "You first," and returned to her ear, her cheek, her throat, her shoulder, each kiss or nip making her tremble. She shuddered when she felt him hardening against the small of her back, and squirmed against him. He breathed raggedly into her neck and squeezed her to him more tightly. She wondered why he hadn't wanted to go first himself. So long as she had him eventually, she supposed it didn't matter.

Austin tugged DeVille forwards by the arm. "Kiss me," she said, just before his mouth closed over hers. His clever fingers delved beneath the bandages she used to bind her bosom, and a moment later she felt another set of hands join in. Cotton fluttered down her sides and to the floor, and for the first time in six years, hands other than her own touched bare skin. She whimpered and sagged back against Harcourt, who cupped and held her breasts for DeVille's hot, delicate mouth.

She twisted in their grip for an eternity, until DeVille muttered something and Harcourt lifted her off her feet, with no more effort than she would have used in picking up a kitten. DeVille, she realized, was yanking off her boots, then her pants. She had just enough presence of mind to grab, but she wasn't quick enough to prevent him from seeing the rolled bandage that provided the other element of her male disguise. He grinned up at her and kissed her right on the quim. "Maybe it's time for those bedrolls," he said. "Harcourt, do take off that blamed knife. And the rest of it, while you're at it."

Austin lost some details after that. Both men seemed intent on making her lose her mind. She had never felt anything so good in her life as strong male bodies pressed both to her front and her back, their hands seeking out every sensitive spot she had. For a long time she did nothing but hold on and respond to whomever happened to be kissing her at the time. She could tell them apart even with her eyes closed: DeVille's artistry and the scrape of his moustache, Harcourt's smoother skin and more aggressive tongue and teeth. Harcourt's hands were more direct, too, which she appreciated as she began to feel more and more wild for release.

His blunt, calloused finger delicately traced down the line between her buttocks, then stroked the folds of her quim. She cried out. The finger pressed upwards, opening her with impossible gentleness. The tip of the finger curled inside, and she cried out again. Harcourt said, sounding out of breath, "I think she might be ready for you, Virgil."

"God damn . . . hold her for me . . ."

She didn't want to wait for anything. Austin grabbed DeVille's cock. "Hurry *up*, you son of a—" She lost her breath as he nudged himself inside, stretching her deliciously; then Harcourt's hands shifted her hips in some small way, and DeVille slid in even more deeply, until there was no more space between them at all. He rolled his hips, rubbing deeply into the centre of her pleasure, and she gasped, "Again!"

"Anything for a lady," he said, and after a little more of this she crested with a sharp cry, clinging to him until the waves of pleasure ebbed. She felt wonderful, but still wanted more. She squirmed between them both, sliding her hands from DeVille's shoulders to his hips and back again. She could still feel him inside her, harder than before, and Harcourt's cock like an iron bar digging into her waist.

DeVille said, tightly, "I need her on her back right now."

Harcourt took her head in his lap. She hadn't had a good look at his cock before now. She rubbed her cheek against it and kissed his velvety skin; after a muttered curse from him and a strained chuckle from DeVille, Harcourt took her shoulders firmly in his big hands and shifted her down, so she could no longer reach. She braced her feet on the blanket for what she expected would be a wild ride. Tense as he'd sounded, though, DeVille took his time, each stroke long and slow and sweet, punctuated now and then by his mouth on her breasts. Austin eased into a trance of pleasure, spiralling around DeVille's cock and Harcourt's gentle fingers playing in her hair and stroking her forehead and lips.

She didn't think she could come this time, but she revelled in DeVille's gasping breaths as his thrusts gradually turned short and ragged. She squeezed her passage tightly on him, on his next push; it felt even better, and DeVille's back arched, his fingers tightening on her hips. She did it again from then on, keeping up the torture until, with a soundless exhalation, he spilled his pleasure inside her. At the end, as he began to soften, he wedged two fingers into her and stroked up and forwards, just enough hardness and pressure to wring another crest from her, this one deeper, seeming to flood her from the inside out.

After that, she drifted, barely aware of Harcourt shifting her more fully into DeVille's embrace, then sliding down behind her and throwing his arm over them both. His cock was soft; she hadn't seen him come, but perhaps he had, while she was occupied by her own pleasure. That was good; it meant there was no rush to satisfy him. She dozed a little then, and she thought DeVille did, too, for when she opened her eyes Harcourt had propped himself on his elbow and was stroking his friend's brown curls. As if he'd felt her eyes, his hand abruptly stilled.

"I was just remembering something," he said, withdrawing his hand and pretending interest in the door of the barn. He shook DeVille's shoulder. "Wake up, lazybones!"

"But she tuckered me out!"

Austin grinned. "I want to tucker *him*, too." She eased her backside against Harcourt and found him ready for her. He growled and grasped her hip, holding her there for a stroke or two. She said tentatively, not sure if he would allow it, "I'd like a taste of you."

Harcourt's breath whooshed out against her neck.

"Lady's choice!" DeVille said, gleefully. "You can't say it's wicked if she offers." Austin was relieved he didn't seem to mind he hadn't received the same; she hadn't even thought of asking until that moment. Maybe after this round, they could—DeVille leaned down and kissed her, smiling against her mouth. "You are one fine woman," he said. He drew his finger down the length of her nose. She couldn't help but smile at him.

Austin turned in Harcourt's arms and said, "Just a little taste?"

His lips parted, but he didn't speak, only nodded. He laid his hand on the back of her head as she crouched and licked the length of his erection. His legs trembled, and his hand fisted in her hair. It was something amazing, to have power over a man like that. Holding his cock steady with one hand, she lapped his balls, then dragged her tongue up his length again and pushed back his foreskin. She traced his rim before pressing tiny kisses on to the head. The slit leaked clear fluid, and she drew it between her lips. He tasted salty. She pressed her lips around the head and sucked. A noise like a howl burst from him, and she jerked back, startled.

"Enough," he gasped. "Virgil, quit laughing!" Harcourt yanked her towards him and kissed her feverishly.

He seemed to want her on top of him. Austin was happy to oblige, stretching out on his muscled length, pressing her bosom to his strong chest and matching up her quim against his rigid cock. She rubbed against him and moaned into his mouth, hungry as if she hadn't already come twice that night. Harcourt kneaded her backside and DeVille stroked the rest of her, from one end to the other. Harcourt's cock was insistent, though, and she began to feel hollow, so she sat astride him, lifted up enough to get a grip on his cock, and slid down. Harcourt reached up and played with her nipples, panting but not thrusting into her. "Lady's choice," he said. DeVille settled on his heels next to them, apparently content to watch for now.

Austin laid one hand on Harcourt's belly, letting her fingers stray down into his curls, and then touching where they were joined. "I want a good, hard ride."

He grinned, a flash of teeth she would've missed if she'd blinked. "That'd be a mercy just now, ma'am, but you please yourself."

Austin found herself smiling. "I'm not aiming to have any mercy," she said, and squeezed her passage on him. She could have sworn she felt the pulse of blood moving in his cock and throbbing against her inner walls. She bit her lip and rocked against him while he steadied her hips with his hands.

DeVille reached between them and laid his warm hand over her mound. His thumb nudged between her folds. "You want a little extra?" he asked.

"Yeah," she said. "And—" Harcourt's hands went to her breasts before she could ask.

Her ride laster longer than she'd hoped. They were all weary, and even with DeVille's skilled touch, her pleasure this time took longer to build, but it was worth it. Her crisis wracked her with spasms from feet to scalp. She cried out and, soon after, Harcourt followed, holding her tightly in his arms. When it was over, he pressed his mouth to her temple and held it there for a long moment. His fingers feathered down her back, and she blinked back tears, though she surely had nothing to cry about. She kissed his mouth softly and rested her forehead against his.

All three of them lay spent for some time, until DeVille said, "That was some pumpkins."

Austin laughed. She didn't want the night to end. She hesitated then decided to ask for what she wanted. When else would she have the chance? "I want you two to kiss. Because I ain't seen it before, and I want to see it now."

Harcourt opened his mouth then closed it again. He didn't look so dangerous with his eyes so wide and shocked.

DeVille grinned. "Come on, Harcourt. Where's your grit?"

Austin touched his face. "You don't mind so much, do you? I've just got a powerful curiosity."

"I noticed," he said, dryly. "All right." He gave DeVille a quick, sliding glance.

DeVille said, "I never thought I'd see the day. They must be sledding in hell right now."

"Maybe I should change my mind," Harcourt growled.

"Don't," DeVille said. He slid a little closer on the blanket, eyes downcast. "Listen to me."

Harcourt's brow wrinkled. "What's all this solemnity?"

"I don't want to joke about this." He looked up, and Austin's breath caught at his steady gaze, though he wasn't looking at her. "You know if you asked me, I'd do just about anything for you, don't you?"

"You don't have to do *anything* for me. If you think *that*—"

Austin put her hand on his arm. "Let him talk."

DeVille went on as if she hadn't interrupted. "I didn't say anything about *having* to. I only—Will you let me do this my way?"

"You're serious about this. You really *want*—Why?"

"There's a difference between us, Aaron. Not colour, or money, or bravery. You had a family, at least you did once. All I ever had was you. I've always wanted you to know that." DeVille caught Harcourt's face between his hands, dragged him close, and kissed him, open-mouthed.

Even weary as she was, it was downright exciting, seeing others engaged in intimacy at such close range, and so emphatically. DeVille's hand snarled in Harcourt's hair almost immediately, as if afraid he would escape; but after Harcourt's first instinctive flinch, she could see his shoulders relax as he let DeVille taste him. Then Harcourt's hand lifted, and she'd never seen anything so tender in her life as when his big square hand fitted itself to DeVille's cheek, his thumb stroking. A moment later, he leaned forwards, moving into the kiss, and DeVille made a tiny sound in his throat.

Austin slid her hand down between her legs. Harcourt reached back, blindly, and grabbed her arm, pulling her towards them. He dragged his mouth away from DeVille's, looking dazed, and kissed her hungrily. Then he turned back and kissed DeVille, who made a sound like a whimper, then Harcourt was tugging them both down to the blankets.

The night wasn't quite over yet.

When morning came, Austin found herself rolling her few extra clothes into a saddlebag, not quite sure how DeVille had talked her into going with them, to make their fortunes in San Francisco.

Blackberries

Nalo Hopkinson

"You want some blackberries?" I asked Tad. "They grow wild all along here."

In fact, blackberry bushes lined the narrow winding road as far as the eye could see. I walked over to the nearest one, where there was a clump of fat, ripe fruit hanging just about level with my mouth.

"You crazy, Shuck?" asked Jamal. "Those things are growing by the roadside with all this pollution! You gonna make him eat those?"

As if to prove Jamal's point, a semi came hurtling down the road, careening around the curves, belching blue smoke. It was huge and it stank, but there were still three cyclists riding in its wake. They had serious gear on, and straddled serious racing bikes. One of them looked sure to overtake the truck at the next bend. I shook my head. Vancouver. Gotta love this city. I'd only been living in her three years, but already she had my heart, with her tree-hugging, latte-sipping, bike-riding ways. Some girls are just like that. I waved a wasp away from the bunch of blackberries I was eyeing and pulled the ripest ones off. They just fell into my hand, staining it a little with juice.

"Here," said Tad. "Lemme try 'em."

Jamal sighed and rolled his eyes at his boyfriend. "Your funeral, sweetie."

Tad smiled and made a kissy face at him. "And I know you'll look hot at the wake, so cute in your tux."

I put one of the blackberries into Tad's mouth, enjoying the warmth and slight dampness of his mouth against my fingers.

Tad had the kind of plump, ripe brown lips I liked. I imagined crushing the berries against them, and licking the juice off. Shit, the things I was thinking about my oldest friend.

Tad bit into the berry. He raised his eyebrows in surprise. I grinned. "The blacker the berry," I told him. He responded with that flirty grin I remembered so well. Oh, gay boys could make me so randy. Gay boys and mouthy femmes.

"Come on, Jamal," Tad said. "You really need to taste one of these. Here." He took a berry from me and waved it in front of Jamal's face. Jamal looked sceptical.

"Just smell it." Tad put the berry under Jamal's nose and winked at me. "You know how they say the way to man's heart is through his belly?"

"That's no belly," I pointed out.

"You know it," Jamal said. "I don't spend all that time in the gym for nothing."

Jamal was wearing denim shorts that looked like they'd been sewn right on to him, and a sinfully tight white tank top. Like many black men, he didn't have much body hair to obscure the view. The white cotton made his skin gleam. His chest was a map of every workout he'd ever done. He was long and lean to Tad's short, rotund muscularity. Ah, so what? I bet my arms were bigger than his. I bet I could take him. I felt the warm pulse come and go in my clit and smiled. That was the thing with me and some guys: this balled-up heat, this combination of competitiveness and good, hard wanting. A lot would satisfy it. Wrestling, maybe. Or . . . no. Shut it, girl. I didn't know if I could flip these boys. Even if I could make them, just for a little while, hard for someone with girl bits, would it be someone like me? Every fag I knew was fascinated with breasts, and I was a little deficient in that department.

Jamal got a good whiff of the blackberry, and his face changed. He practically sucked it out of Tad's fingers. Tad laughed.

Two lanky white guys in surfer shorts and skateboarding T-shirts scrambled around us on the narrow verge, trying not to stare at the tableau of three black folks together in the same space. Not a sight you saw a lot in Vancouver. They headed on towards the entrance to Wreck Beach, the smell of weed tailing them.

I slurped down the rest of the berries. "C'mon," I said. "Let's go." We continued along the roadside.

Jamal and Tad were up visiting me from Seattle. Tad and I had been buddies when I lived there. We'd known each other since school days. Sometime near the end of high school, Tad had come out to me, like I hadn't guessed! With his example to follow, I'd come out to myself – a good obedient black girl from a fine Christian family, engaged to a minister in training – and fled into the arms of outcast women like myself with no plan of ever looking back. Tad and I had stayed fast friends, but we'd stopped the outrageous flirting with each other that we used to do. No need, right? Now that we'd each shown our true colours and didn't need the other as a shield any more. Except, when Tad contacted me a few weeks ago, we'd fallen right back into the sexual innuendo, the teasing. It felt familiar. Tad was my home. I'd invited him and Jamal to visit me and Sula, and I was thrilled when they accepted. The guys had landed at Vancouver airport a scant two hours ago. I'd whisked them off immediately to show them Wreck Beach.

We were at Trail Number Six, the path that led to the beach. "Nearly there," I told them. I took the first few steps down. Tad and Jamal followed me, then stopped to look around. We were in a forest, dark, damp and cool. Lean old maples stretched forever to reach the sky. The footpath angled sharply down in steps hewn out of the earth and shored up with planks. A deep ravine dipped down beside the footpath. It was overgrown with saplings, tangled blackberries and undergrowth. Here and there, a few giant rotted tree trunks jutted up out of it, looking like a giants' caber toss.

"*This* leads to a beach?" said Jamal.

"Yup," I replied. "It's about twenty minutes straight down; ten if you're fit."

"Lawd 'a mercy," muttered Tad. "The child still has a taste for hard labour."

I smirked at him. "Ready to hike?" I said to them.

Shot through with bars of precious sunlight from above, a yellowed maple leaf drifted slowly down into the ravine. The leaf was the size of a turkey platter.

Jamal looked at me, a gleam in his eye. "Ten minutes?"

"For me, anyway," I said. The gauntlet had been laid down. Would he pick it up?

"Betcha I can do it in seven."

"You're on!" I burst past him. He yelled and ran to catch up. I knew this path well; could do it in the dark. I had, one night, with my girlfriend Sula. And when we'd made it to the beach; well, mosquitoes bit me that night in places no mosquito had any right being.

I grabbed a sapling for purchase, slid around that little dog-leg you get to about a third of the way down. I shouted for the joy of it.

"Please be careful, both of you!" yelled Tad.

I stopped, looked up at Tad a few yards above me. He was skating and slipping on the pebbles. He skidded to one knee, grimaced as he skinned it. He'd stopped about an inch from the edge. Jamal looked down. It was a steep drop over the side.

"He's right," I said. "I'll race you, but let's not do anything stupid, OK?"

Jamal measured me with his eyes. I let him look. My sawn-off jeans showed the bulges in my thighs, and my arms strained at the sleeves of my T-shirt. I was a fair match for him and we both knew it.

"All right," he replied. "Nothing stupid. We take it easy. But I bet you I'll be the one to make it down there without breaking a sweat."

"In your dreams." I turned and kept climbing down, Jamal neck and neck beside me.

"Tad, you OK up there?" called Jamal.

"You bitches better slow down!" he shouted back.

"Yeah?" I said to him. "You gonna come down here and make us?"

Tad chuckled. "I bet you'd like that."

I could hear him puffing, his feet landing heavily on the steep stairs, but Tad didn't ruffle easily. Like when he'd come and pulled me out of my parents' house, where my dad had me under house arrest for the crime of being a bulldagger. Dad had reached for the baseball bat he kept behind the couch, but Tad had just grabbed it away from him and calmly told me to pack a bag, he'd wait for me. Been too long since Tad and I hung out.

"I can smell the sea," Jamal said.

"Yeah," I told him. "I love this part. The forest belongs to the land, but as you come further and further down, the sea starts to peek through. You smell it first, then you begin to see it. A few more steps, and . . . ah. There she is."

We were at the landing, just a few yards above the beach. The sand stretched out on either side, with the water just beyond it, its gentle waves licking at the beach. The sea smelled like sex. Off in the distance, the Coast Mountains marched away from us, range upon range, disappearing into the mist.

Jamal stood tall, but he was breathing hard, and I could see the beads of sweat on his face. I bet they tasted like the sea. "Little winded, there, Jamal?" I teased him.

He sucked his teeth. "Don't give me that, girl child. Look at you."

He was right. I was puffing a bit myself, and my T-shirt was soaked. I pulled it over my head. I never wore a bra. Jamal literally jumped. I calmly tucked the end of the T-shirt into my belt. "What?" I asked him. "I told you it was a nude beach." You weren't supposed to get naked until you were actually on the beach, but I was feeling the devil rising in me. Wanted to see how Jamal and Tad would deal.

Tad had caught up with us. He burst out laughing when he saw me. "Susanna Paulette Avery, you're still flat as an ironing board!"

"Don't talk shit, Tad. This a thirty-eight inch chest. I work out hard to get this chest."

"Chest, yes. But where are the titties, girl?"

"On your momma."

Now Jamal was laughing too. He looked relieved. Probably cause he didn't have to look at bouncing boobies on me. Even with my shirt off, lots of people still mistake me for a man. Nipples a little thicker than on most guys, is all.

I pointed to the Johnny-on-the-spot off to one side on the landing. "You guys want to use the facilities before we go down?"

"Nah," said Jamal. "We can piss in the bushes if we have to . . . oh. Excuse me, Susanna. Unless you want to?" He gestured towards the toilet. Damn. Show a little bit of girl parts, and he goes all gentleman on me.

"No." I moved past him and headed for the stairs. "And shut it with the 'Susanna' crap. Everybody calls me Shuck."

"Except your daddy!" Tad sung out. Giggling, he brushed past me on the stairs and raced down to the beach. "He calls you . . ."

"Don't start, Tad!" I ran, caught up with him, tackled him to the sand.

"Ow! Big meanie." Laughing, Tad got me in a chokehold, pinned my back to the sand, one arm behind me. The buttons of his shirt were plucking at my nipples. They swelled. I got my legs around Tad's body. Men have the upper body advantage; women have the lower. I twisted, flipping Tad like a turtle. I sat astride him. Jamal ran up and stood there, watching us both with a shit-eating grin on his face.

"Now," I said to Tad, "*what* does my dad call me? Tell me." And I started tickling.

Tad wriggled helplessly under me. "Bitch! Stop it! No!" He giggled, tried to slap my hands away, but I kept moving them, kept digging my fingers into his tummy, his sides, the bit along the bottom of his belly.

"Here, let me help," said Jamal. He knelt at Tad's head, grabbed his arms. Laughing, Tad struggled, but Jamal held him fast. I kept tickling. Tad started to squeal.

"I think you men need to go to the other part of the beach," said a firm woman's voice.

I looked up. She was pointing to where the gay men usually hung out. She looked part Asian, part something I couldn't identify. She was completely naked, all soft curves, about fifteen years older than me, with a relaxed, amused grin. Just the way I like 'em. I stood up off Tad. "Yes, ma'am!"

"Oh," she said, hearing my voice. "Maybe not." She'd pegged me for a woman.

"Where is it?" Jamal asked her.

She pointed, but I said, "I can show you." I took Tad's hand, pulled him up off the sand. The woman raised an eyebrow at me, but only said, "I'm sure you can," and sauntered off.

I watched her departing behind: chubby and round, like two oranges. I bet that ass felt good in the hands. It was bouncy, too. "Gotta be jelly," I muttered.

"Cause jam don't shake like that!" Jamal finished. We laughed, punched each other's shoulders.

I led the boys further out on to the beach, to a nice patch of sunlight. Sunlight, like black people, was a rare and precious occurrence in Vancouver. Tad and Jamal stared around them. Even in early fall, some people still came down to the water. There was a mound of sand, human height, with a sand sculpture of a naked woman carved into its side. Over to our right, someone had stuck bleached fallen logs into the sand, angling them together into the shape of a teepee. Over to our left an elderly Asian woman and man, nude, sat on towels with their chess game on the sand between them. Three ruddy children and their dog played with a bright green ball. The children's laughter and shouting and the barking of the dog ascended into the cool autumn air and were thrown back from the forest behind us.

"Water? Pop? Smokes?" The vendor strolling the beach was male, stocky, white. He swung a bright red cooler from either hand. He wore sturdy rubber sandals, a money pouch around his waist, a sun visor on his head and a bow tie around his neck, all in the same red as the coolers. Nothing else. Tad's face as he spied him was a picture.

"We don't have anything like this in Seattle," he murmured.

"Hey, Philip," I called out.

The vendor smiled when he saw me, and came over. "Hey, Shuck," he said. "Nice day, eh?"

"Beauty," I agreed.

Tad quirked an eyebrow at me. "Beauty?"

I shrugged. "Been here three years. Starting to talk like the locals." Philip snickered.

"You guys thirsty?" I asked them. They nodded. So I bought some pop from Philip.

"Smokes?" Philip asked again. "I got tobacco and, um, herbal."

"Reefer?" asked Tad. "You selling reefer out in the open like this?"

Philip just grinned.

"Shuck," said Tad, "we're the only black people as far as the eye can see. You know that if some shit goes down with the cops, we'll be the ones doing jail time, not him."

"Just chill, man," Philip told him. The borrowed black phrase sounded odd in a white Vancouverite's mouth. But hell, probably no odder than me saying, "beauty".

"This is Vancouver," I told Tad. "*And* it's Wreck Beach. If the cops start picking people up here for smoking weed, the jail'll be overflowing in an hour."

Tad shook his head. "S'all right anyway, man," he told Philip. "Thank you."

"You guys have a good day, then," Philip replied. He nodded at me and continued down the beach.

I turned to hand a can of pop to Jamal, and my mouth went dry. He'd kicked off his sandals. As I watched, he stripped off his tank top and shorts and slipped out of the skimpy black jock he was wearing underneath. When he bent, the hollow that muscle made at the side of his butt cheek was deep enough that I could have laid my fist inside it. Graceful as a dancer, he flicked the jock off, tossed it on the pile of his clothing, rolled it all up into a cylinder, and stood. Tad gave his lover's body an admiring gaze. Jamal took the can of pop I held out towards him; somehow managed to do so without looking directly at me.

For a while we all just stood, uncomfortably silent. Sucking on the drinks gave us something to do with our hands. I led them to a pile of flat rocks, comfortable as armchairs. We sat and looked at the people around us, looked out to sea, anywhere but at each other.

Not too many people out today; it was early fall, and a little bit chilly for the beach. Two more nudists were playing frisbee not too far from us; both appeared to be in their sixties. He was tanned with a fall of long white hair tied into a ponytail, and elaborate mustachios. Both forearms a rainbow of tattoos. He carried his firm pot belly on his sturdy thighs like a treasure chest. She had long, blonde hair, a beautiful and weathered face, a toughness and pride to her movements. She had knotted a burgundy lace shawl around her hips, not that it hid anything. It seemed to be just for pretty. And she was pretty. Her breasts bounced and jiggled as she leaped, laughing, for the frisbee. She caught it, went and took the man by the hand. Together they walked over to a group of three children frolicking by the rocks. They had a family picnic over there, spread out on towels.

"There are kids here," said Tad.

"Yeah. Everybody comes."

"Doesn't it get a little . . . racy for them to be out here?"

"No. Anybody starts to make out in public, people will stop them."

"Oh." He looked a little disappointed.

"Of course, what happens in the bushes isn't exactly public . . ."

Jamal snickered.

". . . I'm sure there's a lot that goes on that we don't see." Hell, I'd played my own reindeer games here. That night with Sula and the mosquitoes, for example. No one was allowed down here at night, but we'd managed.

Over to our right, a young woman sat fully clothed on the sand, her knapsack beside her. She had a sketchbook. She seemed to be drawing the mountains in the distance. The two surfer dudes we'd seen earlier were skimming wake boards in the shallowest part of the water, hopping on to them and riding parallel with the shore.

"There's nobody in the water," Jamal said.

"Nah, not much. It's cold and there aren't any waves. That's not the attraction of this beach."

"No?" Jamal replied, a teasing tone to his voice. "Then what is?"

Tad gasped and grabbed my arm. "What's that?" he hissed. He pointed out into the water.

Jamal looked where Tad had pointed. "Shit. Is it a dog?"

I smiled. "Seal. Harbour seal."

"For real? A live seal?"

"For real."

The seal had surfaced not twenty feet off shore, only its head visible. Its fur was black and shiny, its eyes large and curious in its big, round head. It was staring at the surfer dudes.

"It's just curious," I said. "Don't make eye contact with it . . ."

Too late. The seal had turned to look at us and had seen us staring. Shy and cautious, it disappeared back into the water.

"Fuck, that's wonderful," whispered Tad.

"Yeah," Jamal replied. He leaned back against Tad's chest with a happy sigh. He leaned over, patted my hand. "Shuck, thank you for letting us visit. Really."

"No problem." They were gorgeous, sitting in a love knot like that. I think that was the moment I decided to see if I could turn them both on to me, just for the afternoon.

"Hold this for me will you, baby?" Tad handed Jamal his empty pop can and whipped his shirt off. He'd gotten a belly since I saw him last, and his arms and thighs were heavier.

"Being in love suits you, sweetie," I told him. "You look good."

He looked embarrassed. "Fat, you mean."

"No, I mean good. Like you'd be good to hold."

Tad raised an eyebrow at me. Jamal chuckled. "Oh, yeah. I just wrap my arms and legs around him and ride all night."

I gave them both a measuring stare. "Yeah, I can imagine." Jamal stared me back down. Tad just looked uncomfortable. Shit. Had I pushed too far? Maybe this was a bad idea. Tad was my friend, had stood by me all these years. Didn't want to ruin that over a fuck. Better ease up a little, figure myself out. I stood up and said, "OK. Let me take you to where the boys are."

Never mind the cooler weather, gay Wreck Beach was hopping. A large man in a small, frilly apron circulated through the crowd, selling Martinis right off the tray he balanced on one hand. There was a volleyball game going on further down the beach, a serious game. I recognized those four guys; they came down here a lot, but I never saw them cruising. They really just enjoyed being naked in the sun. One of them jumped and spiked the ball hard, sending his opponent sprawling when he tried to stop it. A few people watching them applauded. Down by the water, some diehards were trying to swim. Better them than me. They had little triangular purple flags stuck in the sand near their towels. A nudists' club, then. Three women and a dog lolled on the sand. They nodded and smiled at me. I nodded back. A man lay on a towel on his stomach, his perfect bottom upturned invitingly to the sun, and to the eye. A few guys just strolled the beach, alone, their eyes alert for opportunity. And there was plenty. The twinks were twinkling, the bears were bare, and the bushes were shaking. Before winter, certain of the man-handling men of Vancouver seemed determined to get in every last bit of naked cruising on the beach.

It was rockier here. Back at my and Sula's apartment, my shrine had a collection of rocks I'd collected from Wreck Beach, all colours. All worn smooth by the water. We picked our way across the rocks and sand.

The three of us had drawn instant attention the second we crossed the invisible dividing line between the straight part of the beach and this one. No surprise; we had us some permanent tans. Up in the city, being black could get you followed by security guards when you went into stores. But down here, it was a different matter. Most of the guys scoped me for a girl and immediately switched their attention to Tad and Jamal; those greedy two were loving every instant of it.

A hairy man with a tall, thin body gave Tad a melting smile. "Hello," he said as he walked by.

Tad dipped his chin in response. "'Ssup," he growled, all serious and street, but when the man had passed, Tad grinned and gave himself a thumbs up.

Jamal was like to get whiplash, he was working so hard at seeing everything there was to see. "It's hog heaven up in here!"

he hissed at us. He was getting his fair share of appreciation, too.

My shoulders were getting warm from the sun. It wasn't too bright, but it could still burn. I fished the flat plastic bottle of sunscreen out of the back pocket of my shorts and smeared some all over my upper body. Better protect the nips. Then I flipped the bottle at Jamal. "Here," I said. "Put some sunscreen on that pretty behind."

He caught the bottle, looked at the label, sneered at me. "Girl, what you think I need this for? Got me more melanin than alla these motherfuckers out here!"

"All right, but don't come crying to me when your hide gets hard and leathery like somebody's old wallet." I held out my hand for the bottle. Jamal cut his eyes at me, but he put the sunscreen on.

An older man came walking past us. He looked white, but he was tanned a deep brick red. His skin had settled into soft folds on his body, and he clanked when he moved. I spotted a pinkie-thick rod through each nipple, plugs and multiple rings through his ears, and a bunch more rings and rods through his dick. There were probably more I wasn't seeing. Tad shuddered, but I thought he looked really interesting. Had to admire his dedication.

Then I got a better look at one of the men coming out of the water. Could it be? I wasn't sure. He saw us, altered his trajectory so that his path would cross ours. Dragonfly tattooed on his left thigh. Yes, it was him!

As he passed by, he looked Jamal up and down, slowly. "Mm," he said, "chocolate." He walked on, gazing back at Jamal now and again. He flagged down the Martini seller.

"The fuck was that?" said Jamal.

I chuckled. "He didn't recognize me."

"Where you know him from?" Tad asked.

"Shuck," said Jamal, "can we find somewhere to sit that's a little bit private? All of a sudden, I'm not digging on these guys so much any more."

Perfect. Just my chance. "They're not all like that, you know," I said. But I led them to the place I had in mind: a private little patch of sand surrounded by scrubby trees. Good, no one was using it just now.

"Where do you know him from?" asked Tad again.

I pointed to a large, flat-topped rock. "You can sit there," I told them. "It's almost like an armchair."

"Susanna . . . I know you when you get like this," Tad said. "What's the story with that guy?"

I grinned. "You gonna take those clothes off? It's warm down here."

Jamal put his clothing down on the rock and went to undo the fly on Tad's jeans. Tad made a show of slapping his hands away, then submitted. I sat on the boulder that was conveniently near the flat rock and watched. Triumphantly, Jamal yanked the zipper down.

"Wait, sweetie, wait," Tad said. "Gotta take the shoes off first." With a shy glance at me, he sat on the rock, put his balled-up shirt next to Jamal's clothing, and started taking off his runners. To keep him company, I took off my sandals, put them on the boulder beside me. Tad got his shoes and socks off, snuck me a glance again, rocked his jeans off his hips, and pulled his legs out of them. He was wearing black cotton shorts underneath. So modest. He rolled the jeans up beside the other clothing.

"Stand up," I said. "Let me see you."

Slowly, he did. His thighs were thick, his calves full and muscled. "Well, look at you," I told him.

Jamal was smiling at me thoughtfully. Was he egging me on?

"Lover," he said to Tad, "turn all the way around for your friend. Let her look at you."

He *was* egging me on.

"Two of you are shameless," muttered Tad, but, to my surprise, he did what Jamal asked. I took my time admiring his butt, the fullness of his belly. He turned to face me, but I'd barely glanced at his package in his shorts when he sat down. "So," he said, faking nonchalance, "you gonna tell me about that guy?"

"You wanna know what happened, you have to take the shorts off."

He cocked his hand on his hip. "Is the story worth it?"

"Worth seeing you in the full, glorious flesh? It's a high price, baby, but I think I can meet it."

He made a face at me. But he looked pleased, too. This felt good. This felt like the way we used to tease each other. I just wanted to push it up a notch, that's all.

Maybe Tad was thinking the same thing, because all of a sudden he pulled his shorts down, stepped out of them, grabbed them up off the sand, and sat down. He tossed the shorts on to the pile of clothing and turned back to me. "There," he said. He crossed his hands in his lap, conveniently hiding his crotch. "So, tell me the story."

Jamal sat on the warm sand beside Tad's knee.

"All right," I said. "You asked for it."

I settled comfortably on my boulder, leaned forward. "Well, Sula and I have this game, right? Every so often, one of us dares the other one to do something outrageous. If you chicken out from doing whatever it is, you lose, and you have to be the other person's sex toy for a night; do everything they say."

"Oo," said Jamal. "Kinky." He stroked Tad's calf.

I snickered. "You don't know the half of it. One time I lost on purpose. Could barely stand the next day, after Sula got done with me." The memory of that night was making my nipples crinkle up. All those girly pantyhose that Sula owned had made the most fiendish restraints. I didn't know I could bend in some of those positions.

"You're stalling, Shuck," said Tad.

"No, just setting the story up. Cause, this one time, I took her up on her dare. There's this gay bar called Pump Jack's, a men's bar. I'll take you there on Friday. Sula said she wanted me to go in there and get one of the guys to let me jerk him off."

"No!" from Tad.

"Yes. And I did it."

"With that guy we just saw?"

"With that guy."

"How?"

"I went to the bar in drag . . ."

"In a dress?" asked Tad.

Jamal chuckled. "No, silly. She went in guy drag."

Though come to think of it, I pretty much look like I'm in drag when I wear a dress, too. "Yeah," I said. "Little goatee, little bit of extra swagger in the walk. Wore my regular clothes. Walked right in. I mean, I go in there as a chick, so I thought the bouncer would recognize me. He got this look like he almost did, but then you could see he didn't make the connection. I didn't speak the whole time. Ordered a beer at the bar by pointing at the draught spigot. When I started drinking it, I knew I'd have to do something soon, before I needed to go and piss."

Tad was shaking his head. "Susanna, you are something else."

"Susanna left home. I'm Shuck."

"What happened then?"

"I saw this guy looking at me. That guy, the one on the beach. I started staring him down, looking him up and down. If I did that to a woman, she'd probably run a mile. But this guy, he came and sat next to me. Said hi. I didn't answer, just pointed with my chin over to the bathroom. Shit, I didn't think it would work! Figured he'd see I was a woman, and I'd have to pass it all off as a joke.

"But that didn't happen. He just gave me this rude, slow smile. Leaned over and whispered that he'd see me in there. And off he headed, to the john.

"My heart was fucking hammering in my chest, I tell you. But I put down my beer, followed him. He slipped into a stall, and I slipped in behind him. He reached for me, but I didn't want him touching me too much. Women's skin has this soft feeling, you know? Even mine. Didn't want that to give me away. So I pushed his back against the stall door. I sat on the toilet, unzipped him . . ."

"Shit, that's hot," said Jamal. He was leaning forwards, his mouth a little open. His cock was firming up. I was getting a tingle in my shorts, too, telling this story.

"He was hard the second I got his dick out of his pants. I slid my hands up under his shirt, grazed his nipples, pulled on them a little."

Tad swallowed.

"I ran my tongue around the head of his dick. He moaned, kinda low. I held on to his dick, gave it a good squeeze. It jumped in my hand."

Tad got this odd look. He squeezed his knees together and said, "You know, you better stop talking like that, else you might see something you don't wanna see."

Oh, yes. Now we were getting somewhere. Jamal looked up at his lover, gave him an evil grin.

I stared right into Tad's eyes. "What you covering up there, Tad?" I said. Jamal snickered, but I held Tad's gaze like the headlights hold the deer's. "Something I'm saying getting you horny? Something about the way I pinched that man's nipples, and took his dick in my fist and slid up and down, squeezing whenever my fingers went past the head?"

Tad gulped. He cupped his hands tighter around himself, but he wasn't fooling me; those hands were rubbing up and down, ever so slightly.

"You didn't know I did guys, did you? Only sometimes, Thaddeus. Only when the man is as gay as I am, and there's no hope in hell of pretending that the sex we're having is straight sex."

Jamal shot me a look. Was that admiration? I set my focus back on Tad. Jamal could match anything I could dish out, throw the challenge back in my face. We understood each other. Tad was the one I'd have to convince, if this was going to happen.

"Tad," I said.

"Yeah." His voice was raspy.

"You know what I did next?"

"No."

"I had my fist around that dick, feeling the little surging swells as he got more turned on. I took the other hand away from his nipples . . ."

"Aw!" protested Jamal.

"Hush, you," I told him. "I took my hand away from his nipples, slid it flat down his belly, towards his cock. Held the head in one hand, just pumping a little, back and forth . . ."

"Oh, God," whispered Tad. He was openly stroking himself now, hiding the view from me with one hand, sliding the other up and down over his cock and balls.

". . . held that head, and drew my nails, very lightly, up the underside of his cock."

Tad's mouth opened.

"He moaned again, louder this time. He leaned back against the door. He had his hands at the top of the cubicle, hanging on to either side. I could see the muscles straining in his arms."

Tad made a little breathy noise.

"He got a drop of pre-come at the tip of his dick, just twinkling in the eye. I rubbed my thumb in it and used it to moisten the head of his dick."

Jamal moved in closer to Tad, laid his head on Tad's knee. Tad jumped, and Jamal stroked Tad's inner thigh. "Shh, baby, it's OK," he said.

Tad's eyes flicked from Jamal to me, a desperate, needy glance.

Jamal chuckled. He ran his tongue along the outside of Tad's thigh, licked his lips, and said to me, "So, did you suck him off?"

"Jamal!" Tad sat up straight. His hands slipped a little, and I could see his cock: compact, dark like the rest of him, with a pretty pink tip. Nice. "Jesus Christ, Shuck. You're my friend. We shouldn't . . ."

Jamal pressed Tad back against the rock, stroked his tummy. "Don't fret, Daddy. This is fun." Bless the boy. He looked back at me. "So. Did you?"

I shook my head. "Suck him off? Not my thing. You know what I did instead?"

"What?" whispered Tad. Jamal gave him an encouraging smile.

"I spat on the place where my hand and his dick met, got it nice and wet. I started pumping his whole dick, slow."

Jamal ducked under Tad's leg, moved Tad's hands away from his cock and balls, held them out away from his body. "Like this?" he said. He spat on Tad's erect cock. Tad gasped. His hands made clutching motions. Jamal let them go. Tad held on to Jamal's shoulders, threw his head back. "Like this?" Jamal asked again, and started sliding Tad's cock between his fist. Fuck, they were lovely.

"Kinda like that," I told Jamal. "Keep going." I opened my own knees, thumbed my shorts open and yanked the zipper down. I could smell my own musk. I slid my hand between my belly and the spread-open zipper. No underwear; I mostly don't bother with it. The crisp curls of my pubic hair were damp. Jamal dipped his mouth down to Tad's cock, ran his tongue slowly around the head of it. Now both Tad and I were moaning. I splayed my legs wider. My fingers found the folds of my pussy lips. They were hot and slick. My clit was puffy in between them. It jumped at my touch, at the sight of Tad, eyes closed, mouth open, his hand around the back of Jamal's neck. Tad was bucking his hips now, slowly, popping his cock in and out of Jamal's mouth. Jamal, greedy Jamal, kept reaching for more.

"Jamal," I said. I was hoarse. "Can you get to your knees?"

Jamal made a garbled sound of assent around Tad's cock in his mouth. Tad reacted to the vibration with a slight shudder. Somehow Jamal managed to get into position, just like I'd asked. He spread his knees for traction, released Tad's cock from his mouth, only to start licking and tonguing Tad's balls. His perfect ass was displayed to my view, firm and dark as a cherry, two halves with the split between. Fuck. With my three middle fingers I started rubbing my pussy, fast and flat against my clit, fingers just dipping into my cunt with each push. I was creaming up inside my shorts.

There was sweat running down Tad's chest and heavy belly. More of it beaded in his tight, short hair and the beautifully groomed goatee.

"God, you two are hot," I muttered. Tad opened his eyes, saw me looking, squeezed them shut again. He slowed his incursions into Jamal's mouth. I got a flash image of a black-furred head disappearing shyly beneath the water. Oh no you don't, Tad. I wasn't going to let this scene end here.

"So that guy in the bathroom?" I said to them.

"Mm?" mumbled Jamal, around a mouthful of Tad's cock and balls.

"I'm working him up with one hand. I hold the other hand up to his mouth. I'm still not talking, but he gets the idea. He starts licking my hand. Gets it good and wet."

"Shit," whispered Tad. But the rhythm of his hips had sped up again.

"I took that hand, cupped his balls with it. But just for a second." Remembering that forbidden night got me even wetter. I kept working my clit, slipped a couple of fingers on the other hand into my cunt, just at the entrance, beckoning against the front wall. Shit, shit, yeah. "Then," I said, "I slipped my hand past his balls, back, until I touched his asshole. He jumped a little."

So had Jamal. The motion pushed his ass out even further into relief. His little pink rosebud of an asshole winked at me. I could see the curling black hairs that ran from the small of his back down towards it, like an arrow. *Here's the honey. Here.* Jamal had one hand on his own dick, stroking hard.

"I slipped one fingertip in . . ." I said.

Tad started to pant. His eyes were wide open now, fixed on Jamal's busy mouth.

"His asshole squeezed tight around my finger, like a little kiss. Then it opened up for me."

Jamal was making little groaning noises around Tad's cock. I pushed off from my rock, dropped to my knees beside them. Knees would pay for that later. My clit under my strumming fingers felt like a marble in syrup. The fingers of my other hand stroked hard against the spongy ridge just inside my cunt. It pushed back. Soon. "I . . ." My body was shaking, my crotch jutting towards Jamal and Tad. My thigh muscles knotted. It felt good. "I pushed one finger inside him. Then two. He took them both."

"Shuck," muttered Tad, "it's . . . I'm . . ." Jamal had his fist clamped tight around the base of Tad's cock, his mouth working the head. His hand between his own legs was almost a blur. He was screwing his ass around in the air. He looked so nasty.

"I plunged those fingers in and out of him, feeling him clasp them with each push. His dick was hard as iron in my hands."

The letting-down feeling started inside me, muscles starting to push down and forwards. It was like I needed to piss.

"He slammed his shoulders back against the door. His crotch was arched way out. He was calling out for Jesus. He started to come. It spurted . . ."

Tad made this low, deep growl. His body began to spasm. Jamal pulled his mouth away so we could watch the gouts of juice rhythmically pumping out of Tad's cock. He stared, intent, at his lover's crotch, then came himself, hard and roaring.

That put me over the edge. My hand was flying at my clit, my forearms like cables. My own body pushed my fingers out of me, and I let go, and I was flying. I howl and laugh when I come, and I squirt. Lots. When I was done, the front of my shorts was sopping, and Tad's foot and Jamal's knee were in a puddle of girl-juice-soaked sand. I collapsed on to my side, breathing hard. Was going to be hell getting the sand out of my dreads.

I heard a noise behind us. I pulled my hands out of my pants and rolled over. Two eager heads had just pushed through the bushes to see what all the commotion was about. "Oh, excuse us," said the two men. They tromped away, giggling. I heard one of them say, "Was that a *woman* with them?"

Jamal started laughing – a low, slow roll. He put his head on Tad's knee and said to me, "Girl, you are some dirty bitch." He reached out and high-fived me. Our hands made a wet noise as they slapped together.

Tad still looked a little sheepish, but his whole body was more relaxed now. He leaned back against the rock, stroked Jamal's head. "Is this Canadian hospitality, Shuck?" he teased me.

I put my head against the warm sand, reached out a foot and slid it along first Tad's leg, then Jamal's. I was going to have quite the story to tell Sula tonight. I admired our skins, the three shades of brown against the pale sand. "Look at us," I said.

"Three black sheep," Jamal joked.

"Three black berries," I replied.

Tad gave a happy sigh. "And such sweet juice."

Karen Leaves her Husband
for the First Time

Catherine Lundoff

How do you tell your husband you're dumping him for his assistant?
That question was almost enough to make Karen walk out
of the lobby, get back on the train and forget this particular
errand. She didn't have to get on the elevator and go upstairs
to see him after all. There was always the coward's way out: the
note on the table, the carefully removed possessions. But she
couldn't do that to Danny somehow. It didn't feel right. Not
even if Elaine would punish her for it afterwards, just the way
she deserved.

That thought brought a hot flush to her entire body and
her walk slowed to a languorous strut that made heads turn as
she made her way to the elevator. Memories of her last stolen
moments with Elaine filled her head, licked their way up her
thighs and drove hard little fists inside her until she found
herself standing in front of the receptionist's desk in Danny's
office with no idea of how she got there. It took a few seconds
for her to find the breath to get the words past her lips. "I need
to see Danny."

The woman at the desk raised an eyebrow but turned to
check his calendar without making any comment. "I'm afraid
he's in a meeting for the next twenty minutes, Mrs Anderson.
It looks like that's his last one for today though. Would you
like to wait in his office?" She buzzed Karen in after a mute
nod answered her question. Karen walked slowly past her and
inched her way into Danny's office without being noticed by

anyone else. She shut the door behind her with a sigh of relief and collapsed in one of the chairs.

Then there was nothing to do but sit for an eternity and rehearse what she was going to say. She felt a little guilty that she hadn't told Elaine that she was going to do this today; after all, it was Elaine's job on the line if Danny freaked out. Maybe she should just tell him there was someone else and leave it at that. She wiped her shaking hands off on her skirt and eyed it critically. It was too short and too tight for this kind of talk. Then there were the flimsy lace panties under it and the sheer bra under her silky blouse. All in all, she looked like a woman who dressed to be fucked, not to ask her husband for a divorce.

The realization made her groan. Her head had been full of seeing Elaine tonight, not on how Danny would respond to her this afternoon. Besides, Elaine had bought the lingerie set for her and insisted she put it on this morning. Anyway, it had been ages since Danny had paid much attention to her at all so why expect things to change now? He didn't even have a photo of her on his desk. *That's it. Get mad. It'll be easier that way.* She made herself hang on to that thought, adding to it by remembering every slight and argument of the last few months. By the time Danny walked in, she was fuming and her outfit was all about what he wasn't getting any more.

"Hi, honey. To what do I owe the pleasure? You look lovely, by the way." He glanced her over appreciatively and gave her a quick peck on the lips, then strode off to sit behind his desk and shuffle papers around.

"Danny, we need to talk about something important," she began, proud of how dignified she sounded. That lasted all of a minute when it became obvious that he wasn't paying attention. The realization stabbed through her. "Look at me, dammit! You don't feel a thing for me any more, do you? No, don't bother denying it. That's why I'm leaving you. I'm sick of being ignored . . . and neglected." She burst into tears with the last words. It still hurt to say them, even if she was in love with someone else now.

"Oh, honey!" Danny was at her side and pulling her up out of the chair faster than she could have believed. His arms held her tight and he murmured into her hair. "I didn't know you felt that way." He paused for a couple of breaths, filled only by her sniffles. "You're so right, baby. I haven't been appreciating you like I should. But I love you, Karen, you've got to believe that." His hands stroked her back as she sobbed wordlessly into his shoulder, hating herself for breaking down like this. But then he felt so good and warm and safe when he held her in his arms. It was so hard not to respond to him.

Then he tilted her face up and kissed her eyelids, her cheeks, her hair, wiping the tears away. His lips met hers for a long, hard kiss and she could feel her pulse beginning to race. It almost felt like he meant it, like he really did care. He showered kisses down her neck until the breath caught in her throat. If she didn't stop him soon, this would get completely out of hand. Despite her intentions, she could feel herself moisten when she thought about what that could mean.

But she made herself pull away and catch his face in her hands. Looking into his big brown eyes, she forced the words out. "No, wait, Danny. There's more. I'm seeing someone else."

"Are you now? And what's he got that I don't have?" His jaw tightened and she could see the hurt in his eyes. But he still held her close, one hand sliding down her skirt to cup her ass and pull her up even closer to him. A sharp heat went through her and she could feel him harden, feel herself begin to ache with need.

Oh, this is not good. She was supposed to be long over him, long past memories of what his body felt like against hers. Not responding like this. Gasping, she managed to respond, "She. I'm leaving you for Elaine."

His dark blond eyebrows rose in surprise but he didn't let her go. "Really? Well, I can think of quite a few things that she's got that I don't. Which of them won your heart, love?"

Karen stopped crying and wondered what to say next. After eight years together, he deserved an explanation. "She pays attention to me, Danny. I can really talk to her." *And she knows what I need better than you ever did.* A shiver went through her as she imagined Elaine's tongue on her clit, coaxing and caressing until she couldn't stop coming. A drop of moisture ran down the inside of her leg and she bit her lip to hold back a tiny moan. Danny. Think about Danny, not Elaine, she told herself sternly.

He was still looking at her, sad brown eyes inches from hers. She couldn't help noticing that his grip was tightening, not loosening up, while she looked for a way to let him down a little easier. His hand stroked its way over her ass and down her thigh so gently that she almost didn't notice it. Almost, but not quite. Her breath caught in her throat and she whispered something incoherent about still loving him.

His hand went up her skirt and between her legs in a single motion, hard fingers shoving her lace panties inside her. A sound somewhere between a groan and a yelp tore itself from her lips and she pushed feebly against his shoulders. Her body was betraying her and she could feel herself hot and wet against his fingers, soaking the lace crotch of her pants. The lace irritated her clit, making it hard to think clearly. Danny ran his tongue down her neck from her jaw to her cleavage and thrust his fingers deeper inside her. "You were saying," he prompted.

She could feel the desk behind her now, pressing into her thighs and she imagined what it would be like to have him take her right there. He would have done that back when they were first married, back before he got a private office and an assistant. Unthinking, she moaned and buried her fingers in his hair.

Danny tugged his wet fingers out of her and forced her back into an almost painful arch, thrusting her hardened nipples up towards his mouth. He sucked on one, slowly tonguing it through the fabric of her shirt until her whole body trembled. "We were having a discussion, Karen, my love. You were telling me why you were going to leave me for Elaine."

She tried to imagine pushing him away, walking out before this went any further. It was getting harder to picture by the second. That was when he reached up with both hands and ripped her shirt open, buttons flying in all directions. She yelped and grabbed at the tatters of the silky shirt. *What did he think he was doing? I love this shirt.* She tried to look indignant, shocked at this casual brutality.

Danny continued playing with her nipples through the thin lace of her bra. "And I see you came dressed to leave me today, darling. I like the bra almost as much as the panties. Does it unfasten in the front? Ah yes, I see it does."

His teeth closed on her nipple with a hard nip and she yelped, "She . . . she spanks me." Ooops. She hadn't meant to tell him that, hadn't meant to let anything slip about their sex life at all. But then she hadn't expected his hand up her skirt or his mouth on her breast. He knew her body so well it was clear he meant to exploit every nerve ending, every weakness. And she was prepared to let him do it. *It's goodbye, after all. Elaine would understand that. Wouldn't she?*

"Really? I didn't realize you were kinky, darling. But all you had to do was ask, sweetheart. Remember that time you wore your old cheerleading uniform during the Superbowl? You seemed perfectly happy with my performance then." He tugged her panties up sharply so that they pressed in a tight line from her clit to her asshole. "But perhaps you were just faking it." His other hand trailed unexpectedly gentle fingers over her breast and down to the top of her skirt.

"No. I mean yes. It was so hot but, Danny, that was a long time ago." The words tumbled out of her while her hands seemed to have a will of their own. She found she had loosened his tie and was unbuttoning his shirt without even thinking about it. He picked her up and sat her on the edge of the desk while she frantically tugged his shirt out of his pants, her fingers flying past button after button.

She had started to unfasten his belt buckle before he spoke again. "You're right, love, it has been entirely too long." He pulled her thighs up to his hips as he spoke, letting her feel his hard length against her wet pussy. "But I think you've got some responsibility here too. You might have told me what you wanted, been a bit more assertive about seducing me." He reached under her skirt and pulled down her panties, tugging them off over her heels with practised ease. "Ooooh. Did she shave you, too?"

Karen nodded and Danny stepped back. For the first time since she had come in, he looked angry. Also very, very hard and very hot. Karen barely held back the impulse to drop to her knees in front of him and take him into her mouth. Instead she tried to tug her torn blouse closed as he walked around behind her to sit in his chair.

"Come here, Karen." It was not a tone that she could disobey and she stood up on shaky legs to walk to his side. "You know how much I wanted you to do that for me and you always said no, didn't you?" She looked down at the industrial carpet and curved one high-heel inwards before she nodded. "Now pull up your skirt and let me see whether I like it or not."

She vaguely remembered that she had come here to do something else and this wasn't it. But her hands found the edge of her skirt and pulled it upwards anyway. Danny ran his hand lightly over her bare skin, then leaned over to plant a kiss just above her throbbing clit. Karen didn't think she could stand much more. Elaine would have to buy a cat-o'-nine-tails to punish her enough for today. Danny's voice broke into her thoughts. "You've been a very bad girl, haven't you, Karen?"

Her head shot up and she gave him a deer in the headlights stare. This was how Elaine always started out. A single drop ran from her aching pussy down the bare skin of her leg, followed by another. She nodded at Danny as if her head was attached to strings. How had he known? He reached out and caught a drop of her moist desire on his fingertips. Then his fingers were at her lips, insistent with the scent of her longing. She licked her juices from his skin and trembled.

"Assume the position." Danny's voice barked like it belonged to someone else. Unthinking, she stepped forwards and bent over his legs, bracing her hands on the rough carpet to keep her balance. He had never been like this before, never shown her any sign that he would be interested in the kind of things she and Elaine did together. Where, she wondered, was he learning all this?

The sharp sting of his hand on her bare buttocks brought her back. "Are you sorry that you never shaved your pussy for me?" She hesitated and his hand cracked down even harder.

"Yes!" she wailed, not meaning a bit of it. It was different with Elaine. She remembered those deft fingers shaving her down to the skin as her lover slipped her tongue inside her between each pass with the razor. She never would have trusted Danny to do that.

His hand fell again. "I don't believe you. Why don't you tell me you don't love me any more instead?"

That she could do. "I . . ." Smack! She was going to come soon, she could feel it. Just a little pressure on her clit would send her over the edge. Smack! "Don't love . . ." Smack! The skin on her buttocks burned and she was gasping for air. She squirmed desperately against him, wanting him inside her now, filling that awful emptiness. Smack! Smack! Smack! He had fallen into a rhythm now and she had forgotten what she was saying.

He twined his fingers into her and yanked her head back up, twisting it awkwardly so she was looking at him. The angle hurt her neck while his hand kept meeting her flesh, punishingly hard. But it was nothing more than she deserved. She had been very bad, sneaking around with Elaine behind his back and lying to him. Once she even squeezed into the cheerleading uniform for Elaine and let her fuck her ass like she never let Danny do. It took a minute before she realized that she had spoken that thought out loud.

There was a pause and she could see his jaw set in a hard line. He stuck his fingers inside her while she moaned and thrust back against them. Then he began working one finger up her asshole, all the while holding her face twisted upwards with his free hand. "Since it may well be my last chance, I'd better take advantage of this opportunity. Don't you agree, dear?"

She closed her eyes, her hips rolling against his thighs as if he was all she wanted in the whole world. His breath was ragged now and she smiled to hear it. But it wasn't supposed to be like this. She was supposed to be mature and calm and on her way out the door by now. How had she ended up here?

Smack! His hand met her quivering flesh hard again and again. Oh yes, she remembered now. He stopped to drive a finger up her ass, then two. She lost count after that, lost count of the number of times she apologized and begged him to fuck her. She even came once, shaking wildly over his thighs, his fingers in her ass and her flesh burning with the prints of his palm.

That must have been when the door opened and someone came in. Someone who sat down in the chair on the other side of the desk and watched them. Karen tried to look up but the desk blocked her view. "Tell me again that you're not leaving me." Danny's voice was full of menace and the delicious promise of unknown punishments to come.

She melted against him, frantic to feel him inside her. For the next few moments, she begged, she pleaded, she said anything he wanted to hear. She was still babbling when he pushed her off his legs so she dropped to the floor on her hands and knees. He rolled the chair away from her, an odd smile on his face. She followed him, not bothering to stand up, not sure her legs would hold her if she did until he stopped moving and she found herself looking up at Elaine.

Oh shit. "I'm sorry, I . . ." That was when she noticed Elaine's hands were inside her panties, rubbing frantically while she watched them from under half-closed lids.

"Get over there and get busy, Karen. I want to see your tongue on her clit while I fuck your ass. If this is to be our last evening together, you're going to fulfil every fantasy I have and I'm going to enjoy it to the maximum. You want to make that happen for me, don't you, love? Your little farewell gift?" Danny leaned over so his face was inches from hers, his fingers rolling one of her nipples.

Karen jerked away and sat up. Something didn't feel right. "You two set me up, didn't you? None of this was real." She glared first at Danny then at Elaine.

Elaine sat up, a peculiar smile curving her full lips. "My promotion came through today and Danny and I had a little talk. We came to an . . . arrangement. Do you really want to choose between us, love? Danny was betting that you didn't and it looks like he was right. You certainly looked like you were having fun."

Karen scowled. "That's not really the point . . ."

"Isn't it?" Danny was on the floor next to her now, trailing his fingers over the bare skin of her exposed thigh. "I was thinking that you should leave me more often, at least once we're done here. I really need to be done right now. Don't you, darling?" He leaned in close, his lips at her ear making the breath catch in her throat. When she didn't push him away, he trailed his tongue down her neck.

Karen looked up at Elaine, panting slightly through open lips. Could she really have both of them? Elaine dropped to all fours from the chair, like a cat, and moved gracefully across the carpet to Karen's side. Without saying a word, she devoured Karen's lips in a savage kiss that burned away all resistance. "Yes," Karen murmured when they came up for air.

Then she was between Elaine's legs, licking her honeyed sweetness while Danny drove himself inside her. Now it was her tongue coaxing her lover into ecstatic moans, into coming hard, thighs shaking around her head. Danny came moments later, thrusting himself into her until she spasmed around him, shaking and moaning until they all collapsed into a sweaty contented heap.

"I think I'd like to be the straying spouse next time," Elaine murmured in Karen's ear as Danny's fingers found her clit again. Karen was too happy to argue.

Our Friend in Alaska

Olivia London

Funny, the things you remember.

Years ago, when my husband Trevor was still my boyfriend and we were living in San Francisco (a far wilder cry from the hinterland hamlet we reside in now), my man talked me into fucking his best friend. The things we do for love!

I was giving my boyfriend a hand job one lusty night when he stopped me and said, "Erica, honey. I saw the way you looked at Henry when he helped us move into this overpriced apartment. You were practically salivating watching the tectonic shifts of his muscles as he loaded our boxes into the truck. When you handed him a glass of lemonade, you touched his forearm and stroked his fingers. And I sure noticed the way Henry eyeballed your curves. Would you ever consider a threesome?"

I sat up in bed and said, "For the record, I certainly did *not* stroke his fingers. I just wanted to make sure the glass was secure in his hand. Every time we go out partying with him, he spills a drink . . . or two. You know what a klutz he is."

Trev smiled his wicked smile and pointed his cock at me like a microphone. "You still didn't answer my question, love. Would you or wouldn't you?"

Just glancing at my lover's countenance was enough to arouse interest in anything. He had the kind of face that could get a girl peeling off her panties faster than she could change lanes on a highway at dawn. His grey-blue eyes were always alert with a passion for learning new things, which gave women the impression he was sensitive. I was drawn to his sensitive nature, too, but fortunately Trev had enough push in him to take control in the bedroom and his erotic techniques could please even the most demanding connoisseur of love. Just as in any relationship, we'd had our ups and downs, but even though we had been together since college days, I never wanted anyone else. I already had just who I wanted to turn to for a night of arrant bliss. Sure, a woman has fantasies that can put her mind through the darkest labyrinths of desire, but those are reserved for down times at work and blocking out surly faces on commuter trains. Fantasies are the elixir that keeps our fragile psyches from spilling into aisles and tripping people up with our messy wants.

I never thought I'd be tempted to blur the line between fantasy and reality.

When Trev and I watched porn together, we'd always pick a two-guys-and-a-girl scenario and when I was home alone, masturbating, I'd often imagine a third shadowy figure invading our bed. In the latter event, the interloper was typically a stranger who would give me a sound spanking while my boyfriend fondled his erection. One recurring vision I had was of being forced to kneel in front of two men, alternately sucking their cocks until one man came on my chest and the other jacked off on my belly. Just closing my eyes and thinking of more than one hard-on at my disposal was enough to make me wet.

"Hey, where are you?" Trev asked, bringing me back to the present. God, he was gorgeous. He still had the rugged good looks of a hiker though he knew better than to drag me down a trail. Our only fight occurred when he convinced me how fun mountain climbing would be. I forget at what point I stopped breathing properly and started enumerating all the truly fun things we *could* be doing, like sipping cocktails at Vino's or watching movies naked, but things were said that would take a while to be unsaid. It didn't help that a pack of silver-haired seniors briskly passed us by, high-fiving one another in their use-it-or-lose-it momentum.

"I was just thinking about how into you I am. We've been through so much together. Do you really want to invite Henry into our bed?"

Trevor pulled me in for a hug and said, "We can go to his place. He lives alone, you know."

"You've discussed this with him?"

"Sure. If you're game, this Friday would work. Speaking of games, you get to make all the rules. I could just be a voyeur or an active participant. But, reason I'm even asking you to consider this is that Hen says he's had it with city life. The poor sod's moving to Alaska of all places. Moving next week. So it would be a nice farewell gift . . ."

"Yeah, I get it. We screw each other's brains to heaven and back then forget it ever happened. Henry in Alaska, though – I can't picture it."

Trev guided my hand back to his erection and I instantly wondered what Henry's cock looked like. There was the penis before me and the phantom penis, the doppelganger dick. No point in choosing if I was being offered both.

The night of the assignation arrived and I was afraid my boyfriend would notice the extra care I took with my appearance. I couldn't help myself; I was stepping into an erotic wonderland and I wanted to look my best. I brushed my long hair until it shined like chrome and painted my nails oxblood red. My dress wrapped around my body like a winding road of tulle, the material taking to each curve with the smoothest glides and motions. My silk-stockinged feet gladly conformed to the arches of a pair of very expensive stilettos. The delicate lace panties I wore were begging to be yanked off, and, with one muscular pull, they could be. I was ready. More than ready for a phallic overload.

"Wow, you look great," Trev said, backing me against the wall in our hallway and roaming his hands over my breasts and hips. "This is going to be some night."

"So do you. Look great, that is. I love that madras shirt you're wearing. Your casually elegant attire always works for me."

A half-foot taller than me, Trev dipped his head down for a kiss and rattled his keys in an excited fashion. "Well, let's not keep the good man waiting."

Soon we were knocking on Henry's door in Pacific Heights, banging on the door, really. It was always a mystery how our friend could afford an apartment in such a tony neighbourhood, but Trev and I figured that was Henry's business. Our friend had been a house painter for many years, putting himself through college working odd jobs. He was the most interesting, well-read person we had ever met but, for some reason, Henry just never found his niche. The poor guy deserved a break. He certainly deserved to get laid.

When the city's most vaguely employed citizen opened his door, I did a double take. Who was this man?

"Come on in, folks. Let me introduce you to the new Henry." Gone were the painter's long black locks and earrings festooned to his left lobe. No more jewellery. No more hair.

"You shaved your head!" I exclaimed, stating the obvious. It was a good change for him, only it made him look employed, which I knew he wasn't.

Trev and Henry shook hands then, possibly remembering what the night was about, gave each other a hug. Soft jazz was playing in the background, Sade's sex in a voice it sounded like, and I unconsciously started to sway on my stilts. Henry led me by the hand to his wine rack and let me pick out something suitable for our soiree. I picked a grand Merlot.

The first bottle of wine was strictly for conversation and mood setting. Henry spoke of his plans to work on a fishing boat even though he was a resolute meat and potatoes type. In fact, Trev and I could never get Hen to join us for dinner at a seafood restaurant. Our friend was truly a mystery wrapped in an enigma folded into a hand towel.

Halfway into our second bottle of Merlot, I kicked off my heels and let my feet do a little dance. Henry caught one of my peds and began massaging it in expert circular motions. He had graduated from massage school but never got licensed or put up a shingle. Another topic best avoided. As if on cue, Trev started massaging my other foot and I let my head drop on to the sofa as body and soul melted into undulating waves of relaxation.

"Don't get too relaxed," Trev said, then covered my mouth with a deep kiss. When he pulled away, I noticed his trousers were unzipped and his cock was standing sentinel for duty. Without even thinking about it, I went down on him, taking in the length of his penis with long pulls and pausing now and then to canoodle with the bulb on top. A driblet of pre-come glistened at the slit like a dollop of dressing. Perfect complement to every meal.

Suddenly, Henry was taking my face in his hands and moving my mouth to his fully erect penis and I heard him say, "Sure this is OK? With both of you, I mean?" It sounded as if his voice travelled from the end of a tunnel.

It must have been fine with Trev who was now slowly stroking his hard-on and smiling in a blissed-out sort of way. I had to put Henry at ease and what better way than with a blow job?

Taking Henry's cock for conspicuous consumption, while listening to the slapping sounds my boyfriend's hand made as he jerked off and watched, was almost more than I could handle. I kissed Henry's balls, licked the slope of his shaft then pursed my lips around the tip before sucking him all in, all the way down, until it seemed that his cock was exuding out of my very pores. Satisfying as it was to hear Henry moan and curse with pleasure, I ached to have that cock pounding me between my damp thighs.

As if reading my thoughts, Henry guided me to a supine position and pushed his throbbing cock into my wet cunt. Damn, it felt good. Each thrust took my breath away until he had my pussy pinned right where he wanted it and we settled into a rocking rhythm.

I wasn't one to complain, but missionary-style sex sure gets tired fast, so I was secretly grateful when Trev let slip, "Hey, Hen. Erica prefers to be taken from behind."

"Is that right?" our buddy asked.

"Oh, yeah," I said, slightly abashed.

Henry pulled out so I could reposition myself on my hands and knees. For ballast, I sunk my hands in a space between the sofa cushions. I looked over at Trev, who was still smiling and stroking himself, and blew him a kiss. Henry's first thrust in the new position absorbed all the moisture I had left and I may have mentioned how much tighter this posture makes me as I heard Henry bark with mounting excitement. He sped up his delivery while Trev exploded, jacking off on his friend's shoulder and biceps, spackling my hip with a bit of splooge.

Henry's orgasm was quite intense, as was my own. The three of us fell into a heap on the floor and started laughing then crying then laughing some more. We all agreed another dose of wine was in order, but that first a shower would be nice.

Our friend had an old-fashioned tub with a rust stain forming an orange moustache around the drain, but it was a sizeable porcelain beauty and it was in that shower where a long-time fantasy of mine came true. The three of us were clowning around and soaping each other up, when, on a whim, I sat on the edge of the tub and waited for the guys to rinse off. Before anyone could step on a bath mat, I had Henry's cock in my mouth again, only this time just for a moment. I turned my head a notch to suck down Trev's cock then alternated back and forth, going down on two magnificent cocks, listening to the appreciative murmurs of friend and lover as their penile fluids escalated towards fruition. Trevor shot his load all over my breasts. Hen took longer to come but come he did all over my lap and knees. I looked down and was glad I had trimmed my coffee-brown pubic hair that morning. The hair on my head is coffee-coloured too, and Trev liked to call me his ever lovin' cup of cappuccino.

We were all spent after that . . . and starving. Henry suggested going downtown for burgers then remembered my little black cocktail dress. He frowned a little. He disliked going to fancy places . . . unless Trevor was paying.

"Let's grab something in North Beach," Trev suggested, adding, "My treat."

Still scowling, Henry said, "I'd rather we just stay in and order a pizza." So that's what we did.

Despite all the sexual festivities of the evening, I couldn't imagine eating a slice of pepperoni and cheese wearing just my panties and bra. And my dress seemed content where it was scooped into a black puddle near a sofa cushion. Henry went to his room and returned with a long T-shirt for me to wear.

Now it was Trevor's turn to scowl because screwing like mad is one thing, but letting your girl wear another man's comfortable article of apparel is another matter. It's the mundane intimacies that always pose a threat.

Finally, I wrapped myself in a sheet and we sat cross-legged on the hardwood floor with its tasteful brocade carpet and discussed Henry's plans.

"Yeah, well. That Alaska business is all up in the air. San Francisco is where it is . . . where it's always been for me." Henry's face filtered an expression of such unrequited longing that I had to look away.

"Not if you're broke, man. Look, you need to go where the money is. You said someone in Juneau offered you a job and—"

"Anchorage," Henry spat, breaking his friend off. "And all I'm saying is: nothing in this world is ever for certain. Yesterday, I wanted to move to Alaska. Today, I think I might be in love with your girlfriend. Hell, Erica and I might even take off for the wilderness together. Live off the land like that kid in . . . what's that book called? *Into the Wild.* Yeah, like that. How 'bout it, Erica?"

"Oh, Henry. I thought you understood this was a one-time thing. We go way back, but you don't even know me well enough to know I'm not the outdoorsy type."

"She gets winded when we're out grocery shopping."

"Stop it, Trev. And I'm in love with Trevor, your best friend. Hello!"

"Because he's successful."

"How dare you say something like that to me, Hen. Trev has helped you financially through all kinds of creative transitions. I never begrudged that because I think you're a special person. I've never once had a negative thought about you. I thought we were all friends. Good friends. Close enough to fulfil each other's wildest fantasies."

Henry dropped his tonsured head into his hands and sat there thinking for a spell. When he looked up, he said, "You're right. You and Trevor have been the best buddies I ever had, seeing me through messes when no one else would give me the time of day, and here I am trying to spoil it. Sorry."

Trev slapped his friend on the shoulder. "No need to apologise, man."

Trevor always has been quick to forgive, one of the many reasons I fell in love with him. We finished our pizza in amiable silence and went home.

Months later, Trevor and I received a postcard from Anchorage with nothing written on it. Of course it had to be from Henry, but we thought it strange he didn't even sign his name. A year later we received a card from Portland, Oregon. It too was blank. A year after that, Trevor and I left San Francisco, never to return, not that we didn't want to. Real life has a way of kicking in and taking over. We got married and moved to the Midwest to be near Trev's family. Now, the only thing we fantasize about is having a day off from our manifold obligations. Every once in a while though, Trev will look at me with a hint of mischief in his eye and say, "I wonder what ever happened to our friend in Alaska?"

In The Name Of . . .

Isabelle Gray

It started with a black Sharpie pen, as we were lying in bed, drowsy and naked, watching TV. Theo and I had just finished making love, and he was basking in the well-deserved glow of his sexual prowess. "I wonder if I could write your name along the length of my cock," he mused. "Not like, when I'm just getting out of the shower, but if my cock was really long and hard, right before we fuck."

I shrugged, and reached for the Sharpie on my end table. Sliding my hand between the sheet and our bodies, down his soft stomach to his cock, I nibbled on his ear. "Let's give it a try," I said.

It took a few tries to get it right. That first night, fumbling in the blue glow from the television, Theo used large, widely spaced lettering, and could only get half my name along the length of his cock. This initial defeat, however, did not deter him. It, in fact, made this whole thing a quest. Given his days as a teenager, when a good time was playing Dungeons & Dragons, there was nothing Theo loved more than a quest. He would persevere. I would humour him.

We revisited the subject a few days later, while I was in my office grading papers and Theo was sitting on the edge of my desk, playing with the pens and other detritus in my pencil cup. As I scribbled notes in margins and wrote "Great job", over and over, Theo unbuttoned his jeans, and started jerking off. He found a red marker and pulled the cap off with his teeth. Once his cock had achieved what he deemed the appropriate level of length and rigidity, he began, in

smaller script this time, to write my name along the length
of his cock.

I paused, watching him over the top of the paper I was
reading. "You're starting too far from the base," I muttered.
He shook his head, but ultimately, I was right. By the time he
reached the tip, giggling, because the felt of the marker tickled,
he had three letters left. I bit my lower lip and remained quiet,
but I was thinking, I told you so.

When I crawled into bed later that night, Theo was waiting
with a blue marker and, in tiny script, he was writing my
name on the opposite side of his cock. He accomplished his
task, but the letters were so tiny that the overall effect was
underwhelming. I kissed the tip of his nose, before turning
the lights out. "That's sweet, honey," I told him. He turned
away from me, his shoulder muscles tight with irritation, his
cock covered in blue and red ink. My man looked so sad
and defeated that I closed the space between us, pressing my
breasts against his back. I laid a line of kisses across his broad
shoulders. He pretended to ignore me until I slid my hand
up his chest, lightly squeezing his nipples between my fingers,
throwing my left leg over his. Reluctantly, he turned towards
me, his lips turned down in a small pout. I placed a kiss just left
of his lips, then crawled on top of his chest. I slid my tongue
between his lips and slowly lowered myself on to his cock and
apologized properly.

Theo finally got it right when I took matters into my own
hands. Straddling his thighs, and using a purple marker, my
choice this time, I carefully wrote "I S A B E L L E" with
room to spare. When I was done, I took a moment to admire
my handiwork, letting the ink dry, and then I wrapped my
lips around the tip of Theo's cock, suckling softly, and tasted
a thin sliver of salty pre-come. I worked my way down the
shaft, humming so my lips vibrated, until my lips were pressed
against his groin. My throat muscles quivered in protest.

Theo groaned gleefully. "I have no idea why this turns me
on so much," he said.

I tried to reply, but I was occupied and had long ago learned
not to talk with my mouth full. He slid his hands through

my hair and began rocking his hips back and forth. I could imagine the smug expression on his face as he stood there, the muscles in his thighs flexing against my cheeks as he made me swallow my own name.

Sooner than later, I was ready to up the ante. Writing my name on Theo's cock in different colours, across different areas, with different orientations was well and good, but there wasn't a lot at stake. It was an exquisite secret that deserved an audience. Over coffee at a café near the campus where I taught, I stared across the table at Theo, running my sandalled foot up and down his calf. I wondered, not for the first time, what it would be like to see him with another woman. I wanted to see if I could go through with it, surrender that part of myself for a night, see if he would come back to me, see what he would look like thinking of me while fucking her. It was a dangerous idea – such things rarely end well – but I couldn't help myself.

"What are you thinking?" he asked.

I took a sip of my coffee, frowning at the bitter taste, and then I shared my suspect thoughts. Theo coughed and blushed, a light red rising from his neck up through the dirty blond roots at his forehead. He turned his head to the side in that endearing way he does when he's nervous and quickly looked around to make sure no one was listening.

"How do you come up with these ideas?"

I smiled, winked and took another sip of coffee.

For a few weeks, Theo dismissed my idea, but my investment in the notion increased with each passing day. I began to look at every woman who crossed my path in a new light. Theo always claimed that he didn't have a type, but even a casual inspection of the photo album where he kept pictures of his exes demonstrated a theme. It was obvious that he liked his women short, with dark hair, blue eyes and just a touch of crazy. In restaurants, I would point out potential candidates and Theo would either blush, or roll his eyes. While we were having sex, I would offer suggestions from the eligible pool of our mutual acquaintances. When I was at the gym, hunched over the handrail of the elliptical trainer, trying not to pass out, I would stare down saucy minxes bending over yoga balls or stretching out on the mats, imagining what my husband's long body would look like bent over theirs.

Once I had found my "It Girl", I surprised Theo at work, slipping into his office and locking the door behind me. He grinned at me from behind his desk and loosened his tie. "I do love a working man," I drawled as I inched around his desk. Theo tapped his desk, and closed the file he had been reading.

"It's a matter of approach."

"What is?"

"You know."

Theo leaned back in his chair, crossing his fingers behind his head. I stood behind him, massaging his shoulders, flicking my tongue against his ear. "I've found her and now, it's only a matter of approach."

Theo opened his mouth, but I turned his chair around so he was facing me and pressed two fingers to his lips. "Shhh," I said. I dropped my coat and, turning his chair as I walked, I hopped up on his desk, ignoring the papers and pens and the half-empty coffee mug. I slid my shoes off and perched my heels against his shoulders. "We should make the most of your lunch break."

Theo arched an eyebrow, and slid my skirt up around my hips. He hooked his fingers around the waistband of my G-string and slid it down until it was around one ankle. He slid those same fingers inside my cunt and I gritted my teeth, wrapping my ankles around his neck and pulling him closer.

"Tell me I'm right," I said.

"Right about?" Theo began licking my clit, twisting his fingers around in a languorous circle.

"Tell me I'm right that it's fucking hot that your boss is thirty feet away and your wife is spread open on your desk."

Theo groaned softly and stood, then quickly unbuttoned his slacks. I slid my legs around his waist, and he placed his hands on my shoulders, thrusting his cock inside me, hard and deep.

"Tell me I'm right," I repeated.

Theo pulled me up and wrapped his arms around me. He clasped the back of my neck as he kissed me, fucking me fast and dirty. I clenched my cunt muscles and sank my teeth into his neck.

"You're going to leave a mark," he gasped.

I released my grip. "Tell me I'm right."

Theo's hips started rocking faster and then he was coming, his breathing slightly ragged. "You're right," he said, over and over.

I held him inside me, enjoying the moment, enjoying the heat of his body, and the shiver down my spine. "That's all I'm saying."

At home that evening, Theo sat down next to me on the couch, and began tapping his fingers against his thigh. "So who is she?"

Her name was Francesca, and we had grown up in the same Italian neighbourhood in Brooklyn. Back then, she wasn't much to look at, and admittedly, neither was I, but now, she was something else – deep olive skin, icy blue eyes and jet-black hair that cascaded down her back. Her features were sharp and angular in places, round and inviting in others. She wasn't perfect looking, her eyes set far apart, her lower lip slightly crooked, but she had a crafty smile, a loud laugh and ass for days. These were all things Theo would enjoy and I hoped she would be up for it – we were both recovering Catholic school girls after all. Francesca and I got together for drinks every couple of weeks, so it wasn't extraordinary when I invited her to our place for dinner the following weekend.

I served veal saltimbocca, roasted green beans, a Caesar salad and a good Pinot Noir we had picked up in wine country last year. Francesca raved about my cooking, regaled us with a story about a disastrous blind date, and eventually noticed that neither Theo nor I were saying much. "What's up with you two?" she asked.

Theo looked at me, his eyes wide. I set my fork down. "Rather than be coy, I'll just come out with it. I'd love to watch my husband fuck you," I said. "A one-time thing."

Francesca coughed, and refilled her wine glass. "You always were crazy, Izzy."

Theo reached for my hand, and I grasped his fingers, tightly. "Yes, but I'm not kidding."

Francesca nodded, and traced the rim of her wine glass.
"When?"

I cocked my head to the side. "Now?"

I sat in the armchair in the dark corner of our bedroom,
wearing only my panties. I wanted it that way – to watch him
without him watching me. I wanted him to forget I was there,
lose himself until I found him again. There were candles on the
end tables and the dresser – they would add to the mood, we
had decided. Francesca brought her wine glass with her and
sat on the edge of our bed, taking long, steady sips until there
was none left. She unbuttoned her blouse, tossing it towards
the doorway, and shimmied out of her jeans. In the dim light
of the room, I felt a moment's panic as I took in her ample
décolletage and her flat stomach, and the ass that wouldn't
quit. Theo stood behind her, cupping her ass in his hands
and squeezing. Then Francesca slid towards the centre of the
bed, crossing one leg over the other as she leaned back. Theo
undressed quietly, and brought me the Sharpie, hesitating as
he handed it to me. I pressed the palm of my hand against
his heart then wrote my name on his cock. I wrote slowly and
carefully, pressing the marker firmly into his skin. He leaned
down and kissed my forehead, then I turned him around, and
sank into the softness of my chair. I couldn't watch him walk
away. I closed my eyes and ignored the tightness in my chest.

Theo stood at the end of the bed and shyly crawled up until
he was kneeling between Francesca's legs.

"I can't believe we're about to do this," she said.

Theo looked back in my direction. "Neither can I."

He placed his hands between her calves, sliding them up
to her inner thighs as he spread her legs. He kissed her navel
and dragged his tongue along the undersides of her breasts.
When he wrapped his mouth around each of Francesca's
nipples, sucking loudly, she grabbed the sheets beneath her,
drawing her fingers into loose fists. Blindly, Theo reached for
the end table, where earlier he had set a condom. He ripped
the package open with his teeth, and Francesca sat up on her
elbows, helping him slide the condom over his cock. She smiled

at him, her shoulders relaxing, and slid a long, manicured finger into Theo's mouth. He groaned – he loves that sort of thing – and, holding Francesca's wrist, he pulled each of her fingers into his mouth one at a time, then placed a kiss on the inside of her wrist.

I leaned forwards in my seat, my chest growing tighter still, my throat dry, my eyes curiously damp and my pussy on fire.

Francesca sighed and slowly rolled over on her stomach. She smiled back at Theo – an unexpected, surprising and perfect erotic gesture. She arched her back, her perfect ass high in the air. Theo slapped it lightly. Francesca wiggled. "Don't be shy," she said. Theo splayed both hands across Francesca's ass, sliding his thumbs between her ass cheeks, before slapping her ass again, harder this time. "That's what I'm talking about," she encouraged. Theo alternated between smacking Francesca's ass and massaging her backside with his fingers until her skin was bright red, and her thighs were quivering.

She looked at Theo over her shoulder and he paused long enough to kiss her, a crushing, sloppy, hungry kiss that forced me to look away. Francesca reached for him and he worked his cock inside her, my name sliding into another woman's cunt one letter at a time. I could hear how wet she was. The bitch was enjoying this. So was I. I also entertained the idea of each of the letters of my name circulating through her bloodstream and wrapping themselves around her throat, constricting with each breath and moan until she went silent.

At first, Theo teased Francesca, filling her to the hilt, waiting, sliding all the way out, rubbing the tip of his cock along the curve of her pussy before filling her again. He turned to me again, smiling, tapped his heart and pointed to me. Francesca's legs spread wider. She rocked back against my husband, urging him to stop playing games. "Fuck me," she said harshly. Theo grabbed hold of her waist and shoved his cock forwards, deep and hard. They found a rhythm, the two of them, their bodies slapping together wetly, then coming apart, and back together again. Theo grabbed her hair and pulled Francesca's head back, her neck muscles straining. He slid his tongue in her mouth, groaning, the sound, I imagined, echoing into her chest and waiting there. He fucked her harder, the sound of her desire growing slicker, looser, my name reaching further into her body. I sat perfectly still, my jaw aching. My teeth had been clenched for some time. They looked good together – his pale skin against her darker tones, his leanness where she was round, their thighs pressed together, the undulating of their bodies moving in time, their eyes closed, mouths open. I felt myself disappearing into the walls of our home, the rest of the world falling away. And I felt the painful and intense pleasure of watching something I was not supposed to see. I hated myself for it.

"You like this, don't you?" Theo asked, punctuating each word with a slap on her ass. "You like it dirty."

"God, I do."

Francesca began moaning louder until she was practically shouting, her head and her long mane of black hair flying from side to side. She whispered, "I can't believe I'm going to come." She shrieked, once, and buried her head in a pillow, her body trembling. Theo kept fucking Francesca, steadily stroking her pussy with his cock. "I'm not stopping until I'm done," he said, lifting her hips higher. He fucked her until he came, his ass clenching as he gave her one final thrust, so hard that she slid up the bed, her head bouncing against the headboard. He lay on top of her for an uncomfortably long time, then rolled off when Francesca pushed him away and jumped out of bed. The room was filled with an awkward silence. I finally allowed myself to breathe deeply and pulled my knees to my chest, hugging myself.

Francesca started collecting her clothes. "I don't want to overstay my welcome," she said. "But that was wonderful."

Theo smiled, and wrapped a towel around his waist. Once Francesca had dressed and composed herself, he walked her to the door. When he returned to the bedroom, I had blown out all the candles and was standing near the window, watching Francesca drive away. I heard the snap of Theo removing his condom and the soft thud of it being tossed into the trashcan. I couldn't look at him, afraid of what I might see there, not even when he wrapped his arms around me from behind nor when he whispered, "I love you."

I reached back and squeezed his thigh. "I know."

"Are you angry?" he asked.

I shook my head, swallowing hard.

"You sure?"

I took his hand and pulled it around my waist, sliding it beneath the waistband of my panties. He parted my pussy lips with two fingers. I hissed, my clit throbbing and jealous and angry. I felt my wetness slide around his fingers while he stroked my clit. "What does this tell you?" I asked.

Remember This

Shanna Germain

I've had the pill for three weeks now. I keep it folded in an envelope in the nightstand next to my bed and, every evening, I take it out and hold it in my palm. It's so small, almost too small considering what it could do, what it will do, and it's a colour that's not quite blue, not quite grey. Sometimes I only hold it for a moment before I let it fall from my palm back into the envelope. Other times, like tonight, on the eve of my fiftieth birthday, I hold it for a long time, reading the single letter on it over and over. Neither Raina nor Maddox know I have the pill. They would try to get me to give it up, and I can't do that. Not to them. Not to me.

It's too early for me to even have this pill – there are only small signs. Forgetting where I put the keys, or how to make my famous anise cookies. Only once have I forgotten how to get home, back to this place that I love, but that was enough for me to make the appointment. They say I'm overreacting, that there's no way to make a diagnosis yet. Maybe. Maybe not. But I know they see it too. Already I'm forgetting. Not just recipes or directions or birthdays, but the things that really matter: how to strap on the harness that Raina likes so much, the way that Mad holds his balls up with one hand when I suck him, how I sound when I'm coming.

The forgetting runs in the women in my family like bad eyesight. My grandmother. Then my mom. At fifty, my mom didn't just forget things, she forgot herself. She forgot her quiet sense of humour, her acceptance of people, her love of the men she called the Dylan Boys, meaning the poet and the musician. In the end, she swore and raged and pinched.

I'm still holding the pill when I hear Raina come in. I drop it back into the envelope and slide it quickly under the pillows.

Downstairs, Raina slicks off her raincoat and stamps her feet on the rug. "Ana? Anabel?"

"Up here," I call. "In bed."

Raina laughs, her big horse laugh that comes from her belly and booms through the house. Such a little person to make such a big sound. "Of course you are."

It's true. All I want to do lately is fuck. Fuck and be fucked and then, finally, lie in our big wide bed with Raina on one side, Mad on the other. It's like my biological clock is ringing overtime, only it's not for having kids. It's for having orgasms, for having the taste of skin in my mouth, for the feeling of being filled once, twice, three times more.

I lean back against the pillow, listen to Raina's stockinged feet pitter-patting up the stairs. The smell of fall enters the room before she does. Her curly salt-and-pepper hair is damp with rain. "Sleeping?" she asks.

"Not with that loud-ass laugh of yours booming through the house," I say.

"Oh, I'm so sure," she says. Her eyebrows go up – she's caught sight of my new lingerie. A lacy bra that's almost blue, almost grey. I ordered it online and forgot what colour it was until I put it on this afternoon. "Nice," she says. "Birthday gift?"

"Do you like it?"

"Mmm . . ." She sits on the side of the bed and rubs her hands together. Where I am dark and tall and thin, Raina is white and short, shaped like an alabaster violin. Her hair, now more salt than pepper, seems the same colour as her washed-out blue eyes, as her pale skin. She has on a soft orange skirt that I like – one that looks like fall – and I slip one hand beneath the hem, find the top edge of her thigh-highs. Beneath my fingertips, the band is raised in some kind of pattern I can't make out.

She raises the hem of her skirt enough so I can see the top of them – it's some kind of flower – I can't remember the name – and I slip one finger beneath the fabric, feeling the cool of her skin. Raina shivers, maybe from my touch, maybe from the cold she's brought in with her.

"Fucking freezing and pissing out there, all at once," she says. "Lucky you're not out in it."

There's nothing to say to that, so we sit in the silence for a moment. Raina's hands make a fast, scritch-scritch noise as she tries to warm them. I love having her here. Mad and I asked her to move in, once, a long time ago, but she said no. And it's worked this way: me and Mad here; her in her little condo downtown, spending the weekends with us. Although, lately, it's been more than that. I wonder if her biological clock feels something too.

"How was your day?" She wants to know if I forgot anything, but she doesn't ask.

I reach up with my free hand and run my fingers along her eyebrows, notice a bit of grey there too. I don't tell her about the phone, how I tried to call Mad at work and got his old college office, the one he left years ago.

"Fine," I say. "Better now. Even better in about, oh, half an hour?"

She laughs again. It's so big it sounds like it belongs outside. "That when we're expecting the Mad-Dog?" She's called him that since the first time we all had sex, when he ground his teeth and nearly growled out an orgasm. Now we laugh about it, but still when she says it, I get a visual memory of us all that first time, playing like puppies in the big bed, how young we all were, how free. Raina's hair was down to her ass, and Mad had pulled it like reins while he was fucking her from behind. I hope I never forget the curve of her neck when he pulled her backwards into him. Or the way she moaned my name, beckoning me closer.

"Ana?" Raina prods me lightly with a finger.

"Hm?" I'm rolling down one of her thigh-highs, watching the white length of her thigh being revealed bit by bit. I like moments like this, when I don't even know what kind of underwear she's wearing – if any at all – but her thighs are bare and free. Exposed to me and my roving fingers.

"Mad-Dog? Coming soon, yes?" she asks again.

"Oh. Yes," I say. "Half an hour or so."

"Guess I have time for a warm-up shower then?" Raina asks.

I don't want her to leave me, now that she's here, but I nod.

She wiggles her cold fingers at me. "Jack Frost be-gone," she says. "Warm Raina be-back."

"Warm Raina," I say. "Sounds like the perfect weather for a vacation."

When she kisses the tip of my nose, her lips make me shiver all the way through.

Out of the shower, Raina is warm-warm and naked-soft against my back. She spoons me up in the hug of her arms, and we lie that way for a while. My ass fits against the front of her perfectly and her small, round breasts press into my back. She used my lotion, and it makes her smell like oranges and chocolate.

Smells. Lately, I want to smell everything that's possible to smell in the world, to hold it in my mind like the key to a dissolving door. I turn my head to sniff her shoulder, the clean crook of her armpit. I will the scents, those invisible pheromones or atoms or whatever they are, into my nose and brain. I pray for them to stay.

"Shall we wait for Mad?" Raina asks, her palms already sliding over my shoulders, down my arms. Her touch is soft, so unlike Mad's, the small callouses on her palms the only sharp edges at all.

"Since when do we wait for Mad?"

"Thought I'd ask," she says.

I reach around until the globe of her ass is in my hand, and pull her closer to me. "Don't," I say. Meaning: don't wait for Mad. Don't ask. Don't change the pattern. We've never waited for Mad. We're not about to start now.

She kisses the back of my neck, the side of my shoulder. Her hands find the edges of my bra. "Really nice," she whispers, as she tucks her fingers beneath the lace. She makes soft circles around my hardening nipples, and I move so she has better access.

"You should see the thong," I whisper.

"Later," she says, her voice heated around the puckered point of my skin. "Roll."

I roll to face her and then she's kissing me the way she does, her tongue meeting mine. She used my toothpaste too; she tastes like mint and the mochas she drinks. Soy something-or-others.

She unhooks the bra and pulls it off me. Then her fingers start again, circling my nipples until they crinkle.

"So, birthday girl, what's your pleasure?"

"It's all pleasure," I say and, for the moment, it's true. Her warm body here, the way she's touching me, the knowledge that Mad is due to join us any second.

"Hmph," she says. She slides down, runs her tongue along the underside of my breast and then down my stomach. She looks up at me as she moves her tongue between my thighs. I spread my legs to let her in. I'm not wet yet, but the tip of her tongue slipping between my lips is enough to start the flow. And then she presses, laps, opens me. I love the softness of her tongue and lips, how different from Mad's often scratchy chin. She presses, slow rasps of her flat tongue between me, before she edges the very tip lightly to my clit, round and round and round.

I'm so lost in the pleasure of Raina's strokes that I don't hear Mad come in. Suddenly, I open my eyes, and he's there, leaning against the doorjamb.

"Hi, ladies," he says, that half-smile punctuating his words as he watches us, hip canted to the wood.

After all this time, such a beautiful man. Ever the professor, just as he was when we met, dressed in jeans and a brown corduroy jacket. Glasses now, and a bit of salt in his hair too, just at the sides.

"Mad-Dog," Raina says. She slides up my body and takes my nipple in her mouth, then lets it out with a pop. "We started without you."

"You always do," he says. His laugh is the opposite of Raina's, more smile and air than noise.

"Come to bed," I say. I stretch out my hand and he steps forward to take it.

"Should I undress first?" he asks.

"Naw, we'll take care of it," Raina says.

"Shoes too?" he asks.

"No, no shoes," Raina says, between lollipop licks of my nipple. "Dirty."

"Thought that was the point," Mad says in a pouty voice that belies his age, but he sits on the edge of the bed and unties his shoes. "*You* get to wear shoes."

Raina raises her head from my breast. "Oh, yeah, Ana, remember that last pair of pumps I got? The red ones?"

Am I the only one who has a reaction to the word "remember"?

I am. Neither of them seems to notice. Raina has her mouth back around my nipple, teasing the skin with the edge of her teeth. Mad is slipping off his jacket and letting it fall to the floor.

"I remember," I say. They were gorgeous shoes. Not candy-apple red, but something darker. They didn't scream "sex", they whispered "fuck". Like candied apples that had been dragged through the dirt, scuffed and then lipsticked over in a dark bar. Watching Raina walk in them, strutting her stuff, that alone had turned me soaking wet, had forced me to sink a finger between my thighs while I watched.

"I remember," I say again, and my voice is soft. "Come to fucking bed, Mad. Fuck me. I'm tired of waiting."

"Yes, ma'am," he says.

Raina lets go of me, leaves me in the bed alone and strips off the rest of Mad's clothes. In seconds, they're back in bed, cold Mad on one side, warm Raina on the other. Mad takes his glasses off and puts them on the nightstand and then he kisses me, long and deep. He leans across me and kisses Raina too. I like to watch them. Knowing how they each kiss me, I wonder how they kiss each other.

Mad licks his lips like a cat. "You *did* start without me," he says. "You taste like Ana."

"So, what's your pleasure, birthday girl?" he asks.

Raina and I look at each other and giggle.

"What?" he says.

"Nothing," I say. It's not that funny, just the same phrase twice, like déjà vu, but I can't stop giggling. Raina's giggle rises up into her big belly laugh, and then we're all cracking up. I love the sound of us, bundled in the big bed, laughing at nothing much.

When the laughter quiets, I say, "Less laughing, more fucking, please."

"Who fucking?" Mad asks. His cock is already nudging my thigh.

"You fucking," I say to him. I touch the curls between Raina's thighs, and then touch my lips. "You, here, where I can lick you." What the hell? It's my birthday and I'm about to lose my mind, or at least one part of it. I can't have what I really want, but I can ask for something that's almost as good.

I lie on my back in the perfect centre of the bed, feeling like a pampered queen as Raina climbs over me, facing Mad, her thighs on either side of my face. I grab the curves of her ass, force her down until I can find her with my tongue. Taste, smell, taste. River water. Sugar water.

Mad slides his hand between my thighs. "You're so wet," he says. "I love that."

I'd say something, but my tongue is busy licking Raina. She gets a little wetter with each stroke. A little louder too.

Mad pushes my legs apart on the sheets, and rubs the tip of his cock against me. I wish I could see it, watch it harden all the way and enter me. He shaves his balls still, and I love the way they look, soft and vulnerable. For now, the feel of him will have to be enough. He slides in slow, slow, slow, until I'm taking my want out on Raina's pink folds, her tiny clit.

"Jesus, Mad, fuck her already," Raina says. "She's going to make me come."

It's a joke. They both know I like to go last, but Mad drives all the way in. He fucks me steady, long slow strokes that move my whole body on the bed. The kind that bring me to the border of orgasm without actually crossing it, a lazy pleasure that trickles through me, teasing, touching, until I'm gritting my teeth, begging in a hissed, grunted breath.

"Raina, you want?" he asks. I don't hear her answer, but in

a second, I feel her fingers playing at my clit. Each of Mad's thrusts captures Raina's fingers between him and me, locked to stillness before she can break free and start again. It's the just right rhythm of stroke and push, and I want to stay tucked between the two of them forever, locked in this perfect moment.

Mad's strokes become faster, until he's nearly lifting me off the bed and into Raina's waiting fingers. He's finding his voice, the long, low growl that means he's getting close.

Raina's clit tightens and hardens, becomes a small, round pink pill on the tip of my tongue.

"Oh," she says, like surprise. I always forget how quiet she is when she comes.

Her fingers go still, and I feel my clit clench like a heartbeat for a second before she starts up again. She floods my tongue with the taste of her, and I swallow, swallow, swallow, my cheeks wet with her salt. And then Mad goes off, growling and pulsing into me, the warmth of his pleasure filling me, contractions inside me that make my hips buck against him with a wild, unconscious frenzy.

I try to hold it back, the muscle memory, the drives against her fingers and his cock that will bring me to orgasm. I try to take a breath. Hold it, hold it, I think. I want to remember this moment, this sound. I want to hold on to this pre-coming, the way it works up inside me, gathering strength, buzzing its way through my brain and body.

But Raina's fingers work me, work me, around Mad's last final thrusts, and then it's me, my own cries muffled against Raina's skin. There it is, I think, even as I'm coming. That's the sound I make. That low, belly-grunting keen. That's me.

"Happy birthday, baby," Mad says a few moments later, once we can all breathe again, our chests rising and falling in the almost matched rhythm of those who take in the same air. He's on one side of me, Raina on the other. He strokes my belly with a touch so light it almost tickles.

"Yeah, happy birthday, Ana," Raina says. Her voice is sleepy. She'll nap now, like she always does after, and then deny it.

Mad and I will stay awake, talking about whatever it is old, married people talk about after sex.

I slide my arms out beneath both their pillows and settle in between them. Tucked under one pillow, my hand touches a piece of paper. It takes me a moment to remember what it is: the envelope. The pill.

There's another sound that comes then: a low choked sobbing sound. Is that me? I realize that it is. And I'm surprised at how much crying sounds like coming.

"You OK, baby?" Mad asks. He's put his glasses back on and he's leaning up, looking at me. "Want to talk about it?"

I crumble the envelope under the pillow. "No," I say. "I'm OK. Really." Maybe I am. Maybe I have everything I need here, right in the bed: two people who love me, who fuck me with joy and tenderness, and one small pill that gives me some kind of control.

Raina puts her head on my shoulder and brushes my hair behind my ears. "I brought a cake." Her voice is drowsy. "You can make a wish later."

I don't say anything, just close my eyes and inhale all of the pheromones and atoms I can. Oranges and warm skin and salt and sex. Remember this, I tell my body, my brain. Remember as long as you can. It is the only wish I can possibly make.

Wives

Kate Dominic

My Irish Catholic mother had firm opinions about marriage. She'd thump her coffee cup on the table and shake her head at the latest scandalous gossip. "A man who will cheat on his wife is 'a man who will cheat on his wife'! Any woman who thinks otherwise is a fool!" Given Mother's red-haired beauty and fiery temper, and the fact that she'd always managed to keep my wild and carefree father firmly entrenched in her bed, I'd always pretty much taken her opinions on marriage as gospel: men who cheated on their wives were not to be trusted.

I'd often been told I resembled my mother. Unfortunately, I was three weeks into a torrid affair with Jawid when I realized he was married. Not that I'd looked that hard. I'd met his "ex", Nasrin, at one of the routine hospital social functions a while back. She was a few years younger than Jawid, I guessed in her late twenties, and quite beautiful, with the deep, expressive eyes and lithe figure so typical of young Middle Eastern women. She was impeccably dressed in an emerald-green designer suit and exquisitely delicate jewellery that subtly enhanced her warm and ready smile. I'd been delighted to discover the wicked intellect and generous sense of humour she kept so well hidden under her quiet demeanor. I'd liked her.

But when Jawid said he was available – and I did ask him – I assuaged my quick flickerings of guilt with the knowledge that I wasn't a home-wrecker. It had been months since the last time he and I had worked together. Whatever had happened between Nasrin and him had been just that – between them. People's lives changed, especially those of talented doctors as handsome and personable as Jawid. I let myself conveniently forget all about Nasrin. And forgetting was easy.

From the moment Jawid first touched me, I was consumed with passion for him. At work, I constantly battled my almost primal need to be with him. I wanted to maintain my position as a senior administrator. I was only thirty-two, and had fought long and hard to earn the respect and cooperation of my colleagues. So Jawid and I had to be discreet. But his kisses electrified me, and we were both working brutally long hours. When our need became desperate, we indulged in quick, dangerous trysts in my office, the only room available with a locking door. On quick breaks, he lifted my skirts and took me roughly and quickly on the top of my desk, dropping his pants just enough to fuck me, hissing and thrusting harder and deeper when I grabbed his hips and viciously scored his skin.

When we could steal whole lunch hours, I stripped him and pressed him into my desk chair, straddling him naked, riding him slowly and thoroughly. My breasts felt alive against his skin. When he closed his arms around me, my nipples strained towards the soft tickles of the lustrous dark hair on his chest and arms. I opened to him, like a flower, demanding his tender probing, offering the petal-soft lips of my vulva to him. He took my cries into his mouth as we shattered into the sunlight stealing through the closed slits of the window blinds. I was greedy. And so quickly in love.

And so blissfully, naively, unaware of the cultural chasm between my "Americanized" lover and me. Jawid's English was flawless, almost without accent. He'd been in the States since he was fourteen. He seemed thoroughly assimilated, at least for Los Angeles, where celebrating Eid al Fatir is no more unusual than celebrating Christmas. Although I'd never met the large and much loved family he talked about so often, I assumed that was because our whirlwind affair had blossomed so quickly, and because of our hectic schedules. Besides, he and I had so much in common: a love of Renaissance paintings and techno dance music, a dedication to the childhood vaccination programme for undocumented immigrant children that I'd worked so hard to implement. In my hard-headed Irish-

American brain, love conquered all, especially on the day Jawid said he wanted me as his second wife.

Which to me meant he was divorced from his first wife.

Wrong, wrong, wrong!

The light finally dawned when we were rolling on the sheets in my bedroom, celebrating.

"Beloved," he whispered, his dark eyes glazed with passion and his golden skin glistening with the sweat of our loving. He held himself above me, balancing on strong, beautifully rippling arms, gliding into me, hot and slick and demanding. "Oh, my Amanda. Nasrin will love the way you cry out when I am thrusting deep into your woman's heat."

His words flowed over me like the soundless warmth of his breath, teasing my skin. We were devouring each other on the blue satin sheets of my queen-sized waterbed, letting lust and desire rule us on a long, stolen afternoon, celebrating our engagement while we played hookey from a board meeting that had everything to do with politics and nothing to do with our programmes. I cried out, mindless with passion, wrapping my legs around his waist and trying to draw his firm, lean body further into me.

"Nasrin will love the way you squirm when I suckle your breast, the way your musk fills the air when you climax with me buried in your sweet cunt." He twisted like an acrobat and sucked my nipple slowly up into his mouth.

A warning bell rang in my mind, but my thoughts were scattering into impending orgasm. I screamed, as pleasure waves washed over me, my body vibrating like a violin shimmering to the draw of the sweetest bow.

"You will marry me, Amanda," Jawid gasped, his shoulders shaking as he ground into me. "You will become my second wife. I will love you like this for ever."

He thrust once, twice, quickly, and, as Jawid shuddered into me, I suddenly heard what he was saying. I mean, for the first time, I listened to the words themselves, not to what I'd thought they meant. My belly went cold and I opened my eyes to see the final grimace on his beautiful face as he emptied himself into me. Actually, as he emptied himself into the rubber I'd insisted he use. I felt like a bucket of ice water had been thrown over me.

"You're still married." My voice sounded oddly flat, even to my own ears, like someone else was speaking out of my mouth.

Jawid panted above me, his arms shaking slightly, his head hanging as sweat dripped from his thick hair on to my collarbone. As his breathing slowed, he opened his velvety brown eyes and smiled down at me.

"What did you say, beloved?" He leaned down and kissed me, sucking softly on my lower lip. When I didn't respond, he lifted his head and looked at me. "Amanda?"

"I said, you're still married – aren't you, you shit?" I shoved hard at his chest, pushing him off as I struggled free of his hold.

"Am I still married to Nasrin?" Jawid rolled to his side and looked at me with a confused smile on his face. I tried not to think about how sexy he was, lying there with his skin all flushed from our loving, his still tumescent shaft resting on his balls, still glistening with his semen as he pulled the rubber free and tossed it into the trash. He quirked his head at me. " Of course we are still married. Why do you ask? She told me you two got along. It's important that wives like each other."

The confirmation, as unwanted as it was suddenly expected, stunned me more than I'd thought possible. A red wave of heat washed over my eyes. "You son of a bitch!" I yelled, launching myself at him, pummelling him with my fists.

"Amanda? What are you doing?"

His smile enraged me even further. It faded when my nails drew blood down his chest. I hadn't realized how strong he was until I found my shoulders flattened to the bed, my wrists held in an iron grip against the mattress as he fought to avoid my flailing legs.

"Stop it!" he grunted, as my knee connected with his belly. When I again missed my target, Jawid straddled me, his eyes flashing. "What is the matter with you?"

"You're married," I hissed, fighting him for all I was worth. "You bastard! You asked me to marry you, you made me fall in love with you, and you're already married to somebody else!

Why did you do that?" He was too strong for me to fight. I was pinned to the bed like a butterfly on a mounting board. I turned my head towards the wall in frustration and shut my eyes tightly, trying to close him out, trying to shut out the pain, as hot tears leaked out from under my eyelashes. "Why?"

"Amanda, of course I am still married," he whispered. "Beloved, I would never abandon a wife to a real divorce." Still holding me tightly in place, he gingerly clipped my wrists together in one of his hands, then pulled my face towards him. "If Nasrin had objected, I would not have become involved with you. I love her, as I love you. I will honour my wives, always!"

Wives. I sniffled and finally looked up at him. Even through the haze of tears, I saw his concern. Which made me cry all the more. And made me think that maybe I should be laughing instead, at the sheer, ridiculous insanity of the situation. I felt like I was talking to someone from another planet.

"Jawid," I choked, my voice still shaking. "You've lived in this country for almost twenty years. You know polygamy is illegal here. One man, one wife – or at least one wife at a time. My God, what the fuck part of that minor detail don't you understand?" My anger was mixed with overwhelming pain. "Or are you deliberately being an ignorant asshole?"

Jawid's eyes flashed at my language. I was swearing on purpose, partly because the occasion damn well called for it, and partly because I knew how much he disliked it. He pressed my hands into the bed, irritated.

"I have not changed my paperwork because you had not yet said yes – at least, not until today. Now Nasrin and I will get a civil divorce, though not a religious one, of course. After the papers are 'final', you and I can get married." He leaned down and gently kissed my forehead. I turned my head away. "Then Nasrin can move back in with us, and our family will be complete. She will stay with my sisters in the meantime. She wants us to have our honeymoon first, which is as it should be." He rained a light trail of kisses over the bridge of my nose. "We will need some time alone, you and I. To settle in to each other." He sucked softly on my lower lip. "To wear the edge off this frenzy we have for each other, so the three of us may live in harmony."

I bit him. Hard enough to draw blood. His eyes flashing, he pushed me into the bed and slapped the side of my butt – hard.

"Amanda, why are you doing this?"

I don't know what hurt more, the anger or the surprise. His and mine. His stupidity at thinking such a thing could ever work. My own stupidity for still wanting him. I turned my face to the wall, willing my body not to shake any more, taking quick, shallow breaths, so the pain of drawing in air didn't hurt so much. I tried to ignore the heat seeping into me through his strong hands and the thick smell of our sex, knowing I'd never have them again. When I could finally speak, I let all my anger and the cold despair wrapping my heart come out in my voice.

"Get out," I whispered. "Go home to your wife, Jawid, and stay away from me." I took a deep, shaking breath, trying not to feel the waves of pain crashing over me with each word. "I don't want to see you again. Ever." I said it quietly. I didn't move, just stared for the longest time at the afternoon shadows falling across the stark white bedroom wall.

"I do not understand," he whispered. "Amanda . . ."

As his voice broke, a warm, wet drop fell on my cheek, and my hot tears started again. This time, I didn't try to stop them. "Get out," I hissed. "Now!" When he finally released me, I curled into a ball, and stayed frozen in that position until I heard the front door close. Then I hugged my pillow and cried until I was too exhausted to do anything but sleep, for a long, long time.

I called in sick the rest of the week, then spent most of the weekend in bed. Eventually, I called my sister. I didn't go into much detail. She's never left the coal-mining town we grew up in, so I doubted she'd understand a cultural morass I couldn't even begin to explain. I just told her I'd stupidly become involved with a married man. She listened, the way sisters do, and told me I was better off without him. "Remember what Mom always says, 'Once a cheater, always a cheater.' Just pay more attention with the next man, OK, hon?"

I told her yes, though the truth was I didn't want to meet

another man. I was still in love with Jawid. I was still working with him, though our co-workers kindly didn't mention my now icy demeanour towards him. We hadn't told anyone we were seeing each other. But we worked with bright people, whose ability to save lives often depended on their being able to read between the lines. Ours was not the first failed romance at work. It wouldn't be the last. Our colleagues gave us both a wide berth, and tried not to schedule us in the same meetings.

The telephone call from Nasrin came a month later. I was packing for a long weekend out of town. I was still miserable, but I'd decided I'd wallowed in self-pity long enough. It was time to join some girlfriends for an impromptu camping weekend – to force myself to do something, anything, to get my mind off Jawid. Although I was trying not to take any more time off from work, I'd arranged to leave my office mid-morning on Friday. Nasrin's insistence that she had something to discuss with me that could not possibly wait – or be said over the phone – had me wondering if it would all just go away if I hid my head in a basket long enough. But I felt so guilty I finally agreed to join her for lunch on my way out of town.

Her house in San Marino was far away from downtown. I'd assumed Jawid had lied about going to my place because it was closer to work – the same way he'd lied about everything else. As I started up the winding, tree-lined streets of the gated community they lived in, I wasn't sure how I felt about realizing that, at least with the geography, he'd told the truth. When I gave my name, and Nasrin's, the guard waved me through. Five minutes later, I was ringing her doorbell, admiring, against my better judgment, the profusion of exquisite flowers that lined the walkway.

I'd half expected Nasrin to punch me when she answered the door. I was stunned when she hugged me instead, taking my hands in hers and laughing as though we were continuing the conversation we'd started on that evening so long ago. I was still stumbling through my greeting when she linked her arm into mine and started showing me through the lower floor of the house.

"I'm so glad you could make it." She smiled and led me into a music room bright with the noontime sun. Her hair was pulled up in a heavy gold clip that enhanced the open-faced beauty I'd only partially remembered. The flattering drape of her brown and yellow pantsuit made me glad I'd changed my jeans and sweatshirt for dark slacks and a light silk blouse.

Nasrin didn't seem to notice my nervousness. "It's such a beautiful day," she said, leading me along. "I thought we'd eat in the garden. It's this way."

Although I tried hard not to, I could see Jawid, as well as her, in every room we passed through. The pristine white furniture in the immaculate living room emphasized formality, even as it invited me to sit down and rest my feet on an overstuffed hassock. The sofas and chairs were arranged in a large U-shape, to make for easy conversation and to accent an exquisite, thick Persian rug covering the hardwood floor. I recognized the stylized attack helicopters woven in with the ancient vine patterns in the upper corners of the rug, reminders, even in the opulence, of Jawid and Nasrin's shared refugee past. Yet when I closed my eyes, it was Jawid's presence I sensed. I could almost smell the spicy, musky tang of his skin. Even the baskets of ripe fruit resting on the polished tables in the kitchen and dining room reminded me of him. I imagined him biting into one of the oranges he so loved, the juice running sweet and sticky down his throat as he licked his fingers clean. The more I thought about him, the more the walls seemed to echo with the laughter I missed so much. I avoided Nasrin's eyes, letting her running historical commentary blur into the background as I steeled myself against the onslaught of memories that soon hurt too much for me to see or care if she noticed.

If Nasrin picked up on my feelings, she didn't say so. She led me through the house and out into the garden. Fortunately, that was all hers. The wind chimes tinkled in the afternoon breeze, soothing my ears as I inhaled the perfume of her thriving, vibrant roses. She'd set a small table in the shade of a vine-laden archway. I protested that I really shouldn't join her. I wasn't hungry, though I'd been living on coffee and frozen dinners for weeks. But when she uncovered dishes of fresh green salad and roast lamb with pitta bread, my stomach growled loudly. Despite my embarrassed flush, Nasrin laughed and steered me into a chair. The food was delicious, with a honeyed pastry for dessert, and glasses of hot, sugar-laced tea. I began to relax.

"I love how Americans name their roses after famous people." She spoke between bites as I tried to place the elusive spices in the vinaigrette. While Jawid had no accent, Nasrin's voice was thick with the music of her homeland. I vaguely recalled that she'd come to the States as a young adult. "That white one is called a Kennedy, after the President. The smell is so light and fresh. The pink is a Princess Diana. Such lovely blushes on the petals, as befits a beautiful princess, yes?"

"Yes," I said.

Nasrin's face glowed when she spoke about her flowers. "The deep red one with the white markings is a Dolly Parton. Very full-bodied." I almost choked when Nasrin winked wickedly. "And this . . ." She leaned to the side of the table, cupped an exquisite, lavender bloom in her slender fingers, and inhaled deeply. "Mmmm. This is my new Barbara Streisand. She is beautiful enough to inspire song, I think." Her laugh was contagious. "Please." She smiled up at me and motioned for me to sniff. I bent forwards, inhaling the comforting scent, suddenly aware of the faint sandalwood perfume of Nasrin as well. "Ooh," she laughed, turning her hand as a ladybug climbed on to her fingers. She lifted it carefully back on to the leaves. "I try to keep them happy. They're so good for the garden." She waved around her. "Do you tend flowers, also?"

"No," I laughed, looking at the subtly organized riot of vibrant colours that surrounded me. "I just tend to other people's problems." At her raised eyebrow, I shrugged. "I work long hours. That's how I met Jawid . . ." I closed my eyes, a wave of shame and guilt and pain washing over me. I quietly set my fork down.

"I apologize," I said stiffly. "You've been very gracious, Nasrin, but I have no idea why you asked me here. I have no business sitting here talking to you as if we were friends, even though I like you. God knows why, because I'm still in love with your husband." I took a deep breath, my voice trembling. "My behaviour has been inexcusable. I didn't know he was still married, but if you want my apologies, I offer them. Truly. I'm so sorry."

I'd been going to add that if I'd known, I wouldn't have done it, but these days, I wasn't at all sure about that any more. And I was crying again. I wasn't sure I'd really ever stopped since I'd told Jawid to leave.

I was surprised to feel Nasrin's hand on mine, pressing a tissue into my palm. I looked up to see her smiling sympathetically at me.

"Men do not always explain themselves well. But then, they are only men." She patted my hand, and the sparkle in her lustrous brown eyes had me smiling tearily back at her.

"Since you've been working so much, I assume you have not been to the Arboretum lately."

"No," I said, wiping my eyes. "Not at all, actually. It's rather far out."

"Oh, then we will go now," she said. "The gardens are wonderfully healing when one is upset." Before I could say another word, Nasrin took my hand and reached down to collect our purses. The next thing I knew, we were in her Mercedes, heading north towards Arcadia. I gave up and called my friends to cancel. The sunshine felt good, and I decided one more weekend at home wouldn't kill me. At least I was out of the house and away from work, if not away from all memories of Jawid.

Nasrin and I spent hours in the gardens. At first, her arm linking with mine felt awkward. My American sense of personal space was well developed, and I was still uncomfortable with my role as the Other Woman. But the unexpected comfort of Nasrin's touch and her love of the flowers, and the incredible breadth of her knowledge, soon had me holding her hand in awe as we watched tiny lizards scurry beneath the open orchid blooms in the rainforest greenhouse. Through the thick glass walls we could hear the cry of the peacocks outside on the walkways.

"They are such sexual birds," she said, as a domineering male scream echoed through the walls. "Just like human men."

I smiled as a second shrill cry rose in unison with the first. I was beginning to understand that while Nasrin seemed quiet, she was more than willing to voice her surprisingly uninhibited opinions. And I was finally starting to understand a little bit of where Jawid had been coming from with his insane idea of marrying me as well as Nasrin.

"I have always expected that Jawid would take a second wife." We rounded a corner, and Nasrin stooped to trail her long, carefully manicured fingers through a small waterfall between two towering ferns. "I assumed it would happen later." She smiled up at me. "And that she would be much younger than me. Someone who would catch his eye and give him another lifetime's worth of children when I had grown older and more matronly. But one can never tell when love will strike, can one?" She stood up and rubbed her hands together briskly, drying them in the air. "After all, I certainly did not expect to love him."

I stared at her. "Why not?" I didn't care that I was being rude. Despite the soothing moisture of the man-made mists and the perfume of the flowers, and the solace of Nasrin's company, I was still raw inside. She had Jawid, and she hadn't wanted him. It wasn't fair!

She took my hand in both of hers, the warmth of one contrasting starkly with the water-cooled touch of the other. "Ours was an arranged marriage, Amanda. I thought you knew."

"No," I said bluntly. To my mind, arranged marriages only happened in faraway places where women were treated like chattels. Places where men had up to four wives, regardless of how the women felt, and divorced them with the throw of a stone. I sighed heavily. Faraway places like where Nasrin and Jawid were from. I was amazed at how little I'd known of someone I'd thought I'd come to understand so well.

Nasrin moved to my side and again linked her arm into mine, leading me back outside and on to the pathway. The sun was higher now, the call of the birds and the dryness of the afternoon heat stark in comparison to the comforting coolness of the greenhouse.

"My family was dispersed when we left the refugee camps. I went to Germany with my brothers and my eldest uncle." She steered me on to a eucalyptus-lined path, pausing to run her hand over one huge, smooth-barked trunk. "My uncle had a friend whose cousin went to school with Jawid's father. When Uncle got the address, he wrote to Jawid's father, and sent my picture. Jawid approved. So his parents and my uncle and aunt made the arrangements."

She paused to watch a screaming peacock spread his tail feathers in a glorious fan of greens and royal blues. The white eye-feathers seemed to wink at us as he raised and lowered his tail at the plain brown peahen, which was studiously ignoring him.

"I remember sitting for that picture." She hugged my arm to her breast, laughing as she shook her head. "I was so nervous. I wanted to look my prettiest, to look smart, so I'd catch a good husband. My uncle told me to look practical instead, as Jawid was going to be a doctor, so he would need someone to tend to his home, not someone frittering about the garden, tending flowers and flaunting the fact that she could read."

Nasrin wrinkled her nose, and made a sombre face. I laughed.

"I looked like this," she said, "until just as the man's hand moved to uncover the lens cap. Then I smiled." Her grin lit her face. "Uncle was mad, but he didn't have the money to pay for two pictures. So he told me it would serve me right if I ended up married to a poor man who made me hoe other people's vegetables all day." She wiggled her fingers at me, and I saw the callouses from her gardening tools beside the light peach of her nail polish. "Little does Uncle know, but now my orchids win state prizes and bedeck my husband's house. And I grow champion tomatoes!"

She hugged me. Her breast was warm against my arm. I liked her. Even though she was Jawid's wife, and I still ached with the loss of him, I couldn't help liking Nasrin.

"You came to love him, though, didn't you?" I asked quietly, smiling into her upturned face.

"Oh, yes." She smiled. "How could I not?" A pang shot through me as the glow of her love suffused her face. "The moment I saw him, I felt I had known him all my life." She blushed unexpectedly. "And I wanted him in ways I wasn't supposed to know anything about, but I wanted to learn." She clasped her fingers into mine. "Was it the same with you? And Jawid? I know American women do not often come to their weddings as virgins. Was his loving still special to you, the way it was with me?"

The question was so clear, and so open, and I was so stunned by her bluntness, that I answered truthfully. "It was the most wonderful thing in my world." I instinctively tightened my fingers, trying to push back the longing and pain when I thought about him. "I fell in love with him the first time I touched him. We were working on separate projects. I'd been offsite, doing research, and I hadn't seen him in many months. My project ended, and I needed his signature on a document. The clinic was full of people, total chaos. As I handed him the papers, a small boy ran into me, and I literally fell into his arms." I looked at her, squaring myself for her reaction. "I felt like I'd been struck by lightning."

I don't know what reaction I'd expected, but her laughter wasn't it.

"How wonderful!" She grinned. "But then, Jawid is an excellent lover." She blushed all the way to her hairline.

I must have looked as stunned at her reaction as I felt. Nasrin led me quickly to a bench in the shade and we sat down, still holding hands. She took a long drink from the water bottle she was carrying and passed it to me. I drank deeply, ignoring the occasional stares from people walking by, noticing again, even though I didn't want to, how beautiful Nasrin was, then suddenly realized that I didn't care what people were thinking. I wanted the support of her touch too much to let go.

"Jawid truly would like you to be his second wife."

I just stared at her, jerking when she reached up and gently stroked the hair from my forehead. "Jawid tells me you are older than I by four years, and that due to your work, our children will likely all come from me, rather than you. But he wants you still." Her hand cupped my cheek, her palm warm and accepting. "He loves you, Amanda. And you love him. You would make him a good wife." Her thumb stroked lightly down the side of my face. "And you would be a good companion to me."

I shook my head, pulling away from her. Only our hands stayed linked, where her tender grip refused to let go. "Nasrin, that's not possible."

"Why not?" She laughed. "He can obviously support us both."

"That's not the point," I said, shaking my head. "Jawid knows that. In this country, it's one man and one woman, to love, honour and cherish, forsaking all others, 'til death do us part. There are no provisions for fucking around with men who are already married to someone else. Personally, I'd shoot any son of a bitch who ran around on me!" I blushed when I realized what I was saying, and how vehemently I was saying it. "I'm sorry. I shouldn't have said that."

Nasrin waved her hand, dismissing my ramblings. "You are talking secular marriage laws, Amanda. Jawid explained how to work around them."

"Nasrin," I said, exasperated. "If he divorced you, you'd lose all your rights. I couldn't live with that. And I'd never trust him to do right by me if he did that to you. I'll have no part of his divorcing you, and I'm certainly not converting to a religion that requires women to live with their husband's mistresses!"

She shook her head, smiling, and stood up. "We will talk more about this later, my friend. Perhaps there is some way we can yet work things out. Look, the peacock is fanning again!" Her delight was contagious, and we put aside our discussion to tiptoe behind a bush and watch the proud and noisy bird's display for the whimsical little brown peahen.

We left before the traffic got heavy. Nasrin had purchased some seedlings in the gift shop. I carried them on my lap on the way home, balancing them precariously while trying to learn the dance steps Nasrin insisted on teaching me at every stop light. It was early enough that I felt comfortable going back into the house. I knew Jawid would still be at work. When we'd deposited the new plants in the potting shed and cleaned up, Nasrin herded me into the kitchen and handed me an apron.

We spent the rest of the afternoon with her showing me how to cook potato *boulani* and meat rolls and rice with raisins and sauces with names I couldn't pronounce. As I prepared the green salad, I forgot that I was making something that Jawid would later eat. I savoured the unexpected blend of tastes on Nasrin's fingers as she fed me a sample of rice. I was licking her fingertips clean when her hand went still.

I closed my eyes, taking a deep, calming breath, knowing without looking that Jawid was there.

He wrapped his arms quietly around us both. "So, my loves. You have had a good afternoon?"

Nasrin's smile lit her face. "Yes, my heart. You were right. I can easily love Amanda. For herself, and as a wife to you."

The honesty and selflessness, and, to my mind, stupidity, was almost more than I could bear. "Excuse me," I whispered. "I'll be going now. Thank you for a wonderful afternoon, Nasrin."

Nasrin's grip held me. "Amanda, that is enough." She shook my arm lightly. "You love him. I love him. We can grow to love each other. What is so wrong with that?"

"It's not . . . right," I stumbled. Things weren't so clear any more. I wanted to resist. Over the course of the afternoon, Nasrin had become a friend, and I was betraying her by my very presence, lusting after her husband. I had no right to love him."

"Of course it's right." Nasrin pulled me closer, so that her arms encircled me. I was erotically aware of her body, and stunned that I didn't want to resist her touch. I inhaled shakily and leaned into her embrace.

Jawid's arms tightened convulsively around us. "Have you reconsidered my offer, Amanda? Will you become my second wife and join our family?"

Nasrin squeezed my fingers reassuringly.

"This is insane," I whispered.

"The law is insane, but since it is a law, yes, we will have to go around it." He held me tightly to him and slid the fingers of his other hand up Nasrin's arm to stroke her cheek. "I hadn't realized how much I would love my first wife," he said quietly.

"Despite what Nasrin believed, I hadn't planned on taking another wife, not once I had her. I did not expect to fall in love with you." His glance slid over me. I shivered, my skin humming as his fingers travelled up my arm. "That is why I needed her approval, and your acceptance of her role as first wife."

Nasrin slipped her arm around my waist, hugging me, smiling, and rested her head on my shoulder. Her fingers joined Jawid's, tracing down my back in tandem with his.

"Knowing all this, will you still marry me, Amanda?" he whispered, licking the curve of my ear. "I love you."

"God, I hope it's not cheating if we're married," I whispered. Clutching them to me tightly, I took a deep breath and threw myself to the winds. "All right, Jawid. I'm certain I've lost my mind, and, for the record, I still think this whole idea is insane. But I can't help loving you. I will be your second wife. I won't convert, and I'm keeping my condo and I have no idea what I'll tell my family. And you'd better believe we'll have some iron-clad legal agreements."

That's as far as I got before Jawid crushed his lips on to mine. I kissed him as if he were air saving me from drowning, giving myself over to pleasure. Nasrin licked my collarbone and sucked softly on my neck.

We kissed until dinner was ready. Then we ate. Nasrin insisted, saying we would need our strength later. I barely noticed the food, despite the aromas tickling my nostrils, but I was glad for the energy suffusing my body and the warmth as I downed yet another glass of tea. I dropped my fork when Jawid took my hand and gently bit my fingertip. My legs trembled when Nasrin kissed me and gently led me upstairs to get me ready.

Halfway up the steps, I turned and saw Jawid, facing the fireplace, his tea cupped in both hands as he stared into the flames. In the light, he looked so civilized, yet so sensuous, raw and wild – and so handsome, kind and quietly strong. Perhaps he was strong enough to accept both my world and his. Perhaps we all were. I turned and followed Nasrin up the stairs.

The bedroom was through the first door on the right. Nasrin adjusted a dimmer switch, bathing the room in a soft, golden glow. I curled my toes into the deep greens and burnt orange patterns in the thick Persian carpet. Nasrin clicked on the stereo, and hauntingly erotic music filled the air – tambours and stringed instruments I couldn't identify. Then she turned down the covers on the king-sized bed. Even from across the room, I could see the softness in the pure, white cotton sheets. Nasrin smiled at me as she reached up and undid the clip in her hair. Her thick tresses fell almost to her waist in silky black waves.

"Your hair is beautiful," I said, nervously wiping my palms on my thighs, shifting my weight from one foot to the other. "I've always wanted long straight hair."

"Thank you. I've always wanted short, carefree hair, like yours." She walked over to me and took my hands. "Red hair. It seems so wonderfully exotic." Her thumbs stroked my palms. Then her fingers glided up to my neck, stroking lightly, toying with the curls, weaving one around her finger. "It would give me great pleasure to prepare you for Jawid, Amanda." She cupped my cheek. I leaned into her hand, nodding in spite of the butterflies in my stomach.

Her fingertips stroked my cheek and she kissed me. Her breath smelled of raisins and honey and lemon. I didn't resist. I'd never kissed a woman before, but the moistness of her parted lips felt so right. I wanted her, as part of Jawid, and for herself.

Still, I trembled when her fingers started unbuttoning my blouse. She slid my clothing off, one inch at a time, stroking the newly unveiled skin with her fingertips while she gently sucked my tongue. When I was naked, she took me into the bathroom and slathered my legs with depilatory cream. Her foam-covered hand slid between my legs, and I gasped.

"I . . . I didn't think the women in your country shaved there."

"They don't," she said. "But Jawid likes it. Do you mind?"

I shook my head, surprised that I was excited rather than bothered by having Jawid's wife, his first wife, I corrected myself, teaching me new things about him. The cream tingled, but I tried to ignore it as I brushed my teeth and watched Nasrin strip. Her body was as beautiful as her face. Her nipples were a dusky rose, softer and fuller than my tight pink tips. I blushed when she noticed me watching her. Unembarrassed, she stretched her arms high over her head, then ran her hands down the length of her lithe, supple body. Her palms circled her nipples, causing them to perk up into hard tight peaks. Her hands moved lower, sliding between her naked labia as she spread her legs wider, stroking over the flash of gold metal exposed between her legs.

"Are you pierced?" I stammered.

Nasrin winked. She opened her legs and tugged on the shiny bar pierced through the hood of her beautifully protruding clit.

"This is also not traditional. It took me a long time to convince Jawid that I would not damage my sex with the piercing." She flicked the bar and shivered. "After much discussion and research, he accompanied me to the piercers. He held me down, so the needle would strike true." Her breathing quickened and a flush suffused her chest as she tugged again. "I was more afraid than the night when I gave my virginity to Jawid. But I begged him to let me do it. He held me flat to the table, and he kissed me, giving his tongue to suck as the needle pierced me. I screamed." Suddenly, she panted and blushed, shuddering through a shimmering orgasm. When her breathing slowed, she smiled at me and stretched again. "Jawid came in his pants. But the piercing is wonderful. Sometimes, I climax just from walking."

She moved to my side and kissed my shoulder. "Our stroll through the Arboretum was especially wonderful today. But that was as much from the pleasure of your company as it was from this wicked, nasty bar." She marched me into the shower and rinsed my legs and vulva with quick, businesslike motions. Then she led me from the steaming shower and into the huge, sunken tub that took up the entire far corner of the room.

My muscles turned to putty as she washed me, massaging the tension from every inch of my body. At her insistence, I leaned back and concentrated on nothing but my breathing, the warmth of the water, and the incredible sensuality of her touch. She kissed her way down my breast and tenderly sucked my nipple into her mouth.

"Nasrin," I moaned, unsure if I wanted to pull away or arch towards her. "Is th–this also traditional?"

"No, love," she murmured. "But I want to do it." She peppered me with kisses. "You will appreciate Jawid's ministrations more if your nipples are already swollen with passion when you enter his bed. Now hush, and let me prepare you, so this is a night of most exquisite pleasures."

Her lips moved to my other breast, and I leaned back and let the warm, scented water surround me. Nasrin's lips were pure, luscious torment. I shuddered each time I looked down and saw her full painted lips surrounding my areola, slowly and deliberately suckling the light cream of my breast. She sucked me until I was tender to even the lightest flick of her tongue. Then her fingers stroked down over my belly, and rested on my newly denuded and exquisitely sensitive mound.

"Grab the bars above your head, so I can prepare the rest of you."

I obeyed without thinking, letting myself float on the water as Nasrin moved between my legs and her strong, warm hands lifted my hips. I felt the heat of her breath on my pubes. Then I gripped the bars and held on for dear life as Nasrin lowered herself into the water, neck deep, placed my open thighs on her shoulders, and slowly swiped her tongue up the length of my slit.

"Oh, God!" I groaned.

"You taste sweet," she said.

I cried out as her tongue flicked my clit. My newly shaved skin registered even the lightest of touches. I writhed as she licked and sucked and probed.

"This nub, too, should be tender and swollen." She sucked me into her mouth, dipping her fingers deep into my cunt. "Your juices are sweet, Amanda. Jawid loves the taste of a woman's passion. He will be so hard and hungry when he pleasures you."

An orgasm was building deep within me. It had been so long since I had made love with Jawid. I'd been too depressed to even masturbate. I arched up into Nasrin's face, groaning with need and frustration. She sat back.

"Please," I begged, squirming in the water. Memories of Jawid licking between my legs blurred into the desire for more of the flailing female tongue that had also sucked him to orgasm. "Do it more, Nasrin."

"No," she laughed, shaking her head. "My task is to prepare you. Your orgasm is your gift to Jawid." She massaged my legs and took my foot in her hands. "I will relax you for a while, then I will prepare you some more."

When my body had calmed, Nasrin helped me from the tub and towelled me dry. Then she took my shaking hands and led me to the bed. Three more times she brought me to the brink of orgasm. I was almost insane with lust when I looked up to see Jawid watching us. He had changed into traditional garb and was leaning against the wall, smiling at us, his dark eyes glittering with desire. His erection tented out the front of his loose cotton pants.

Our eyes met and I reached for him, trembling as he took my hand and gently sucked my fingertips. He climbed on to the bed and pulled us both up to him, kissing first me, then Nasrin, until the cunt juices glistening on her face were sticky on all of us. Jawid smiled as he carefully licked her lips. When he was satisfied, he pulled free of Nasrin, licked his finger, and slid it between my swollen pussy lips. I shook at the exquisite torment of his thumb on my engorged and tender clit. Nasrin had done her job exceptionally well. Still, when I heard her gentle, approving laugh, I flushed and looked away.

"Don't, Amanda," Jawid whispered, sliding another long, slender finger into my hungry cunt. "I have told Nasrin how much you like my hands in you. Let her see you take your pleasure." He kissed me deeply, and I tasted my juices on his tongue.

"If you say his lips don't feel good, I won't believe you."

Nasrin's hand cupped my breast, kneading gently, then holding it on her palm for her husband to play with. Their hands clasped together, holding each other, as Jawid stroked his thumb over my nipple. My skin was so tender and engorged, even that light touch was a mixture of pleasure and pain.

Jawid pulled his clothes free and lifted me on to his lap, turning me so the heat of his erection pressed into my back. He kissed the side of my neck, licking and sucking and biting. I couldn't stop my tears. I sank back against him, into the touch I'd been certain I'd never feel again.

"Shhh, love, don't cry," he whispered, wrapping his arms around me. I was vaguely aware of Nasrin stuffing pillows behind him, so he could lie back against the headboard. Then he spread my legs wide and lifted me. I cried out, high and keening, as the hot, thick flesh of his swollen, unsheathed shaft slid into me, filling me, deeper and deeper. When he was inside me, naked and hot and unprotected, when I was so full of him I throbbed at the exquisite, unrelenting pressure of his cock against the centre deep inside my cunt, he again took my breasts into his hands and slowly, deliberately, milked my swollen nipples until I was writhing in his arms, desperate for the climax that was building inexorably.

Nasrin opened my thighs and moved between my legs. I mewled as she licked her way up my slit.

"You are so beautiful, beloved." Jawid's voice was thick with passion. "Will you come like this for me? Will you pull the seed from me, with just the walls of your wifely woman sex, until we are one in our orgasms and my semen bathes your womb?" The tip of his penis twitched deep inside my cunt. I trembled uncontrollably.

"Please," I whispered. "Please . . ." I wasn't sure what I was asking for, I only knew that I needed their touch more than I needed to breathe. Jawid rocked me against him, groaning as my pussy walls spasmed around him. Nasrin laughed and flicked her tongue over me, then sucked my clit into her mouth. I shrieked as the orgasm gushed from me, clenching my cunt muscles as tightly around Jawid as I could, leaning into him. He arched into me and cried out, his body shaking as warm rivers of semen spurted into me and ran down his shaft. Nasrin licked us clean while I shook in Jawid's arms.

I collapsed on to the bed, rolling on to my side, rousing myself only to suck the beautiful, dusky rose nipple that brushed hungrily against my lips. Nasrin held herself above me and cried out her pleasure as Jawid buried his face in her vulva and brought her to climax after climax.

That night, I slept like I'd never wake up again, wrapped in both their arms, warm and safe and happy.

I don't know why I feel so married now. I mean, it's still not legal. And even if it were, I have no interest in converting – given the rights I'd have as a woman in Jawid's home country, I'd certainly never go back there with him. With them. But some time between that day and now, I've gradually moved most of my things into the house. The three of us eventually had a feast with our closest friends and colleagues and Jawid's family. My family came, too, though they don't even pretend to understand. But my mother says that as long as I'm happy, she can live with the scandal.

"After all," she said loudly, clucking her tongue as she dabbed ceremonial henna on my hand, "if it's OK with God, who am I to argue? Just keep the condo, dearie, for you and Nasrin. Any man who can live with two wives bears watching. Keep him on his toes."

From the other room, I heard a muttered comment about mule-headed and non-traditional women. Nasrin and I laughed. My mother shook her head and joined us.

The Minyan

Lawrence Schimel

Simon felt self-conscious as he walked down East 10th Street. He wondered if everyone could tell that he was going to a sex party, which was a ridiculous thought since it was a private party being held at someone's apartment. It wasn't as if he were going to one of those clubs where anyone watching him enter or leave would know what he was up to.

Still, he felt like it was obvious. Which may have simply been because he was nervous. He didn't usually go to sex parties, but one of the guys from Congregation, Uri, had invited him. Simon had spent the rest of the service wondering which of the other guys Uri had invited as well. He found himself mentally undressing the men around him, wondering what they would look like naked, how big their dicks were, if Isaac was hairy all over, thick mats of fur covering his body. He'd imagined them in all sorts of sexual poses and situations.

As if he didn't feel that these thoughts – so improper in *shul* – were sacrilege enough, Simon had been embarrassed by his body's behaviour, by the fact that he'd had a hard-on pressing its way outwards in his pants every time he stood. He'd felt like he was back in high school, getting a woody on the way to class and holding his schoolbooks in front of his crotch, as if everyone – especially all the other guys – didn't know what that meant. The instinct to shut the *siddur* and hold it protectively in front of his crotch, to shield his erection from view, was still strong, but Simon resisted. He recited the responses from memory, his vision blurring as he nervously glanced to his left and his right, trying to see from the corners of his eyes if anyone had noticed his arousal. He was grateful for the fringe of his *tallis*, which hid his boner behind its white veil, although he was afraid that his hard-on was making the fringe stand out as well.

Although he was not certain who among the congregation was also invited – the way one did not know who exactly the *lamed vavnik* were – Simon had skipped services two nights ago because he felt too ashamed about seeing those men there and knowing what they planned to do this evening. Or what he imagined they planned to do; Simon wasn't quite sure what it would be like, since he didn't often go to this sort of party. In fact, he'd never been to one like this, although he had once been to a "sauna" when he was down in Puerto Rico on vacation. He'd been fascinated to be in the presence of sex, to watch men around him sucking and fucking in public, but he was too nervous to let anyone touch him, let alone do anything more. Men did touch him sometimes – the rules seemed to be touch first, ask later – but Simon always shied away from the groping hands, and the men who tried to sink to their knees before him. He'd fingered his own dick behind the protective curtain of his towel, too afraid to show it off in public despite the naked bodies all around him, and he came almost immediately, shooting into the terrycloth fabric. He went back to his little cubicle and turned the towel inside out, so that the come-stained side was not against his skin, all sticky.

But he did not leave.

He had felt a compulsion to stay as long as his time would permit and to watch as much sex as he could. It had taken days of rationalizations and justifications to talk himself into coming to the sauna, and he'd done it only because he was so far from home – practically in another country, though it was technically a territory of the United States. He'd always been curious about the sex clubs back home in New York, but he was always afraid that if he went to one he'd run into someone he knew. It didn't matter that they would both be there for the same reason; Simon would just die of embarrassment if that were to happen.

So now that he'd convinced himself to finally visit one, he stayed in the bathhouse in Old San Juan for hours, pacing the halls, exploring every room and alcove, always watching, silent, not talking to anyone – whether they spoke English or not. He just wanted to be there.

Hours later, in a back room that was pitch black, Simon did let them touch him. He didn't know how many men there were – he couldn't see them, couldn't see anything. Somehow, as long as he couldn't see them, it was OK. It was like his friend Eric who talked faster and faster whenever he lied, as if he hoped that somehow God wouldn't hear his falsehood if he spoke so quickly.

It didn't make any sense, Simon knew, but he stopped thinking about it. When a hand had touched him in the darkness, he did not jump back. He let it explore, slowly working its way down his chest to the barrier of his towel, tightly wrapped around his waist. The fingers pulled on the flap tucked away, and Simon grabbed the towel before it fell to the floor, clenching it in his hands – to give him something safe to hold on to as the fingers continued to explore, and touched his cock.

Because he couldn't see anything, Simon was able to imagine whatever and whoever he wanted. He was too afraid to do anything to anyone else, although he did from time to time reach out with one hand to feel the bodies of the men around him, the invisible men whose hands and mouths were touching his body, and there were always too many hands or mouths on him, always more than one man. His fingers would venture forth (the other hand still tightly clutching the towel like his own version of Linus' blue security blanket) and touch flesh, drop down to feel the man's cock, then retreat back to the safety of the towel, wiping off the droplets of pre-come that clung to his palm.

Simon had wanted to pull back, before he came in someone's mouth – he didn't know whose – thinking, This is unsafe, you shouldn't do this, you don't know who I am. But it was too late. Before he knew it, he had crested over into orgasm, his hips bucking his cock deeper into the stranger's mouth, and the man grabbed his ass, pulling Simon towards him, not letting go until his body had quieted again and his cock had begun to grow soft in the guy's mouth.

Stumbling over the bodies around him in his hurry to get out of there, Simon had practically run to the showers and scrubbed his body pink, then went back to his hotel. That was all nearly two years ago now, and he had never been involved in any sort of group sex before or since. Until tonight.

Because he was nervous and had built up this moment in his mind for so many days now, Simon was sure that everyone could tell that he was on his way to have sex.

He was also horny. He hadn't jerked off for the past two days, even though he normally jerked off at least once a day. But he had this sort of superstition about not jerking off on the night before he was going to have sex, or when there was the possibility of his having sex, such as if he were on a date. Or going to a sex party.

Part of it was simply performance anxiety. By "saving up" he felt more secure that he would get hard quickly, no matter how nervous he was, and also that he would have an impressively thick come.

He arrived at the building and stood before the door. This was his last chance to turn back.

But Simon wanted to be here tonight. For all his wanting a boyfriend, looking for a mate who'd be his life partner, for all his reticence at the sauna in Puerto Rico, Simon knew that he could easily become addicted to such promiscuous sex. There was a part of him that craved that wild abandon, to have sex with many men in a single night, to not know or care who they were or if he would ever see them again.

He hoped that tonight, among these men he knew and who, moreover, were his people in so many ways – fellow Jews, all with the same sexual desires he felt – that he'd be less nervous, more willing to let himself try things he'd only fantasized about. To be part of the groupings of bodies he had only witnessed last time.

Simon cleared his throat, hoping his voice wouldn't crack when he had to say his name, then pressed the buzzer. After a moment of waiting, he heard the click of the door being electronically unlocked, without anyone asking him who he was.

This made Simon a little more nervous. Just how many men were invited to this party that they let anyone up? Or was he simply the last invitee left to arrive?

As he rode the elevator he wondered if men were already having sex or if they'd waited for him before starting. Staring at the floor numbers going up and up, he shifted his hard-on in his jeans, willing it to go down. He thought it would seem improper to have one before he arrived and disrobed, as if he were so hard up and desperate that he couldn't control himself.

Arrows indicated which wing each set of apartments was in. He pulled the invite from his pocket and checked the number, then put it away again. He stood before the door and rang the buzzer. Simon could hear men's voices inside, chatting. He wondered if soon the neighbours, anyone passing by the doorway, would be able to hear their sounds of sex.

Simon heard the flap on the eyepiece being lifted. He smiled, although he always felt he looked ridiculous through those warped fisheye lenses. He took his hands out of his pockets. Uri opened the door.

It's strange to be greeted at the door by someone you know only casually who's wearing nothing but his BVDs. Especially when you're not used to seeing the person in this state, such as if you went to the same gym and saw each other in the locker room all the time.

Simon couldn't help looking him over, up and down, staring at Uri's body. He was short but solid, with thickly muscled arms and legs. His skin shone like burnished bronze, and he had wiry black hairs in a line down his chest and covering his legs, like sparse grass poking up through desert sand. He'd grown up on a kibbutz in Israel before moving to the US five years ago.

"*Shalom!*" Uri cried, leaning forwards to kiss Simon on the lips in the typical gay greeting. "The party's just getting started," he continued, "come on in."

Simon reached out and kissed the mezuzah on his way into the apartment. Uri lived in a nice one-bedroom condo. He had a large abstract painting over the living room couch, under which sat three men, also naked except for their underwear. They all looked sort of nervous, sitting separate from each other even though they were all on the same sofa; nowhere did skin touch skin. Simon nodded to Benji, who he knew, and then looked away, blushing because of how Benji was (un) dressed and what they were planning. He had to suppress a barely controllable urge to giggle.

There were other men, also in only their underwear, standing with their backs to Simon, looking at the books on Uri's shelves. Two of them had kipahs on, pinned to their dark hair.

Uri led him into the kitchen. "Take your stuff off," he said, pointing to the stacks of neatly folded clothes on the countertop. "What do you want to drink?"

At other apartment parties, everyone took their coats off and left them in the bedroom, then congregated in the living room. But tonight, the bed was going to be put to better use. And so, for that matter, was the living room.

There were six other guys there so far besides Simon and Uri. Simon knew three of them from *shul* – Howard, Stanley and Benji – although he'd never seen any of them naked (or nearly naked) before. They hadn't been among the guys he mentally undressed that night Uri gave him the invite, but they didn't look bad without their clothes on, just sort of average: dark-haired, dark-eyed, Slavic Jews who didn't get much sun.

Of the rest of them, there was one guy, Darren, who Simon had met before at a gay Yeshiva dance. He was tan like Uri, but his body seemed hairless. It was only later, when Simon was closer, that he realized Darren had shaved it, even his crotch.

The other two guys, Ezra and Joshua, Uri knew from when he lived uptown and went to the gay congregation there. Joshua was a redhead whose arms looked too thin. Not at all Simon's type, but then he never understood the fascination many men seemed to have for redheads. Ezra, on the other hand, was the kind of boy who might catch his eye on the street, with his dark eyes and goatee and v-shaped torso. It was a surprise to Simon to learn that Ezra was shy and unsure of himself, sort of nerdy, hiding behind his glasses the way Simon felt that he, too, did quite often.

Everyone was in their late twenties or early thirties. And they all seemed nervous or unsure of what they were or should be doing. Everyone except Uri, the mastermind of this little get-together, who walked about with complete comfort, unconcerned about his near nudity and the sex that was on everyone's mind. He played the host but also seemed completely at ease, chatting with his friends as if this were any ordinary get-together.

Since few people knew each other, no one really knew what to talk about.

"It's funny," Howie said. "My mother is always after me, since all my boyfriends are blond and blue-eyed. If you have to have sex with other men, she asks, couldn't you at least find a nice Jewish boy? And here I am, in a roomful of guys she'd approve of, only not about to do anything she'd approve of!"

It was the wrong thing to say, really, Simon thought. No one wanted to be reminded of what their parents would think of what they were about to do, for all that everyone there was eager for it all to begin. But what would happen when they ran into these men again in their regular lives? How could Simon ever go back to *shul* if he saw Stanley, tonight, with a stranger's fingers up his butt? He would never be able to see these men again without remembering what they looked like naked.

The silence stretched on uncomfortably.

Darren told a joke: "So this kid comes home from school and says, 'Ma, Ma, I got a part in the school play!' And the mother says, 'That's nice, dear, what part did you get?' So the kid tells her, 'I got the part of the Jewish husband.' The mother stops what she's doing and looks at her son. 'What's the matter,' she says, 'you couldn't get a speaking role?'"

Everyone laughed.

The buzzer rang. All noise stopped suddenly and everyone turned to stare at the door, even though whoever it was had to come all the way upstairs before they got to the door. They were all wondering the same things, Simon knew: would it be someone familiar or a stranger? What if this new guy was ugly? What if he was unbearably cute?

Even though only Uri knew everyone there, it was like they were all tired old regulars at some bar, just waiting for fresh meat to show up. Was that how things would happen: one time someone would come in and catch someone's eye and make their move, breaking the ice for everyone else to start having sex? Who would be the first to do something?

Uri looked through the peephole of the door, then opened it. Simon could see from where he was that there were two people on the other side of the door frame.

"Aaron," Uri said, "what a pleasant surprise. You should have told me you were bringing someone."

"It was sort of a last-minute thing," Aaron said. "Jorge, meet my friend Uri. Uri, this is Jorge." He smiled at Jorge, then looked back at Uri and winked. "We met at Escuelita last night."

This was one of those moments of sex party etiquette. Or perhaps simply party etiquette. What to do if someone brings someone who hasn't been invited? At a normal party, this sort of behaviour is usually more forgivable.

Uri looked over Aaron's friend and evidently decided he made the cut. He invited them both in and led them to the kitchen to unclothe.

The whole nature of the party seemed to change with Jorge there. It was the presence of foreskin in a roomful of circumcized gay men. It was the presence of a non-Jew.

Simon remembered how his uncle Morty used to always joke, "*Shiksas* are for practice," whenever he asked if Simon had a girlfriend yet.

Simon didn't doubt that this *sheggitz* would get as much practice as he wanted tonight, since every guy there seemed to be utterly entranced by Jorge's smooth dark skin as he stood in the doorway of the kitchen – to show off? – and peeled out of his clothes.

Once stripped down to their Calvins and 2(x)ist briefs and holding their cocktails, they came back into the other room. There were ten men now crowded into the small area, sitting or standing around awkwardly.

"Hey, we've got a *minyan* now," Howie said. You could tell he was happy to be the first one to notice.

"Actually, we don't," Ezra said. And technically he was right; Jorge didn't count.

But that was for prayer. For a sex party, ten bodies – regardless of their religion – was enough critical mass to get things going. Uri circulated, introducing people and drawing them into conversation. Not everyone could fit comfortably in the living room – at least, there weren't enough places to sit. So some of the guys had drifted into the bedroom, where they'd started to get it on while no one – at least, not everyone – was looking.

Of course, the moment one of the living room group noticed, everyone rushed to the doorway of the bedroom to watch.

Somehow this didn't seem to be the right sex party etiquette, but it didn't stop anyone.

Simon watched the back of Joshua's head bobbing up and down before Stanley's crotch, as if Josh were *davening*, and perhaps this was like prayer for Joshua, lost in a trance of cock-sucking.

With all of them crowded there at the door, growing hard from their voyeurism if they weren't already, it didn't take long for the rest of the guys to start touching one another as well. A hand on thigh or belly, fingers cold with nervousness. A hand cupping an ass cheek through the fabric of his underwear. Simon didn't really know who was who but it didn't matter. His heart beat faster, he felt a tight constriction in his chest from nervousness, then he took a deep breath and relaxed into the sensation of his ass in some man's palm. He thought for a moment back to that bathhouse in Puerto Rico, where even though he'd wanted to he hadn't done anything except in the concealing darkness of the back room, as if sex were something too shameful to be seen. Among these ten men, these other gay Jews gathered together for the worship of the body, he no longer felt guilty about his desperate yearnings for sex with other men, as he had on the walk over here and on so many occasions previously. He looked around him, at the men who were so like him, now lost in their pleasure, the giving and the receiving of it, and he smiled. He was not alone, and he was glad to be part of something bigger than himself, this *minyan*, which for him is what it was even if one of the men was not Jewish. A *minyan* of desire, men who no longer needed to congregate in clandestine secret to worship, but who could love and pray without shame.

"Amen," he whispered, and pressed himself back against the man who cupped his ass, no longer holding himself apart.

Glossary

Daven: The ritual bending of the knees during prayer that causes the body to sway back and forth.

Lamed vavnik: The term for the thirty-six people who are so pure of heart that God does not again destroy the world with flood or fire or so forth. Because no one knows who these thirty-six are, Jews are taught to be kind and offer hospitality to all, in case they are one of the *lamed vavnik*.

Minyan: The minimum number of adult males (ten) necessary to maintain a temple and pray.

Shiksa: A derogatory term for a non-Jewish girl.

Sheggitz: The male form of *shiksa*.

Shul: The Hebrew word for temple.

Siddur: A holy prayer book.

Tallis: A ceremonial scarf.

Rebecca's Place, 1978

Susan St Aubin

Hal's stomach growled loudly as he and Evelyn followed her lover, Rebecca, up the stairs to her apartment. Now he was annoyed rather than excited, as he had been before Evelyn had decided they should all leave their bed for Rebecca's. Something about a jewel Rebecca usually wore in her pierced tongue, which she had taken out and left at home. Evelyn wanted her to wear that gold frog with tiny rubies for eyes. It made no sense to him. Rebecca had even brought Chinese food for them, which Evelyn had taken out of their oven, where it was keeping warm, and packed back into the shopping bag she now carried. He felt like he was in a cave when they got inside Rebecca's place – the ceiling seemed so low he ducked reflexively. Once Rebecca switched on the light, it wasn't as low as he thought, but when he saw the loft bed he realized he probably wouldn't be able to sit up straight there.

"I demand food now," Hal said. Since this seemed to be an evening of demands, why not make his known? He was ready to spank Evelyn if she didn't agree; in fact, imagining the feel of his palm smacking her flesh excited him. It could, he thought, work as well the other way around, with Evelyn feeling her flesh smack against his palm. As you hit, you are hit. Or maybe Rebecca should be the one to spank Evelyn; she needed retribution for this sudden change in plans, as well as for the spanking Evelyn had given her back at their place. He surprised himself with this sudden desire to watch Evelyn be punished by another woman, who would also be punished by the flesh smack-back, but the Herald, as Evelyn liked to call his cock, was twitching as if He knew this scene and was eager to get on with it. Hal himself had another hunger that was more pressing. He grabbed the bag of food from Evelyn and began putting the lukewarm containers on Rebecca's tiny kitchen table.

"We should heat them," said Evelyn, turning on the oven while Rebecca lit the gas heater in the corner.

Hal reached over to swat Evelyn's rear. She'd set the stage: what she gave Rebecca, he could give her. He was satisfied with the sting of her ass on his palm.

"No time," he said, opening a random container, which seemed to be chicken in some sort of sauce. "I want it cold. Now." He wolfed it down until his mouth and throat were on fire.

Evelyn handed him a glass of water. "That looks like Kung Pao chicken, Rebecca's favourite. North Chinese, hotter than a curry."

The water actually seemed to increase the burning sensation at first, although as he drank, his mouth gradually became numb.

Rebecca was eating fried rice out of another container while Evelyn patiently waited. "Aren't you hungry?" Rebecca asked her.

"Nope," Evelyn responded. "First things first. Rebecca, go put your gold frog back in your tongue."

Rebecca obediently disappeared into her bathroom, where Hal heard her brushing her teeth, then gargling. In the long silence that followed, Hal imagined her wrestling the frog into her tongue. He couldn't quite understand how it was fastened in there. The whole idea of tongue piercing made him gag.

Evelyn opened another container. "Mmmm. Mongolian beef," she said as she nibbled. "The trick is to take very small bites." She passed the box to Hal, who, his mouth still numb from the chicken, shook his head.

Rebecca came out of the bathroom and stuck out her tongue. "See?" she announced. "It's in."

Hal felt uneasy looking at it, but Evelyn poked him in the ribs. "You'll like it, really." She gathered the food containers and stuck them in the oven, then stepped over to the cushions piled in a corner beside the loft bed, and took off her jeans and sweater.

Hal, seeing a flash, turned to find Rebecca holding a camera, which made a strange grinding noise as a picture slid out of the front. Of course, a Polaroid, ideal for sexy pictures which no photo-processing employee would have to see.

"Perfect," said Rebecca. "I got a great back shot, Evelyn."

Hal watched the photograph gradually turn from grey to shades of brown and pink as Evelyn's ass surfaced, a process that was, he thought, a bit like watching someone come to life. Caught in the act of slipping off her jeans, she seemed real in this picture, even though she was playing a role Hal wasn't familiar with.

Then, another flash as Rebecca took Hal's picture looking at the picture of Evelyn.

"Clothes off, everyone," Evelyn ordered, clapping her hands like a teacher.

Rebecca handed Hal the camera so he could take a picture as soon as she was undressed. He carefully framed a full frontal shot of her with one hand on her hip, her mouth closed to hide the frog. Then Evelyn grabbed the camera while he undressed, and took a shot of him and Rebecca sitting side by side on the cushions, knees modestly held to their chests.

"Now stick out your tongue," she told Rebecca, moving in closer to capture the frog on film. "Look at her, Hal. Look at the frog."

Hal wondered what they would think of all this when they saw the pictures in twenty years. He saw the flash, watched Evelyn put the camera down, then felt her hand confidently stroke the Herald, and wondered why He rose to meet the lips of this stranger, formerly his lover. Hal felt left behind. He'd barely had time to get to know Rebecca, and now even Evelyn seemed unknowable.

Flash. Rebecca got a close shot of Evelyn's mouth around the Herald, while Hal blinked in the sudden light. Evelyn sat up, took the camera away from her, then guided the Herald into Rebecca's mouth. If we're a triad, thought Hal, then the Herald must be the hypotenuse, the line that ties it all together. I'm the base, Evelyn the right angle, Rebecca the side. My hypotenuse is what everyone wants. Thinking this made him feel less like a bystander. He was the base, in control, the beginning, and the end; he would conquer that frog. He felt the Herald thrust deeper into Rebecca's soft and willing mouth, and was relieved to sense the jewel as a small but intriguing firmness. His eyes closed as he listened to the whirr of the camera as Evelyn took pictures.

Rebecca felt her tongue, weighted with the frog, as something apart from her with a life of its own as it danced over Hal's penis, which didn't seem a bit bothered by the worried look on Hal's face. Her tongue kept going, increasing the pressure of the frog as it slipped over and around the cock. She liked the notion of separate body parts functioning at will, full of surprises for the main brain/mainframe. She'd picked that word up from Hal, the computer expert: mainframe, the brain of the whole computer system. Suddenly she saw each body as a system, with interconnected yet separating functioning parts, and thought people must have designed computers in their own image. She made her tongue move carefully so as not to injure either the part or the mainframe, and began thinking mathematically about the triangle of Hal, Evelyn and herself. Where would the jewelled frog fit? An angle, or one of the lines connecting the angles? She couldn't remember the geometric terms, but she knew her jewel was the connection that had first attracted Evelyn to her and, through Evelyn, she'd met Hal. It was Evelyn's desire for the jewelled frog that had brought them here, to her place; the frog was the connection that held the three angles together.

Evelyn took pictures, framing and creating what she watched. "Take him out of your mouth," she said, and Rebecca obeyed, laying her tongue, jewelled frog up, beside the pulsing Herald so Evelyn could shoot a picture. "Better let him rest a bit," Evelyn whispered in her ear, licking the rim. Rebecca lay still a minute, then tentatively kissed the Herald before she sucked him back inside.

Evelyn watched herself, too, wishing for even more distance from her body so she could photograph the three of them. She remembered wanting this, her two lovers together, but that memory felt distant, as if it belonged to someone else. But who would that be? Her, and yet not her. As she watched Hal and Rebecca together, she could recall wanting to eat experience, inhale it, and pictured her past self with each of them. But now these memories frightened her. She put down the camera to rub her palms together, still feeling the sharp slaps they'd given Rebecca's ass back at home, slaps to her as well as from her, like fire on her hands. She didn't need any more pictures.

She wanted to be alone with Hal, to kiss him, to hold him, to guide the Herald into herself instead of Rebecca. She wanted Rebecca to vanish. Is this love, she wondered, this act of exclusion? She had always imagined love expanding to include everyone, every experience, but never this contraction to a couple, rotating through the universe together yet always somehow pulling on each other, never completely satisfied, stuck in a claustrophobic sort of balance.

Meanwhile she felt bound to play her part. What was wrong, she decided, was Rebecca, who seemed to be dividing instead of connecting, Rebecca who was not letting her in now to share the Herald, Rebecca who would keep going unless Evelyn pushed her aside. Rebecca was ignoring Evelyn in favour of doing things two by two instead of three.

Hal was amazed at how good Rebecca's frog actually felt, how warm and smooth yet with a bit of roughness to those ruby eyes that sent the Herald over the top before He knew what hit Him. Rebecca drank hungrily – well, he thought, she must be, late as it was and no real dinner.

She lay down beside him and whispered in his ear, "See? It's a gentle frog." She gave one last delicate lap to the Herald, who rolled away, satisfied.

Hal didn't want to say he'd feared the frog would slice him open, because the Herald, who wasn't such a coward, had welcomed the frog, as if the two of them belonged together.

Hal wanted to be included in his own triangulation of Herald, frog, Hal.

Since they seemed to be going in pairs, Evelyn cleared her throat to remind them it was her turn. Of course sex is exclusion when you have to wait in line. Her fantasy had been about something beyond waiting your turn.

Hal raised his hands to her shoulders. "You're tense," he said, with a tone of surprise.

"Yes," Evelyn agreed, thinking, Who wouldn't be after watching your boyfriend make it with your lover right in front of you. But then she remembered a former self, who would have wanted this experience. Perhaps what was wrong with this scene was her own reluctance.

She let Hal rub her shoulders while she lay on her back with her head in his lap, the Herald limp beneath her cheek. Great, she thought. My turn and he's dead.

But that was exactly the problem: this wasn't supposed to be about turns, and it was up to her to change the action. With one foot she nudged Rebecca, who had picked up the camera. "No pictures," she whispered.

Rebecca looked puzzled.

"I want the three of us together," said Evelyn.

"A picture of the three of us?"

"No, the real three."

Her mind moved quickly. Intercourse wouldn't do because clearly that would only work for two. Hal's hands moved to her breasts, fingers circling the nipples until they hardened, helped by Evelyn's own remembrance of Rebecca's ass, whipped pink and glowing. She rubbed her foot on Rebecca's hand until Rebecca finally bent her head to Evelyn's clit, moving her jewel tongue over and around it.

"Turn around," Evelyn whispered. "I want to see if your ass is still pink."

"It can't still be." Rebecca laughed as she turned and straddled Evelyn, never taking her tongue away.

Evelyn reached a hand to Rebecca's ass, stroking one cheek, then the other, enjoying the smooth, loose texture like a pudding, like a risen soufflé, looking almost like something rich she could plunge her hands into, except here she couldn't because flesh was resistant; unlike baked concoctions of milk and egg, it was alive. She put a finger in Rebecca's creamy cunt, then two, then three, pressing her thumb to the button of the clit. Rebecca's tongue froze, the jewelled frog resting on Evelyn's own swollen gem for a moment before resuming its circumrotation.

Evelyn rolled her head over the Herald, who was gradually rising again. She lifted herself, reaching for Him with her free hand, but this was awkward and made her neck ache. She closed her thighs on Rebecca's head.

"Rearrangement!" she called. With three people someone had to give orders.

Rebecca and Evelyn disentangled themselves and sat up. We need a map, thought Evelyn, and suddenly laughed out loud.

"What?" asked Hal, his hands empty at his side.

"All right, I'll direct this shot. But no camera," Evelyn warned Rebecca, who appeared to be reaching for it again. "Now, let's get into, like, a circle." She was improvising, but she didn't want them to suspect because she understood that what she was enjoying most about this evening was the sense of being in charge. Under her control, nothing bad would dare happen. "A triangle in a circle. Rebecca, on your knees behind me. I love that frog so I wanted you to press it into my cunt. And I'll be on my knees behind Hal. And then Hal . . ." She arranged him so that he lay on his side with one hand on Rebecca's mound. Now Evelyn could take the Herald between her lips, but could give no more orders. She concentrated on sucking while simultaneously feeling Rebecca's jewelled tongue nudge her clit-button, then dip to the buttonhole.

She was amazed this was working. Every once in awhile Rebecca would suck in her breath and pull out her tongue, which meant Hal was doing his part. She could hear them all breathing in unison, incredibly, unbelievably coordinated, three bodies moving as one. She wondered if this could happen with five people, six, an infinite orgy, the whole world coming at once in a giant circle, one orgasm that would end war, poverty, starvation; human meanness forever wiped from the globe.

Hal felt Evelyn's mouth, firm and warm on the Herald she knew so well, and realized he'd never properly introduced him to Rebecca, not by name. The Herald hadn't seemed to think that was important so neither did Hal, who was now at one with his Herald, moving slightly in Evelyn's eager mouth. He pulled his finger from Rebecca's cunt and sniffed its strange sweet scent, something like an oatmeal cookie, a yeasty vanilla. Evelyn, he reflected, was more smoky, earthy; he remembered sitting outside by his grill, smoking a salmon while thinking of her. He ran his fingers from Rebecca's clit down to the opening and back, finally sliding in four fingers, moving them in and out while his palm pressed her mound in a rhythm to match the motion of Evelyn's tongue, reflecting how the part and the whole of him were also pulsating rhythmically together.

Hal came first, the Herald squirting deep into Evelyn's throat, and while she swallowed she felt a rush of warmth across her stomach as her own contractions began, exactly like Hal's but with nothing coming out except the liquids already swimming between her thighs. Rebecca still kept up the rhythm of their former joint breathing until with one large exhalation, she stopped, collapsing on top of Evelyn, who waited for her to start breathing again.

"Well," Evelyn said. She wanted to give linguistic form to their success, but she couldn't get her tongue to move. She thought that she had, finally, learned something, though she wasn't sure what. That three could be as good as a pair? That it was perfectly fair for Hal to have two orgasms because the first had been for the Herald, the other for him? She lay between Hal and Rebecca, holding their hands. "Reach over me and hold each other's hands, too," she said, adding, "please," so as not to appear to be ordering them around. But when they did clasp hands, she realized this was a circle, not a triad. It was an enclosed, fluid shape, without angles, that could function with many, or just two. The circle drifted, the circle slept as one.

Hal woke by habit at dawn, warm enough on the pile of cushions because the gas heater still hissed across the room, but hungry, no, starving. The food in the oven was probably dried crispy; he didn't even want to look. He extricated himself from the two women, and shook Evelyn's shoulder.

"Wake up," he whispered. "When do you have to be at school?"

She grunted as she sat up. "It's morning?"

He searched around for their clothes and they quietly dressed. Evelyn put on jeans that were way too long because they were Rebecca's, so she had to take them off again and feel around under the cushions until she found her own. Together they tiptoed out of the apartment.

At home in the shower as he soaped Evelyn's breasts while she washed her hair, Hal asked, "So, was last night what you wanted?"

She let the water run over her head and cascade down her breasts, carrying sweat, soap and dirt. "Yes, it was," she said. "I think we're learning what to do with three, don't you?"

"It worked," he said. "I liked it. But this is nice, too." He soaped her breasts again, rubbing his palms in circles over them.

She sighed as she placed herself under the flow of warm water again. "I'm glad it worked out, I just wouldn't want to lose track of this, though. Us. The pair."

"I don't think we ever would," he said. "It's just nice to have variety, someone like Rebecca, a different taste. I'd like to have many different tastes to share with you.'

"What?" she said, stopping with her hand on the faucet. She felt a physical shift, as though they had momentarily uncoupled and changed directions before rotating together again.

"You seem surprised. But you were a different person, too, with Rebecca there, and that was really interesting. Maybe confusing at first, then just exciting." He began to whistle, which Evelyn realized she'd never heard him do before.

"We have time for boiled eggs before I have to leave," she said, turning off the faucet, and grabbing a towel off the rack.

Rebecca woke alone. She'd heard them leave earlier, as she'd known they would, but had preferred not to let them know she cared about being left alone, calmly rolling over and drifting back to sleep so they wouldn't realize she'd been awake. Why fuss about it? She pulled a large cushion over herself, thinking of moving out, finding a bigger place, a better job, a lover who wanted only her.

"Enough of these screwed-up sex fiends," she mumbled to her pillows, including herself in that description because she had to admit last night had been a charge, until they'd left her. If she had the energy, she'd climb up to her loft bed for the rest of the day, but no, she decided it would be better to clean out her cupboards, throw out that Chinese food, probably rancid by now, and invite Hal for lunch. The best part of last night, she decided, was when she'd had him in her mouth, shutting out Evelyn, even the mainframe of Hal, just his cock in her mouth, like everything she'd ever wanted.

She dialled their number, knowing Hal would be working at home alone by now. "Hi," she said when he answered brusquely with a single "Yes?" no doubt expecting a call from work.

"I loved last night," she said after a pause. He didn't recognize her voice, after all that?

But then he said, "Rebecca!"

She listened to his breathing quicken. "I was just thinking, you guys left so suddenly I didn't even wake up to say goodbye! Would you like to come over for lunch?"

"Well . . ." He sounded doubtful. "Evelyn's at school, so I don't think she could make it."

"She used to come over for lunch all the time," said Rebecca. "But I guess she's having a busy day today."

"Yeah," said Hal after a pause that made Rebecca smile to herself. "She sometimes serves lunch at the Culinary Institute's restaurant. We should go there, it's a great deal."

"And let student cooks practise on us?" Rebecca protested. "No, I'd rather have you to myself today."

"We'd have to make reservations in advance anyhow, it's really popular. So, OK, I'll come over. Not for that old Chinese food, I hope."

"Oh, God, no, I tossed that out. How about soup? Tomato soup with cheese? We called it Blushing Bunnies in Girl Scouts. Hardly gourmet, but good."

"Blushing Bunnies?" he laughed. "Sounds as good as your blushing behind. I'll be there."

Well, well, she thought as she got ready, putting blush on her lips, her cheeks, and thinking about doing her ass, too, but that would probably just rub off on her clothes. She didn't think he'd be ready for a nude greeting at the door, but maybe soon. She found two cans of tomato soup in her cupboard, and some rather hardened cheese in the fridge, but grated and melted it would taste fine. At least it wasn't turning green.

When the bell rang at noon, she buzzed him in and greeted him at her open door with a kiss. "Back so soon?" she murmured, then, daring, slipped a hand over his cock, which rose beneath his jeans in a greeting of its own.

Take Me to Carnevale

Maxim Jakubowski

They had arranged to meet in a small café on the left hand side of Campo Santa Maria Formosa, right opposite the church and the hospital. It was February. It was Venice. A thin morning mist still shrouded the city, floating in from the lagoon, like a shimmering curtain of silk, half obscuring the old stones, the canals and the normal sounds of the floating city.

The connection had been made over the Internet.

He hadn't even brought his laptop with him on this Venice trip, but the apartment they were staying in, which he had agreed to house-sit for friends travelling in India, had a computer in almost every room and a wi-fi connection and it had been, for both of them, almost too much of a temptation. Like allowing their fate to be decided by the vagaries of electronic availability.

Emma had been sitting on one of the sofas, half reading and half daydreaming, while he listened to music on his iPod. Right then the soundtrack by Nick Cave for *The Assassination of Jesse James*, he would remember later.

"I don't know," Emma had said, and he had known exactly the precise words she had uttered, just from reading her lips behind the threnody in his ears. It was something she often mumbled when things were not quite right.

He'd switched off the music and turned towards her. "What is it?"

The green of her eyes emerged from a sea of sadness. "You know . . ." she replied.

He knew. Oh yes, he knew. They were just going nowhere, and no earnest conversation could put them back on track. Even in Venice.

They had reached the city a week or so earlier, arriving at Marco Polo airport. To save money, they had not gone to the extravagance of taking a water taxi but, instead, the bus which took them across the Ponte Della Liberta to Piazzale Roma where they had caught a vaporetto down the Grand Canal to the Rialto Bridge stop and, following the map they had been emailed by his friends, had somehow made their way on foot to the apartment, dodging the customary labyrinth of small bridges and lesser canals.

By now they had seen a multitude of churches, several handfuls of Titian and Canaletto paintings, eaten too much exquisite food to jade the best of palates and suffered an indigestion of baroque and classical architecture and the silences between them were growing longer.

From their bedroom window, they could see St Mark's Place and the Doge's Palace and the Campanile across a bend in the Canal. But the weather was cold and humid and the old building's heating was stuttering at its best and they'd had to wear sweatshirts most of the time both inside and outside.

Maybe he should have chosen the Caribbean where they could have lazed naked on a beach and the warmth might have seeped into their mood. But Emma had never been to Venice and he had promised her he would take her anywhere she wanted, and she was aware that Roberto and Marta had offered them the apartment here should they ever wish to visit. Geoff had been to Venice several times before and, to be frank, had never been too much of a fan. In summer, the canals smelled and he disliked being just an anonymous part of the tourist crowds. In truth, he was not a great traveller.

Emma, on the other hand, was twenty years younger and always sported an enthusiasm for new places and experiences that he no longer could pretend he had. And he secretly knew he'd never possessed the joy or curiosity even when he had been younger himself.

Although it remained mostly unsaid they both knew to a different degree that their relationship was doomed. The age difference, the opposing temperaments, the cultural differences, the weight of his own past, her own ambitions in life. But love still bound them. His, full of despair that she might well happen to be the last great love of his life; hers, full of wonder that Geoff had somehow become the first great love in her life but with her mind, her imagination nagging her daily about the roads not taken and all the future roads that were still to be reached.

In an effort to combat the due date on their affair, they had come to Venice. In her mind, she had wanted to confront beauty. In his, it was just a melancholy vision of past literary memories of Thomas Mann, Byron, Dickens or Nic Roeg, which resonated in the greyness of his soul, the delusion that a trip to a new place could repair the stitches that were coming apart in their affair.

"Carnival begins tomorrow," he had pointed out to her.

"Really?" she had exclaimed, her eyes widening in anticipation.

"Yes."

"Will you buy me a mask?" Emma had asked.

"Of course."

"And I will get one for you," she suggested. "Something darkly romantic, that would just suit you."

"Why not?"

"And we acquire them separately, and they remain secret until the first evening we go out and wear them. A surprise!"

"A lovely idea," Geoff had readily agreed, the fleeting thought of Emma quite naked except for a delicate white Carnival mask shielding her face, and her green eyes peering through the disguise already warming his heart and suggestible loins.

His finger lingered on her knee, and he shuddered. The electricity between them still worked.

"Can we go online and read all about the Carnival?" she asked.

"Of course," he said. They made their way to the guest bedroom where the nearest connected computer stood on a rickety trestle table their host often used to mix his paints on.

Above it, by coincidence, hung slightly crooked on the wall by the window, was a gaudy painting of a woman in chains wearing only a black mask which obscured her eyes. Roberto's latest BDSM variation.

They surfed freely for the next couple of hours, learning all about Carnevale and its origins, the stories of Casanova, the types of masks and their significance. One link led to another and yet another until an aimless stroke of the keyboard took them to the website where out of sheer prurient curiosity they arranged for the meeting in the bar on Campo Santa Maria Formosa the next day.

At first, Geoff had been somewhat hesitant, but Emma's enthusiasm had swayed him.

"It will be an adventure," she said.

"I suppose so," he answered.

"Don't be so old," she added.

Geoff smiled wryly. She always knew how to silence him.

"Yes, it's all because of Attila the Hun."

They were sipping espressos at the back of the small café. The man was in his fifties and had silver hair and was explaining how the earliest inhabitants of Venice had been exiled all the way to the lagoon by the invasion of their native lands by foreign hordes.

"Fascinating," Emma commented.

"And the bridge that connects us to the Italian mainland was only built by Mussolini under a century ago. Before that we were isolated and you could only reach the city by water."

Geoff ordered another round from the hovering waitress. Mostly San Pellegrino mineral water; neither he nor Emma could cope with too much coffee at this time of day.

"It's a party," the man who called himself Jacopo said. "But we try to organize matters so that we adhere to all the old traditions of the Venice Carnevale, not the diluted versions that have sadly evolved over the years since Carnevale's heyday."

"We understand," Geoff said. Emma looked him in the eyes, and nodded.

"It is strictly by invitation, of course," he continued. "Normally, we try to restrict attendance to pure Venetians, but as you know, there are fewer of us now. The younger generations are all leaving the city. So sad."

He looked at Emma. Her dark hair shone glossily; she had washed it just before they had left the apartment to walk here. When wet, her curls ironed out naturally and her hair extended then to the small of her back. Geoff observed her, too. She looked luminous. Already excited by the prospect of the party they were being informally interviewed for. As if a fire was rising inside her, bringing light to her features, heat to her hidden senses. Geoff recognized that gleam in her eyes. It was invariably present when she had been fucked. He kept on watching, transfixed as Jacopo's words swept soundlessly over him. The man with the silver hair also kept on observing Emma, as if weighing her in his steady gaze.

Geoff returned to reality, reluctantly abandoning his vision of Emma's fascinated attention to the man's words.

"Naturally, you remain masters of your destiny. A polite 'no' will always be an acceptable response to overtures, although it is hoped that all guests will participate freely and openly in the proceedings."

Again, Emma nodded, her chin bobbing up and down.

Geoff sighed discreetly.

It was true that they had often discussed the remote prospect of others joining in their games, their lovemaking. But they had never reached the stage where they had actively done anything about it.

Something inside him – something rotten or diseased? – had always imagined what it would be like to see Emma mounted by another, harboured the curiosity to witness how another man would touch her, make her moan. Because he found her so beautiful, part of him felt she should be shared with the whole world, so that all and sundry could truly understand why his love for her was so strong and overpowering. But it was a long road from thoughts to the realities of the flesh.

She had even asked, "Would you be jealous if it happened?" and he had been obliged to dig deep into his thoughts and had finally answered quite truthfully "I'm not sure, maybe if I could watch. I wouldn't want you to fuck another man behind my back, that's for sure."

"Wonderful," Jacopo said as he rose from the café table. "You are a lovely couple. I think you will enjoy our parties a lot."

They had jointly agreed to attend the opening of Carnevale the next day. He had slipped over a piece of paper with the address.

"Every party takes place in a different locale," the man with the silver hair had said. "They can only be reached by the canals, so you will have to make arrangements accordingly."

They all shook hands and he departed.

Left alone, Geoff and Emma looked at each other. He tried to smile, but couldn't raise the right rictus. He knew already that they would go. Emma had always been a woman of her words and once a decision had been taken, only hell and high water could ever change her mind.

"Well," she said.

"Hmmm . . ."

Emma was dressing.

"Don't wear panties," Geoff suggested.

"Really?"

"Yes. I think it would fit in with the spirit of the occasion."

Emma chuckled softly. "If you say so. Anyway, the dress is quite heavy, so I shouldn't feel the cold . . ." She gave him a twirl. He applauded theatrically.

"Flattery will get you everywhere," she said.

They had been shopping in Mestre. In Venice, the prices were much too unaffordable. She had found him a sleek black silk suit made in Thailand, which Geoff wore with a black shirt and a scarlet bow tie.

"My prince of darkness!" Emma laughed. As if he now reminded her of a vampire.

In contrast, the dress they had acquired for tonight's event for her was white and made from thick linen, falling from her bare shoulders to her ankles with ornate elegance, thin, almost invisible straps holding the dress up above her small, delicate breasts, unveiling just a discreet if appetizing hint of gentle cleavage. Underneath she wore just dark hold-up stockings reaching to mid-thigh, their black veil as sharp as her luxuriant pubic hair. A perfect conjugation of nights, when she cheekily raised the dress to her midriff, exposing herself to him.

God, she was stunning! Her lipstick was fiery red and she had surrounded her eyes with a grey circle of kohl.

In the end they had gone shopping for masks together at Mondonovo, on Rio Terra Canal, near the Campo Santa Margherita, where masks could still be found that were replicas of the old historical, traditional models, and were different from the traditional fare on offer to gullible tourists in search of local colour.

For Geoff, in his black outfit, they had chosen a *larva*, also called a *volto*. It was white, made of fine wax and should have typically been worn with a tricorn and cloak, which he had of course absolutely no intention of doing. After all, this was the twenty-first century! The shape of the mask would allow him to breathe and drink easily, and so there was no need to take it off, thus preserving anonymity.

Emma, on the other hand, had been coaxed by the old wrinkled lady at the store to select a *moretta* instead of the more traditional *bauta*. It was an oval mask of black velvet that was usually worn by women visiting convents. Invented in France, it had rapidly become popular in ancient Venice as it brought out the beauty of feminine features. The mask was finished off with a veil, and was normally secured in place by a small bit in the wearer's mouth. As this was not appropriate to participate in a modern party, Emma's model had been modified so it was held by a clip at its apex that was attached to her mountain of curls.

"*Bella*," the old woman had said when Emma had tried the mask on.

"*Bellissima*," Geoff said in turn, with a painful stab of fear coursing through his stomach, as Emma stood, fully attired in dress and mask, and the jungle of her curls peering impudently above the formal mask.

"*Grazie mille*," she laughed.

There was so much more he wanted to say to her. Like "Do you really want to go?" or "What will you do if another man proposes to you?" or "Do you still love me?" but the gondola they had booked had just arrived. They walked down to the waterside entrance of the building. The night air was cold and the sky full of scattered stars whose reflection glistened over the waters of the small canal like a million phosphorescent fish.

Geoff read the address out to the gondolier in his French-accented Italian.

"It's party time," Emma said.

The half-abandoned palazzo dominated the Grand Canal halfway between the Ponte del Rialto and the Ponte dell'Accademia, with the Campo San Polo visible from the ornate balconies on the landside of the building.

The tall man who wore the white mask with the elongated beak, similar to the head attire medics had worn in the years of the plague, when pepper had been lodged into the furthest reaches of the bird of prey-like beak to shield its wearers from the illness, had been hovering near them most of the evening. They had briefly been introduced by Jacopo, earlier on in the festivities. Occasionally the man would approach them with new glasses of champagne and would whisper in Emma's ear, or casually allow his leather-gloved hands to brush against her bare shoulders. His English was nigh perfect, albeit with West Coast American inflections. Geoff couldn't remember his name. Real or otherwise. They had been introduced as Byron and Ariadne.

As neither Emma's nor Geoff's Italian was fluent enough, they had been isolated in the margins of the party and its flowing conversations. They had both drunk too much by now. Which meant Geoff was retreating, as he did, into longer and longer silences, whereas her demeanour was becoming looser, more joyful by the minute. How many times now had she wondered at the sheer elegance of the evening and its incomparable setting, the candles illuminating the cavernous, marble-floored rooms, the gold dishes laden with fruit, the never-ending flow of booze. She was intoxicated by both the alcohol and the sense of occasion. Was this the adventure she always claimed she was seeking when he would raise any questions about the future?

A hand took hold of his. Geoff turned round. A woman in a red velvet dress and a white powdered wig pulled him a metre or two towards her. He looked up at her. She had endless legs enhanced by thin six-inch heels. Behind her mask, he could see her eyes were the colour of coal.

"You are English, no?"

"Indeed," he answered.

Her scent was sweet, cloying almost.

"So you like our Carnevale?"

"Absolutely," he responded, ever polite.

Her purple lipsticked lips moved into the shape of a kiss. "Is it your first time in Venice?" she asked.

"Not quite," he answered. "But the first time I've been here at Carnival time, though."

"Ah . . ." She moved nearer to him.

He realized they were now alone in the large room; the woman with purple lips, Emma, the tall guy and him. Somehow all the nearby partygoers had drifted out silently into the other neighbouring rooms, leaving faint echoes of conversations and the tinkling of crystal glasses sort of suspended in the tobacco smoke-infested air.

He took a step back.

"Oh . . . Shy?"

"No," he muttered.

"So?" She extended her left arm and her fingers swept across his dry lips.

"Your woman isn't as shy, I see," she remarked.

Geoff's heart dropped all the way down to his stomach as he glanced round. Emma was now being embraced by the tall stranger, who held her tight against the far wall of the room, his hand burrowing under her dress, his face muzzled into hers. Her eyes were closed.

"Come," the woman with the white powdered wig said,

taking him by the hand and leading him to a low couch at the opposite end of the room.

He followed, as if in a trance. Time slowed down to a crawl.

Her cunt tasted of exotic spices. Pungent, strong, savage. His tongue lapped her generous juices with quiet and studied abandon.

She spread her legs wider apart and pressed his head down firmer against her. Geoff gasped momentarily for breath.

"Lick me harder," she ordered him.

Once she had tired of his worshipping the thick folds of her labia and the invisible radiating heat pulsing through her opening all the way from her innards, she pulled him on to the worn-out couch and slipped his trousers downwards and began sucking him off.

Somehow, even though she was talented and imaginative, he failed to get totally hard, and she gave up within a few minutes.

"No worry," she said. "It happens."

Red-faced, he looked her in the eyes, attempting to find out how old she might be behind that mask. Her skin was spotless and taut and her unending legs were those of an athlete at the peak of her form. He gulped and recalled instantly the taste of her and its striking flavours. She had been on her knees and rose to her feet. He just stood there, his black silk trousers bunched around his ankles.

"Undress," she said. It was more of an order than a suggestion.

He meekly obeyed.

He wanted to turn around and see where Emma was. And the tall man. Their own noises had been muted, distant, but nevertheless insidiously present all the while he had been involved with the purple-lipsticked woman. She sensed this.

"Do so as you are. Don't turn," she said, unclenching the black leather belt that circled her thin waist. "Look down to the floor as you undress."

He noticed the smudged purple stains of lipstick on the mushroom tip of his cock, like dried wine against the ridged flesh of his masculinity. He pulled the trousers down over his laced shoes. Then kicked the shoes off and quickly slipped off his socks. Surely there was no more ridiculous sight than a naked man wearing just black socks? He then pulled himself up and began unbuttoning his shirt. As he did so, he saw the woman reach for her matching red handbag, which had been lying on the couch and pull a devious contraption, all leather straps and ivory trunk from it.

His stomach froze.

There was a faint cry from the other end of the room.

He was now naked.

The woman pulled her ruched dress upwards and belted the strap-on to her waist. The artificial cock jutted ahead of her like the prow of a boat. Hard, inflexible.

"Maybe this will give you a hard-on?" she suggested. "Legend has it that English men are much appreciative . . ."

He knew he could say no, and just leave the room with no further words of protest. But the word wouldn't pass his lips. And then he knew he could not leave Emma here alone anyway.

The woman indicated the couch and how he should bend over its sides and she positioned herself behind him.

Now, through the corner of his eye, he could finally see Emma and the other man. She had also been stripped naked, and wore only the hold-up black stockings. The pallor of her body was unbearable to look at, as was the shocking contrast between her skin and the dark as night material of the stockings.

The other man's cock was thick and dark pink and was ploughing her roughly and systematically, pulling out of her almost all the way with every stroke and then digging back into her up to the hilt with every return thrust. Machinelike, metronomic, like a deadly instrument of war. Emma's face rhythmically banged against the wall with every repeated movement in and out of her.

Geoff felt the pain explode through his own body as the woman's artificial member breached him with one swift movement. He swallowed, almost bit his tongue

As he did so, he realized why Emma was so silent. A red handkerchief had been stuffed into her mouth. He couldn't help noticing the handkerchief was the exact same shade of red as the lipstick she had decided to adorn herself with to attend the party.

Also, her hands were tied behind her back with brown fur-lined metal cuffs.

She must have agreed to this.

There was another huge stab of unbearable pain as the strap-on began stretching him and he felt himself being filled like he had never been filled before. For a brief moment, he feared he was going to defecate, as the pit of his stomach went totally numb, but the pressure against his inner walls soon reasserted itself and the pain slowly began to recede. Not that being fucked in this manner gave him any pleasure. He felt as if was becoming detached from his own body as it was being defiled.

And his eyes kept on hypnotically watching the abominable movements of the other man's massive member inside Emma, the way the tight skin around her opening creased inwards and then outwards again as she was being implacably drilled, and the eyelet of her anus winked open and shut with every movement below it. There was sweat dripping from her forehead. Her calves tightened, her ass cheeks shook, her hair was undone, her curls spilling in every conceivable direction as if moved by an invisible wind rising from the nearby lagoon and flying over the Giudecca to shroud the city on its way to the marshes and Trieste.

From the tremors mechanically coursing through her body, Geoff knew Emma had come. The stranger had succeeded in raising her senses, playing her like Geoff had rarely been capable of doing.

But the man did not cease.

He would continue fucking her until she begged for him to stop.

Would she ever?

Back at the apartment, they at first could not bear to look each other in the eyes. They went to bed in total silence, still coated by the dry sweat of their exertions, of their shame.

They slept late into the morning.

After breakfast, they took a vaporetto to the Lido and later to the Isola di San Servolo – a trip they had agreed to undertake a few days before they had stumbled across the website which had lured them to the party.

Over dinner in the San Polo district, they began communicating again.

"Talk about an adventure!"

"I suppose you could call it that . . ."

"Regrets?"

"No."

"Sure?"

"Absolutely not."

"Were you jealous?"

"A little, I suppose."

"You?"

"No. It's . . . how can I put it . . . life . . ."

"Certainly one way of putting it . . ."

They tried to go for coffee at Café Florian, but it was closed on Tuesdays in winter. They made their way back to the apartment. There was no power. They tiptoed their way through darkness to the bedroom.

"It doesn't change anything, does it?"

"I don't know," she replied, spooning against him.

It was at that precise moment Geoff knew he was about to lose her.

That it was too late to plea, beg, affirm his love, however impure it now was.

He didn't sleep that night. He stayed awake in the darkness, listening to the vague sounds of the Canal delle Due Torri lapping against the building's rotting stone facade and the imperceptible melody of her breath, as her chest moved peacefully up and down against him under the duvet.

He smelled her, listened to her as if trying to fix these memories in his brain once and for all. What he would one day be left with.

Geoff finally succumbed to sleep around seven in the morning.

When he awoke, she had left the apartment.

The morning went by. He tried to read, but couldn't concentrate on the text, whether a week-old newspaper or an anonymous serial killer thriller.

Emma returned at the beginning of the afternoon. She was wearing that black skirt he had once bought her in Barcelona and which held so many memories. The one with the giant sunflower patch sewn into its flank. And a T-shirt he had once loaned her in the early days of the affair when their lovemaking had proven a tad rough and messy and he had left compromising semen stains across the blouse she had been wearing that day. The T-shirt that advertised "Strangers in Paradise" across the Aubrey Beardsley-like face of a woman.

He was sipping a glass of grapefruit juice at the kitchen table.

He welcomed her.

"Had a good walk?"

"No."

"Oh . . ."

A shadow passed across the room shielding her eyes from his examination.

"I saw him again," Emma said.

The pain inside returned.

"Have you fucked him again?"

"No."

"I see."

"There is another party tonight. A different palazzo this time, near the Campo San Silvestro. He's invited me. Wants to introduce me to some of his friends . . ."

"Do you want to go?"

"Yes."

"Without me?"

"Yes."

"Why? I still love you, you know."

"I know. But love is not enough. I need adventures, you see. On my own. I don't want to be owned . . ."

"I've never tried to own you, you know that. You're too much of a gypsy to be kept in a cage."

Emma smiled. "You can come, if you wish, I reckon. As long as you'd promise not to interfere and allow whatever happens to happen . . ."

"I don't think so," Geoff said. "Don't much care to repeat the other evening's foursome. Just didn't feel right to me somehow."

"I understand."

She walked to the bedroom they had been using; she was holding a large Rinascente canvas bag.

"What have you got there? Been shopping?" he asked.

She looked away. "No . . ." She hesitated then came clean. "It's the outfit he wishes me to wear tonight."

"Can I—"

Emma interrupted him. "I'd rather you didn't see it, Geoff."

That evening, he left the apartment to wander the narrow streets and have several coffees in a row to allow her to dress in privacy.

By the time he returned, she had already left for the Carnevale or had maybe been picked up.

She did not return that night or the following day.

His days and nights were haunted by obscene visions of her with other men, and the abominable images of alien cocks of all shapes, sizes and shades invading her. Her mouth, her cunt, her arse, her hands. Orgasmic flush invading the delicate pallor of her skin. The indelible marks of hands, ropes, whips and paddles across the familiar geography of her body. And the sound of her voice just saying, "Yes", "Yes" and "Yes" again, like Bloom's Molly. And the grateful acceptance of her smile, of her eyes.

Finally, she reappeared halfway through Carnevale.

She looked radiant. More beautiful than ever.

"You haven't shaved," she remarked. "It's so grey."

"Couldn't be bothered," he said. "So, you're back."

"Not really," Emma said. "I've just returned to pick up my stuff, my clothes and all that."

"I'm sorry," Geoff said.

"It's the way things are," Emma remarked. "After Carnevale ends, Master has promised me that the adventure will continue.

He wants to take me to Mardi Gras in New Orleans and also the carnival in Rio one day . . ."

"How exciting," he said bitterly in response.

"Don't be like that, please, Geoff," she protested. "You should be happy for me. Respect what I am doing, surely."

"I find that difficult, Emma. I would have given you everything. Surely you realize that."

"I know, but it would never have been enough. You know that. I'm young. I have a life to live. My life. "

Her skin shone in the pale light coming through the window, the curls in her hair like the gift of Medusa.

Geoff closed his eyes. Promising himself he would not open them until she had left with her belongings.

He never saw Emma again. He stayed in Venice until the end of Carnevale. At dinner one evening, he met another woman, a legal interpreter from Arizona. They had a few drinks together and he was pleased to see that he could still chat up a woman, be reasonably witty and seductive. But when he took her back to the apartment and undressed her after some willing fumbling and a cascade of mutual kisses, he wasn't capable of fucking her. Just couldn't get hard enough, despite her assiduous ministrations. Lack of inspiration or wrong person, he wasn't sure.

The next day as he sat at a café by the Rialto Bridge, he caught a glimpse of a small water cab racing down the Grand Canal. A woman was standing at its prow. For a brief moment, he thought he recognized Emma. Same skirt and T-shirt, but the embarkation was moving too fast for him to be certain it was actually her. At any rate, she was alone on the small boat, standing erect behind the driver, facing the breeze.

Shortly after, his friends returned from India and he quickly made his way back to London.

He left the two masks they had worn on that fateful evening behind. Not quite the sort of apparel you could wear for the Notting Hill Carnival.

He would never go back to Venice.

The Epicures

Marilyn Jaye Lewis

It was called Petrograd in honour of the opulence of czarist
Russia. Its interior brimmed with ostentation and the owners
didn't care; attracting the proletariat was not their aim. The
average working stiff could hardly afford the cocktails at
Petrograd, let alone anything from its tasting menu. We,
however, always ordered from the tasting menu, blind, with our
wine flights selected especially for us by Sergei – who was not
really Russian, or if he was, it was from so many generations
ago as to make any Tartar roots in him undetectable beneath
his Brooklyn accent.

In those days, we savoured every moment of our affluence
because we recalled too keenly how it had felt to be among the
starving class. Our riches were so new to us in fact that poverty,
it seemed, still lay in wait for us up the block, wondering when
we might return. We weren't sure. All we knew was that good
fortune had alighted on us at last and we planned to wring the
most from it – starting with haute cuisine and vintage wines –
before good fortune evaporated into the ether and left us poor
again.

Every booming market goes bust eventually, and to survive
it you have to prepare for the inevitable in advance. Our safety
net was our loft apartment in Tribeca; we'd paid cash for it in
early 1982. It belonged to us. We were determined not to be
homeless again and we turned that cavernous, once-industrial
space into a lush cocoon. That was where our hedonism went
unleashed for many years, right there in the bosom of our
sanctuary.

Paulina moved in with us in March of that particular year (was it '84, '85?). We'd met her at Petrograd in early December, when everyone in New York was already tipping extravagantly and bursting with Christmas cheer. She was a coat check girl there, an immigrant. Illegal, for all we knew, but it wasn't important to us. We liked her enormously. She was saucy with a dry sense of the absurd. Yet when we welcomed her into our home that first frosty evening, we discovered quickly that all her worldly urbanity fell away from her when she was kissed – along her collarbone, say, or on her lips, her neck, across her pale shoulders; she melted under the tenderness.

Paulina's legs were long and parted so easily, but she was not tall. She gave the impression of being tall, however, because she wore those very high Italian heels that made her legs look even longer.

Her breasts were full, her waist was narrow and her hips wide, and although she was curvy, she was also slender. When not in her coat check uniform, she dressed in the height of fashion. She was fastidious about her appearance. And truth be told, so were we. I guess you could have called us vain and not been far off the mark. Still, at least we could kid ourselves about it. Perhaps it was that unexpected dash of humility that kept us from being too insufferable. Whatever it was, we were always greeted by the staff at Petrograd with welcoming smiles. We were made to feel at home there.

Bertrand, my fiancé, was what one used to call "a salty dog" – an experienced man with a rather wanton libido. Far from satiating his appetites, however, good food and good wine only made his carnal cravings more pronounced. He didn't have to say a word. When an item from the blind tasting menu was brought to our table and laid before him, I could tell by the merry gleam in his eye of which delicate or yielding, straining or supple quality of a woman's body he was most reminded. Five years we had been together, and in that brief time, I had come to learn his lascivious thoughts well. I knew he could say the same about me.

As luck would have it, we were both fond of women as sexual playmates; of servicing them, of testing their limits, their capacities, delighting in their raptures. Bertrand's easy glide between the sights, smells and tastes of food, and the idea of devouring women (metaphorically, of course), was not lost on me. His appetites filled my eager mind with irresistible pictures – a fleshy rear end, a succulent thigh; a hole stretched to accommodate my lover's unflagging lust. I often drank my wine a little too freely at Petrograd; the atmosphere there crackled with barely concealed promiscuity. The wine going to my head, the heady mix of Bertrand's pronounced tastes and the spectre of the dinner crowd's insatiability – set off so flatteringly by candlelight; all of it served to glut that river of longing in me until the waters threatened to overflow all over the seat of my chair.

Paulina would flirt shamelessly with us when we left the restaurant in our inebriated state. I believe I was the one who slid to her our address, scribbled on the inside of a Petrograd matchbook cover. "Do they ever give you a night off around here?" I said.

She half smiled and replied, "Sure. We're closed on Sundays."

"Ah," Bertrand chimed in, content in the afterglow of a Petite Sirah Port. "The Lord's day. What could be more fortuitous?"

Paulina and I regarded each other quizzically, neither of us entirely sure what Bertrand meant. Still I said, "Well, by all means, join us some Sunday evening. Come for dinner. We're excellent cooks."

"We're modest, too." Bertrand helped me into my winter coat.

Paulina laughed politely. "No reason to be modest, you know. No one would fault you for crowing a bit. Most of your attributes are readily discernible."

Bertrand slipped her a handsome tip. "You shovel it all so seamlessly," he said sweetly.

She winked at him and stuffed the tip in her pocket.

It had been two weeks since we'd last been to Petrograd, so Paulina was not uppermost in our minds when our downstairs buzzer bleated loudly early one Sunday evening just prior to

Christmas. The noise startled us from our mindless gazing at the oversized television screen.

Bertrand stretched and said, "Who could that be?"

"Shall we buzz it up and see?"

He said, "Why not?"

We got up from the comfy couch and then buzzed up our visitor.

We couldn't have been more pleased when we saw Paulina – dressed in her Sunday best – step off the old freight elevator out in the hallway.

"It's Paulina," I said happily.

"So it is. Well, come in, Paulina. Make yourself at home."

She came inside. "You neglected to give me your phone number, so I took it as a sign."

"Of what?" I asked curiously, helping her out of her lovely coat in our entryway.

"That I was welcome anytime. That calling ahead would have only been a formality."

Bertrand and I smiled at each other. He said to her, "How right you were, love. You know, you have quite a good grasp on the English language."

"I know," she said pertly. "Now, what are we drinking? Are we going to get festive with it being so close to Christmas?"

"Around here," Bertrand said, "we even get festive on Arbor Day. Why don't you ladies relax in there by the fire and I'll whip up something wonderful in the kitchen."

"Like what?" I asked.

"I'll think of something. Maybe something frothy or steamy, or creamy – I don't know. I only know that it will be brimming with possibilities and there will be plenty to go around."

"And then what about dinner?" I wanted to know. "Should we plan on ordering up?"

"No," he said. "Let's cook, the three of us, together. Can you cook, Paulina?"

"Not really," she said. "But I can follow directions; I'm easily taught. You know, I grasp things well."

"I'm sure you do," Bertrand said, eyeing her perfectly manicured fingers. But beneath her high-toned appearance,

she was just a little tart, Paulina was, and Bertrand and I
enjoyed it thoroughly – the aural bait she was dangling. "We'll
definitely work those pretty fingers of yours to the bone," he
went on. "We're excellent teachers. I'm sure the three of us will
concoct something memorable."

I took Paulina by the hand and led her into the living area.
Our loft had not come with an actual fireplace; we'd had a
quasi-one designed for us, though. It was elevated on a brick
platform, with a bronze vent above it and encased in bevelled
glass. There were logs on a grate and amber flames; it looked
impressive. But it was more an elaborate Sterno pit than a
source of any real heat.

"How cosy," Paulina purred. "And for such an enormous
room. Not an effect that's easy to achieve."

"We had time on our hands," I assured her.

"And money, I'm guessing."

"That, too. Shall we sit?" Without a moment's hesitation,
even in her expensive skirt and sweater, Paulina stretched out
on the rug by the fire. I sat down beside her. "Where are you
from?" I asked her.

"Oh, far away," she replied vaguely. "Lots of ice and snow,
you know, that sort of place."

"And what did you do there?"

"A little of what you do here, I should think."

"Here, as in America? Or here, as in our apartment?"

She looked up at me. "Your apartment," she said coyly.

I leaned over and kissed her, just a quick kiss, on the side of
her face. Her skin was soft. She smelled pretty. "Fascinating,"
I said.

"What is?"

"You, your secret world."

She shrugged. "And you don't have any secrets?"

"None," I said quietly. "There's been nothing that's been
that important."

"What about him?"

"Bertrand?"

"Yes."

"An open book – ask him anything, you get an answer. Not

always the answer you're hoping for, but an answer, an honest one."

"And he likes to cook?"

"We both do. We love food – the pleasure of it. There was a time when we didn't have much."

"Pleasure or food?" she asked.

"Food," I said decisively. "Between us, there has been no lack of pleasure."

"And yet you're both so thin. The hedonists I knew in my country were always on the fleshy side, and, sadly, always in such a hurry to get undressed and show it off."

Hedonists? The word made me laugh. "Your vocabulary is certainly impressive, Paulina."

One of her perfectly manicured hands reached up and lightly stroked my cheek. "And you're pretty, too," she said. "They aren't always as pretty as you."

Bertrand came into the room carrying a pitcher and some glasses. "We've a rum punch for starters," he announced. "Is that festive enough?"

"Rum punch!" I enthused. "It goes perfect with Christmas fudge. I'll go get a tray from the kitchen and bring some in."

In the mere moments it took me to arrange the fudge on a glass tray and bring it into the living area, Bertrand had managed to remove Paulina's pretty Italian shoes and was gently massaging her feet through her stockings down there on the floor by the fire. Her stockings were black with a pretty, all-over lacy pattern.

"Wolford," I said, sitting down next to them with the tray of fudge in hand. I set it down on the floor.

Paulina said dreamily, "Pardon me?"

"Your stockings – I recognize the pattern – Wolford hosiery. I saw those at Bergdorf's." Bertrand had filled our glasses with the rum punch and they were lined up in a neat little row on the elevated hearth in front of us. I leaned over Paulina and reached for a glass. I added, "Being a coat check girl must pay *very* handsomely to afford Wolford."

She said slyly, "You'd be surprised."

"Nothing surprises us any more, does it, dear?"

Bertrand, content for the moment to be rubbing Paulina's feet and driving her quietly into ecstasy, said, "No. Nothing does. Not any more."

Moaning softly, Paulina barely left her reverie when she mused, "I would have liked to have known you both then."

"When's that?" I said. I was the only one among us who was not immediately heading into some type of swoon. I helped myself to a piece of fudge.

"Back when things surprised you," she said.

Bertrand smiled at the remark. He parted Paulina's legs and stared at whatever it was he could see up under her skirt.

"I was right, you know," I said, though no one seemed to be noticing me. "About the fudge, I mean. It goes great with the rum punch, if anyone's interested: sugar on top of sugar, you know. They complement each other. Of course, a little goes a long way."

Bertrand leaned over and grabbed Paulina by her hips and slid her down the rug closer to him, her skirt sliding up around her waist as he did so, revealing that her expensive stockings were the stay-put kind. She was not wearing garters. But she was wearing a tiny pair of silk panties, ruby red with a black lace pattern overlay. They looked stunning against her bone-white skin. A half-moon-shaped scar on her pelvis peeked out at the top of her panties. I ran my finger lightly along the scar.

"I had a baby once," Paulina said. "They took it out of me there." The scar did not look new. She said, "Are you surprised?"

I looked at Bertrand and said, "A little – how about you?"

"Actually, yes," he agreed, sitting now with Paulina's legs spread before him and practically wrapped around him. She had draped her legs over each of his arms. "I am a little surprised by that news. You're so young."

"I was even younger then. I wanted to give birth the real way, but the doctor wouldn't let me. Things became complicated. He was afraid I was going to die. But I was looking forward to childbirth; now, I won't have any more babies."

We didn't ask about the fate of the one baby she'd had. If she were a mother, it would come out in good time. If she wasn't, well . . . her private world wasn't really our business yet; we barely knew her.

Bertrand slipped a roving finger inside the crotch of Paulina's silk panties and gently stroked the hidden lips. "Will you be with any of your family at Christmas?" he asked her.

"No. I'm alone in America."

"Do you miss your family?"

"Not much," she said. She pulled aside the crotch of her panties to give Bertrand better access to her lips.

"Wow," he said quietly. "You're beautiful."

She looked at me. "Does he say that about every girl?"

"No," I assured her.

"Have there been many?"

"A few," I said. Bertrand pushed a finger into Paulina's vagina. Her eyes gleamed when he did it. She looked intoxicated – in that amorous way. I added, "But none of the others were as pretty as you are."

She moaned contentedly and rocked on Bertrand's probing finger. She was a girl who liked being told she was pretty, even though there was likely no doubt about it in her own mind. I leaned down and kissed her on her mouth.

"You taste like sugar," she said.

I smiled at her. I broke off a tiny corner of the fudge and fed it to her. She didn't so much eat it as let it melt in her mouth. Then her eyes sparked. "That *is* good. Did you make it yourself?"

"Yes," I said quietly. "I made it this morning."

Bertrand, having lost Paulina's undivided attention for now, reached for his cocktail and scooted closer to us. He helped himself to a piece of fudge. He said, "What would we like for dinner tonight?"

I was too busy feeding Paulina, and kissing her neck, kissing her across her collarbone, to answer him right away. I was on all fours, leaning down to her. Bertrand rested a hand on my rear end then let his hand roam all over my tight slacks. He said quietly, "I'm thinking ratatouille; something with something else, and then ratatouille on the side."

"But that's a summer dish," I said distractedly. "And it takes hours."

"We've got hours . . . haven't we? Paulina, do you have to be anywhere?"

By this time, Paulina and I were kissing, our lips pressed together, our tongues meeting. She moaned something guttural that sounded like "no". Her reply reverberated in my mouth. The thought of having hours with her further excited me. I felt my way down between her legs while we kissed. Her legs were still parted, the lips down there still exposed – and they were slick. She was already aroused. I stopped kissing her and said softly, "Do you want to play with us in our kitchen?" Two of my fingers pushed into her hole and felt the tight, slippery walls push open to accept me. I wanted to pull her panties down, get them all the way off and out of my way. But she planted her feet on the rug and pushed her hole down hard on my fingers; she wanted to stay connected. She took my fingers past the knuckles; her canal was deep and it gave me so many ideas. "Yes," she finally said, a little breathlessly. "Let's play in your kitchen – whatever that entails."

We're fond of the baby eggplant, Bertrand and I: its perfect shape, its deep purple colour; the substantial heft it has when one holds it in the palm of one's hand. In the vegetable world, they are small works of art. Baby eggplants are always in our kitchen, along with every colour of bell pepper, and yellow squash, zucchini, onions, tomatoes, potatoes, garlic. We never run out of carrots, or celery, or cucumbers. In the spring and summer, there is no shortage of asparagus, green beans, or broccoli in our kitchen, or fresh fennel bulbs, chard, or leeks. And fresh herbs – we love herbs, and sea salt, both fine and coarse. We love peppercorns of every colour and, of course, olive oil.

Bertrand dons his chef's apron. It is pure cotton and bleached white. We are on to the wine now, a Font-Mars, for starters; it is deep red. The colour of it excites me when Bertrand pours it into our glasses. But it is not a wine to be hurried; in an hour or two, it will taste even more intoxicating than it would now. Since we have all evening, I concentrate instead on seducing Paulina out of her clothes, right there in our kitchen.

"In front of all these windows?" She is disinclined to do it – at first; until she sees that we do have window shades. Enormous ones: the windows are tall and wide and comprise one entire kitchen wall. Bertrand, with his glass of Font-Mars in hand, tugs the cord that brings the shades gliding down. We are now completely alone in a city of so many millions.

Bertrand is over his initial idea of preparing ratatouille. I have no idea, yet, what he has decided upon instead, but as Paulina steps out of her skirt and pulls her sweater off over her head, Bertrand prepares to concoct a simple *amuse-bouche* to have with our wine.

Paulina's bra matches her panties; it is the same ruby red silk with a black lace overlay. It pushes her ample breasts together, offers them up enticingly. She is stunning. Her dark hair frames her face angelically. Her dark eyes are quite large and expertly made up to appear as if she were wearing no make-up at all. I reach behind her to unclasp her bra, but I wait for the unveiling of her tits. I let her do that part by herself. I reach for my wine and I glance at Bertrand. I know how much he loves to see a woman's tits spill out of a lacy bra. He's eyeing Paulina with rapt attention, but I notice also that he's eating Brie! And he hasn't offered *us* any. What happened to our *amuse-bouche*? I catch his eye and he shrugs, smiling sheepishly. He takes a sip of wine and then his attention goes back to his chopping block. He's chopping away at herbs. For now, I am more interested in Paulina's breasts – which are luscious, perfectly formed – than in chiding Bertrand over his hoarding the Brie. After all, there will always be Brie, but how often does a gorgeous foreigner strip out of her expensive underthings in one's kitchen?

Paulina is now clad in just her panties and those expensive stockings from Bergdorf's. She scoots up on to one of the kitchen counters. Since she is not tall, this height is perfect for having her lovely tits almost even with my face. Her legs part as she reaches for my hair, pulling me gently to her, encouraging me to latch on to one of her nipples. They are the plump kind, meant for suckling, or for tugging on. My mouth sucks one of her nipples in eagerly and I am surprised by how intensely she moans, by how her hips writhe on the countertop, by how insistently she pulls me closer to her, pressing my head flush against her breast. I wrap my arms around her then, I hold her and let the full power of those erotic sounds she is making wash over me while I suck on her tit. It is a primal feeling, and it happened so quickly. I am very aroused myself. I can feel her nipple swell against my tongue from the pressure of my mouth and, as the nipple swells, her moans become urgent whimpers. It fascinates me; how sensitive she is. It's as if I'd never sucked a nipple before. Certainly never one that was this responsive. The act of suckling her and listening to her ecstasy becomes my entire world; I am lost in it. My pussy is soaking inside my slacks. Soon Paulina is writhing against the counter so much that I am beginning to wonder if she is going to come. I let her set the pace of it; when she wants me to stop, we'll stop. If she wants me to keep at it until she comes, I will do my best to keep up with her rhythm. I've yet to make a woman come without touching her clit, though. It would be a challenge; still, it was one I was willing to take.

It's not long, however, before I realize that Bertrand is standing right next to us. He nudges me over so that he can have one of her tits, too. I release my hold on Paulina; I make room for Bertrand. Paulina leans back a little, enough to give us room. We each suck on a nipple and it is almost more pleasure than she can stand – judging strictly by the whimpering that issues from her then.

I am trying to keep up the pressure on Paulina's nipple, thinking that this is going to make her come; that this is the object of our foreplay. But Bertrand is overcome with lust. Pushing me aside completely, he picks Paulina up in his arms and moves her over to our kitchen island, shoving aside the many canisters of utensils and baskets of vegetables and fruits to make room for her to lie down. He tugs her panties off her, pushes her legs open wide and plants his mouth right on her pussy. Bertrand is usually the type of man who is the first to have his cock out of his trousers, sticking it wherever a woman is willing to take it. But with Paulina, his mouth did not seem able get enough of her.

I watched the two of them, locked in their lusty syncopation. It aroused me to see them like that. Paulina, naked except for her black stockings, writhing, tugging on her own nipples, lost in a swoon, her knees hiked high while Bertrand had his face buried between her legs, his sizeable hands pushing down on her slender thighs, holding her open.

Just then, Paulina's eyes opened; she focused on me. She looked drunk with lust. Almost inaudibly, she pleaded, "Find something to stuff up me."

It was jarring. I looked at her, momentarily confused. "What do you want?" I asked her. "Do you want Bertrand to fuck you now?"

"No," she said, trying to catch her breath but still pulling like mad on her nipples. "Stick something up me. Something big, that I can really feel, you know?"

I thought I knew. I looked around at our countertops; there was food everywhere. I wondered: what would I want to fuck if I were in Paulina's position, out of my mind with lust and needing to really *feel* something?

I grabbed a zucchini. It was thick and long. I held it up to her. "This?" I said.

She shook her head no. "Something bigger than that."

"Bigger than this?" I said. I wasn't at all sure I could handle the zucchini up my own hole, yet she wanted something bigger. "What? Are you into fisting or something?"

"No," she insisted, losing patience with me, sounding as if she was nearing a climax. "Something wider – to stretch me open, you know? *Fill me up.*"

I felt a bit frantic, as if I had to find this pleasure tool to stretch Paulina open before Bertrand managed to make her come in his mouth. I picked up a yellow squash. It was wide at the bottom but had a slender neck, like a handle. Maybe that would work, I thought. I showed it to her. Her eyes gleamed again. "Yes," she said. "Try that."

"Do you want Bertrand to put it in you?"

"No," she said. "I want you to do it."

I was thrilled. It was my turn to nudge Bertrand aside. He'd been nearly oblivious to us, though. At some point while he'd been feasting on Paulina's pussy, he'd taken his cock out of his trousers and had begun jerking himself off under the white chef's apron that he was still wearing. "Move," I told him gleefully. "This is my spot now." I showed him the yellow squash.

"Oh yes," he said quietly, the reason for the squash dawning on him. He moved aside. In fact, he went and got his glass of wine and then came back and pulled up a kitchen chair.

At last, I was getting a good look between Paulina's legs. Her pussy was indeed as gorgeous as the rest of her. I understood, now, Bertrand's uncharacteristic oral need. The outer lips were only lightly covered with black hair; the inner lips were glistening wet, and deep red now and fully engorged. It was a pussy that was without doubt ready for fucking. Bertrand had done his job well.

But her hole looked really small. I looked at the yellow squash; surely she wouldn't want the neck going in her first? "Are you sure you want this?" I said.

She was propped up on her elbows, watching us. Her feet planted on our countertop, spread wide apart, bracing her. "*Yes*, I'm sure."

"OK."

Bertrand took a sip of his Font-Mars and savoured it in his mouth. For some reason, I was very aware that he wasn't swallowing.

I pushed the wide, bulblike end against the opening of Paulina's vagina. She was very wet, so lubrication was not the issue. The squash simply seemed too big compared to the size of her hole.

"Push," she said. "Come on."

I pushed, steadily. And she pushed against me.

"*Ah*," she cried out. "Keep pushing. Don't stop."

I kept pushing; I didn't stop. She bore down on it and, sure enough, her hole started to open. She began to pant lightly. I looked at Bertrand and said, "This thing is huge."

He still hadn't swallowed his wine. He only nodded his head in agreement. From the look on his face, he seemed to be in heaven.

"*Ah*," Paulina cried again. But she was taking it. Her hole had opened but it was a snug fit. Then all at once it had been sucked right up her. Even the neck of the squash had gone up.

"Now what?" I cried. "I lost it."

Bertrand swallowed finally and looked startled.

Paulina was a step ahead of us, though. She grunted determinedly, bearing down. "Grab it," she said haltingly. "Get it before it pops out."

Bertrand and I watched as the hole pushed open. Her pussy looked incredible. Straining, spreading, then the neck of the squash began to emerge. "Grab it," she said again. "Don't let it pop out. I want to get fucked with it."

I managed to grab the squash by its neck but it was slippery now. I had to dig my nails into it to keep it from sliding back up her. I fucked her with it slow at first, amazed that her pussy was so resilient. Easing it down her canal until the widest part of the squash was wedging her hole completely open, I then held it there, stuck in her. Its bright yellow colour looked even brighter squeezed on all sides, as it was, by the deeply engorged lips. When I did that, she cried out; she sputtered a bunch of "Oh gods" and "Oh, yes. Fuck." And Bertrand groaned appealingly into his glass of wine.

Then I pushed the squash deep into her, as deep as I could get it while still holding on to it. I fucked her with it fast and hard, until her cries sounded more like she might hyperventilate. But I only stopped the fucking motion to ease the widest part down the canal again to thoroughly open her hole. Paulina groaned low: "Oh. Yes – God." And she held it there, its widest part stretching her open; her knees raised and completely spread. Nothing obstructed our view. Bertrand said softly, "I can't believe this. This is incredible, isn't it? Christ, dinner will *never* be ready at this rate . . ." While Paulina panted and grunted and sounded like she was giving birth.

And then I realized what this was all about for Paulina: she'd wanted to experience giving birth but they'd forced her to have a Caesarean delivery. I had an idea. I eased the squash out of her completely. "Hey!" Bertrand said, and Paulina looked at me in shock, her hole gaping open, empty.

"Wait," I said. "Don't panic. I have an idea. I'll be right back, I promise."

I came back with a baby eggplant. "Want to try this?" I said, holding it out to her.

Bertrand looked at Paulina and me wide-eyed, clearly hoping that she was going to consent. She did, without even batting an eye.

The stem end would have to go up first this time. There wouldn't be any fucking; she was simply going to give birth to the thing. She braced herself. The stem end easily opened her right up, but the bottom of the eggplant was significantly wider than the squash had been. She took a few breaths – she was really concentrating. Bertrand had done away with sipping his wine and was now swallowing it in mouthfuls. "It's not going to go," he said. "That thing's too big."

Paulina breathed sharply and said, "No – I'll do it. I will. *Ah!*" She pushed hard. But then she squirted us, accidentally. A quick stream of piss flew out of her. "Sorry!" she said urgently. Her voice sounded high-pitched now and overwrought. "I'm sorry!"

"Don't worry about it," Bertrand assured her. "In fact, do it again if you have to."

His insatiable lust amused me, but still, I was on a mission. This was about giving birth to an eggplant; it wasn't about his fondness for water sports. "Make yourself useful," I told him. "Go pour yourself some more wine."

"But I don't want to miss anything," he protested.

"We're right here. We aren't going anywhere. This is going to take a minute."

But it didn't take a minute. Suddenly, she'd opened up and the rest of the eggplant went in, and then the hole closed immediately around it once it was securely up the canal.

"Holy Christ," Bertrand said.

"Wow," Paulina said, breathing heavily. "Wow." Then she added, "I'd like a little wine."

Bertrand did the honours and brought us our glasses of wine. He topped us off with more Font-Mars and then we clinked our glasses in a toast. "To the baby eggplant," I said. "Cheers, Paulina."

She took a few sips of wine and then set her glass aside. She stripped off her stockings then scooted her bottom to the very edge of our kitchen island. She planted her heels wide apart and propped herself up in a half-sitting position. She bore down hard, until her anus was pushing open. She pushed and then pushed harder still. She grunted and groaned. She held her breath at times; then let her breath go and panted hard. She spit on her fingertips and began rubbing her clit. But it wasn't coming. She let her clit alone and pushed some more.

I privately worried that the thing was stuck in there and would never come out; then what would we do? Take her to Beth Israel? It was the closest hospital . . .

"Oh shit," she finally squealed. "Yes."

And we saw it, big and purple and round, crowning in her hole.

"Oh God," she groaned deeply, her whole body relaxing. But then it disappeared again. It *still* wasn't coming – it had slipped back up the canal. For a moment, Paulina did nothing. She was pacing herself, it seemed; she caught her breath. Then she bore down again and there it was, pushing her vagina open, really coming out now. She cried out and the pitch of her cry made my heart race. And then, for a few moments, she didn't move and the eggplant sat there, right in her hole, opening her impossibly wide. I realized then that I was holding my breath, my mouth was filled with wine; I couldn't swallow. I looked quickly at Bertrand and understood him a little better then. His eyes were glued to the sight of Paulina's stretched vagina; he wasn't swallowing either but his right hand was back underneath his apron.

Paulina gave a final grunt, a final push and, to our relief and delight, the eggplant popped out and headed straight for the kitchen floor.

The bottle of Font-Mars was long gone; we'd moved on to a Cavalchina Bardolino. Bertrand had settled on grilled brined salmon fillets for dinner with a fresh dill and fennel relish, roasted stuffed onions, green beans and chive and parsley mashed potatoes. Our *amuse-bouches* had turned out to be delightful: mesclun and ricotta *salata* on grilled garlic toasts. The wine suited it all to perfection. We ate leisurely, sitting in the overstuffed chairs by the fire, our plates spread out on the large coffee table before us.

Rather than putting her clothes back on, Paulina passed the remainder of the evening in one of Bertrand's white, button-down shirts. Of course it was much too big for her and she looked adorable in it. The shirt held the added advantage of falling to the floor in a heartbeat, as well. It wasn't long after our meal that we were feeling amorous for one another again. We were more subdued after two bottles of wine and a good meal (light as it was) than we'd been earlier in the kitchen, but we still had a grand time.

Understandably, Paulina was too worn out for traditional intercourse, so she and I concentrated mostly on using our mouths on each other. Until Bertrand wanted to have her the back way and she was game. It aroused me no end – watching the two of them together. They enjoyed their passions so thoroughly; they made such noise. Paulina was a good sport all the way around. She spent most Sunday evenings at our apartment after that, usually spending the night. We didn't always start out in the kitchen on her nights with us but when we didn't, it was solely because we were dining in bed . . .

In the many weeks that followed, we experimented with all sorts of vegetables, helping Paulina give birth to quite an unusual selection. We had such great times with her, in fact – that and she'd lost the lease on her pricey uptown apartment – that in March, we asked her to move in and were delighted when she did.

One rainy night when we were feeling contemplative – the dinner had been heavy: a beef ragout with a Saint-Emilion – Paulina lamented once again that she had never given birth the real way. "I never got to breastfeed my baby," she said. "I really wanted to experience that, too."

As usual, Bertrand and I glanced at each other, reading each other's thoughts. Paulina's breasts were so full and exquisite, her nipples so responsive, that nursing would likely have sent her into orgasmic bliss in record time.

"In my country," she assured us, "women can give milk without being pregnant. It is not necessary to be with child in order to give milk."

We were sceptical, Bertrand and I. The following day, over the telephone, we consulted with some fetishists we knew on East 9th Street and they, in turn, assured us that it was true. The trick, they said, was to fool the pituitary gland into thinking Paulina had an infant to nurse.

Really? This was certainly news to us. But intriguing news; exciting news!

"It would require constant suckling, of course, maybe even for a couple of months. Do you think you're up for the task?"

Constant suckling at Paulina's breasts, her ecstasy so contagious that it would nearly make us come, as well? We hung up the phone. Our mission was clear: we would suck on Paulina's nipples, night and day, until the milk came out. It was a mission that suited us thoroughly. And as luck would have it, in late spring, when Paulina's milk finally came, I found myself with child. Bertrand and Paulina couldn't have been more pleased. With Veuve Cliquot, they joyously toasted the baby's conception. Though no less joyous, I abstained, however, from the champagne and thought instead of the moment of birth, contemplating ecstasy.

Darlene's Dilemma

Andrea Dale

Darlene had surreptitiously squirmed her way through breakfast, trying to no avail to find a comfortable position on the chair. She was stubborn enough not to want to admit there *was* no comfortable way of sitting in public when there was a butt plug buried in your ass.

Of course, the wriggling around made it worse, made her more aware of the silicone toy inside her. It wasn't terribly big – she wasn't into harming delicate tissue – but it was *there*, and it brought a flush to her face any time Jaden or Sienna lubed it up and told her to bend over.

They allowed her to wear panties to breakfast, because they had a respect for the hotel's antique chairs and didn't want her staining the cushion.

Sienna was wearing a plug, too, but somehow she managed to look completely unconcerned and entirely comfortable. She didn't find it as deliciously humiliating as Darlene did.

Sienna was playing on the bottom today, kinky switch that she was. Darlene was pretty much always a sub – it was just her nature – although occasionally she could be persuaded to punish Sienna if Jaden thought Sienna needed two people topping her. Darlene did enjoy that, because it meant she could do all the things to Sienna that Sienna did to her. Turn about was fair play, after all.

It was a perfect arrangement for all of them: Jaden Powell, rock star extraordinaire; Sienna, his creative wife; and Darlene herself, their willing girlfriend.

Jaden had reached middle age with a grace that everyone

envied. It pissed off a few people, too. Exercise and eat right, and still watch things sag. Live a life of decadence, of drugs and booze and wild nights, and continue to look like a god. He no doubt had a portrait in a safe-deposit box somewhere.

His sexiness had something to do with that British accent, still apparent even after years of living in homogenized, sun-drenched Hollywood. His voice had a way of reaching out and caressing you, stroking over your skin, teasing its way into your panties . . .

The blue eyes, craggy features, wicked grin, devil-may-care tousled brown hair that had graced a thousand posters didn't hurt either.

Jaden was in rare form this week. Their trips to the Victorian spa always involved some new game, something nasty and creative that Jaden dreamed up. (Or sometimes that they all dreamed up together.)

After they'd gotten settled in yesterday, he announced that Darlene could have all the orgasms she wanted for the duration of their stay. He might manipulate them a little, hold them off to make them more intense, but otherwise it was no-holds barred.

The catch was, she could have them any possible way *except* with the benefit of something in her pussy. No cocks, no dildos, no internal vibrators. No fingers or fists either.

"It'll be a fun experiment," he'd said, his sensual mouth curving into a wicked smile. "Let's see how many ways we can make you come without something inside you."

Darlene's cunt had promptly spasmed at the thought. Immediately she felt bereft, felt like she needed nothing more than something deep inside her, stretching her out, massaging her G-spot.

Of course, she'd promptly started getting wet, too. Most kinds of play talk got her wet and, right now, her excellent imagination was coming up with all sorts of ideas about how she could be brought to climax with tongues and fingers and vibrators, by nipple play and butt play.

She didn't realize just how desperately she'd miss cock until she saw Sienna getting some earlier. Sienna, with her face and chest blushing the same colour as her strawberry-blonde hair as she came.

Yes, Jaden was in quite a mood this morning. After they'd had a little time to relax after breakfast, he went to work on the two of them.

First he'd had them remove each other's plugs. Darlene had removed Sienna's first, which she regretted soon after. She'd simply popped it out, whereas Sienna took her own sweet time, fucking Darlene's ass with the plug before slowly removing it, bit by excruciatingly arousing bit.

Whistling cheerfully – one of his own hits, Darlene recognized – Jaden helped her into a soft leather dildo harness, complete with a bright purple dildo that had a strong upwards curve to it. The end of it in the harness had a vibrator that snuggled up against Darlene's clit, which poked out between her shaved, glistening lips.

Oh, this could only be good, right?

He turned on the vibrator to its lowest setting, just enough to make her dance a tiny bit.

Around her waist he buckled a strap with cuffs on either sides for her wrists. He strapped an identical one around Sienna's torso.

Hmm. Getting interesting.

The low hum added to the excitement from the butt-plug breakfast.

He had Sienna stand with her legs spread apart, instructing her to hold herself open. At his command, she dipped her fingers in then fed her glistening juices to Darlene.

Sienna tasted sweet, like thick sugar water. Darlene would have been happy to go down on her, both because she enjoyed it and because she usually got a nice reward for a job well done, but that wasn't in Jaden's current plans.

"Put the dildo into her," he said to Darlene. "Slowly, now."

Darlene bent her knees to bring the head of the dildo down to the right height, and nestled it between Sienna's parted lips. Slowly she stood, pressing the fake cock up into Sienna's cunt by measured degrees. Their difference in height meant that when she was standing straight again, the dildo would be comfortably up Sienna.

Her thighs trembled, but only a little. All those Pilates classes were paying off.

Sienna panted as the cock filled her. Darlene's own pussy felt empty by comparison, reminding her that she wouldn't be getting the same treatment. She tried to console herself with the fact that she had the vibrator on her end, but it was only a partial victory.

Jaden secured Darlene's right hand into the cuff on Sienna's waist, then Sienna's left hand to the cuff attached to Darlene. It forced them to stand close together, forced the dildo deep into Sienna and the vibrating end harder against Darlene's clit.

"Hold on to the bedpost," he said.

So that's why he'd left their other hands free.

Darlene looked at Sienna. They both wanted the same thing, and they'd been together long enough that they didn't need words. By unspoken agreement, they both moved their hips. Even this close, they were able to part a little bit, pulling the dildo a short way out of Sienna, then shoving it back in as they bucked close again. It wasn't nearly like the full range of fucking, but from the way Sienna's nostrils flared, it was obviously good for her.

Jaden's hands flew to each of their necks, his fingers weaving through the hair at their napes and tugging. They both froze, heads back to avoid the pain of having their hair pulled.

"I didn't say you could move," he said.

They waited, achingly aroused but unable to do anything about it, while he rooted around in their luggage.

Finally he found what he was looking for: a pair of nipple clamps and a chain that attached them together. Sienna had pierced nipples with rings, something Darlene had never been interested in doing. But her own nipples were very sensitive, and Jaden often used that to his advantage – like now.

He snapped the clamps on to Darlene's nipples. She sucked in her breath at the fiery pain that slowly transmuted into a deep, aching throb. Then Jaden showed just how wickedly inspired he was today.

He threaded the chain through the hoops in Sienna's breasts and connected the ends to the clips on Darlene. The short chain forced them to stand even closer together, pressing their breasts against each other, their hard nipples further aroused by the contact.

If they tried to pull away, their sensitive buds would be stretched and tugged.

A fresh wave of moisture and desire rippled through Darlene's empty pussy.

Jaden made sure they were both comfortable (under the circumstances), then stepped back to admire his handiwork, caressing their asses, checking on the vibrator and bumping it up a notch.

And then he brought out a bright red leather slapper, the kind with holes in it for an added sting.

Darlene squealed under her breath, and Sienna moaned. Darlene loved getting spanked, but Sienna had something of a love-hate relationship with it. She enjoyed it, but tended to squirm all over the place to get away.

She wasn't going to be able to do that now. Not unless they were both willing to put up with some serious sting in their breasts.

God, he was inventive!

"You can kiss each other if you want," Jaden said. "In fact, I'd like that very much."

It was as good as a command, and they both welcomed it. Darlene loved the way Sienna's soft lips and small tongue teased and caressed her mouth.

He started on Darlene first, with warm-up blows that didn't do much more than tingle. She knew that wouldn't last for long. She was just starting to feel the heat when he switched to Sienna, spending a little more time on her to bring her up to the next level.

What Jaden loved most about that particular slapper was its colour. His goal, he always said, was to make their asses the same vivid hue of scarlet.

He generally achieved his goals.

Back to Darlene. Now her ass started to sting. There was no escaping the blows. He mostly concentrated on her butt, which meant many of the hits were right on top of each other, not giving her sensitive flesh time to recover from the last slap. She bit down on Sienna's lip, keening lightly.

It hurt, but it was a good hurt, and by the time the sensations made their way from her brain and back down, they'd turned to pleasure. The bump of the vibrator against her swollen clit still wasn't enough to bring her off though. Not yet, at least.

Darlene was mostly able to stay still, but the same wasn't true of Sienna. She flinched with every blow when Jaden returned to her side, which tugged at the chains connecting their nipples, sending streaks of painful pleasure through Darlene.

It was all Darlene could do to keep hold of the bedpost. Her ass was on fire, her nipples were on fire, and the excruciatingly light buzzing between her thighs wasn't enough to tip her over the edge. She could smell her own arousal, could smell Sienna's, and it only made her hornier. She tried to distract herself by kissing Sienna, but then she thought about how good Sienna's tongue was when it was between her legs, licking her.

Jaden tossed the slapper aside. He caressed both their butts with his large hands, and although his touch was barely more than a light brush, they both yelped.

He laughed at them. He disconnected the chain, although he left the clamps on Darlene, and unhooked their wrists from each other's cuffs. Then he had Darlene pull the dildo out of Sienna. As it emerged with a squishy *pop*, Sienna whimpered.

At least she'd *had* something inside her. Darlene inwardly pouted.

Still, she had the vibrator on her side. Jaden positioned Sienna at the side of the bed, bending over, her crimson ass wiggling in the air. Jaden gave it a couple of slaps with his hand, causing her to cry out against the bedspread.

"You want me to fuck her?" Darlene asked.

Sienna mumbled something that sounded suspiciously like "Yes, please."

"But of course," Jaden said. "Sienna, open wide."

Sienna reached down and spread her shaved, glistening lips. Darlene set the tip of the dildo between them.

"Hold on," Jaden said.

She stopped, and he reached between her legs to turn the vibrator on full force.

"Have fun, you two," he said, amusement dancing in his voice. They both knew what he meant – it was their cue to come, and come again.

Darlene was so on edge that she knew it wouldn't take long. It took only a few short moments before she felt the familiar surge rising inside her, focusing down and centring on her clit.

Closer . . . closer . . . oh God . . . there!

Her climax grabbed her like a vice, then shook her into a million pieces.

The orgasm made her pump her hips in a flurry of motion, which tipped Sienna over the edge as well. Their cries mingled as they shuddered through their releases.

When they'd recovered, Jaden unbuckled the harness from Darlene because her hands were still shaking too hard to manage the clasps. Sprawled on the bed, he had them lick and suck him, using their mouths and hands to bring him to his own completion.

They collapsed on the bed in a happy puppy pile. Darlene thought she might have even dozed off for a bit, before Jaden stirred again.

"How about a soak in the baths before lunch?" he asked cheerfully.

Flash Fire

K.D. Grace

"I just don't see how I can fit it in," Liz said as Ian led her into the gaping maw of the firehouse. She could just make out the shape of a lone truck in the darkness like the skeleton of some dinosaur at a museum.

"It's for a good cause."

For the past two years the firemen had put on an event for the Home Planet, an environmental organization educating people to do their part for the health of the planet. There had been a car wash, and a slave auction, but the pin-up calendar was the most ambitious and daring undertaking the firemen had come up with so far.

Ian ran one caressing hand along the flank of the huge truck and the other came to rest on Liz's bum. Everyone at the firehouse knew Ian's sometimes girlfriend, sometimes fuck buddy was a photographer. He pulled her close and gave her neck a nibble. "We want the best for this job."

Of course, that was her. She'd already made up her mind she would volunteer herself. Still, she was mercenary enough to wait and see what Ian was willing to do to persuade her.

"You'd be photographing barely clothed fireman. And I know you like a man who knows what to do with his hose." He pinned her against the truck, lapping at her mouth and tongue until she no longer protested his efforts. "I'll make it worth your while." His right hand moved to cup her breast. Ian was a tit man, and Liz's more-than-a-handful rack was well displayed and easily accessed in a strappy summer top.

"Besides," he added, "You said it yourself, firemen make you horny."

This fireman certainly made her horny, with his dark curls, brown sugar eyes that would melt steel, and an olive complexion that caressed a lean, hard body. He lowered his mouth to suckle at her breast through her thin vest until the fabric clung to her engorged nipple. Then he guided her hand to the front of his jeans, shifting his hips until she felt the familiar shape of his erection ready for action. Her cunt was suddenly wet, as she thought of him getting her off in the crowded tube last week. They were on it for the long haul, and packed in like sardines. He had a seam-busting erection and her pussy was thrumming. No one had noticed his hand under her skirt, or the way he rubbed himself against her . . .

"It would be good for all of us." He slid his hand up the inside of her thigh.

"Stop it." She pushed him away. "What if someone catches us?"

"So what if they do?" His voice sounded guttural in the cavernous space. "Besides, I know how much you always wanted a ride in the fire truck." He reached a muscular arm up and opened the door. Before Liz could protest, he lifted her on to the seat and, in a movement befitting a magician, he slid her knickers off and let them drop to the floor board.

"What the hell are you—" Her protest died in her throat with a gasp as he pushed her skirt up and buried himself face deep in her pussy. Liz suddenly didn't care where they were, or who might be watching, as long as his tongue and her clit were getting on so deliciously. She had lost her Manolos when he hoisted her into the truck, so she rested bare feet on his shoulders and arched her back until he could slide his hands under her to knead and stroke her bum. He manoeuvred until one thumb circled her arsehole, increasing in pressure as it homed in on the centre and began to push in and out gently, yet hard enough to make her rock back and forth against him, willing him to probe deeper, and when he obliged, she came, bucking and bouncing against the seat. His breath was hot against her inner lips as he nibbled and licked. He stopped his magical tongue dance long enough to pant. "I promise you, Lizzie, you'll be well compensated for this little shoot. In fact, we thought we'd give you a bonus right up front."

Just then the door on the other side of the truck burst open and she squealed with surprise. She just managed to make out Ben Clark's face before he laid an upside-down kiss on her that sent more heat down to her slit, which was doing its best to return Ian's kisses.

Ben and Ian had been best friends for years. With his corn silk hair and silver blue eyes, Ben was the white hot to Ian's dark and steamy. He was taller, leaner of build, with muscles that rippled like flowing water. Ian knew that she lusted for his friend. She'd even made offhand comments about what a great threesome they'd make, but she never thought he'd take her seriously.

Ben spoke, coming up for breath. "We'll make sure you're well compensated for your efforts." She didn't protest as he pulled her vest off over her head and shoved at her bra working his way towards her nipples.

"And there'll be regular bonuses for work well done." Ian gave her a wicked grin just before stepping on to the running board and pushing into her slippery pussy.

Ben slid out of a pair of athletic shorts, which appeared to be the only thing he was wearing. She gasped at the size of his heavy penis. It was even bigger and thicker than she'd imagined. He took her open mouth as an invitation, sliding in and out of her suckling lips carefully until he was sure she could handle his equipment. Then he slid his index and middle finger into his mouth, and when they were slick and glistening with his saliva, he arched his beautifully sculpted torso over her to stroke and circle her clit.

"It tastes as good as it looks," Ian said, pulling out long enough to give his friend a chance to suckle her pouting lips, while he watched, stroking his cock.

The thought of Ben's tongue where Ian's penis had been only seconds before was too much, and Liz came again, uttering a muffled cry around Ben's erection. Then Ben gave way and Ian slid his cock back inside her, this time inserting two fingers into her backside, moving them with a gentle stretching motion. The sensation sent more shock waves of pleasure across her vulva. She tightened her grip on both cock and fingers and heard Ian grunt in response. As he inserted yet another finger, he gave Ben the nod.

Ben pulled his cock from her mouth and crawled in behind her, easing her up off the seat, first her head, then shoulders, until his muscular thighs were splayed around her, and his penis, still wet with her saliva, pressed against her back. For a delicious few seconds, he lingered there, cupping her breasts from behind, tweaking her swollen nipples.

Then Ian lifted her upwards and towards him, further on to his cock, his fingers still stretching her pucker hole. Another nod between the two men, and Ian removed his fingers, but held her arse cheeks splayed as Ben positioned himself. She held her breath. Fantasy was about to become reality. Someone's fingers spread her juices to lubricate her anus, then Ben carefully pressed into her.

"That's it, just relax, Liz." His voice came in harsh little gasps as he exercised exquisite control. "This is gonna feel so good. Just a little more, that's it. I'm almost in." He grunted, gave a little push, and he was fully inside.

A brief flash of panic quickly gave way to intense pleasure laced with just enough discomfort to be exciting. The two men quickly found their rhythm. Liz gripped them both in a haze of heat. Probing tongues and groping hands only enhanced the relentless, delicious pounding between her legs and up her arse. Their passion rose until she was sure the whole fire truck would tip over as she was hammered and pumped. And when she could take it no longer, there was an explosion of light behind her closed eyes that matched the explosion in her pussy, then she was gripped from both sides in a bone-crunching embrace as both men came.

When the three of them began to breathe again, she spoke. "You win. I'll do the bloody calendar. But this—" she gave both of their cocks a stroke "—is just the down payment. I don't work cheap." She was sliding her knickers up over her hips when there was a noise of something being knocked over. They all jumped, and turned just in time to catch a flash of red hair and a slender body disappearing out the side door.

"Bloody hell, was that your intern?" Ian asked.

"If it was she definitely got her virgin eyes full," Ben said. "Has she ever even seen a cock?"

"She has now." Liz watched Ben wrestling his penis back in his jeans.

He chuckled. "Must have been frightening for her seeing the monster in action."

Teri Dalton was from a conservative, well-moneyed family in Texas. Against her father's better judgment, her aunt had paid for her to take an internship in the heathen wilds of London so she could see a bit of the world she'd been sheltered from. Liz had taken her on in spite of her puritan upbringing because she was a good photographer. Ian and Ben had an ongoing bet as to whether she was a virgin.

"I told her she didn't have to help with this shoot since it might be uncomfortable for her. I wonder why she was here."

"You didn't tell me you were doing porn." The intern forced a brittle laugh as she clanked two mugs on the break-room table and slapped tea bags in them. Before Liz could respond, she continued, "The dark-haired one, the one who was . . . giving you oral sex," she spoke the words through barely parted lips, "he's your boyfriend?"

"Wait a minute, Teri. How long were you there anyway?"

Her face turned as red as her hair. "No one was there, and I was about to leave when I saw you two."

Liz couldn't hold back a chuckle. "You naughty girl. You didn't want to leave, did you?"

"Please don't tease me. It's not funny." Just then the kettle shut off, and Teri busied herself making tea. Liz was struck again by how sexy she was. She was shorter than Liz, and she was curvy, with high full breasts and a mounded backside that filled her jeans to perfection. Today she wore a summer skirt and the silky fabric of her red vest barely disguised nipples and areolae at full salute.

When she finally spoke, her voice trembled. "I'm sorry. I shouldn't have watched."

"Why not? I would have." Liz pushed the girl's hair behind her ears, admiring her yummy green eyes. "Did you masturbate while you watched?"

The intern stepped back and straightened herself. "I would never. I've never touched myself."

Liz held her gaze. "Then you've never come."

Teri's full lips quivered.

"Teri, are you a virgin?"

"I was taught to save myself for my husband. That's what my parents expect." She forced herself to meet Liz's gaze, and her eyes filled. "But I'm not so sure any more. What if I never get married? What if I die not knowing . . . what it feels like?" The girl burst into tears and threw her arms around Liz's neck. "It looked so exciting, the way they touched you, and you were all so—" she choked back a sob "—so hot. I just don't know any more."

Liz patted her back and tried not to notice the press of the girl's breasts against hers. In her distress, Teri wriggled closer and began stroking Liz's arm solicitously.

"You came, didn't you? You came lots." The stroking against Liz's arm became a caress.

"Yes. And I'm sure you'll find—"

Liz's words were lost against Teri's lips. The total surprise of the kiss was quickly mitigated by the warmth of those full, pouty lips. The girl may have never come, but she sure as hell knew how to snog. If the kiss was a shock, what happened next was even more so.

Teri's breath was a wisp against Liz's mouth as she spoke. "Show me."

"What?"

"Last night I wanted to be you, but I wanted to be the guys too and touch you like they did."

"Teri, you need to think about this, you need to understand—"

"I'm an adult, Liz, and I know what I want. I want to enjoy sex like you do without someone telling me it's wrong." Teri's hand slid from Liz's shoulder to just above her breast.

It made sense. If anyone could teach a woman how to come, who better than someone who knew exactly what felt best? Who better than another woman?

"Please, Liz. Please can I see you down there." She brought her hand to rest fully on Liz's breast.

In the back room where the camera was set up for portraits, Liz led Teri to a sofa.

She slipped out of her panties and sat down, feeling the cool leather on her bare bottom. Teri knelt in front of her, eyes bright, pupils dilated. Then she awkwardly shoved at Liz's skirt like a child unwrapping a pressie, and Liz opened her legs to the intern's gaze.

"You're like a flower," the girl gasped

She sat for a long time letting Teri admire her pussy, then she led her to the long mirror used for last-minute touch-ups before portraits. "Now, take off your knickers."

The intern nearly hyperventilated. "I can't."

Liz moved in front of her. "Don't be shy. Just relax." She ran trembling hands up under the intern's skirt. There was no protest. "That's right. That's a good girl."

Teri breathed a childlike sigh as Liz slid panties over the roundness of her arse cheeks and down silken thighs. Then she parked her on a stool in front of the mirror and pushed up the girl's skirt, holding her breath, feeling the anticipation tingling down through her own cunt.

"Open your legs for me," she said soothingly. "We're going to look at your pussy together." Once she had exposed Teri's neatly trimmed muff, she moved so they could both see the view. Teri opened her legs and shifted her hips and her pouting cunny was displayed like ripe fruit ready for the eating. Liz whispered, "Makes me want to touch you." She caught Teri's entranced gaze in the mirror. "You must want to touch too."

"I wanted to last night, but I didn't know what to do."

"I'll show you," Liz whispered. "It'll feel so good."

Liz guided Teri on to the floor and into a pile of cushions she used for shoots. Then she positioned herself so they could both see the other's pussy. "Your fingers are your best friends," Liz breathed. She fingered her own slippery pout, making tight circles over and around her charged clit. She heard the resulting gasp, but Teri didn't touch herself. She still needed some coaxing.

"Your clit is lovely, Teri, – so full and round." Liz leaned forwards and slid her fingers over the intern's pussy. "You're so swollen and slick. You need to come so bad, don't you, hon?" While Teri squirmed against her fingers, Liz opened her blouse and freed her aching breasts, cupping and kneading herself with one hand while stroking Teri's cunt with the other. "Play with your tits, Teri. A great sex toy – breasts. I play with mine often. And you should yours too."

Teri obliged. Her nipples were large and pink set against stiffening areolae that rose to the stroking and pinching of her fingers.

Liz began stroking her own pussy, mirroring what she was doing to Teri. "It feels nice, what I'm doing to you, doesn't it?"

Eyes glued to Liz's cunt, Teri nodded and gasped, bearing down against Liz's hand.

"Good." Liz took her hand away. "Now you do it. Go on. Trust me, you'll know exactly what feels good for you."

Teri needed to come too badly to refuse Liz's advice. Soon her own fingers circled her slippery clit. No doubt she'd have rug burns tomorrow the way she bucked and writhed. Then she began to pant. "I think I'm coming, I think . . . Oh God!" She arched against the cushions and convulsed, breasts heaving, legs straining.

Liz could see the spasming muscles of Teri's slit, just as her own explosion spread like a flash fire, and then she had an idea.

There was no answer that evening at Ian's door. He was expecting Liz, but maybe he was showering. They had always managed to stay friends whether they were dating or just fuck buddies, so they both kept keys to each other's flat.

Anxious to tell Ian her idea, Liz unlocked the door and stepped inside. The shower wasn't running. She was about to call out when grunts and moans coming from the bedroom made her stop. It wasn't the first time Ian had fucked another woman, though it had been a while. They had an open relationship and had gotten past jealousy long ago. She was just turning to go, planning to call him later, when she stopped in her tracks. She was very familiar with Ian's sex sounds, but the other sounds were also distinctly male.

Holding her breath, she tiptoed down the hall closer to the sounds of heat. She could hear heavy breathing then soft laughter and an occasional muttered curse. As she peeked around the open bedroom door she recognized the sex sounds of the second male. She'd heard them just the other night in the front seat of the fire truck. Sure enough, Ben sat naked on the edge of the bed. Ian knelt in front of him deep-throating his best friend's cock. With one hand, he gently kneaded Ben's balls, while the other slid up and down the length of his own erection.

She watched in aroused fascination, wondering how the hell Ian could get so much of Ben's monster cock into his mouth.

For a second, she desperately wished she had a camera. The hard planes of male flesh, the contrast of pale and dark, the textures of pubic curls against smooth straining penises would have made for a phenomenal photo.

Ben's fingers were curled in Ian's hair. He watched, through half-closed eyes, as Ian took more and more of him into his mouth. With each suckling and tonguing of his penis, Ben's face contorted in that wonderful look in which pleasure and pain meet and become one. On the bedside table were a half-empty bottle of Cabernet Sauvignon, two glasses, several condoms and an open tube of lube.

They had been naked together in the fire truck, but Liz was sandwiched between them, preventing any embarrassing male-on-male contact. But now, even she had to admit, the sight of hard male muscle straining so intimately against more hard male muscle was both exciting and touching. The two blokes had been best friends for ever, but until this moment, she had no idea they were more than that. For a second, she felt hurt. She thought she and Ian had gotten past the need to keep secrets. Knowing her so well, he couldn't have possibly thought she'd think less of him.

Most of her girl friends admitted they had at least fantasized about sex with other women. Liz had always felt that it was neurotic of men to fear what she saw as their natural attraction to each other. She shouldn't be surprised. After all, Ben and Ian were two of the least neurotic people she knew. She wondered if the two had been doing each other while they made plans to sandwich her.

As she watched, Ben guided Ian to stand before him and the roles were reversed, as Ben took Ian's cock into his mouth, his arms sliding around to caress and cup the magnificent arse cheeks with which Liz was so familiar. Then he slid exploring fingers to the cleft in between, stroking and pressing until Ian shivered and moaned. Ian had always liked his anus stimulated when they made love, but then so did she.

Her back hole clenched and her pussy twitched at the memory of having the same thing done to her so recently. Very carefully she lifted her skirt and eased her hand down into her knickers. The slick warmth grabbed at her stroking fingers as her pussy muscles tensed as she watched.

Without losing his considerable rhythm, Ben reached for the lube on the nightstand, and when his fingers were slippery, he began stroking and stretching and thrusting, causing Ian's arsehole to clench and expand against his probings until Ian found his own rhythm, thrusting first against Ben's mouth, then back on to his fingers.

"I can't stand much more." Ian's voice was breathless at the back of his throat. He pushed his friend away from his cock and took his mouth with a hard, probing kiss, as he reached for a condom, which he expertly slipped on to Ben's anxious cock. Then he turned and bent over the bed, offering Liz a perfect view of his gorgeous backside.

Liz forced herself to stillness lest she come before she was ready. She wanted to make it last.

"Not like that," Ben said. "I want you in bed."

The two men tumbled back on to the bed. Ian positioned himself on his stomach with his arse and hips raised, Ben panting behind him.

"I need your cock. I need to come now," Ian gasped, holding himself open while Ben pressed the head of his penis home.

The ease with which they worked together told Liz this was not their first time. "Oh fuck, that's good," Ian moaned as he bucked backwards against Ben's thrusting.

Ben's hand snaked under Ian's belly and stroked his best friend's penis in rhythm to his own thrusts. The sound of flesh slapping against flesh, of grunting and pushing drove Liz to thrust against her fingers circling her clit then dipping deep into her pussy. Liz would have thought them too intent on their own pleasure to notice her muffled groans and gasps as her lust built. She was wrong.

"Lizzie," Ian lifted his head and called out, "if you're going to watch, then at least return the favour."

She didn't wait for a second invitation. She dropped her bag by the door and left a trail of clothing across to the chair. There she plopped down so the two lads got a primo view of her cunny twitching from the action on the bed.

The room was electric, permeated with the salty sweet smell of pussy, and the more meaty smell of sweating cocks. They were all thrusting and grunting and moaning, straining nearly to the breaking point. Ben's hand was jerking at Ian's cock as though there was a battle going on, and his engorged balls were slapping ever harder against his friend's arse with each thrust. Liz matched their hammering with her own strokes, amazed at how in tune they all seemed to be with each other's rhythm, so in tune that they all three came together. Ian spurted like a fire hose against the headboard of the bed, Ben convulsed against Ian's arse nearly flattening him, and Liz practically fell off the chair when her orgasm hit full force, shuddering up through her cunt, across her belly and breasts, surging over the top of her head like a tidal wave.

"How long has this been going on?" she asked afterwards, when the three of them were snuggled together in the big bed.

"Not long," Ian said. "We thought maybe showing you might be better than telling." He offered her a wicked smile. "It wasn't ever anything we planned. One night there was a big fire, and after, we came back here, watched a little telly, some porn rubbish. I don't even remember. We were a little drunk when we started talking about, you know, what it felt like to be with a bloke. Then one thing led to another, the next thing we knew it just happened."

Ben continued the story. "We laughed about it in the morning, but we both knew we'd do it again. Doesn't mean we don't like chicks," he added quickly.

Liz chuckled. "I sort of figured that much." Then they both listened while she told them her idea.

At last, Ian spoke. "Let me get this straight, you want us to make Teri Dalton come?"

"Both of us?" Ben asked.

"It's not like she hasn't seen you with your cocks up. You two are my last shoot, late in the evening. No one else will be around. I've asked her to help out. All I'm saying is, if things head in that direction, just follow her lead. She just needs to boost her sexual confidence, that's all."

Ian nodded. "Any decent bloke would do what he could for her."

Ben agreed. "Can we bring toys?"

"You always want to bring toys," Ian observed.

"Just be nice and be gentle. She's very innocent, but enthusiastic. We want this to be a good experience for her, not a scary one."

When Liz agreed to shoot the calendar, the firemen allocated the adjoining garage for the project. It housed extra equipment and an obsolete fire truck. The men had rigged up lights, hoses, a fire pole and several other props to make the photos look realistic. Teri was already busy checking equipment and setting up lights when Liz arrived. She looked angelic in a white vest and a pink cotton skirt, but Liz suspected this little angel could be very naughty.

Right on cue Ian and Ben showed up for the last shoot in nothing but boots and waterproof trousers with braces. They stood by the fire truck, displaying broad chests and thick biceps like super heroes. Even Liz was breathless at the sight.

"OK, lads, we'll start with a nice shot of you two relaxing against the truck after a fire. Teri, there's stage make-up on the table. These two need to look like they've just come from a fire. Would you mind?"

Teri took the make-up and handed it awkwardly to Ian.

"No, hon." Liz came to her side. "They can't reach to put it on their backs. You'll have to help. I'll show you." She took a gob of black greasepaint and smeared it first on Ben's cheeks, then across his chest and down his torso, watching his stomach tightening as her hand neared the waistband of his trousers.

"Here, I'll hold this and you can give me a rub down." Before Ian could take the make-up from her, Teri tensed and a large blob of black greasepaint erupted from the top of the tube on to her vest.

"Oh dear." Ian produced a handkerchief from somewhere and wiped at the spot just above her left nipple, his strokes expanding to a cupping caress that spread the black across the whole of her now heaving breast. "Don't worry. I'm sure Liz knows something that'll get that out."

Flustered, Teri tried to push his hand away, but Ian folded his fingers around hers and brought both their hands and the blackened handkerchief to his belly, wiping a large smear all the way down to where the dusting of dark hair began just beneath his navel. "There, that's perfect." He smiled reassuringly. "If you could put a little down my chest and back and—" The handkerchief fell to the floor and Ian gasped in surprise as Teri slid her hand into the top of his trousers. "I don't think I need make-up there."

"You have an erect—a hard-on." She looked up at him wide-eyed. "It must be uncomfortable."

"Getting that way, yes." He grunted, shifting against her hand. "Would you like to see?"

She nodded. Her cheeks flushed. Her breath quickened.

He caught Liz's eye where she stood frozen with her smudged hand low on Ben's back. She nodded approval. Then he offered the intern his wicked smile. "First take off your vest."

"What?"

"You show me yours; I'll show you mine. Shall I help?"

She lifted her arms as he slid off her vest, then unhooked her bra. He took his time, admiring her, ignoring her impatience. Then, at last, he undid his zipper.

Before Teri could do more than stare at his penis stretching stiffly towards her, Ian pulled her close and lifted her skirt. Trembling against him, she whimpered and her eyelids fluttered as he eased her legs open and slid his hand inside her panties.

"You're wet." He nipped her ear lobe.

"Fire safety." She gasped. "Wet things don't burn."

He chuckled. "Wanna bet?"

Liz had been so intent on watching, she was surprised by the sudden press of Ben's erection against her hand.

"I could use some help with my hose. Would you mind?"

"Always glad to help." Liz stroked and Ben thrust, groaning his pleasure.

Teri looked on wide-eyed, while Ian fingered her slit with one hand and caressed her tits with the other.

As Ben undid Liz's jeans and slid them down around her ankles, she had to admit the watching was almost as good as the playing. He guided her hands on to the fender of the truck. "Bend over and give us a look." She heard both Teri and Ian catch their breath as Ben gently teased and exposed her pussy lips, then he knelt and helped her out of her jeans and knickers.

A glance over her shoulder told Liz the intern was a captive audience. She understood why when Ben's tongue replaced his fingers between her slippery pussy lips. His mouth closed around her distended clit, and he began to suckle. She braced against the truck as her first orgasm broke over her.

"Would you do that to me?" Teri asked Ian, sounding a bit like a child asking for a pony ride.

Another look over her shoulder revealed a changed scene, and Liz could see Teri was now bent over, hanging on to the fire pole with both hands, her cunny undulating against Ian's accommodating tongue.

Tension crackled through the room. Clearly Teri Dalton was enjoying herself, but it was only when she bellowed, "Oh my God, I'm coming!" and collapsed in a breathless heap at the base of the fire pole that the tension truly broke. She scrambled to her knees and gave Ian's cock a deep-throated kiss, nearly gagging herself before she came up laughing. "I had no idea it could be like this. Why didn't anyone tell me?"

The two men nodded to each other, and Ben stopped communing with Liz's quinny and whispered in her ear. "Time to give Little Miss a proper initiation into womanhood. Follow our lead." He reached into the truck and pulled out a penis-shaped vibrator.

Then Ian lifted the surprised intern on to the hood of the truck. Both men scrambled up after her, and Ben handed the vibrator to his friend, and donned a condom.

"You've been eyeing Ben's big cock ever since he first unwrapped it," Ian said. 'Would you like a test drive?'

Teri was already guiding Ben's erection into her dilated pussy. With the first gentle thrust, her gasp was tinged with pain as she stretched to accommodate him. But pain quickly gave way to purrs of pleasure as Teri wrapped her legs around him and thrust back.

"I saw you eyeing Lizzie's pussy," Ben grunted between thrusts. "You'd like a taste, wouldn't you?"

Ian was already helping Liz on to the truck. Liz was more than a little surprised when the intern grabbed her by the hips and pulled her down snug against her enthusiastic mouth. She was a quick study, lapping and tugging at Liz's labia and clit with a tongue that must surely be double-jointed. Then the two men nodded to each other again.

"I want you on top," Ben said, pulling out and shifting until Teri was sitting on his belly riding his cock.

"Do you like toys, Teri?" Eyeing Teri's arse, Ian revved up the vibrator.

"Don't you dare," Liz gasped.

"No, I want it," Teri protested. "I want to know what it feels like to have . . . something up there." She held Liz's gaze. "You seemed to like it."

"You heard the lady, Lizzie. Would you do the honours?" He lifted the vibrator to Liz's mouth and, for the sake of Teri's tender arse, she gave it a good licking.

"That's a girl. Now, Teri, I'm going to show you another great way to come." He pressed the head of the vibrator against Teri's tight anus. She squirmed and groaned, but instead of pulling away, she licked her fingers until they were dripping with saliva, then began to probe and stretch at her own arsehole.

"Put it in me," she gasped.

"You sure?" Ian asked.

"I'm sure. I'm ready." She leaned forwards over Ben.

Ian obliged.

The intern screamed and bucked hard. At first Liz mistook her orgasm for pain until she cried out, "Oh God, don't stop. That feels so good! So good!"

Then Ian guided Liz's hand to the vibrator. "You do the honours, Liz. After all, she's your intern." He winked at her.

Liz took over the controls. "I've saved the best for myself," Ian grunted, as he lifted her hips and slid his penis into her wet snatch. "Your cunny's still the best of the best, Liz. I can't get enough of you." He nodded to the vibrator. "Keep the pressure on. Our student needs the practice." Liz was pretty sure Teri would be sitting carefully tomorrow.

They were all properly smeared with greasepaint and covered in a fine sheen of sweat. The wet sounds of sex filled the room along with the thickening scent of arousal. Hands groped tits and arses, mouths and tongues probed and suckled all to a soundtrack of thrusting and grunting and the low buzz of the vibrator up Teri's arse.

They were all close, so close. Ben's muscles looked as though they would shatter from the tension increasing with each thrust, and Liz was pretty sure Ian had been holding his breath, riding the wave so near the crest. She clenched tight as another orgasm raged through her, and that was enough to send Ian, who gripped her arse and groaned. She could feel his cock convulsing inside her. Seconds later, Ben followed suit, and suddenly Teri cried out her own release.

Later, when they were dressed and had finished the shoot, Teri nodded to the set. "If all the shoots were like this we'd never get this calendar finished." Then she gave Liz a tonsil-deep kiss, followed by a good feel up of her tits. "But we'd have fun, wouldn't we?"

As the intern left, the two men each put an arm around Liz. "Are we squared on our debt now?" Ian asked.

Liz pushed them away. "I'd hardly call something you both clearly enjoyed so much payment of your debt, would you?"

"Then what did you have in mind?" Ben asked.

Liz looked down at her watch. "Well, it is Friday night. None of us has to get up early tomorrow. I really could use a bath after our exhausting little shoot."

The two men looked at each other. "You want us to give you a bath?" Ben asked.

"For starters. Then we'll see what comes up."

"But we'll enjoy that too," Ian said. "At this rate, we'll never get out of your debt."

"Now you're getting the picture." She gave them both a quick stroke of the cock through their jeans and headed for the door, with both blokes close behind, and anxious to service their debt.

One Last Fling

Kristina Wright

"We're Vegas bound," Douglas said, helping me into the back of our sleek, black limousine.

The neon lights outside Club Europa reflected off my silver-sequined minidress, causing it to sparkle like a disco ball. I made a half-hearted effort to preserve my modesty as I climbed into the limo, tugging my dress with one hand while I held a glass of champagne in the other. I wasn't particularly successful at either, as I felt a cool breeze on my ass and the trickle of champagne on my wrist. I fell into the back of the limo in a fit of giggles and waited for my entourage to join me.

"Oh, but I'm not finished dancing!"

Alex got in beside me, his long limbs tangling with mine as we made room for two more. "It's three hours to Vegas and the girls are waiting for you. You'll dance the night away tomorrow night."

"Fuck the night away, is more like it," Douglas said, as he and Neil climbed in and sat across from us.

Neil tapped the partition between the driver and us. "We're ready," he called. "Let's get the bride to Vegas."

The limo pulled away from the kerb in front of my favourite dance club and I waved goodbye as if I would never see it again. I was giddy and tipsy and very cosy in the back of the limo with my three favourite men – besides my fiancé Simon, of course. What can I say? I've always been a tomboy and that has translated into deep, meaningful – and sometimes even platonic – friendships with men. Not that I don't have female friends, I do. They were waiting for me at the Bellagio in Vegas and in the morning we'd be getting massages and pedicures and talking about boys before I walked down the aisle. But I had wanted my last night as a single woman to be spent with my three closest male friends.

It had been Simon's idea for my bachelorette party to end up in Vegas, where we were to be married the following evening. Now, I was floating happily along thanks to the beautiful, bubbly champagne that kept flowing into my glass from endless bottles provided by my attentive staff of three. I was dressed in sparkly sequins and smoky mascara, looking very much the part of a party girl out for a night of dancing and debauchery. I smiled like the proverbial cat that has eaten the cream and curled up contentedly on the leather seat next to Alex.

"Well, lady, did we show you a good last night?" Alex asked, refilling my glass yet again.

I giggled as I sipped the expensive champagne. "Absolutely. We made quite a scene on the dance floor."

It was true. We'd popped into three clubs over the course of the evening and caused a bit of a stir every time as I led the men out to the centre of the dance floor. Gyrating with three men is likely to garner a lot of attention. Not that I minded. I loved having all eyes on me and my boys. Alex, at six-four and with almost white-blond hair, often caused enough of a stir on his own. But throw in former football-playing Douglas with his rugged good looks and Neil, with the lean, muscular body of a runner, and I was certain every woman in every club was jealous of me. The best part was the safe feeling I had surrounded by men who knew me at least as well as Simon did. I snuggled against Alex's shoulder and sighed. Douglas and Neil sat across from us, drinking beer from the well-stocked limo fridge.

"I could get used to this, if I wasn't getting married tomorrow."

Douglas winked at me. "Why would you trade in wild nights of dancing with your own personal harem for boring married life?"

"Aren't harem boys usually eunuchs?"

"Definitely no eunuchs here," Alex said, gruffly.

We laughed at that. Alex's sexual conquests were almost as legendary as, well, my own. I'd tested those waters a time or two and decided he had earned his reputation as a cocksman. Of course, Douglas wasn't a slouch in the bedroom, either. The only mystery for me was Neil. Bedroom-eyed, soft-spoken Neil was a big question mark to me. I glanced at him now – wondering things probably better left unknown.

The limo turned a corner a little too sharply, which pressed me a little closer to Alex. "Hey, Mr Limo Driver," I called through the darkened partition. "Please be careful! I'm getting married tomorrow."

The partition lowered enough for me to see blue eyes staring at me in the rear-view mirror. "Yes, ma'am. My apologies."

I giggled. "Is OK."

"It's official," Neil said. "She's drunk."

I harrumphed in a very unladylike fashion.

"I am not drunk. I'm just a little bit tipsy."

Alex's hand, which had been on my knee since the corner turn, seemed to have accidentally slid up my thigh. "Well, I'm drunk."

As if to prove his intoxication, he stroked my thigh seductively. His fingers felt warm on my bare skin. I couldn't tell if he was messing with me or being serious. The possibility that he might be serious was exciting – and also proof that I was most definitely a little drunk. I made a low murmur of pleasure and the three men laughed. I didn't like that at all. I was the bride, damn it! I wanted to be pampered and coddled and . . . other things.

"Uh-oh. Watch out, Alex," Douglas said. "You know how she gets when she's drunk."

I tilted my head and finished the last of the champagne in my glass before holding it out for another refill from Alex's bottomless bottle. "Do tell, Douglas. How do I get?"

"Oh, love, you know how you get," Alex answered good-naturedly as he refilled my glass. "Don't you?"

Alex, more so than the other two, always knew how to calm me down from one of my bitchy moods. I looked into his twinkling green eyes and smiled. I covered his hand with mine, wondering if I dared move his hand just a couple of inches higher. The thought made me squirm and sigh.

"Oh yeah. I remember now." I licked my lips, noting the way his gaze followed the tip of my tongue from one corner of my mouth to the other. "I get very *needy* when I'm drunk."

"Very needy," Alex said. "That's certainly one way of phrasing it, babe."

"She's *needed* me on more than one occasion." Douglas smirked, giving Neil's shoulder a nudge as if the whole thing was a big joke. "Haven't you, doll?"

I pouted. "I don't remember."

"I remember." Alex topped off my champagne glass. "Douglas' birthday, three years ago. You did naughty things with his birthday cake and then you disappeared into his bedroom for a good half-hour—"

"It was an hour," Douglas interrupted.

"Fine, a good hour. And when you came out you had birthday cake in your hair—"

Douglas laughed. "Among other places."

"I did not!" Of course I had, but I felt like I needed to defend my feminine honour in the face of their laughter at my exploits.

"Then there was that night we got thrown out of that club – what was the name of it? – because you pulled me into the bathroom. The *women's* bathroom," Alex went on.

I glared at him. "My zipper broke on my dress."

"Before or after he went into the bathroom with you?" Douglas asked.

Neil had remained quiet through their ribbing, but now he finished his beer and shook his head. "You've never *needed* me."

I opened my mouth to say something, but he was right. All of my drunk fooling around over the years had been with Alex and Douglas, mostly because I knew they didn't take it more seriously than what it was. Neil was different, though. I always suspected he had a bit of a thing for me and while I adored him and thought he was sexy as hell, his attraction was purely physical. I might play with the boys, but Simon had my heart and I felt like that was the one part of me Neil might demand if I let things go too far. But, like earlier, I was starting to wonder what I had missed.

"My loss." I gave Neil a sad smile. "You know I love you anyway, right?"

"I don't think we're talking about love here," Neil said, looking away as the limo moved through the quiet city streets.

The mood had shifted in the limo and I looked at Alex with dismay. Sensing my discomfort, he offered, "Well, the night's still young – and she's definitely drunk."

The men laughed, even Neil, and I relaxed a little. It was hard to think about Neil's hurt feelings with Alex's hand making slow, sensual circles on my thigh. I wriggled against him, which moved Alex's hand just a bit higher on my leg and under the edge of my dress. He was so very close to touching my pussy I considered how much more I could slide down before I would be on the floor. It was a fleeting thought – and an unnecessary one. Alex spread his fingers on my thigh. His long fingers. Then he wiggled them lightly against the edge of my panties. I bit my lip to keep from moaning.

"Guess she's feeling needy," Neil said. "Is the bride-to-be wet already?"

I made a face at him. "That's rude."

"Yes, it is," Alex agreed. "And I don't know if she's wet."

They laughed at me again. I couldn't help but laugh with them as I enjoyed the feeling of Alex's finger rubbing lazily against me. "You are all bad," I said. "And I love it." Alex leaned down to whisper in my ear, "If you spread your legs just a bit, love, I promise you will love it even more."

How can a girl say no to that? I did as he suggested, spreading my thighs far enough apart that my dress rode up to my hips and gave Douglas and Neil a glimpse of my lacy white panties. I watched them watching me, getting more and more turned on by the way the night was going. Alex cupped my panty-clad pussy and gave it a gentle squeeze. I gasped, Douglas groaned and Alex made an appreciative sound low in his throat. Neil just stared, his heavy-lidded eyes watching me. I looked past him and saw another pair of eyes staring at me from the rear-view window. I smiled and winked, thoroughly enjoying the attention.

"Oh yes, the little minx is quite wet," Alex confirmed. "Despite your little white virginal panties, I think you're the bad one, Victoria."

I nodded in agreement. "Oh yes, I'm quite bad."

"Should I stop then?"

By way of an answer, I covered his hand again and pressed it to my pussy. "You'd better not."

"We're almost to the highway," the driver announced. "Shall I make one last rest stop before the drive to Las Vegas?"

Just then, Alex slipped a finger under the edge of my panties and pushed just the tip into my pussy. "Yes," I gasped. Then, quickly added, "No, no! That won't be necessary."

"Excuse me, ma'am?"

I met the driver's eyes in the rear-view mirror again, wondering just how much of our back-seat antics he could see.

"I'm sorry, we were talking about something else," I said breathlessly as Alex pushed his finger inside me just a little bit farther.

Douglas and Neil exchanged amused looks.

"This is the best conversation I've ever had," Neil said, seeming to have recovered his sense of humour. I liked him better this way – my familiar old friend instead of the one who might have gotten away.

I stuck my tongue out at them. "Just drive, please."

"Certainly, ma'am," the driver said. "We should be in Las Vegas in a little under three hours. Let me know if you need anything."

"I wouldn't mind doing a little less talking," Douglas said. "I think actions speak louder than words."

I heard something in his voice that promised pleasure. For me. The combination of champagne and familiarity had left me utterly without inhibitions.

"What would you like to do, Douglas?" I asked, raising my hips to Alex's questing hand. Alex obliged me by sliding his hand down the front of my panties and giving my bare pussy a squeeze.

Douglas slipped to his knees on the floor of the limo. "I'd like to have my mouth too full to talk."

"Seems like she's already occupied," Neil commented. Whatever his feelings for me, he was clearly enjoying the show.

As if by silent agreement, Alex withdrew his hand from my panties and pulled the lacy fabric to the side. My bare, bikini-waxed – and increasingly wet – pussy was exposed to Douglas' view. He moved forwards between my legs, pushing my knees apart with his hands. I squirmed on the seat, my pulse quickening in anticipation of what was to come. But Douglas made me wait. He stared at my exposed pussy, nostrils flaring as if he was taking in my scent. He was so close that I could feel the warmth of his breath on my aroused flesh. The silence in the limo was almost tangible – even the road sounds seemed to have faded beneath the pounding of my heart.

"Lick her," Alex said, giving voice to my silent plea. "She's dying for it."

Douglas looked into my eyes, one eyebrow cocked, as if seeking my permission.

I nodded. "Please."

His tongue felt like velvet on my engorged sex. With the broad flat of his tongue, he lapped at me. I moaned, raising my hips to his mouth, wanting more. He licked me slowly, as if we were alone and had all the time in the world, his tongue dipping between the valley of my pussy lips and up over my swollen clit. Again and again, he licked me with those slow, methodical strokes designed to torment me even while they gave me pleasure. I moved my hips against his mouth, seeking more.

Alex slipped the strap of my dress over my shoulder, exposing my breast. Then he dipped his head to suck my nipple into his mouth. I moaned, tugging the other strap down and cupping my breasts, offering them to Alex's lips. Douglas shifted lower, hooking my legs over his shoulders as he devoured me with his mouth.

I looked at Neil. He watched the three of us, his expression one of barely controlled lust as his hand moved slowly over his crotch. It excited me to know he was watching – an observer rather than a participant. I wanted more, though. I wanted to see him stroke himself. I opened my mouth to say just that, but Alex chose that moment to flick my clit with his finger as Douglas dipped his tongue between the lips of my pussy. I moaned, the combination of sensations driving me out of my mind and to the brink of orgasm. I tucked my head against Alex's shoulder, my eyes fluttering closed as I pushed my aroused body at the two men who pleasured me.

"She's going to come," Alex said. "Lick her faster."

Douglas' tongue licked along my wet opening while Alex stroked my clitoris with his fingertips. I clutched at Douglas' hair and tightened my thighs around his bent head. Every muscle in my body went taut, my damp skin feeling hypersensitive in my arousal. Then Douglas sucked my clit – and Alex's finger – into his mouth and I came.

"Oh, yes!" I gasped, nearly sliding off the seat as my orgasm slammed into me. "Oh God!"

"You naughty little girl. Come hard for us," Alex whispered in my ear. "Come on his tongue. Show us what a very bad girl you are."

I rode wave after wave of orgasm as Douglas nursed gently at my throbbing clit. Alex rubbed his wet fingertip over my nipple and sucked it into his mouth again, his soft moan telling me just how much he was enjoying the experience. When I gently nudged Douglas away from my sensitive clit, his mouth shiny with my wetness. He grinned and licked his lips. "Delicious."

"Thanks," I said, feeling a little light-headed.

Alex squeezed my pussy again.

"So juicy. I don't think you're done."

I shook my head. "I don't think so either."

Douglas moved my legs off his shoulders and shifted on to the bench seat beside me. Now, Alex and Douglas sat on either side of me while our silent observer sat across from us. If Neil felt left out of our debauchery, he didn't show it. He smiled, sipping his beer and looking from my face to my still spread legs.

I took a steadying breath, my pulse still throbbing. "This is turning out to be quite a bachelorette party."

"If you were a guy, we would be at a strip club right now buying you lap dances from pretty girls pretending to get off," Alex said.

"Pretty girls stripping for me." I contemplated that for a moment. "That wouldn't have been so bad. But sexy boys stripping and getting off for me would be infinitely more fun, I think."

For the first time – perhaps ever – I think I shocked them. Alex and Douglas went very still on either side of me. Neil glanced through the tinted window at the darkness racing by. I giggled at their sudden incongruous modesty.

"C'mon, you have seen each other naked at the gym countless times," I said. "What's the big deal about getting naked for me?"

There was a lot of throat clearing and looking anywhere but at me, while I shook my head in feminine disgust. Men who thought nothing of revealing the naughtiest, kinkiest details of their sex lives, not to mention watching me expose myself and writhe in pleasure in front of them, were suddenly shy schoolboys when it came to stripping down in front of each other.

Alex was the first to break the awkward silence. "Naked and, er – *naked* – are two different things." He gestured towards his lap where his erection made an impressive tent. "I wouldn't want to intimidate these guys, after all."

"Yeah, right," Douglas snorted. "That's the reason I don't want to strip in front of you – I'm intimidated by your enormous dick."

"Mmm," I murmured, running one fingertip along the hard ridge of flesh in Alex's pants. "Enormous dick. I vaguely remember . . ."

Alex snorted. "Vaguely? I'd think it would be etched in your memory."

While the three of us were joking around, Neil watched and kept silent. I studied him as Alex and Douglas continued to trade barbs about the size of their equipment. Though his body appeared relaxed, with his legs stretched out in front of him and his arms across the back of the seat, he was staring at me hungrily. I liked the way he looked at me, as if I were the only thing that could satisfy him. It reminded me of Simon.

"You're awfully quiet," I said. "What do you think, Neil?"

He shrugged. "It's your party, babe. If you want me to get naked and jerk off, I'll get naked and jerk off."

Suddenly, I lost all interest in Alex and Douglas. They were familiar, predictable. Men's men. Or boys' boys. They'd goad each other into doing something neither of them would willingly do on his own. On the other hand, Neil – whom I had always assumed to be the more prudish of the three – was willing to do whatever I wanted without coaxing or bribery. I loved it.

"That would be . . . delicious," I said, searching for just the right word. "You'd do that for me?"

Neil nodded solemnly. "If that's what you want."

"I guess Neil is the only one who wants to make me happy," I teased.

Douglas and Alex were quiet, sitting on either side of me like silent bodyguards. I could almost feel the tension in the confined space as they contemplated what Neil was agreeing to do – and what they didn't want to do. Neither wanted to back down, especially when they thought they had the upper hand over Neil, who had missed out on the fun thus far. Their desire for whatever kinky games might transpire once they were naked was still outweighed by their heterosexual drive to be the only man in play.

While they considered their options, Neil made the first move. If he was embarrassed to strip down while the three of us watched, he didn't show it. He only had eyes for me as he loosened his tie and unbuttoned the cuffs of his shirt. While there is a certain pleasure in watching a man undress, I found myself anxious for him to hurry. I had never seen him naked before. I had never even kissed him, much less touched his bare chest. Suddenly, I was sure the look in his eyes was mirrored in my own. Desire. Need. A pull so strong it was almost physical. I wanted him. And since this was the only time I would ever have him, I wanted to take my time enjoying him.

Part of me felt guilty for ignoring Alex and Douglas as Neil stripped off his shirt to reveal a lean torso and finely sculpted muscles. These two men had been my friends and play partners in the past and there was no reason to exclude them now, even if my attention would be focused on Neil. Of course, it really depended on whether they would participate, but I fully intended to give them the chance.

"Well, boys, what about you?" I asked them, resting a hand over each of their crotches. Their arousal turned me on almost as much as Neil arching up off the seat to tug off his trousers.

"What about us?" Douglas asked, sounding almost offended, even as his cock twitched beneath my gentle stroking.

"Neil isn't the only one who is going to get naked, is he?"

At that moment, Neil stripped off his confining boxer briefs, revealing a thick, heavily veined cock. He sat back down, his hand curling around his erection as he looked at me for instruction.

"That depends," Alex said, his voice thick with lust. "What's in it for us?"

I laughed. "Like the man said, it's my party, *babe*. You'll just have to get naked and find out."

Then there were two more men undressing in the limo as it headed for Las Vegas. I felt drunk on more than champagne as I watched them reveal themselves for my pleasure. I was dizzy trying to look from one to the other, watching as Douglas stripped off his shirt and exposed that muscular torso I had once rubbed against until I had a very wet orgasm. Then I was staring at Alex as he unfastened his pants, revealing the fabric of his underwear stretched tautly over his erection.

"I guess we know who the *bigger* man really is," Alex conceded, glancing at Neil. It was true – even without a measuring tape it looked as if Neil had a couple of inches on both of them. Not that it mattered to me, but I was excited to know they were looking at each other too.

I stroked Alex's cock through his pants. "It's not the size of the ship—"

"—it's the motion of the ocean," he finished with a grin. "I remember rocking the waves pretty hard a time or two."

"Oh yeah," I breathed as he lowered his mouth over mine.

We kissed hungrily, tongues tasting of beer and champagne. I freed him of his pants and squeezed his cock until he moaned into my mouth. He returned the favour by fondling my breasts, tweaking my nipples hard just the way I liked.

"Hey, what about me?"

Eyes closed, I shifted to kiss Douglas. The taste and texture of him was different from Alex – rougher, more nipping of teeth than caressing of tongues. Alex continued to pinch and squeeze my nipples as I used my other hand to play with Douglas' erection. A cock in each hand, my breasts being played with while I kissed each in turn – I felt like my senses were being overloaded. I couldn't find a rhythm because each man's attention was different. Alex was slow and languid; Douglas was quick and intense. I was caught between their desires, my own building to an almost painful need. I crossed and uncrossed my legs, my pussy sadly neglected.

I remembered Neil and pulled my mouth away from Douglas to look at him. He was angled in the corner, one leg stretched out along the seat, the other bent at the knee. He fisted his heavy cock as he watched us, a thoughtful smirk on his face. I wondered what he was thinking as he made long, slow strokes up the length of his erection. I not only wanted his body, I wanted inside his head.

"Let me know when you're ready for me," he said, when he saw the direction of my gaze.

Those few words were enough to make me whimper in need. I watched Neil while I continued to play with the two cocks on either side of me. I mimicked his strokes, feeling some strange pull towards him that I had never had – or never admitted to – before. While Douglas and Alex made guttural sounds of pleasure, Neil remained silent, that enigmatic smile in place as he showed me how he pleasured himself.

"I want you," I whispered. "Now."

Everything changed between us with that proclamation.

Neil's smile was pure satisfaction, as if he had already gotten the sexual release he craved. "Anything the lady wants."

"What about us?" Alex asked, closing his hand around mine as I stroked him.

"I want Neil."

Douglas whispered hoarsely, "Just don't stop touching me."

Neil followed Douglas' lead from earlier, slipping to his knees in front of me. I spread my legs, offering myself like a gift. He dipped his head between my thighs and licked me – softer than Douglas, like he was licking foam from a latte. I sighed, shifting forwards on the seat to give him full access. I could feel wetness trickling between the cheeks of my bottom and I was sure I was leaving a puddle on the limo upholstery, but I didn't care.

I spread my legs over Alex and Douglas' legs. Each of them put a hand high on my thigh, as if framing my pussy for Neil's pleasure. I met the bemused gaze of the driver in the rear-view mirror and winked at him before closing my eyes and giving myself over to the pleasure of Neil's slow, infuriating licks. He nibbled my labia, sucking each plump lip into his mouth before circling my clit with the tip of this tongue. When I didn't think I could bear the teasing any longer, he took my swollen clit between his lips and sucked it.

I gasped, whimpering, "Oh, I can't take any more! It's too much!"

He ignored me and continued sucking, as if intent on drawing every sound and sensation he could from my body. I reflexively tried to close my legs, but Alex and Douglas held me open, spread for Neil's enjoyment. I still held their cocks in my hands, squeezing and stroking them in rhythm to my own pleasure. I squirmed, aroused beyond measure at the feeling of helplessness and the overwhelming pleasure that seemed to border on pain. I knew I could end it at any moment, but though it was almost too much to take, I didn't want it to end. I never wanted it to end.

Just as I felt the first tremors of orgasm low in my belly, Neil pulled away.

"No," I gasped. "Please!"

"I'm going to fuck you," he said simply. "But I don't have a condom."

"No problem, dude," Alex said, fumbling with his discarded trousers. "Here."

Neil took the proffered square with a grin. "Always prepared."

Alex breathed in sharply as I ran my thumb over the glistening tip of his cock. "Yeah, but I thought I was the one who would be using it."

The rip of the condom packet made my pussy ripple. "Hurry," I said. "I need you."

"I need you, too," Neil said, and then he was inside me.

From feeling open and vulnerable, I was suddenly, almost impossibly, full. I took a deep, steadying breath as Neil slowly pushed inside my wetness. He stared into my eyes and the intimacy was too much. I tilted my head back against the seat and closed my eyes, whimpering when his cock was fully inside me.

"Look at me," he demanded. "Watch me fuck you."

The tone of his voice demanded immediate compliance. I jerked my head up, staring first into his hard, almost unfamiliar face, then looking down to where we were joined, his olive skin looking so much darker against my paleness.

"That is so fucking hot," Douglas said softly.

I looked at him and saw that he, too, was staring between my legs and watching Neil fuck me. A quick glance on the other side confirmed that Alex was equally mesmerized by the scene before him. My orgasm had subsided enough for me to regain something of my control and I began to slowly stroke the men on either side of me in time to Neil's strokes. I was fleetingly reminded of a horse and jockey, both moving in tandem, joined in a powerful race to the finish.

Neil gripped my ass, pulling me down hard on his cock even while Alex and Douglas still held my legs open. "So fucking tight," he growled.

I moaned, that pain-out-of-pleasure sensation cutting through me like a dangerously sharp knife. I kept my eyes on Neil, letting him see what he was doing to me. He fucked me in long, deep strokes, withdrawing his cock until the head was just inside my opening before slamming inside me again.

Every motion brought a moan to my lips and a plea for more. My skin was damp with sweat and I felt dizzy from the heat of our bodies moving together.

"Come on my cock," he demanded. "I won't come until you do."

I felt as if a knot of tension unwound low in my belly. I undulated against him, rocking my hips for my own pleasure, squeezing and stroking Alex and Douglas as if they were extensions of my body. I felt wetness on my hands, but I didn't know if they had come or if it was sweat. I didn't care. They would tell me to stop when they were ready, but none of us was ready for it to end. Not yet. Not quite yet.

Neil pulled back, thrusting shallowly just inside my pussy, the head of his cock stroking my sweet spot. I gasped, going tense and still. Then, suddenly, I was coming. Hard. My orgasm rocketed through me like an explosion, causing me to scream out my release. My body, still a moment earlier, went into motion, rocking on Neil's cock as if I would milk him dry.

Neil's answering groan as my pussy rippled around him was softer than mine, but the expression on his face told me the pleasure was no less intense. He flexed his hips one last time, his cock throbbing inside me. We stayed like that for a long moment, sweat-slick bodies joined together, until my orgasm subsided. Neil was still breathing hard as he pulled free of my body. I gasped, then giggled self-consciously, feeling suddenly bereft at his absence.

Alex cleared his throat. "You can release your death grip now," he said gruffly.

My giggle turned into a full-fledged laugh. In my excitement, I had been holding on to Douglas and him for dear life. Now I realized that both were going flaccid, having certainly enjoyed the moment.

"Sorry," I said.

Douglas stroked my thigh softly. "Don't be. It was pretty amazing until about five minutes ago when I started considering we might end up eunuchs after all."

I shifted on the seat, wincing at the stiffness in my thighs from being held apart for so long. "Sorry, sorry," I said.

I realized Neil hadn't spoken and I searched his face for what he might be thinking. That smile was back in place – the one that was a little too serious to be amusement.

"You OK?" I asked, as if we were alone in the limo.

He nodded. "Just grand."

"Thank you." There didn't seem to be much more to say except, "You are truly amazing."

"Back at you, babe," he said rakishly. "That was a dream come true."

The driver spoke up before I had time to contemplate the meaning of his words.

"We've arrived at the hotel, ma'am."

I looked out the window and saw the lights of the Bellagio sparkling like an oasis just outside the window. The night had passed and I would be getting married soon. Reality came rushing back like a splash of cold water in the face as I considered all the things I still needed to do. I was hardly in any position to get out at the moment, however.

I watched in drowsy detachment as the boys hurriedly dressed. Now that the party was over, they were anxious to beat a hasty retreat. I giggled. The champagne buzz had worn off, but the sex buzz was still going strong.

"Remember, what happened in the limo stays in the limo," I said conspiratorially.

"Right," Alex said. "Good to know."

Douglas grinned and shook his head at me as he tugged his trousers on. "Only you could get me to do that, lady."

I smiled. "I know."

"Aren't you going to get dressed?" Neil asked.

I nodded. "In a minute. I'll let you guys get out of here so I can straighten up in peace."

"I can wait for you," Neil said, still looking out for my needs.

The driver responded, "I'll make sure the lady gets to her room."

The guys exchanged looks, Alex raising an eyebrow at me. "Is that OK with you?"

"I'll be OK. Find the girls and tell them I'll be there in about an hour."

Douglas grinned, as if he knew something. "It looks like the lady's evening isn't finished, boys."

Alex and he laughed, but Neil just stared at me. "You've had too much champagne. I'm not leaving you alone with the limo driver."

I laughed. "It's OK, Neil." When he still didn't budge, I leaned forwards and whispered in his ear, "Trust me. I'm safe with the driver."

Something in my tone made him turn around and look over the partition. He nodded. "I see."

Alex gave me a hug and a deep, soulful kiss before opening the limo door. "See you tomorrow, babe."

"Get some sleep," Douglas added, giving me an equally intense kiss. "It's going to be a busy day tomorrow."

Then they were gone and Neil was still watching me. "I don't know what to say."

I kissed his cheek. "Thanks for this memorable night. Truly."

He started to speak and I could see in his expression what he was going to say, so I kissed his mouth. He pulled me to him as if he would never let go, but after a few moments he did. "See you tomorrow," he said before slipping out of the limo and closing the door behind him.

I waited until he had disappeared in the same direction Alex and Douglas had gone before saying, "OK, you can come back here now."

The driver's door opened and closed and then the door closest to me opened and he settled beside me, his black hat at a jaunty angle. I tossed it on the seat across from us and mussed his wavy brown hair.

"Quite a night you had, Mrs Rhodes," he said.

"I'm not Mrs yet, Mr Rhodes."

He angled me sideways on to his lap, brushing my hair from my damp cheeks. "Was it all you wanted it to be?"

I smiled, happy but also a little wistful. "And more. How about you?"

He chuckled. "Fantasy satisfied, though I wish I could have seen a bit more of *you*."

I stretched my arms out. "You can see me now."

His gaze roamed over my body and I was instantly conscious of what a picture I must present. Naked except for my dress bunched around my waist, my hair a tousled mess of blonde curls, my smoky mascara smudged beneath my eyes.

I smiled. "Like what you see?"

He nodded. "You look like one very satisfied woman."

I wiggled on his lap, feeling that urgency building in my vein again. "Almost. Not quite."

"You want *more*?" His mock surprise only made me laugh. "What an insatiable wench you are."

I slid to my knees and nudged his legs apart. He stared down at me as I unbuckled his belt and worked his zipper down over his heavy erection. I felt my pussy – still tender from earlier, but already wet – tighten in response to his arousal.

"Aren't you happy you're marrying me?"

He groaned as I freed his cock from his pants and gave the tip a lick. "You are definitely a dream come true – *my* dream come true. Are you happy you're marrying me?"

I thought of Simon indulging my last fling with my three best friends while he fulfilled his fantasy of watching me. It didn't seem possible that two people could be more perfect for each other. I sighed in blissful abandon. Just before I gave Simon his last single guy blow job, I looked up into his eyes and whispered, "Absolutely."

The Good Samaritan

Dorianne

"They're at it again," Marlene said as Jenny came out on to their deck carrying three beers.

"Fucking or fighting?" asked Marlene.

"They just finished fighting now they're fucking," Dan told her.

"Aw, I missed the foreplay fight? Damn," said Jenny.

From the deck of their place they could see directly into the apartment across the alley. The couple that lived there had never noticed the three housemates spying on them. They never seemed to notice anything but each other and they never seemed to exhibit anything other than lust or anger at each other. This provided Jenny, Marlene and Dan with hours of entertainment.

"I'm so bored of them though," Marlene announced.

"What are you talking about?" said Dan with a sniff. "They're like a soap opera and a porn all rolled into one. It's awesome."

"They're so . . . white bread," complained Marlene.

"They certainly are white," observed Jenny. The couple next door had classic Aryan good looks, unlike the three of them who came in varying shades of brown.

"Their whole shtick has gotten old," said Marlene. "They scream and slam doors and if we're lucky we can make out enough words to know what trivial thing they're fighting about. Then they go at it, which is fun for sure, but they only ever use the two most standard positions and their sex never gets, you know, interesting."

"Not everyone can be freaks like us," stated Jenny, watching the other apartment fixedly, absentmindedly twirling one of her dreadlocks.

"Why not?" asked Marlene. There was a pause as they all gazed at the male neighbour's thrusting buttocks.

Marlene didn't know the other two were even contemplating her offhand question until Dan remarked, "Why not indeed?"

Jenny absently rubbed her nipple and said, "Hmmm . . ."

Katie was just arriving home from work when a black girl on a bicycle took a hard fall on the road beside her. The bike fell on top of the girl and blood spurted from her knee. "Oh my God, are you OK?" asked Katie. She seemed in shock.

"I don't know, I mean, ow," said the girl. She looked imploringly up at Katie. "Do you have a Band-aid?"

Feeling a rush of Good Samaritan pleasure, Katie said, "This is my place right here, I've got Band-Aids and Polysporin, why don't you come in?" They locked the bike up to the fence surrounding the building and went inside.

As Katie was getting out her first-aid kit the girl's cell phone rang. "I hurt myself," she said into it. "I fell. A pretty lady is helping me with my cut but can you come and help me get my bike home? It might be broken." She covered her mouthpiece and said to Katie, "Can my friends come help me?"

Katie was blushing – she wasn't used to being called "pretty" by random strangers. "Of course," said Katie. "Tell them to buzz 106."

There was a silence as the girl played with one of her dreadlocks. Then Katie remembered her manners and, like a good hostess, offered her guest a drink.

When Marlene and Dan arrived at apartment 106, just around the corner from their apartment where they'd been waiting for the call, Jenny and Katie were drinking wine in the kitchen. The kitchen was a cute little affair, painted cornflower blue with every available space used to handily house the usual kitchen instruments. Pots hung above the stove, a spice rack topped with a large set of rather phallic salt and pepper shakers was set into the counter, a set of oven mitts decorated to look like piglets hung from a hook by the stove.

"For the pain," Jenny said as she raised her glass at them and offered a slight tilt of the head in acknowledgment of their Machiavellian plan.

Katie said, "Welcome, welcome, you two! Your friend here took quite a tumble. She was a little shook up so I thought some wine might help her calm down. Well, the bottle's open now, would you like a glass?" Marlene and Dan accepted and sat down around the kitchen table. Marlene was wearing a shirt that was very low cut, exposing a suggestive bounty of her smooth Sri Lankan skin.

"Jenny was just telling me about your, um, unconventional lifestyle. It's really interesting! Of course you always hear about things like that but you don't usually meet people who actually live it."

"Well, you need to be honest with yourself about what you want out of life and then make that life happen," stated Marlene. She was unsure which part of their "unconventional lifestyle" Jenny had revealed but was sure that statement was broad enough to cover all bases. She also enjoyed the delicious irony of claiming honesty when the circumstances behind the three of them being in this apartment were entirely falsified.

"Oh, yes, yes, of course. I'm not sure I ever considered, you know, polyamory as an option. I love my boyfriend but a lifetime is a long time to be with just one person. Who knows what I'll want in ten years?" Katie mused.

The look that passed between Marlene, Jenny and Dan indicated that none of them was willing to wait ten years. Luckily Katie's blonde head was bowed and she didn't see their non-verbal exchange.

Katie looked up, confused. "But what I'm not sure of is . . . so which of you is dating the other? Like do you," she addressed Dan, "just have two girlfriends and they both date you? Ha, I can't wait to tell my boyfriend, he'd be so jealous! What guy doesn't want two girls?"

Dan leaned to his left to kiss Marlene, then leaned to his

right to kiss Jenny. "Yeah." He smiled at Katie, a winning, charming smile. "Life doesn't get much better than this."

Marlene hoisted herself into Dan's lap. "But," she said, "it doesn't end there. Can't let Dan have all the fun." And she leaned over and kissed Jenny.

While Dan's kisses had been soft and intimate but quick, Marlene meant business. She forced Jenny's lips open with her own and plunged her tongue deep into Jenny's mouth, ensuring the angle was right for Katie to see.

Katie was blushing right to the roots of her hair. Her face was scarlet, her eyes bright. She got up to get another bottle of wine. When she turned around from the counter with the opened bottle she couldn't help but notice all three of them had been looking admiringly at her ass. She almost dropped the bottle but managed to collect herself a bit and sat down. She filled all their glasses and downed most of hers in one gulp.

"So you're . . ." She trailed off.

"We all are," Dan stated, his cock stiff, Marlene still in his lap. Katie's eyes widened and Dan hoped she had meant what he thought she had meant. He knew from their spying that now was about the time of day that Katie's boyfriend arrived home from work.

"I hope you're not freaked out," Jenny said with concern.

"Oh no, not at all!" exclaimed Katie. She reached out to place her hand on top of Jenny's. "I've never encountered it before, but it's nice, you all seem so normal."

"We're not freaks," said Marlene, flexing her ass muscles against Dan's cock. "We just like to enjoy life – and to help each other to enjoy life."

Dan exerted effort to keep his smirk to himself. "Freaks" was exactly what they were and they all knew it. And loved it.

"To help everyone enjoy life," Jenny said seriously. One of her hands was on the table underneath Katie's; the other hand she placed lightly on Katie's thigh underneath the table.

Katie looked down, then up at Jenny. She looked across the table at Dan and Marlene. Marlene smiled and Dan hugged his arms around Marlene's abdomen, a gesture which happened to also lift her breasts up prominently. Katie couldn't help but stare at Marlene's cleavage. As she stared she felt the hand on her thigh move upwards. She turned her head only to end up with her mouth against Jenny's. Jenny was now out of her seat, kneeling on the floor with her wounded knee, between Katie's legs. Katie gave up thinking and leaned into the kiss.

Bill was in a bad mood. Work was frustrating. The coffee shop had been out of croissants. He had forgotten his cell phone in his desk. Nothing was going right today. He knew that on days like today Katie always found some way to provoke him further. He hoped today would be different. He didn't feel like a fight right now. Except that he did love the passion of the post-fight sex.

What he found when he came home was certainly different than what he had been expecting but no less provocative. Katie was in the kitchen, her shorts around her ankles, and some girl was kneeling with her head between Katie's thighs. Katie's face was buried in the cleavage of another girl who was on the table on all fours. Her skirt was flipped up to her waist and some guy was behind her, sticking his fingers deep inside.

Bill was stunned for a minute and for that minute no one noticed him at all. They just went on licking and sucking and probing each other. Then Bill got angry.

"Katie, you fucking slut!" he roared. "What the hell are you doing? Who are these whores?"

Katie lifted her head from between Marlene's tits. "Oh honey," she said, confused, "you know how you said we should try new things in bed . . .?"

"In bed with each other, not in the goddamn kitchen with a crew of mangy perverts!" he yelled, his voice becoming more constricted. His arm flung out threateningly, knocking the spice rack to the floor. "I'll show you to fuck around on me!" He moved forwards with malevolence. Before he could take a single step, however, Dan was on top of him. They crashed down to the kitchen floor in a flurry of violence.

Katie screamed. Jenny held her tight. "It's OK," she said. "Dan's very good at this." Marlene adjusted her position on the kitchen table to watch.

Dan was a master wrestler. He had been a wrestling

champion in university and he kept it up, practising multiple times a week in various ways. Every time Bill tried to go for Dan's throat, Dan ducked underneath and bent Bill's arm backwards. Every time Bill tried to get up, Dan would knock his legs out from under him. Bill was angry, bent on inflicting pain. Dan was enjoying himself, bent only on his own amusement. Dan flung himself on Bill's back and they crashed to the floor again. Bill hit the linoleum face first, smashing his nose, which began to bleed. Dan snuck his arm quickly under Bill's chin and secured it.

"This," he announced, "is a rear naked chokehold." Then he said, lower, into Bill's ear, "Too bad we're not actually naked." Dan knew Bill must be able to feel Dan's hard cock resting between his butt cheeks.

"It's OK, Katie," Marlene soothed the distraught woman. "Now we can talk to him."

Jenny got down on the floor, face to face with the immobilized Bill. "I'm Jenny," she said. "That's Marlene and Dan. We're not dangerous." Dan sniggered. "Well, not *very* dangerous," amended Jenny. "We just want to make Katie feel good. And you too if you want to. Do you want to?" Bill's eyes were watering. His jaw worked but no words came out. "Your girlfriend's very lovely, it's a shame for you to keep her for yourself."

Katie blurted out, "How come you never call me lovely?" in Bill's direction. She looked startled to have spoken.

"You never tell her she's lovely, Bill. How is a woman supposed to feel good if you don't tell her that she's lovely?" Jenny stroked Katie's breasts through her shirt. "I want to make your girlfriend feel good. Don't you want me to?"

Marlene, perched far above on the table, asked, "Katie, does Bill have any porn?"

"Yes . . . it's behind the James Bond movies," Katie admitted. Marlene hopped down and exited into the living room, coming back with an armful of movies.

"*Chicks Licking Chicks, Booty Babe Bacchanal*, yep, he's certainly got some girl-on-girl stuff in here."

"Well then," cooed Jenny. "He must like to watch that sort of thing." Her hand reached for Katie's exposed cunt. Bill's eyes widened. Jenny stroked Katie with one hand and removed her own shirt and pants with the other. She was wearing a black and red lacy set of matching bra and panties. She removed Katie's shirt and bra, leaving her completely naked. She rolled Katie back up on to her shoulders, her cunt arching towards the sky, and she began to eat it in earnest. She spit huge wads of saliva into Katie's open hole and put two fingers in, then three, then four. She teased Katie's clit with her tongue until Katie begged for more, then took it away to plunge her whole hand deep inside. Katie moaned and wailed.

Bill watched, transfixed. Dan still didn't want to let his guard down, though, so he caught Marlene's eye. Marlene knew just what to do. She left the table to get down on the ground beside Bill. She stroked his face. Bill's breath caught and he forced his eyes away from Jenny and Katie to look at Marlene.

"No, no, don't look at me, love," said Marlene. "You watch the show. I'm just here to help you." Dan rolled over on his side, pulling Bill with him, leaving his front exposed to Marlene. She unzipped his pants. "Hard already," she announced. "Are we surprised?"

Dan chuckled. "That makes two of us," he whispered into Bill's ear as Bill's cock disappeared into Marlene's mouth.

Now that Bill was occupied and overstimulated, watching his girlfriend get fucked by a girl while his dick was getting sucked, Dan felt comfortable adjusting his hold. He pulled Bill's arms behind Bill's back so he could secure them with just one of his own hands. This left his other hand free to unzip his own pants and pull out his cock. He stroked it for a bit, waiting, watching.

Katie and Jenny were reaching a fevered pitch. Katie's moans echoed all around them. Jenny's fingers were moving fast and furious inside Katie . . . but her head was upright and her eyes were roaming around the kitchen floor. Jenny was looking for something. Triumphant, she reached out and grabbed the pepper grinder, left on the floor from Bill's upset of the spice rack. She leered at Bill as she put the pepper grinder in her mouth. Then she turned back to put the circular knob at the top of the grinder into Katie's pussy. Katie screamed but did not try to scramble away. She stayed on her shoulders, her cunt up in the air and the pepper grinder sunk deep inside her, the end sticking straight up. Jenny put her hand on it, pushed it away from her, forcing Katie's body up further on to her shoulders, her pussy higher up into the air . . . her asshole now facing Jenny. Jenny flicked her tongue at it and Katie howled. Jenny pushed down hard on the pepper grinder at the same time as she stuck her whole tongue in Katie's ass. Katie started shaking all over and making sounds both high and low at once, like two cats fighting.

Marlene chose this moment to use her impressive deep-throating talents. Bill's moans joined Katie's and his eyes bugged out in her direction. Dan decided this was the time to get his pleasure out of this twisted situation. He released Bill with his arms, trusting Marlene's mouth to hold him in place. He pulled Bill's pants down and slapped Bill's ass with his cock. Bill arched up against it, reacting now to any touch. Dan reached back and happily found that he could reach the fridge, from which he extracted the margarine. He greased his cock up with it and placed its head against Bill's virgin little anus. Bill bucked, startled, seemed to come back to himself. Dan wrestled him to the ground again, still on his side. Marlene's amazing mouth never left Bill's cock. Dan wrapped his legs around Bill's, pulling them back and apart. He placed his cock back at Bill's anal entrance.

Katie came, shivering and shrieking, the pepper grinder flying out of her with the force of her cunt muscles clenching.

"Did I tell you you could come?" yelled Jenny, slapping Katie's ass.

Bill grunted, though whether it was a yes or a no and whether it was directed towards Dan's oncoming attempt at sodomy or at the abuse of his girlfriend was unclear.

"Yes," said Jenny, calm now, looking in his direction. "Your little slut is still coming." It was true. Each blow that landed on her ass sent another paroxysm of pleasure through Katie's body. "I think you'd better help me out with that."

Jenny flattened Katie's body down on the kitchen floor and

slid her towards Bill, helped along by the slipperiness of the floor which was covered in Jenny's saliva and Katie's pussy juice. She pushed Katie till her cunt was right under Bill's mouth, being sure not to dislodge Marlene down below. "Eat it!" she demanded. Bill complied. Katie whimpered. "You have been making altogether too much noise," Jenny told her. "What will the neighbours think? I think I should keep your mouth busy." Jenny pulled her panties to one side and sat on Katie's face. She didn't have to tell Katie to eat it – Katie knew what was expected of her and eagerly sucked and licked at Jenny's swollen pussy.

Bill's mouth was full of cunt and his cock was being sucked – he must be too busy to even notice, reasoned Dan, knowing full well that Bill would still likely notice a cock in his ass. He did. Still, the full head of Dan's cock was wedged up in there before Bill pulled away from his girlfriend's crotch in protest.

In reaction Marlene stopped. She slid up towards his face. "Don't you fucking stop eating that pussy," she growled at him. "I'm gonna keep sucking your cock and you're gonna keep eating that pussy and that's what's going to happen." She slapped his face once, hard, then slid down again.

Bill lowered his face again. He moaned into Katie's cunt as Marlene nibbled on his balls. He grunted into Katie's cunt as Dan thrust deeper into his ass. Katie moaned into Jenny's cunt and Jenny moaned into the air. They were all getting off now ... except for diligent Marlene, still hard at work on Bill's cock. Dan, always conscientious about other people's pleasure, at least as much as he was about his own, grabbed the abandoned pepper grinder and stuck it into Marlene's pussy. She thrust up into it even as she continued to swallow Bill's dick. Dan shoved the pepper shaker down into her even as he thrust his cock into Bill. Now they really were all getting off.

Jenny was a squirter, a fact which neither Dan nor Marlene nor Jenny herself had felt the need to warn Katie. When Jenny came it filled Katie's mouth and splashed down her naked torso, hitting the top of Bill's head. She choked on it, coughed it up, came again herself. Jenny collapsed on the floor. Katie pushed herself away from Bill and slid back into Jenny. Jenny wrapped her arms around her, pinching her nipples, and they stayed like that watching Marlene and Dan and Bill.

Marlene's head moved quickly then languidly, teasing Bill along, then even harder and faster than before. Bill's body jerked from the force of Dan's thrusts but Marlene still kept her expert mouth wrapped around his dick. As Dan's movements became more urgent, so did hers. Suddenly Bill froze. His eyes rolled up into the back of his head and he went limp. Marlene crawled forwards, turned his face up, and spat a long stream of his jism into his face. She was just in time to get out of the way as Dan pulled out from Bill's ass and pulled himself up to come all over Bill's face, Dan's jism mixing with Bill's own.

Dan fell over Bill's chest, finding enough energy in himself to slam the palm of his hand hard into the pepper grinder sticking out of Marlene's pussy. It drove deep into her, almost disappearing. When she came she toppled forwards on to Bill's sticky face.

Jenny, Marlene and Dan recovered more quickly than Katie and Bill, which was to be expected – they were well versed in debauchery and thus more used to the exertion involved. They dressed quickly and left, not wanting to find out if Bill would recover his anger along with his awareness.

Jenny came out on to the deck, stretching and tying her locks back, to do her daily morning yoga ritual. As she was saluting the sun she saw Katie in the window across the alley, staring straight at her. It was bound to happen, of course. Now that the couple knew the freaky threesome, how could they not notice them across the way? Jenny smiled her most guileless smile and waved. For a long moment Katie just stared at her, then, slowly, held her hand up in a still facsimile of a wave. Jenny smiled again and then continued with her salutation, gracefully folding over at the waist.

Now Katie and Bill must know where they live. Perhaps they'll be over to exact their revenge, thought Jenny. We can only hope.

The Twelve Fucking Princesses

Kendra Wayne

Once upon a time there were twelve princesses, and every night . . .

What? Did I *ask* you to stop me if you'd heard this before? Because you might *think* you've heard it, but you don't know the real story. You know the watered-down, sanitized, safe-for-children version.

The truth isn't really appropriate for children, trust me.

You really think it's about twelve princesses dancing their shoes to tatters? Have you never heard of euphemisms?

C'm 'ere. Let me tell you what really happened.

Yes, there were twelve princesses, but they weren't sisters, because if they were some of them would be too young for this story. They were at a finishing school, and they were supposed to be sweet virginal things, and the headmaster couldn't figure out where they were sneaking off to every night and half-destroying their clothes.

And smelling suspiciously like certain bodily fluids – both women's and men's.

Not that the headmaster could admit that to their parents, oh no. How could he? He'd get flogged – and not in a way he'd enjoy it. He had to get to the bottom of this before anyone else found out.

He tried locking the door and sitting outside. No go. He tried hiring chaperones to stay in the young women's communal dorm room (because he certainly couldn't), but they all ended up refunding the money and wandering off looking, well, smug. Self-satisfied.

W.T.F., right?

So word got out about the headmaster's problem – I'm not saying he was advertising, but you know how these things go. And one of the people who heard the word was . . . let's call him John, shall we? John, not to put too fine a point on it, was an ass. Sure, he wanted the money (by this point, the headmaster was getting a little desperate), but he also figured if he played his cards right, he might get his hands on a little bit of princess treasure, and I'm not talking about gold and jewels.

What do you mean, how do I know all this? Just shut up and let me tell the story.

OK, I'll wait while you make a joke about pearl necklaces. Let me know when you're done.

John, focused on the allure of money plus potential princess pussy, got the brilliant idea to disguise himself as a woman in order to infiltrate the finishing school and get the currently vacant chaperone job. Normally he would cast aspersions, as they say, on a man dressing in such a fashion, but he told himself it was for the money. And the booty.

Luckily he had a swimmer's build and was blond enough that his body hair wasn't as obvious. A wig and a dress and falsies and heels, and he was there.

Go ahead, snicker. He was an ass. He deserves it.

So, the princesses. Brianna, the eldest, was the de facto leader of the group. Gabrielle was the youngest, and she tended to kowtow to Brianna even though she was pretty sharp herself.

The rest aren't crucial to the story, but because I know you'll ask, their names were Juliana, Simone, Marguerite, Lianne-Marie, Charlotte, Talia, Faris, April, Rosalyn, and Philippa.

Brianna looked at John (who introduced himself as Jonette) and smiled a little smile that would've made him hard if he hadn't tucked his peen back to avoid, er, outing himself.

"I'll be honest," John said. "You know I've been hired not just to give you comportment lessons, but to find out where you're off to every night." He knew saying something that was truthful would disarm them, distract them from his mountain of falsehoods.

"Of course you are," Brianna said. "And you will."

So then it was all about a hidden passageway and crossing an underground lake on a boat (like *that* isn't a metaphor). Gabrielle made sure she was sitting next to Brianna, and she whispered, "Something's not right about Jonette."

"You're a goose," said Brianna. "She's just like all the others."

"Her fashion sense is deplorable, and not in a low-country kind of way," Gabrielle pointed out. "And I just don't like the way she looks at me."

"You won't have to deal with her after tonight," Brianna said. "She'll leave just like all the others."

Brianna never mistreated servants, but she did kind of think they were all the same, interchangeable. Gabrielle sighed and stopped protesting, although she *was* going to say, "I told you so," later because she wasn't perfect and Brianna *was* going to deserve it.

But I'm getting ahead of myself.

John had no idea what he was letting himself in for. Now, I should mention that the fact that the princesses came home each night reeking of various fluids wasn't something the headmaster had shared with *anyone*. If word of *that* got out . . . Yeah. Not so much.

Given the stories of torn clothing, though, John was expecting some kind of rave, maybe. For all his nasty thoughts, he really didn't have a clue.

They disembarked on a wide, whitewashed dock. Two men came forwards and held the boat as the princesses and John jumped out. He trailed behind them into the room so he could keep an eye on them.

Then he was inside, and saw what the princesses were really up to every night.

"Oh, goody." Talia clapped her hands together. "Slave Augustus here. I've been itching to blister his adorable ass."

"And he cries so prettily when you do," Simone said.

"Shall we tag team?"

"Yes, let's!"

They skipped off together, headed for a buff man wearing not much more than some straps criss-crossed around his chest, a posing pouch and a collar, all made out of burgundy leather.

Swiftly, they tied him down on a spanking bench while another slave gathered implements for them. Because a princess can't mar her pretty, soft white hands, now can she? Talia was rather fond of paddles herself, but Simone chose a flail, and ran her fingers through the strands while she watched her friend go to work on the slave's ass, which was indeed quite adorable, and getting hotter by the moment.

Slave Augustus murmured his thanks after every blow.

Charlotte and Faris had also chosen to share a slave, but to more direct benefit. Charlotte reclined on a feather bed full of pillows while the slave licked her and Faris played with her nipples.

Meanwhile, Rosalyn indulged her slightly subby streak with two men, preparing herself (and them) for an exquisite double penetration. She had a cock in each hand and alternated between sucking them – but skilfully not letting them come just yet.

Subby, yet always in control.

"What's wrong, Jonette?" Brianna asked. "You don't have to be all dom if you don't want to. April and Philippa are as vanilla as they come." She pointed to where each princess was squirming and squealing under the attentive ministrations of an accomplished man whose sole purpose was to give her as many orgasms as possible. "The slaves are just here for our pleasure – you can have them do whatever you want them to do to you."

"Uh, Brianna?" Gabrielle said, because she was starting to figure things out. "I think maybe he—"

"Ohhh!" Brianna said. "Are you a lesbian? There are female slaves here, too." She beckoned to one of the men, who stepped forwards, hands clasped behind his back. He was naked except for a short gold chain around his neck.

"No, I . . ." John panicked.

Then he felt his skirt being pulled up and, before he could react, delicate hands plunged between his legs.

"I *thought* so!" Gabrielle cried. "She's a *man!*"

Something clattered to the floor, and she snatched it up. "And he has a camera," she said. "Spying on us. Probably planning to blackmail our parents."

And then it was too late for John.

The princesses (the ones who hadn't already gotten distracted, that is) pinned him down and, with the help of some of the slaves, had his clothing off, his wrists cuffed to a belt around his waist, and a spreader bar keeping his ankles apart faster than you could say your safe word. He would've protested, except for the ring gag they slipped into his mouth.

"I think we should let the slaves have some fun for once, don't you?" Brianna asked.

"Excellent idea," Gabrielle agreed, having already thought of it anyway.

Because you know, don't you, that John was very much the type of man to not just be heterosexual and leave it at that? He had an abhorrence of anything that might remotely involve the faintest whiff of homosexuality. (Unless it came to girl-on-girl action, of course. That was entirely different. Charlotte and Faris over there, kissing and fondling each other while Charlotte bounced on the slave's cock and Faris ground herself against his mouth? Hot. Very hot.)

The only thing worse than that? Having anyone he knew suspect *him* of such perversion. Which is why that camera of his came in so damn handy.

They got pictures of him being enthusiastically screwed up the ass by a lucky slave. They got pictures of him wearing a penis gag with an anonymous princess (it was Lianne-Marie, but for obvious reasons her features weren't visible) bouncing up and down on him – because, of course, the princesses weren't going to let the slaves have *all* the fun. They got pictures of him crying as he was whipped on an X-frame, having his face splashed with come from a circle of slaves, being forced to suck a whole line of men.

Worst of all, they got pictures of him achingly aroused by all of it. His penis straining erect, his balls shaved and bulging around a cock ring. Slaves licking his cock and balls and ass while he writhed and struggled.

A lovely video of him pumping his hips futilely against empty air, ungagged so he could beg to be allowed to come. That was the *pièce de résistance*, the ultimate piece of blackmail.

They debated leaving a vibrating butt plug shoved up his sorry ass, but in the end agreed that permanent damage wasn't really necessary. They *did* lock him into a chastity belt and toss the key into the lake on the way back, so he'd have that special added humiliation of asking someone for help removing it.

John slunk off in shame in the middle of the night, never to be heard from again.

And the princesses? Well, let's just say they all went home, got married and became the power behind the thrones.

Except for Gabrielle. She runs a porn empire. She always did have a head for business.

Those Daaaaaancing Feeeeeeet!

Nick Mamatas

Reg found it extremely difficult to choreograph an orgy in these days of Mannerist decadence and increasing ticket prices. There was the challenge, of course, of avoiding heteronormative slot-tab type things: a girl on all fours, a cock in her mouth, one in her ass, a guy under her slacking while she ground her pussy down on him. Even the formulation – one cock, two cock, fill all the holes – tended to dehumanize everyone. Then there were the "show-time"-style stunts: handstands and toes tucked into assholes, streams of semen shooting in fine arcs like an Italian fountain. Clever stuff, hard to pull off, but about as sexy as the cramped interior of a circus clown car. Well, that was probably somebody's kink ... but Reg digressed, as he often did when amidst a forest of limbs, some hard with muscle, others flabby and warm.

"From the top," he called out after he lost his own erection, and the twists of arms and legs and tits came undone. There were ten in all, seven men and three women, including Reg. Daniela smiled at him and walked over on her tiptoes, her back arched and little lemon tits sticking out.

"Reg," she said, "maybe if—"

"—the genders were even, yes, I understand. But *everyone* does that."

"Or more women than men!" José called out. He was wiping himself down, a towel under the crease of his belly.

"It'll work fine," Reg said. "We just need to loosen up." He waved his arms. "Qigong, everyone." And the players lined up and lifted their arms and began their deep breathing exercises.

There was just enough room on the cramped stage for everyone, especially with arms outstretched and eyes closed, but Reg kept his eyes open. On the skin of his cast – pink and brown and dark – he could see the traces of his handiwork. Impressions of limbs and hand in the flesh. Then he had an idea.

Here is how it went. José on all fours, Jeanette squatted on to his back, her ass plump and back curved. Her face was buried in Lindsey's shockingly hairy bush – shocking as Brazilians were in season; hair was the new "ethnic" and ethnic was in, Reg supposed – and her hands pressed against Lindsey's fat breasts. José had Don's odd brown cock in his mouth, and worked his throat till his nose was buried on Don's pubic hair. Don held on to the back of José's head for a moment to balance himself. He spread his feet, sunk his weight on to his heels and then bent over backwards. Little Daniela straddled Don's gymnast torso. Reg waved his arms and the Wong twins, Lee and Henry, took up position on either side of Daniela. She grabbed their dicks and started pumping them, then turned to kiss Lee hungrily, then Henry. Reg himself slipped behind Henry and stuck his tongue up Henry's ass, lubing it for the cock to come. Only when satisfied did the last two men – the burly bear Kenneth, all blond fuzz and beer belly, and a stocky fire hydrant of a man named Russ, take their places. They grabbed Reg's ankles and wrists and held the choreographer up and on his side. It took a few long moments for Reg to penetrate Henry, and he nearly lost his erection, but sucking the sweat from Kenneth's big balls helped with that, and soon enough he was in. Finally, they were all in position. Reg hummed, giving Kenneth the signal. Kenneth blinked twice.

That was the cue. Lindsey slid to the left, Jeanette still attached to her cunt. Under Jeanette, José grunted but his strong arms and thighs were up to the task of holding her weight. He moved from Don's cock to his outer thigh, licking it all over and hunting for ass. Daniela put her arms around Henry and Lee and lifted herself up to spread her legs. Russ shifted Reg's legs to his own shoulders and bent over to suck on Lindsey's toes. The Wongs reached between that mass of bent bodies and jerked one another off. Freed from Daniela's cunt, Don's cock glistened with slick syrup. He lay down for a moment, but Kenneth reached down and lifted the other man up by the cock. Still on his side, wedged between several men, Reg wondered if this was still all too Hollywood, but he would only know at the final bow.

The sad fact, Reg thought to himself during his smoke break, is that people don't come to see Broadway fuck shows for the choreography or even for the musky smell of the sex. They like the fog pouring out of the smoke machines and the beams of light arcing overhead, ones that look so solid you could reach up and touch it, hang off it. Older women enjoy the songs and the first act teases – that first flex of bicep or expense of abs. The legs or the flick of a hip. They even dig the improbable show tune rhymes: "Oh when will Mister Lee So Yung/ decide to finally have some fun/ and put my pudenda/ on his agendaaaaa!" Reg often found himself fuming by the stage door as the audience members wandered by humming that crap.

The other problem is that orgy choreography is just like driving a car or running the United States – everyone thinks they can do it, but most people who actually try are friggin' morons. Reg liked to tell his cast, "And everyone is half right." That would get a laugh. Competition was keen, and nobody wanted to take it up the ass any more. Prima donnas, all of 'em. Reg stubbed his cigarette out on the heel of his shoe and went back to the dressing rooms to tell Donald to go easy on the mahogany tonight. Speaking of prima donnas.

"Are you *kidding*?" Don asked.

"Nope. I want everyone pale."

"Under those lights? I'll look like a fish fillet." Don sucked in his little belly. He was an older guy – late forties but looked maybe a decade younger. Only he wanted to look two decades younger. "What's this all about? Are you going to tell the Wong brothers to 'lighten up' too, or are you just looking to make sure I don't get any more callbacks?"

"Don't be an asshole. Just do it."

Don muttered something about the union and amateur-hour horseshit, but Reg just walked out, ignoring him but still nervous. About how it was going to go, not about that cocksucker's empty threats. Soon enough the curtain went up. People laughed when they were supposed to – Daniela sodomizing Kenneth to bring out the falsetto in his voice, Russ facing down the Wongs in a three-way cock duel that ended up with all the players tumbling into the orchestra pit. They gasped at Lindsey hanging from her labia (and unseen, from her waist and ankles) thanks to clamps and string while she drank water and told a few jokes about coming to New York on a two-day bus trip from South Dakota. Lots of applause for Russ' touching solo spoken-word piece about wishing he could invite his grandparents to see his show, but how they likely wouldn't understand. (The audience plant, an older woman, nearly missed her cue when she rose from her seat to blow Russ kisses, but that clumsiness just gave the whole thing a bit more verisimilitude.)

Then the finale. Reg could barely get hard, not even after a bit of surreptitious frigging. Forget the peeled ginger in the bum, it was the applause that did it. He was out there and hard and so it went well. There were giggles and quiet smiles between the players as they dropped to their knees or spread dry mouths and wet snatches. It had been two hours under the lights with nothing but the occasional draft from the wings, but Reg still had goosebumps. He wasn't the only one. And they fucked. Boy did they fuck. The Wongs coated Daniela like she was a pastry of some sort; Jeanette's face and chin were drenched. The cunt juice ran down her neck and stomach to mix with her own perspiration. That just made the effect better though, when they all lined up to take their bows.

Yes, the effect. Ten figures, all standing hand in hand, with big smiles and bow, with the traces of one another's bodies pressed into the skin. Impressions of arms and ass cheeks, flanks and thighs red from being pressed into the boards. Across the expanse of skin, there was left a picture – a man and a woman, too many limbs and stretched across thirteen feet of glowing actor, entangled in the act of physical love.

Departures

David Findlay

My sister Cecilie was the last one home. By the time she arrived, we'd stacked forgotten aunts and brand-new cousins in the front room and master bedroom, Uncle Ron and his frightened-looking third wife in my old attic room, and me in back of the upstairs library. In the frenzy of relocation someone even moved my mom's ashes in their ugly urn from the obscurity of her old study to the sill of a stained-glass window overlooking the front stairway. The guests just kept on coming, but I wasn't going to consider letting anyone else stay in my sister's room.

At midnight on the eve of the funeral, Cecilie arrived with an unexpected retinue: a leather-clad room-mate I'd never heard of and a quiet young person of indeterminate gender who held the door for both of them, then disappeared into the bathroom. Cecilie's wardrobe took up three bags, each of them as heavy as I'd been when I worked security. I helped their grateful driver to prise each case one at a time from the boot and the back seat, feeling a little bit heroic as I bore the brunt of the weight. The room-mate was lovely. Her outfit was so distracting that it took me a moment to realize she was the same height and build as my sister, with the same waist-length blonde dreads and the same cat's-eye red glasses. Her dog collar and air-soled boots were pink, accenting the shiny black surface of her miniscule outfit. She bounded out of the cab, shook my hand and began bustling packages to the porch while I held my sister. Cecilie and I hadn't ever really given each other physical comfort before, and I didn't want to let go.

"It's crazy, CeeCee. Glad you're here."

She smelled like lube and lavender, and her hair tickled my ear. In her usual insanely high heels, my little sister was far taller than me. Cecilie pulled slowly away, kissed me on the cheek and whispered, "Bet you've got it totally under control, big bro. Isn't Izzy a peach?"

The rare compliment found its mark and for a moment I felt like a responsible adult. Izzy? If Izzy was the room-mate, "peach" didn't begin to describe her. I watched her ass flex beneath the tiny, too-tight skirt as she wheeled one of my sister's bags across the expanse of lawn to the front porch. Dancer's thighs, grey translucent stay-ups . . . a guy could get obsessed with that kind of shape. I allowed myself a moment's fantasy of lifting her skirt and sliding my hands up the back of her thighs, cupping her cheeks, lifting the skirt higher, higher, all the way up until . . .

"How far up?"

Izzy was asking me about where to take the baggage, and I'd been caught ogling her posterior before we'd even got her into the house.

"Um, yeah, second-floor landing, then to your right. Cecilie's the first door on the right next to the little washroom. Or would you like a hand with that?" I had almost caught up when Izzy popped the most massive bag over her shoulder and trotted across the porch. Her skirt crept higher, showing another hint of her muscular, round rear.

"I'm fine, Graham, but maybe you want to watch from the bottom of the stairs just in case I fall?"

I looked down, chastened, and imagined the view from a tongue's length away.

"Someday when you're moving slower, maybe?"

Flirting with my sister's room-mate(?) new girlfriend(?) was probably not a brilliant idea, given that Cecilie would be a handful to keep in line even if I were on her good side. Maybe Izzy would help? She certainly seemed capable of being a distraction. As I struggled with the other bags, their mute, androgynous companion came out of the bathroom. The three of them unpacked nonchalantly into Cecilie's room as if it were the most obvious thing in the world that they'd all share her ancient twin bed. I tried not to imagine what they'd get up to beneath the quilt Gran Amble made. I tried to think myself calmly through the question of whether they were actually doing any harm by ignoring customary small-town decorum when every gossipy relative in the world was camped at our place. In Abercrombie, one doesn't usually advertise three-way gender-queer liaisons as blithely as all that . . . unless you're Cecilie.

When everyone was settled down, I brought a six-pack upstairs, spread my bedroll in the copyright law section and stripped down to my long johns. The moon was almost full, and the library was aglow with reflected light. Done with stressing about funeral arrangements, my brain turned to happier thoughts. I imagined Izzy's ample cheeks spread around my stiffness, grinding on my face. The house creaked as only ancient oak can, and I kept wondering if I heard my sister's bed over the other household sounds. It took many hours and a lot of beer to get to sleep.

When I woke the moon had dropped to the east and there were long shadows in the hall. One of the horde of relatives had spilled something foul in the downstairs kitchen. I cleaned up, nibbled at an excellent curry from the day before, and tried to get excited about reading an antique monograph on ownership and origination. There was plenty more beer in the back of the fridge, and there isn't really a wrong time for beer. Time passed.

Our house has only been in the family since the sixties, but it was built long before the advent of indoor plumbing. The master bathroom is an opulent afterthought, with marble and tile hiding the odd angles, copper pipe girdled to the inside wall, and custom brass mermaid fittings that Mom found at some estate sale. An inset tub opposite the window allows an unbroken view of the disrepair behind our house, dilapidated outbuildings and unploughed fields matching the neighbours' equally decrepit acreage. I had spent my first few days back alone, wandering the broken stone half-walls at the property edge during the daytime and soaking by candlelight in that huge, stained porcelain tub every night. Up to my neck in makeshift decadence while overlooking ruin, it was a good vantage point from which to remember the drama, trauma and comedy of growing up in Abercrombie. The luxury of that room was now usurped by relatives, so I tiptoed back up to the second-floor toilet, which is carved into a slant-ceilinged cupboard next to CeeCee's room and as narrow as the master bathroom is wide. I slipped in just as a lithe shape grabbed the door.

Dad's plaid bathrobe was tied loosely at her waist, flapping open as she pulled the door closed. I recognized my sister's panties: gauzy pink silk that shouldn't still have been intact. Flooded with shame, I remembered sneaking those and additional handfuls of her underwear from the laundry hamper, making off with them to this very bathroom. Smelling them, touching them, touching myself as I inhaled her scent, bringing them redolent and sticky back to the laundry room on days when it was my turn to do the household wash. Even if I hadn't been exponentially increasing the wear on them, they should have long ago been outgrown and discarded. CeeCee goes through clothes like most people go through Kleenex. She would be thirty in days, and I first jerked off in those panties when the two-year gap between us felt like aeons, when she and I were snarling teens who barely spoke to each other at school. Nobody keeps underwear for seventeen years!

"I guess she was right."

"I beg your pardon? Sorry, you're welcome to use the bathroom, I can wait . . ."

"She must have been right about you and her underwear. You look like you're witness to the ghost of puberties past. See something you like?"

Izzy untied the robe. Her areolae were large and light brown, puckered with the chill. Her hips were wide, straining thin fabric. She reached into the pockets and drew out threadbare brassieres, more small panties, all of them familiar. I must have made some incoherent sound.

"Don't stress, honey. It's OK. It's OK if you're the kind of depraved twistoid who gets off on his little sister's smalls. I won't tell anybody." She snickered. "Apparently it's still working for you."

Physically trapped, confronted with my own unforgivable behaviour and full of beer past my bladder's capacity, I should not at that moment have been painfully, pointedly tumescent, but there it was. My erection was aimed through my long underwear, across the bathroom and directly at my sister's gorgeous girlfriend's snatch.

I blame the beer. I've never been exactly a model of restraint and impulse control. I've never been one who tries to resolve social awkwardness by grabbing for somebody, either, but that's just what I did. I could feel my movements as if they were instructions to a faulty robot waldo: I flexed my shoulders and stepped forwards, reaching for the nearly naked woman before me. Izzy smiled and let my weight pull me past her, tugging my forearms to the left as she nudged my hips off balance. Her bare left foot did something subtle and sweeping and she caught my shoulders, effortlessly taking my weight so I didn't hit the bathroom floor too hard.

"Careful, big boy."

Standing over me, relaxed and apparently unfazed, Izzy tested the resilience of a flowered cotton bra. It tore, as did the cotton panties she tried next.

"Take those off." She gestured to the long underwear tented around my slightly diminished stiffy. "Off!"

Izzy seemed mildly surprised that I hadn't immediately, unquestioningly obeyed her. I was too shocked by the whole pattern of events not to obey. I wriggled out of the long johns and the hardwood floor was cool against my back. "What did you just do there? I'm sorry. I mean, what happened?"

Izzy ignored my questions. She bent closer. "Put your hands together up beside the cold water pipe."

I complied. Far too easily, she used another familiar twist of silk to bind my wrists above my head.

Far too fast, I found my ankles secured with old bras to the radiator and the sink. Izzy immobilized me with the same smiling ease a flight attendant brings to their safety spiel. I was waiting for her to point out emergency flotation devices and air masks, but instead she knelt directly over my face. I nearly passed out from a sudden mixture of joy and shame-tinged desire. I could feel the blood streaming into my cock, feel it pulsing with each heartbeat. "What are you doing? Where did you get these?"

"On eBay. Where else? What does it look like I'm doing, pervert?"

It looked like she was putting her hand slowly down the front of the too-tight panties, taking her time, relishing my response. She was going to wake up the rest of the house if she kept talking so loudly. I saw her expression change as her fingers found sensitive tissue. I bucked against the air behind her. I felt the way I had after I got my first piercing, or when they pulled me out of what was left of my first car. Floaty. Unreal. A little out of synch with the outside world. She opened her eyes and stared me down, laughing. Her breasts did amazing things when she laughed. She stood again.

"Breathe, Graham. Inhale. You'll pass out otherwise."

From the robe pocket she tugged a piece of fabric that wasn't actually underwear – a red silk scarf. It, too, had been a regular part of CeeCee's wardrobe, and it, too, had been the target of my adolescent onanism. Once.

How had she known?

"I can explain!" I sounded like an idiot.

"No you can't, and you shouldn't try. This morning's theme is going to be 'honesty'. Can you handle that?"

I nodded.

"Speak up, Graham."

Izzy gave orders with a gentle, certain authority I had never encountered before.

"What? Ummm . . . sure. I can handle honesty."

"Excellent. I knew you could. Raise your head."

The praise made me glow. Why should I care what this stranger thought? Why would I let her do this to me? Obediently, I raised my head and let her tie the scarf around my eyes, doubled over itself and wrapped twice around my skull. The world went dark. My cock bobbed stiffly and my bladder ached.

Izzy laughed quietly again. "Your reaction is very gratifying, Graham. Are you ready to be honest?"

"Yes."

"I like honesty, Graham. I'll reward honesty. Would you like to be rewarded?"

Her voice was close, now. She smelled of lube and lavender.

"Yes, please."

"Were you watching my body this morning, Graham?"

"Yes."

Izzy knelt at my waist, the heat of her cunt bright and sudden on my pelvic bone. I bucked reflexively.

"Be still! Were you thinking about touching me?"

"Yes."

Izzy's nails stroked the skin just outside of my nipples on either side. I fought to control my movements.

"Good little boy!"

I stilled my reaction and stored away a little piece of anger to use on her later. I let my face show calm and contentment.

"Sorry!" Her apology was instantaneous. "I gather that's not a good word combination. I'm sorry, Graham. No insult intended."

I wondered who had trained her. I wondered if she had a weapon. Without any obvious external movements, I tested my bonds. Solid. Tight. With her astride me, I couldn't even muster leverage to tug at them. Five minutes too late, I realized how completely Izzy had me.

"Really, Graham, I'm sorry."

Her lips were tender on my nipple, and her crotch pressed harder on my hip. She stayed that way, kissing softly, as my body gradually relaxed. Belatedly, I realized that she was taking much of her own weight on the outside leg. I wasn't used to any of this, least of all the experience of a stranger's gentle consideration while utterly powerless on my own bathroom floor. I wanted to cry again.

"It's OK, honey."

She kept saying that. It wasn't. She was wrong.

"When you wanted to touch me, what part of my body did you want to touch?"

"Ah . . . everything!"

"Honesty, Graham. Remember?"

"Your ass. Your thighs." I tensed again.

"Thank you."

Izzy slid a tiny bit lower and more towards the centre of my body. The change was dramatic. Her weight was an unbearable pressure on my bladder and her rear was an unbearable teasing near-friction against the tip of my cock.

I tried to flex my abs to take her weight, and then to twist away.

"Still!"

"Bitch!"

"Yes, Graham. Your cock is very hard, Graham."

I was silent. The house creaked.

"May I mark you, Graham?"

"Yes."

I felt her teeth at my neck, at my nipple. I heard her breath, felt her hot cunt shift on me again. I went way inside to a wordless, hungry place and stayed there. I went way outside to fantasies that nobody should have, and stayed there too. Her bites were cruel. Her tongue teased. I needed to piss. I needed to come. The combination was fucking with my brain in delicious, wrong ways. I needed to scream. I whispered, "Please."

"Please what, Graham Edward Gryn?"

"Please . . . give me more."

"More questions? Certainly."

I groaned quietly. She raked her nails along my chest, brushed my balls with her fingertips and left her hand lingering by the underside of my bobbing cock.

"Do you masturbate?"

"Sometimes."

"Do you have a girlfriend?"

"I have lovers."

"Where?"

"In America."

Her hand drifted away.

"Chicago, and just outside Chicago. Three women. They know about each other, but don't know each other."

"Thank you." Her hand was back, stroking my cock with a feather touch. "Have you ever been to a prostitute, Graham?"

"Once."

Her hand paused.

"A few times. Once that was good."

She chuckled. It wasn't an unpleasant chuckle. "What made it good, Graham? In detail."

She squeezed, once, bending low and grazing my chest with her nipples.

"She was beautiful, and funny, and she got really wet. She . . . spread and let me watch while she played with herself."

"Nice." Izzy's hands were insistent, varied, attentive.

"She, um she had really pretty tits. Like yours. She told me about her fantasies, and listened to mine. She sucked me long and sloppy, with lots of slobbering and no condom."

"Did you come in her mouth?"

"No."

"Did you fuck?"

"Yes."

"Did you come in her pussy?"

"No."

"In her ass?"

"No."

"In her face?"

"No."

"Did you come on her pretty tits, Graham?"

"No."

Her hand slowed, teased. "Tell me."

"We fucked for a long time. We were in the kitchen at a place I was renting, and it was a Saturday morning. I made us a pot of coffee, and we drank it naked while she sat on my cock. She took two sugars and one cream. She kept her glasses on."

"You like girls with glasses?"

"Yes!"

I felt her turn around, felt her adjust her knees beside my shoulders. Izzy's hands were both on me now, slow and steady. Her pussy was over my face. I strained up towards her.

"Did you come, Graham?"

"Yyyes. I did. I came in my hand."

"Yes?"

"We fucked for a long time, and she let me suck on her titties, and then she fingered her ass while I watched, and she asked me if there was anything else I wanted."

"And?"

"And . . . I said there was. I asked her to lie on the kitchen table on her back."

"Yeah?"

I felt fabric brush across my lips. Her pussy smelled like water tastes after a day of dehydration.

"I asked her to play with herself again while I licked her asshole."

"You what?!"

"I rimmed her while she wanked, and then, when she was ready . . . she peed. She pissed all over my face, and I came in my hand licking her butt hole and drinking her piss. And I liked it."

"I bet you did! Dirty, dirty, fucker. Nasty perverted man. Thank you for telling me that, Graham." Her hand held my cock at the base, and I could feel her breath on me. "I bet you wish I'd let you do that, Graham."

I said nothing.

"I bet you wish you could let go, too, don't you?"

Her lips were wet and warm and suddenly around the tip of my dick. I nearly passed out. The sensation was gone just as suddenly. Slicked, her hands moved more urgently, pumping my cock.

I groaned again. "Please!"

The house creaked alarmingly. Something, probably her tongue, reached out and joined her hand, twirling big, wet circles around the head . . . then it stopped again.

"Are you a filthy pervert, Graham?"

"Yes."

I felt the shift of her weight, then I could hear her fingers in her cunt right over my face.

"Are you a sick, depraved fucker, Graham?"

"Yes!"

"Will you do whatever I ask you to?"

I felt the first warm drops on my face before I answered. "Yes! Yes!"

For a while, there was just sound and taste and sensation. Her hand on me kept pumping, slowly, erratically. Izzy's piss hissed out into the panties through her fingers, on to my face. She made it last: stopping, releasing, grinding against my lips, pausing, then letting it flow again. Her mouth would descend on my cock for a second then she would pull back. As her stream in my face subsided, she leaned forwards again. It took me a while to figure out that the smooth, soft pressure was her sliding my cock between her tits.

"Let it go. Now, Graham. Soak me."

I heard her hands moving faster and I heard her breathing accelerate again.

"Come on, Graham. Do it."

I tried. Nothing happened. I relaxed. Nothing happened. I thought about holding her by the hair, kneeling in front of me with her mouth open, and I did it. Izzy shook and was quiet while my piss spurted between her breasts and down between us. Her fingers danced a constant, constantly changing pattern. Relief and pleasure and permission to experience both at once threatened to split my head open. The last few gouts splattered her chest and mine, and I felt her mouth on me again for a brief, tantalizing second.

"Wow. That was good, Graham. So good. Do you want my mouth now?"

"Yes!"

"Do you want me to suck it?"

"Yes, please."

"Tell me to suck it."

"Suck it."

"Say 'Suck it, slut.'"

"Suck it, slut."

"Say 'Suck it, CeeCee.'"

I froze.

"Say it!"

"Suck it!"

"Say it!"

"Suck it already, slut!"

"Say it! Tell me!"

The floor creaked.

"Suck it, CeeCee. Suck the piss out of your brother's dick. Take it down your throat, little whore, and gag on it. Suck it and don't stop sucking on it . . . Oh! Cecilie!"

There was a pause while I waited for the world to end.

The house creaked again, loudly. Izzy's mouth was extraordinary. Her tongue laved the underside of my cock while she took it deep in her throat, and she held that depth for an impossibly long time. She licked and sucked and slobbered and smacked so loudly I was certain she would wake the entire house, and her hand didn't for a second stop frigging her juicy pussy above my face. Eventually, I felt her do something I'd only heard about people accomplishing with their lips.

"Was that what I think it was?"

"Yeah, some people don't even notice. Do you mind?"

"Hell no! Does that mean you're going to sit on it?"

"Beg me."

"Please, Izzy, put my dick in your beautiful, sweet-smelling pussy? Please?"

"Nicely done, but that's not what I want to hear after all. Tell me."

I was so hard in her hand that the band of the condom was biting me.

"Sit on it, girl."

"Tell me."

"Sit on it, slut. Fill your pissy slit with my dick. Sit on it, bounce on it, stuff it up your coochie and come on it! Damn it, Izzy!"

"Tell me!"

"Fuck! No."

Izzy laughed. "If you won't give it, I'll just take it. You've just forfeit the use of your mouth, Graham."

The panties were rank and wet. I tried to bite her when she stuffed them in my mouth. Her first slap felt as if it loosened some of my teeth.

On the second slap, I opened my aching jaw and my mouth was full of warm, salty, sodden panties.

She was already sliding down on my cock by the time she took off the blindfold. I was almost disappointed to see her there. The locked door had not opened. There literally wasn't room to open it. The woman sitting on my cock was not my sister. I had now in spirit broken every trust with CeeCee, but she was safely asleep in her bed, and this tramp, this impostor had not won . . .

"You're a good brother, Graham. Shoot it. Come for me. Come for me and pretend you're not thinking about fucking your little baby sister. Come in my wet, wet cunt and pretend you don't wish it were CeeCee squeezing the jizz out of you. Shoot it, big brother! Shoot it, Graham, come in me. Come in your sister. Come for your sister . . ."

I came. I came. Oh Lord, I came.

We looked at each other. She pulled a penknife from the robe and sliced silk from my ankles and wrists. Tenderly, she rubbed circulation back into my extremities, pulled the panties-that-weren't-CeeCee's from my mouth. I hadn't expected her long, sweet kiss. I hadn't expected her incredible, wordless gentleness as she sponge-bathed me, held my cock again as I pissed more of the beer, pulled the long underwear on my exhausted body and walked me to the library. At the door, she put my father's bathrobe over my shoulders. I watched her step back, naked, down the single flight of stairs. I watched her, confident and quiet, her hands full of shredded underwear, avoid the creaking board on the landing and slip into my sister's room. Crying felt almost as good as coming had, and I slept through sunrise for the first time in weeks.

The actual service was ridiculously huge, bolstered by a silent phalanx of burly business associates, two teams of lawyers from competing firms and another last-minute influx of relatives and faux-relatives. Dad was not the most social person on the planet on the best of days, and there was no way his quiet printing business should have merited the attention of so many bigwigs. I kept wanting to check if the self-important strangers from the city were at the right funeral, but Abercrombie doesn't tend to have more than one a month.

Something had changed in the years I was away, and Dad's new associates had an odd similarity about them, as if they were all part of the same strange club. I was genuinely flummoxed. A clump of my suddenly paunchy, greying school friends had paid their awkward respects, determinedly overcoming our decade's absence to stride up and shake our hands; murmur their best wishes for us. Their dignity and genuineness was a gift, and for the first time I was glad to be back.

Cecilie squeezed my hand. We were standing on raised earth by the grave, with our hometown's mist starting to obscure the departing guests. She was characteristically inappropriate in an impossibly form-fitting black ball gown, the plunge of its neckline accentuated by a spill of lace veil. In the context of that presentation, her push-up bra was the kind of overkill that challenged all of anyone's best instincts. This was not the time for another sibling battle. I was speaking sternly to myself, repressing both the instinct to stare and the annoyance I always felt when my little sister's appetite for attention outdid her good sense. Atop these familiar responses was a new terror about what her lover might have said, what she might have heard. Cecilie looked at me with big, trusting brown eyes and squeezed my hand again.

From the greyness behind us, an ursine bruiser whose nose had more than once been reshaped by non-surgical means approached us. An oversized umbrella danced in his nervous paws, twirling like a silken mushroom as he spoke to my sister.

"You, ah, intimate with the deceased?"

His accent was hard to place, but my first guess was Russian with a Glaswegian overlay. His meaning was harder to parse.

"I beg your pardon?" Cecilie was as confused as I.

"You were his girl? *Eë kurtizánka*? Accept please my condolences. Of me the name is Jimmy. You will be need someone to look after you of now. It appears you are like a nice girl."

He held out his arm in a way that suggested she should take hold. The gesture came perfectly naturally to him, however insanely presumptuous it might have seemed to us. He *so* did not look like a Jimmy, and the accent overlay was sounding more like Israeli. It still took us both a while to pull meaning from the elegant oddness of his sentences, but Cecilie recovered first.

"His girl? No, Mr Jimmy. Yes, I am his . . . I was his daughter. Daughter. *Doch'*. Not *prostitutka*."

He turned red at the same time I figured out "*kurtizánka*". I'm not a violent man, and I have never been the kind of "chivalrous" lout who hits people in protection of anyone's reputation. It surprised me greatly to discover that I had backhanded Jimmy. It surprised me more to discover that he was still standing. This did not bode well. Even someone twice my mass and a half-metre taller should have the grace to collapse when I whack them that hard. His blush faded, while the left side of his face remained an angry red where my hand had struck. He flexed his own oversized hands, dropping umbrella and overcoat just as twin rugby tackles at waist and ankles spread him flat on the dewy grass.

Christian Hail, captain of 1989's most feared ball team for miles, was breathing heavily, grass stains on his too-tight grey suit. There was a grim smugness to his expression as he sat on Jimmy's chest, going slowly through the much larger man's pockets. Michael and Manny Caruthers each held one massive leg, while Edmond Arrigakar, younger brother of my first steady girlfriend, pinned Jimmy's head and shoulders.

"He's got a piece! The fucker's got a piece! What kind of idiot thug brings a cannon to a blessed funeral?"

"Watch how you pull on the man's gun."

Cecilie watched the portly ex-ballplayers tugging a tiny, elegantly chromed weapon from Jimmy's waistband.

"That's the safety you just turned off. You're pointing a loaded, cocked pistol at your mate's knee, Manny."

Cecilie took the weapon from Manny's shaking fingertips. She yanked a lever on the top, tapped a rounded black clip out of the handle and tossed both into her purse.

"What the fuck was Dad doing for these goons, and when did *you* turn into a pugilist?"

I had no answers. More of the old team was showing up, comfortingly boisterous now that they had a more familiar task. Someone passed me a flask. Fog hid time's work on the living as we stood among the dead. They let Jimmy stand, resembling cygnets around a limping, lumpy swan as they marched him away.

When I squinted, I could just make out clusters of unfamiliar mourners trying not to stare at us through the fog. My hand hurt.

"Whaddya say we hijack the lawyer's limo and see if they'll give us a lift home?"

Mimicking Jimmy's gesture, I thrust out an arm for Cecilie to hold. She took it gratefully, managing not to lean on me too hard as her heels poked plugs in the graveyard turf. I still held the flask. I wanted to get home and get properly soused so I didn't have to think about what my dad had been working on, or about my sister absently, happily stroking the pistol in her purse.

She wasn't going to let me have a quiet drink.

"So while you were defending my honour, had it occurred to you to wonder how I paid for law school?"

It was my turn to blush. I looked up at the roof of the car, wondering how many bugs would be standard issue for a lawyer's limo.

"You didn't have to . . ."

"No, I probably didn't have to. I could have done less interesting things for less money. I did have a choice. I still do."

"I don't want to talk about it."

"Bollocks. You want to lecture me about being foolish and reckless and mad."

"Not now I don't. You've taken all the fun out of it. What are you going to do with this hard-earned new law degree, miss?"

Cecilie beamed. "Nothing, probably. I don't half hate law."

I thought about getting out and walking home. I thought about her girlfriend's mouth. I thought about the glimpse of elaborate gartered and stockinged thigh my sister's gown displayed, and I thought a lot about the Christian notion of hell. If it existed, maybe I'd see my father there.

"Mr Gryn retained us in the early eighties when his clientele began to ask him for jobs that were not entirely, er, within the realm of traditional printing practice. We helped him to find offshore locations for that aspect of his business, and to keep his dealings within the legal frameworks that those nations required. The environments to which he moved proved a phenomenal source of new work for an artist of his abilities, and soon we were handling a few million pounds of business traffic every month. You two (and Ms Gryn's mother, should we succeed in tracking her down) are the sole heirs of a fortune that far exceeds the GNP of Chile for last year. Do you understand?"

I did not understand. Cecilie seemed to.

"We're rich, bro. Filthy, stinking rich."

"Huh?"

Cecilie was already asking the important questions. "What's the current legal standing of our father's enterprise?"

"Perfectly legit. We had a visit from two Dutch government agents a couple of years ago over suspicions your father's enterprise was printing passports, but . . ."

"Were they?"

"No, Ms Gryn, the last of that side of the operation was phased out for good in 1991, on our advice. On paper it never actually happened and the only records we retain are those that keep people like Jimmy on their best behaviour."

"You were there? By the grave today?"

"Our representatives were. They may not know firearms, but they have other skills."

Out the office window of Hannaford & Locke, I watched as two tugs dragged an oversized barge too far starboard in the twisting, narrow waters beneath Burnsey Bridge. The barge hit a piling and the entire bridge tilted alarmingly. A semi on the bridge skidded across two lanes and stopped with the cab dangling over the water. I couldn't see the driver. As I watched, cranes, ambulances and a flittering black helicopter arrived at the scene. My sister crossed and uncrossed her legs beside me. The stockings were pearl-grey fishnet, with at least six elaborate catchments for garters.

"Mr Gryn? Graham? Are you all right?"

"Just fine, thanks. A little distracted is all."

"Of course, Mr Gryn. Trying times, and a great deal of information to take in." Indeed. Cecilie put her hand on mine.

"I think my brother could use a drink. I know I could. Do you people keep any whiskey here?"

My father's oily solicitors didn't bat an eye between them. Nor did they offer us a choice of whiskies, as some younger employees of newer firms might have. The heavy crystal goblets they produced brimmed with a liquid that had too much peaty, potent golden musk to have been created by mortal hands.

I signed something that acknowledged our commitment to keep seeking CeeCee's mom and to set aside a third of the assets in her name, excluding the house but including a property in Scotland we'd never seen or heard of. I signed a dozen more documents, handed the sheaf of paper back across the desk, and looked back out the window. Then they gave me the whiskey.

Mr Locke smiled in a thin, careful way. "I've met Ms Flowers. It will be my deep and abiding pleasure to locate her and hand her the keys to her ah, new Scottish castle."

"Castle?!"

"Yes, ma'am. Parts are in poor repair, but it's doing well for a fourteenth-century structure. Do you wish to reconsider ceding ownership to your mother?"

CeeCee looked at me. I shrugged.

Cecilie cleared her throat and sat up straight. "No, when you find her, it's hers. But a castle? Really? Wow. How? Oh, never mind. Weirdness."

There was a tiny alarm clock tattooed in green on her inner thigh, with thin, coiled black cables running up from it towards . . . I drained my whisky and looked out the window again.

The helicopter had left. My stomach didn't like me. I didn't like me. I wanted more whiskey, but Cecilie walked me out of the office, hailed a cab and held my tired head to her shoulder for most of the ride home. I had this doomed, horrible premonition about walking back into the house, but she walked me up, under Mom's ashes, past her door, past the bathroom, and tucked me in to my nest in the library.

"Sleep it off, Graham. You did good. Thanks for being there, big brother."

The Cecilie I grew up with would never have said that. I slept. I dreamed. Time passed, as it will.

At some point they took me out to get fitted for a tux. I spilled curry and whisky on it at a strange wake. The whole room was full of fawning strangers and distant cousins who reminded me how their names were spelled. None of the respect for the dead you might expect at a funeral, but none of the raucous reminiscence by actual friends and family a real wake would have. I might have made an inappropriate comment or two. At the point when I tried to start fisticuffs with a guy who could have been Jimmy's larger twin, my sister's silent partner cut suddenly between us and steered me into a beige alcove of the bland, "pub-style" chain restaurant in which the whole ill-conceived event occurred.

I stared. "Are you bonking my sister?"

"Absolutely. Are you too blotto to be out in public?"

"Unquestionably. How come you never talk? What's your name?"

"Pauline."

"Really?"

"Really. I swear on a stack of original Batman comics."

"All right then, Mr Pauline. How do we get out of this benighted place? Where's CeeCee?"

"She's in her car, waiting with Izzy."

"Whose car? We're Gryns. Nobody'd give us a licence!"

Pauline cracked a small smile full of sharp-looking teeth. "They assigned you guys a car, a driver and a bodyguard, but even together they wouldn't be wide enough to stop that ambulant mountain you were insulting. Come back to the house. All your relatives are gone . . . and there's more whiskey."

"I see why she likes you, Pauline. Common sense and clear priorities."

"Naw, it's probably my good manners and small hands. Step this way."

The driver didn't speak, but he got us home in eighteen minutes and his limo smelled of fresh cedar.

I stared out the window, which meant watching the reflection of my sister and her double making out while Pauline stared out the other window. The bodyguard's name was Fidel. He checked the house from top to bottom and gave us his number before departing. Pauline and the girls skipped upstairs.

I headed to the kitchen in search of liquor. I wished for a Chicago whore and a pot of coffee. The bed creaked. I wished for a less active imagination. It was hard to decide between beer and whiskey, so I chose both. After my first two beers and midway through my first triple shot, Pauline came downstairs. I didn't stare or fall over, but I did choke a little. Pauline wore combat boots, a grin, and more piercings than I was aware one small body could accommodate. It was oddly embarrassing to be staring at the shaved, multiple-pierced pussy lips of a person I had defaulted to treating as male. I redirected my gaze upwards.

"You're adjusting to the temperature in Abercrombie?"

"No, I'm cold as fuck, but your sister figured this would get your attention."

"Uh-huh."

"If you come upstairs, I can get under a blanket with a hot-water bottle and you can get your dick sucked. Again."

I wondered if conversations before my dad died had made more sense, or if that was just an error of memory.

"You're down here naked to offer me head on Izzy's behalf?"

"No, Graham, I'm offering my own mouth, which is reasonable skilled and salivating a little bit at the prospect of being wrapped around your big, juicy meat."

"What if I turn out to have a soft, tiny wiener?"

"Come upstairs. I'll work on the softness *and* I'll show you how I know it's not tiny."

"What if I like how stiff your nipples are right now? What if I'd like some of your mouth right here?"

Pauline knelt and crawled towards me. Crew cut. No visible tattoos. More muscular definition than on any body I had previously seen in real life. Tiny, pointy tits pierced by vertical bars and rings placed horizontally. Big brown eyes. I watched those eyes approach. I looked into those eyes as Pauline quietly, deliberately began to massage my balls through my trousers with a strong tongue. When my sister's no-longer-quite-so-androgynous companion turned, stood and walked upstairs, I followed.

On the second floor, I got to the door of my sister's bedroom and hesitated.

"Don't worry, Graham. Come on in. It's just you and me."

"How about we go up to the library?"

"No, I promised to show you how I know your dick size. Besides, my hot water bottle's in here."

Pauline sat on the distended rubber bubble and pulled up Gran Amble's quilt. I thought about personal pronouns. I thought about unzipping my pants and standing on the bed. This last thought carried me to action, and I found myself looking into the cupboard nestled in the crook of my sister's ceiling while Pauline got energetically to work on my cock. The cupboard housed CeeCee's volleyball trophies, a stack of my old girlie magazines(!) and two exhaust vents from the adjacent bathroom. One vent curved up and through the roof, one stopped midway to the ceiling and ended . . . in a mirror. The water bottle squished and gurgled. The floor creaked. The bed creaked. Pauline sucked back another inch and the bathroom light came on.

"You're kidding!"

They weren't. Pauline choked a little. The reflection was inverted, and it took me a second to realize what I was seeing.

Their backs were to the bathroom vent, and I had a crazy moment of realizing how hard Izzy and my sister had worked to emphasize their similarities. Even next to each other, the resemblance was striking. CeeCee was bustier and wore more ink. Izzy was more muscular and had a more upright posture, but their hair was identical, their asses were the same generous roundness and their gestures moved at the same even pace as they stripped off each other's bra. It was obviously a well-rehearsed show. I was watching their regular routine, something they did for money, for strange men. I tried to step away from the vent, but Pauline grabbed my ass and kept me in place, in mouth, in range to see my sister undressing from above. The implications of this view were starting to sink in. Pauline passed me a bottle.

I was not going to think about CeeCee watching me come all over her panties, year after year. I was not going to think about her watching me sitting on the john jerking it to these very same magazines that were now inches from my nose, their pages still stuck together. Whiskey burned my throat on the way down. Pauline's throat was hot, too. I leaned into the heat. CeeCee grinned up at me. Pauline choked again, and I wondered if I was going to weep or come.

"Are you going to come, bro?"

Her voice was as clear as if we were in each other's arms. Pauline did something astounding with that tongue piercing.

"Are you?"

CeeCee spoke directly to the vent, up to me, breaking the fourth wall. Izzy lapped whiskey from between her spread legs. Their pubes matched. For the hundredth time that week, I thought about waking from a nightmare that had become sexual in all the wrong ways. Pauline slurped and licked at my balls, humming happily.

Cecilie smiled and pushed Izzy's face lower. I dealt appropriately with the spectacle of my sister frigging herself while her doppelganger ate her ass, which is to say that I yelled, pushed Pauline away, ran out of the room and stood hyperventilating on the landing with my dick still flapping out of my pants.

My three tormentors came out of the bathroom and from CeeCee's bedroom next to it in uncanny synchronicity, each of them bearing a litre of whiskey. Pauline wore the quilt, too, but appeared to have abandoned the hot-water bottle. CeeCee spotted me, smiled and fell over. The other two caught her and her bottle, propped her up and advanced towards me.

"This has been a long time coming, Graham." Izzy was slurring her words a little.

"Where did all this booze come from?"

"Our lawyers. Isn't that sweet?" Cecilie staggered slightly, but the three of them kept coming. It was like a horror movie, or a porno, or the scariest elements of both combined. I could not move. I knew it was going to be sick, bad and wrong, but I could not budge.

Pauline reached me first, handed over the bottle and knelt before me.

CeeCee and Izzy dropped to the edge of the landing, watching us. Their hands were busy at each other's cunt, but their eyes were fixed on the wet, slippery juncture of Pauline's lips and my improbably stiff cock.

"Did you put Viagra in the whiskey or something, Pauly? How come he's so hard?"

"Maybe he's still into watching his sister."

Izzy slipped a slick forefinger into CeeCee's butt. I wondered if I would go blind immediately or during subsequent months of reliving this moment. There was something both performative and very genuine about the way they were together. I imagined they were an amazingly successful duo. I imagined that maybe they were so good at performing that they didn't have to actually touch their clients. My wishful thinking isn't any more hampered by realism than anyone else's.

CeeCee licked her lips. "Are you going to save some of that for me, Graham?"

I struggled not to spit up a mouthful of impossibly good whiskey and wondered if I could drink myself into impotence before the unthinkable became more thinkable.

"This firewater, sis? No, you've got your own."

"The cock, Graham. I want some. I want you to fuck me."

Izzy and Pauline pulled their respective hands from various orifices and applauded. I gaped and sputtered. Pauline kept sucking.

"About time you asked clearly for that, honey. About time you got it, too." Izzy was saying exactly the wrong thing. The world was not behaving. Dad would have blamed me.

CeeCee stood, wobbling, near the edge of the landing, precariously close to the edge of the last long flight of stairs down. All of a sudden I saw the drunken tragedy about to happen, pictured her losing balance and tumbling to her death down these same stairs. I pulled away from Pauline for the second time in one night, miraculously avoiding being maimed by all those pretty, perfect teeth. I stepped forwards too late, saw the slow-motion collapse begin, and threw myself across the landing to intercept CeeCee's fall. Even in the haze of my rush to catch my sister I noticed the calm of Izzy's placement, carefully bracing herself against the banister, poised. Even as I tripped on my own ankle-bound trousers, I noticed Pauline snapping into place on the other side of the landing, also braced and waiting. Almost as if they had rehearsed it . . .

I fell atop Cecilia, saw her head expertly caught and pillowed in Izzy's lap, and only knew for sure I'd been bamboozled when Pauline landed heavily on my back, sandwiching me on the landing atop my naked, squirming sister.

"Watch it!"

Izzy slapped the falling urn out of the air just above my head, dashing it against the stairs above us. Grey powder and slivers of ceramic spattered us all. CeeCee gasped, looked horrified, and dabbed a splinter from her bleeding cheek.

"Oh shit." She sounded suddenly, perfectly sober.

I spat my mother's ashes into her face and started to laugh. "Get off me, Pauline. Now."

There were little stinging punctures all up my neck, bleeding into the tux shirt. Ashes and spilled whiskey made a vile, bumpy mud that showed brown-grey on my jacket. I wondered how much it would cost to replace the whole bloody, crusty mess, and then I remembered the insanity of our meeting with Locke and Hannaford. One ruined tux was not going to send me to the poorhouse, one skanky sister wasn't going to melt my brain and one mouthful of my mother was not going to ruin my night. I stood, pulled off the uncomfortable dress shoes, yanked off the red-streaked white bow tie, tore off the jacket and shirt and wiggled out of the trousers. Blood dripped from a cut in my forehead, pooling around my eye and dripping on CeeCee's perfect knockers. She looked like an extra from an X-rated zombie film.

"Got a rubber, Pauly?" I might have had rubbers in the tux pants, but everything else was punctured by shards of ceramic, and it didn't seem the right situation to risk holed condoms.

Cecilie pulled her knees up around her ears and looked at me. "This time, Graham . . . this first time I want skin on skin. Do it." Gone was her uncertain slur. I had been duped by a master.

I knelt. I pressed the head of my cock against the delicious, sticky wetness of my sister's pussy. I wondered if I could stay hard through this impossible, mad, stupid moment. Cecilie canted her hips up, reached down for my cock and pressed it against her asshole.

"Do it. Now. Before I change my mind."

I did.

Sometimes ass-fucking feels like a scary struggle. Sometimes it feels like the smoothest, sweetest wrongness a guy could do to his gorgeous, plump-bummed, spread-wide-open little sister. This was one of the latter times. I pressed slow, steady. I realized midway through opening up her butt that I couldn't really feel my own cock. I'd gone numb from excitement and feeling overwhelmed. We looked at each other, my sister and I, and we laughed as I pushed into her ass a little deeper. Pauline appeared with a pump jug of lube and applied it liberally. Those really were small hands. Most of Pauline's left hand slid into CeeCee's pussy and her eyes crossed. Izzy tapped gently at CeeCee's clit, and the four of us began to build a rhythm.

Sensation returned to my cock as I relaxed. My cock sunk further into CeeCee as *she* relaxed. As I pushed in the last few inches, she made a noise I've never heard another human utter.

Izzy looked at me. "What was that?"

"Er . . . I hit bottom."

"Hit it again! Three years of boffing this hottie and she's never sounded like that. Give it to her!"

I did, looking down at her skin distended around me. "Change your mind, yet, sis?"

Cecilie smiled beatifically. "Just stuff it in me, Graham. Like I've wanted you to since I knew what fucking was."

"You're kidding. You hated me."

"Not really. Thought about this every night and watched you every day . . ."

I slid in again, slow, deep, slippery with lube into my sister's impossible tightness. "Filthy, sneaky little voyeuristic princess. You know it was you I was thinking about. Still is. I can't believe I never figured out that vent."

"Who are you calling filthy, Graham? Fucking panty sniffer! Pervert. Fuck me, Graham. Just like that!"

I watched Pauline's hand push CeeCee open and open again, timed my own strokes to alternate. Izzy and I were breathing in tandem. She looked smug and euphoric. Izzy had set this scene up, I was sure of it, and I was grateful. In her expression, I think I saw how much she cared and how much she would risk for my sister. I tried not to feel competitive. I pushed in a little harder, and CeeCee's breasts bounced with the impact. I wanted to be in her always. My perfect, pretty, sneering little sister had become this horny, warm, wet woman who wanted me. "I love you, Cecilie."

CeeCee blinked. Ashes, blood and sweat mixed on our skin with fragments of ceramic. The effect was surreal. "I know, bro. I can feel it."

I reached for somebody's whiskey bottle, took a pull of it and got a mouthful of lukewarm tea.

"You didn't need to set up all this elaborate game, but I'm glad you did. You both make pretty convincing drunken sluts." I spat the tea into CeeCee's face, grabbed her ankles and pushed in again. Hard. She squealed.

Izzy slapped a little more emphatically at my sister's clit. "Are you going to come for us, honey? Come around your brother's big, hard cock?"

"They both should." Pauline stroked and tugged at my balls. I wasn't in any hurry to orgasm, and I was feeling so full of liquor and beer that I probably couldn't anyway. This time when I reached for a bottle it was pure whiskey. CeeCee clenched around me, wiggled her rear and leered. "Give it to me! Graham, you're the brother everyone should have. I love you too."

She laughed as she came, her asshole spasming around me and her face reddening. "Holy shit! Yes! Yes!"

Pauline's guffaw joined in behind me. "You guys are amazing. I don't believe you're actually fucking."

CeeCee held me close, made sure I didn't pull out. "This is so fucking sick. It doesn't get any nastier. Damn!"

For a moment, we both believed that was true. I relaxed, pushed in further and concentrated on releasing the valve that should be shut when one fucks. It took a moment, and then the floodgates opened. I breathed deep, looked into my sister's eyes and waited for her to notice I was pissing up her ass.

The Queening Chair

Kate Dominic

One doesn't have to be a queen to enjoy a queening chair. One does, however, need to have a retinue of lusty men available, ready and able to wear their tongues out on the queenly nether regions presented on the opened seat of the low stool beneath which each royal retainer will lie.

Max loves eating my pussy, but it will be a cold day in hell when he slides beneath a queening chair. We're both hardcore dominants with no interest in seeking out non-existent submissive sides. Fortunately, by the time we met, we'd been in the BDSM scene long enough to have learned how to negotiate getting our sexual and emotional needs met. We go to BDSM play parties together, spend the evening topping other people in bondage and spanking scenes, then come home, compare notes, and fuck each other senseless.

Neither of us was comfortable with penetrative sex with others – at least, not yet. When I realized how much I really wanted to try a queening chair, though, he thought about it, then said even though a tongue sure as hell could penetrate – we both knew his did! – to him oral sex wasn't the same as fucking sex. He bought me the queening chair, invited three trusted male submissive friends from our group over to entertain me, and went off to play poker with his non-kinky buddies.

When Max had gone, I took my time getting ready. I'd programmed my MP3 player with a selection of slow sexy songs, all sung by men with deep, rough voices. I shaved my pussy silky smooth. I piled my hair on my head in my favourite jewelled clip and slid into a deep, scented bubble bath. Then I leaned back on my bath pillow and let those crooning sandpapery voices glide over my skin while my pores opened.

It wasn't long before my hands were sliding through the warm, slippery bubbles, stroking my breasts and my belly, moving down between my open thighs until I was so horny I couldn't help wiggling my fingers into myself. With my thumb on my clit, my index finger in my pussy, and my middle finger up my ass, I masturbated until my skin was flushed and I was breathing hard. Finally, I was so close to coming I just lay there, my fingers motionless inside me, concentrating on the feel of the air moving in and out of my hypersensitized body as the bubbles popped around me.

However, I had no intention of coming before I was seated on my queenly chair. By the time I climbed out of the tub and wrapped myself in a thick thirsty towel, I was primed for an evening of talented male mouth performance.

I'd chosen a black leather bustier, short gold velvet skirt and thigh-high leather boots for the evening's festivities. As I finished styling my hair, I could hear my submissives arriving downstairs, greeting each other as they disrobed and set up the living room per the detailed directions I'd sent them during the week. I had no doubt they'd be naked except for their cock rings by the time I made my entrance.

It's so lovely playing with well-trained submissives. When I walked in the room, the queening chair was in the centre of the carpet – low to the floor, the well-oiled leather of the padded arms and back bar forming a C-shape around the opening in the middle. Below that opening, the cylindrical neck pillow hung from silver chains that gleamed in the firelight. I had no doubt it was already adjusted to position the mouths of my servants at exactly the right height to service me. Next to the chair was an antique end table, covered in a pristine white linen cloth. On it rested a glass of sparkling water in a crystal goblet, a just-opened box of Godiva chocolates, the TV remote, the latest issue of *Cosmopolitan* and my cell phone.

The only sound in the room was the crackling of the logs in the fireplace. I lifted my skirt just enough for it to clear the arms and back of the chair. Then I squatted down with my boots just outside the chair legs and adjusted myself until I was comfortable. It took me a minute. Although the chair supported my weight well, my knees were bent deeply. The position spread my pussy lips and my anal crack deliciously wide, though. I snapped my fingers, picked up my glass and the remote, and turned on the TV.

Those wonderful men had set the station on the Food Channel. A special on angel food was just beginning. I picked up a bonbon, biting into a juicy cherry truffle as the lusciously muscular and spectacularly hung Darin slid his head beneath my skirt. The women in our club considered him an Adonis, and he was a masochist to his core. He was usually naked in my presence – my submissive in many percussion scenes. I had never before allowed him access to my pussy.

He appeared determined to show himself worthy of the honour. His erection stretched above his belly button, the gleaming red head so stiff it had pulled completely free of its cover. His forehead bumped my thigh as he positioned his head on the pillow. He kissed the spot in apology. Then his hands gripped the chair legs and his hot, wet tongue slid like silk the entire length of my newly shaved slit.

I shivered so hard I almost dropped my glass. Max was no slouch at tonguing me to orgasm, but Darin was worshiping my pussy. With each tender, delicate swirl, my clit seemed to reach for his tongue. I drew in a deep breath, my hand shaking so badly I could barely set my glass back on the table. He swiped full length again. I arched my back, pressing my pussy into his mouth as I imagined my exquisitely sensitive nub growing more engorged with each taste. I imagined it puffing and stretching out from under its tiny hood, displaying itself in a way that invited even more dedicated attention.

Darin rose to the task. As pre-come drooled from the long, deep slit at the tip of his penis, he flicked his tongue mercilessly over my clit. He wasn't even stopping to breathe, just ruthlessly flailing with a constant steady friction that seared sensation beneath and over and around – and deep up into the exquisitely tender area that so rarely peeked out of its protective cover.

The orgasm stunned the air from my lungs. I screamed. Screamed again, thrusting my pussy down hard on to his face. He wrapped his lips around my clit and sucked. I shrieked and came again.

Even through my shaking, I could feel Darin's face sliding on my juices. When I finally leaned forwards to rest, he went back to long, slow swipes up my slit, no doubt licking up the evidence of my orgasm before passing the tongue baton to his colleague.

With my hand still trembling, I picked up my cell phone and speed-dialled Max. He answered with a gruff, "How's it going?"

"I have just had the most incredible orgasms of my life!" My breath was still unsteady. Darin's quick kiss to my clit was too unobtrusive to have been anything but respectfully polite, but I was learning the nuances of his lips on my pussy enough to know he was smiling.

"Better than me?" Max was laughing. I didn't answer. When he asked again, his tone of voice was guarded. "Babe?"

"Darin—" I shivered as Darin's tongue swiped again "—is highly motivated."

"And I'm not?!"

The stifled snicker from behind me told me Max's ire was carrying across the room.

"You're not under a queening chair, tonguing my pussy to ecstasy."

As Max harrumphed into the phone, the tongue on my clit again started flicking. I moaned with pleasure.

"What's going on now?"

"Darin is tonguing my clit again. You know how I like it – fast and steady, even though your tongue gets tired really fast. But he's not wearing out."

Darin's tongue had been slowing, but as I spoke, the speed picked up with renewed vigour. Over, under, around. Flick, flick, flick.

"Ooh! He's licking way up on top! You know – that special spot that's usually hidden under my clit hood." Darin took

direction like a charm. "Right there. Don't stop! Oh, fuck, yes
– DON'T STOP!"

I screamed as I came, right into the phone. Darin kept his
tongue dead on, flailing his target as I bucked and howled and
my pussy juice squirted on to his face.

"Oh, God!" I shuddered, pressing my pussy down on to his
lips. "I just squirted!"

"No shit!" Max was laughing now. I had no doubt his pride
was more than a tad bruised. But Max was a pragmatist. If
something worked, it worked, and he was the first to admit it.
"You're taking notes for me?"

"Of course." I had no doubt I'd have plenty of tips for
him, when I finally quit coming. With my pussy once more
humming, I lifted my left foot, touching the pointed leather
toe to the tip of Darin's deep red, jutting shaft. He groaned
beneath me, his lips closing around my clit, sucking the
tender little hood against the flesh beneath as I dragged my
toe downwards. Suddenly, he bucked beneath me, moaning
against my skin as come spurted from his cockhead. I smiled
as my pussy shuddered again.

"Darin is going to stop now, though." His lips immediately
stilled. "He just came all over my boot. So he's going to clean
it up. And he's going to rest his marvellous mouth so it can
service me more later. In the meanwhile, Richard is going to
take his place beneath my queening chair. Richard will no
doubt strive to live up to the precedent his colleague has set."

"I'm going to listen."

I didn't respond, just watched the neck and torso still
trembling at the edge of my skirt. Darin kissed my pussy
goodbye and slid out from under me. His handsome face was
smeared with my juices and flushed a beautiful dark red. He
looked thoroughly sated.

"Babe?"

I don't take orders from anyone, including my husband.
I watched Darin wiping my shoe for a moment. "You were
saying . . .?" I purred into the phone.

I could almost hear Max gritting his teeth. Finally he
snapped out, "I was saying I'd like to listen, sweetheart, while

Richard eats your pussy." When I still didn't answer, he growled, "Please."

I smiled into the phone, waving Darin over to the couch for a well-earned break. "Of course, sweetheart. Richard's sliding into place now. I'm used to seeing his pretty dark curls bobbing while I flog him. This will be quite a new experience, seeing only his legs and torso and his lovely short thick cock waving above him while he worships my pussy."

I gasped as Richard's tongue swiped slowly upwards. His tongue was different from Darin's – short and stocky, like Richard overall. He licked sweetly up, circling my clit with the flat of his tongue until I was trembling. Then he moved slowly back down. Down. Parting deep between my labia – and sliding in. His tongue wasn't long enough to probe very far. But it was fat and hot and talented. I had no doubt he was going to play that magical first inch of pussy wall in ways I'd only dreamed of.

"Babe?"

"Wait, Richard." His tongue instantly stilled. "Max, I'm putting the phone on the table beside me. You may listen, but don't interrupt. Richard is going to tongue-fuck me until I scream. I don't want any distractions."

I ignored Max's sputtering as I stretched my arms high, reaching for the ceiling as I grinned and resituated myself on the chair again. I ate another bonbon, this one butter cream, and glanced at the TV long enough to see we'd now moved on to preparing a dinner party for twelve on twenty-four hours' notice. Definitely not something I'd be doing without the services of a talented wait staff. By the time I'd taken another drink and set my glass down again, the sputtering from my cell phone had gone silent. But the light was still on. I knew Max too well to think for one minute his voyeuristic streak wouldn't have his ear glued to the phone. Richard's breath teased lightly over my pussy lips.

"You may begin."

I'd always thought a long, agile tongue was a prerequisite for proper pussy eating. Richard's short and stocky tongue was eating my pussy into fits. He started where Darin had left off, swirling the broad, flat top of his tongue over my clit until I was once again trembling above the mouth below me. But where Darin had used his supremely agile tongue to tease my engorged clit to poke up free of its hood, Richard licked and stimulated those overloaded synapses against the exquisitely sensitive nerves lining the inside of my hood.

Once more, I yelled when I came. But unlike when Darin had been licking directly on my clit shaft, this time I wasn't too overstimulated for continued friction as I came. Richard was able to continue the lovely, orgasm-inducing laving through every glorious wave.

When my trembling finally slowed, his hot thick tongue licked slowly downwards. He worshipped my outer labia, then the inner, working his way down my pussy. When he reached the opening where my pussy juice dripped out wet and slick, he licked until I was certain he'd lapped up every clear, tangy drop. Still licking, he slid his tongue inside.

My husband's tongue is talented. But no way was Max's tongue wide and stiff enough to emulate a short, thick dildo the way Richard's did. Once again, Richard used friction, pure and simple, to stimulate me. He was tenacious as a bulldog, concentrating his entire being on that first magical, nerve-rich inch at the opening of my pussy.

He moved slowly at first, then faster and faster, then slowly again. I pressed down onto his face, panting and moaning as his tongue slid up and down around the inner walls of my pussy entrance. Then he started a slow, deep circling. His touch made me so hungry – hungry for tongue and cock inside me; hungry for taste and smell and sensation. I pressed down harder, moaning as his tongue slid deeper. My breath was coming heavily. My nipples were pebbled hard against my bustier. I was *hungry*!

I plucked a bonbon from the box; sweat beaded on my breasts as I popped a dark round chocolate in my mouth. I bit. Cherry juice spurted across my taste buds as Richard's relentless tongue finally drove me over the edge again. Chocolate-flavoured cherry juice slid down my throat as I tipped my head back, smiling and swallowing and groaning

– pressing my pussy down on to Richard's face to keep his supremely talented tongue firmly inside me until I finally quit quaking.

I looked down at my lap, at the hairy chest sticking out from under the hem of my gold velvet skirt. Richard's stocky, drooling cock waved up towards his belly button. I lifted my legs, shivering as Richard's tongue speared even deeper into me. His whole face was buried so far in my pussy lips I didn't know how he could breathe.

From the condition of his cock, I didn't think I was going to need long. I caught his shaft between the inner sides of my boots. He lifted his hips, moaning and fucking his tongue into me fast and furiously as my boots pumped him. Four, five, six times. Groaning loudly, he spurted all over my shoes – much the way Darin had, though I was stunned at the sheer quantity of semen pouring down Richard's shaft.

My boots were going to need some serious care, but I figured I'd send one home with each of them and, at our next group play party, flog the one who'd done the best job. I slowly lowered my feet to the floor and sighed.

"That was delicious, Richard. You may rest now." I picked up the phone, sighing as Richard tenderly kissed both sides of my pussy lips, then my clit, and slid free.

The green "active" light still glowed on my cell phone. "Max," I said, stretching languorously. "Are you still there?"

"Yeah," he growled. He sounded disgruntled, though not truly upset. "You were being awfully quiet there."

My husband was jealous! I smiled as I realized I was enjoying that. Not that Max really took our sex life for granted, but the heat had been fading a bit. We both liked spice. Sometimes hot, stinging spice. Maybe it was time to add a sprinkle of cayenne. Our relationship was solid. So was our communication. Max knew I was being serviced in my queening chair tonight. A bit of spice would make for some interesting negotiations later on.

"Richard's tongue is like a short, fat dildo," I purred. "It was exquisite."

Max growled into the phone. Richard blushed and inclined his head respectfully. I snapped my fingers at Carlos. His dark eyes glittered with mischief as he lowered himself and slid beneath me.

"I didn't know you liked dildos."

"Sexual innovation is always exciting. It keeps things from getting dull."

Max's breath exploded into the phone. "Are you saying our sex life is dull?!"

The little green monster was definitely biting Max's butt. I shivered as Carlos licked the insides of my thighs. Light kisses, then licks, moving slowly upwards. Oh, yes – this man's tongue was long and agile!

"I've never tried a living dildo before. It was quite exceptional. Thick and stiff. Not deep, but wonderfully able to sense my responses and adjust position and rhythm accordingly. The constant friction made for an extraordinary orgasm. If Richard could bottle his tongue, he'd be quite rich."

I inhaled sharply as Carlos' tongue swiped hot and fast over my clit. Carlos had a reputation for being competitive. I had no doubt he would go out of his way to surpass both Darin and Richard – and to please me enough to really rile Max.

"You're breathing hard."

I smiled at my husband's waspish comment. Despite his annoyance, his voice held the bossy timbre that said he was getting turned on.

"Carlos is licking my clit. His tongue feels like a living vibrator." I groaned and picked up another bonbon. Chocolate butter cream. My favourite. I let the sweetness slide over my tongue. "Mmmmm."

"Now what?!"

I gasped as Carlos' tongue lashed down my slit.

"What's going on?!"

"He's licking into my pussy." I groaned and Max sighed loudly. Carlos' tongue flicked in and out like a snake. "Ooh, he's talented!"

I froze as Carlos' tongue swiped further back.

"Babe?" Max caught the change in my breathing. "Are you OK?"

Carlos' tongue slipped lightly into my crack.

"Yes," I whispered. Carlos was laving the length of my crack. Touching. Tasting. Stroking the virgin skin. I'd been fucked in the ass before. But no one had ever worshipped me there. I gasped as his tongue swirled over my anus.

"Honey? Are you all right?" There was real concern in Max's voice now. "Answer me, dammit!"

"He's licking me," I whispered. "Back there." I licked my lips, searching for the words as Carlos' tongue washed over me in wide, slow circles. "He's licking my . . . anus."

Max's chuckle was low and sexy. "Do you usually like that?"

I stiffened as Carlos' tongue probed into the centre. "I d-don't know," I panted. "Nobody's ever done it to me before."

Carlos' tongue stilled.

"No shit?" Max was laughing now. "I never knew that. Damn, honey. You're in for a real treat!" He paused. Then his voice got quiet. "Does Carlos know it's your first time? Make sure you tell him. He needs to know to make this really special for you."

Carlos kissed my anus. So sweetly and tenderly I couldn't help smiling. "He knows. Now."

Carlos was licking again. Washing again. Starting over. This time he was circling slowly from the outside in, then licking back out, long swipes from the centre out to the edge, working his way carefully around my entire anal ring. I moaned in pleasure.

"Is he doing right by you?" Max's voice was back to normal – straightforward, possessive and determined to have me enjoy myself. "Lots of spit? Lots of foreplay?"

God, I loved that man. "Lots of spit and foreplay," I panted. "It feels really good!"

Carlos' tongue probed into the centre again. This time, though, I was too relaxed to tighten.

"He's sticking his tongue . . . in my a-anus!" I moaned and dropped the phone. I could hear Max yelling, but what Carlos was doing felt too good for me to think about anything else. He was slowly working his tongue into me. I wasn't tightening. Not really. But I was too stunned to do anything but sit there and enjoy the feel of his tongue pressing in.

Suddenly, Darin was next to me, picking up the phone.

"Beg pardon, sir. Mistress can't talk right now. Yes, sir. She's fine. Yes, she definitely appears to be enjoying herself."

Enjoyment didn't begin to describe what I was feeling. The tip of Carlos' tongue was flat against me, then it pressed down and in. Hot flesh slipped between my anal lips. I groaned and thrust against him.

"Ma'am, sir says to bear down, like you're having a BM. If it pleases you to do so, ma'am."

I obeyed without thinking, bracing my feet against the floor. I gasped as Carlos' tongue slid in deep. He kept it there, rooting around, slowly licking the sides of my anal ring. Getting me used to the feel of his hot wet tongue flesh fucking me. Fucking my ass.

"Beg pardon, sir. I know you didn't say 'if it pleases you to do so, ma'am'. But I have to say that, sir. I'm her submissive!"

I looked up to see Darin grinning at me, his eyes sparkling as he held the phone far enough away from his ear to keep from being deafened by the tirade of swearing issuing from it. I narrowed my eyes at him.

"Give me that phone. No – hold it by my mouth." Carlos was sucking the side of my ass lip. It felt so good I could hardly breathe.

"Dammit, Max! Stay the fuck out of this! If you want to listen, fine. But I don't want to hear one more word out of your mouth unless it's to say something that's going to make me come harder!"

Darin covered his mouth, hiding his snicker. Richard was beside me as well, though his head was turned and he was wiping his lips. Carlos loosened his grip just enough to move up a bit. Then he was sucking on the next section of my anal lips. I bore down again, my groans getting louder as he took even more of me between his rhythmically pulling lips.

"Yes, sir." Darin moved next to me, nodding as he dropped to his knees. "By your leave, ma'am, when you're ready, your husband wants me to suck your nipple. And he wants Richard to finger your clit, so you get a really good come while you're asshole's being licked." He held the phone out to me, but close to my mouth, rather than my ear. "And he wants to listen, ma'am. When you're coming. He said if he can listen to you come while your asshole's being licked, he'll keep his big fucking mouth shut."

Darin's face was so close to the top of my bustier, I could feel his breath. But he didn't move closer. Richard's hand rested on the hem of my skirt, but he didn't lift it. "If it pleases you, ma'am. Your husband would like to hear you scream when you come."

Max was such an asshole. But I wouldn't deny either one of us sharing my virgin analingus orgasm. I nodded and reached beneath myself, gripping the edges of the chair. Darin moved the phone right up next to my lips. With his other hand, he opened the top of my bustier. He lifted my breasts free, then bent his head to my nipple. He licked as my hem lifted. Richard's fingers slid up my leg, dipping down in front, sliding on to my slick, swollen clit as Darin sucked my nipple into my mouth.

Carlos was licking in circles again, gentling my anus to relax, seducing it to open further.

"If it pleases you, ma'am." Darin's breath was hot on my wet, pebbled nipple. "Your husband suggests you bear down hard when Carlos really starts tongue-fucking your asshole. He says that'll open you wide enough for him to get in really deep. He says it'll let you come so hard you'll see stars." Carlos was probing again. Darin kissed, blowing softly just before he latched on again. "Your husband respectfully requests you come so hard your scream blows out the microphone on the fucking cell phone."

My laugh came out somewhere between a moan and a cry as Carlos' tongue once more pressed flat on my anal gate. This time, though, when he pressed in, I pressed out to meet him. His tongue slid in deep. Then it was out. And in. And out. I bore down hard, again, reaching for his tongue with my asshole as he once again slid in deep – and stayed. As I pressed against him, he licked the inner walls of my sphincter. Then he was tongue-fucking me again.

The pressure was starting deep in my belly. Darin's talented lips on my nipple and Richard's equally talented fingers working my clit were beyond exquisite. But the orgasm was starting deep in my asshole. Starting where Carlos was fucking my asshole with his tongue. As the splendour raced up through my body, I screamed, "Don't stop! Please, don't stop! PLEASE!"

I wailed as the orgasm tore through me. Darin's lips were locked on my nipple, sucking hard as Richard's hand kept up its relentless pace. And Carlos' tongue – Carlos' exquisite, perfect, angelic tongue – was buried deep in my asshole, wiggling but not pulling out as my spasming sphincter clamped down like a vice around him. Something hot and wet hit my leg. My asshole clenched so tight I was certain I'd push him out. But Carlos' tongue stayed deep, letting me glory in the ecstasy of my first true anal orgasm. When he finally pulled back and kissed my quivering anus, I was still shaking so hard, I almost fell off the chair.

I looked down at the torso beneath me. This time, I wasn't going to have to take my boots to the man beneath me. Carlos' chest and belly and Richard's arm and my leg were covered with glistening white puddles. A final line of semen dripped from the head of Carlos' now only half-hard cock.

I lost track of how many times I came – and how many times they changed places. Eventually, I told Max I'd talk to him when he got home. I hung up and watched a chick flick he hated and ate more bonbons and drank my sparkling water and even some champagne Darin brought me from the kitchen. I called my girlfriends. There's nothing in the world quite like sipping bubbly and watching movie stars with tight butts making slow tender love to their women – all while chatting up a play-by-play of the movie with my totally vanilla best friend from college. With each breath I took, an anonymous tongue beneath me worshipped my quivering pussy or my equally tingling anus.

Max got home shortly after I'd sent the others on their way. I fucked him so long and hard, I even wore him out – no mean feat for a man renowned for his stamina and horny beyond belief from listening to me come over the phone. He rolled me over on my tummy and slid his lube-slicked cock up my still hypersensitive ass. I screamed and came again, milking the juice from his cock as he grunted and growled and told me he loved me.

The next day, I was still so horny, I jumped his bones before he was even all the way awake. Max didn't get the reputation he has in the pussy department by being a slouch. He took me out to dinner in a classy restaurant, we renegotiated our sexual agreements, and by the next Friday night, he'd arranged for his three now wildly enthusiastic friends to join us again at the house.

This time, it was definitely going to be "us". Max still wasn't going to climb beneath the queening chair. But he was going to feed me peeled grapes and tell me dirty stories and kiss me and suck my tits when I came. When he got too horny, he was going to jerk his dick, but he wasn't going to let himself come until after everyone else had gone home. Then he was going to fuck me in every orifice I wanted. No matter how many times I'd already climaxed that evening, he was going to pleasure me enough to be sure I came at least one more time – with him.

Goldberg Variations

Lisabet Sarai

Harvey and Al stood in the chill drizzle beside the muddy grave.

"Damned inconsiderate of Richard, dropping dead without any warning," Al commented.

"I'm sure that he didn't do it deliberately. Certainly he would much rather have attended one of our funerals than vice versa," observed Harvey.

"No doubt. He only cared about himself."

"Well, to be fair, he put a lot of effort into the trio."

"Right. *His* trio, he used to call it."

"Whatever. It's been our bread and butter for twenty-two years, so don't knock it."

"Sure, but what are we going to do now? There's no work for a violin/viola duo."

Harvey sighed. "Obviously, we've got to find another cello. I'll put an ad in the *Times* next week. It shouldn't be too difficult; there must be hundreds of starving musicians in New York."

"Yeah, but can they play Bach? We don't want someone whose repertoire is restricted to 'Yesterday' and 'Endless Love'."

Harvey had a pounding headache, and the rain was beginning to drip down underneath the collar of his topcoat. His brother's negative attitude was all too familiar. "We'll just have to see, Al. We've got a full schedule for the next few months. We'll make do with what we can get."

He glanced over his shoulder at the chauffeur, waiting under an umbrella beside the hired limo. "Let's go. Everybody's probably back at the house by now."

The two-storey Brooklyn row house was packed with a boisterous, hungry crowd of relatives and friends. Harvey offered some obligatory greetings and accepted routine condolences. Finally, he managed to escape upstairs to the study.

It had been their father's space, first, and then, since he had been the trio's business manager, Richard's. The walls were decorated with autographed pictures, their father shaking hands with Yehudi Menuhin and Pablo Casals. Then there were posters from some of their tours ("The Goldberg Trio, Live at Pittsburgh Symphony Hall") and replica covers from their four recordings (*The Goldberg Trio Plays Classical Favourites*).

Dad would have been proud, mused Harvey. Wouldn't he? It was hard to know.

On the bookshelf stood a picture of the three of them with Dad. It had been taken at Coney Island, not long after Al's mother died. Everyone was trying valiantly to appear happy.

The three boys didn't look much alike, but that was hardly surprising. Dad had divorced both Richard's and Harvey's mothers. Al's mother, sweet, red-headed Emma, had been taken by cancer.

When Dad died of a heart attack only a few years afterwards, he left the row house to his three teenaged sons. The half-brothers had made it their home ever since.

Harvey realized Aunt Nelda was calling him. His father's sister was frail but the years hadn't diminished the piercing quality of her voice.

"Harvey? Where are you? Some of the guests are leaving, and Al seems to have disappeared. Harvey?"

Before he left the sanctuary of the office, he grabbed two aspirin from the bottle Richard kept in the desk. He chewed them without water, relishing the bitterness. Noticing Richard's planning calendar in the drawer, he flipped through the pages to October. God, their next appearance was two weeks from tomorrow. A reception at the Mayor's mansion, yet!

Harvey swallowed his panic and headed downstairs. Somehow it would work out. Things always worked out, one way or another.

* * *

Al was hiding out in the tool shed at back of the lot, smoking a joint. I'm some hip cat, he thought sourly, forty-nine years old and still getting high. When his rust-coloured hair had begun to thin, he had shaved it all off. Now he had the look of a bald scarecrow, long-limbed, skinny and awkward. Only when he tucked his violin under his chin and began to play did he achieve some kind of grace. Those were his happiest times, in fact, when he could lose himself in the music, in harmony for once with his brothers.

The rest of his life seemed empty and hollow, eaten away by envy, fouled with the nasty taste of decayed dreams. Richard had been the lucky one, the good-looking one, the one who had a solo career before the time of the trio. Richard had even had a lover, Al remembered, a pretty Barnard girl who used to come over and listen to him practise. Sherrie, Al dimly recalled.

What had happened to Sherrie? She had drifted away, it seemed, like all their hopes, leaving them marooned in this house full of ghosts, wandering through life as lonely and embittered as ghosts themselves.

The pot was making him maudlin. He dug a hole in the dirt floor with his toe and buried the roach. Now Richard was gone, a real ghost, leaving him and Harv behind. Al wasn't sure whether he still envied Richard or not.

Harvey's ad attracted a raft of responses. There was the jazz cellist who wanted to "broaden his horizons", the spinster who had been teaching cello for forty years out of her home in Queens, the high-school kid who bragged about being "first cello" in the school orchestra. Harvey sighed as he reviewed the alternatives.

After all, the Goldberg Trio had a reputation. The *Times'* Art and Culture columnist had speculated in Richard's obituary on the future of "one of the city's most persistent musical institutions". Harvey had fumed briefly, then shrugged his shoulders. He couldn't afford to waste his energy on some catty member of the press.

The latest response, though, was intriguing. It had a formality of tone that reminded him of an Edith Wharton novel.

Dear Mr Goldberg,

I am writing in response to your advertisement of October 9 in the *New York Times*, seeking an experienced cellist to join your chamber music ensemble.

I would be honoured if you would consider engaging me for this position. Currently I am employed on the faculty of the Berklee College of Music in Boston. However, I have become quite frustrated with teaching, and had been seriously considering a return to performing even before I saw your advertisement.

I have attached a copy of my CV. If you are interested in auditioning me, would it be possible for you to come to Boston? I have a very heavy schedule during the next week, but after that I can disengage myself more easily. On a longer-term basis, I have no objection whatsoever to relocating to New York.

Thank you for your consideration.

Yours sincerely,

Deidre Rasinovsky-Corbatta

Ms Rasinovky-Corbatta's résumé was impressive. Training at the St Petersburg State Conservatory and the Conservatorio de Santa Cecilia in Rome, six years as a soloist with the Moscow Philharmonic and three touring on her own, then a Masters from Julliard and four years at Berklee, arguably the best music school in the country.

Harvey read her missive one more time. How had she known how to address him? Presumably she had heard about Richard's demise and made a calculated guess. It sounded as though she was sharp, as well as qualified.

How would she interact with the two remaining Goldberg brothers, though? Harvey understood that the trio's success over the years had been based on a delicate balance of personalities as much as on a shared dedication to music. Wouldn't bringing in a stranger, and a woman at that, upset the balance?

There was no help for it, though. Richard was gone, and anyone they found to replace him would be a stranger. Harvey hated making phone calls, but he swallowed his nervousness and dialled Ms Rasinovsky-Corbatta's number. With a gig in less than two weeks, he couldn't afford to indulge his fears.

The Amtrak train chugged through the wilds of Connecticut. Al stared gloomily out the window at the yellowing vegetation, drooping damp under an overcast sky. Harvey sat snoring in the next seat, his round face slack and relaxed and his mouth open. His glasses had slipped down his nose. Gently, Al reached over and returned them to their proper place.

Al had a sense of foreboding about meeting this cellist. Sure, she had fabulous credentials, but he just couldn't imagine having a woman join their trio. Women were trouble, irrational and demanding. Women made men behave irrationally.

Of course, Richard had been demanding, too, a real prima donna at times, but he and Harvey had known how to handle Richard. After all, they had years of practice.

Maybe he and Harvey should simply give up and dissolve the trio. With Brooklyn continuing to gentrify, they could sell the house for a tidy sum and start over.

Start over doing what, though? Al visualized himself on stage, in the spotlight, soaring through one of the solos from *L'Estro Armonico*. He knew it would never happen, though. He was too old, too tired, spoiled from playing too long with the same group. Too lazy to try, you mean, a mocking voice whispered in his head. You could have been great, but you've never been willing to make the effort.

Al shook his head. Why did all his musings these days degenerate into depression? He manoeuvred his way past Harvey's knees, careful not to wake his slumbering sibling, and headed towards the café car. It was past three, surely not too early for a cocktail.

They got out of the taxi in Back Bay at ten to five. Their appointment was for five thirty.

"Ms Rasinovksy-Corbatta is in Practice Room 5 on the second floor," the receptionist volunteered. "You can go on up, if you'd like."

Harvey and Al bundled their instruments up the stairs to a long hallway that smelled of dust and rosin. Room 5 was at the end. The door was ajar. Light and music spilled through the opening.

Harvey grabbed Al, who was about to push the door wide. "Wait," he whispered urgently. "Listen."

The melody swirled around them like smoke, mysterious and difficult to apprehend, shifting form and mood in each moment. Harvey recognized Bach's masterful D minor Partita, rendered with a purity and restraint that made Harvey ache. He closed his eyes and allowed the music to invade him, to overwhelm him. The notes soared heavenwards, until he felt breathless in the thin atmosphere, then sank into low, throaty tones that vibrated deep in his gut.

He knew the piece well – could remember Richard performing it, to enthusiastic crowds – but now it seemed as though he had never truly heard it before. The playing was formal and precise yet somehow the control only heightened the emotional intensity. Pensive, questing, triumphant then subdued, the music ebbed and flowed in the darkened corridor.

"She's good," Al whispered.

"Shh!" Harvey felt momentary rage at his brother's interruption, then the emotion washed away in the tides of Bach's creation. She was more than good. She was great, clearly a far more talented musician than any of the Goldberg brothers. Even Richard.

Why in the world would she want to be part of their group? What could they offer to induce her to join them? Harvey fretted briefly. Then the music raised him up again and carried him along, until the last mournful note trailed away into silence and set him free.

The two of them stood motionless for a long moment, looking at each other. Harvey gave a gentle knock.

"Come on in." The voice was low and well tempered, with the faintest trace of an accent. Harvey led the way into the practice room.

"Ms Rasinovsky . . ." he began. He was unable to continue.

He didn't know what he had expected, but the woman facing him with the cello cradled between her thighs was a shock.

Her red-shading-to-magenta hair made a spiky halo around her head. Her plump lips were painted to match. Wedgewood-blue eyes blazed in her long, pale face. One ear was pierced by half a dozen silver hoops and every finger of the hand that clasped the bow was decorated with a silver ring.

She wore a tight black jersey that zipped at the neck. The zipper was pulled down low enough that Harvey could see the tiny rose tattooed on creamy skin of her throat and the shadowy chasm between her full breasts. Her matching skirt was slit up the front. Harvey was grateful that she was wearing opaque tights.

When she smiled, put down her bow and stood to greet them, Harvey noticed her pointy-toed, high-heeled, Wicked-Witch-of-the-West boots.

No, there was no way this woman could have created that music! He swallowed hard, and tried again. "Ms Rasinovsky," he croaked. "I'm Harvey Goldberg, and this is my brother, Albert."

"It's a pleasure to meet you both. Thank you for coming all the way to Boston."

Al's eyes gleamed. He stepped forward and took the slender hand the cellist offered. "The pleasure is ours, Ms Rasinovsky. I haven't heard that piece played so well for many years."

The woman laughed, deep in her chest. "You flatter me. And please, call me Deidre."

"Al is telling the truth – Deidre. Your performance was astonishing. Not only was it technically perfect, it was very moving."

"I appreciate the praise all the more, coming from a musician of your reputation, Mr Goldberg – I mean, Harvey."

She made his name sound like music. Harvey suddenly felt as though somebody had turned on a sunlamp. His wool suit was unbearably hot. His necktie was strangling him. He burned with embarrassment as he imagined how she must see him: a dumpy middle-aged man, balding and a bit dishevelled, blushing like a girl. He needed to take control of this interview, but somehow he couldn't organize his thoughts enough to utter a coherent sentence.

To his surprise, Al stepped into the breach. "I can see why you'd want to get back on the stage, Deidre. Your talent is wasted on students. What I don't understand is why you're interested in joining us. Because, honestly, we're not of your calibre."

There was that laugh again, vibrating through Harvey's body like a low G drawn from her bow.

"I've had a solo career, Albert. It is a lonely life. The spotlight isolates you from your fellow musicians. I am familiar with the fleeting fulfilment of applause and the acid of my colleagues' envy. I don't want that. I want to belong to a community of music, a collaboration where our creation is greater than what any of us could achieve on our own. A musical family, if you will. And I sense, from listening to your recordings, that you could be offering what I am missing. That sense of belonging."

"Do you have a husband?" asked Harvey, struggling to gain a foothold in the conversation. "Children?"

"I was married once, briefly. It rapidly became clear to both of us that despite the intense sexual attraction we shared, no man could compete with music for my affections."

Harvey blushed again. How could they possibly contemplate performing with this post-punk siren, when simply talking to her turned him back into an awkward, tongue-tied teenager?

Al, on the other hand, seemed to radiate poise. "After hearing your Bach, Deidre, I hardly think we need to give you an audition. However, it seems like we should try playing together. To test out the chemistry, if you know what I mean."

"Of course. Why not now? I see you've brought your instruments. How about K563? One of my students has been working on it, so I have the music here."

She extricated two scores from a pile on the table beside her, and handed one to Al. "I only have two copies, though. Do you and Harvey mind sharing?"

"I think we can manage," Al reassured her. He adjusted the music stand so that he and his brother could both read the page.

Deidre settled back on to her stool and embraced her cello. Her long pale fingers caressed the flowing curves of the body, then danced lightly up the frets. Her gestures were so sensual that Harvey found himself becoming aroused.

This was unbearable. He fought an urge to stand and run out the door, back to Brooklyn, back to the dreary but familiar confines of his normal life. There was something dreamlike about this encounter, or perhaps nightmarish. He needed to escape, but this exotic, disturbing woman rooted him to the spot.

Al had busied himself tuning his violin and rosining his bow. Harvey tried to hide his nervousness by doing the same.

"Shall we try the Allegro first movement?" Deidre asked. "Or would you rather tackle one of the minuets?"

"The Allegro's fine." Al positioned the violin under his chin. "Ready?"

Harvey and Deidre prepared themselves. Al nodded the signal, and they launched into the piece.

The attack was perfect. Mozart's sprightly melody filled the room, light as summer, free as running water. Harvey felt it flowing effortlessly from his instrument, entwining with the voices of the others. Laughter rose in his chest, bubbling and threatening to spill over. First one instrument and then another danced away from the ensemble, gambolling up and down the scales before rejoining the harmony. It was as wonderfully careless and playful as the composer had intended.

He glanced over at Deidre. Her painted lips were parted, her eyes sparkling. Al wore a smile for the first time in weeks. Harvey felt as if he were levitating six inches above the floor. He forgot to be embarrassed or self-conscious.

He knew that they still had a lot of work to do, reviewing the schedule, rehearsing, figuring out the money part. The most serious obstacle, though, seemed to have evaporated. It was clear that Deidre could become part of the trio. In fact, it felt as though she already was.

It had been Al's idea to move Deidre into Richard's room. They were spending six hours a day practising together, why waste time having her travel back and forth to a hotel? Of course, there were considerations of economy as well. Plus, Al admitted to himself, he enjoyed the thought of the glamorous cellist inhabiting Richard's space, sleeping in his bed. If Richard were haunting the place, he'd be eating his heart out. After three days, though, Al was beginning to wonder whether he'd made a mistake. Rehearsals were going well for the most part, but when they weren't playing, he was finding it difficult to concentrate.

Her sharp patchouli scent lingered in the hallway. Her lace brassiere hung in the shower. Yesterday morning he had pushed open the half-ajar bathroom door, thinking the room was empty. Instead, he found her clad in a screaming red satin kimono that clashed with her hair, with one foot perched on the toilet seat, shaving her legs.

She glanced up and smiled at him, obviously unfazed. He backed out of the room mumbling an apology. Later though, the scene haunted him. His momentary sensory impressions elaborated themselves into detailed images: the fine curve of her arch, the creamy skin of her thigh, the glimpses of rounded flesh where her robe fell open at the throat. The amused gleam in her sapphire eyes. The welcoming smile on her harlot-red lips.

Al cursed his imagination. He was becoming obsessed. Each time he lay on his bed stroking himself, the images became more vivid and intense. The release was fleeting. Before an hour was gone, he found himself wanting her again. He considered a quick visit to the girls at the Peacock Club, but he doubted that would help.

He hated himself for his weakness. His father wouldn't approve. Richard would silently mock him. His inconvenient lust was starting to affect his music; during practice today, he had missed two cues in the Beethoven C minor. Deidre had given him a sympathetic look. He had simply wanted to drop dead. If he couldn't even impress her with his playing, what was the point?

There was a soft knock at his door. Hurriedly, he replaced his cock in his trousers and sat up. "Come on in," he called, expecting Harv. When the door swung open, though, he was face to face with the object of his fantasies.

She was dressed in her usual black. Rather than the form-fitting, Emma-Peel-like costumes she mostly favoured, tonight she wore something delicate and flowing, with a scooped neckline that showed off her exquisite shoulders. Her lipstick was softer, cherry instead of fire-engine red, and she was barefoot.

"Good evening, Albert." He cringed. No one had called him by his full name since his mother died. "Can I come in? I need to talk to you."

"Um, sure. Come on in, like I said. What's up?"

She sat herself on his bed, her garment swirling gracefully around her. His nose twitched as the air filled with patchouli. "I know that I'm being nosy, but I'm concerned about you. You seem terribly tense. So tense that you're making mistakes in your performance, mistakes that I know you wouldn't normally make."

"I'm really sorry about today. I don't know what was wrong, but it won't happen again." Al felt as guilty and miserable as a kid caught stealing from the cookie jar.

"I'm not blaming you. I just want to help." She gestured towards the entrance. "Why don't you close the door, so that we don't disturb Harvey? And then I have something here that I think might help you relax."

Al recognized the earthy smell of marijuana before she even produced the joint. He hastened to follow her instructions. Harv didn't approve of drugs.

He found a lighter in his bureau and applied it to the joint until the tip glowed red as Deidre's hair. She inhaled a lungful of the sweetish smoke and held it for thirty seconds. At the same time, she held him with her gaze. Was she challenging or inviting him?

Al felt his cock swell uncomfortably inside his trousers. Deidre passed him the smouldering butt, her fingers brushing briefly against his in the process. It was only the slightest touch. He shouldn't jump to conclusions, he told himself. It could be completely innocent.

Yeah, right. Here she was in his bedroom, sitting next to him on his bed, with the door closed, wearing something that looked more or less like a negligee. Innocent? Hardly. But she was the one in charge, that was clear. He didn't dare to make the first move.

Trying to ignore his throbbing hard-on, he took a big hit of the pot. The harsh smoke seared his lungs. As he released it, he felt the drug rush through him, lifting him like a strong breeze. "Mmm. Good stuff. Thanks. But I wouldn't have expected someone like you to – indulge."

Deidre laughed, that low, sexy laugh that made his balls tighten to aching rocks. "There's a lot that you don't know about me, Albert. Here, take another toke."

Al obeyed her. He figured that he would always obey her. The second lungful was more powerful than the first. He closed his eyes, floating on a cloud of lust and THC.

The next thing he knew, her hands were in his crotch. "What have we here?" She laughed again. "You seem to be already unzipped and ready for me."

Oh God! He must have forgotten to zip up after he jerked off. Embarrassment welled up briefly, but the drug soothed it away. Her hands were precise and knowing. Her fingers danced along the length of his shaft with the same power and skill that he had noted when she fingered the neck of her cello. She plucked a pizzicato rhythm on the sensitive ridge underneath the head of his cock, then played him with long lingering strokes that arched up his spine. His groans were a new kind of music, as she brought him ever closer to crescendo.

Dimly, Al smelled scorched cloth, where the forgotten roach was burning itself out on the bed. He concentrated instead on the odours of his sweat and her musk. He could smell her true scent now, oceany and dark, overpowering her herbal perfume. She's excited, too, he realized. She's not just doing this out of charity, or for the benefit of the trio. His cock leaped in her hands at the thought.

Marijuana alters the experience of time. He could appreciate every detail, every sensation: the rough callouses on her fingertips, the soothing warmth of her palm, the rustling of her garments, the rush of her ever-quickening breathing.

Blood pounded in his swollen penis. His heart pounded in his ears. Her fingers drummed against his flesh, a primitive jungle rhythm that drove him wild.

At any moment, he was sure, he would explode, and yet it went on and on, an endless rise and fall, eternal as a Beethoven sonata.

Suddenly, there were new sensations, wetness and heat, organic and irresistible. Al's eyes flew open. Deidre's head of tangled purple locks was buried in his lap. Her painted mouth engulfed his cock. She sucked at him as though to consume him.

Al had a raw, hyper-clear image of scarlet lipstick smeared all over his penis. A choked scream tore itself from his throat as he emptied himself into his colleague's welcoming mouth.

As the vibrations died away, he smiled to himself, feeling both silly and self-satisfied. Perhaps having her on the premises had been a good idea after all.

Deidre brushed her sticky lips against his. "Now, Albert," she purred, "why don't you help me to relax?"

Harvey had never considered himself to be highly sexed. He would go weeks or even months without masturbating. He found images of half-naked nubile girls selling blue jeans embarrassing and in poor taste. He knew that Al visited "gentlemen's clubs" occasionally, but personally he had no interest. Harvey's diversions tended to be on a different plane: music, art, literature, the occasional movie.

Since Deidre had joined the trio, though, Harvey had been feeling like a randy eighteen-year-old. Her mere presence was enough to harden his cock to the point of pain. When she spoke to him, her sultry voice full of soft Russian vowels, he felt his own power to speak escaping him. Her always assertive gaze was a ray gun that froze him in his tracks, or perhaps more appropriately, melted him into a featureless lump of swollen, aching flesh.

It wasn't just the aura of blatant sexuality that surrounded her. It had something to do with her music, her cool, controlled technique that contrasted so strongly with the passion flowing from her instrument. It was intense, visceral. Each vibrant note penetrated his flesh to settle in his groin.

Most of the time when they played together, Harvey managed to concentrate on the score and execute his part in a manner that was competent if not inspired. If he happened to glance over at her, though, he was lost. He saw the way she clasped the belly of her cello between her thighs, and imagined himself in its place. He watched her fingers travel over the sounding board and saw them dancing across his flesh.

This morning he had messed up the second movement of the Schubert B flat so badly that they had to start over.

Al hadn't made any comment. Harvey had been surprised to find sympathy in his brother's look, rather than the expected scorn. On the other hand, Al seemed to be playing exceptionally well today. His blunders of yesterday did not repeat themselves. His solo passages soared with a new lyricism. Harvey noticed that Deidre was smiling at Al, her face alive with pleasure and approval.

For the first time that he could remember, Harvey felt jealous of his brother.

Al was not generally the perceptive type. Still, he couldn't miss the fact that Harv was turned on by Deidre. The moment Harvey walked into the practice room this morning, Al had noticed the swelling in the crotch of his brother's baggy trousers.

When Harvey stumbled over one of his passages, Al could identify. Poor guy was probably having the devil's time focusing on the music, with Deidre's lush body and spicy scent so close by.

Al was aroused himself, but now that he was confident that he'd get relief, the erotic tension seemed to elevate his playing to a new level. The phrases flowed effortlessly from his violin, immaculate, sublime. In her presence, he felt possessed by genius.

Whenever his eyes met hers, electric sparks arced through the short distance that separated them. Everything about her demeanour was full of future promises.

Harvey went upstairs to get a glass of water. Deidre put aside her cello. "Come over here, Albert." There was a clear invitation in her voice. Al ached to obey her, but he resisted.

"We've got to be careful, Deidre. We don't want Harv to get suspicious."

Deidre parted her legs more widely. A whiff of her scent rose in the basement practice room. Al grinned, realizing that she had probably omitted to put on panties this morning. In his honour, he assumed.

"Don't worry about Harvey. He'll be fine. I guarantee it." The cellist stood and came to him, pulling him into a voluptuous kiss. Capturing his thigh between her own strong limbs, she began rubbing her crotch against his corduroy pants.

"Deidre, please! I can hear him on the stairs."

They broke apart seconds before Harvey entered. He looked miserable, his round face pink and damp with sweat. "Do you mind if I open a window?" he asked. "It seems terribly hot in here."

"Sure, Harvey, go ahead." Al was feeling indulgent. "It is a bit close."

Al figured that Harvey would get over his infatuation eventually. After all, his brother had never been that interested in sex. In the meantime, he didn't want to cause Harvey any more pain than necessary. He and Deidre should try to be discreet.

Harvey found himself in the midst of a strange, vivid dream. He was dead, it seemed, lying on a satin-draped bier in a candlelit room. The air was heavy with the scent of roses.

No, thought Harvey, in confusion, it's Richard who died, not me. He tried to sit up, but though he could breathe in the floral atmosphere and enjoy the smoothness of the satin against his skin, his limbs were cold and unresponsive. A seductive languor held him still. The room itself was pleasantly cool. He wondered vaguely if it was a crypt.

The only part of him that was warm and alive was his cock. It pointed straight up from his motionless body, straining towards the shadowy ceiling. Harvey didn't wonder at this, or at the fact that he was naked. His cock had been a hot spear of swollen flesh for as long as he could remember.

He heard a rustling, of silk, or wings, or nameless creatures moving in the dark corners. Then he saw Deidre standing beside his couch. How he saw, through closed eyelids, was not clear. It didn't matter. He sensed her presence, a concentration of heat vibrating near him.

She was naked as well. The candles painted gold motes on her alabaster skin. She held a scarlet rose in the hollow between her breasts. She brought it to her lips, which were painted the identical colour, then bent over him as though to place it in Harvey's clasped hands.

Suddenly she drew a sharp breath. From some omniscient perspective that he couldn't explain, he saw several drops of her blood, scattered over his mostly hairless chest.

"Oh, Harvey, I'm sorry," she whispered. She sank to her knees, leaned over and gathered the ruby droplets with her tongue. The sensation was exquisite, her muscular warmth a shock to his passive coolness. His cock pulsed in time as she lapped at his skin, energetic as a mother cat cleaning her kitten.

The blood was gone, but she did not stop. She flicked at his nipples until the cold nubs woke into bright points of flame. She trailed her mouth wetly over his belly, leaving a path of fire in her wake. She took a mouthful of his grizzled pubic hair and gently pulled. His cock danced wildly, threatening to spray fire all over the immaculate bier.

"Harvey," she murmured, her voice kindling him further. "Forgive me." With the same economy of movement she used in handling her cello, she straddled him and sucked his rigid cock into her pussy.

Pleasure overwhelmed him, pleasure too acute to be endured. The dream world shattered into liquid fragments along with his cock, red as blood and roses, white as satin.

No, thought Harvey, panicked, fighting to wake. Please, I don't want to have a wet dream. All the awkwardness and embarrassment of his youth came flooding back, pushing him up out of the well of sleep.

The chilly, rose-scented vault was gone. The candle glow was replaced by the wan light of dawn filtering through his old curtains. Yet the dream had not fled.

Deidre still rode him, clutching his plump hips between her long white thighs. She moved deliberately, giving him time to savour every inch of her slick heat sliding over the stretched skin of his cock. Blood surged into his swollen organ with every stroke, sending shudders of pleasure through his body.

Despite his fears, he hadn't come. He was still hard, granite, steel, monumental, irresistible. He began to move with her, arching his back to drive his cock as deep into her as he could. He groaned as she tightened her cunt muscles around him.

Deidre smiled. "Good morning, Harvey," she murmured, squeezing him again. He grunted and rammed his cock into her. She gave a little cry and stopped talking.

They rocked together, faster now, Deidre allowing him to set the pace. He grabbed her lush buttocks in both hands, seeking leverage to plunge still deeper. She moaned at the bite of his fingernails and ground her pelvis against him, lewd, abandoned, forgetting everything but her own pleasure.

Leaning forwards, she used her arms to brace herself against the bed. She slammed herself down on his cock, again and again. Her ripe breasts dangled inches from his face. Without his glasses, the world was fuzzy, but he could see that her mouth was a grimace of lust. Her eyes were squeezed closed. Her nipples were crinkled purple pebbles.

Straining his neck to reach, he took one of the tempting nuggets in his teeth. At the same time, he stabbed upwards, burying himself completely in the luxurious wetness of her flesh.

Deidre wailed like a cat. Fierce spasms shook her body. Her cunt contracted with terrific force. He yelped at the unexpected pressure, then yelled in triumph as her crisis infected him. Waves of come surged up his stalk, one after another, each one breaking into a froth of pleasure in the shallows of her still-shuddering cunt.

The explosion of his climax triggered a fresh round of spasms inside her. Harvey lay in helpless ecstasy as she twitched and trembled around his exhausted penis.

Gradually, the aftershocks died away. The delicious weight of Deidre's body rested on his chest. His bedroom smelled of sex, mixed with essence of rose. Harvey buried his face in her neck, breathing in the remnants of perfume from her damp skin.

"Harvey," said Deidre, turning her head to look him in the eye, "I hope you don't mind. I don't normally force myself on men."

"Mind?" Harvey felt like giggling. "Do you know how much I've been wanting you?"

She grinned mischievously and gave his cock an affectionate squeeze. "Well, I had some idea. But you were so shy, I really didn't think I could seduce you while you were conscious. So I decided to take advantage of you when your guard was down."

She paused to kiss him, her tongue dancing playfully in his mouth. He returned her kiss with an ardour that transformed play into passion. He could feel the heat beginning to build again where his crotch was close to hers.

"So am I forgiven?" she asked after a time, blue flame flickering in her eyes.

Filled with new confidence, Harvey rolled her over on to her back. He let his hands wander for a while over her lovely, cello-shaped body. Leaning over, he brought the tip of his tongue to the rose tattooed in the hollow of her throat. "Well, that depends . . ."

Two days to go. Al could tell they were ready. The timing, the phrasing, the harmonies, they were all perfect. Even the Borodin, so technically demanding, they had mastered. The music flowed from their instruments without any conscious effort. Their communication seemed instinctive. They could play for hours, without a word, without a mistake.

Al had never felt so inspired as when he played with Deidre. Somehow, even as they bowed and fingered their instruments, he felt that she was making love to him. With her beside me, he mused, I really could be great. For once the dream did not seem completely ridiculous to him.

He noticed gratefully that she was being especially kind to Harvey. His brother seemed more comfortable, too, less flustered and more serene. Probably he had grown out of his crush on Deidre, and could now relate to her as a colleague instead of an object of desire. The fact that their rehearsals were going so well had probably helped, too. Harv could be a worrier sometimes.

When the chips were down, though, you could always depend on him. After all, it was Harvey who had found Deidre. Al would have to remember to thank him someday, when the time came for Al and Deidre to share their secret with him.

Harvey couldn't believe how good he felt. With Deidre's morning visits, he should have been exhausted, but in fact he'd never had more energy. Not bad for an old geezer of fifty-two, he thought, as he tried on his tuxedo in preparation for the concert. The formal costume fitted him well. He looked taller, thinner, more distinguished than he remembered.

What will Deidre wear? he wondered. He could imagine her showing up in black leather or see-through lace. But she was a professional, as surely as he and Al were. He trusted her to understand what was appropriate for a gathering of politicos and international dignitaries.

Over the last few days, rehearsals had gone so well, he had suggested they all take a day off before the gig. They were going to lunch in SoHo and then to visit the Cloisters, one of Harvey's favourite places. He couldn't wait to see Deidre's flaming hair and graceful form against the backdrop of medieval stone and stained glass.

They'd have to work hard to make sure that Al didn't feel left out. Harvey understood that his brother thought of himself as something of a lady's man. It would be a real blow to Al's ego to discover that Deidre had chosen Harvey as her lover.

He'd have to figure out some way to break the news gently. After the concert, of course, nothing could interfere with the return of the Goldberg Trio to the musical scene. The New Goldberg Trio, he corrected himself mentally, imagining Deidre naked with her cello between her legs.

Wouldn't Richard have been surprised?

*   *   *

The concert was a triumph.

In some sense, the trio was just sophisticated background music for the Mayor's party. When Al led them into the first movement of the Beethoven C Minor, though, the murmur of voices and tinkling of glass died away. The guests, cultured, urbane, even jaded, stood enchanted by the trio's magic.

Deidre, resplendent in a classic black velvet gown, laid bare the passion hidden under Beethoven's intellectual facade. Al's playing was so pure and perfect it literally brought tears to Harvey's eyes. Meanwhile, his viola seemed unreal, unnecessary. Surely the music flowed from his heart, through his fingers, and out to the world, without the mediation of any physical mechanism.

At one point he caught Deidre's eye, and felt the connection, as tangible as a physical caress. The intimacy of that look sent shivers up his spine. Al glanced at him, and then at Deidre, a beatific expression making his narrow features glow. The music swelled around them, moving them, changing them.

Harvey forgot about the audience. He was aware only of the music and of his fellow players. He could sense their heartbeats driving the melody, feel their breathing in his own lungs. The strands of music wound around them, binding them together, closer, and closer still.

During the interlude, Harvey wandered among the glitterati, sipping champagne. Deidre was surrounded by eager admirers. He couldn't get near her. Their eyes met across the room, though, kindling a familiar fire in his belly.

The music critic from the *Times*, the one who had covered Richard's funeral, strolled by. Harvey nodded to him amiably. No one could deny that tonight belonged to the New Goldberg Trio.

It was after two when the limousine deposited them back at the house. Still in their coats, the three of them collapsed into the overstuffed living room chairs.

After a moment, Deidre pulled a bottle out from under her cloak. "A toast!" she exclaimed. "To the Goldbergs!"

"Deidre!" Harvey sounded shocked. "You didn't filch that champagne from the Mayor, did you?"

"Consider it to be part of our compensation," she said with mock dignity. "They can hardly claim to have paid us what we are worth."

She shrugged off her cape and began to wrestle with the cork. Al brought glasses from the corner cupboard.

Although she had consumed at least two glasses of champagne at the reception, she didn't feel even slightly tipsy. With the first sip from this bottle, though, the alcohol hit her full force. She giggled like a girl of seventeen.

"To us," she intoned, raising her glass.

The two brothers were both staring at her. "To us," Harvey repeated softly.

"To us," echoed Al. "And to many more successes together."

"Together, yes, definitely." Deidre drank deeply before setting her glass down. "I want to thank you both for giving me the chance to experience what I felt tonight. Thank you for welcoming me into your midst. Thanks for putting up with my quirks."

"Hey," said Al, deliberately offhand. "You put up with us."

Harvey was looking uncomfortable.

"No, seriously. I will always cherish tonight's memory, our first performance together." She reached across the table and took Harvey's hand in her own. Al's face darkened until she held out her other hand and he accepted it.

"I told you when I met you that I was looking for a special kind of community. A union that was more than the sum of its parts."

She looked from one man to the other: lanky, angular Albert, sharp as the high C on his own violin, hiding his vulnerability under a veneer of cynicism; pudgy, self-effacing Harvey, the sensible worrywart with the soul of a passionate romantic.

"That is what we are, the three of us. A communion of music. A family."

Her voice broke. For a moment she was on the verge of tears. "Thank you," she whispered. "Thank you both." She bowed her head for a moment. Al and Harvey looked at each other, equally unprepared to handle a weeping woman.

When she looked up again, though, her face was bright. "Well, it has been quite a night. I think it's time for bed. Don't you agree, Albert?"

Before he could answer, she sealed his mouth with her own. His palms cupped her breasts; hers snaked down to cradle the growing bulk in his crotch.

She heard Harvey stand up, shuffling his feet. Afraid that he would flee, she broke away from Albert and hastened to erase the horror and pain on Harvey's face with an equally passionate embrace.

"What the hell? Deidre, what's going on?" Al sputtered in disbelief.

"I'm inviting you into my bed," she responded, when she and Harvey finally came up for air. "Both of you."

"Both of us?" Harvey looked shocked and incredulous. "You can't . . . we can't . . ."

"Why not?" She put her hands on her hips in mock exasperation. "Don't you think I can handle you?"

"Yes, but . . . he's my brother," said Al carefully, trying to work out the implications.

"Would you rather that Harvey and I just go off by ourselves, then?"

"No, of course not . . ."

"Well, then, come along, Albert."

"But, Deidre . . ." Harvey began.

"Yes?"

"Well, I . . . you know that I love you . . ."

"And I love you, silly boy. But I also love Albert. So the two of you will just have to share me."

She headed up the stairs, the velvet train of her gown trailing behind her. The two men remained where they were, each unable to take that first fateful step.

Halfway up, she turned to look over her shoulder. "Please," she said, "don't disappoint me. Remember our music. Remember what it's like when we play together. And imagine the possibilities, the improvisations. The infinite variations."

Al and Harvey stood there in the darkened living room, staring at the floor, for at least sixty seconds.

Harvey sighed, finally, and turned towards the stairway. "Last one up," he said wryly, "is a rotten egg."

The Gift

Saskia Walker

Lowering my eyelids, I wait with bated breath for Chloe's instructions. I'm sitting on the edge of the bed, naked and ready. More than ready – my body is desperate with longing, my nipples growing hard as she approaches. As soon as she says my name, I look up at her, her willing doll as she applies my mascara.

That's when Mac walks in.

"Don't mind me," he says, nonchalantly. He struts across the room – wearing a black T-shirt, leather jeans and boots – carrying three glasses of wine. His presence multiplies the tension in the room tenfold. I was already struggling to retain my composure, but now he is here and the seal is on the deal. We're going to do it, the three of us.

I'd picked up the whispers at work. *They're swingers. They like to find a new playmate once in a while.* When I heard that, it all fell into place. As a couple they intrigued me. Mac watched on while Chloe was the social butterfly, chattering, hugging and kissing her friends. The people who whispered had no clue that it would heighten my interest. It turned me on. Being bi, it was bound to. Besides, I'd had a crush on Chloe since the day I met her. Once I met her boyfriend I couldn't get the pictures out of my head – erotic images of them together, and me getting in on the act. When Chloe asked me to come round to their place to prepare for club night with them, my libido and my imagination knew no bounds.

Mac sets one of the glasses down on the dressing table next to Chloe and then hands me the other. I swig from it gratefully, my blood pumping fast. He looks down at me, his eyes possessive as he surveys my naked body. Chloe undressed me while blithely informing me I was going to wear something of hers.

"Does Mac being here bother you?" She asks the question casually, but I know this is about my consent, consent to whatever follows.

I smile his way. "No, he doesn't bother me. Not in a bad way, at any rate."

Mac lifts his glass in my direction, apparently pleased by that. A sense of expectation exudes from him tonight. His eyes are hawk-like, not missing a thing, and his dark hair has been closely cropped, making him look even more mercenary than he normally does.

"Wonderful." Chloe inserts the mascara wand back in its shiny silver tube, and then runs her fingers through my shoulder-length hair. "Are you ready to get dressed?" Her kohl-lined eyes are bright and simmering with suggestion. "I always think the right clothing can make you feel even more *undressed*," she adds, suggestively.

I nod. I am *so ready*. Ready for it all. I want to touch her, hold her and taste her. I want to have her man climbing the walls because of what I'm doing to her.

Mac is pleased. "It's like a ritual for you women, getting dressed up to go out."

"I guess it is." If this was a ritual, was I the sacrifice?

Chloe chuckles. "He likes the way I get turned on about dressing up."

"That's understandable," I murmur, and Mac nods at me, silently exchanging the knowledge that we have in common.

Chloe walks to the wardrobe and opens the double doors with a flourish, the sleeves on her red silk kimono sliding against her beautiful pale skin. Chloe is all about fabrics: silks, velvets and leather. Their bedroom is a palace, decadent with sensual fabrics. Erotic prints punctuate the walls, offering suggestions for sex, everywhere. With one hand, she runs her black-lacquered fingernails over the club gear lined up at one end of the wardrobe. Her sleek black bob looks good with the red silk kimono, turning her into a 1930s silver screen diva. The kimono swings open and the soft pale skin of her cleavage, abdomen and bare pussy is revealed to me. It makes me want her more with every passing moment.

I watch as she flicks through the clothes, apparently deciding what to dress me in. We are near enough the same size, although I am not as luscious as Chloe. Mac moves and rests on the bed behind me, up against the headboard, while I sit naked between him and his girlfriend. I feel his gaze on me; hear the creak of his leather jeans at my back.

After some deliberation Chloe pulls out an outfit, clutching it against her, stroking the shiny surface to her breasts, her eyelids drop as she revels in the feeling of the luxurious, soft leather corset. "What's the golden rule?" she asks.

"Boots first, then corset." My naked skin tingles as I say the words. It was one of the first things she ever said to me, when I admired her boots on her first day in the office.

Chloe nods, grabs another hanger and steps over to the bed with them. She places the chosen items next to me. I stare down at them as she goes back to the wardrobe. Two black, boned corsets. One laces at the front, the other at the back. Mac makes a sound behind me when I stroke the leather, a sort of approving growl. My skin tingles with anticipation. Looking at Chloe I see that she is bending over, rooting about amongst the many pairs of boots piled at the bottom of the wardrobe. The red silk dips between her buttocks and thighs, gravitating into the heat there. I want to walk over, kneel down and rest my tongue against her pussy through the fabric, to wet and darken it with my mouth, making it stick to her groove. I could just picture how the damp silk would look clinging to her there.

She stands and walks back, carrying two pairs of boots. "You first," she says and drops one pair, unzipping the other pair one by one. "Left foot."

Resting my hands flat on the bed either side of my thighs, I lift my left foot, obediently watching as my damson-painted toenails disappear into the boot. When she puts on the second boot, she gestures at me and I stand. Turning me around, she instructs me. "Bend over, and I'll do them up for you."

I'm facing Mac now, and he looks like a dark master lazing nonchalantly against the pillows. I can't help noticing the bulge at his groin. I bend over, hands flat to the bed so that she can zip the boots up the back of my legs, all the way to my thighs. The sense of vulnerability I experience makes me dizzy. My bottom is facing Chloe, my breasts on display to the man of the house. I feel like Chloe's doll, and it's incredibly arousing. I drop my head, my hair trailing over my face.

The sound and bite and clutch of the zip as it pulls the leather tight around my legs race through my senses. She moves from one leg to the other, humming softly as she does, her hand stroking the leather on to my skin. Her breath is warm against the back of my thighs as she moves, and I long for it higher still. My clit is already painfully swollen in the folds of my pussy, and I fight the need to squirm and rub myself.

She stands up behind me, drawing me upright too, holding my arms steady as I find the measure of the tall, spiked heels, lifting one and then the other as the leather settles against my skin. Her hands curve round my buttocks and she squeezes them tightly, resting a kiss against my shoulder blade before she ducks down to pick up the corset. She's giving me the one that laces at the back, and I stare at Mac as she moves the garment around me, fleetingly squeezing my nipples between her finger and thumb. Mac watches all the while, his gaze hot. I have to close my eyes as I sway, delirious, savouring the touch of fingers and eyes on my body.

"You're so horny tonight," she murmurs against my ear, in a breathless voice that tells me how aroused she is too.

"Circumstances," I respond, and laugh softly. When I glance Mac's way, I find myself wondering what his cock looks like. The moment is surreal, but the fact that it's happening is making me so hot and slick that the tops of my thighs are damp.

She pulls the corset into place, lacing it quickly. Mac watches, and the bulge at his groin is getting bigger. My nipples practically burn with pleasure. The leather is hard against my skin, so tight.

"I want you to dress me now," she states.

She thinks this is dressed? No wonder it makes her feel even more undressed. Wearing only a pair of boots and a corset can do that. She shrugs her shoulders and her kimono falls to the floor, then she stands sideways to the bed. I kneel at her feet to zip her boots. They are PVC knee length, 1960s chic with massive, futuristic platforms. Dressed, she will look like a glossy manga diva. She is a chameleon, immediately at home in whatever time period she decides to adopt.

My hands shake as I zip the boots along the inside of her legs. With my hands around her PVC-clad calves, I glance at her shaven pussy, the urge to touch her there overwhelming. She's looking down at me and responds with a naughty smile.

"Is my girlfriend aroused?" Mac's question makes my stomach flip.

"Yes, very aroused. I think she likes this," I say from my place at her feet. I have such a crush on her that I am aching from it.

"Do you think she would like you to touch her, to make it better?"

"Maybe just a kiss," I whisper, the words catching in my throat.

"Naughty girl," Chloe says. She covers her pussy briefly with her hands, playfully, and then puts her hands back on her hips. I stare up at her as I kiss her pussy, sinking my tongue into its groove to seek out her clit. Her body grows taut, and she moans. That sound makes my hips roll and I close my eyes, revelling in the taste and feel of her in my mouth. Her clit is swollen and her folds slick. She wants this; the knowledge of that fact sends shivers through my core.

"Corset now," she murmurs, but I can see that it's taking all her effort not to break with her plans – because they are plans, I sense that now.

I stand and take the garment from her hands, lean in and wrap the leather around her torso. She holds it loosely in place while I begin to lace it up from the waist. As her breasts are gradually pulled tighter, and higher, I sigh. "You look so hot."

"So do you." She points at the full-length mirror on the wardrobe door.

I glance over. Yes. We look strangely obscene and powerful, with shiny black boots and corsets, our naked pussies proudly on display. I can see Mac on the bed in the background, sipping his wine, watching us. Instinctively, I move closer to Chloe, moulding against her.

"Ladies, you're not even laced up yet," Mac chastises mockingly.

I reach for the laces again. Oh, but squeezing her breasts tight in the leather is hot. It takes a while, but when we are done, Mac nods and smiles. "Now you're properly prepared."

"Prepared?" I repeat.

Chloe looks coy all of a sudden and she nibbles on her bottom lip quickly before speaking. "It's my birthday, and you're what I wanted."

My body tightens then liquefies inside a heartbeat. "Is that why you unwrapped me as soon as I arrived?"

She clutches at my elbows, holding me steady, which is just as well. Concern shines in her eyes. "Do you mind?"

"No. I'm honoured."

"When Mac met you, he thought you might want to be here."

Mac – the watchful one – he knew that I was interested, right back then. Perhaps they weren't swingers after all. Perhaps they were just looking for their third? I hoped so; I wanted that.

Leaning in, I kiss her. Her lips are so soft and they part easily, her hands closing around my naked hips as she melts into me. Pressing closer, I feel her bare pussy touch mine, and the shock-pleasure is too intense, like electricity sparking over my mound. I push her down on the bed and I'm on my knees in a flash, between her thighs, my mouth on her pussy, my hands stroking her PVC-covered calves. Her clit rears up from the swollen folds of her pussy. I circle it quickly, before nudging it back and forth.

"Oh . . . don't stop."

The thrill of hearing her say those words lights me. I reach out and flatten her on to the bed, my hand splayed beneath her breasts, my tongue barely breaking contact with her delicious pussy.

She lets out a cry of delight, her hips undulating. Sucking her off is hot enough to make me come, but she wants it all. Her hand lands on my head, and she pushes it up a little to lift me off. With the other hand, she clicks her fingers and moves two of them in a walking movement. I drop back, wiping my mouth with the back of my hand, licking her juices off my wrist while making her wait.

She purses those gorgeous lips of hers. "Oh you're so bad, no wonder I want you. Now get up here and 69 me."

Mac watches avidly, and I wonder if he's just going to observe, or get involved. I guess I'll find out soon enough. My heart throbs out a fierce rhythm. Climbing over her, I kiss her mouth, long and hard. Her lips part under mine as she relinquishes her strength to me.

"Let me have you," she urges.

My heart aches for her, and that's not all. Moving fast, I climb over her, turning as I do so, getting into position. The smell of leather and PVC and sex is ripe in the air. Hovering over her, I gasp when she latches her hands around the back of my thighs, where my boots end. My head drops and I breathe her in, my face between her thighs, my leather-covered breasts crushing against her. The combination of soft flesh and shiny black is so hot; my pulse thuds wildly in my groin, my nipples hard as nuts inside my corset.

Her mouth latches to my pussy, her tongue stroking me fast. Wild fire burns through me. My mouth on her clit, hers on mine, we are engulfed in each other. We move in time, leading each other on. Even as I sink into the total delirium, I'm aware of the movement on the bed. Mac is prowling. I feel his hands on my hips; he's behind me. When he pushes a finger into my gaping slit, I react, shoving my tongue inside Chloe.

I hear the sound of a condom wrapper, and I know he's going to fuck me from behind while this is happening. Chloe will be watching his cock going into me, and that makes my body squirm and my tongue move faster. Chloe's hips buck under me, and when Mac eases his cock inside me, she answers with her own assault, as if it's turning her on even more. She bites my flesh before ringing my clit with her tongue. Mac begins to thrust, hard and fast, filling me. Strung out on multiple sensations, I plunge my tongue inside her, my chin rubbing her clit as I do.

I hit home, my clit throbbing and my core in spasm. I hear Mac groan, and his cock jerks, his fingers tightening on my buttocks. Chloe's thighs tremble with pleasure on either side of my head. I lick her liquid heat as it dribbles from her, and she shudders to completion. When Mac pulls his cock free, I roll on to the bed beside Chloe, and keep her fingers loosely knotted in mine as we catch our breath.

Mac strips off his T-shirt before he lies with us. Quietly, we explore each other with curious touches and hungry kisses.

"Enough for you?" Mac teases, eventually.

"No, I want to do this all night, preferably in front of the mirror." I shouldn't have said that. This was their party.

"I've got a camcorder, if that would help," Mac offers.

"Oh, you say all the right things," I tease, and smile his way. He gives me a subtle nod as I continue to stroke Chloe.

She stares at me, her eyes warm with affection. "I've wanted to do this with you for weeks, so has Mac."

"Really?"

She nods. "Really."

Mac kicks off his boots. "I take it we're not going out tonight?"

"Why spoil a wonderful evening?" Chloe purrs, fondling my breasts where they are lifting from the corset

Mac is at my back, and he kisses my neck, grazing me with his teeth. I arch in response. "It's my birthday next week," he says, breathing against my skin.

"Sure it is," I respond.

"Oh, it is," Chloe confirms.

"Do you want me to come back then, gift wrapped?"

Mac thinks about that for a moment, and I feel his cock getting hard against the back of my thighs. "I think you should just stay with us, all week."

"Sounds good to me," I say, and settle between them, and it's right where I want to be.

More Than a Mouthful

Rachel Kramer Bussel

Sometimes all I want is a good fuck – or a good suck, I'm not picky. I know that as a modern woman, I'm supposed to ask for the whole package – a kind, sensitive, man who does his share of the housework and is gentle and patient, who also knows what to do with his dick – but there are moments when his package alone will do, and the bigger, the better. I just want it somewhere inside me, anywhere to quench that seemingly insatiable, overwhelming urge, the kind that can only be satisfied by a dick that's aching just as powerfully for me. Yes, there are times when I want to make love, to luxuriate in the sensation of skin on skin, of hard and soft, of his hands and lips grabbing me, taking me. Other times I just want it down and dirty, I want to be a whore of the highest order. Usually I get exactly what I want, but sometimes things don't go quite according to plan. What happened last week was an example of the latter.

I had just tried to wake long-term boyfriend, Hunter, up with a blow job. That's one of my favourite times to suck his cock, when he's sleeping like a baby, blissfully unaware of my intentions, and I get to take him from resting to aroused. I never feel more powerful, more full of womanly wiles, than I do when he hardens between my lips. Sometimes I just stare at him sleeping, his big body scrambling for air, loud snores wracking his frame, like he's afraid to settle into the true peace sleep can offer. I can stroke his shoulder or even plant a soft kiss on his back without him noticing. His dick and I do our own private dance as he stays in dream world until eventually the excitement awakens him. But sometimes, my oral approaches are less than welcome.

"That feels great, baby, but it's OK," he mumbled, pushing me off and turning over, the quilt clutched more tightly around him, shielding him from me. "I've got to get to work." He rolled away from me, shuddering as if something utterly distasteful had just occurred, or at least, that's how it felt to me. He rose and, without looking at me, pulled on boxers and a T-shirt and made his way across the room.

He didn't seem to notice the clear disappointment on my face, the way I stared up at him, not pouting, just hurt, rejected. And I didn't say a word. I just stumbled into the bathroom, sat on the toilet, and let silent tears crawl down my face while I listened to him boot up his computer.

I vowed that that would be the last time I'd try to wake him in such a way. If he wanted his cock sucked, he knew where to find me; by then I wasn't even sure his was the cock I wanted to fill me up. I stormed out of the house filled with pent-up sexual frustration and anger that I had let myself fall for someone so uninterested in sex he could reject me like that. I was better than that, deserved more from the person I'd pledged my heart and body to, damn it. My anger was all well and good, but it didn't lessen my desire to have my mouth stuffed, filled, used. The more I thought about it, the more I realized that not getting to be the good little cocksucker I can be was a deal-breaker, and if I couldn't get it from him, I was going to find someone to give me what I craved. I've always required some kind of oral stimulation, always found it exciting beyond belief to let a man trace his fingers over my tongue, to lick my way along a salty forearm, to tease an inner thigh with my teeth, to suck a finger (or two) when I'm getting fucked.

After that first morning of stomping down the street in my tallest heels with a pout on my face, slamming things around at my office – I run my own time-management consulting firm – I didn't stress about it any more. I felt a sense of calm wash over me. It wasn't an obsession so much as something I knew would happen when the time was right. After all, women like me who live for going down don't often go neglected for long.

Plus, the more I was made to wait, the more I'd appreciate it when I finally got that fat, juicy cock in my mouth – and, boy, was I right. My chance didn't come until four months later, an agonizing time during which I did my best to keep things cordial but never over-the-top with Hunter. We fucked, but in an understated way; we didn't paw and claw each other when we walked in the door. We were content to wait, where we hadn't been before. If he missed our more passionate days or thought I was in any way aloof, he didn't say anything, which only solidified my intention to sate my hunger elsewhere.

And elsewhere turned out to be a Caribbean cruise – a work thing, as it turned out. I was asked to speak to a group of business executives about time management. The pay wasn't great, but since it included a free trip, and I was overdue for a vacation, albeit a working one, I figured I couldn't say no. I did ask if Hunter could get comped along with me, but his boss said no, and part of me was relieved. I needed some time apart from him, to see who I could be without him clinging to me, a sensation that had been plaguing me since before the blow-job incident. I certainly wasn't about to pay for him myself, and he seemed more than happy to let me go by myself – much happier than I'd have been about unleashing him on a group of strangers for a week, all trapped on a confined vehicle, save for the times we'd be frolicking on sunny beaches in skimpy outfits (even work-related cruises have their downtime).

The week before the cruise flew by, and I gave Hunter only a kiss on the cheek as he slept through my early-morning departure. I kept largely to myself for the first two days, not wanting to get too chummy with anyone and then be caught off guard if I spied them in the audience, preparing my speech and wondering just how many hook-ups were happening on-board at that very moment. The crowd was mixed and while wedding rings abounded, I knew as well as anyone that didn't necessarily mean anything. I hoped someone was getting some, anyway; all I had was my hand and the little clit-stimulation vibrator I'd brought with me, one I'd found worked much better with penetration than without.

I also worked out in the gym on-board, sweating away the stress and the sexual tension, pumping iron and jogging until I returned to my room spent. When it came time to give my speech, I was mellow, focused, fully prepared and, to be immodest for a moment, I can safely say that I nailed it. I wowed them, making them laugh at all the right moments, seeing nods of recognition, smiles of excitement as I promised them that they too could have everything they ever wanted, fulfil every wish, if they only took a stronger command of their schedules. You can learn to be punctual, organized and on top of things, but some of us need more training than others. I shared my own journey, and finished to a rousing round of applause, followed by a line twenty-people deep waiting to talk to me.

After about an hour, only two people were left – two very hot guys, both tall, muscular, exuding testosterone, who seemed to know each other well. One was a redhead, his shock of bright locks glowing from the light while the other had a round, bald black head. Together they looked almost comical, but they were friends from Seattle, both in charge of their own successful start-ups, but concerned that they spent all their time on work, with little left for play. And it seemed that both of them were more than happy to ignore my wedding ring as they chatted me up. The cruise director came over and thanked me, and I figured, while I wrapped up my business with him, my new friends, Sean and Rick, would take off, but they were waiting for me when I finished things up.

"Want to get a drink?" Rick asked, touching my arm and sending heat running along my skin. Then Sean touched my other arm and the twin forces seemed to race to meet in my centre.

I looked from one to the other, then smiled a tiny smile, realizing that far from home, way out at sea, I was very likely about to get my chance to avenge the misbegotten blow job, to redeem my cock-sucking skills in a way I had never imagined.

We went through the usual social niceties, save for the alcohol on my part, which surely would have helped get this particular party started. Without it, I was reminded yet again that one of us would have to make the first move, and while they were sitting on either side of me, their barstools as close as could be, neither had mentioned anything about going back to my room, or one of theirs. So finally, as I saw the last customers other than us leave the bar in favour of bingo and dancing, I turned to Rick and began stroking his sexy, bald head. "I've never been with a . . . bald man before," I said, because it was true. Then I leaned forwards and kissed him, our lips meeting briefly as equals before his swallowed mine. I hoped Sean would get my silent message that kissing Rick was in no way meant to exclude him. Already, I knew I'd found the men who'd provide me with much more than the mouthful of cock I'd been craving. When I felt Sean massaging the back of my neck, his fingers kneading me there, making me moan against Rick's lips, I knew we'd each gotten the message loud and clear.

I was sure one of the bartenders was about to tell us to get a room, and didn't want those I'd just lectured to about to-do lists and next-action items to see me sandwiched between two men, as hot as they were, so I extricated myself, stood up, and simply offered a hand to each of them, leading them down the hall to my suite, grateful that a quirk of fate had gotten me a king-size bed rather than a twin.

Some women would take the opportunity to get naked with two hot guys as the perfect time to try double penetration. But I could do that with a butt plug and a big fat vibrator, and I do, often. That wasn't what I was looking for, not tonight, anyway. I had something even naughtier in mind, and I was going to make sure they were both so turned on they wouldn't dream of saying no. I may have been cheating, but I felt like I deserved it – plus, when would such a glorious opportunity come my way again?

The two men followed me, as if that had been their plan all along. Who knows? Maybe it had been. Maybe they were used to taking a woman home with them together. Maybe they were the kings of threesomes and often found women who were more than willing to double team them. But I had a feeling this was as new to them as it was to me, the latter a secret I hoped to never reveal. For tonight, I didn't want to be some sheltered girl who was trembling with nerves, at least, on the outside. I wanted to be the kind of red-blooded woman who craved not just cock, but cocks. Who was so adept at sucking them that she could take two at once, easily, one whose offers were never rebuffed because she was just that good.

My mouth watered – as did my pussy – as the image of me with their dicks in my mouth simultaneously filled my head. There was no room in my body for the hot shame of tears I'd felt earlier that morning, even though if I tried I could feel that gentle push on my shoulder, feel Hunter moving me along as if I were some unwanted obstacle in his path to success, some annoying girl with her incessant demand for blow jobs rather than the one he'd told me was the only girl for him. I guess technically I still was; he'd said he loved me, not that he wanted his dick sucked in the morning, though to me, those two were inseparable.

I knew rationally that his universe was the mixed-up one, because in real life, men should be drooling, begging, utterly undone when faced with a woman who can't wait to take their cocks all the way down her throat, then wish she had more to choke her with. But be that as it may, I needed to be shown, not just told by the voices in my head, that I was the best cocksucker in the world (or at least, one of them), like the way after a break-up friends tell you to get back between the sheets straight away. To erase the sting of oral rejection, I had to get back in the game, big time.

Soon there was a hand on each of my ass cheeks, manly fingers squeezing and caressing, and in the elevator, each man reached beneath my dress. Fingers on each hip slid my panties down just enough for the cool air to reach my lips before they began exploring my wetness. We were headed to the penthouse and had a ways to go before reaching the climax of our ride, and I humped those fingers back as they slid inside me while the other pair circled my clit hard with a thumb.

I could tell they thought one particular thing was going to happen; they were going to fuck me, either together or one at a time. I was going to lie there and let them, maybe arch up into them, moan a little, have an orgasm or two. But they'd be the ones taking me, penetrating me, and I let them think that. "Face the mirror," said Sean, his red head appearing behind mine as he pressed my hands flat against it. Then Rick's dark skin was before me, his fingers dipping into my already low-cut blouse, exposing my nipple. Seeing the pink bud there in the mirror made it all more real, and I was lucky that we arrived at our floor when we did, otherwise I might have been caught mid-act in front of strangers who may or not have been pleased to see a woman with two cocks in her mouth. As wild as I may be, that was for behind locked doors.

In moments, that's where we were. Rick turned on the radio and I moved into Sean's arms. I wanted to take control but he had his hands on my ass, kneading my cheeks, and then Rick was behind me, lifting my dress up. Sean pulled it all the way up, then over my head. I watched it land on the floor as Rick pushed my panties down while Sean began stroking my breasts, holding their weight in his hands. I stared at his erection, hoping I'd get to see it unveiled soon. Rick's fingers slipped between my legs and I trembled, arching against his touch despite myself.

"What do you want, Carla?" Sean asked as he pushed my breasts together, then sucked both my nipples at once, his mouth providing both relief and a tease. It had been a long time since they'd been more than briefly caressed. What they were doing felt so good – Sean's lips there, Rick's fingers there – that I was hesitant to call a halt to their ministrations just so I could get down on my knees. But then I turned around to look at Rick and the outline of his dick made me gasp. It was huge, straining against the front of his pants, and I reached for it.

Then I turned so I could touch each of them, a cock in each hand. "I want you both to get naked, and then sit down next to each other on the bed. I'm going to give you the best blow job of your life. Please, don't say no. That's part of why I took this gig – to find a man who'd let me use my mouth the way God intended, to fill me up so deep. And now there are two of you." I couldn't talk any more; I was so wet, so horny, but underneath, also tense, wondering if this hunky pair would prove to be just like my man, the one I'd thought was full of as much testosterone as I could stand, but who was proving that bed death isn't just a lesbian thing.

"Do it for me. Let me." I stepped back, not wanting to beg. Sean looked at my body longingly, running a hand from my cheek down my neck and shoulder, his fingers warm as they travelled along my skin.

"Give me a second," said Rick, and I watched his chocolate-brown fingers slide between my legs, pressing upwards. He made a show of entering me, then pulling out so we could all see my dew coating him. That brief touch felt so good, but this wasn't about my pussy any more, but my pride. I needed to avenge myself as a girl who knows her way around a dick, not simply gratify my basest needs. And besides, fucking is always, 100 per cent of the time, better once I've swallowed a man's come, once I've worked my way up. Sex should be a reward for a blow job well done, a reward I'm well primed for by virtue of being on my knees, savouring his essence. When I don't get to put my taste buds into action, I feel deprived, like we're skipping some essential step in the process.

And going home without having done the deed, even if I got pounded by these two studs, would've meant I'd somehow failed. I needed those dicks in my mouth, and I needed them there now. Rick raised his fingers and I shut my eyes and opened my mouth, and he fucked me with them. There's a big difference between a man letting you suck on his fingers and fucking your mouth with them, all the difference in the world, really. When he simply places them there gently, he allows you to take over, to lift your tongue to the salt of his skin, to wrap your lips tightly around his fingers, to mould yourself around him. When he fucks your mouth, he claims it as his own, lets you know that your mouth is for his use, not yours. It's the rare man who really knows how to fuck a woman's mouth with his hand like that; most of the men I've been with get too excited by the way it feels, too aroused by the warm wetness, the reminder of its similarity to her pussy, the promise of what might happen.

But Rick read me perfectly. He got me ready, had me rocking my head back and forth in time with his thrusts, as my juices slowly dribbled down my thighs, my legs trembling.

Then he abruptly took them away. I lifted my head, opened my eyes, and watched them undress. Rick proudly pulled down his zipper, his giant cock popping free, while Sean was slower, as if he had some reason to be ashamed (he so didn't). He looked down at his cock, then up at me, and finally, at Rick. I didn't know if either had been in a situation quite like this, one where it wasn't just about getting a girl off, together, but about the energy passing between three people.

After all, I wasn't about to let their dicks touch in my mouth without making them kiss each other first. I took off my bra, stepped out of my panties, but kept my heels on. I like to feel them pressing into my feet when I'm on the ground, curling against me, reminding me that I'm servicing a man, even when it feels like he's servicing me. I walked towards Sean, turning him and marching him towards the bed. I peeled back the covers and pushed him down, then crooked my finger at Rick to join us. They sat so close they were touching, their dicks standing at attention, all for me. I stood, my breasts in front of their faces, then reached for Rick's cock while I kissed Sean. Rick reached up and grabbed my ass, and once again, I had to remind myself of my mission. I could've easily straddled either man, sank down in one fast motion, switching off my mouth's salivating instincts and telling my pussy to take over. But I resisted the lure of that luscious dick for a few more moments.

I stood and pushed their faces together into one of the hottest kisses I've ever seen, slow and hot, manly and sensual at once. "You two are so gorgeous," I said. "You could make a lot of money renting yourself out to horny rich women. Or just photographing these two cocks." I pushed them together, rubbing the pre-come-laden heads against each other. They pulled apart and stared down at their now-joined cocks, as if they'd never seen such a beautiful sight. Maybe they hadn't; it wasn't the time to ask.

Even more than I loved simply being in the room with two naked men, I loved manipulating them, knowing they were at my mercy. I liked the idea that they were straight, for the most part, yet would do this favour for me, would let me have my fun by joining them together. I knelt down before them, never surrendering an inch of that feminine power as I pressed their dicks together, one white like mine, one brown, both equally gorgeous. When I tried to wrap my mouth around both heads at once, to my disappointment – but not theirs – I couldn't. I opened as wide as I could, but still, they were too big for me. Maybe two smaller cocks could've made it, but I didn't want anyone else's.

Instead, I made sure they both got a treat. I licked each head, alternating so neither man would feel left out. I shut my eyes and tried to forget which dick was which, because it didn't really matter. I slid my thumb along the wet slit of one as I pressed my mouth down on the other. Sean and Rick each murmured their encouragement, as invested in our oral ménage-à-trois as I was. When I opened my eyes at one point, I was faced with a wall of cock, both flush against the other, and it seemed less like I was going down on them than that we were all having sex with one another.

I shifted down to lick their balls, something I used to find odd but have grown to love, those tender sacs the opposite of the hard poles I held in my hands. Knowing I could get two men off made me feel invincible, like I could handle – and enjoy – an army of men. When I said to Rick, "I want to swallow your cock," he groaned and guided my lips to his dick.

Sean stroked my hair, encouraging me, and when I looked up at him, he said, "I'm next." Satisfied, I started in on the best part of a blow job: deep-throating. It's not for everyone, but to me, it's the greatest test of my sexual skills, and the surest way to make my pussy ache. Often, it gets me in trouble, because I suck a guy off so well he's spent for a while, leaving me wanting. But I had a plan: I'd suck Rick, then Sean, to climax, then take a ride on each of them.

I concentrated fully on Rick's huge dick, which stretched my mouth and meant I had to fully focus on what I was doing. But even with such steady focus, I could feel Rick breathing, stroking, observing. It made me all the more excited, like this was meant to be. If Hunter hadn't pushed me aside, maybe I wouldn't be getting this luscious opportunity. I sucked in as much air through my nose as I could while letting Rick invade my mouth. There was a point at which I surrendered some of my power, let it melt on my tongue until Rick was fucking me, fucking my mouth as surely as he'd later fuck my pussy. "That's it," he said, and our eyes locked as I rose up and down under his guidance. With one hand wrapped around his shaft, I reached for Sean's leg, needing to hold him too as Rick started to thrust harder into me, until all of a sudden, he was coming. He announced it with a yell, and soon his semen was flooding my mouth. I eased up enough so I could swallow as best I could, though some of it dribbled out.

I panted, my eyes glazed, as I finally slid off him. He thanked me by roughly pinching my nipples, making me pant and then bite my lip. And he didn't stop. No, Rick kept right on toying with my nipples as I shifted my attention on to Sean. At first, I thought this wasn't really fair. How could I be expected to give another sensational blow job when my body was being distracted, tormented and teased? Well, somehow I did, and I think what I lacked in finesse I made up for with the sloppy fervour with which I swallowed Sean's cock. He could see that Rick was fingering my pussy, then hear him smacking my ass, then sense that he'd put his head between my legs. I didn't talk dirty to Sean, didn't tell him how delicious his cock was, how even though it wasn't as fat as Rick's, it was long and hit that spot at the back of my throat that makes me cream.

He stopped me before he could shoot down my throat. "No?" I asked, disappointed.

"I want to come on your face," he said, his voice husky and serious.

"Oh my God," was all I could say as I shut my eyes. He slapped his dick against my cheek, as I once again submitted, this time to two men at once. I could tell Rick was hard again and he teased me by slapping his dick against my ass as Sean rained come down on my face, then slid down so he could kiss me.

I was ready for anything by that point, as long as it involved me getting fucked. Rick handed me a condom and with trembling fingers I unrolled it on to his dick, which seemed even bigger than it had earlier. Instead of having me face him, though, he lay down and positioned me astride him, facing away – reverse cowgirl. This gave Sean the chance to play with my tits, to suck on my clit, to look at every inch of me, and he took all those chances and more. The two fucked me in tandem just as well as if they'd been doing double penetration. As the sensations swept over me, I grabbed Sean's hand and stuffed four fingers in my mouth, that needy orifice begging for more. His stray hand roamed his friend's body, adding to the erotic current between us. I may have bitten his fingers as I came, I don't really know. I lost it there at the end, shaking and trembling, overwhelmed by Rick's giant cock, his hands slamming my hips up and down, Sean's hot tongue flaming against me. All I know is that I came and saw lights in front of my eyes, then leaned back so I was resting against Rick's chest as he pumped me up and down before coming again.

It's hard for me to believe sometimes that I'm an expert in time management, when sex – good sex, that is – is enough to make me forget that time even exists. I spent every free minute of the rest of the cruise with the two men, and though we exchanged numbers and email addresses, I knew we weren't going to try to take this off the boat.

Oh, and when I got home, I split up with Hunter, making a clean break. No more sex, and the great irony was that as I was leaving, he begged me for one final blow job. "Find another girl. I'm busy," I said . . . and, for the rest of the night, I was. It's not too difficult to find a man who likes his dick sucked if you're a girl like me, but I'd forgotten that for a while. I'm grateful to Sean and Rick for reminding me.

Gift Exchange

Sommer Marsden

Evan brought it up as we were decorating the tree. I think he truly believed that, if he caught me off guard, I would agree without hesitation.

"You know what would make a great Christmas gift?"

I fully intended to say, "No," but had to appreciate his creativity. "Dare I ask?" I laughed, hanging a tiny carved stone angel on the tree.

"My fantasy. You could make my fantasy come true for Christmas. Number five is a year to celebrate, don't you think?"

"So, since this is our fifth Christmas together, you'd like me to give you the gift of infidelity?" I took a delicate glass shamrock from the box of ornaments.

"It's not infidelity if I ask for it," he said, smiling. He looked a little crestfallen, though. Perhaps he had fully convinced himself his scheme would work. "It's only cheating if you do it behind my back. I want you to do it in front of me."

I stared at his face, set in stubbornness and hope. "Fine. I'll do it. But you have to play, too. Not just with me. With him." I only realized my words once they were out and a line of anxiety snaked through my belly. Where the fuck had that come from?

Evan's look of hope turned quickly to shock. "What?"

I threw my shoulders back and swallowed hard. Apparently, I had a few kinks of my own. No backing down now. "You heard me. Here's the deal – I'll do it. You start him off. Prime the pump, so to speak." I couldn't resist the evil smile that stretched across my face. No way would he go for this. "And

I'll take him home. Right there in front of you. Whatever you want."

Evan let the string of lights fall to the floor and sat heavily on the misplaced sofa. We'd had to slide it to the middle of the room to make way for the tree. Lucky for him. I think he might have just hit the floor had the sofa not been there.

"Allyson, I'm not gay."

"I never said you were." I calmly selected another bauble and placed it on the tree. That was that. I was off the hook.

"But wouldn't that mean I was?" His face had gone a floury white with the exception of his cheeks. A red flush flamed across his cheeks like a brand.

"No. Don't be ridiculous. It's the means to an end. That would turn me on and allow you to get what you want. You'd get your fantasy and provide me with mine."

I was very proud of myself. I had not only discovered one of my secret desires, one I had no intention of acting out, I had also found a way to put Evan's fantasy to rest. I smiled to myself, feeling quite smug, as I started to hang the glass pickle from Germany near the highest bow.

"OK, I'll do it."

The pickle shattered at my feet. *Damn.*

"What?" I turned around to find him smiling at me. My stomach did a flip that reminded me of being on the roller coaster as a kid. Sick and excited at the same time.

"It's only fair. You're absolutely right. Fair is fair. We both win. I can do that for you. I would do that for you."

I let the conversation go until dinner. Even as I cooked, a swirling of excitement and dread rolled through my body. The dread was from being caught in my own trap. The excitement was over the prospect of actually doing this with Evan. *For* Evan. I hadn't even considered the idea that I would actually like to see him with another man until I had blurted it out. I had most certainly never considered the idea that I would actually go through with something like this. Yet, as I cracked a nice bottle of Shiraz for dinner, I knew I would.

In the pit of my stomach the excitement burned brighter. A moisture started between my legs, insinuating itself into the soft fabric of my panties. I laughed out loud wondering if I would even make it through dinner before I fucked Evan senseless.

"What's so funny?" he asked, poking his head in the kitchen.

"How hungry are you?" I asked, pouring two glasses of wine. Red like blood. Red for sacrifice. Red for desire.

I would sacrifice a long-held value for him, and him for me. I would give him his desire and he would fulfil mine. My nipples puckered under my blouse, my pulse slammed in my throat. I was blushing so fiercely my face burned.

He stared me dead in the face. Read my expression. He grabbed my hand. "I can wait."

We made it to the landing. At that point, location didn't matter. Not a lick. I shoved Evan to the floor where he landed with a startled "Ooph!"

"Sorry, sorry," I murmured, but I really wasn't. I was too busy yanking the top button of his button-fly jeans. After the first one heeded to my brutal yanking, the others followed suit. I took his cock in my hand and let my body slide down several steps so my mouth was even with him. I was suddenly ravenous for him. Just to have him in my mouth. Feel the slide of his warm, engorged cock against the inside of my cheeks. Over my tongue. I sucked him in as far as I could, relaxed my throat, took him in as deep as I could. The thought of what we were considering burned under my skin like a fever. Could I? Would I? What would it do to us? All of this flitted and capered in my mind as I worked him. Swallowed him.

"Christ, what's gotten into you?" he mumbled and shoved his hands into my hair. Sifted his fingers through it so black strands brushed against my face. Tendrils got trapped in the moisture on my lips, slid along his length along with my mouth. I sighed against him and cupped his balls. "It's this whole thing, isn't it? You're getting excited about it, aren't you? Me doing that for you. Letting you see me do it. Now do you understand what I want?"

Part of me wished he would shut the fuck up. Part of me prayed he wouldn't. I needed to hear this. Needed to know that he wanted it just as badly as I did. I was still reeling from the fact that I wanted it at all and if he told me he was OK, told me he wanted it, I might not question my sanity. Or my devotion. Or my love for him.

I nodded but didn't release him. He wrapped my hair around his hands and pulled me in a little harder. Forced his cock a little deeper. I sucked in air through my nose and closed my eyes. The scent of him seated deeply in my sinuses. The feel of him making me crazy.

I felt him tense and laughed just a little around his cock. I loved that feeling. The feeling of pushing him right up to the edge and then shoving him right over it. Making him come for me. Evan had other plans. He pushed my head back and released himself.

"Evan . . ."

"Over. On your back, Allyson. Now." His voice was much deeper than normal and my body responded instantly. Extra moisture between my thighs. Hair standing at attention along the nape of my neck, like a sizzle of electricity shooting through all my nerve endings simultaneously.

He hauled me up the steps, flipped me on my back and undid my jeans. "Help me. These goddamn things are so tight I don't know how you breathe in them."

I lifted my hips, wiggled. When they were down around my thighs, he hooked his fingers in the sides of my thong and yanked that along with the jeans. Both items were flung down the steps.

No words. He was gone from words. His cock so hard and ready it was imposing. His eyes, usually brown, were nearly black. He shoved my thighs apart roughly and thrust three fingers into me so quickly I gasped. Then, grabbing my hips, he pulled me forwards and drove into me.

"Fuck," he hissed in my ear. "Are we really going to do it?"

I rocked up as he pulled me against him. Two forces with the same objective. Wrapped my legs around his back to hang on. Felt my eyes roll back as the first forceful ripple of orgasm ripped through me. I rode it out. Let it flow. It spiralled out, a seemingly unending coil of pleasure. "Yes," I sighed as I let my body go limp even as he clutched at me.

At the word, Evan came. His voice half growl, half sob. I'd give him his gift, and he'd give me mine.

When we finally sat down to dinner, I sipped my wine and then asked, "So who's the third party?"

Evan shrugged and attacked his spaghetti, apparently famished. I laughed and he looked up and smiled. There was a tiny speck of sauce on his chin and I wiped it off. "We could scout someone out this weekend," he said.

"What's this weekend?" I hadn't touched my food. I was perfectly content with my glass of wine and the speculation.

"The community block party. A Christmas jamboree." He laughed. "We can see if anybody catches our interest then."

I nodded, stirred my noodles but didn't eat them. "Sounds good." Now that he had put the thought in my head, I already had a possible candidate.

I hadn't shared the information. I had somehow managed to keep it to myself despite some covert spying on the new neighbour. The more I watched him, the more I thought he would be perfect. I think my fear was that if I came right out and said it, instead of letting the idea come from Evan, he would think I desired this man more than him. That wasn't the case. But the fear of him thinking so was enough to make me keep my mouth shut.

"Ready?" Evan pulled on his suede jacket – the one with the shearling lining. I joked it was his Marlboro Man jacket.

"As I'll ever be," I laughed. It was slightly high. Slightly hysterical. Not a calm laugh, but one full of anxiety and excitement. I cinched the tie on my leather jacket and fluffed my hair. "Let's do it."

The winter block party was about to begin. Much like a summer block party but the street was peppered with chimineas instead of barbeque grills. Most houses were open to guests. People congregated out in the cold, warming their hands and chatting around the small fires, or wandered in and out of each other's homes for lovely buffets and booze aplenty. Any door that was open was an invitation to the open house within.

"You sure you don't have any ideas?" he asked. His face said he thought I might. It was a gentle question, though, not an accusation.

I took his hand and gave it a squeeze. It was solid and warm and familiar. A hand that had run over every inch of my body, given me untold pleasure, knew me inside and out. I squeezed again and tried to stay as close to the truth as possible. "I've considered a few. Some of them are definitely out; some are possible. We just have to be careful. We need someone discreet, preferably unattached. Open-minded." I sighed and stood on my toes to kiss him.

Evan kissed me back. He cupped my face with those big warm hands as his tongue played around my own. I shivered despite the jacket. We were really going to do this. We were scouting for a lover. He would start; I would finish. Another shiver worked through me and he laughed. "Nervous?"

"A little."

"Excited?"

"A lot." This time it was my turn to laugh. I took his hand again and pulled him forwards. "Come on, then. He's not going to come find us. We have hunting to do."

I saw him before we were even halfway up the block. Christopher Sweet had moved in just two months earlier. He was just a guy. Not too pretty, not too slick. A normal guy with normal-guy looks. The only thing that really made him stand out from the crowd was the way his eyes lit up when he laughed, and the laugh itself. Slow and warm like thick syrup dripping from a bottle. The sound of that laugh was enough to warm me from the inside out. Starting deep between my thighs and spreading up and out like a starburst under my skin. There had been an attraction the moment I had introduced myself the day he moved in. I had ignored it. I knew it was human nature to feel attraction even in a committed relationship. Human nature to flirt, even. If I was honest with myself, though, if there was going to be a third party, I wanted it to be Christopher.

I felt Evan watching me watch Christopher. Then he turned to look too. "Is it him?" he said.

Before I could answer, Christopher spotted our combined stares and raised his hand in a friendly wave. He grabbed three beers from a snow bank and started our way.

"Allyson, he's coming. Is it him?"

I was afraid to answer. Afraid of the feeling in the pit of my stomach. The trembling flutter of my pulse in my throat. What were we doing? This was crazy. I loved Evan and I was risking it. This would ruin us. Ruin everything. I would lose him.

Evan squeezed my hand again and then he smiled. That warm open smile that had made me fall in love with him. A smile that always let me know everything would be OK. "Allyson, it's OK. If it's him, it's OK."

So I nodded and smiled back despite an aching urge to cry. "It's him," I breathed just as Christopher arrived.

"Hey, guys. Happy holidays! What's going on?"

"Not much," Evan said, accepting a beer with thanks. "We were just discussing what we were going to get each other for Christmas."

I accepted a beer and my numb lips nearly lost the liquid as I drank. The only thing that kept me from dropping the green bottle and running was Evan's warm arm around my shoulder. His fingers paling gently in my hair. Something that always calmed me. I laughed at a joke Christopher told and when he laughed along with me, I felt my insides warm a little. Some of the fear ebbed away and was replaced with a smoky curl of desire.

We wandered the street, the three of us, stopping to warm ourselves at the outdoor fires, laughing, chatting the way neighbours should. On beer three, Evan took the lead. Once the sentence was out, I felt a shock ripple through me. No turning back.

"Do you want to come home and have a real drink with us?" Evan asked, his gaze sliding to me for just a second. His smile was warm and comforting. "I'm getting a little cold, and judging from the look on Allyson's face, she's half frozen."

I nodded, knowing full well that half of the cold blanketing my body was from nerves. "We have that nice bottle of Merlot."

Christopher smiled and gave a good-natured shrug. "Sure, why not? I don't know most of these people real well anyway. I could go for defrosting all my fingers and toes."

We started up the street together, the two men ahead of me. Christopher taller and blond. Evan closer to my height, with thick dark hair. Two sets of broad shoulders. Two men walking side by side. For just an instant, my mind supplied another picture. Evan on his knees before Christopher. His mouth around Christopher's cock. Moving. Sucking. I shivered again, but not from the cold. I had never realized how badly I wanted to see something like that. What it would do to me. How it would make me feel. In the next half-hour I should know if it was a possibility. At least with Christopher.

"Wow. I love the colour." Christopher touched the newly painted wall in the dining room. I had chosen the colour. A pale buttery yellow. New England yellow. I watched his hands trail over the wall I had painted just two weeks before. My skin prickled as if he were touching me. A flush crept up from between my breasts to heat my face.

"Thank you. I had to choose a colour that wasn't too girly." I laughed, flashing a fake look of frustration at Evan.

"Well, you did a good job. Elegant without being too feminine. Enough colour to add to the house, but not overwhelming. Great choice. And it makes the furniture stand out. Really makes the old pieces look that much more elegant."

I knew Christopher made furniture. His praise of my grandmother's pieces was touching. I cleared my throat. "I'll go get that wine." I moved a little too quickly into the kitchen. Evan might have noticed the urgency in my gait, I doubted Christopher did.

I was wrong. I heard him say, "Is she OK? Should I leave?"

I strained to hear Evan's response as I grabbed three glasses and the corkscrew. It was fading, though. He was leading Christopher into the living room where we had built a fire. I uncorked the wine and realized my hands were shaking just as I nearly lost my grip on the corkscrew. It clattered to the counter and I put my head down to breathe. What would I find when I walked into the living room. What look would be on that nice man's face? Disgust? Confusion? Fear? My stomach flipped again and I sucked in a breath as if I were drowning.

"You'll never know unless you go in," I whispered to myself. I glanced out the tiny window over the sink. The sky was darkening and I could just barely make out the fact that it was snowing. A beautiful light snow that danced on the fading light. Elegant and peaceful. I stared for a moment. Let my heart rate slow, listened to the sound of the blood rushing in my ears fade. I would be fine. We were asking. The worst he could say was "No."

Gathering the glasses and the wine bottle, I took a few slow steps towards the dining room. Let myself grow even more calm. Then I walked out to see if Evan was making any progress.

I walked in and both sets of eyes were on me. Two beautiful men. One blond and blue-eyed, the other with gorgeous dark hair and startling eyes the colour of chicory-laced coffee. Both were smiling. Easy smiles. I felt a spark of excitement lick up my skin, raising goosebumps in its wake. Those two smiles on me were as intense as two sets of hands sliding along my skin. That intimate. That intense. I almost lost my grip on the glasses.

"How about Christmas Eve?" Evan asked, standing quickly and relieving me of my burden. He poured three glasses of wine and handed them out until we each had one. "The day after tomorrow?"

I cleared my throat to steady my voice. "It's fine," I said. Then I laughed. Another high, twittering laugh so unlike my normal throaty laugh. "You're OK with this?" I asked Christopher. His eyes travelled over me, soaked me in, and again I had the overwhelming sensation of being physically touched.

"I am."

"And Evan explained it all? *All* of it?" I said a little too forcefully. I could see Evan nodding in my peripheral vision. I knew Evan. Knew he had. Of course he had. I still had to ask.

Another slow nod from Christopher and another easy smile. As easy and slow and sweet as that laugh of his. "I get it. He starts, you finish. I'm the odd man out. Or in. I guess it depends on how you look at it. Either way, it's fine with me."

I nodded and tried to sip my wine. Instead I managed to down almost the whole glass in one gulp. "You OK?" Evan said in my ear. His breath hot on my skin and familiar. Safe. He filled my glass and handed it back. "You can change your mind. You don't have to do anything you don't want to do. You're more important to me than anything. That includes this fantasy of mine."

But I realized as I cautiously sipped my refill that his fantasy had become mine. I loved him. Wanted to make him happy. I also wanted what I wanted. What I had asked for and he was willing to give me that. Fear of the unknown would not eat this dream whole, I decided. If we got through this in one piece, still together, we could be that much stronger for the experience. The exchange. The giving and receiving could be the best thing that ever happened to us. Or it could destroy us. I knew this, too; I wasn't a fool. But I was willing to take the risk and hope.

Christopher sat on one end of the sofa, watching me. Judging my reaction. I swallowed hard and fought off the cold finger of fear that trailed up my spine. I would be fine. We would be fine. Better than fine.

Evan took my hand and led me to the sofa. I took a final sip of wine and put the glass on the coffee table as I sat. Right next to Christopher. Close enough that my thigh pressed up against his. Evan sat on my other side and rubbed my arm. "You sure about this?"

I nodded not trusting my voice. Then he leaned forwards and kissed me. I tightened up for just a second, second-guessing something that is normally the most natural thing in the world for me. Kissing Evan. In public, in private, it didn't matter. I did it easily. Now, though, feeling Christopher's eyes on us as we kissed, I felt suddenly stiff. Then Evan's tongue pressed against the seam of my lips. Licked me gently. I loosened, felt myself go soft and opened my mouth to him. The kiss deepened, he pushed his tongue into me further, probing gently and warmly with his. My body responded – years of pleasure, years of enjoyment. My nipples tightened. And, as the kiss continued, I felt hands that were not Evan's on my breasts. Hands that I had looked at, wondering what they would feel like on my body. Now I didn't have to wonder. A slow tremble worked through me, and I gasped into Evan's mouth.

Christopher's hands were bigger than Evan's. His touch was firm but gentle. Unfamiliar and intoxicating. I arched up into the kiss and into the hands that were on me. Pressing against two different points of contact that mingled into one vortex of pleasure. I felt Evan reach over my lap, heard Christopher draw a startled breath. Not breaking the kiss, I opened my eyes just a bit, just enough to peek. Evan's hand slid the length of Christopher's denim-clad erection. Each sweep of his hand defined the other man's cock through his jeans. I watched, mesmerized. The kiss went on. Christopher's fingers plucked my nipples. The sight of Evan stroking another man was . . . A moan escaped me. I wasn't even aware it was coming. I shifted on the sofa – the moisture pooling in my panties was both pleasant and torturing.

I watched Evan run his thumb over the head of Christopher's cock, heard the scratchy whisper of denim being stroked. Then Evan broke the kiss. Christopher left his hands on my breasts. Then, after a long moment of warm contact, he removed them. Evan pulled his hand from Christopher's lap, and we all regarded each other.

"Are we all still OK with this?" Evan asked in his normal, no-nonsense tone. There was just a touch of trepidation in his voice. Only I would notice.

I nodded. "I am." My voice was small but firm. My heart was banging restlessly away in my breast. I felt just a tiny bit light-headed.

"I'll be back night after tomorrow," Christopher said, and stood. He brushed his hand along the length of my hair. Stroking me as if I were made of glass. Then he shook Evan's hand.

"We'll see you then," Evan said with a small smile.

"I'll be here with bells on." His rich liquid laugh filled the room for a moment and I held my breath at the sensual sound. Then he dropped me a wink and left.

"Bed? At least for a while?" Evan smiled. His eyes wandered my body, never staying on one spot for too long. I flushed under his gaze. He took my hand and led me to the bedroom without another word.

Sunday afternoon finally arrived, and I was already exhausted. Saturday had taken a hundred years to pass. I'd already had countless arguments in my mind both for and against what we were planning to do. One moment the anticipation and excitement nearly stopped my breath, the next the fear of it did. I would gasp. Unable to breathe. Panicky and unsure of my mental state. And then, for just a moment, I would see Evan. Unaware that I was watching him. Humming. Reading. Puttering in the yard. And I would think of how much I loved him. How much I wanted to give him this thing he had wanted for so long. To be the woman who finally said, *Yes, I love you enough to do this for you and give you something you desire.* And I would be OK, before the cycle started again.

Dinner came and we had an hour to go. I was too nervous to eat. I drank my wine and pushed my food around on the plate.

"Not hungry?" Evan's eyes were kind. Worried even. They were that mocha colour that always made me stare a beat longer than I normally would. Flecks of green and gold and blue. Like looking at a picture within a picture, those unusual striations were one of my favourite things about him.

"Nope. Not even a little. I think I'm just a little anxious." I ran my hands over my jeans. I mentally ran through what was on under my clothes. Black silk thong, black lacy bra . . . and me. That was it. Simple, but hopefully effective.

"You can change your mind. I want to say that one more time. I won't care." He set his fork down and took my hand. "Just say the word and we call it off."

I shook my head and tried to plot an answer. The truth was, I wanted it just as much as he did. Maybe more, I was shocked to find. How could I explain that it was simply fear? A black, sinister fear that I was throwing it all away. "No. I don't want to call it off."

He nodded and started to clear the table. "I love you, you know that. I don't think I can quite explain why I want this."

It was my turn to nod. "I can. You want to know that I would do it for you. I want to know that you would do it for me. The ultimate test. How far will you go for me? To give me what I want? To prove that you are mine?" I went and put my arms around his waist, talking out my own feelings under the guise of trying to explain his. "To prove your love and your desire to see me happy . . ." I trailed off, absorbing my own words.

He put the dishes back on the table and stroked my jaw with his hands. "Wow. I couldn't have put it like that if I'd tried. But that's it. Here's how far I would go for you."

And I kissed him. It was the sweetest kiss we'd ever shared. It only stopped when the doorbell rang.

The moment had come. Luckily, I was expecting it. That deer-in-the-headlights moment. The urge to simply get swallowed up in the panic and flee. Instead of capitulating, I simply poured drinks and did deep breathing. I never thought that yoga would come in handy during a threesome situation. I could hear the two men talking in low voices. Most likely about me. And "Would I go through with it? Was I OK?" I smiled at that thought. At least we had chosen a third party who was considerate. Kind. A good man. I gathered the drinks and went in, even though my heart was beating so erratically it hurt.

"Here we go," I said, the cheerfulness only partly forced. "We should do a toast." I laughed. "Something to honour the occasion."

Christopher took over in a blink. "To good friends, new experiences and a lovely holiday. May your gift exchange be everything you want it to be."

That sealed it. I clinked glasses and took a huge sip of my wine. Then I set it down and threw up my hands. "OK, let's go. Let's get this started."

Both men stopped, glasses halfway to their lips and stared at me.

I stared right back. "What? Let's just go. Down your drinks and let's get upstairs." My voice was high. My throat felt too small and my chest hurt from an invisible pressure that had settled there.

A small smile curved Evan's full lips and he tried to stifle it. He knew exactly what was happening. "We can't finish our drinks?"

I shook my head so hard my vision went wild for a moment. "No. Now. Let's go." The fear had pushed me to the point of annoyance. I was impatient and throwing a hissy fit.

Christopher laughed and ran his hand through his hair. "OK. Well . . . Are you sure you're OK with this? I can leave. You seem a little . . . worked up."

I sighed and suddenly felt so stupid I wanted to melt into the floor. "I'm sorry. I didn't mean to flip out. There just isn't a graceful way to do this, you know?" I regarded each one calmly. I wanted them to see that I was settling down. "It's the anticipation and the build-up that's driving me crazy. We all know why we're here. I just want . . . It would just be easier . . ."

Evan took my hand and beckoned to Christopher. "I think it would be easier on Allyson if we just skip the preliminaries and the niceties."

That invisible weight in my chest lightened and then seemed to drift away. "Yes," I sighed gratefully, "much easier. Let's just go."

Christopher followed us up the steps and I could hear that thick honey laugh. "You are a very strange woman," he said. Another laugh spiralled up the steps and curled up my spine like smoke, stimulating each nerve as it travelled. "I like you very much."

I smiled in the dark.

The moment we hit the bedroom, I started unbuttoning my blouse. No time to waste. Do or die. Move or run. I was going to do one or the other. I knew myself too well. I chose move.

"Um, Allyson?" Evan said slowly, watching me with that bemused look of his.

"What? A slow seduction? Is that what you're asking?" I let my hands drop and blew out a breath. "We either do this, or I run screaming from the room. I want to do this, so . . ." I shrugged and attacked the last two buttons. "Let's do it."

The two men shared a look and, finally, Evan nodded. By then, I was down to the thong and the bra.

"Now?" Evan asked, just a hint of a laugh in his deep voice.

"Yes, now! Who's first?" I demanded as my pulse slammed in my throat. My skin was hot despite the fact that I was nearly naked and the room was cool. I pinned each one with my gaze in turn. I almost felt angry but the arousal bubbled just below the surface. I focused on that. Then them, and finally closed my eyes and the mental image from the winter block party popped into view. Full colour, full view. Evan on his knees *for me* in front of Christopher.

They both stood staring at me. Now who's the deer in the headlights? I thought and actually laughed out loud. "Are you two just going to stare at me all night? You—" I pointed to Christopher "—ditch the pants. You do the same, Evan."

Another shared look and then both started to shuck their pants. Christopher's khakis came down first, as did Evan's faded button-fly jeans. The briefs quickly followed. The shirts came off without request. Just whispers of fabric in the silence. Again they stared at me. Apparently, I was in charge. At least for the moment.

"Evan, would you . . .?" I was losing my nerve. It was one thing to see it in my head. A completely different thing to articulate it. Out loud. In front of a third party. But he was irrelevant really. Nothing more than a cardboard cut-out, not to put too fine a point on it. This was about me and Evan. About us. So I pushed the words past my lips. "Would you get on your knees in front of Christopher . . . please? For me?"

I shed my thong and sat on the bed. I didn't think I could stand for this.

And he did. Dropped to his knees without a moment's hesitation. Without my asking, he leaned forwards, because he *knew* what I wanted. I held my breath, watched, felt my heart go all erratic in my chest again. The moment his lips touched Christopher's cock, starbursts of heat exploded under my skin. I could barely breathe as I watched Christopher's cock sliding in and out of Evan's mouth. Lips that had kissed me a million times sliding over another man's erection. I didn't let myself blink. I wouldn't miss a second. Not one second of what he would do for me.

I watched Christopher watching Evan and my skin seemed to shift. Like mercury heating up and shifting form. When he placed one big hand on top of Evan's head to guide him to go deeper, a small sound escaped me. A tiny sound that was nothing but desire. Without thinking, I touched myself and my fingers came away wet. Not just wet, but slick. Just the one quick flick against my clit made me feel as if I hung right on that edge. I could come with one stroke, maybe two. Just from watching Evan do what I had asked. What I had discovered was, for some reason, important to me. So he did it.

Evan couldn't see me – I was watching him in profile – but his shoulders dropped just a little at the sound I made, as if he had been somewhat tense. Did I like what I was seeing? At that sound he knew how I felt and the tightness in his broad shoulders went away. He was fluid and moving slowly. No indication that he was uncomfortable or unhappy. And I let the next sound escape me as it welled up so he would know. Know how much I appreciated his gift. It was nothing more than a soft sigh but it slid out of my throat like a silk ribbon. On a breath, I managed one word: "Deeper."

And he went deeper. His neck muscles were more defined, his features sharper in the half-light. Christopher's head tipped back and he growled just a little. Just enough to make my skin feel raspy as if it had been rubbed with sandpaper. My nipples peaked, and the fluid that had left my fingers slick now pooled on the bedspread between my thighs. When Christopher's other hand slid into Evan's hair and joined the hand already there, I had to grip my thighs to keep my hands from my clit. To resist the urge to slide them in and out of my weeping entrance. Despite this, I felt the tightening, oh so familiar, start in my cunt. A torquing of flesh that wants what it wants – release.

I watched Christopher's cock disappear completely as Evan's nose nudged the dark-blond pubic hair at the base. I felt my eyes well up just a little watching him in that submissive position before another man, for me. Doing something that most men would never consider because what would it mean? Nothing, really. Just that he loved me. Trusted me. Could give me that and let me watch, and know that I would not judge. One more long slide, one more glimpse of his throat working over Christopher's erection. I heard him suck in a long breath through his nose, something I heard myself do too many times to count, and I let it be the last.

"OK." That was it. That was all I said and they broke apart. Both looking slightly dazed. Evan checking my face for acceptance and then smiling when he found it. Christopher checking us both for approval. His cock stood out, fully erect and nearly purple. I licked my lips as I looked at Evan and laughed a little. Now it was my turn.

I didn't trust my legs or my voice so I just used my hand to motion Christopher over so he stood before me. I could see Evan's saliva, still wet and shiny, on his skin even in the dim light. I stroked it with my palm and his cock jumped. I circled the head with my finger and inhaled deeply. I could smell the scent of Evan that still clung to this man's skin. Then I took him in my mouth and picked up where Evan had left off. I could taste him on Christopher, too. A distinctive taste I took away from every kiss. We all have a scent, we all have a taste. This one was familiar and comforting to me, considering I hadn't done this for another man in five years.

"Allyson, go slower baby." Evan's voice, off to my left. I glanced out of the corner of my eye as I slowed my pace. He wanted to see. He wanted me to see everything and now I understood this. So I slowed down. An inch at a time, moving with care. It was probably maddening to poor Christopher, but this wasn't about him at all. His hands found my hair, too, but he didn't draw me in closer or faster. He just twined his fingers in my hair as I sucked him. I watched from the corner of my eye and the tightness inside of me intensified as I saw Evan stroking his cock, saw the length of him slide in and out of his closed fist.

I took a deep breath and played my tongue along those mysterious ridges that are different on every man. Each dip and swell new to me. When I heard Evan suck in a breath,

I did it again, arching my tongue out, careful to run just the rigid tip along the shaft. I could hear them both breathing. Two men, breathing hard and fast in this room. For me. Because of me. But only one mattered. Both were exciting but only one mattered.

"Say no if you want," I heard Christopher mutter, and then he was pushing me back. Gently, but backwards. Big hands on my shoulders as I seemed to recline in slow motion. "Somebody say 'stop' and I will," he warned again. His face had gone to dark, his eyes hooded, his voice always heavy now so thick it didn't even sound like him. He was positioned over me, between my thighs. His big legs were pressing against my smaller ones, and forcing them outwards. The blunt head of his cock was right at the tight portal that would let him into my body.

This was not in the script, but I found that I wanted it. That strange slide of another man. That first startling stretching of soft tissue around hard tissue. The electrical current of someone unfamiliar entering you for the first time. My eyes darted to Evan. I wasn't close enough truly to read his eyes, but I saw the brisk nod. A decisive nod. If he didn't want me to, he would have hesitated. I knew that for certain. I arched up and pressed the moisture between my legs against the head of Christopher's cock. Inviting him. With another low growl he took me up on it. And slid into me.

One quick thrust, and my breath left. Then it was movement. Sweet and effortless. I was so wet it was like dancing. His body dancing into mine. Intoxicating. But my eyes never left Evan. The sight of him stroking himself. Eyes pinned on us as Christopher fucked me. Pinned on my face, moving to my hair, taking in the way my breasts rose and fell. The way Christopher bent – still sliding into me, out of me – and nipped my breast through my bra. Worked his tongue over the stiff flesh, forcing the lace of my bra against the sensitive tip. I groaned and saw Evan's head tilt back, his eyes drift shut. A look I knew. He was close. Right there. And then he seemed so far away.

My cunt was so tight I thought I might scream with the heat that builds before an intense orgasm. I was wetter than I ever remembered being. It was all there, and Evan was a million miles away. And I hated it.

"Come here, Ev. Please. Hurry."

Again, he did it instantly. All he needed was to hear my plea. Hear my voice and he responded. As he always had. As he always would. Now I saw that. He came. Knelt on the bed and waited for me to tell him what I wanted, what I needed from him.

I pulled at his thighs, pulling him over my head. He continued to stroke his cock, his eyes locked on the place where Christopher and I were joined. Mesmerized by each thrust and each retreat. I could read his eyes now. Could read the look. Magical. He had my trust, and that could never be questioned again.

Christopher's movements intensified, nearly jerky. His breath tore in and out of him and his eyes were fixed on some distant point. A lock of hair had fallen into his eyes and I had the urge to brush it away, but then the first sweet curl of pleasure shot through my belly, blazed a trail through my cunt. And, without thinking, I cried out, "Oh, Evan."

Evan growled, and Christopher became more frantic, pushing into me almost brutally hard. His movements drove me closer to Evan, under him, and I watched as that beautiful hand worked that beautiful cock. It jerked, Evan cried out, and I grabbed his hand and opened my mouth. His come was like a baptism. And, as soon as the hot liquid hit my face, my orgasm burst apart inside me. I came. Another man in my body. The man I loved over me. Bright sparks of blue and purple behind my eyelids as I gave myself over to two points of pleasure. Two points that were only relevant in one context. Giving.

There was no three-way post-coital tangle on the bed. That had been made clear to Christopher, and he was fine with it. He left shortly after, and was just as friendly and kind as when he arrived. I had no worries that we had ruined a friendship with him or alienated him in any way. The mission of the evening now accomplished, I simply wanted to be with Evan.

With a bottle of wine and two glasses this time we went to the bedroom. He wrapped himself around me in normal fashion. Holding me as close as ever. Trying to press all of his skin against me at once, which usually earned him teasing. Tonight it earned him the same. I tried to have every part of me against him at once. If I could have crawled into his skin with him, I think I would have.

He kissed the nape of my neck, his fingers playing slowly in my hair. Gently. Barely a touch. Enough to make me drowsy and happy.

"We're OK?" he asked and kissed my ear. I could hear in the tone, he already knew the answer. He just needed me to say it.

"Better than fine. Thank you." I kissed his fingers one by one and, as was my usual joke, sucked on his index finger until he groaned.

"Why are you thanking me?"

"You gave me something I wanted. You had the courage to give it to me," I said and kissed his other fingers in turn.

"Shouldn't I be thanking you? You did the same."

"That was the point," I said. "We did it for each other. With each other." Then I kissed his palm and closed my eyes. I was suddenly very tired. I relished the feel of his warm mouth against the back of my neck. So familiar and now even more treasured.

"Do you think you'd ever want to do it again?"

"I don't know," I whispered. "Do you? Think you'd ever want to do it again?"

"I don't know either. I guess we'll find out," he said and then yawned softly.

"Together. We can find out together." I let myself drift off. I was safe. I was cherished.

Peace de Resistance

Kris Cherita

Linsey winced as Brianna kneaded her back. "Jesus, girl," said the masseuse, "you are a fucking *mess*. What the fuck have you been doing?"

"Just working."

"Why doesn't that surprise me?" her friend asked rhetorically, with a hint of a sigh. "Why did you take that job, anyway?"

"They forced money into my hand," said Linsey wryly. In truth, she'd been offered the position of principal of Maria Goretti College, over many colleagues with seniority, because of her excellent track record as a teacher. She'd accepted it in the hope of being able to improve the school as a whole, and had scored some minor victories, but only by micro-managing as much as possible. "Ow!"

"You getting any exercise?"

"No."

"Getting laid?"

"No!"

"Thought not. When was the last time?" When Linsey started doing the maths, Brianna shook her head. "Not since Phil left, right?"

"No," she admitted, with a slight twinge. While her ex-husband had had many faults, he was undeniably good in bed – a vast number of beds, unfortunately. She'd been hugely inexperienced when they'd started dating, but he'd soon changed that; he was a silver-tongued actor and dancer with the ability to arouse her to the degree that she would agree to almost anything. "I've been on a couple of dates, but none of them . . . well, you know. None of them turned me on."

"How much of a chance did you give them?"

"What?"

"Did you try talking about anything other than your job?"

"I don't know. Maybe."

Brianna nodded.

"I don't get many opportunities to meet anyone—"

"Bullshit," said Brianna. "There are plenty of people out there, and you still look damn hot – OK, not in that straitjacket you were wearing when you came in, but you do now. Pretty face, big tits, nice curvy butt, good legs . . . you just have to learn to show them off a bit. All it takes is some effort and a bit of imagination."

"I can't go cruising the bars, or anything like that. I have my position to think of. I'm having enough trouble at the moment with parents trying to sack one of my best teachers for saying that abstinence-only sex education isn't enough, and we should tell the girls about alternatives, including contraception and masturbation."

"Maybe you should take that advice yourself. Start thinking about alternative and different sorts of position. Do you masturbate, at least?"

"I've tried that. It doesn't work for me, either. I can't . . ."

"Let yourself go?"

"Something like that."

Another sigh. "You always were a control freak. You've got to learn that sometimes you have to make the choice to let someone else take control instead; always being in control fucks you up almost as bad as never being in control. Then you can decide when to take control again, because you want to or need to, not because it's just a habit."

Linsey didn't reply.

"OK,"Brianna said, after a moment's thought. "It's your birthday next month, right? And I owe you something for introducing you to Phil in the first place. What say I arrange a party for you, out of town, so you don't have to worry about meeting anyone with daughters at your school?"

"I don't know . . ."

"Did I ever tell you about the time I worked in a brothel?"

"You did *what*?"

"Just as a receptionist. I needed the money – besides, I wanted to play Blanche DuBois, and this seemed like a good chance to watch the working girls. Anyway, I found out some interesting stuff – for one thing, a lot of our clients were lawyers or judges. And after a while, I learned what their kinks were."

"I'm scared to ask."

"Judges, and a lot of lawyers who'd just won a case, wanted to be dominated, even tortured. Restoring the balance, if you like: they'd meted out punishment, and wanted to be punished for it. They'd taken away someone else's control over their own lives, and they wanted to surrender control themselves, if just for a few minutes. It sounds to me like you should try doing the same thing."

"I'm not into S&M," Linsey said sharply.

"I'm not so sure. Taking that job might be considered masochistic. So what *are* you into?"

The limo that arrived to pick Linsey up on Friday night had tinted rear windows, so dark that she could barely see outside, and the chauffeur warned her not to wind them down. "You don't want to spoil the surprise, do you?" he asked cheerfully. "Help yourself to something from the bar, if you like."

"No, thanks." She stopped trying to keep track of the corners they turned, then blinked as the TV came on. The sound was turned down, but it didn't take her long to realize that a man in a sea captain's cap was directing four couples into an increasingly intense orgy.

The next scene began with a blonde nurse in a latex uniform, who teamed up with another equally unlikely looking nurse and a male doctor to remove a long dildo that had become lodged too far up another woman's ass for her to extract unaided.

The third scene began with an Asian woman in a maid's uniform being summoned to her blonde mistress' bathroom; the limo pulled into a garage just as the maid began licking her mistress' soap-slick slit. The sound cut out as the garage door closed behind her, and Linsey began to wonder whether she'd made a horrible mistake going along with Brianna's plans. Despite this, she stepped out of the car when the chauffeur opened the door for her, and was escorted down a hallway into a small office. The woman sitting behind the highly polished desk looked her up and down as the chauffeur left, then nodded at a side door. "There's a bathroom in there," she said. "You can change in there. I don't know what the friend who paid for your session here has told you, so I'll just run through the basics.

"Firstly, there's nothing here to sign: I don't know your name, nor does anyone else here, and we don't need to. For tonight and tomorrow, if you want to stay that long, you're Roberta Stepford; a sex robot, a living, walking, talking fuckdoll." Linsey's eyes widened in alarm, but the manager gave no sign of noticing. "How much personality you choose to display is up to you, but you must obey all legal orders you are given. The most important thing you need to know is that we do not allow anything illegal or unsafe, though you can simulate it if you wish. Your sponsor has given us a list of what you won't allow." She reached into a drawer and removed a sheet of pink paper, which she handed to Linsey. "The other participants have been told this, of course, and they will be removed if they break any of the rules. The next most important thing is that if you wish the games to stop, you only have to say your safe word, and you'll be taken to a room where you can dress and recover, and someone will drive you home again. Your safe word is 'overtime'. Do you understand?"

"Yes," said Linsey. Her mouth was dry and she wasn't sure her voice was audible, but the woman merely nodded.

"However, once you use that word, everything stops. No line-item vetoes here unless someone else breaks the stated rules. If that happens, your sponsor will receive at least a partial refund, and you can then decide whether to continue, or to return another time."

"Who are the . . ."

"Other participants? Some are employees here; some are . . . volunteers, but they have all been very carefully vetted, and understand that if they break any rules, they'll be heavily fined and then permanently blackballed. OK?"

Linsey nodded.

"Excellent. So, if you'll go in there, please, and get into your outfit, I'll send one of the maids in to help you with your make-up, give you your enema, and help you shave."

The bathroom contained a shower stall, towel rack, hand basin, toilet, folding massage table, inflated bondage chair and a TV mounted in one corner. Linsey looked at the costume laid out on the table – a silver lamé corset that stopped just above her hips and below her nipples, and silver boots – with some alarm and more than a little amusement.

She stripped, showered, and was reaching for a towel when the door opened. A pretty woman in her mid-twenties, wearing black latex gloves, spit-polished slut shoes and a maid's outfit only slightly less revealing than Linsey's abbreviated corset, walked in and looked at her appraisingly. "Nice," she drawled. "OK, let's get you ready. Lie down on the table."

When Linsey didn't obey immediately, the maid shook her head. "What part of 'lie down' didn't you understand? Do you speak English?"

"Yes."

"That's 'Yes, Mistress Abigail' to you."

Linsey blinked, but echoed, "Yes, Mistress Abigail."

The maid smiled. "That's better. Now say, 'I will do everything my mistresses and masters tell me.'"

"I will do everything my mistresses and masters tell me."

"You're a big-titted robot fuckdoll. What are you?"

"I . . . I'm a big-titted robot fuckdoll."

"Mistress," the younger woman reminded her.

"I'm a big-titted robot fuck doll, mistress."

"Better. OK, now get your butt up on that table. Roll over on to your side. Now, grab your cheeks and spread 'em." Linsey obeyed, then gasped as she felt the cold, well-lubed enema nozzle being pushed up against her anus. Abigail chuckled, then reached around between her thighs and began gently rubbing her clit. "Relax," she said, making it sound more like a suggestion than an order. "You're a fuckdoll. Fuckdolls take bigger things than this up their nice hot asses. And you want to be clean for your masters and mistresses, don't you?"

"Yesssss," came the reply, through gritted teeth.

"Mistress."

"Missstressss."

"That's good." When Abigail was satisfied that the nozzle was firmly in place, she began lathering up Linsey's honey-coloured pubes, tantalizing her with the brush and her fingers. "Pretty hair," she mused. "Seems a shame to get rid of it, but orders are orders. Right?"

"Yess, mistress . . ." Linsey's senses were beginning to reel. Phil had taught her to enjoy anal sex, and it felt as though she were being flooded not just with warm water but with happy memories. That, combined with Abigail's expert ministrations, were bringing her close to orgasm, but there was still something niggling at the edge of her consciousness, something that stopped her . . .

If Abigail was disappointed by Linsey's failure to come, she didn't show it; she simply finished trimming and shaving her pussy, then wiped it clean and leaned back to admire her handiwork. "OK," she said, then returned the shaving gear to the drawer under the sink, and produced a butterfly vibrator, a G-spot stimulator and a remote control for the TV. Abigail strapped the butterfly vibe over Linsey's clit, then sat in the bondage chair and began using the G-spot vibe on herself while she watched a scene of two women decorating a third with frosting until she resembled a cake – which they then proceeded to devour. The next scene showed a blonde woman cheerfully taking on four men, and Linsey realized that the vibrator on her clit was sound-activated, responding both to the soundtrack of the porn movie and Abigail's squeals of pleasure. I'm not in control any more, she thought, and moaned as she let herself be overwhelmed by the delightful sensations. She opened her eyes a moment later to find Abigail standing over her and grinning. She smiled back weakly.

"Happy little fuckdoll?"

"Yes, mistress."

"Good," said Abigail, producing a collar and leash from the pocket in her apron, "'cause that was just an appetizer. Wait until you see the entrée."

When Linsey was prepared to Abigail's satisfaction – silver eye shadow and nail polish, scarlet gloss on her lips and nipples, lubricated silicone anal beads in her ass – she was led down the corridor to meet her new masters and mistresses. "Remember to show proper respect," said Abigail, before she opened the door. "Don't speak until you're spoken to, smile and say thank you whenever you think it's appropriate, and don't look anyone in the eye: it's best if you don't look any higher than their crotches unless you have to. Are you ready?"

"Yes, Mistress Abigail."

"What are you?"

"I'm a big-titted robot fuckdoll, mistress."

"Good." Abigail opened the door, and led her into a large room dominated by a huge bed and a plasma TV screen. Assorted strangely shaped chairs and sofas were positioned along the walls, and six people – four men and two women – were standing around with drinks in their hands. "Ah," said the shortest of the men, who was wearing a tuxedo jacket with no pants, "the new toy. Bring her here so we can take a closer look."

Abigail shut the door behind her, and guided Linsey into the centre of the crowd. "Good flesh tones," said another man, as he reached out and cupped one of Linsey's breasts, hefting it as though trying to guess its weight. "Feels natural, too." Linsey's nipple stiffened as he rubbed his thumb around it. "Very convincing. I approve."

"They are impressive, aren't they?" said a slender Chinese woman. She grabbed the other and squeezed it, almost hard enough to cause pain. "It's remarkable that she walks as well as she does without overbalancing."

Another man, half-dressed like the first, with his cock already rising to parallel the floor, chuckled as he walked around to look at Linsey's back. "I doubt she spends much time standing up," he opined, running a finger between her buttocks, then turned to Abigail. "Fully functional, I hope?"

"Yes, of course."

"I can't get over how well she moves," said the short man, relinquishing her breast. "Can she do jumping jacks?"

"I'm sure she can," said Abigail, unfastening the leash from the collar. "Well, Roberta? You heard your master."

"Yes, mistress," said Linsey, trying to smile. The people stepped back to watch her breasts bounce as she did a series of star jumps. After the sixth, the short man told her to stop, then went up to her, grabbed her breasts again, and sucked a nipple into his mouth. "Hmm," he said, his voice muffled. "They even taste like the real thing. Wonderful!"

The other woman – dark-skinned and dark-haired, wearing a sari that left one beautifully shaped hard-nippled breast free – nodded approvingly. "Good work, Professor," she said to a bespectacled man wearing a white lab coat. "But is she flexible enough to touch her toes?"

The "professor" raised an eyebrow, and Linsey bent over, straining to reach her toes – something she hadn't done in years. She'd come within a few inches of succeeding when lab coat said, "All right. Stop."

Linsey looked up, and realized that he meant her to hold that position. The short man was still sucking on her right breast, refusing to be dislodged, and was patting the other back and forth, making it sway. The Chinese woman walked behind Linsey, fondled her wet cunt, then sniffed her fingers. "Not bad," she said grudgingly, then slapped Linsey on the ass, hard enough that she nearly toppled over. "Very good," she said, as she spanked the other cheek. "Nice convincing wobble, and they turn a lovely shade of pink, too. You're an artist, Professor."

"This I have to see," said the Indian woman, walking around to stand behind Linsey. The two women took turns in spanking her, until they were joined by the second man, and soon she was being smacked on each cheek while another hand gently rubbed her pussy. The beads in Linsey's ass, on their flexible shaft, shifted with every smack; they weren't as thick as Phil's cock had been, and they felt more like a wonderfully long finger probing and caressing her, but they were yet another reminder (as if she needed one) of the overwhelmingly intense orgasms she'd had from being masterfully sodomized. The recollection, combined with the rhythm of the spanking, the tingling of her cheeks, and the wonderful feeling of so many hands and mouths on some of the most sensitive parts of her body, soon had her on the verge of coming again. Go with it, said a voice in her head.

It's humiliating, a vanishingly small part of her brain replied. *Who the fuck cares? When was the last time something felt this good?*

That was all it took; soon, she was shaking and shrieking with the force of her orgasm, while the people fondling her propped her up and kept her from falling. She thought she could hear laughter and applause, but she wasn't sure, and she wasn't sure she cared.

When she could focus again, she saw a hard cock being waved invitingly in front of her face, and she opened her mouth wide to let it in without wondering whose it was. It had been so long since she'd sucked a dick that she'd forgotten how much she enjoyed it, how good it was to turn someone on and feel and taste the proof of it. The spanking had stopped, but there was still a hand between her thighs, and now both of her breasts were being sucked. She wasn't sure how long it was before the cock in her mouth erupted, but she relished every second.

She felt the softening dick pop out of her mouth, and waited for it to be replaced by another; instead, she heard the Chinese woman say, "Were you *told* to swallow his come, fuckdoll?"

Linsey tried to think. "I wasn't told to spit it out," she replied, numbly.

The Indian woman laughed. "She has a point, Ting. You've programmed her well, Professor."

"Except that she forgot to say 'thank you'," said the tallest of the men, reprovingly.

"Thank you, master," Linsey gushed. "Thank you for letting me suck your cock, and thank you for coming in my mouth, master."

"Hmp," Ting grunted, and removed her little black dress,

showing herself to be naked underneath. "Does she eat pussy as well?"

"As well as I can, mistress."

This time, she was sure the laughter and applause were real. "Show me," said Ting, lying down on the bed with her legs spread. Linsey dropped to all fours and crawled towards her, slowly kissing her way along one thigh to her crotch; it had been many years since she'd gone down on another woman, but she felt confident that she still remembered how to do it. As Ting began to purr, she also remembered *why* she'd done it, and began hoping someone would think to do it to her – if not Ting, then maybe Abigail or the Indian woman. Cunnilingus had been another thing Phil had done well . . . almost as skilfully and eagerly as Brianna had, back during their brief affair. Linsey found herself wishing Brianna were here, and fuzzily wondered whether offering to eat her out would be considered a suitable way to thank her for this wonderful gift.

She heard the professor muttering something about viruses and nanobots, then the sound of a condom wrapper being torn open, and a few seconds later a cock slid into her cunt. The man fucked her slowly, allowing her to concentrate on licking Ting, for which part of Linsey's brain was weirdly grateful; she was vaguely convinced that a good fuckdoll would make sure that Ting's pleasure came before her own. She was gratified when Ting climaxed, allowing her to concentrate on the delightful sensations she was getting from the dick in her pussy and the beads in her ass – which rapidly intensified as the man fucking her picked up the pace and grabbed the ring at the end of her anal toy and proceeded to pull it out slowly. Her sphincter expanded and contracted as the beads popped out one by one, perfectly synchronized with the peaks of her own orgasm.

She lay there for a moment, face down between Ting's silky thighs, unaware of anything but immeasurable pleasure and the hope that her now empty ass would soon be filled by something larger, preferably a cock. Instead, the short man grabbed her and turned her over on to her back as Ting wriggled up the bed. "I've wanted to do this since I saw you," the man said, squeezing a bottle of lube into his hand and applying it to his dick.

"Thank y—" Linsey began, but to her surprise, the man grabbed her breasts and pushed them together, then thrust his slippery – but unsheathed – cock between them. Linsey's eyes widened in amazement. She'd heard of tit-fucking, had even seen it on porn movies, but had never tried it; Phil had always been more of a butt man, and her other male lovers had been too inexperienced to think of it or too shy to ask for it.

"Nice big fuckable funbags," Shorty grunted. "Every fuckdoll should have beautiful boobs like these. Ohhhh, that feels *fantastic!*"

Linsey blinked. To her, it felt only mildly pleasurable, but she found that she did enjoy seeing the purpling head of Shorty's long dick appearing between her breasts, just within reach of her tongue, and she began licking it as it emerged.

Shorty obviously wasn't a control freak: unlike the slow fucking she'd just received, the tit-fuck lasted less than a minute before she saw the come start spurting out of his cock – a sight she'd never previously witnessed, and found utterly fascinating. Without waiting for orders, she opened her mouth to catch as much of his semen as she could, then licked the rest off her face. "Thank you, master," she said, surprising herself with the sincerity of her tone.

"My pleasure," he said, kissing her on the forehead. "You are a *fantastic* fuckdoll."

"Thank you, master!" She looked around, and saw that Ting and the Indian woman were lying on the bed on either side of her, obviously enjoying the show.

"Impressive," said the Indian woman. "How was her cunnilingus?"

"Pretty good," said Ting, wiping a stray drop of come from Linsey's face and licking it, "but I think she could benefit from more practice."

"Hmm. Is she programmed for rimming, too, Professor?"

"If I remember the specifications correctly," said the man in the lab coat.

"I am, mistress," said Linsey, as the woman unwrapped her sari and lay prone on the bed.

"Then lick my ass."

"Yes, mistress. Thank you, mistress." With an enthusiasm that she no longer even wondered at, she parted the woman's beautiful brown buttocks and buried her face between them, her tongue running along the crevice until it found the hot little starburst between them. As she began rimming her, she felt another pair of hands – Ting's, she rightly suspected – part her own cheeks, and a large dollop of lube being applied to her asshole. After some precautionary and thoroughly pleasurable probing with his slippery fingers, the professor slid his latex-sheathed circumcised cock easily into her butt; she felt her sphincter contract again and close around the shaft after the acorn-shaped glans had entered, and began coming. Her tongue slipped inside the Indian woman's anus, and soon she was tongue-fucking her in synch with the cock reaming her ass.

They're using me, she thought. I'm just a fuckdoll, a sex machine, I don't even know their real names and they probably don't know mine, but fuck, it feels so fucking *good*!

After that, the rest of the night, and the next day, and the next night, were something of an erotic blur. She did have a clear memory of jerking two of the men off so she could watch them come on her breasts, and then licking as much of their jizz as her tongue could reach before the other women finished the job of cleaning her up . . . and of Shorty returning for a second go at her tits, this time facing her feet while she licked his ass as avidly as she'd rimmed the Indian woman's, or Ting's, or Abigail's . . . and of being blindfolded and ordered to guess whose cock was in her mouth, with the "threat" of a spanking if she guessed wrong, and of coming as the "threat" was carried out . . . and of being fucked and sodomized by all of the men, and by Ting with a strap-on, though she couldn't remember in what order . . . but as she woke up Sunday morning, her body still glazed with come and other juices and covered with lipsticky kisses in four colours, the most important thing she remembered was how much pleasure her body, too long ignored, had given her and seven other people.

She lay there in what Abigail had called the "recovery room", still slightly dazed, and wondered whether she should ask the chauffeur to stop at a church so she could go to confession on the way home – at a church where no one knew her, of course. She'd gotten less than halfway through listing her encounters of the weekend before reaching for one of the vibrators Abigail had thoughtfully left on the nightstand.

Linsey kept her expression neutral as she listened to the secretary of the PTA drone on reprovingly about the teacher who some parents thought was being too frank about sex in biology classes. The woman was only a few years her senior, and as Linsey looked at her prim, even severe, appearance, she realized that she was what she might have become without Brianna's gift.

Maybe I'm judging her too harshly, she thought. Maybe she has a girlfriend as well as a husband. Maybe she has an impressive collection of piercings and tattoos under that Dior suit. Maybe her ass isn't really so tight that it doesn't regularly accommodate a nice hard cock, or so hard that it doesn't jiggle a little when it gets spanked. Maybe she likes to go to sex shop movie booths in some other town and suck cocks through a glory hole. Maybe—

". . . do the girls even need to learn biology at all?" the woman asked, bringing Linsey out of her reverie. "Unless they decide to go into medicine, what use will it be to them later in life?"

Linsey stared at her for a moment, and seemed to hear Brianna's voice in her head. *You can choose when to be submissive*, it said, *and that means you're choosing when not to be.*

"The course stays on the curriculum," said Linsey, firmly. "Biology is not some shameful little secret; there's a reason they call it a life science. And I am *not* going to fire a teacher for doing her job, answering questions and encouraging curiosity. Yes, we will tell the girls that abstinence is safest – but if they ask about alternatives, any alternatives, I expect the teachers to answer the questions as honestly as they are able and let the girls make informed decisions about their own lives. How do you put it? 'Teach the controversy?'"

The woman turned red, and stood. "I hope you're ready to defend this position at the next meeting, when I suggest to the other parents that we pull our daughters out of this school."

Linsey resisted the urge to make a joke about withdrawal not being a particularly effective alternative. "You're free to do that," she said, "but I'm not apologising for the position I've taken. Is there anything else you wish to say?"

Clearly there wasn't, as the woman stood up and stormed towards the door. Linsey looked at her ass for a moment, fantasized about having it bent over her desk ready for a thorough spanking, then reached for her cell phone. "Brianna? It's Lin. What're you doing this weekend?"

Wish Girls

Matthew Addison

Max opened his bedroom door, and there they were, his wish girls, sitting primly on the bed with their legs crossed, looking up at him through lowered lashes. Allison (the blonde) and Stephanie (the brunette), wearing the modified cheerleader outfits that made him cringe with inward embarrassment now whenever he saw them. The wish girls were fresh and perky and eager as always. "Hi girls," he said, tossing his coat on to the chair and dropping his bag. He'd had a hard day at the bookstore, and more than anything he wanted someone to listen to his troubles and make him dinner, but those were two things his wish girls wouldn't do, couldn't do, hadn't been made to do, so he'd have to be satisfied with the services they did offer.

Stephanie and Allison were seventeen years old, and had been for the past fifteen years, never changing. They wore yellow-and-red uniforms, which resembled the ones worn by cheerleaders at Max's old high school, but altered to titillate the perpetually aroused fourteen-year-old he'd been when he wished them into existence. The tops of the outfits were tight and thin and clinging, and Allison and Stephanie's ever-erect nipples stuck through visibly. There was a round keyhole cut out in each bodice, revealing the full side swells of their firm high breasts, and the skirts were so short they hardly qualified as garments. The wish girls wore no panties, and even with their legs demurely crossed he could see the curling of their pubic hairs, blonde and black. They wore knee socks over their smooth, lithe legs, and Max felt a bit like a dirty old man for admiring them. The wish girls had been older than him when they first appeared, but they hadn't aged as he did.

"Strip," he said. "Then go into the bathroom and shave." He lingered to watch them undress one another, with many shy glances and coquettish looks at him, peeling off one another's tops, shimmying out of their skirts. Their bodies were perfect, fine tits, taut bellies, round firm asses, the fantasy amalgamation of all the girls he'd lusted after as an eighth-grade loser. Their bodies were identical, both the same height, both with pink nipples, breasts the same ample size, and he wished for the thousandth time that he'd given one of them brown nipples, at least, or made one of them 5'9" and the other 5'2" (they were both 5'7", done something to differentiate them, but he'd only wished for one blonde and one brunette, and that was the full extent of the variation. Even their faces were identical, *Seventeen* model faces, with full lips, big blue eyes, high cheekbones.

The wish girls were undoubtedly lovely, but they'd been lovely in exactly the same way for a long time.

They finished undressing, and he stepped aside to let them into the living room. His apartment was too small for three people, but the wish girls didn't live with him, exactly – sometimes he fell asleep with them in his bed, but they always disappeared by morning, and they didn't use the bathroom or cook meals or do anything to take up space. There was a time, even a few years ago, when watching them undress one another would have aroused him enough to make one of them kneel and suck him off, but he found that more elaborate steps were required to excite him now.

Max made a microwave pizza while the girls shaved one another in the bathroom, and sat eating on the couch when they emerged, arm in arm, cunts freshly shorn. "Position sixteen," he said, and the girls knelt before him, facing one another. Each put a hand on the other's hip, and each slipped a hand into the other's always wet cunt, fingering one another, and they tilted their faces together, eyes closed, and kissed, lips parted, pink tongues moving gently. Max slipped off his pants and his boxers and sat back down, tugging his cock while they made out. "Pinch her nipple, Allison," he said, and the blonde reached out and tweaked, bringing a moan to Stephanie's throat. "Harder," he said, and she twisted, but Stephanie didn't make any sounds of pain. As far as Max could tell, they didn't feel pain, which made his forays into S&M less satisfying than they might have been, and made him wonder if they truly felt anything. "Gasp like it hurts you," he said, and Stephanie did, making high sounds of distress. "Slap her tits, Allison," he ordered, and watched for a while, but even this wasn't doing much for him.

"Position thirty-nine, variation b," he said, and the girls turned, facing away from him, first getting on all fours, then lowering their heads to the carpet, leaving their asses in the air. They crossed their arms behind their backs at the wrists – that was the "variation b" part – and Max took two silk scarves from the table by the couch and used them to bind their wrists together. He went to the tall red tool chest in the corner, which contained years of accumulated sex toys and supplies, and took out lube and a pair of clear acrylic butt plugs. Returning to the girls, he squirted lube on to their pink rosebud assholes and rubbed with his fingers. They moaned and moved against his touch – he'd taught them to do that – and gasped as he slipped the plugs into them. Once he'd filled their asses, he wiped his lube-slicked hand on a towel and began spanking the girls, alternating between Stephanie and Allison, full-palm swats that made their beautiful asses bounce. Their skin never bruised or reddened, no matter how hard he hit, and he'd never broken their skin. The wish girls were the product of adolescent fantasies that hadn't gone much beyond groping, blow jobs and vague misconceptions about fucking, and they weren't well equipped for some of the kinks he'd developed since then. Still, they gasped and cried out and begged for mercy, as he'd instructed them to do, until he was sufficiently turned on to slip his cock into Stephanie's tight, welcoming cunt, while fingering Allison with one hand. When he was close to orgasm, he pulled out. "Position eight," he said, and pulled them into upright kneeling positions. They put their faces close together and looked up at him worshipfully, licking their lips, and he tugged his cock until he shot come on to their smiling faces.

Once spent, he sat back on the couch, feeling empty. He liked coming on their faces, visually, but didn't find it as physically satisfying as coming in their mouths, cunts or asses. They kept kneeling, attentive, waiting for any further orders, but Max shook his head. "I'm done. I'll call if I need anything." The wish girls unbound their own hands, removed the butt plugs gracefully, and slipped back into the bedroom. They would disappear now into whatever place they went when he wasn't using them.

Max sat on the couch, flipping channels, until he got lonely. He called "Stephanie!" The brunette stepped out of the bedroom, clad in her cheerleader costume and with her full complement of pubic hair again, reset to her default state. "Put on the nightgown," he said. She stripped off her uniform, dropping the garments to the floor, where they would remain for as long as Max looked at them, though they would vanish the moment he looked elsewhere. She went to the toolbox and took out a sheer silk nightgown, which was, relatively speaking, modest. "Position 115," he said, and she sat beside him, one hand resting on his leg, her head leaning against his shoulder, a warm and intimate nuzzle. Sometimes having her act like a girlfriend – like he imagined a girlfriend would act – made him happier, but tonight it just made him sad and even lonelier. "Position forty-three," he said, sliding down a little in his seat, and she lay sideways on the couch, head resting on his belly, and she sucked slowly, almost meditatively, on the head of his cock, until he built towards orgasm again. He grasped her head in his hands and thrust his hips, his cock hitting the back of her throat again and again, until he came in her mouth, and all the while she made moans of exquisite pleasure.

Letting go of her head, he said "OK," and she sat up, swallowing and licking her lips. "Kiss me goodnight," he said, and she did, sweetly, softly, and then he sent her away for the night.

*　　*　　*

Max worked in the genre fiction section at a big chain bookstore, shelving mysteries, romances, sci-fi and fantasy. That morning he held a purple trade paperback with a golden Aladdin's lamp on the cover, the second book in some series about a wisecracking genie, and he tried to remember what, exactly, the circumstances of his wish had been. He knew he'd been in the woods behind his childhood home, and found . . . something, a ring, a bottle, a coloured stone, and he'd been given a wish, though now he couldn't remember if some spirit or being had spoken to him, or if the knowledge of the wish had simply appeared in his mind. That was part of the wish's defence, he understood, to make the memory of its genesis vague, because then it would be harder for Max to tell other people about it. Whatever the specific circumstances had been, Max had held the wishing object in his hand, or he'd buried it in the dirt, or he'd broken it open, and he'd made his wish, voicing one of the many elaborate fantasies he concocted in his narrow bed each night, and then Allison and Stephanie came to him. He'd spent the next three years slipping away to the woods every chance he got, on weekends and afternoons, even some days when he cut school, going to a secluded clearing beyond earshot of his house and waiting for Allison and Stephanie to step out of the trees. They'd done everything he wanted, and in those years he did everything a young man could think to do with two girls, and watched as they did everything two young girls could do to one another – at least, without the help of props and accessories and costumes. Max's grades fell, he stopped seeing his friends, he didn't take part in sports or theatre or band, and he didn't ask girls out – why should he, with two lithe nude eager wish girls waiting for him in the woods? They'd been like a drug, he understood now, like heroin, and everything in his life became secondary to the pursuit of the pleasure they gave.

Someone tapped him on the shoulder, startling him. He turned to see a woman, about his age, with short copper-coloured hair and round-rimmed glasses, and he automatically compared her to Stephanie and Allison, as he did with every woman he saw – her face was round, her eyes startlingly green, she had a pimple above one of her eyebrows, and her expression seemed amused even at rest. "I'm the new girl," she said. "Just transferred from the downtown branch. What's your name?"

"Uh, Max," he mumbled, looking down at the book in his hand, uncomfortable standing so close to her.

"Nice to meet you, Max, I'm Kira. I used to work in genre at my old bookstore, but they stuck me with photography and art books here. Let me know if you ever want to trade."

"Uh," he said. "No, I, uh—"

"Just kidding, Max, I'm not going to poach your section." She patted his shoulder and said, "See you around."

He turned and watched as she walked away, and he noticed her curves, her hips. She probably weighed fifty pounds more than Allison or Stephanie, and was four inches shorter than them, but it looked right and proportional on her – Kira didn't have their willowy waists. Max turned back to his shelving. Why had she made him so nervous? Spending fifteen years with Allison and Stephanie had rendered him incapable of interacting with women normally. He'd never been on a real date, and didn't have any close friends, didn't go out to bars – and why would he? The other guys at the bookstore went out, drank and tried to pick up women, but Max didn't need to pick up women. He had the holy grail at home, two hot girls who couldn't get enough of him. His life was perfect. He'd blundered into magic, and his life was magical as a result.

So why didn't he look forward to going home any more?

Max had expected things to change with the wish girls when he got his own apartment. Once he'd moved in, out on his own for the first time, he'd called the girls, and they'd emerged from the bedroom, seeming happy, as always, to be summoned. "This is our place now," he said. "You never have to leave or disappear, no more going to the woods, you can just stay here." Their smiles didn't falter, but they didn't seem to absorb what he said, either. They could talk, and they understood the often-complicated tasks he set for them, but they never truly conversed with him. Beyond a certain basic repertoire of phrases – "Yes, please, God" – he'd had to teach them whatever he wanted them to say.

"Allison, position one," he said, and she knelt before him, unzipping his pants and pulling out his cock, stroking it to erectness and then licking the shaft slowly, from bottom to top. "What do you think of the apartment, Stephanie?" he said, while Allison tongued the vein beneath the head of his dick.

"It's so big," she said. "It feels so good inside."

Max frowned. The words made superficial sense, though they weren't exactly accurate, and they were, of course, things he'd taught her to say under other circumstances. He wondered how intelligent they were, really, these wish girls of his, and it was something he would come to wonder again and again in the coming years.

Over the next weeks he tried to make them understand that his home was theirs, but they kept disappearing when he was done with them each night. He kept running up against the limits of their capabilities. Once he tried to teach Allison to wash dishes – after all, if they were his willing slaves, why shouldn't he use them for something other than fucking? He'd explained everything required to wash dishes, and told Allison the chore was her responsibility from now on. The first night, she'd emerged from the bedroom and changed into a frilly white apron, four-inch spike heels, and nothing else. She'd filled the sink with soapy water, then leaned over the counter on her elbows, breasts in the suds, ass lifted invitingly, and Max had been so turned on he'd come up behind her and pounded her hard, pulling her hair and squeezing her soapy tits while he thrust into her. It was only later that he realized she hadn't done the dishes at all, even when he was done fucking her, and all his later attempts to get them to do anything non-sexual ended that way – he'd fucked Stephanie from behind while her head hung in the toilet after he tried to teach her to clean the bathroom, and while they were more than willing to let him eat off their bodies, they never prepared food for him. They were happy to dress up in maid's uniforms – that was one of the first mildly kinky things he'd done with them once he had his own apartment – but not to act like maids.

He'd had great plans for their life together, but most of them hadn't panned out. Once when he was desperately short of money – car broken down, dental bills overdue – he'd tentatively asked if they were willing to fuck other men, thinking he could pimp them out. They'd shaken their heads in unison, almost sadly. Another time, he'd wanted to go out on the town and impress people with the hot women hanging all over him, intending to strap them into butt-plug harnesses, dress them in tight tops and skirts and stripper heels, and let them follow him around bars and nightclubs, squirming from the plugs in their asses, but they'd refused to cross his threshold. They wouldn't let anyone else see them. That was probably his own fault. Max couldn't remember the precise wording of his wish, but hadn't there been some element of the grasping and the selfish? Some phrase like "only for me, just for me", when he'd wished for Allison and Stephanie? He'd been young, and hadn't thought through all the ramifications of his wish.

"I wish you would talk to me," he'd said one night that first year out of high school, hungry for conversation, wishing for something more than the endlessly physical.

Allison and Stephanie gazed up at him. "We belong to you," Allison said. "You can do anything you want with us," Stephanie said. "We love you," they both said. Just like he'd taught them to.

Max lay in bed and fondled his cock and balls, thinking of Kira, fantasizing about the softness of her belly against his cheek, the weight of her body upon him, imagining birthmarks and freckles – he'd been with the wish girls for so long that he'd begun to fetishize blemishes. He stroked and tugged himself towards orgasm, the first time in years he'd jerked himself off – why masturbate when at a moment's whim he could have a perfect, sweet-faced cheerleader giving him a hand-job or sucking him off? But now he was thinking of Kira, and he imagined her face, those green eyes, that half-smile, as he came, spurting hot come over his fingers and on to his stomach.

As he lay in the dark he thought, Maybe it's time I started dating.

A week went by, and before Max could work up the nerve to ask Kira out, she asked him if he wanted to get a bite after work. "Sure," he said, and they went to an Ethiopian place near the bookstore, where they ate spicy and savoury food, scooped up with hot soft pieces of *injera*, Ethiopian flatbread. They talked about working for the bookstore, why she'd transferred to his branch (hers got downsized), about books, and Max managed more or less to think of her as a person rather than a woman, and gradually his anxiety diminished. She was cute, funny, and interesting, and he did his best to keep her entertained and interested in talking to him. It was surprisingly easy to do. They liked the same books, hated the same movies, and Max eventually realized she was flirting with him. They started talking about fantasy novels and stories, and without much conscious thought Max steered the dialogue towards wishes. "What would you do with three wishes?" he asked.

Kira sat back against the cushioned booth, hands laced across her stomach, under her breasts. "I always thought three wishes were too many. With three wishes, you can ask for wealth, eternal youth and top it off with world peace, and feel like a big hero for the last one. I think it's more interesting to ask what you'd do with one wish. That's how you can tell the selfish from the generous. So tell me, Max, if you had one wish, what would it be? World peace, or strippers and blow?"

Max thought it over. He knew what he'd done with his one wish, but he'd been fourteen at the time, and by definition almost sociopathically self-centred. If he had the wish again, now . . . "I'd wish for happiness," he said, and it felt true, like something he wanted very much.

"Selfish, but abstract," Kira said. "I'd probably go for the strippers and blow myself. I've read too many stories to think that even well-meant wishes would turn out the way I wanted."

They finished the meal, and Max walked Kira back to her car. "We should do this again sometime," he said. "Soon."

"We should do more than this sometime," she said, and leaned up to kiss him. Her breath tasted of *timatim fitfit* and after-dinner mint, and his surprise made the kiss awkward, but there was something behind it, a warmth and pressure of a sort he'd never felt with the wish girls. "Soon," she said, and that was goodbye for the night.

Max wanted Kira, wanted to make love to her, but he couldn't. He had other means of release, however. He drove home from dinner and found a package on his doorstep. He took it inside and opened it on the kitchen counter, smiling as he drew out the tangle of leather straps and D-rings. It was the strap-on harness he'd ordered from an online erotica catalogue, along with a nine-inch black silicon dildo. "Girls!" he called, and after they appeared he directed them to shave, put on red cocksucker lipstick (they appeared fresh-faced and without make-up by default), and be back in the living room on their knees in ten minutes. "We're doing scenario twenty-one, variation c," he said. "Stephanie's top, Allison's bottom."

"You heard him, you little bitch," Stephanie said, and slapped Allison's ass. "Get in there and get your clothes off." Allison hurried away, eyes downcast, hands held behind her back.

Max leaned in the bathroom door and watched them get ready, Stephanie cajoling Allison, slapping her tits, and promising her humiliation and violations. For her part, Allison was obedient but frightened, her lower lip quivering as she put on mascara, which she would cry off in act two while Stephanie flogged her.

"Come get dressed, Stephanie," he said, and took her into the bedroom. He laced her into a black leather under-bust corset that lifted her tits even higher than normal, and she put on knee-high leather boots. He gave her a wicked riding crop, which she lashed through the air experimentally. "I just got this for you today," he said, and showed her the new strap-on harness. She oohed and ahhed appreciatively, the way she always responded to the sex toys he brought home, a sort of automatic erotitropism. He helped her into the harness, taking great pleasure in pulling the leather straps tight around her hips, the black dildo rising impressively erect from her crotch. "You like being top, Steph?" he said, and she nodded. He grabbed both her wrists, wrenched her arms over her head, and forced her down to her knees. He twisted her wrists, and when she gasped he shoved his cock into her mouth, thrusting hard. "Just remember, I'm the one who's really top," he said. "Tell me you love it. Tell me you love the taste of my cock." He adored the way she sounded, trying to speak while he fucked her mouth, and it took all his will power not to come then. He pulled out, and looked down at her, where she knelt, breathing hard, breasts heaving prettily, arms still held over her head.

How could she be so perfect, with her teeth never brushing his cock no matter how hard he used her, never sweating, never belching, never having a headache or having her time of the month? Never . . .

Never surprising him. Perfect, and perfectly familiar. She was exactly what he'd wished for, and every night he spent with his wish girls was a night of incredibly sophisticated masturbation, and nothing more.

Well, fuck it. Pleasure was pleasure, and there was something to be said for the familiar. At least Allison and Stephanie didn't make him nervous.

"Get up," he said. "Let's get Allison trussed up. I've got a new mouth harness I want to see her in. I'm thinking, after we whip her, we can lay her out on her back across the dining room table, and you can fuck her ass while I fuck her throat. Sound good?"

"Whatever pleases you, Max," she said.

"I can tell you're the shy type, Max," Kira said, pouring him another glass of sangria. "And I don't mind being aggressive, but I want to know my advances are welcome. I don't want to make an idiot of myself. Are you interested in me?"

Max sat on Kira's couch, and she passed him his drink, then sat beside him, tucking her legs beneath herself with casual grace. "You move so beautifully," he said, the two glasses of sangria already inside him relaxing him enough to say such things.

She looked at him over the rim of her glass, sipped, and said, "I studied ballet when I was a kid, but I didn't have the body to keep it up – not thin enough, too zaftig by half. I was crushed at the time, but in retrospect, I'm glad I don't live a life of glamorous starvation and crippled feet."

"I think you look wonderful," Max said, but he looked down into his drink, shy. This was nothing like talking to the wish girls. "I'm sorry. I do like you a lot. I just . . . haven't gone out much. I'm nervous. I've only been with a couple of women in my life."

"That's OK," she said. "That just means you won't have as many bad habits to unlearn." She grinned, a twinkling, mischievous look of a sort he'd never seen on the faces of the wish girls, and she plucked the drink from his hand and set it aside.

Kira leaned into him and they began kissing, and she took his hand and pressed it against her silk shirt, against her breast, which was large and full and shaped differently from those Max was used to. Her hand touched his thigh, then slid up to squeeze his cock. She kissed his neck, stroked his leg, slipped a finger into the waistband of his pants, her fingernail brushing through his pubic hair, making him shiver and tingle all over. Max's heart hammered, pulse throbbing through him and making his cock twitch, and he felt weightless, unmoored – he didn't know what she was going to do. Kira was an independent operator, an ongoing surprise. Her hair smelled of strawberry shampoo, and there was a hint of sweat, and her skin – the wish girls smelled almost of nothing, a little bit of baby powder, nothing else. This was intoxicating and, for the first time, it occurred to Max that sex could be a collaborative act.

"Bedroom," Kira said, and tugged him by his waistband into her cluttered room, walls decorated with painted kites, a double bed with a white comforter. They fell into bed together, touching one another urgently, and she stripped off her shirt and bra, revealing pale breasts with large brown nipples. Her left breast was slightly larger than the right, and this amazing human variation made Max moan and push her down on the bed, bowing his head to take her nipple in his mouth and suck. She made a sound like a contented cat and lifted her hips against him. He stopped kissing her breast and pulled down her skirt, taking a moment to admire her panties – black lace, hardly there, she must have planned all along to take him to bed — and then he pulled them down, too, and buried his face between her legs. Oh, the smell, sweat, and wetness, and something unmistakably feminine – the wish girls were nothing like this. He'd gone down on them countless times, and they'd never had a scent like this, just that baby-powder neutrality.

What had he been missing all this time?

He tongued her, slipped a finger inside her, was surprised to find she wasn't very wet yet. Another way she differed from the wish girls. He licked her, bottom to top, and she said, "Oh, that's right, warm me up, Max." When she was wetter, he slipped a finger into her and moved it while tonguing her clit, and this went on for a minute or so before she touched the top of his head. "Max, sweetie," she said, "your heart's in the right place, but your finger isn't."

He looked up at her, his hand unmoving, and realized that all the thousands of hours he'd spent fucking the wish girls had taught him nothing at all about women. "Tell me what to do," he said, and she gave him that grin again.

She guided him. "There, press your fingers up towards the, yes, right there, now swirl your tongue, to the right, no, my right, yes, there, keep it up." Max did as she said, though his wrist got sore and his tongue got tired. He'd never spent so much time going down on Allison and Stephanie, just enough to satisfy his own urge to taste and finger them, but this was something different, something more worthwhile, and after a while Kira got much wetter and bucked against his hand and tongue. She trembled, almost silently, with none of the theatrical orgasms Max had seen in porn films and taught the wish girls to emulate.

He kissed her belly, and she stroked his hair, and he said, "Can I fuck you now?"

"You'd better," she said, and he rose up and pushed her legs apart, and she said, "Whoa, Max, not so fast, condom first." She reached to the bedside table and lifted a square foil-wrapped packet.

"Ah, right," Max said, suddenly terrified. He'd never worn a condom in his life.

"I'll put it on you," she said, and rolled him on to his back. She grasped and tugged his cock, then put it briefly in her mouth, and he swelled to full hardness. She tore open the package and deftly rolled the condom – cold, strange – on to his cock, then swung one leg over to straddle him and eased herself down, guiding his cock up into her warm wet cunt. She rocked on top of him, reaching down to tweak his nipples, slipping a finger into his mouth for him to suck. Her weight, her spontaneity, the way she moved, it was all so different and, if not for the condom acting to dull the sensation a bit, he might have come in her right away. A euphoria grew inside him, spread through his body, suffusing his limbs with out-rushing lightness. Max had never felt so good. She lowered herself, breasts against his chest, cheek against his cheek, her breath in his ear, and he reached down to take hold of her ass in both hands, thrusting his hips against her. Her breath quickened as she thrust back, and soon they were rocking together, headboard slamming against the wall, moving faster and faster, until he felt himself starting to come. He squeezed her ass harder and thrust away, the two of them moving in wonderful concert, and she gasped in his ear and shuddered, trembling. He couldn't tell whether his orgasm had excited her into her own, or vice versa.

Afterwards, she didn't disappear, and he was glad.

"We should do this again sometime," he said, tentatively, afraid she'd turn away.

"Soon," she said. "Take me to your place next time?"

"Of course," he said.

Max knew better than to think it was true love. Oh, maybe it was, but Kira could just as easily grow bored with him, or more likely he would fail her in some way, since he had no experience with romantic relationships. But he'd turned a corner. Even if he didn't stay with Kira for ever, there would be other women, other relationships. He'd discovered how things could be, now, and there was no going back. He'd finally grown up.

But he hadn't grown up so much that he didn't want one last fling, for old time's sake.

The next morning Max called in sick to work, and summoned Stephanie and Allison. He dressed them in black stiletto heels and knee-pads and nothing more. "Stephanie, kneel there, legs spread, and reach behind you and grab your heels. Don't let go of your heels, no matter what." She did as she was told, and he fastened a leather and plastic ring gag around her head, a mouth-harness that held her jaws open for constant access. She gripped her heels, breasts jutting out beautifully, and he slipped his cock through the gag into her warm wet mouth, sliding it back and forth. "Keep looking up at me with those wide eyes of yours. And you, Allison, kneel behind me and lick my asshole."

He fucked Stephanie's face for a while as Allison tongued him. He could have come on them then – Stephanie had never looked more fetching – but he wanted to run the gamut today. He put collars and leashes on them and led them around the room on all fours, lashing their rumps with a riding crop. He leaned them both over the couch, lubed their asses generously, and pounded first one, then the other. He lay down and had Stephanie straddle his cock while Allison sat on his face, and they kissed and fondled one another while he tongued and fucked them. He had Stephanie put on the new black strap-on, and they double-penetrated Allison, who whimpered as Max thrust into her ass, begging him to do it harder, harder. Then he had Allison put on the old strap-on harness, and let his wish girls fuck him – he went down on all fours, Allison sliding a smaller dildo in and out of his lubed ass, Stephanie shoving her big black dildo in and out of his mouth. After that he spanked them, whipped them, fondled them, caressed them and fucked them every way he could think of. By day's end he was exhausted, sweat-soaked, and trembling from the exertion. His cock felt drained dry from the day's several orgasms. The wish girls, of course, seemed as calm and well rested as always.

"I'm letting you go," he said.

Allison and Stephanie looked at him, then looked at each other. They frowned, in unison. He'd never seen them frown before, except when they were playing Harsh Mistresses, and even that was a different, more theatrical expression.

"I appreciate all you've done for me," he said. This was harder than he'd expected. "You've made my life wonderful. But . . . I don't think this is good for me any more. I've met someone . . . well . . . It doesn't matter."

"You're setting us free?" Stephanie asked.

Had Max ever taught her to say that, as part of some bondage role-play scenario, maybe? He didn't think so. "Yes. You can go."

"Turn your back while we get dressed," Allison said.

Max knew he'd never taught her to say that. He'd seen her in every conceivable state of disarray – even now, his come was drying on her breasts. But modesty, he suddenly understood, was a privilege of the free. He turned his back.

"OK," Allison said a moment later. He turned to find them dressed in jeans and grey sweatshirts, not outfits he'd ever have chosen for them, clothes they'd conjured for themselves. They stepped towards him in unison, each kissing one of his cheeks. "Bye, Max," Allison said.

"We didn't think you'd ever get to this point," Stephanie said. She patted his cheek.

The wish girls left. They didn't disappear; they just went out the front door. Maybe they'd get to be real people now, and make choices of their own. He didn't know.

Max spent the rest of the evening filling heavy black garbage bags with sex toys, bondage gear and lingerie, then tossed them all into the big dumpster behind the apartment complex. The garbage men were sure to get a kick out of that. Maybe he and Kira would start playing with toys eventually, but he'd buy new ones for that. Even Max's vestigial sense of gentlemanly conduct told him that was the appropriate thing to do.

Two days later, Max sat on his couch, and Kira knelt on a pillow between his feet, sucking his cock. He looked down at her closed eyes, the expression of tender concentration on her face, and he was overwhelmed with happiness. She was doing this because she wanted to, because she liked him, because she wanted to make him feel good. And because she knew he'd return the favour.

Kira's teeth brushed against Max's cock. It hurt, a little. He'd never been happier.

The Spark

Cecilia Tan

Glory picked a bad moment to check out on us. We were booked on Autarie- - one of those self-contained orbital casino resorts with nowhere to go but around and no easy way on or off – for six simulcasts. Lots of money, and every "night" a different time zone with no travelling or loading out for us. Sweet deal. Or it would have been if not for Glory's sudden departure the night after the first show.

I suppose it was a trick of fate that I was the one who found her and not one of the others. There she was, stretched out on the coffee table in her suite as if it were a mortuary slab, her fingers cold and stiff around the neck of her trademark vintage Walker original. Her skin was all pastel shades of violet and blue, except where her black lipstick and eyeliner were smeared, as if at the end she'd shed a few tears for herself. Most don't go so gracefully – history is full of those who went on wild rampages, died in flaming vehicles, collapsed of overdose in public places, or choked on their own vomit. But she just lay there, beautiful and dead.

She'd lost the Spark, and the grief I felt seeing her there, alone, cut off from us for ever, was at least partly for myself. I knew someday I might go to a similar fate. And with her gone . . . my day seemed like it might be closer at hand than before. My mind was starting to fill up with details: our unfulfilled six album contract with Warner-Sony, tour cancellation . . . and then some tears came and blurred away all the business thoughts for a moment.

Calla was the next to come in. She'd heard me sob and come to see what was up – she probably thought Glory, in one of her mercurial moods, said something horrible to me, made me cry. But then she saw what lay on the table and she took me by the hands. "Oh, Luna, Luna, I'm so sorry," she said and it took me a moment to realize she was talking to me. My lover – in name if not in function recently – was dead.

I coughed a little but the tears had dried up already. "Shit, Calla, what are we going to do now?"

She leaned against the sloping, non-rectilinear wall and rested her eyes on her hand. She looked remarkably undebauched given last night's events. Her blonde hair gelled into a neat twist and her face fresh and make-up free above her resort-issue bathrobe. She was a double-x realgirl, like me, her eyelashes blonde in the artificial light. "Did you guys have a fight?"

"Yesterday. Twice. You were there."

It had started out a bitch session and ended up a screaming fit for Glory. She'd been going on and on about how a gig on Autarie was the ultimate ignominy. I'd tried to point out, as our booking agent had, that doing orbital simulcast was economical and easier on us. "But Autarie!" she'd screamed. "It's like fucking Vegas!" At the time I'd assumed that "Vegaz", as she said it in her Saturnál accent, was an ex-lover of hers who'd sucked in bed. Now little pieces of rock and roll history bounced through my moon-raised brain and I recalled an old interview I'd read with Mick Jagger – or was it Sting? – saying he'd never play Las Vegas and the meaning came clear: home of the has-beens. No one had been listening to her but me. Once she would start to go hysterical the others would tune her out. I suppose I only listened because I was the one trying to argue with her. "Oh, fuck," I murmured. Even if I had caught the reference, though, what good would it have done? I couldn't have stopped her, could I? She was gone.

Calla went over and knelt in front of the body. "It looks like she just . . . lay down and died."

"She did."

"What do you mean?" Calla had been with us a year, a great bass player, but neither Glory nor I had been sure she would stick with us. So she didn't know about the Spark.

"I don't know," I lied.

"Well, we have to get a doctor in here, find out what happened . . ."

I held up my hand. "No, no doctors."

"But Luna . . ."

"Not yet." My mind tried to come up to speed, but last night's party and the shock of seeing her there like that kept me partly paralysed. "Huiper. First call Huiper and figure out what to say about it."

I put my head against the doorjamb and sighed. It was the end of Glory, the end of the Seekers in all likelihood, possibly the end of all our careers. Replacing a drummer or back-up singer is one thing, replacing the lead singer and founder is another thing entirely. I felt cold and lonely and sick and I sank down there in the doorway and almost wished it could have been me instead of her.

Basil almost tripped over me when she came in waving hard copy of a review of last night's show. I liked Basil, even if I wasn't sure if she was a double-x or some form of genderqueer. Those things never mattered to the omnivorous Glory. For me it was good enough that she used a female pronoun. She was about to begin crowing the good bits of it aloud when she caught sight of the spectacle on the table. I couldn't bear to watch her face crumble into grief. So, I looked at my own whiter-than-white hands, and at Glory's, still streaked with the indigo and violet of last night's stage make-up, clamped tight around the neck of the guitar. I supposed that the Walker was mine now, but I couldn't bring myself to prise it out of her grip.

I heard my own voice. "We can't have her photographed like this, like some funeral or something." Oh Glory, couldn't you have lived up to your name and gone out with a blaze of it?

Calla did not turn around, but said in a weak voice "Was she . . . with anyone last night?"

I looked up at the two of them. Basil was taking it well. If anything she looked a little pissed off, and when she heard

Calla's question she stiffened. Young and spurned. "Not me. She took off during the party and didn't come back . . ."

Until after we were all unconscious. Poor Basil, the newest of us, she'd only been playing with the Seekers for about six months and Glory had been leading her on for most of it. She cursed under her breath. Glory had liked her youthful fire, her defiance. Perhaps she saw a little of herself there, or perhaps someone else she knew. She would have been a good vessel for the Spark, too, but Glory had held back passing it on. "Baz, could you get Huiper on a secure channel?"

"I'll try," she said, and went into her room to boot up a terminal.

Calla had left the room, too, leaving me alone with my dead lover. Ex-lover in any case now, I supposed. Although neither of us had taken up with someone else – we hadn't "broken up" – we hadn't had sex in a long time. A year, maybe two. And the fights recently had been worse, hadn't they? I'd wanted to believe that Glory's irritability, irrationality, and general out-of-control bitchiness was just a periodic magnification of her lead-singer prima donna persona, just a phase that we'd work out. But all along she had been suffering. The burning out. The end.

And I hadn't even felt it. Could I have helped her? Saved her? She'd been so distant from me, I doubted it. When the Spark is lost, there's no getting it back.

The first one I'd ever seen was just a month after I'd joined the group. Glory's ex-lover Saffron had split off to form his own band, but he came back once in a while to jam with us. His band wasn't doing very well. The critics were lambasting them for repeating the formulas of the past, and even I thought his music was kind of dull. He went out with a super cocktail of drugs and stims. Repeating the formulas of the past, as it were. We found him with the injector still in his hand at one of Glory's penthouse suites on Triton.

That one was easy for me to handle. I didn't know him that well, I was in love with Glory, and I was so young and new to the Spark that I didn't really connect Saffron's fate with mine. Huiper, our publicist, did a pretty good job of spreading the dirt around about the wild rock and roll boy who didn't know when to stop, and even made him into a kind of small-time martyr among his few but loyal fans. That was Huiper's job. But what would he say when he heard about Glory?

He would, of course, look for an angle that would generate maximum publicity and make Glory into a posthumous legend. That wouldn't be hard since she was already a legend when she was alive. We all were. It was all a part of the Spark, the magic. We were stars in the celebrity skies of the whole solar system. But Huiper didn't know why or how she really died and this time I didn't have a story to feed him. Mysterious cause of death unknown is what the headlines would have to say. The powers that be took her too soon, they'd lament. Or, maybe she died of a broken heart? Had our love really died? I shuddered at the thought. Huiper wouldn't implicate me in such a thing, would he? A sordid affair of lost love and betrayal?

The first fight we'd had yesterday was at sound check. The kind of spat that turned the mills of tabloid rumour, and all too typical. One of those fights that started as a bad mood, became a disagreement, then a full-fledged argument, and finally that hands and skin and bodies roughness that comes all too naturally with those who have been lovers. I had been tuning my guitar while she picked at the catered food backstage. Artificial gravity always screwed up her stomach for a couple of days but I didn't see as how that was any excuse for her to treat us all like shit. So when she brushed past me and bumped my tuner I griped at her loud enough for everyone to hear. I would have, stupidly, made even more of it if Maynard, our stage manager, hadn't called for everyone to take places for sound check.

Glory was the first one out of the room but the last one to climb on to the riser and sling her guitar over her shoulder. We were only on the second verse of "Tears" when Glory called for a halt. "I need this monitor up, less rhythm guitar."

I tried to talk into my mic but it was off. I waved at Maynard to up it and everyone heard me say ". . . can't do that. I won't be able to hear myself and you'll get off strum and you know it."

"Don't be ridiculous." She put her hands on her hips, the guitar hanging loose over her middle. Even under the house lights her skin had some hints of the lavender and blue that were her trademark colours. "You're so loud I can't hear the backing vox."

"Glory," I said, walking closer to her so she could hear my unamplified voice. "That's what you said at our warm-up gig on Metassus and your solo was completely off . . ."

I saw her jaw clench as she made a little starting/stamping motion. "You deaf wretch!" She took a step towards me, swinging the Walker off her shoulder and brandishing it in one hand like a sceptre. "You wouldn't know a good solo if it split your skull." Her voice had gone shrill and Maynard modulated it through the PA to save all our ears. "Which one of us is the lead here?" And then she broke down into hurling epithets at me in Saturnál.

I didn't hear what she called me; I started to shout back, "Fuck you, you egoistic bitch." But all I got out was "Fuck . . ." and then I threw off my head-mic and put my guitar in its stand and started to stalk off the stage. I couldn't be reduced to calling her names. I had to walk past her to the stairs and, as I did, she pushed me on the shoulder. My arm flailed back and connected with her cheek and then she was trying to grab me by the hair and strangle me and bite me all at the same time. Then the road crew, uniformly burly, uniformly imperturbable, were pulling us apart. She'd scratched my arm hard enough that bright crimson blood began to trickle down my skin, lurid on the paleness of flesh that never sees sunlight. And she said, "You ungrateful bitch! Without me you'd still be rotting on your ass in moondust! You'll never be anything more than a second-rate fill-in back-up stringer!"

I was gone before I heard any more – I didn't need to. Fact is without her I'd never have been in this band or for that matter ever made it away from suburban Luna. Fact is I mostly believed the rest, too. Sometimes she told me I only had that one good song in me, and sometimes I believed her. We never recorded another one of mine after "Tears", that's true. Huiper, the paparazzi, the fan sites, were always making up stories about us. Sometimes it was hard even for me to tell truth from fiction. The legend they tell about me is that I sneaked backstage at a Seekers show on Luna with a demo in my back pocket, and, when she heard it, she fell in love with me. In some versions she is heartbroken over Saffron leaving, and that's why she swore off men, and fell for me.

The true story is not like that. First of all, Glory's heart never broke. And second, although I did go to that show on Luna, it hadn't been my intention to meet her. My own band had just broken up from the force of apathy and neglect. I'd been ready to sell the guitar, maybe move to Earth where my parents wouldn't have any more say about me, but I decided to spend at least one night forgetting all of that, suped up and dancing like a banshee at their show. It was at the Dome, huge crowd, thousands at the biggest gathering space on all of Luna. It was being simulcast all over Earth, a big event. I was in the general admission section down front where I elbowed my way to the stage. I can only speculate that she saw me then, and liked what she saw. Halfway through their final encore one of their road crew pulled me out of the crush at the front, over the security wall into the tech pit. I couldn't make out what he was saying but I got the vague idea that I wasn't being busted but invited to some kind of party. There were some others there, dressed like fans, looking lost too, so I figured we were all either equally safe or equally endangered.

It was a party. A tremendous party at the Lunar Grand Hotel. We were all a part of the entourage and never before had I felt so welcome wearing ragged black denim in the retro-look of the times. We were ushered into a grand ballroom where food and swirling lights were already in attendance as if the inanimate party had already begun. And at some point I recall being near her, Glory, and wanting to tell her something about how much I had enjoyed the show. Maybe I did tell her. Anyway, she led me to the true party within the party, an inner sanctum penthouse where the band members and all manner of miscellaneous wildlings were lounging, boozing, orgying and so on. And eventually she pulled me even deeper into things, and we were in her own room, and in her own bed, in the dimness, as I traced the curve of her stomach by the shine of the glitter there and she breathed hot on my sex and we did not sleep until well into the next morning.

I only remember that night in snatches now. I remember lavender lips and the way she closed her eyes when she kissed me. I kept mine open to watch the way her mouth moved, then closed them as her hand sought deep into my jeans. I remember her left hand seeking between my legs and I imagine that I even felt the callouses on her fingers as she dragged them over my slick clit. I remember being on my back on the expanse of her bed, her body pressing mine down as her tongue hunted in the forest of my bush and I stared at the cleft of her ass, her cunt, pistoning above my face until I reached out with my own tongue. I remember what seemed like hours with my legs over the edge of the bed, and her quick fingers playing over my clit again and again, and sinking her hand into me, first the cone of her fingers, and eventually her entire hand, balled inside. There was probably more, but it has been obliterated by time and drugs and overlayers of bad memories.

It wasn't until after we woke up that afternoon that she began to ask me about myself. Or maybe I should say tell me about myself. I played guitar, right? And I sang. And I wrote about what was black and dripping in the human soul. "How do you know?" I must have asked, my jaw flapping as she ran her fingers through my straight black hair and remarked how even my lips were moon-dust pale. And she started calling me Luna right then. She hinted that she was very good at reading people through sex, though of course now I know it could have been the Spark.

Then she told me she wanted to hear me play. She forced the Walker into my hands and made me play. I was too nervous to sing, but I let my fingers go by themselves, through riffs I'd fought with Derel over before we'd both begun to act like we didn't care about the band or each other. And at the end of the song, the one that would later become "Tears" when I wrote words for it, she did have tears in her eyes and she told me she knew just how it was with me.

There is nothing like making love with your lover's tears wetting your face. She kissed me then, and laid the guitar aside, and pushed me back on the bed, and it is not like we were wearing clothes anyway. She dragged her cunt along my thigh, hot and slick like her tear-stained face, until she came, and then I flipped her over and fucked her with my fingers and ate her at the same time, until I don't know how many times she came, piling orgasm on top of orgasm, until she turned the tables and did the same back to me.

That was probably the last time I had been in charge at any time in our relationship. Because when her fingers were still inside me, after my third or fourth orgasm, as she sank her other hand into my hair, she asked me if I was interested in leaving Luna, and joining her as rhythm guitarist.

That's the real story of how I got whisked away. Because of course I said yes. Had she already passed the Spark to me? I think she had. I think it happened when she fucked me right after I had played. What would have happened if I had said no? Would the Spark have died, and me with it? I just didn't know. There was too much we didn't know. I know that through the fire and heat of music and sex and losing ourselves in both she passed it to me, but even ten years later, I knew very little more than that.

Calla and Basil had not had such an initiation from her. They were still waiting.

I should have realized when Saffron died that I might be in over my head. But I was so caught up in her, and in music, in finally devoting my life to someone and something that I enjoyed, that I felt I was born to do, that I didn't worry about how the Spark worked. It was just the lifeblood that fed us, that kept each of us going, writing, composing, playing. Some nights, when we'd played to a fever pitch, it boiled over, and there were always wildlings around to party with, to soak up that energy and go home tired and exhilarated both in the morning. Groupies don't know it, but it's the Spark they are attracted to, addicted to. Maybe they figure it's just the drugs, or the excitement, they feel it during the sex we have, that thrill singing in their veins. But unless they have music in their souls, it can't hurt them. It passes through them just like the drugs. It's only people like me that it takes hold of and doesn't let go. And Saffron. And Nura and Rose, who were both gone now for years, replaced by a string of studio musicians of Glory's choosing, until now Calla and Basil . . .

I had started to shiver, there in the doorway, as if the coldness of her flesh was making me chilly. There was also the fact that I was wearing just an old show T-shirt and underwear. I felt cold and empty, and the shaking became worse.

Calla was there, then, dressed in show clothes. Anticipating a press conference, I guess. She wrapped her arms around my shoulders. "Oh, Luna . . ." she started. "Be strong."

But I wasn't shaking with sobs. Glory had told me once that the Spark runs its course like a fever – oh sure, it could be years and years, but the hotter it burns the more likely it is to burn you up. At some point it burns out and leaves you high and dry and unable to function.

She had waited until after I'd accepted her offer to spell all that out for me. When she told me, it felt almost like it wasn't anything that I didn't already know. Some hacks can go on for ever because they never had it in the first place. But those who really had it . . . I didn't have to hear her name out the others. The agonizing slow death of Elvis, who staggered on long after the Spark had abandoned him, trying to replace it with amphetamines and sycophants until both failed him. Janis Joplin, whose own insecurities about her talent strangled it and forced her into drugs also. Kurt Cobain. The murderous rampage of the octogenarian Paul McCartney outside Buckingham Palace.

My body was wracked with spasms. And suddenly it made sense to me. The Spark was going to go out for me if I didn't do something about it. The flame needed to be fed, stoked, with music and sex with other people who had it. Was that what killed Saffron, ultimately? Being cut off from her, and being unwilling to share it with others for his own survival? I wished I had known him better. Had he been losing it already, starting to burn out, when he left the Seekers? Had Glory and I been killing each other with the fighting and "creative differences"?

The passion had turned to anger long ago, is that what made her burn up or gutter out?

"What happens now?" I asked Calla, who was squeezing me harder now, as I clenched my jaw to keep my teeth from chattering.

I hadn't meant her to answer, but she did. "Luna, you're sick. We have to get you to medical."

"No!" What would they find? The Spark was a secret not even Huiper knew about. Who could I turn to? I had met very few others who I knew beyond any doubt had it. Bowie, still going in his thirteenth decade, reinvented once again. But I didn't know how to reach him and couldn't imagine the conversation we would have.

Looking at Glory there on the table, I considered the traditional ways out for a moment. But I couldn't see myself drowning my "sorrows" in chemicals or crashing my flyer while "under the influence". I took a deep breath and got the shivering under control for a few moments.

There was really only one choice. Pass the Spark on to Calla or Basil, or die. "Calla," I said, trying to work up the nerve to say something.

But then Basil was there. "Huiper's not reachable. We can try him again at four, though." I looked up to see Calla take her hand, and I suddenly knew the two of them had slept together last night.

No, they were about to. They had each been waiting, hoping, to be the one that Glory took up with when she took up with someone again. Now she was gone, and they could see each other clearly for the first time. They looked into each other's eyes, a kind of wordless connection strung between them.

They looked up at the first sound of the guitar. I had crawled over to where Glory lay, and slid the Walker from her hands to cradle it in my lap. I had no pick and just used my fingernails to strike a chord, the first of a descending series starting up on the neck and working my way down until it felt right. From there, I fell naturally into a minor key riff, alternating the strum with finger-picking.

I could almost hear the parts that would go along with it, a cello, with a deep, rich bowed voice, and hand drums, a doumbek maybe. I kept playing. There were no words. I didn't know what to tell them, what I wanted to say about her or me or my life. I just kept playing.

But eventually the song came to a close, as it cycled down and my energy flagged. When I finished, I saw they were both crying. I laid the guitar aside and went to them, and hugged them.

Exactly how that turned into me kissing Calla, I'm not sure. Her mouth was hot in mine, her cheeks wet and scarlet. Her breath came fast and hard. My hands travelled down her sides, over her hips. I felt her weight shift, as she reached out to Basil. Then she was kissing her, too, and in the back of my head I tried to pause. I had done many wild sexual things since leaving my quiet life on the moon. Some of them had been with Glory, some not. But I did not know what Basil had under her jeans and to some part of me that mattered.

The Spark did not much care for my squeamishness. The pang of fear I felt transmuted into thrill, and then my attention went back to Calla and I felt desire flare. I pulled her towards me, Basil trailing along like the caboose, on to the smooth, hospital-cornered bed. I began peeling off the clothes she had just put on. Basil took her other side, and very shortly Calla was naked there on the coverlet between us. Basil and I exchanged a look, then each of us took a nipple in our mouths and Calla gasped. In perfect harmony, we each slid a hand up the inside of her legs, teasing her. Then Basil's fingers cupped over her mons, her labia, and then spread, opening her for me. I used the tip of my index finger to skim the cream from the edge of her vaginal opening, spreading it liberally around her clit. She moaned. I continued to move gently, my touch light, until she ground her hips upwards towards my hand. But she could not move much, as Basil and I kept sucking her nipples, and I lifted my hand away from her.

She whimpered and Basil chuckled low in her throat in response. I played with her lightly until she bucked again and this time I let her impale herself on my fingers, my index and middle fingers curving into her, my thumb extended over Basil's hand and then sliding between her fingers to where her clit swelled. One of her hands clutched at Basil's jeans and I gave her a little nod. I had her cunt to myself then, and I took the opportunity to position myself there, my cheeks between her thighs. But as I licked her with long strokes, at first softly but then with urgent energy as her voice rose to a wail, I had one eye fixed on Basil. Under the jeans she had plain white briefs, with a noticeable bulge. My stomach tightened. Then she slipped those off, too, and I almost laughed with my tongue plastered in Calla's cunt. Basil's protuberance was a technocock of some sort, form fitted and wired to her nervous system, rising rapidly in response to the arousal signals her brain was sending. The skin was imbedded not only with millions of nanosensors, but with accompanying lightglow effects. Right now the base was a deep red but the tip was glowing white like an iron left in the fire.

Calla tugged at Basil's brightly coloured cock then and silenced herself as she pulled the slender machine into her mouth.

Baz gasped and steadied herself on the bed with one hand, as Calla's tongue worked. It felt to me like I was licking her, too, as if somehow, through Calla, Basil's cock and my tongue were connecting. "Kee-rist . . ." she breathed, the only one of the three of us whose mouth was not busy, and yet she could barely speak. "Wow . . . it's . . ."

Calla paused to grin up at her. "Is it as good as they say?"

Basil nodded, then must have read the questions in my eyes. "It's new. She . . . paid for it . . ." and that was all she could say as Calla's mouth went back to work. It made sense now, the way she kept expecting Glory to invite her to bed. I felt Calla's clit spasm under my tongue and knew she was close to coming. I increased my pressure and she came while Basil thrust into her mouth, into the fleshy side of her cheek where I saw it bulge. Then I closed my eyes and concentrated on making her come once more, two fingers spiralling in and out of her while my mouth drew her clit in and I clicked my tongue on it. She rewarded me quickly, wailing again as Basil popped free.

I sat up and Calla looked at me, pleadingly, both of them did, and it was easy to see she wanted more of the technocock. Basil and she giggled a bit as we swapped positions, and I shifted around until Calla was sitting up, her back against my chest like two kids on a gravity toboggan. I reached around with my hands to brush her nipples and she arched just as Basil thrust in. Soon she had established a rhythm, and I let the waves of sensation come through her body and into my own cunt. I had tucked my head next to hers and she could turn her head to kiss me on the lips. I closed my eyes and kissed her and rode the wave of Basil's backbeat for a while. Then she broke away and kissed her, too.

I was startled out of my reverie then by Baz's lips on mine, her tongue searching urgently for something in my mouth. The Spark flared up to meet her hungrily. And then somehow she was climbing past Calla, and the two of them together climbed on to me. Calla lay along one side, kissing my neck and stroking me from breast to the top of my bush, while Basil crushed the erect technocock into the crook of my hip with her body.

"Luna," she whispered, her throat tightened by desire. "Luna."

I quivered under her, the echo of the shivering fit I'd had before starting again. I knew if I paused too long ... I knew I didn't want to pause too long. Glory and I had played with dildos, the low-tech kind, from time to time – she liked sticking things into my cunt as a way to prove she was in charge – but never anything like this and not in a long time. I crooked one knee up and there was the tool, now glowing blue and green and casting an undersea look on Basil's face, bumping up against the flesh between my legs. It had looked so slim before as she had pumped Calla's mouth, but now I wondered if it would hurt when she put it in. I clutched at her sweaty back with one arm, the one that wasn't trapped by Calla, craving it and fearing it all at the same time, which only stoked the Spark hotter. Calla's free hand then, it had to be, reached between my legs and opened me wide, and Basil thrust upwards through the slippery juices, then she adjusted her angle and sank into me.

I cried out, not from physical pain but from the sudden memory of the shape of Glory's hand stuffed into me. Basil's technocock was nothing like that, conveniently shaped for pleasure but not the rock heart that her fist had been.

Calla moved then, letting Basil push my knees up, and straddled my face. I licked at her between gasps as she dug her fingers between our bodies to get at my clit. She soon had the loose skin of my labia and bush stretched up taut towards my belly with one hand while the other jabbed in double time over the hard nub. Basil's thrusts mashed her hand even harder into me and I thrashed my head from side to side. "Harder," I said through clenched teeth. My body wanted violence, needed it to break through the tense wall of pain that separated me from them. The wall that Glory's death had erected.

No, I realized. The wall that Glory and I had built bit by bit over the last few years. Basil and Calla obliged, fucking me and frigging me as hard as they could, until I felt the edge of Calla's finger claw over my clit. "Yes!" She crooked her finger more and I bucked hard against her, Basil now the one along for the ride. The orgasm seemed to radiate along my skin as well as through my insides, doubling back and cresting for a second time as they continued their motions until I went limp.

I was amazed that Basil had not come, but what did I know about how the technology worked? Maybe she had a way to turn it down. She pulled out of me, the tool glistening wet and now throbbing a deep purple, and Calla nearly leaped upon it. Baz obliged, falling on to her back and letting Calla seat herself with the cock deep inside. She moaned and fell forwards for a moment, then sat up erect. Now I could again circle her with my arms and get my fingers on to her clit and nipples.

I don't know how long it was before she succeeded in making Basil come. All sense of time had long since fled. The three of us were just in a groove, where Calla would peak, then I would, using my own fingers when I had to, until eventually she arched and cried out and gripped her by the hips for two last thrusts that set Basil finally into a spasm, while I thrust my own fingers into my empty vagina, trying to remember what Glory's callouses had felt like.

The two of them were then on me again quickly, Calla burying her face in my muff while Basil hugged me from behind. Then, as Calla drew another orgasm out of me, as I beat my palms on the coverlet, I shouted, "Enough, enough!"

They fell away from me as the sensation ebbed. There weren't many cases, but there were a few, where people were fucked to death. The Spark can burn out a host, too. It was time to get it back under control.

I think it was some time later that I began to speak. I'm not sure if I blacked out or not, but when I came to, they were still there. The three of us were lying on top of the bed and I had no way of knowing if we'd been there for a minute or an hour. "We're going to play tonight," I said.

"What?" Basil sat up at the sound of my voice and rubbed her eyes.

"We're going to play tonight. A tribute concert for her. Just like we did here. Improvisational, cooperative." Not like anything we'd done before. As I described it to them, I could see the idea catching fire, the memory of the song I had played stirring faintly. "And there's something else I have to tell you." And I told them, about the Spark, about Saffron, about Glory, Rose and Nura, and all I knew. "I'm sorry," I said as I finished. "I should have told you before. For some it becomes a curse . . ." I looked at Glory, still lying in state on the low table. "But it is a gift, too."

In response, they came and kissed me, both together. I already had the sound in my head of the music we could make together.

Celtic Tongues

Jacqueline Applebee

They said a creature lived here. I breathed in deeply, inhaled a thousand shades of green into my lungs. I breathed out, opened my arms. I welcomed the new world. I was in Scotland, in the Highlands that surrounded the legendary Loch Ness. The lure of a monster in the deep waters had piqued my interest, but what had finally drawn me hundreds of miles from my home in Bristol was the thought of quiet, peace and tranquility.

Nine glorious hours on a train had left me in the city of Inverness, the capital of the Highlands. A short bus journey had brought me to my destination: a collection of chalets in the tiny village of Invermoriston, where I would be staying for seven days.

I made my way to the reception area, but nobody was there. I went back outside, my feet crunching on the decorative gravel that formed a border to the building. I was in no hurry to check in. I could have a leisurely walk around the sprawling grounds first; acclimatize myself before I settled in.

A figure approached me from the pathway, a young man who was tall, lean and tanned. The sun broke the clouds, and shards of light glinted across his bare chest. I saw his toothy smile from some distance. I found myself grinning as he moved closer.

"You OK there, hen?" he asked. In my journey from the West of England to the North of Scotland, I'd been called "mate", "love", "hen", "pet" and "wee lass". I was starting to become accustomed to the variety of endearments used by complete strangers; it was quite sweet when I thought about it.

"I was supposed to be checking in, but I guess I'm early." I tried not to look at the young man's nipples, but he was quite a bit taller than me, so his chest was literally in my face.

"Well, my ma's just on her way over." He picked up my heavy suitcase with one hand.

I inhaled clean sweat as he moved, but was riveted by the sight of lean muscles that flexed beneath his skin. He looked hard and solid. I licked my lips without meaning to.

I tore my eyes away from his delicious body, as a woman of my age came trotting up to us.

"Hello there!" she called in an accented voice. "You must be Molly."

We shook hands. I glanced discreetly between the mother and her son. "I see you've met Adam." She nodded to the object of my desire and sudden dread. "He's helping me out today. Would you believe he's just graduated from university, but the lazy boy won't go out and find a proper job?"

"I consider this a proper job!" Adam called out over his shoulder as he walked to the nearest chalet.

"Ach, young people," his mother said with a melodramatic sigh. "Do you have any children yourself?"

I shook my head. I'd never been able to conceive. After a few years, I'd stopped trying, got on with the rest of my life.

"He's a good laddie really." She ushered me to the chalet. Adam leaned against a wall near the door. He didn't move as I squeezed by. All those good looks were obviously a veneer for a cocky attitude. He knew the effect he was having on me.

Adam's mother explained which keys opened what doors, where the recycling bins were, when the launderette was open. But I heard little of what she said, as my eyes and my attention kept being drawn to her son as he moved around the small chalet. At one stage, he reached up to unscrew a light bulb from a ceiling lamp. I watched his jeans slide low over his hips; I glimpsed the tan line over the swell of his buttocks. He glanced down at me, shook the bulb gently.

"I'll get ye a new one." Two buttons on his fly were open. A bulge was outlined against the denim. "I'll pop by later, if that's OK?"

I nodded, unable to speak. That would be more than OK.

They left me alone after I completed the paperwork. I had just started unpacking when a polite knock at the door signalled Adam's return. I let him in, making sure that I stood at a discreet distance, but it was hard work. Something dark stirred in the depths of my belly; I felt desire move like a creature inside me. I wanted to reach out to stroke over his fine tanned skin. I wanted to get on my knees, and blow him. Why couldn't the man take pity on me, and wear a shirt? I was going to get myself into trouble if this went on for much longer.

"Do you have any plans now you're in our wee neck of the woods?" he asked, tilting his head. "I don't know if it's your thing, but there's an event in Inverness tomorrow night. I'll be performing there." He pulled a little stool from beneath a nearby table, and then stood on it to get at the light fitting with ease. Once again his worn jeans drooped over the top of his hips. Against my better judgment, my murky mind took a plunge into an obscene fantasy. I pictured Adam stripping in front of a gaggle of screaming women, throwing discarded items of clothing into the fray. I swallowed, willed my voice to remain calm. I was forty-two, old enough to be the man's mother.

"Can I ask what sort of performance it will be?"

Adam looked at me. His eyes were green, unblinking. "It's Nos Ur."

"Nos Ur?" I repeated, puzzled.

"It means 'New Style' in Scots Gaelic.'

"You speak Gaelic?"

"Aye, I speak it, I sing it and I love it." He screwed in the bulb, fixed the light shade in place, and hopped off the stool.

"Impressive."

Adam stepped up to me, invading my space completely. "I could only use this language, once I knew I had it." His voice was low, husky. "But sometimes words do me no good at all." When his lips brushed against mine, I breathed in a thousand shades of green. Adam tasted of the wild land. His tongue met mine, and his fingers gripped my arm. I felt drawn in to his world.

"Ma will be around with cake in a little while."

"What?" My eyes had trouble focusing.

"She does it for all the new visitors – cake for your first time, a bottle of wine for your second."

"I don't drink," I said stupidly. "Anyway, I'm sure this won't be my only visit here."

"So will you come to Nos Ur?"

I nodded, smiled. The door to the chalet opened just as Adam took a few steps away from me. His mother carried a covered plate in her hands.

"Cake for the new guest," she said with a smile. She set the dish on the table, and swept away the cloth to reveal what looked like a small fruitcake. "I hope Adam hasn't been bothering you?" She shot him a look that meant she knew exactly what kind of bother he could cause.

"No he's been very helpful."

"We'll give you some peace then." She beckoned to her son, who gave me a wink before he followed his mother out.

The next evening I went to an upmarket venue in the heart of Inverness. Tall pine trees that framed the dark loch had given way to grey stone as the small city opened out, but I still felt that I was deep in the Scottish Highlands.

Nos Ur had brought some serious crowds to the concert hall. Ten bands would be playing, each one in a different Celtic language. There would be a vote for the favourite, and they would then go on to a bigger event that would be held in the Netherlands later in the year.

At Nos Ur, there were bands that performed in languages that I had never heard of before, like Cornish and Lowland Scots. However there were also some that were more familiar to me, like Welsh and Gaelic from both Scotland and Ireland. I was struck by the way the music united all the different languages and dialects. At one stage I even started singing along with a happy tune sung in Lowland Scots, which was the closest language to English. I wondered if this was how the world was before Babel. I didn't have a hope of translating all the tongues I heard, but somehow I just knew what every song was about. I felt the magic of the area start to permeate my skin.

Finally Adam's band came on. Two women played violins, a man played keyboard and Adam sung like a force of nature, howling into the microphone with passion. My eyes travelled over my young friend, taking in his unusual outfit. Adam wore what looked like very baggy trousers. I peered closer, leaning forwards in my seat to see that they weren't trousers. Adam wore a skirt: a long black garment that swept the ground with every move. I'd expected to see men wearing kilts in Scotland, but not skirts like that. I knew where my vote was going tonight.

I may have voted for Adam, but a Welsh band got the majority, and they would be going on to the finals. I felt a little sad for Adam, but his music was so good, I just knew that a record producer would snatch him up real soon.

I found Adam after the closing ceremony. He looked somewhat down, but he still smiled as I approached.

"I thought you were great. Thank you for telling me about this." I stroked his back.

"The Welsh boyos were grand. I voted for them myself," he said.

"Really?"

Adam nodded, holding up a little disc. "I've even bought their CD."

We both laughed until we doubled over.

I awoke late the next day with the River Moriston as the only sound in my world. I walked around the local area after my breakfast, trudging up pathways that led me through a dense pine forest. Little sparkling streams ran alongside me as I climbed higher, enjoying the fresh air, the peace and all that green. I imagined mysterious woodland creatures danced just out of view as I made my way through this special place.

When I returned to my room several hours later, I felt as if I had slipped back in time. Everywhere I looked was lush emerald grass, the curve of high mountains speckled with purple heather. Everything was just perfect.

Later in the day, I made myself a cup of tea, and sat out in the grassy area outside my chalet. The sound of running water enveloped me – the River Moriston flowed beneath the banks that formed a green steep drop. The clear water bubbled over rocks and small boulders, but as I peered into the distance, I saw how the river widened further on, streaming over bigger obstacles to become Telford Falls, which in turn fed into Loch Ness. I wondered if the Loch Ness Monster had ever been sighted this high upstream? I wondered if the creature that had spawned myths and legends was truly real.

I finished my tea, and then I walked along the riverbank to where a crumbling stone bridge spanned the rushing water. The sun was setting, but there was still enough light to see a couple on the bridge, enjoying the view to the sound of some ambient music. I watched intrigued as a man sat on the edge of the bridge – it was Adam, looking gorgeous in the waning light. A man danced with his back to me. The sensuous moves were hypnotic, but I was left in no doubt that he and Adam were an item. As if to confirm my thoughts, Adam reached out and ran a hand over the dancer's back, stroking his neck. Adam's partner leaned into the embrace briefly, and then stepped away.

The man picked up a strange object, and then he began dancing with it. Soon I spied a band of light that span in a wide circle with streaks of gold, red and blue. I watched amazed as he twirled a glowing rod in time to the music. He turned, still spinning the staff, gyrating slim hips to match the movements. I finally recognized him as the keyboard player from Adam's band. I realized that the dancer was smiling at me. Light dazzled my eyes. I smiled back.

"Hello, Molly." Adam raised his hand in greeting.

"I didn't mean to interrupt," I said weakly, as I clambered on to the stone bridge, now aware of how precarious it was: rubble was scattered down one side, and the low walls seemed incredibly fragile. "Your friend looked really interesting. I've never seen anything like that before."

"Molly, this wee lad is Cerise," Adam said, pulling the dancer closer into an affectionate hug. Cerise glanced at me shyly before looking down at his feet. Adam punched the young man playfully on the shoulder. "Molly was paying you a compliment, idiot," he teased.

"*Tapadh leat*," Cerise mumbled. "Thank you." I wondered how someone could be shy after moving with such open abandon earlier.

"What is that?" I asked, pointing at the wooden implement he held.

"It's a glow staff," Adam replied. Cerise handed the staff to me. I twisted it in my hands, but it only looked like an ordinary piece of wood in my grip. "Cerise is great with poi and the like," Adam explained, but I'd never heard of poi before.

Cerise trotted over to the far end of the small bridge, where a black rucksack lay. He rummaged around for a moment before he came back to us, carrying an armful of objects.

"Poi." He held up what looked like two long socks that bulged from the bottom. When I didn't make any comment on the strange items, he took a step away from me. He rotated his arms, and the poi swung easily around him. Time slowed down as he began to move the rest of his body, and soon I was treated to the sight of an impressive routine. The poi were mesmerizing as they circled in front of my eyes.

I became aware of a presence behind me: Adam stood close, pressing against my back and my bottom. "There's a little trick you can do," he whispered in my ear, moving his hands down to mine. "Like so," he continued, lifting my hands straight out in front of me. Cerise grinned, moved closer, and let the poi wind their way around my forearms. The solid feel of the poi restrained me, pulling my hands together in a sudden clinch. Cerise twisted the poi, tying it securely in a quick movement. My breath faltered in my throat. I stood sandwiched between the two men, helpless to escape.

"Nice trick," I whispered. My voice was hoarse. My whole crotch began to pulse and spasm. The two men moved closer to me, squashing me slightly as they leaned forwards. They exchanged a long kiss over my head. I felt twin erections against me, from the front and from the rear.

"*Ceutach,*" Cerise crooned. He licked along the side of my neck.

"Beautiful," Adam translated the Gaelic into English.

Adam's hips moved against mine, rubbing his length against my bottom. Cerise nosed the skin around my bound arms, mouthing across to my elbow, and then back up again.

"Do you want us to stop?" Adam asked, as if my humping his legs wasn't enough of a clue.

I bit my lip, whined as he stroked my front, brushing fingers across my chest. I felt the play of muscles against me as Adam wrapped his arms around my waist. Cerise leaned over once more to kiss him, his dark hair brushing against my face. I was hungry, longing to be kissed too, but I couldn't reach either of them. I gasped, stood on tiptoe, but the men just pulled me back down again, and resumed kissing each other instead. Just when I had given up on getting any attention, the two men directed me to where the canopy of a tree spilled over the side of the bridge. We tumbled into the bushy leaves, balanced on the crumbling rock of the old bridge. My eyes fluttered shut as fingers reached into my knickers, tugging them down in three short pulls. The material of my panties lay twisted around my ankles, restraining me even further.

Adam ran his thumb over my mouth. "Suck it," he whispered.

I licked and slurped on his thumb, drawing it inside, enjoying the feel as it invaded me. My tongue swirled over the whorls of his thumbprint, memorizing the unique feel of his hard skin. Abruptly he pulled it free, but then I felt calloused hands cup me, whilst Adam's wet thumb circled my arsehole from behind. Even in this pursuit, the two men were affectionate with each other; their fingers joined as they stroked and caressed my pussy and my arse. The pounding water from the River Moriston sped around me. I felt awash in the stream as my breathing grew faster. And then suddenly the whole world tipped to a strange angle as Adam leaned back, holding me with one hand whilst the other was buried in the crack of my arse. Cerise bent to latch on to my protruding nipples, biting right through the fabric of my sweater to make me hiss with pleasure. A small part of my brain wondered what on earth I was doing, fooling around on a dangerous bridge with a couple of young men. However most of my mind was just satisfied with the way Cerise's fingers tweaked my clitoris, how Adam's thumb had wedged inside the tight entrance to my arse. I could beat myself up about this some other time.

I heard a low moaning sigh, but this wasn't the sound of a mythical creature that swam far beneath us. The noise came from my own throat as Cerise unzipped his trousers, and then dragged his cock against my thigh. Adam held my skirt in bunches as he helped his lover enter me.

"That's my wee lad," Adam crooned to the man above me. "My beautiful boy." His thumb hooked into my arse, a solid weight that made every nerve ending sing with delight.

Cerise said something in Gaelic that sounded like it meant, "Good." He thrust inside me, surging into my pussy that was wet and willing. I had been waiting for this for the past two days, although I had thought that it would be only Adam and I. I wasn't going to complain though, not when Adam's thumb made my arse sparkle with pleasure. I wouldn't say a bad word when Cerise's cock nudged my clit with every thrust he made. The younger man practically climbed on top of me as his movements became harder, less fluent. I felt shudders beneath me. I prayed that it was Adam shaking, and not the bridge that was falling apart. The sound of the torrent that thundered below grew loud in my ears, but I knew that if I fell, tumbling into the water, I would not be alone.

Cerise angled his hips, slamming against me, touching a spot deep inside that made all my fears dissolve into pure pleasure. I came, surrounded by two Highlanders, with my voice wild and free. The words I uttered were the first moments of Babel, where the single human language splintered into a thousand dizzying tongues.

Cerise cried out too, and then he slumped against me. His hair was soft against mine.

"You might want to let me up now," Adam squeaked from behind.

The music came to an end. The two men stepped away, leaving me bound and breathless, a heap on the crumbling bridge. I didn't know what I was supposed to do. I wriggled in my restraints, but could not get free until Cerise kindly unwrapped me.

"Do all your guests receive such a great reception?" I rubbed my arms until the blood began to flow freely once more.

"It's the latest thing," Adam replied, picking up his small stereo.

"Nos Ur," Cerise chimed.

"Plus mature women do something to me," Adam confessed with a shy smile. "I couldn't help it."

"Scots Gaelic is really a beautiful language," I said dreamily.

"Aye it is," Adam whispered before he helped me to climb back over the broken portion of the bridge.

"Do you think you could teach me some?"

Adam looked at Cerise before he spoke. "Meet us here tomorrow night, and we'll see what we can do." Adam gripped Cerise's hand in his. He drew him farther into the growing dark.

Ivo

Alana Noel

When my friend Micah was too old for a babysitter his parents hired one anyway to stay overnight with him. Giselle lived in the neighbourhood. His dad knew her dad, something like that. What Micah remembered about Giselle was she had whip-long hair pulled into a tight cord over one shoulder, and she'd painted her fingernails purple, fingernails she dragged across the kitchen counter when they were alone; and she'd ordered him to make her some scrambled eggs. Micah said he felt that drag of nails across his soul, like his electrodes shifted, and he tried to make those eggs perfect. Except he fucked them up or so she said he did. Giselle yelled at him, and the more this chick shouted at him in the kitchen by the stove, the harder his cock got. Micah said he beat off in the bathroom later. He jerked off reliving the heat of Giselle's breath beating him in the face.

Now we were in a hotel room, Micah and me, and you could say the room was swanky because Ivo had class. The air in the room smelled like flowers, and the furniture was plush in that upscale hotel kind of way. The bed was huge. A picture window overlooked Portland, a gleam from the Willamette River. Out on the balcony you could smell rain, just the smell though; the sky at the moment was clear and dark like a bruise.

Micah had started on the champagne. He continued looking at me over his shoulder. "What do you think she's going to ask us to do, dude?"

"You know what she'll ask us to do."

"OK, so will you take it up the ass or will I? We should figure this out."

I shook my head. No way. "We do whatever she says."

"Yeah, yeah," Micah said. And then he got back to the champagne.

Three months ago, I answered an ad. *Woman seeks beautiful bisexual boy to do what he's told. Apply with a phone number and photo.* When I sent off my photo to a post office box, I didn't expect a reply.

It was a Wednesday night, and I sat in an apartment I shared with Micah and watched him fast-forward through a porn tape looking for a girl who could squirt come from her cunt. "She ejaculates, man!" Micah was excited.

The cell phone in my jeans pocket vibrated, agitating my boner. I looked at my phone: caller unknown. Meanwhile, Micah couldn't find the girl with the squirting cunt.

"Fuck, she was here." His jeans were open, and his cock poked out.

I hit the answer button on my phone. "Yeah?"

"Tyler?"

"Uh-huh . . ." My voice trailed off. Feminine voice. Unfamiliar. "Who's this?"

"Who do you think? Elmore Park, one hour. Bench by the water fountain."

"OK."

She clicked off. I looked at Micah.

"I'm about to find her," he said.

I stood from the couch and zipped up. Shit, sweating already, an adrenaline rush, something. I felt dizzy. "Hey, I've got to go."

"What are you talking about? I'm about to find the chick who squirts."

I dropped my phone in my pocket then went to a mirror and looked at myself.

There was this actor, Jonathan Brandis, big eyes and darkish-blond hair, who did a show about the sea or something, and chicks often said I looked like him, so I figured, Hey, a good thing. Except I heard this guy had gotten depressed about his star falling out of the sky, losing his fame or something, and so he'd killed himself, and I'd imagine a supernova when I thought about this actor guy, a star that burns real bright before it's gone, and then I got sad about it. Weird feeling.

Behind me in the apartment our TV glowed with an eerie silver-blue light. Micah liked to set a mood. I pushed my hands through my hair then turned my head side to side checking my face in the mirror. Heck in this light, I glowed.

Micah had settled in his chair, cock like a kickstand in his hand. "Look at this chick's ass. God, I'd like to fuck that ass." He yanked another second then said, "You ever fuck a chick in the ass, Ty?"

"No. Listen, I'm going now."

"You suck, dude."

"I know, see you later." I waited for him to ask where I was going so I could tell him.

"Fuck," he said. "I want some pussy!" Micah yanked harder. I went for the door. "Hey!" Micah yelled behind me.

"What?" I looked at him, waited. He'd twisted around in his seat.

"The chick *squirts.*"

I waved at him then bolted. Later, I'd give him the details.

Outside, the sky was the colour of an old bruise. Sitting inside my car, a Mustang I'd painted and reupholstered in high school, I stared out the windshield and got a case of the chicken shits. What if I bailed? *Beat off, Ty; get it out of your system.* Get what out of my system? A woman wanted to tell me what to do. And I wanted that. Simple. Like, use me, fuck me up. I figured we'd bring Micah into it eventually. A woman would lift the veil, force me into a full-on gang bang with straight sex, gay sex, all of it. I experienced a jolt to my crotch then almost cried. I leaned my head against the steering wheel then drifted, which I used to do in school.

I had a teacher in a high school, Ms Ryn. She got to me. Ms Ryn used to come up behind my desk while I daydreamed in class then slap her hands together, which made me jump so hard I'd hit my knees on the desk. Sharp pain.

When I'd look at her she wouldn't smile, but her eyes would look glacial bright. "I want you to stay after school," she said one day.

I didn't ask why – for daydreaming, whatever, didn't matter. My friends complained. "Bitch."

I shrugged. "Yeah." What I didn't say was, *That bitch turns me on.*

After school, Ms Ryn gave me a stack of paper and one pencil and then instructed me to write: "I will pay attention in Ms Ryn's class. I will pay attention in Ms Ryn's class. I will pay attention in Ms Ryn's class." I wrote until my hand cramped, until the callous in my middle finger was indented and I had lead under my fingernails. Maybe the punishment was . . . elementary, demeaning? I don't know; it wasn't to me. I mean, it was those things, but I had a hard-on the whole time I wrote those sentences.

And Ms Ryn . . . she was tall and reed thin, burning red hair, and a few wrinkles around those eyes she'd cast over me like I was . . . beneath her.

Oh, fuck, I was.

An hour later, Ms Ryn put her hand on my arm. "Stop."

I dropped the pencil then covered my lap. My arm, where she'd touched me, was intensely warm.

"Will you pay attention in my class, Tyler?"

"Yes, ma'am." God that felt good. What if I got on the floor? My cock twitched. I wanted nothing more than to jerk off at her command. If only she'd tell me to do it. Call me a fag then say, "Jerk off," until I shot a load, which accidentally got on her shoe, so she'd tell me to lick it.

Ms Ryn eyeballed me like, almost, something passed between us, recognition or acknowledgment, something. "You may go."

You may go. Loved how she talked like that. I stood holding my backpack in front of me but then didn't move or couldn't or didn't want to, something. Ms Ryn had walked to the front of the room then noticed I was still there. "Is there something else, Ty?"

A lot else, but how did you say that to a teacher?

That night in the shower, I jerked off imagining Ms Ryn. Writing *You will pay attention in Ms Ryn's class* while she breathed in my hair before she pushed a hand inside my shirt to pinch my nipple hard. I came a bucket of jizz. And I groaned so loud I slapped a wet hand over my mouth worried maybe Mom might have heard me.

In high school, I used to skip school to smoke cigarettes with these other jerks, and of course we had no idea why we skipped school and smoked except we needed to appear tough. That was important: look tough to the chicks. Except I fantasized a woman who led me into all kinds of things: handcuffs, rim jobs, dildos up my ass and hitting me if I said no. And I do mean slapping the shit out of me.

Once, while a chick gave me head in the front seat of my car I said, "Would you hit me? You know, across the face, hard as you can?"

She'd shown me this google-eyed stare. "What?" You really would have thought I was the biggest moron on Earth by the look on her face.

"I don't know. Never mind." I'd pushed her head down and focused on the sensation of her mouth on my cock, but mostly on a voice in my head, which was supposed to be hers. *"Sissy little piss ant, don't you dare come."*

"Oh, fuck, fuck." I'd shuddered, shoved my hips forwards, and then held the girl's head as I'd shot off inside her wet mouth. *Fuuuck.*

"Geez, Ty, you could have told me." The chick had twisted away to wipe her mouth. Maybe she'd been mad, thought I was scum.

"Maybe you should, you know, pay me back or something, punish me."

The girl had sighed. "Just tell me next time, OK?"

It wasn't Mom. I know that would be an assumption: Mom knocked me around, under-mined my self-esteem, something. Mom was tough; she had to be. She raised me alone, and for a while we were dirt poor until she clawed her way into a good job. I respected Mom, thought the world of her actually, but there wasn't a Freudian connection. Mom never did anything out of line with me.

I didn't chicken out that Wednesday night. I drove to Elmore Park. Straight there. Into the arms of Fate. In the parking lot, I shut the car off then pocketed my keys before working my hand around my phone, bit of cold warmed by contact with my body. When I got out of the car, I inhaled oak trees, my own anticipation, then started across a stretch of grass. I walked fast, almost like it was a race. I knew where the fountain was. The sky was dark now, and the moon was a sliver, which reminded me of a woman's fingernail.

When I got to the bench I sat. Then waited. When I looked at my phone, I saw I was twenty minutes early. Then I was on time. Then she was ten minutes late.

Fuck, had somebody snowed me? I started to think of ways Micah could have orchestrated the whole thing then imagined getting back to the apartment and him waiting there so he could laugh his ass off then say, "Whatever, asshole, sit down and jerk off."

I pulled my phone from my pocket, ready to call him, laugh it off, hide my disappointment, never admit he'd nailed my *exact fucking desire*, and then I saw something near a light pole. A woman. Yeah. Leggy. Yeah, just over there.

"Hey," I tried to say, but nothing came out.

"Hi, Tyler." Same voice from the phone but clearer – not syrupy or husky either, just calm and collected. She stayed by the light pole looking at me, I guessed; therefore I couldn't make her out like I wished I could – just a leggy figure with a backdrop of light.

"Hi." Finally I found my voice.

The enigma stepped closer. She wore a leather jacket, pants and boots with a heel. Her heels clicked the pavement. I had no idea what else to say, so I stared at her, probably with my mouth open.

"You're cute," she said.

"Thanks." Relief, she thought I was cute. "Chicks tell me I look like this actor, Jonathan Brandis, but he's dead now; anyway, I get told there's a resemblance."

"He committed suicide," she said.

"Yeah." I swallowed.

"So what did you have planned before I called?"

"Just hanging out with this guy I live with, Micah."

"Did you tell him you're here?"

"No, not really, no."

"Do the two of you fuck each other?"

Bam. I liked that. But sure, I got nervous. "Nah, I mean we haven't yet."

"You want to, though, don't you? You like boys."

"Well, I haven't ever been fucked by a guy."

Silence.

"We jerk off together a lot."

Silence.

"I'll do whatever you tell me."

"You will?"

"Yeah."

She stepped a couple of feet closer. "You go to college?"

"No. I mean, not yet, maybe later." I swallowed again, harder. She smelled like something sharp . . . and sweet . . . like apple cider in the sun.

"You work?"

"Yeah."

"Doing what?"

"Nothing cool, just deliver pizzas."

"You make good tips?"

"Well, sometimes."

"Have you ever delivered a pizza to the wrong house?"

"Once I did."

"Did she punish you?"

"Huh? Oh." I laughed, or my voice cracked, something. "No, it was a dude."

"What happened then?"

"Well, the right house was just around the block, so I got there on time."

"His pizza wasn't late?"

"Nah, I'm usually early."

"I noticed that."

"Yeah well, that's me." I laughed again, incredibly nervous. "Hey, you want to sit? You can sit if you want." My voice had just cracked again. *Shit*.

"I have to go," she said. "But there's a restaurant on Franklin Avenue, Three Brothers, know the place?"

"I've heard of it, nice place."

"Be there tomorrow at eight. Dress nicely and comb your hair."

"OK."

"When you get there tell the host you have a reservation; give him the name Ivo."

"Your name is Ivo?"

"Listen." Her voice had taken on an edge.

"Sorry." My skin got a chill. My cock twitched.

"A young man will bring a basket of bread to the table and a pitcher of water."

"Cool."

"That's all you'll be having."

"No problem."

"Don't request anything else."

"OK."

Ivo was silent, a sinewy shifting silhouette with a blade of light across part of her face. I said what popped in my head next. "The name Ivo, it's very cool."

That's when she laughed, and the sound of it was like fork tines dragged across my ass. Then: "Shut up," she said. "And . . . get the fuck out of here."

I jumped off the bench and went; I was very turned on.

When I got back to the apartment the place was dark and quiet except for the ten-gallon fish tank across the room. The tank light was on, giving the water a violet hue, and the filter gurgled like a fountain. I stood at the tank a minute and stared at the fish, mostly mollies and neon tetras, but we also had a betta in there. Naturally solitary and very aggressive, the betta was blue with flamy feathery fins. It glided among the rest of the fish as if totally disinterested. Then it approached the glass, and I would have sworn it looked at me as it opened its mouth. I'd heard they had tiny razor-sharp teeth.

I went down the hall, dropped my clothes, and then slid into his bed next to Micah. He was slim as a knife in there. I touched his back with one hand, scooted closer, fitted my body against the length of him then wondered what it would be like if he fucked me up the ass. I couldn't ever ask him.

Micah fidgeted, woke up. "What?' he said, sounding irritated, half out of it.

"Nothing." I turned over then heard Micah yawn.

"You get some?" he asked.

"Nah. She's into bi guys though."

"She told you that?"

"Yeah."

"What's next?" Micah moved close enough his cock touched my back.

"I don't know," I said. "I'm going to see her again tomorrow. She's amazing, dude, I mean it." I cupped my hand around my cock. "Older than us, totally dominant."

"Think I'll meet her?" Micah shifted his body again; his cock bumped my ass.

"I don't know, that would be cool, you know if the three of us . . ." I wanted Micah to jerk off while Ivo orchestrated how and when he moved his hand before she gave the word to unload on my back, or in my face even.

"What's she look like, dude?"

"Tall, very leggy, she wears boots and leather."

"Dude, I love leather."

I felt how his cock rested in the crack between my ass cheeks. I turned over.

"Let's jerk off," he said.

Nervous as shit the next night getting ready. I put on the only pants I had that weren't jeans and a button-up shirt.

Micah stood in the doorway to my room checking me out. "You meeting her?"

"Yeah."

"Where?"

"Three Brothers," I said, and then I looked at him. "I've never been there."

"Place is totally overrated." He eyeballed me. "Dude, you gelled your hair."

"So?"

Micah smiled. He actually had a cool smile, attractive, like beguiling or something. I looked in the mirror again. "Do I look all right?"

"Yeah, good. You rub one out already?"

"I'm fine."

Micah shook his head. "Ty, man, you've got to rub one out before you go."

I checked myself again. Should I button all the way or leave the top button open? Shit, I'd already sweat on the shirt. What if I changed? Except this was my best shirt.

"Ty," Micah said behind me. "If you bang this hot older woman and come too fast, you'll never see her again."

I looked at him.

"I've got a chick who *squirts*, dude, you know the *movie*."

Time on my phone gave me an hour. "Yeah, OK," I said.

We sat on the couch, pants opened and cocks out. The chick in the film ejaculated from her cunt in a fan of nearly invisible rays. I'd never seen anything like it. My balls were full and about to blow, but then I realized I didn't want to get jizz on my shirt. "Fuck," I said aloud then looked at Micah. "Do me a favour?" He passed me his shirt. I came in it.

At Three Brothers I told the maître d' or whatever, the host, I had a reservation under Ivo. The guy, who had white hair although he really didn't look older than thirty, gave me the most condescending look I'd ever seen; he swept his blue eyes over me like I wasn't even a fly in shit – whatever. And then he led me to a table at the centre of the room before he pulled out a chair and swept his hand in front of him like, *sit, dweeb*. He gave me a menu.

"Thanks," I said.

The guy laid another menu on the other side of the table then left. The place was pristine: soft lighting, piano music and autumn-coloured flowers on every table. People were dressed to the nines, so I must have looked like I was playing dress-up. Another guy showed up with bread in a basket and a pitcher of ice water, just like she'd said. He asked if I wanted a wine menu. I said sure. He came back and presented the menu like it was the biggest deal in the world to give someone a menu. I tried not to smile too much.

"Would you like recommendations?"

"Actually, I'm waiting for someone; I'll wait for her."

He left, and I sat there. What did I know about wine? I checked out the dinner menu: no prices. Anyway, I was having bread and water. My cock went stiff. Then my phone vibrated in my pocket. Micah. I hit ignore. Waited some more. I'd stay hungry all night. A woman appeared at the front of the restaurant: tall and narrow and older, black hair. I knew who she was and got scared.

Her name was Ivo. She had hair like Uma Thurman's in *Pulp Fiction*, smooth and blunt and black. She was older than me. I don't know how old: ageless. Her face killed me. Strong mouth, small nose, crooked teeth when she smiled, eyes like sky through an icy window. Crow's feet and freckles.

I'd never seen a woman less perfect or more gorgeous my whole life.

Reason I got scared that night: I'd go through with it. That's why. Up until that moment, no one had given me what I'd wanted, and as soon as I saw Ivo in the restaurant, full glory, in motion, I knew she'd give me what I wanted, and it was like when a person who was supposed to happen in your life was about to happen and then you knew your life would change for ever, and I'd do anything she wanted even if it turned out I'd be stripped of all my secrets, games up, make-believe, pretension, shot to oblivion.

"Did you always do what your mother told you?" she asked at the table, hand around a glass of white wine. Something bitter she'd said, with bite.

"I tried."

"Teachers?"

"Pretty much."

"What about lovers?" She ordered pasta with grilled salmon and a white dill sauce. Ivo ate everything put in front of her. Her mouth gleamed from the sauce and wine and from her licking her lips.

"Well . . . I've only had a few. But the girls I've known, they never told me what to do, they always asked me, what do *you* want to do?"

"How'd you feel about that?" Later, Ivo asked for a dessert menu. She ordered sorbet. My stomach gurgled with serious intensity. I felt light-headed too.

"Bored, I guess, not happy."

"If I tell you what to do will it make you happy?" The way she spooned the sorbet into her mouth, you would have thought it was the best thing ever to happen to her. I wanted to lick her bowl, the inside of her mouth if she let me.

"Absolutely."

"Even if it hurts?"

"Yeah."

"Why?"

"Because . . . it's hard to put into words."

"Try."

"I'm not a strong person."

"You're not?"

"Well I don't *feel* strong. I feel more like . . . I don't know what I'm trying to say."

"You feel more like a girl?"

I laughed a little. "Hmm. I don't know. Maybe. If feeling like a girl means feeling subservient. I know there are, you know, women who aren't subservient, who are strong and in control, and I've tried to find them, you know, because I want to be in a situation where I'm a guy but not in control, because feeling helpless turns me on. A woman hurting me, demeaning me, using me, turns me on. Fuck." I put my face in my hands. I'd never articulated it before like that and now . . . Bam. "I want you to rip off my guise like when the school nurse ripped off

a bandage once and all the fucking skin came off, and I could
see my own flesh." I shuddered.

"Tyler, that's . . ."

"Dumb? I fucking know." I stared at my hands, dizzy or
something.

"Honey," she said. "Look at me."

I did. And my vision cleared for one stark moment.

"Don't cut me off again." And then Ivo hit me in the face
and everything swam.

When I could see again, Ivo motioned for the bill.
Men at other tables looked at her. She ignored them. My
stomach churned like you wouldn't believe. I grabbed a
piece of bread and chewed on it to calm the churning. I
had to shift in my seat to give my boner as much room
as possible, although it was suffocating in there, and the
men in the restaurant looked at me like I was a joke or a
fucking riddle. *What the fuck is she doing with him?* But the
women, they smiled. Ivo reached across the table and took
my hand. I felt heat all the way up my arm. She told me to
wait outside.

That was the night I saw a shooting star, standing outside
the restaurant; I mean the sky was full of stars and this one
bolted, took a dive. It was beautiful; I almost cried. I saw Ivo
through a window. She spoke to a man. He was distinguished
looking or whatever, more the type you'd think she'd be with,
and when the man put his hand on her arm then leaned over to
kiss her ear or something I thought, That's right, I'm chopped
liver, and then I stood there like she'd told me, and Ivo pulled
away from the man.

Meanwhile couples came out of the restaurant; the men
would speak to a valet while the women glanced at me.

Ivo came out. I stood with my hands in my pockets. "Hi,"
I said.

"Hi yourself." She let one side of her mouth curl. Like
a sneer. Like she hated me. Then her eyes lit up. "Come
here."

I went.

"Closer," she said.

I got closer, an inch away. Ivo tilted her head. I tasted the wine on her breath, the pasta. I felt heat. My hands itched to touch her. Anything.

"Never mind," she said.

Ivo's apple-cider smell brushed past me. Ivo was across the room again. She told me to look at her. I did. She walked back and forth a few feet away, and her body became a musical as she dropped her clothes on the floor and swayed like a cattail in a breeze; her skin reflected light while her eyes burned like the blue on a flame.

"Fuck," I said. "You're amazing."

When Ivo opened her mouth, one side curled back further than the other, and I caught a glint of sharp tooth before she said, "You ass." Ivo was closer to me now; I reached for her, one second of cool smooth flesh, her narrow, boyish hip, and then she turned on me screaming. "Prick!" She wailed on me full throttle, palms across my head and face.

"Fuck, sorry, I shouldn't have touched you, sorry."

I dropped to the floor. I liked this game, a lot. My face felt like army ants had gone at it, and my ears rang. Meanwhile, my cock throbbed so much I thought, This particular boner is never going away; it's fucking permanent.

Ivo smiled at me. "Tyler, take off your shirt."

I did.

"You have a beautiful body, so skinny. Open your pants."

I did.

"Let me see it."

I pulled my cock out. Already oozing pre-come.

"Sit over there."

I sat.

"You know what you're going to do for me?"

"No." I shook my head, holding my cock.

"You're going to take that friend of yours, Micah, to a hotel."

I swallowed. "OK." I noticed a flush spreading across Ivo's chest.

"I'm going to meet you there later."

"That sounds good."

Ivo smiled, one side of her mouth, showing me that tooth again – one hell of an incisor. "I want to watch Micah fuck you, Ty."

"You do?" At this point my cock had gone so stiff it was like a body with rigor mortis. I was terrified and turned on beyond belief.

"Jerk yourself off."

I did. Ivo sat on a table in front of the chair where I sat; she opened her legs, so I saw wiry hair, meaty pink cunt lips. I stared at her, swallowing, using my hand on my cock. "Slower," she said. I slowed down. "Faster," she said. I got a cramp in my elbow. Her nipples were hard. The flush had spread to her neck and face.

"I'm going to come, is that OK?"

"No," Ivo said.

I took my hand away from my cock then sucked in a breath.

Ivo slid her hand over her cunt. With one finger she moved the meaty lips around and then open. I watched her sink one fingernail into her cunt, and then her finger disappeared up to her knuckle. Ivo closed her eyes. "Jerk yourself off," she said.

I started again.

"Want to fuck me, Ty?"

"Fuck, yeah."

I watched Ivo fuck herself with her finger. She pulled it out after a while then rubbed her clit in tight, concentrated circles.

"I want to fuck you," I said. "Can I fuck you?" I was about to blow.

"Stop," Ivo said. She opened her eyes, glacial bright. She moved her finger over her clit and stared in my eyes.

"Fuck," I said "Fuck." I gripped the sides of the chair. A drop of come oozed free of my cockhead.

"I'm coming," Ivo said. Her body gave one definitive shudder.

She arrived in the hotel room: leather pants and a white shirt you could see her nipples through. She had tight tits and quarter-sized nipples. Right away I caught my breath. Her lips were the colour of blood when the scab comes off, wet and bright. The rest of her face was pale and freckled, crinkles around her eyes. She'd tucked her hair behind her ears. She had big ears, actually. No jewellery. Ivo regarded us without a word. The air became humid with what I guessed you'd call sexual tension.

Micah stared at her, looked at me. I met his eyes. "Feel her power, dude?"

"Yeah."

I went to my knees. This was the night of all nights. Micah swallowed so hard I saw the lump in his throat bob. "What are you waiting for?" Ivo said to him.

Micah looked at me then seemed to register I was on my knees. He knelt too.

Ivo walked around the room. She inspected the empty champagne bottle Micah had left in the ice bucket. "Did you enjoy it?"

Micah nodded then met my eyes again. Ivo looked at me.

"Take off your clothes, Ty."

I remained kneeling as I took everything off. There I was, skinny and naked.

"Stand up," Ivo said. We both did. "Not you," she told Micah.

He dropped to his knees again.

"Bend over," Ivo told me.

After a minute I did.

"Did you hesitate?"

"Yeah, sorry."

"Look at me."

I met her eyes. Two pools of ice in a snowdrift. Ivo hit me so hard in the face one side felt as if it had split like ice over a pond.

"Shit," Micah said.

"Shut up," Ivo told him.

I looked at Micah through water in my eyes. He had his hand over his crotch.

"Let's try again," Ivo said. "Bend over."

I did. My cock throbbed like a stubbed toe.

"Open your ass for me, Ty."

I pulled my ass cheeks apart. I felt her move closer; she burned me there with her eyes until my own vision blurred as I stared at my feet.

"You'd like your friend Micah here to fuck you in the ass, wouldn't you?"

I bit the inside of my arm then said it. "Yeah." Good thing I couldn't see Micah. Had no idea how'd he feel about what I'd just said.

"I'd like that," Ivo said. "And you'll do it for me, won't you?" I knew she spoke to Micah, but I didn't hear him answer. I felt Ivo touch my ass cheek. She rubbed it in a circle with her palm then dragged her nails across my skin. I bit my arm again.

Micah said, "Can I yank on myself?"

"No," she answered. I felt her finger on my asshole; she rubbed my hole in circles until it felt good. Until blood rushed to colour my skull. "Come here," I heard her say.

I felt Micah stand then come over.

"Touch him," she said.

"Where?" Micah sounded anxious.

Ivo hit him. Smack. "You know where," she said.

Micah fingered the edge of my asshole.

"Rim him," Ivo said.

I felt my asshole flower. Oh fuck. Fuck me. Yeah. That felt nice. I'd never had a tongue at my hole before. Shit. That was so nice. I felt Micah lean over me, gripping each side of my bony ass with his hands while he rippled his tongue through my crack then concentrated on the brown flower of my hole. Fuck. Jesus. That was good.

Ivo said, "The bed." We all went. "Take off your clothes," Ivo said, meaning Micah. My friend looked as skinny and white as me. His cock was short and fat. I'd seen it before. Now I let myself really see it. "Together," Ivo said. Micah and I scooted together. I felt the taut reed of his leg against mine, the brush of short hairs. Ivo looked pristine in her clothes. She wanted me on my back, Micah on top. For a second our cocks were like two rulers side by side. Then she gave Micah lubricant and instructed him to oil up. His cock glistened. He didn't meet my eyes.

"Gentle at first," she said as Micah pressed the head of his cock to my ass.

"Shit," he said, like he didn't want to fuck me but really did.

Ivo leaned over me then kissed me like I'd never been kissed before. "You're so sweet," she said into my mouth. Then she kissed me all over my face, and I kissed her back, tongue in her mouth, my hands in her hair. First time I'd ever touched her like that.

I felt the head of Micah's cock in my ass. I felt how I opened. "Easy," Ivo said.

Micah moaned, sank deeper, fucked me. I grabbed Ivo. I was like a butterfly on a pin. She kissed my ear lobe. "Deeper," she told Micah. "Come in his ass." His face had twisted above me. The word "Shit," broke from his lips, and then I felt jizz bust out of my cock like pus from a wound. You know how that is after, right?

I woke with spunk leaking from my ass. Micah was asleep under the covers, pillow to his face, a familiar stranger. I smelled that apple-cider smell of Ivo, but she wasn't there. I figured she had another life opposite of what she'd left in the hotel. After Ivo, Micah and I were like what you'd find through Alice's looking glass. I was cracked open, naked as an egg. Happiness is totally scary like that.

Kimberle

Achy Obejas

"I have to be stopped," Kimberle said. Her breath blurred her words, transmitting a whooshing sound that made me push the phone away. "Well, OK, maybe not have to – I'd say *should* – but that begs the question of why. I mean, who cares? So maybe what I really mean is I need to be stopped." Her words slid one into the other, like buttery babies bumping, accumulating at the mouth of a slide in the playground. "Are you listening to me?"

I was, I really was. She was asking me to keep her from killing herself. There was no method chosen yet – it could have been slashing her wrists, or lying down on the train tracks outside of town (later she confessed that would never work, that she'd get up at the first tremor on the rail and run for her life, terrified that her feet would get tangled on the slats and her death would be classified as a mere accident – as if she were that careless and common), or just blowing her brains out with a polymer pistol – say, a Glock 19 – available at Wal-Mart or at half price from the same cretin who sold her cocaine.

"Hellooooo?"

"I hear you, I hear you," I finally said. "Where are you?"

I left my VW Golf at home and took a cab to pick her up from some squalid blues bar, the only pale face in the place. The guy at the door – a black man old enough to have been an adolescent during the Civil Rights era, but raised with the polite deference of the previous generation – didn't hide his relief when I grabbed my tattooed friend, threw her in her car, and took her home with me.

It was all I could think to do, and it made sense for both of us. Kimberle had been homeless, living out of her car – an antique Toyota Corolla that had had its lights punched out on too many occasions and now travelled unsteadily with huge swatches of duct tape holding up its fender. In all honesty, I was a bit unsteady myself, afflicted with the kind of loneliness that's felt in the gut like a chronic and never fully realized nausea.

Also, it was fall – a particularly gorgeous time in Indiana, with its spray of colours on every tree but, in our town, one with a peculiar seasonal peril for college-aged girls. It seemed that about this time every year, there would be a disappearance – someone would fail to show at her dorm or study hall. This would be followed by a flowering of flyers on posts and bulletin boards (never trees) featuring a girl with a simple smile and a reward. Because the girl was always white and pointedly ordinary, there would be a strange familiarity about her. Everyone was sure they'd seen her at the Commons or the bookstore, waiting for the campus bus or at the Bluebird the previous weekend.

It may seem perverse to say this but every year, we waited for that disappearance, not in shock or horror, or to look for new clues to apprehend the culprit: we waited in anticipation of relief. Once the psycho got his girl, he seemed pacified, so we listened with a little less urgency to the footsteps behind us in the parking lot, worried less when out running at dawn. Spared, we would look guiltily at those flyers, which would be faded and torn by spring, when a farmer readying his corn field for planting would discover the girl among the papery remains of the previous year's harvest.

When Kimberle moved in with me in November, the annual kill had not yet occurred and I was worried for both of us, her in her car and me in my first-floor one-bedroom, the window open for my cat, Brian Eno, to come and go as she pleased. I had trapped it so that it couldn't be opened more than a few inches but that meant that it was never closed all the way, even in the worst of winter.

In my mind, Kimberle and I reeked of prey. We were both boyish girls, pink and sad. She wore straight blonde hair that moved in concert and had features angled to throw artful shadows; mine, by contrast, were soft and vaguely tropical, overwhelmed by a carnival of curls. We both seemed to be in weakened states. Her girlfriend had caught her in flagrante delicto and walked out; depression had swallowed her in the aftermath. She couldn't concentrate at her restaurant job, mixing up simple orders, barking at the customers, so that it wasn't long before she found herself at the unemployment office (where her insistence on stepping out to smoke cost her her place in line so many times she finally gave up).

It quickly followed that she went home one rosy dawn and discovered that her landlord, aware that he had no right to do so but convinced that Kimberle (now four months late on her rent) would never get it together to legally contest it, had stacked all her belongings on the sidewalk, where they had been picked over by the students at International House, headquarters for all the Third World kids on scholarships that barely covered textbooks. All that was left were a few T-shirts from various political marches (mostly black), books from her old and useless major in Marxist theory (one with a note in red tucked between its pages which read: "COMUNISM IS DEAD!", which we marvelled at for its misspelling), and, to our surprise, her battered iBook (the screen was cracked though it worked fine).

Me, I'd just broken up with my boyfriend – it was my doing, it just felt like we were going nowhere – but I was past the point of righteousness and heavily into doubt. Not about my decision, that I never questioned. But about whether I'd ever care enough to understand another human being, whether I'd ever figure out how to stay after the initial flush, or whether I'd get over my absurd sense of self-sufficiency.

When I brought Kimberle to live with me she hadn't replaced much of anything and we emptied the Toyota in one trip. I gave her my futon to sleep on in the living room, surrendered a drawer in the dresser, pushed my clothes to one side of the closet, and explained my alphabetized CDs, my work hours at a smokehouse one town over (and that we'd never starve for meat), and my books.

Since Kimberle had never visited me after I'd moved out of my parents' house – in truth, we were more acquaintances than friends – I was especially emphatic about the books, prized possessions I'd been collecting since I had first earned a pay cheque. I pointed out the shelf of first editions, among them Richard Wright's *Native Son*, Sapphire's *American Dreams*, Virginia Woolf's *Orlando*, a rare copy of *The Cook and the Carpenter*, and Langston Hughes and Ben Carruthers' limited-edition translations of Nicolas Guillén's *Cuba Libre*, all encased in Saran Wrap. There were also a handful of ninteenth-century travel books on Cuba, fascinating for their racist assumptions, and a few autographed volumes, including novels by Dennis Cooper, Ana María Shua and Monique Wittig.

"These never leave the shelf, they never get unwrapped," I said. "If you wanna read one of them, tell me and I'll get you a copy, or xeroxes."

"Cool," she said in a disinterested whisper, pulling off her boots, long, sleek things that suggested she should be carrying a riding crop.

She leaned back on the futon in exhaustion and put her hands behind her head. There was an elegant and casual muscularity to her tattooed limbs, a pliability that I would later come to know under entirely different circumstances.

Kimberle had not been installed in my apartment more than a day or two (crying and sniffling, refusing to eat with the usual determination of the newly heartbroken) when I noticed that *Native Son* was gone, leaving a gaping hole on my shelf. I assumed that she'd taken it down to read in whatever second I had turned my back. I trotted over to the futon and peeked around and under the pillow. The sheets were neatly folded, the blanket too. Had anyone else been in the apartment except us two? No, not a soul, not even Brian Eno, who'd been out hunting. I contemplated my dilemma: how to ask a potential suicide if they're ripping you off.

Sometime the next day – after a restless night of weeping and pillow punching which I could hear in the bedroom, even with the door closed – Kimberle managed to shower and put on a fresh black T, then lumbered into the kitchen. She barely nodded. It seemed that if she'd actually completed the gesture, her head might have been in danger of rolling off.

I suppose I should have been worried, given the threat of suicide so boldly announced, about Kimberle's whereabouts when she wasn't home. But I wasn't, I wasn't worried at all. I didn't throw out my razors, I didn't hide the belts, I didn't turn off the pilot in the oven. It's not that I didn't think she was at risk, because I did, I absolutely did. It's just that when she told me she needed to be stopped, I took it to mean she needed me to shelter her until she recovered, which I assumed would be soon. I thought, in fact, that I'd pretty much done my duty as a friend by bringing her home and feeding her a cherry-smoked ham sandwich.

Truth is, I was much more focused on the maniac whose quarry was still bounding out there in the wilderness. I would pull out the local print-only paper everyday when I got to the smokehouse and make for the police blotter. I knew, of course, that once the villain committed to the deed, it'd be front-page news, but I held out hope for clues from anticipatory crimes.

Once, there was an incident on a hiking trail, two girls were approached by a white man in his fifties, sallow and scurvy, who tried to grab one of them. The other girl turned out to be a member of the campus tae kwon do team and rapid-kicked his face before he somehow managed to get away. For several days after that, I was on the lookout for any man in his 50s who might come in to the smokehouse looking like tenderized meat. And I avoided all trails, even the carefully landscaped routes between campus buildings.

Because the smokehouse was isolated in order to realize its function, and its clientele fairly specialized – we sold gourmet meat (including bison, ostrich and alligator) mostly by phone and online, though our bestseller was summer sausage, as common in central Indiana as Oscar Mayer – there wasn't much foot traffic in and out of the store and I actually spent a great deal of time alone. After I'd processed the orders, packed the UPS boxes, replenished and rearranged the display cases, made coffee and added some chips to the smoker, there wasn't much for me to do but sit there, trying to study while avoiding giving too much importance to the noises outside that suggested furtive steps in the yard, or shadows that looked like bodies bent to hide below the window sill, just waiting for me to lift the frame and expose my neck for strangulation.

One evening, I came home to find Kimberle with my Santoku knife in hand, little pyramids of chopped onions, green pepper and slimy octopus arms with their puckering cups arranged on the counter. Brian Eno reached up from the floor, her calico belly and paws extended towards the heaven promised above.

"Dinner," Kimberle announced as soon as I stepped in, lighting a flame under the wok.

I kicked my boots off, stripped my scarf from around my neck and let my coat slide from my body, all along yakking about the psychopath and his apparent disinterest this year.

"Maybe he finally died," offered Kimberle.

"Yeah, that's what I thought when we were about fifteen, 'cause it took until January that year, remember? But then I realized, it's gotta be more than one guy," I said.

"You think he's got accomplices?" Kimberle asked, a tendril of smoke rising from the wok.

"Or copy cats," I said. "I'm into the copy-cat theory."

That's about when I noticed Sapphire angling in unfamiliar fashion on the bookshelf. Woolf's *Orlando* was no longer beside it. Had I considered what my reaction would have been any other time, I might have said rage. But seeing the jaunty leaning that suddenly gave the shelves a deliberately decorated look, I felt like I'd been hit in the stomach. I was still catching my breath when I turned around and saw Kimberle. The Santoku had left her right hand, embedding its blade upright on the knuckles of her left. Blood seeped sparingly from between her fingers but collected quickly around the octopus pile, which now looked wounded and alive.

I took Kimberle to the county hospital, where they stitched the flaps of skin back together. Her hand, now bright and swollen like an aposematic amphibian, rested on the dashboard all the way home. We drove back in silence, her eyes closed, head inclined and threatening to hit the windshield.

In the kitchen, the onion and green pepper pyramids were intact on the counter but the octopus had vanished. Smudged paw tracks led out Brian Eno's usual route through the living room window. Kimberle stood unsteadily under the light, her face shadowed. I sat down on the futon.

"What happened to *Native Son*, to *Orlando*?" I asked.

She shrugged.

"Did you take them?"

She spun, slowly, on the heel of her boot, dragging her other foot around in a circle.

"Kimberle . . ."

"I hurt," she said, "I really hurt." Her skin was a bluish red as she threw herself on my lap and bawled.

A week later, *Native Son* and *Orlando* were still missing but Kimberle and I hadn't been able to talk about it. Our schedules failed to coincide and my mother, widowed and alone on the other side of town (confused but tolerant of my decision to live away from her), had gone to visit relatives in Miami, leaving me to deal with her cat, Brian Eno's brother, a daring aerialist she'd named Alfredo Codona, after the Mexican trapeze artist who'd killed himself and his ex-wife. This complicated my life a bit more than usual, and I found myself drained after dealing with the temporarily housebound Alfredo, whose pent-up frustrations tended to result in toppled chairs, broken picture frames and a scattering of magazines and knick-knacks. It felt like I had to piece my mother's place back together every single night she was gone.

One time, I was so tired when I got home I headed straight for the tub and finished undressing as the hot water nipped at my knees. I adjusted the temperature, then I let myself go under, blowing my breath out in fat, noisy bubbles. I came back up and didn't bother to lift my lids. I used my toes to turn off the faucet, then went into a semi-somnambulist state in which neither my mother nor Alfredo Codona could engage me, *Native Son* and *Orlando* were back where they belonged, and Kimberle . . . Kimberle was . . . *laughing*.

"What . . .?"

I sat up, water splashing on the floor and on my clothes. I heard the refrigerator pop open, then tenebrous voices. I pulled the plug and gathered a towel around me but when I opened the door, I was startled by the blurry blackness of the living room. I heard rustling from the futon, conspiratorial giggling, and Brian Eno's anxious meowing outside the unexpectedly closed window. To my amazement, Kimberle had brought somebody home. I didn't especially like the idea of her having sex in my living room but we hadn't talked about it – I'd assumed, since she was supposedly suicidal, that there wasn't a need for that talk. Now I was trapped, naked and wet, watching Kimberle hovering above her lover, as agile as the real Alfredo Codona on the high wire.

Outside, Brian Eno wailed, tapping her paws on the glass. I shrugged, as if she could understand, but all she did was unleash an even more high-pitched scream. It was raining outside. I held tight to the towel and started across the room as quietly as I could. But as I tried to open the window, I felt a hand on my ankle. Its warmth rose up my leg, infused my gut and became a knot in my throat. I looked down and saw Kimberle's arm, its jagged tattoos pulsing. Rather than jerk away, I bent to undo her fingers, only to find myself face to face with her. Her lips were glistening, and below her chin was a milky slope with a puckered nipple . . . she moved to make room for me as if it were the most natural thing in the world. I don't know how or why but my mouth opened to the stranger's breast, tasting her and the vague tobacco of Kimberle's spit.

Afterwards, as Kimberle and I sprawled on either side of the girl, I recognized her as a clerk from a bookstore in town. She seemed dazed and pleased, her shoulder up against Kimberle as she stroked my belly. I realized that for the last hour or so, as engaged as we'd been in this most intimate of manoeuvres, Kimberle and I had not kissed or otherwise touched. We had worked side by side, a hyaloid membrane – structureless and free.

"Here, banana boat queen," Kimberle said with a sly grin as she passed me a joint. *Banana boat queen?* And I thought: Where the fuck did she get that? How the hell did she think she'd earned dispensation for that?

The girl between us bristled.

Then Kimberle laughed. "Don't worry," she said to our guest, "I can do that; she and I go back."

In all honesty, I don't know when I met Kimberle. It seemed she had always been there, from the very day we arrived from Cuba. Hers was a mysterious and solitary world. I realized that one winter day in my junior year, as I was walking home from school just as dusk was settling in. Kimberle pulled her Toyota next to me and asked if I wanted a ride. As soon as I got in, she offered me a cigarette. I said no.

"A disgusting habit anyway. You wanna see something?"

"What?"

Without another word, Kimberle aimed the Toyota out of town, past the last deadbeat bar, the strip malls and the trailer parks, past the ramp to the interstate, until she entered a narrow gravel road with corn blossoming on either side. There was a brackish smell, the tang of wet dirt and nicotine. The Toyota danced on the gravel but Kimberle, bent over the wheel, maintained a determined expression.

"Are you ready?"

"Ready . . .? For what?" I asked, my fingers clutching the shoulder belt.

"This," she whispered. Then she turned off the headlights.

Before I had a chance to adjust to the tracers, she gunned the car, hurling it down the black tunnel, the tyres spitting rocks as she swirled this way and that, following the eerie spotlight provided by the moon . . . for a moment, we were suspended in air and time. My life did not pass in front of my eyes how I might have expected; instead, I saw images of desperate people on a bounding sea; multitudes wandering Fifth Avenue or the Thames, the shores of the Bosporus or the sands outside the pyramids; mirrors and mirrors, mercury and water; a family portrait in Havana from years before; my mother with her tangled hair, my father tilting his hat in New Orleans or Galveston; the shadows of birds of paradise against a stucco wall; a shallow and watery grave, then another longer passage, a trail of bones. Just then the silver etched the sharp edges of the corn stalks, teasing them to life as spectres in black coats . . .

"We're going to die!" I screamed.

Moments later, the Toyota came to a shaky stop as we both gasped for breath. A cloud of smoke surrounded us, reeking of fermentation and gasoline. I popped open the door and crawled outside, where I promptly threw up.

Kimberle scrambled over the seat and out, practically on top of me. Her arms held me steady. "You OK?" she asked, panting.

"That was amazing," I said, my heart still racing, "just amazing."

Not even a week had gone by when Kimberle brought another girl home, this time an Eastern European professor who'd been implicated with a Cuban during a semester abroad in Bucharest. Rather than wait for me to stumble on to them, they had marched right in to my bedroom, naked as newborns. I was going to protest but was too unnerved by their boldness and then, in my weakness, seduced by the silky warmth of skin on either side of me. Seconds later, I felt something hard and cold against my belly and looked down to see Kimberle wearing a harness with a summer sausage dangling from it. The professor sighed as I guided the meat. As she licked and bit at my chin, Kimberle pushed inch by sitophilic inch into her. At one point, Kimberle was balanced above me, her mouth grazing mine, but we just stared past each other.

Afterwards – the professor between us – we luxuriated, the room redolent of garlic, pepper and sweat. "Quite the little Cuban sandwich we've got here," Kimberle said, passing me what now seemed like the obligatory after-sex joint followed by the vaguely racist comment. The professor stiffened. Like the bookstore girl, she'd turned her back to Kimberle. Instead of rubbing my belly, this one settled her head on my shoulder, then fell happily asleep.

"Kimberle, you've gotta stop," I said. I hesitated. "I've gotta get my books back. Do you understand me?"

Her head was buried under the pillow on the futon, the early morning light shiny on her exposed shoulder blade. With the white sheet crumbled halfway up her back, she looked like a headless angel.

"Kimberle, are you listening to me?" There was some imperceptible movement, a twitch. "Would you please . . . I'm talking to you."

She emerged, curtain of yellow hair, eyes smoky. "What makes you think I took them?"

"What . . .? Are you kidding me?"

"Coulda been the bookstore girl, or the professor."

Since the ménage, the bookstore girl had called to invite me to dinner but I had declined. And the professor had stopped by twice, once with a first edition of Upton Sinclair's *Mental Radio*. Tempting – achingly tempting – as that 1930 oddity was, I had refused it.

"I'll let Kimberle know you stopped by," I'd added, biting my lip.

"I didn't come to see Kimberle," the professor had said, her fingers pulling on my curls, which I'd found disconcerting.

Kimberle was looking at me now, waiting for an answer. "My books were missing before the bookstore girl and the professor," I said.

"Oh."

"We've got to talk about that too."

Down went her head. "Now?" she asked her voice distant and flimsy like a final communication from a sinking ship.

"Now."

She hopped up, her hip bones pure cartilage. She shivered. "I'll be right back," she said, headed for the bathroom. I dropped on the futon, heard her pee into the bowl, then the water running. I scanned the shelf, imagining where *Mental Radio* might have fit. Silence.

Then: "Kimberle? Kimberle, you all right?" I scrambled to the bathroom, struggled with the knob. "Kimberle, please, let me in," I pleaded, imagining her hanging from the light fixture, her veins cascading red into the tub, that polymer pistol bought just for this moment, when she'd stick its tip in her mouth and . . . "Kimberle, goddamn it . . ." Then I kicked, kicked and kicked again, until the lock bent and the door gave. "Kimberle . . ." But there was nothing, just my breath misting as I stared at the open window, the screen leaning against the tub.

I ran out and around our building but there was no sign of her, no imprint I could find in the snow, nothing. When I tried to start my car to look for her, the engine sputtered and died. I grabbed Kimberle's keys to the Toyota, which came to life mockingly, and put it into reverse, only to have to brake immediately to avoid a passing station. The Toyota jerked, the duct-taped fender shifted, practically falling, while I white-knuckled the wheel and felt my heart like a reciprocating engine in my chest.

After that, I made sure we spent as much time together as possible: reading, running, cooking venison I brought from the smokehouse, stuffing it with currants, pecans and pears, or making smoked bison burgers with Vidalia onions and thyme. On any given night, she'd bring home a different girl to whom we'd minister with increasing aerial expertise. At some point I noticed *American Dreams* was missing from the shelf but I no longer cared.

One night in late January – our local psychopath still loose, still victimless – I came home from the smokehouse emanating a barosmic mesquite and found a naked Kimberle eagerly waiting for me.

"A surprise, a surprise tonight," she said, helping me with my coat. "Oh my God, you smell . . . *sooooo* good."

She led me to my room, where a clearly anxious, very pregnant woman was sitting up in my bed.

"Whoa, Kimberle, I . . ."

"Hi," the woman said hoarsely; she was terrified. She was holding the sheet to her ample breasts. I could see giant areolae through the threads, the giant slope of her belly.

"This'll be great, I promise," Kimberle whispered, pushing me towards the bed as she tugged on my sweater.

"I dunno . . . I . . ."

Before long Kimberle was driving my hand inside the woman, who barely moved as she begged us to kiss, to please kiss for her.

"I need, I need to see that . . ."

I turned to Kimberle but she was intent on the task at hand. Inside the pregnant woman, my fingers took the measure of what felt like a fetal skull, baby teeth, a rope of blood. Suddenly, the pregnant woman began to sob and I pulled out, flustered and confused. I grabbed my clothes off the floor and started out of the room when I felt something soft and squishy under my bare foot. I bent down to discover a half-eaten field mouse, a bloody offering from Brian Eno, who batted it at me, her fangs exposed and feral.

I climbed in my VW and after cranking it a while managed to get it started. I steered out of town, past the strip malls, the corn fields and the interstate where, years before, Kimberle had made me feel so fucking alive. When I got to the smokehouse, I scaled up a back-room bunk my boss used when he stayed to smoke delicate meats overnight – it was infused with a smell of acrid flesh and maleness. Outside, I could hear branches breaking, footsteps, an owl. I refused to consider the shadows on the curtainless window. The blanket scratched my skin, the walls whined. Trembling there in the dark, I realized I wanted to kiss Kimberle – not for anyone else's pleasure but for my own.

The next morning, there was an ice storm and my car once more refused to start. I called Kimberle and asked her to pick me up at the smokehouse. When the Toyota pulled into the driveway, I jumped in before Kimberle had the chance to park. I leaned towards her but she turned away.

"I'm sorry about last night, I really am," she said, all skittish, avoiding eye contact.

"Me too." The Toyota's tyres spun on the ice for an instant then got traction and heaved on to the road. "What was going on with your friend?"

"I dunno. She went home. I said I'd take her but she just refused."

"Can you blame her?"

"Can I . . .? Look, it was just fun . . . I dunno why everything got so screwed up."

I put my head against the frosty passenger window. "What would make you think that would be fun?"

"I just thought we could, you know, do something . . . *different*. Don't you wanna just do something different now and again? I mean . . . if there's something you wanted to do, I'd consider it."

As soon as she said it, I knew: "I wanna do a threesome with a guy."

"With . . . with a *guy*?"

"Why not?"

Kimberle was so taken aback, she momentarily lost control. The car slid on the shoulder then skidded back on to the road.

"But . . . wha—I mean, what would I do?"

"What do you think?"

"Look, I'm not gonna . . . and he'd want us to . . ." She kept looking from me to the road, each curve back to town now a little slicker, less certain.

I nodded at her, exasperated, as if she were some dumb puppy. "Well, exactly."

"Exactly? But . . ."

"Kimberle, don't you ever think about what we're doing – about *us*?"

"Us? There is no *us*."

She fell on the brake just as we hurled beyond the asphalt but the resistance was catalytic: the car twirled a double ocho as the rear tyres hit the road again. My life such as it was – my widowed mother, my useless Cuban passport, the smoke in my lungs, the ache in my chest that seemed impossible to contain – burned through me. We flipped twice and landed in a labyrinth of pointy corn stalks peppered by a sooty snow. There was a moment of silence, a stillness, then the tape ripped and the Toyota's front end collapsed, shaking us one more time.

"Are you ... Are you OK?" I asked breathlessly. I was hanging upside down.

The car was on its back. In a second, *Native Son*, *Orlando* and *American Dreams* slipped from under the seats, which were now above our heads, and tumbled to the ceiling below us. They were in Saran Wrap, encased in blue and copper like monarch chrysalids.

"Oh God ... Kimberle ..." I started to sob softly.

Kimberle shook her head, sprinkling a bloody constellation on the windshield. I reached over and undid her seat belt, which caused her body to drop with a thud. She tried to help me with mine but it was stuck.

"Let me crawl out and come around," she said, her mouth a mess of red. Her fingers felt around for teeth, for pieces of tongue.

I watched as she kicked out the glass on her window, picked each shard from the frame and slowly pulled herself through. My head throbbed and I closed my eyes. I could hear the crunch of Kimberle's steps on the snow, the exertion in her breathing. I heard her gasp and choke and then a rustling by my window.

"Don't look," she said, her voice cracking as she reached in to cover my eyes with her ensanguined hands, "don't look."

But it was too late: there, above her shoulder, was this year's seasonal kill, waxy and white but for the purple areolae and the meat of her sex. She was ordinary, familiar, and the glass of her eyes captured a portrait of Kimberle and me.

Wild Roses

Mary Anne Mohanraj

It started with a phone call. Sarah had been expecting the call, but it was still a shock. She had learned over the last few years, as friends succumbed to old age, and to one or another disease, that there were limits to how well you could prepare for death. It was usually cancer, of one type or another. Cancer had gotten Daniel, too. It was hard when it was someone you'd loved.

"He's gone."

"I'm so sorry, Ruth."

"Can I come out? Tonight?"

"Of course."

"The next flight down arrives at 8.30."

"I'll meet you at the airport."

Sarah put down the phone, meeting Saul's calm eyes as he walked out of the studio, wiping paint-stained hands on his pants. She bit back brief irritation at his calm. He and Daniel had never quite gotten along, though they had tried, for the sake of the women. Saul had been quietly pleased when Daniel's career had taken him to Seattle, though not so pleased when Ruth joined him there, a few months later. Saul had locked himself up in his studio and painted huge dark canvasses, ugly compositions in a dark palette: black, indigo, midnight blue. But Ruth had been happier with Daniel than she had ever been with them, happier married and with children on the way. Eventually Saul had bowed to that truth.

Old history.

Sarah said, "I'll pick her up. You go ahead and finish."

Saul nodded, stepping forwards and leaning down to kiss her forehead gently. "You OK?"

Sarah managed a smile. "I'll be all right. Ruth didn't sound good, though."

"No." He opened his arms then, and she stepped into them, heedless of drying paint. She rested her cheek against his chest, wrapped her arms around him, desperately glad that he was healthy. Some arthritis, a tendency to catch nasty colds; nothing that couldn't be fixed by keeping him out of the studio for a few days. After this many years, she could manage that, at least, even if she had to scold like a shrew to do it. She rested in his arms a moment, breathing in his scent, cinnamon sugar under sharp layers of paint and turpentine. He kissed the top of her head, and then let her go.

"I'll make up the bed in the guest room," she said.

Saul nodded, turned, and walked back into the studio, quietly closing the door behind him.

Sarah waited at the Alaska Airlines gate window, her face an inch or two from the cold glass. It was raining outside, a cold hard rain, typical for Oakland in January. The baggage handlers drove their little carts back and forth, luggage covered by dark tarps. The plane had been delayed, leaving her with nothing to do but wait and remember.

The last time she had made love to Daniel, they had been alone. He was leaving in the morning; Ruth had already said what they all suspected would only be a temporary goodbye. Sarah knew her own would be a final one, and so she had taken this last night alone with him. She had planned for it to be tender, sweet and slow. That had seemed appropriate for a goodbye. But instead, Sarah had found herself biting his neck, raking his back, riding him until they were both exhausted, until she was trembling with tiredness. Daniel hadn't been gentle with her either, had dug his fingers into her ass, had bitten her breasts. They had left marks on each other's bodies, dark and brutal and bruised. They had kissed until their lips were puffed and sore. And it was only in the morning, with the long night giving way to a grey sunrise, that their pace had slowed, that they had settled into a hollow of the bed, his hand stroking her dark hair, her fist nested in the curls on his chest. He had asked her then to come with him to Seattle. She had let silence say no for her, and he hadn't asked again. Sarah had gone to Saul the next night with Daniel's marks on her body. He had been gentle with her that night, and for some time afterwards.

The passengers were walking off the plane, some into the arms of family or eager lovers. Ruth walked down, wearing a dark dress, her eyes puffy and red. She had been crying on the plane. Ruth had never cared what people thought about little things. She cried freely in public. She had occasionally tried to provoke screaming fights in parking lots and malls. She had been willing to have sex in the woods, in open fields, had teased and persuaded them all until they joined her. It was only in the big things that she was at all conventional.

They had once travelled east together, two couples in a car, perfectly unremarkable to all outward eyes. They had stopped in Wisconsin, had decided to camp that night instead of staying in a motel. Two separate tents, and the night sky overhead. While Daniel and Saul finished washing the dinner dishes in a nearby creek, Ruth had taken Sarah by the hand and let her into the woods, searching for fallen branches to build a fire. Sarah had dutifully collected wood until Ruth came up behind her, lifted her skirt, then knelt down on dirt and twigs and grass. Sarah wore no underwear in those days, at Ruth's request. So when Ruth's mouth reached for hers, Sarah had only to shift her legs further apart, to try to balance herself, a load of wood resting in her arms, eyes closed. Ruth's tongue licked under her ass, tracing the delicate line at the tops of her thighs. Ruth's tongue slid up over her clit, then back again, sliding deep inside her. Ruth's hands held on to Sarah's hips, her fingers gently caressing the sharp protrusions of hip bones, the skin that lay over them. Sarah was usually quiet, but in the middle of the empty woods, she let herself moan. Ruth's tongue flickered over and around, licking eagerly until Sarah's thighs were trembling. Her heart was pounding, and just as she began to come, waves of pleasure rippling through her, as the wood fell from her arms, Saul was there with her, in front of her, holding her up – his mouth moving on hers, his chest pressed against her breasts, and his hands behind her, buried in Ruth's hair. Then they were all falling to the ground, Saul and Ruth and Sarah and Daniel too, a tangle of bodies, clothes discarded, forgotten, naked skin against dirt and moss and scratching twigs. Leaves and starlight overhead, and Ruth laughing in the night, laughing with loud and shameless delight. It had always been that way with her.

Ruth paused at the bottom of the walkway, eyes scanning the crowd, passing right over Sarah. It had been over a year since they'd last seen each other. Between Christmas and New Year, Sarah had gone up to Seattle for a few days. Saul had originally planned to come as well, but had gotten caught up in a painting and changed his mind. Sarah had come alone into a house full of children and grandchildren, a house full of laughter. Ruth had cooked a feast, with her daughters and sons helping. The grandkids had made macaroons, and each one of them had begged a story from Auntie Sarah. Sarah had left their house a little envious; Ruth had built exactly the kind of home that she'd dreamed of. And while it wasn't the kind of home Sarah herself had ever wanted – still, it was lovely. It wasn't until the following March that the cancer had been diagnosed. Sarah had always meant to go up and see Daniel again – but she hadn't, in the end.

She stepped forwards, raised a hand to Ruth. There was the blink of recognition, the momentary brightening of eyes. Ruth looked lovely despite puffed eyes, slender and fair in her button-down dress, a raincoat over one arm. Her hair had gone entirely to silver, a sleek and shining cap – like rain in moonlight. Ruth came down through the thinning crowd, paused a few steps away. Then Sarah held out her arms, and Ruth walked into them, her eyes filling with tears again. Sarah held her close, sheltering her in the fragile privacy of her arms, until the crowd had entirely dissolved away.

Saul met them at the door. He'd changed out of his paint-stained clothes. Ruth dropped her raincoat, letting it fall in a wet puddle on the floor, and threw herself forwards, into his strong arms. She had calmed down in the car, had been able to talk about the last week with Daniel. He'd gotten much weaker towards the end; in the last few days, he hadn't really spoken. Sarah's chest had ached a little with various regrets. Ruth hadn't cried for most of the ride, but now she was sobbing, great gasping sobs, catching the air in her throat and letting it out again. Saul held her, looking helplessly at Sarah over Ruth's head. Sarah shrugged, put down Ruth's bag, and bent to pick the raincoat up off the wood floor. She turned and hung it neatly on the rack, while Saul gently led Ruth into the living room. Sarah waited in the hall, listening to them walking across the room, sitting down on the sofa. Slowly, Ruth's sobs quieted again. When it was silent, Sarah walked into the room. Ruth was nestled in Saul's arms, her eyes closed. His eyes were fixed on the doorway, and met Sarah's as she entered. She hadn't expected that, that he would be looking for her. She should have known better.

"Do you want some coffee, Ruth?" Sarah asked.

Ruth shook her head, not opening her eyes. "It would just keep me awake. I haven't been sleeping much this last week. I'm so tired . . ."

"Dinner? Saul made pot roast for lunch – there's plenty left."

"No, I'm OK. Just bed, if that's all right?"

"That's fine, dear. Come on – I'll get you settled."

Ruth hugged Saul once more, and then got up from the sofa. Sarah led her into the guest bedroom, turned down the sheets, closed the drapes while Ruth pulled off her clothes and slid into bed. She had always slept nude, Sarah remembered. Sarah came back to the bed, and stood over it, hesitating. Ruth looked exhausted, with a tinge of grey to her skin.

"Do you want me to sit with you a bit? Just until you fall asleep?"

"No, no – I'll be OK." Ruth reached out, took Sarah's hand in hers and squeezed, gently. "Thank you."

Sarah leaned over and kissed her gently twice – once on the cheek, once, briefly, on her lips. "It's nothing, love. Sleep. Sleep well." She stood up then, turned out the light, and slipped out the door, closing it behind her.

They sat at the kitchen table, cups of coffee nestled in their hands, not talking. Just being together. Sarah remembered the day when she realized that she would rather be silent with Saul, than be talking with anyone else. They hadn't met Ruth yet, or Daniel; they'd only known each other a few weeks. They'd just finished making love on a hot July night and were lying side by side on the bed, not touching. It was really too hot to cuddle, too hot for sex. They had both ended up exhausted, lying on the bed with waves of heat rolling off their bodies. Saul was quiet, just breathing, and Sarah lay there listening to his breaths, counting them, trying to synchronize them with her own. She couldn't quite manage it, not for long. Her heart beat faster, her breath puffed in and out of her. But being there with him, breathing was a little slower and sweeter than it would normally be. Being with him, not even touching, she was happier than she'd ever been.

Sarah finished her coffee. "I'm going to go to bed," she said. "Coming?"

"I'll be there in a minute. I'll just finish the dishes."

Sarah nodded and rose from the table, leaving her coffee cup for him to clear. She straightened a few books in the living room as she walked through it, gathered his sketches from the little tables and from the floor, piling them in a neat stack. She walked into the hall, and then paused. To her right was the hall leading to their bedroom. Straight ahead was the hall leading to the library, to the studio, and then to the guest room. She almost turned right, almost went straight to bed. But then she walked forwards down the long hall and, at the end of it, heard her. Ruth was crying again. Sarah stood there a while, listening.

When she came back to the bedroom, Saul was already in bed, waiting for her. Sarah stood in the doorway, looking at him. He lay half covered by the sheet, his head turned, looking at her. She knew what would happen if she came to bed. She could tell by looking at him, by the way he looked at her. He would pull her close, and kiss her forehead and eyes and cheeks. He would run his hands over her soft body; he would touch her until she came, shuddering in his arms.

"Ruth's crying." It was harder than she'd expected, to say it. It had been a long time.

His eyes widened, the way they only did when he was very surprised, or sometimes during sex, when she startled him with pleasure.

"You should go to her." That was easier to say. Once the problem was set, the conclusion was obvious. Obvious to her, at any rate.

Saul swung himself slowly out of bed, pulled on a pair of pants. He didn't bother with a shirt. "You'll be all right?" It was a question, but also a statement. He knew her that well, knew that she wouldn't have raised the issue if she weren't sure. He trusted her for that. Still, it was good of him to check, one last time. It was one of the reasons she loved him so. She nodded, and collected a kiss as he went by.

Sarah let herself out of the house, walking barefoot. It was a little cold, but not too much. The rain had stopped some time ago, and the garden was dark and green in the moonlight. She wandered through the garden – its neat paths, its carefully tended borders. Saul took care of the vegetables; she nurtured the flowers and herbs. At this time of year, little was blooming, but the foliage was deep and rich and green. Winter was a good time for plants in Oakland; it was the summer's heat that parched them dry, left them sere and barren. She carefully did not approach the east end of the house; even through closed windows and shades, she might have heard something. She also refrained from imagination, from certain memories. If she had tried, Sarah could have reconstructed what was likely happening in that bedroom; she could have remembered Ruth's small sounds, her open mouth, her small breasts and arching body. Saul's face, over hers. She could have remembered, and the memory might have been sweet, or bitter, or both. But she was too old to torment herself that way. There was no need.

Instead, she put those thoughts aside, and walked to the far west end of the garden, where the roses grew. It was the one wild patch in the garden, a garden filled with patterns, where foxglove and golden poppy and iris and daffodil, each in their season, would walk in neat rows and curves, in designs she and Saul had outlined. But the roses had been there when they bought the house, the summer after Ruth had left. Crimson and yellow, white and peach, orange and burgundy – the roses grew now in profusion against the western wall, trimmed back only when they threatened the rest of the garden. Wild and lovely. She had built a bench to face them, and Saul often sat on it, sketching the roses. Sarah liked to sit underneath them, surrounded by them, drowning in their sweet scent. She went there now, sitting down in the muddy ground, under the vines and thorns.

There were no roses in January, but they'd come again, soon enough. She'd be waiting for them. In the meantime, it was enough to close her eyes, feel the mud under her toes, and remember Daniel. The way he laughed, bright and full. The way he would return to a comment from a conversation hours past. The way he had touched her sometimes, so lightly, as if she were a bird. The scent of him, dark and rich, like coffee in a garden, after rain.

The Gift

Lewis DeSimone

Jesse would have burned the dinner if I hadn't been there to save it.

"What are you doing?!" I cried, opening the oven door and pulling out the rack. He had set the temperature to 450°F; I quickly turned it down and left the door open for a while to cool it off. Fortunately, the lasagne had been inside for only a few minutes, but already it was bubbling around the edges and some of the cheese on top had started to brown, long before the rest of the dish was even warm.

"You have to handle these things delicately," I said. "The lasagne will be done when it's done." The oven thermometer now read 375°F, so I slid the rack gently back in and closed the door.

"You're just anxious," Jesse said. He was pulling silverware out of the drawer —the good stuff, the set he'd inherited from his mother. Clutching yellow linen napkins in his other hand, he stepped around the counter and began to set the table.

"I am not anxious," I told him. I was still fingering the potholder, looking for a safe place to put it among the clutter.

It was the kitchen, with its Mary Tyler Moore window, that had sold me on the apartment. Jesse had been more partial to the view of the Charles River from the living room. When I was a kid, I'd fantasized about living in Minneapolis, imagining that all its apartments had those shutters over the kitchen counter, shutters I would throw open to converse with my guests as I whipped up dinner. But this was not Minneapolis, and reality was not a sitcom. Since moving in, we'd had surprisingly few dinner parties. Kim was our first guest in months.

"I just want everything to be perfect tonight," I said. "I want her to feel comfortable."

"Nick, she'll be comfortable," Jesse said. "We don't need to impress her." He adjusted the centrepiece, an opalescent blue ceramic vase with daffodils spilling out of it. I'd chosen daffodils because of their height and simplicity – I didn't want some huge, overdone bouquet blocking our view of one another over dinner, obstructing conversation.

I gazed through the cloudy window of the oven at the glass casserole dish, the layers of pasta, sauce and cheese. I always made my lasagne just as my mother had taught me, with loads of ground beef and even ground veal on special occasions. But not tonight. In the layer where the meat should have been, there was a thick spread of spinach in deference to Kim's vegetarianism. To compensate, I'd had a hamburger for lunch. I thanked God she wasn't vegan.

Jesse's arms suddenly encircled me, his head burrowing into my shoulder. "It's going to be a beautiful evening," he whispered. "I promise."

Our image reflected hazily in the glass, his brown head nuzzling against my neck, a complement to the thinning blonde hair that spilled over my own brow. Within a few years, most couples we knew became clones of each other – sharing their clothes and hairstyles so that sometimes you could hardly tell them apart. Perhaps with us the pieces had just fit together better from the start, no need to shave off an edge here and there to squeeze the puzzle into place.

"Well, she's *your* friend," I said, closing my eyes. It was better that way, of course. I couldn't have gone through with it with someone I knew too well.

"Are the wine glasses on the table?" I asked.

"Knew I forgot something," he said, his breath rippling my shirt. But he didn't move until the doorbell rang a few seconds later.

I glanced up at the clock above the oven. "Well, she's prompt," I remarked.

"Timing is everything," Jesse said with a smile, pulling away and heading for the door. "Especially tonight."

I darted across the room to turn down the Schubert, then busied myself pulling wine glasses out of the cupboard. I was lighting the candles on the table when I heard the voices in the foyer. There were no cries of welcome, just murmured hellos, and Jesse followed Kim into the room. She held a bottle of white wine in front of her and laid it gently into my hands as she leaned in to kiss my cheek.

"Oh, it's chilled," I said, my fingers tingling.

She laughed and drew away quickly. "Sorry. I should have warned you."

"I should have known you wouldn't show up with a bottle of warm Chardonnay," I said with a smile.

She had trimmed her hair into a neat bob that drew attention to her face – the slightly upturned nose and high cheekbones. I'd always thought of Kim as pretty, but tonight she looked quite beautiful. Her eyes were bright blue, like Jesse's.

"Can I help with anything?" Kim asked as I led the way into the kitchen.

Jesse slid past her to pull a serving bowl from the cupboard. "You're doing quite enough already," he said.

Kim blushed, a healthy pink in her cheeks. She didn't look like the other vegetarians I knew – pasty, unnaturally thin. Kim had an athlete's body – slender but strong. It showed in the way her feet held the ground, the subtle biceps that appeared when she bent her arm to brush a lock of hair behind her ear. She worked out regularly, she ate right, she didn't smoke. She was a catch. It was a wonder some man hadn't swooped her up by now.

She had been one of Jesse's closest friends in college. They'd even dated briefly. And later, she was one of the first people he came out to. After school they had gone their separate ways, Kim bopping around the country in search of herself. It was pure coincidence that she was here at all. She'd come back to town a few years ago, for graduate school, and we'd bumped into her in line at the movies. If it hadn't been for Woody Allen, this night might never have happened. We might have been standing here with someone else right now, someone neither of us knew very well at all.

While I opened the wine, Jesse made the salad. Salads he could handle – there was nothing to burn.

"So how's school?" he asked, slicing into a tomato. The seeds spilled on to the cutting board, and he brushed it all into the bowl before moving on to the cucumber.

"It's great," Kim said. "As soon as this class is done, I'll be free to work full-time on the dissertation."

I handed her a glass of Chardonnay. "That's wonderful. Congratulations."

Jesse turned and took the other glass. "To Kim's dissertation. And other projects."

"To Kim," I said, smiling.

Our glasses clinked together, a perfect little triangle.

I checked the lasagne, which still had a while to go. We settled down at the table to start on the salad first. It was past seven, but watery gold sunlight was still falling through the window.

"So what's your dissertation about again?" I asked.

"Kate Chopin," she said. "She's not terribly well known these days, unless you're an English major."

"Any relation to Frédéric?"

"Not that I know of. But it might be interesting – finding parallels between the writing and the music."

Jesse laughed. "Wouldn't that be nice," he said, "something we could both read." He leaned towards Kim. "In case you haven't noticed – all the books in this house are mine, and all the CDs are Nick's."

"That's not strictly true," I argued.

"I stand corrected," said Jesse, fork waving in mid-air like a baton. "All the books about music are Nick's."

Kim laughed. "I'd say you guys complement each other very nicely," she said. She looked at us both in turn. "An old friend of mine used to say, differences are gifts; they give us a chance to expand our horizons.'"

"See, sweetie?" Jesse said, patting my hand. "Remember that the next time I leave the cap off the toothpaste."

Kim caught the gesture and smiled. "Seven years?" she asked. "And no itch yet?" She laughed again, a mischievous, throaty laugh.

"Well," I said, "we're not saints. It's all a question of how often you scratch."

"But you're great together. You know that, right?" There was a depth to her eyes, and I realized suddenly that this wasn't just about Jesse and me. She had a stake in it, too. She needed us to be stable. She needed to know she could rely on us.

"Of course," I replied, squeezing Jesse's hand. "We're very lucky."

"Is that all there is to it?" she asked, pushing a carrot slice around on her plate. "Luck?"

"It plays a bigger role than you'd think," I confessed. "It's not as if I deserve this guy, you know."

Head still bowed over his plate, Jesse looked up at me – through the chestnut hair that grazed his forehead. I called it his "come hither" look, but I'd never told him that.

"It's not a question of deserving," he said softly. "Love comes when you're ready for it." He was talking to Kim, but still gazing at me.

"Well," Kim said through a self-conscious laugh, "then I guess I'm still not ready."

"You are," Jesse replied, breaking the connection at last and turning to face her. "But maybe he's not."

"Who?"

"The man you're destined to be with."

Her laughter morphed into a nervous giggle. "Ooh, destiny. That's a little scary. So far I've just been destined for jerks."

"That's not destiny," I told her. "Most men *are* jerks."

"Well, I've met them all," she said. She took a gulp of wine, a period on the remark. "I did get close once or twice – or so I thought. The grand passion that fizzles when reality sets in."

"Preaching to the choir," I said, raising a hand to the sky.

She went on, in a sort of reverie now. "It's amazing how many times you have to learn the same lesson. I keep thinking it's going to be different this time: *This guy* means it. *This one* can open his heart as easily as his pants." She laughed at her own joke and took another sip. "But even when they do . . . they seem to hate it, you know? It's like their nerves are suddenly stripped of their protective coating. They love the feeling at first, but then it becomes too much and they can't stand it. They have to close up again –zip their hearts back up and leave." She smiled delicately, mysteriously. "Men can do that," she whispered. "How do they do that?"

"Some of them feel like they have to," Jesse said. "To survive."

"It takes courage," I added, "to be vulnerable. You know that."

"Were you afraid?" Kim asked, eyes wide.

"Terrified," I said.

Jesse gripped my hand again – warm, one finger wrapped around my knuckle. "It takes work," he said. "You push through the fear. Again and again."

"And if you're lucky," I said, "you find someone who's willing to do that with you."

"There's that luck again," she said, grimacing facetiously.

"Destiny," Jesse said. "You have to have faith that it will happen."

She arched her eyebrows. I saw in her eyes that Jesse was speaking a foreign language.

"It's luck," I told her. Somehow, luck seemed more reassuring. Luck wasn't anyone's fault.

The timer rang and Jesse started to rise.

"No, no, no," I said, tossing my napkin on to the table. "I'll take care of it. You entertain our guest. You're the charming one."

The lasagne was perfect, golden in the middle, brown and slightly crunchy around the edges. I carved into it with the spatula and pulled out three large squares. When I returned with a steaming plate in each hand, Jesse and Kim were laughing together. They looked remarkably comfortable, as if this were any other evening. As if they were still in college, the whole world just a figment of the future.

"I hope it's not me," I said, settling Kim's plate before her.

"No," she said, "don't worry. I was just telling Jesse about one of my students. He was under the impression that Virginia Woolf had written *Who's Afraid of Virginia Woolf?*"

"And how did you disabuse him of that notion?" I asked, turning Jesse's plate as I laid it down so that the garlic bread was on the left, where he liked it.

"Very delicately," she said. "You have to be careful with their precious little eighteen-year-old egos."

I went back for my own plate and fetched the bowl of freshly grated Parmesan. "Will you be happy to be done with teaching for a while," I asked, taking my place again, "or do you think you'll miss it?"

"Oh, I'm sure I'll miss it," she said, slicing into the lasagne. A burst of steam escaped, and she put her fork down to wait for it to cool. "But I'll be back in the classroom eventually. Shaping those little minds."

"What about the really little minds?" I asked. "You won't miss that?"

She lifted her glass and looked into it contemplatively. "I've never felt called to raise children," she said. "This isn't about that."

"I'm sorry," I said. "I guess I need to hear it. Again."

"That's understandable." She drained her glass and reached for the bottle.

Jesse, in mid-crunch on his garlic bread, suddenly perked up. "I, on the other hand, am a completely different story. My biological clock has been ticking since I was six."

"Six?"

"Oh you should have seen me, stealing my sister's baby dolls away. Whenever she wasn't looking, I'd kidnap one of them and start sprucing up its outfit."

Kim laughed and turned to me – wide-eyed and curious, like Oprah.

"I was more into Barbies myself," I admitted. "I liked glamour, not diapers."

"You'll get used to it," Jesse said with a wink.

Kim sprinkled cheese over her lasagne, shaking the spoon gently to get an even layer.

Jesse was right: I *was* anxious. I tend to blurt things out when I'm anxious. "I get tested every three months," I said to break the silence, "like clockwork."

Kim smiled and bowed her head. "I know, Nick," she replied. "Jesse told me."

"I just wanted to make sure you knew," I said. "Clean bill of health."

Jesse rolled his eyes. "We've already had this conversation, honey. We've covered all the bases." He had such a firm jaw, almost square, with a delicate cleft that was nearly impossible to shave properly.

I nodded. They had had the conversation already. She'd asked all her questions; Jesse had asked all of ours. I should have been satisfied with that. But when Kim had called yesterday, telling us it was time, I suddenly regretted being only a vicarious part of the discussion. I wasn't vicarious tonight, and I wasn't going to be vicarious later on, either.

I put my fork down and took a deep breath. I'd learned that much. I'd learned how to shut off the racing of my mind. But at times like this, it seemed like a full-time job. I refilled everyone's glass as an excuse to drain my own.

I fetched another bottle from the sideboard and poured. The Pinot felt smoother on my tongue than the tart Chardonnay. It went down more easily.

"I just want the experience," Kim said at last, her features softened by the third glass of wine. "And time's slipping by. I'll be thirty-five in June, you know. I just want to know what it's like. Is that crazy?"

"No," Jesse said. "That makes total sense. Hell, if I could do it, I would. I'd love that experience."

I laughed. "Honey, if you could do it, we wouldn't be having this conversation."

Kim still had a crush on Jesse – that much was obvious. The way she looked at him now, the way her eyes glowed when she turned from me to him didn't help my anxiety at all. It was as if there was an understanding between them, an agreement that I hadn't signed. I took a deep breath and told myself that I was not the third wheel this time.

As if reading my discomfort, Jesse looked up from his plate and smiled at me, his eyes bright and hopeful. I unfolded my leg beneath the table and touched his foot with my own. His smile broadened.

"It's time for dessert," he said, rising from the table. He gathered the plates into a pile, Kim deftly scooping in one last bite before it vanished from in front of her.

I sat back in my chair. I hadn't eaten much. Even though my stomach was churning with hunger, I hadn't been able to get down more than a few bites. I took another sip of wine. My insides would be all liquid before long.

Jesse returned in a moment and settled dessert plates in front of us – our casual set, the ones with lithe dancers drawn on them in silhouette, striking various ballet poses. Each plate bore an eclair from our favourite neighbourhood bakery, huge chocolate-drenched pastries that ordinarily made my mouth water. I took another breath to avoid throwing up.

He unscrewed a bottle of orange muscat and began pouring it into liqueur glasses. I picked up mine as soon as he'd lifted the bottle away, but he gently slapped my hand. "Not yet," he said. "We have to toast."

I dutifully put the glass down. Kim was already digging into her eclair, the cream oozing on to her plate, obscuring the extended leg of a ballerina in arabesque.

"To the gift of love," Jesse said, his glass in mid-air. Kim and I lifted ours towards him and clinked.

I've always hated double entendre.

I sat. I drank. I waited. The éclair sweated, untouched, before me.

"Well," said Jesse at last, wiping a drop of cream from his lip with a napkin, "now what?"

I stared into my glass – through it, to a world painted orange.

Kim giggled and settled her fork on to the empty plate. "You boys are so coy," she said. "Can't we just say it, for heaven's sake? We all know why we're here. It's the most natural thing in the world."

"Not for me," I said, still gazing into the muscat.

She laughed. "But you have done it before, haven't you?" She paused. "Sleep with a woman, I mean."

"Longer ago than I can remember," I replied. "I think it was the Pleistocene epoch."

"Otherwise known as high school," said Jesse.

"And even then," I said, "it took a great deal of effort. I swear, I must be a Kinsey 6."

"Not even a 5?" she asked. "For me?"

Jesse chuckled from the other side of the table. "Between the two of us," he said, "I'd say it averages out to a 4, so you're in luck."

Kim pushed her plate away and stood up. "Come on," she said, reaching for me. "It's like riding a bike."

Her hand hung delicately in the air, waiting. "I was never particularly good at that, either," I said, finally taking hold of her fingers. They were long and full of energy, and I recalled Jesse telling me that she'd played piano as a child.

And then we were all standing, spooling away from the table and across the room, holding hands like a chain of children on their way to recess.

It was dark in the bedroom, but thankfully no one bothered to flick on the lamp. The light from the living room filtered in hazily, just enough to turn the blackness to grey.

Jesse stood behind me, hands on my shoulders, chest pressed against my back – warming me, keeping me safe. Kim, before me, had kicked off her shoes, and now the top of her head barely reached my collarbone. I marvelled at how "the most natural thing in the world" could happen between such mismatched creatures.

She stood a foot or so away and lifted her hands to caress my chest. The fabric of my shirt crinkled softly against my nipples and I let my head drop back, into the crook of Jesse's neck as she worked on the buttons, as her fingers found their way inside.

Jesse nuzzled me. His tongue flicked teasingly against an ear lobe, and then his mouth moved down, kissing my neck, closing softly against the skin and sucking. I called it his vampire kiss, pulling life from my throat. It was usually all I needed to give in to him completely.

Kim's hands, cold at first against my skin, began to warm as she traced her way down to my belly. She unbuckled my belt, undid the button on my jeans, and a shiver rode my spine. I closed my eyes and breathed in the darkness. The zipper was just a sound in the night, the falling of my jeans just a burst of cold air against my skin.

She held me, still soft, in her hands – patiently, the way I held eggs to warm them before placing them into boiling water, to keep them from breaking against the heat. Her lips were full when she kissed me, opening against me to give me their warm undersides. Jesse's teeth bit gently against my ear and suddenly I felt electricity around me, and my cock flickered to life.

And then, as if by magic, we were all naked, all on the bed – six hands softly caressing whatever they found, three pairs of lips gently kissing in turn. Jesse continued to kiss my neck, as his fingers roped their way through my chest hair, down to my navel. He clenched my cock in one hand and kissed me as Kim's fingers followed his lead, tracing circles around my nipple.

I lay back and Jesse planted himself above me, holding his body aloft with outstretched arms, and smiled down at me as Kim took me back into her mouth. He lowered himself slowly, as if he were doing push-ups, and kissed me delicately on the lips.

We moved spontaneously around the bed, our gestures fluid, changing with no apparent reason – like children again, always in the moment, always ready to be surprised. At one point Kim lay back against the pillows, knees bent in the air, and Jesse sidled up between her legs. He buried his face against her, and she moaned, tossing her head from side to side. I stroked her face to gentle her and dropped my head to her breast. It was my turn to suck now, my turn to return to the buried memory of my own first nurturing. I licked the hard nipple hungrily and drew it into my mouth. Suddenly, this spot became for me the most erotic, the most essential place in the world.

She arched her back and I noticed that Jesse had slid away from her crotch. He was kneeling before her now. I looked up and saw the concentration in his eyes.

He scooted slowly forwards, hands resting on her thighs, and his cock – the head purple, fully engorged – flicked against his belly as if in invitation. He pushed against her, into her, inch by inch, as her gentle murmurs turned into moans, cries – the growing pleasure I so easily recognized. I knew what she was feeling, had felt it, lived with the incessant craving. I watched her face as the breath came faster, her cheeks flushing, her eyelids fluttering against her skin, and I knew at last what my face looked like when Jesse became a part of me, when he held me this close, when he pulsated inside me.

Kim pulled him closer and ran her fingernails down his back, cupped his ass cheeks with both hands – pushing him deeper into herself. Jesse arched his back in response, and suddenly we were eye to eye, our faces only inches apart. He pulled me with one hand against him and pressed his lips on to mine. His tongue forced its way into my mouth, fucking me as his cock fucked her. He groaned deeply, in that way of his, and my arm against his back traced the bucking of his body as he came.

I held him like that for a minute or so, until the last shudder, our lips still sealed against each other, our hearts pounding.

When I drew away, when he pulled out, Kim was rocking gently beneath us, like something bobbing on the waves of a once turbulent sea.

We rested for a while, the three of us, holding one another, leaning our heads together, sharing the warmth. We said nothing for a long time, until Kim rolled her face towards mine and leaned in close. "I need *you* now," she whispered.

It was my turn. We were taking turns.

It was a shock at first – the moistness, the effortless way Kim and I moved together. I had forgotten how different it felt – those soft folds of female flesh, the way they mould themselves around a man.

We were using her, I thought suddenly, uncomfortably – not for sex per se, but for the anticipated result.

It was her gift to us, she'd said. An anniversary present, a love offering.

You guys are meant to be parents, she'd told us the night she'd first made the suggestion – planted the seed, so to speak. *You'd certainly be better parents than me. And you love each other,* she said, *you should conceive your child in love – not with a turkey baster.*

I lifted her towards me, her ass warm as I pulled it away from the sheets. I rocked with her, sliding myself in and out of her – slowly, tenderly. I was afraid to do it as forcefully as I fucked Jesse, afraid she might shatter beneath me.

She closed her eyes and threw her head back, a smile warming her face. I looked up, and it was now Jesse's face I saw – Jesse's blue eyes just inches away, his lips open in that familiar ellipse of passion. And he leaned forwards, pressed his lips against mine again, reached around my neck to hold my mouth close to his.

Someone's hand stroked my side, another squeezed a nipple, still another gently swatted my ass. I kept kissing, kept fucking, eyes closed. It could as easily have been Kim I was kissing, Jesse I was fucking. In the darkness, it didn't matter. In the darkness, we were simply making love. Literally *making* love – as if love itself were a thing, a product of sex, something we created together in the act of fucking. We were making this thing called love, this creature that would one day cry us awake in the middle of the night, skin a knee on the pavement outside, borrow the car and keep us up all night with worry, hold our hands years hence and let us go.

Jesse's fingernails dug into my neck. His teeth closed gently on my lower lip, and I cried out – coming, pouring out my love, coming into the spot still wet with his own seed, mine now mingling with his, my sperm racing his for the prize. I was panting and sweating and smiling, imagining them all, millions of them, swimming together – a team, cheering one another on, not really caring which one made it to the finish line as long as one of them did. They – we – were all in this together.

Hot Springs

Carol Queen

It was Sunday morning before I finally got out of the city, leaving the piles of books and notes that were my dissertation on my desk and closing the apartment door firmly on them. By the time I'd driven an hour north into the valley, I'd begun to relax. The leaves on the grapevines were beginning to turn, great clusters of soon-to-be-harvested fruit everywhere, but the October day was hot as summer. It was beautiful, and got more so as soon as I'd left the valley towns behind and began the drive up the old wild mountain, the road narrow, one switchback after another, and a slightly hazy vista of hill and valley and hill at every turn. Little enough traffic up there that I could take the mountain curves fast, two-handed, my car and I like one creature. I love this feeling, that I'm half man, half machine. Soon I reached the hot springs.

I was ready for a two-day soak, ready to sleep under the mountain stars, ready to be away. The springs were old sacred land, one place where the vast geothermal soup bubbling under the mountain broke through to the surface, appropriated lately as a kind of New Age resort. Still a powerful place, though, and its proprietors now tried to reinforce that sense of the sacred by dotting the place with little shrines, a Buddha here, a goddess there. Its specialness was most apparent in the demeanour of its visitors, all of whom seemed to sense and respect that it had been a healing place long before any of us were born. I lost no time in choosing a place to camp and then sliding into the warm pool, and my dissertation, already well out of mind, retreated a little further still.

I'd left the water to sun myself on the nearby deck when I saw her, unloading her car with her companion, probably her lover, by the way she spoke to and touched him familiarly, almost absently, for she seemed more absorbed in her surroundings. Perhaps a newcomer here. I caught her eye, and she let a small, wary smile slip; then they climbed the steps to the lodge. Not campers, then. I watched them leave their room to explore, strolling the grounds, locating the pools and the showers, passing me once or twice. Then they went back inside. I imagined them undressing, falling on to the bed.

But he was out before long and in the pool, and it was an hour or more before she emerged, clad in a towel. Their room key hung from one of her hoop earrings, and when she turned or shook her head, it grazed her neck, making a tiny jingle, I imagined, that only she could hear. The pool was so deep that the key's tip touched the water, making a little wake as she glided through.

She stood alone for a while, eyes closed, feeling the warm silken water of the mineral springs on her skin. He saw her and moved to join her. Heads close together, they talked quietly for a moment, then left the pool for the sauna. I watched the door swing closed behind them.

She was probably still inside, probably lying flat on the smooth, hot wood of the benches, the heat searing into her with every breath, sweat pooling between her pretty little breasts – she had a tattoo on one, but I hadn't been able to make it out from a distance – when he returned to the pool. He came in slowly, pearls of sweat on him, too, surveying everyone. Seeing me, he moved towards me through the water. Had he noticed me watching them?

He smiled, said hello, began to chat. He was gregarious but somehow sweet, with big blue eyes and the smile of a cherub. He asked my name, told me his, found out within a scant few minutes where I was from, where and what I studied, the topic of my dissertation, how soon I hoped to be finished, and what I wanted to do next. He and the woman were indeed first-time visitors to the springs. He talked about his work a bit – he was a nurse who cared for AIDS patients – but more about hers.

She was a sex educator, he said, who also did AIDS-related work, teaching people about safer sex. He'd been talking about her for a full five minutes when she emerged from the sauna, prompting an overly bright, "Well! There she is now!" from him.

She moved with the languor of one surrendered to relaxation. I could see the sheen of sweat on her eyes in the deepening twilight, and she carried her towel in her hand, not bothering to cover her nakedness as she approached the pool. The key swayed from her ear as she moved. Others in the pool were watching her, too.

Did I imagine the look of pleasure when she saw that he was talking with me? She slid into the water and moved towards us, laughing. "You're such a friendly thing, honey." When he introduced us, her attention turned to me. He told her what he'd learned about me; she asked me to tell her more about my academic work, more keenly interested than he had been.

Serious, intense green eyes. She reached to touch him but kept her eyes fixed on me. Her tattoo shimmered below the water. I thought I could make out the images of a moon and a star. Maybe I'd ask her about it later.

"I understand your area of interest is sexuality," I said, imagining the leering way she must have heard it said before, hoping I sounded nothing like that.

"He's been talking behind my back again, eh?" she said. She smiled at me, arched her eyebrows at him, and he laughed like a kid caught at a game and said, "Yes, I've been telling him all about you."

"I used to read Kinsey out loud to my friends when I was seventeen," she said. "The study of sex always fascinated me, but it didn't seem a serious enough area to specialize in . . . too lightweight, too dilettantish. Until recently," she added, with a little frown.

"Until AIDS?" I asked.

She nodded. "Now it's too real, it's crucial. People seem to have a lot of trouble adjusting to safe sex, or else they're in such fear that they risk losing touch with their sexuality altogether."

What a funny pair they were. He was listening to our conversation with satisfaction, blue eyes laughing, looking first at one of us, then the other, not seeming to respond much to her great seriousness. Some sex educators manage to make the juiciest pleasures sound dry and academic. Not her: she talked about sex like it was the grail, a higher calling – passionate yet earnest, like a Marxist talking about revolution. Tempted to make a wisecrack – "Well, I bet you excelled at your labs" – I decided instead to meet her devotion to her subject with the kind of respect I'd want anyone to show about my own work.

"I have to confess I've had some of those problems myself," I said. "It can be so difficult to know when to talk about safe sex, and I can't really say I like to use condoms." It seemed perfectly easy to talk to her about it. But he was quicker to reply than she was: "You're in luck – we give lessons!" he said with a big grin. Her smile flashed back but she pretended to ignore him, saying, "The real key is having a casual experimental attitude, especially at first. Take it too seriously and it'll seem like work, not pleasure."

I pretended I hadn't heard him, too. I regarded them. Were they coming on to me? Her earnestness in talking, her lack of flirtatiousness threw me off, though he was certainly forward enough for the both of them. Was she a participant at all? Surely this was not just an ingenuous act. I determined to wait until she extended me an invitation to decide whether to take it.

I didn't have to wait long. He moved behind her as she and I continued to talk, and lifted her. He held her up with one hand – easily, she was buoyed by the water – and traced her body with the other. She sighed and settled back against him. She was more near my eye level now, her breasts above water. I could see the tattoo clearly, and even in the dimming light, I could see her nipples growing hard from the touch of the cool air. It was not immediately clear whether this was a show for me; I felt a little uneasy, not knowing, nor knowing how to proceed. Was I going to be a part of this scene?

He moved a couple of steps closer to me. She was now so near that if my cock were erect – which it was beginning to be

– its tip would touch her. She looked me full in the eyes, silent. I wondered what she was thinking.

"What about it?" he said at last. "Do you want a lesson?"

That made her laugh again. "You amaze me, boyfriend," she said to him. "You move so fast. Sometimes I think you move too fast." And to me: "Well? Since he asked – would you like to come with us?" Her eyes said, Come with us.

Decision instantly made. I touched her then, running my fingertips up her belly, across her breasts, over the tattooed crescent. She made a low sound. "I would love to come with you," I replied, and he stepped closer again, so that she was held up by the pressure of our bodies on her. I felt four hands on me, and one of her nipples rubbed one of mine. She squeezed my cock between her legs for a second, then made way for his hand. She sighed deeply. Her fingertips slipped through the hair on my chest, freeing scores of tiny bubbles trapped there; they effervesced between us. He had my balls, holding with just enough pressure to make me want him to squeeze. I sighed, too. I wanted to kiss her.

"Let's go before we get scandalous," she said.

We carried her through the water, submerged hands still caressing. She led us back to the room, detaching the key from her earring as she walked, and led us inside.

Plain room, bed in centre, their things strewn about. The covers already down – she'd been napping earlier – and while she was pulling them down further, he caught her from behind, tumbled her on to the bed, and so I had to wait for my kiss. But from their embrace she reached for me.

I knelt over them, wondering where to start. The muscles of his ass were rhythmically tightening as he began to thrust against her, and she writhed against him in response. As he moved down her body, his mouth now on her breasts, she pulled me down to replace him in the kiss. Such hunger. She held my head, one fist curled in my hair and the other pulling my beard, biting my lips, tongue finding tongue.

I might have lost all awareness of everything but that kiss: teeth and tongue and lips, licking and sucking, tiny bites, feeding the heat and the hunger. But he reached for my cock and, in a couple of strokes, it swelled to fill his hand, splitting my awareness between her and him, kiss and cock. As she sucked my tongue harder, he began rubbing my cockhead with its foreskin. Wet with pre-come, it felt almost enveloped by another mouth; involuntarily, ecstatically, I thrust harder into his hand, moaned into her.

Feeling me respond to him made her hotter. She answered my moan, though I felt it vibrate in my lips and tongue more than I heard it, for my mouth was still on hers, my fingers teasing her nipples. Her hands did not stay in one place for more than a few seconds at a time; she scratched softly at my chest, tugged my hair, clutched my arms as her arousal heightened.

I broke the kiss when I felt his absence, and looked over my shoulder to find him rooting around in one of their bags. "Accoutrements," she said, and in a minute he was back, smiling hugely, and rolled a condom on to me and one on to himself – his erection, by now, making him look more like Priapus than a cherub. And took my cock into his mouth.

And sucked, near-perfectly. Like an angel. It was just right, and I moaned again, couldn't help it. He was jacking himself off as he sucked – I could tell he was keeping us both at the same rhythm, too slow to come, our hearts probably beating in tandem, too. His eyes were closed in concentration and bliss.

Hers were open wide, watching like a cat as the shaft vanished into, then slid out of, the tight circle of his lips. Each time the glans hit the back of his throat, I shuddered with pleasure, and she saw that, too. My fingers had moved to part her labia, slipped inside her sweetly slick cunt, and she sighed and spread her legs to me, but didn't take her eyes off her lover, lost to his cock sucking.

"Do you like this? Do you like watching him suck me?" I whispered. I began a slow thrust into her cunt, pushing into her at the same pace he was devouring me, all hearts beating together now.

He heard me, came back to earth a little. Still squeezing my cock, he motioned me to my knees and moved up to her; she saw what he was doing, spread her legs to him and reached for the lube, and I watched as his rubber-covered dick disappeared into her. Once in, he turned back to me, mouth ready for my cock again. His sucking wasn't quite so perfect now – he had more than one task to concentrate on – but that was more than made up for by the pleasure of watching him fuck her. She met his strokes, thrusting up, still raptly watching the cock-and-mouth dance, sighing and murmuring and moaning softly, and I watched the pink mist of her sex flush spread across her breasts and up her throat, watched her eyes widen and flutter closed as he stopped sucking me and began to fuck her seriously, harder and faster as her orgasm neared. Poised above both of them, I thrust against him, following his rhythm, imagining we were both inside her, our cocks rubbing together, held so tightly by the silky, wet muscles of her cunt. Maybe she imagined the same thing; she'd licked her fingers to moisten them and was making fast, purposeful circles on her clit; she was climbing, obviously climbing. I stopped my pretend fuck and reached between their spread legs, forming a V at the entry to her cunt, adding to the pressure on her labia, and giving him more tightness to push through. Her shut eyes opened wide for a second, acknowledging the extra sensation, and then she reached the top of her climb and rocked and released into orgasm, crying pretty cries. When she was done, I was there to kiss her.

He began his own climb after rolling her on her side, one leg drawn up to her chest, fucking her even faster, and she knew the signal, for she began a whispered litany as he tensed and bucked: "Yes, honey, oh yeah, come on, come on, baby ..." And in a soundless orgasm he collapsed on to us, grabbing for my cock again as soon as he could move, kissing both of us at once, which made her laugh.

He rolled off us, and she squirmed more firmly underneath me. At a glance from her, he pulled off the rubber he'd dressed me in before and slid on a fresh one. Then he took my cock and began to slide it up and down her cunt lips, across her clit (I could feel it hard against my sensitive glans), teasing us both by putting it in just a little way and then, just as we began to thrust, pulling out. But he could feel how badly we wanted the fuck; he didn't toy with us for long. She moaned when I entered her, slowly, thrusting deeply in, maintaining the low song until I began to withdraw, resuming when I pushed in again. She wrapped her legs around my waist, arching up to meet me, wanting to be filled. She reached behind her head to grasp my wrists, leaned up to kiss me, hard, and the look she gave me, articulate as any words, said: Fuck me!

Slowly, to tease us both, but I wanted her hard. I could feel her nails imprinting the skin on my wrists; I shifted so that I held her wrists, and she caught her breath, moaning, "Ohhh, man . . ."

If she had anything more to say, I didn't hear it; my mouth was on hers again, and she sucked my tongue like he had sucked my cock, and her eyes didn't leave mine. I read her arousal in them like a meter as I took her the way I wanted her: as hard, as fast as I could without shooting too soon. We were electric, thrusting into each other wildly and eyes not parting, and I wanted it to last, freezing time with our heat.

I slowed down long enough to release her wrists and raise her legs to rest on my shoulders. She took my whole weight – and the length of my cock – as deep into her as I could plunge, and she was not silent for an instant now, crying out at a particularly hard thrust, moaning and sighing, saying, "Yes, oh, oh, yes, oh man, fuck me, fuck me . . ."

She slid her right leg off my shoulder so she could reach her clit; she climbed fast. I slowed my stroke a little to make it last. "Ohhh! Oh baby, don't stop, don't, don't . . ." Of course I didn't, and, deep inside her, I felt her cunt begin its fast, hard squeeze. She whimpered, clawing my shoulder, and I didn't slow, thrusting through the hard contractions, seeing her eyes register the pleasure of the first stroke after orgasm, as she began to climb again immediately, gasping and then crying out. I rode her through three comes before I lost control and shot, holding her tightly and feeling her cunt throb around me like a tight, wet fist.

He lounged next to us on the bed, jacking off. The spectacle had gotten him hard again.

Acting on a decision I didn't know I'd made, I reached for a condom. I hadn't had a cock in my mouth since middle school;

I suppose I hadn't given much thought to whether I ever would again. But I was clearly embarked on the sort of erotic adventure with these two that I could never have foreseen and, what's more, I trusted them. What had she said? A casual, experimental attitude?

"Use an unlubed one," she said when she saw what I was up to, and I managed to get the rubber on him while she watched, that cat-on-the-hunt look coming into her eyes again; I heard her sharp intake of breath when my lips touched his cockhead. I didn't much like the taste of the latex – had a moment of regret for the loss of naked cock skin, even as long as it had been since I'd tasted it – but my mouth slid down the length of it, and I concentrated on the sensations, his cock so hard and hot against my lips. I glanced up; his head was thrown back and he was breathing deeply; she was absorbed in the vision, her fingers almost absently slipping up and down the length of her cunt lips. My cock was starting to stiffen again already; it responded to the look in her eyes as she watched me. How keenly I felt the heat of her arousal under my own skin. Energy built between us even as I felt on my lips his fast pulse beat.

He reached for my cock. I reached for her, pulled her down to join me. Together we ran our tongues up and down his shaft, kissing around him, trading our attentions from cock to balls. I played with her breasts, tugging on the nipples, feeling her response. He jacked me off with long, slow strokes.

He wanted to fuck her again. So did I, but I could wait. This time I watched for a while, hand on my dick to keep it as hard as he had left it (I wanted to be in the minute he was out). I took advantage of the lull to change condoms. When I saw her hand move towards her clit, I slipped a finger into her cunt, still thinking of both of us in her at once. So hot and tight, wet with sweet, salty cream. She got tighter when I put a second finger in her, then a third. When I began to move them in and out, her cunt stretched with his cock and my fingers. She began her whispered orgasm song again, arched up in a perfect Reichian curve, climbing, climbing. I wanted her full, fucked like she'd never been, this tattooed little sex priestess.

She held her breath, mouth open in an inaudible cry, until she came, but nodded, eyes wide and on me. "Yes, yes . . ."

And came hugely, once, twice, not enough, and then he stiffened with pre-orgasmic tension; I felt him slow his thrusting the instant before he came.

The minute he pulled out, I was on her, in her, enfolded. And we fucked slowly, tight in each other's arms, soul-kissing, soul-fucking, a long time, a long time.

I rolled her over so she was astride me, and I could watch as my cock slid out of her pussy, and she thrust down on it again. She braced her hands on my chest and rode me, my hands cupping her ass. Then I had her on her back again, closer, faster, to finish.

Have I only just met her? I thought. She, silent and intense, gazed at me, engaged in her own wonderings.

They did this all the time, he told me as we all lay in each other's arms, talking, letting the intensity ebb in preparation for my getting up, going out of the room, leaving them.

She had me understand it had been another calibre of experience this time, that it did not always feel like this. Her fingers stayed tangled in the fur on my chest, just over my heart.

Would I leave my number with them, he asked. Could we all meet again?

Of course.

Anyway, it was only Sunday night. We were all staying until Tuesday. Time to play like slick fish in the effervescent water of the warm pool, to meet under the shine of the stars, to talk, catch up in words to this deep knowing. In each other's arms, in the arms of the holy mountain.

Don't Be Mad at Me

Adriana V. López

I don't usually come on to authors I interview. But the baby-fine hair peeking out of the young Spanish writer's open collar was breaking my concentration.

I had devoured his book in one lonely weekend. It was a sophisticated exploration of alienation in contemporary Barcelona. At the novel's centre is an unsuccessful young author who's hired by an enigmatic older woman to write her life story.

When I finished it, I stared at his author photo, looking for the depth in his welcoming eyes that had led to this work. I had to see him in person. I researched the controversial underground Barcelona literary journal he and his cohorts founded named *Crack*, and I found my angle. I decided he would make a good feature on the Spanish avant-garde for *Publisher's Forum*.

David Canetti happened to be in New York for a few months on a writing scholarship. He responded to my email immediately. This is what I love about being the international editor at *the* book review magazine. It's "meet the author" all the time.

David and I were sitting below a Moroccan-style ceiling fan struggling through the leaden humidity of a mid-August night. I told him to meet me in the Lower East Side at a café bar called the Red Pony. Seven p.m. I'd be the girl carrying an emerald-green book tote that said "Reading is Radical". I told him I was tall, with short black hair, and would be wearing a sleeveless turtleneck dress.

After our initial Spanish two-cheek hello kiss and some nervous prattle about the similarities between New York and Barcelona, I got down to business. I asked him about his sales. I could see the creases taking centre stage on his smooth forehead.

I focused on his large, hazel eyes as he attempted to save face. They were encased in a thick set of dark lashes that made him appear as if he were wearing chocolate-coloured eyeliner. I furrowed my brow a little and nodded, feigning concentration.

"Few people actually read the novel today," he lamented in strained English.

"Yes, it's a problem for all authors. It's tough to keep up with the shorter attention spans."

Like a Modigliani painting, his face and nose were long. His fingers were long, too; he had them wrapped around a short glass filled with the amber-coloured whiskey we'd both ordered.

I was as drawn to him as I am to unreadable books.

His eyes remained glued to mine. He took a sip of his whiskey and sat back in his chair and grinned at me.

"So you're family is Latin American?"

"Yes. My mother is Colombian, and my father is a Spaniard. But I was born here." My delivery was flat. I've been told that I can come off as cold, a little arrogant.

"Aha! I thought you were too attractive to be just American. Do you prefer English?"

"Spanish is fine. I need to practice."

"You have a slight accent to your Spanish. It's very cute."

"Thanks," I said, tensing at the dig.

"But it's much better than my English. Nobody in Spain worries about their English."

Of course he had the linguistic advantage. I only got to practise my Spanish with my parents and a bunch of stiffs in my prep school classes on the Upper East Side. Or on the dreaded occasions my parents dragged me to visit my humiliatingly snobbish families in Bogotá and Madrid.

"OK then, Spanish it is," I said in the tongues of our mothers. The *r*'s rolling from my tongue gave me a whole new sexy persona. I felt like I had tapped into that dormant nineteenth-century *maja* I had in my veins.

"*Bueno,*" he concluded.

My cell phone was sitting on our table. I pretended to check it. I needed to divert my eyes from his intensity. I acted as if I didn't see him staring at me.

"I'm expecting a call from the office," I mumbled. "A never-ending edit I've been trapped in all week."

My face was getting hot. I have the kind of skin that easily reddens in the heat or when I get nervous or excited.

I downed my whiskey too fast.

"So what are you reading now?" he asked.

"Well," I began hesitantly, "I just finished reading you."

"Thank you, that makes a whole ten people."

I smiled. If ten had read his last novel, that meant less than five poor souls in the New York literary world would have read my own pathetic attempt at experimental fiction a few years back.

"Did you hear about Samuel Reverte-Ferrante's latest novel?" I blurted, without pausing to think about the book's racy subject matter.

"About the Italian talk-show host who goes to bathhouses to fuck adolescent boys?"

He said the word "fuck" in Spanish. I was surprised at how my nipples hardened with the release of that single word. *Follar.* Just to pronounce it forces one to clench one's teeth and snarl.

"Did you read it?" I asked.

"No. Read about it. It's caused quite a stir, no? Everyone thinks Reverte-Ferrante is gay now, though he's happily married to some big-shot editor."

"Everyone is thinking: How could someone write about it and describe it so well if he hadn't done it himself?"

"Men have been writing about the female orgasm for centuries, Anna. What do they know?"

It was the first time he addressed me by my first name, so soon after saying fuck. *Ah-na.* He pronounced it softly, as if he were stroking the back of my neck with his words.

"Too true," I said.

"I say good for Samuel!" David said suddenly. "What's the big deal really if he screwed some guy in the name of good research? Flesh is flesh, no?"

"Sure." I shrugged, though I didn't really agree. I decided to give him a taste of my New Yorker attitude. "But screwing your wife's brother is crossing the line, don't you think?"

"Perhaps. But haven't you ever crossed the line in a close relationship?" he asked.

"Of course, but ..." I replied, wondering how I could change the subject.

We were coasting quickly into unchartered waters for your standard *Publisher's Forum* interview.

"Really?" he said playfully. "What, with a friend or something?"

He was as excited as I was, hanging on every careless word that flew out of my mouth. David was sitting up straight, resting his hands placidly on the tops of his spread thighs. His head was tilted low and slightly to the side. He was my captive audience.

I took a breath and told him about my room-mate at Vassar, even though I couldn't believe what I was saying. I remembered the drunken night when things went too far with Natasha for the first time. The smell of Johnson's baby powder exuded from her belly button as I pulled down her panties.

Our friendship had reached that point of overwhelming curiosity. She asked if she could kiss me. I couldn't say no to a girlfriend. We were both each other's first, and we took it seriously. We left our usual fits of cackling laughter out of it.

I was larger breasted than Natasha, but just as malnourished. We both lived on cigarettes and Diet Coke. We rolled around my twin dorm bed kissing. I told David that her small pointy breasts and bony hips barely touched mine. I said that Natasha moaned too loudly and overdramatically for what I was doing beneath her perfectly manicured landing strip of a bush. (Mine in comparison was an untidy patch of overgrown ivy.)

Shocked at how dirty I was talking, I stopped myself. His face had turned red.

"This conversation has gone way past any chance of professionalism, hasn't it?" I told him. But I relished the macho bravado of my words.

"I'm enjoying myself immensely," he said with an earnest smile. "Do you still talk to this Natasha?"

"No, her husband doesn't like me much."

"Fool." He tsk'd.

"So, what about you?" I shot back, downing another gulp of whiskey for support.

"My turn, huh?" he said.

"Come on. I just revealed a little too much information to you. Offer me something as good. None of this will be published, I swear."

He let out a tinny laugh. I couldn't tell if it was nervous.

"OK then. You've heard of Sergi Canetti, right? The writer who wrote the historical novel about Hadrian, the Roman emperor?"

"Yes, you and he and some friends started *Crack*. You two related?"

"By father. We grew up together. Our father had moved us to Paris when we were boys. He was just opening his bookshop at the time. We were lonely, awkward looking and had no friends. Our French was poor, and we felt like outsiders in that city. We spent a lot of time alone together. One day we just decided to experiment on each other."

"What do you mean, experiment?" I asked.

"We gave each other our first blow jobs."

I nodded.

"This is quite common for boys you know, at least in Europe," he said. "I don't know about American boys."

"How old were you?" I asked.

"Sixteen or so."

"Here, boys feel each other's cocks at sleep-away camp," I said. "But no one dares to talk about it. It stays in the woods, with their campfire tales."

He laughed at my attempt at being funny.

Then he suggested we try another place.

★   ★   ★

I chose this divey basement bar on Mott Street. It was called Double Happiness, and I found the name cynically comforting. The light from the hanging red paper lamp in our corner booth ruddied our sallow cheeks to a much-needed healthier glow. It seemed we both shared a dislike for healthy outdoor lifestyles.

We sat close to one another. So close that our knees kissed, though they were still separated by a hairline crack. This proximity interfered with making conversation. So I pulled my knee away slightly to concentrate on what the hell I was saying, and hopefully, to seem a little out of reach. If that were still possible.

We jump-started the dialogue by discussing new book releases we thought important (always an ice-breaker for book people), when David mentioned one that I had read by a Mexican American journalist. It had just been translated into Spanish. It was about little boys in Mexico who cross the border by themselves to look for their labourer mothers in the United States. The boys leave their country with only a few pesos in their shorts and an approximate address. They try dozens of times to sneak over, only to die like stray dogs in the desert.

My heart had begun to beat faster and I felt the blood drain from my face. The mere mention of that book brought me back to that terrible time in my life.

"So you haven't read it then?" David asked.

"No, I have." I responded, sounding stiff.

"Oh. It didn't look like it registered with you." He looked confused.

I hadn't wanted to tell him about my mother. I preferred not to talk about her with anyone. But the sad man trapped in his eyes told me to. Despite his generous smiles, he had a sombre look that made me think he understood the incomprehensible, like death, or why we fall in love with the wrong people.

"That book takes me back to a hard time in my life recently," I said. Then it all came out. The alcohol was making me emotional. "It's been two years since I last had sex with a guy, you know."

I was suddenly insane with an urgency to talk about it. It was like I was a bottle of Coke he kept shaking, lifting the cap to watch me splatter. He took a sip of his Scotch and placed it down slowly on to the coaster with the Chinese Double Happiness symbol.

"Wow." He paused, taking a deep breath. "Why?"

"My mother died two years ago. It closed me up to the world, made me hate it. Hate love, mistrust men, everyone."

"I'm so sorry. What she die of?"

"Oh, a bad case of sadness. She overdosed on sleeping pills. Her long-time lover announced that he was going back to Rome for a younger woman he had met while on business. She never wanted to get out of bed again."

"Oh God, Anna. I'm so, so sorry." He widened his eyes and shook his head.

"Thanks," I shot back as if he had just passed me the salt shaker. "I'm OK, don't worry."

I concentrated on carefully taking out my pack of smokes from my bag and lighting a cigarette. I inhaled and exhaled dramatically; it was a necessary release. He placed his hand on my right thigh. He didn't squeeze or press. He just rested it ever so lightly. His long fingers splayed open like a starfish.

As he rested his limb on mine, I noticed what a feminine wrist he had, despite the generous layer of fur encasing it. It was the first time he had placed a hand on my body, other than to tap me on my arm, guiding me away from an oncoming waitress back at the Red Pony.

I had to explain how I got to that point from the mere mention of that book, even though his heart was coming out of his eyeballs with sympathy. I began telling David about the whole experience with a certain peace I hadn't felt in years. His whole being was an open receptacle to my feelings.

"After my mother's suicide I hadn't been able to read for pleasure, something I relied on since childhood to block out the world or my parents' high voltage fights. I showed up to the office a few days after the funeral and dived into my work as usual. It saved me. I had just recently broken off a seven-year relationship, and I hardly saw any of my friends."

"Shit."

"Yeah. It was one of those brutally cold New York winters," I explained. "I would sit on my couch curled up in a blanket desperately trying to escape into another world."

"You mean, through books, yes?"

"Exactly. But it wouldn't work. I would start to read the sentences and a voice in my head would interrupt telling me I wasn't reading. The words . . . I couldn't absorb them; they couldn't get through all the other noise in my head. I lived in a kind of panic that I would never be able to enjoy reading again. But this book broke through. It took me out of myself for once. Its words spoke a simple truth, and I could follow their trail. The pain of these abandoned little boys in the book finally allowed me to privately mourn my mother's vanishing from this earth. I mean, those little boys just wanted their mommies. And I could understand that."

"I couldn't put it down myself," David said. "That journalist really took you there, all those sordid details about eating out of garbage dumps to survive."

"I *know;* it's just terrible," I added.

I felt self-conscious again. I took another sip of whiskey, and my hand trembled as I brought it up to my mouth. I knew I was acting strangely, telling him about my mother and about not having slept with a man for a while. This isn't what you're supposed to do when you first meet someone, especially an accomplished author whom you're writing about.

I let out a nervous guffaw.

"God! Doesn't talking about death just kill a mood?"

He gave me a smile more warm and generous than any I'd ever received. "I'm not uncomfortable talking about it, Anna. Go on."

"You're probably regretting ever having mentioned that book or saying yes to me interviewing you. See what you did! You unleashed my inner monster." I was back to flirting shamelessly.

"She's a wonderful little monster," he matched, responding quickly.

"Oh yeah?" I thought for second, then went for it. You only

live once. I wanted the air, the light around him. "You want to see where I live?"

"I'd love that. But on one condition." He grabbed my thigh and gave me a serious look. "We need to get some slices of New York City pizza first. My little monster of a stomach is growling."

He slid out of the booth and excused himself to go to the bathroom. I looked around the room to see if anyone was looking. No one was. I pocketed a darling little red ashtray that the barman had just placed on our table.

It would complement the other souvenirs I had accumulated over the years, little mementos from places where something memorable had happened.

The Lower East Side at midnight bustled with street action from every living, breathing walk of life. And something about its energy must have gotten under David's skin, making him stop short in the middle of the street.

Without warning, he grabbed my hand and pulled me into the darkness of lonely Eldridge Street.

"What are you doing?" I asked even though I knew.

"*Déjame*, just let me," he said like a boy who wanted to stay up later than his bedtime. He took my two hands and raised them over my head, pushed them up against the rough red bricks of the tenement building I had my back on. I was his prisoner as he breathed on my face, slowed himself down to smell me, and pressed his wet mouth on to mine.

Here was our chance to rise, to overcome the heavy gravity of respectable, dignified social interaction. We took our time exploring each other's mouths, opening them slightly, then pulling back and beginning again, deeper and deeper the next time in, for anyone who cared to watch. I remember opening my eyes and seeing his closed so sweetly, tasting the booze and cigarettes on our saliva, smelling the cheese. All the pores on his naked face reeked of the slice of pizza we inhaled walking and giggling on the way to my place. On my ex, Jonathan's, face I had hated the smell of cheese, but on David it was delicious. Like a sampling of his body's baser smells to come.

We raced up the five endless flights to my apartment and panted like porno stars from severe shortness of breath. Fucking cigarettes! Still insanely aroused at just listening to his heavy breathing, I fumbled placing the key into the hole.

Once we were inside, I flicked on the dozen little lamps in my place, and David found his way into my bedroom. That's where all my books were, in disorganized piles all over the floor. I had never bothered to get bookshelves or nightstands, so my books became my flat surfaces for glasses and candles. Now he was sizing me up, like all book people do, by what I had or didn't have in my collection. I usually never felt self-conscious about the process but with him, I felt instantly exposed.

I took my time and slowly walked into the bedroom. He was sitting on the edge of my bed reading *Death in Venice*. He didn't acknowledge me. Looking very studious, he was either ignoring me or enthralled with the passage he was reading.

I sat next to him and stared at his perfect Roman profile, and then I leaned into him and kissed his neck. He continued to read without looking up at me, and I kissed it again.

"Can't you see I'm reading?" he said, without looking at me. The sides of his mouth twitched with abstained laughter.

"Uh-huh. I can see that."

I got on my knees and unbuttoned his shirt. I placed my hands on the centre of his chest and massaged that hair I had so admired earlier. His skin was sticky from a night's worth of sweat. Without saying a word, I pulled at his left sleeve. He threw his shoulder back and held the book out with his right hand. He did the same in reverse when I was ready for the right sleeve.

Shoulders hunched over, legs spread apart, he continued to read, as I sat kneeling on the Persian rug in front of him, taking him in. He was thin but perfectly T-shaped. Bigger on top, narrower towards the waist. His trail of dark body hair mimicked his shape and thickened in the belly area. As I stared at his torso I could sense him eyeing me over the edge of the book.

He was waiting for me. I leaned forward and kissed his stomach gently. Through the hairs, his skin smelled of sweet milk. Like the sticky remnants of a summer day's ice-cream cone on some sweet child's cheeks. I licked the area around his belly button. Now I tasted salt. He twitched and grunted softly. Then I inserted my tongue right into it, his inny, and he pushed me away from him. His face morphed from shock to lust in a millisecond.

"Take off that dress," he said, indignant.

"No." I said. "You."

His face bore no expression.

He lifted my dress up over my head in one smooth movement. And I was left in a pair of Gap yellow underwear. Not even the thong kind. I forgot I was wearing them.

"Are those boys' underwear?"

I shook my head no.

"Turn around," he said, still sitting on the edge of my bed. He lowered my underwear and sat silently looking at me.

Then he grabbed my hips and pulled me closer to him, sticking his tongue right into the crack of my ass. No man had ever gone there first.

I could hear him unbuckling his belt, unzipping his fly. Then he stuck his fingers into my sex and turned me around.

His long, thin cock was sticking out of his jeans, waiting. "Sit down."

I lowered myself on to him.

He broke through pubic hair, tissue, blood vessels, pride, sadness, desire, me.

Then, there wasn't any room left for air in my lungs. I came pools on to his dark-blue jeans.

My cigarettes called. I left him lying on my bed with one hand behind his head, the other resting on his stomach, smiling big as he caught his breath. His limp dick twitched as it rested outside his open zipper.

"Bring me one too," he said. "And that little red ashtray you stole tonight."

Later, when I had been lying there awake watching him snore, his hands clasped over his chest, like my mother in her black beaded dress the day of the funeral, I imagined his life back in Barcelona.

I thought about this half-brother, Sergi Canetti. I wondered if Sergi was gay. Did David consider himself bisexual? Did it just happen once?

I got up to go to the bathroom, closed the door, then placed my hands over the cold edges of the sink and pressed my face up to the mirror for a reality check. The whites around my brown eyes were bloodshot and smudges of faded black eyeliner streaked the tops of my cheekbones. My lips were chapped and redder than usual. My classmates had called me "Bubble Lips" when I was a girl, but now those bubbles were extra puffy from an entire night of David's love nibbles. "I love your mouth. I love your lips," he'd said to me as I sucked his cock before we went at it again. He made me feel beautiful, alive again. I laughed at myself in the mirror, gave myself a wink. The man I had stared at so intently in an author's photo was now snoring loudly in my bed.

We decided that David should move in after our third date. We couldn't be without each other, and his time in New York would dwindle away fast.

When he first brought all his things over from the dingy little studio he was renting in midtown Manhattan, I was taken aback by how light the man travelled. For a four-month scholarship trip he had brought his laptop, two dress shirts, two T-shirts, one V-neck wool sweater, two pairs of shoes, a pair of dress slacks, a pair of jeans (which I had soiled) and a black blazer. The pairs of underwear and socks he had brought (less than a week's worth) he hand-washed daily in the nude and hung out neatly on the circular metallic ring around my shower to dry.

The only things that weighed him down were the seven books he intended to read or use as references for his writing. We hardly socialized or saw anyone for that first month and a half. Though I liked to blame our antisocialness on David's less-than-perfect English, I really just wanted him all to myself.

David was a social animal by nature. His mother had told him that as a child he opened his arms for everyone to hold him. He made her nervous, thinking he'd embrace a stranger *con malas intenciones* one day. Unlike most of the misanthropic writers and editors I had come to know and sympathize with over the years, David genuinely liked people.

As time went on, I got used to losing him and his attention at those publishing-world events he did eventually want to go to. In conversation, his whole being was absorbed in the plight of other people's pain, just like he had become absorbed in mine. He was a charismatic empath, and both women and men alike were taken with his boyish charm. Most hadn't heard of his work, but they pretended they had when I introduced him as one of Spain's current avant-garde.

He would perk people up like wilting flowers. I even found myself feeling jealous during a genteel dinner party given by a power editor at Random House. Dressed in a low-cut, very transparent blouse, Elaine Williams was just recently divorced. She had allowed her six-year-old daughter Chloe to play with the adults, and both wouldn't stop flirting with David. While Elaine told him all about her horrendous break-up, the girl kept lifting up her frilly dress like a little whore trying to get his attention.

He pinched Chloe's little stomach and turned back up to Elaine's big batting eyes as she continued telling him about her loneliness. Yes, I'm ashamed to say, I felt like strangling mother and child right there.

I studied him with other people: complete strangers, new acquaintances, good friends of mine, it didn't matter. I knew his look so well, because it was the way he looked at me that first night, and thereafter, and I fell in love with him for it. I felt safe and special in that tolerant gaze of his. When he shared it with others, I began to grow resentful.

But he was all mine at home. David worked methodically on his novel while I checked into the office every day and counted the hours until I could rush home and have him again. He inspired me to kick-start my second novel, despite my first's disastrous reviews, and for the first time in years I felt confident and creative again. I wanted to write screenplays with him, edit anthologies, and co-edit another literary journal with him. I was mad with creative energy.

One beautiful fall morning, David invited me to go live with him in Spain. After that, coming home to him in the evenings involved a whole new mindset of possibilities for a future together.

When Sergi Canetti entered our lives, he shook our very foundation. I came home at around seven the night it happened, the time I usually arrived. I'd been thinking about David the whole way home. When I walked in, I immediately stripped in the vestibule, knowing he would follow my lead. We met naked in the centre of my living room, under the low-hanging antique chandelier with small ivory roses I took from my mother's apartment. With all our body parts saluting the other at attention, we wrestled over who would suck the other first. I won the fight, and I kneeled before him in haughty victory.

Then he regained his power, becoming serious in order to sit me down gently on the rickety wooden chair by the kitchen window. I smoked my after-work cigarette, complaining about the idiots I worked with. He knelt at my mound, opened my lips, and suckled my clit until I felt faint. I told him to stop. He stopped his sucking and leaped up on to his feet and put on his best society lady posture. "Yes, my queen," he said, bowing before me.

With one eyebrow raised abnormally high, he pranced around the room speaking Briticisms, his hands fluttering like butterflies, while his bright red penis pointed the way. I laughed as I studied him. He was beautiful in his girlie man sort of way, and I tackled him on to the bed. He played hard to get until I mounted him, pinned him down. I could do that; we were practically the same size.

He lay helpless beneath me, eyes closed, moaning away as I squeezed and rode his dick like I had learned to ride a horse as a wannabe child jockey at our house upstate. English style, back straight, propped up on my feet, legs bent at my sides. I'd push myself up and down, up and down. I concentrated and stared at him below me, leaning back and turning around to caress his delicate balls. They felt cool to my hands, like little plastic bags of sand to play with.

I looked down and saw his feet. His long toes were curled in arthritic pleasure. It was the pleasure of being encompassed by my insides. He was my captive animal, trapped beneath my long, strong legs he loved so much, his *chaleco de salvavidas*, as he liked to call them.

Wanting to somehow participate, he lifted his upper torso to my left breast and sucked me, the saliva popping loudly in his mouth. He'd look up at me occasionally with one of my reddened nipples in between his teeth. I liked it when he did that, with that look of complete submission. At that moment I was Mother Mary giving milk to her baby Jesus. I was omnipotent and feverish, on a sort of low-grade heroine haze. And then suddenly I tired and alighted off him, lying down and spreading myself out for him. I felt shaky, anaemic.

He tried to eat me again but my body couldn't take any more, and I captured his eager head in between my hands like the saviour and lifted it to give him my breath. We kissed furiously, mouths stretched open to their full capacity, teeth knocking, unfurling our tongues like safety ropes.

Then his cell phone rang. I hated that thing. He stiffened for a bit, as if feeling a change in the air. He looked over at it, contemplated getting it, then thought again. He looked at me instead. Then he let himself inside me elegantly, as his eyes peered into mine. It was like he was looking right through me, intuiting my life's accumulation of sadness. I tried holding my eyes right back to his like I usually did, my lioness instinct. But this time I wanted to hide. I didn't know why, but I felt shaken by the way he looked at that phone. I lowered my lashes instead.

The urge to cry was rising in me fast. I thought of my mother, her pain in love, her long-time fear of ageing, of dying alone. I thought of how she finally decided to face this fear by violently making it come true. I felt myself shrinking in his sentient gaze. As he pumped me, his eyes were welling up with tears along with mine. I held back and fought the demon. I didn't want him to know how much I loved him yet or how happy I really was despite my current state. How I wanted to become part of his world and abandon mine!

Deep within me, David twisted and coiled himself, sensually taking in the texture of my inner walls. Then he stopped and said, "Let's get on our sides. But keep me inside of you."

I went with him, face to face, as he grabbed my left buttock, and carried me into a half-turn on to our sides. Never disconnecting ourselves, David had somehow managed to go even deeper in that new position. We rocked back and forth tensely; his cock massaged my clit, our bodies aching in perfect symmetry. There was so much moisture. He pulled out, buried his head at my breasts again, allowing for us to dry off a bit.

When he re-entered me, he pulsed three times and whimpered at the sensation. That was all he could stand and I was ready too. We came in muted silence, and I allowed myself one stray tear to travel down my face as David shut his eyes and rolled over on his back. I quickly wiped it off.

"You OK?" he asked, catching his breath. He stared up at the white glare of my high antique tin ceilings. I had always thought they looked like dozens of tiny breasts lined up in quadrants. He placed a hand on my leg for reassurance. He wasn't one to touch after sex, too busy recoiling into himself.

"I thought about my mom and got emotional," I mumbled.

"You want to talk about it?"

I tried to decipher his tone before answering. Then I thought about the phone call he received during sex. Who could it have been? Why did he even consider stopping to answer?

"No, it's OK. It's passed now," I lied.

"Some water?" he asked.

"Oh yeah, parched is an understatement," I answered.

I forced myself up with him and went for a cigarette while he took his phone with him into the bathroom. It was probably Sergi. I had heard David whispering on the phone with him late at night. When he came out of the bathroom, I asked him who had called.

"It was Sergi. He likes to reminisce when he's drunk."

It was 3 a.m. Spain time, 9 p.m. ours.

"Doesn't he have anyone else to call?"

It wasn't just the question, but the way my voice shot it out. It had a tone of desperation. I felt threatened. It was the tone that my mother had used a million times on my father when he told her he wouldn't be coming home for dinner or that he had another important business trip.

I was envious of a something I couldn't even put into words or quite understand about him and Sergi. It was just a gut feeling I had. There was nothing I wanted more than to be proven wrong.

He was calm. "A mutual friend of ours is arriving into town tomorrow, Anna. That's what he was really calling about. Miguel Velásquez. He's an old friend of the family who's here on business. He's an art dealer."

"Great," I said, trying to keep my sanity. "Where shall we take him?"

We arranged to meet Miguel the next night at a high-end, big-chef restaurant on the newly reformed Clinton Street. We went through three bottles of South Africa's finest wines, since this was thankfully on Miguel.

It was my first time seeing David with a close friend, riding down the green, comforting path of memory lane. Miguel was jet-set handsome with perfectly styled salt-and-pepper hair. He was married to a rich Catalana who stayed at home and raised their two boys while he frolicked around the globe. He was cordial to me but didn't go beyond the niceties to make me feel like part of the old clan.

His attention was all on David. He had a fountain of questions about David's work and about his mother and her health. Miguel asked if she had remarried since David's father passed away. Like a pair of old women, they unearthed fresh and hardened dirt about themselves and their mutual friends.

Sergi's name was splattered over practically every adventurous tale there was to tell. *Remember when you and Sergi had that party for ... or when Sergi and you and those girls ... You and Sergi disappeared with those Swiss dudes ...Whatever happened to them!*

It was obvious the Canettis were the life of the party.

"Yeah, whatever happened to them?" I interjected, giving him a shove and raising an eyebrow.

"Nothing!" David said and laughed. "Nice purple mouth you got there, Anna. Why don't you have some more wine?"

My teeth and lips tend to suck up the tannins. I must have looked like a fool. And he was trying to change the subject.

"Aw come on, man," Miguel egged on. "Those guys were like in love with you and Sergi. You guys were such the cock-teasers!" said Miguel. He glanced over at me to try to detect a reaction.

My blood was boiling, but my face muscles were contained.

Their banter was so drenched in homoeroticisms, they might have as well been fencing with their dicks.

I changed the subject to something neutral. I asked about the art Miguel was viewing in New York. Mentally, I prepared myself to confront David when we were alone.

I knew that I was quieter than usual on our walk home.

After we saw Miguel into a cab uptown, David tried a million times to jump-start conversations about Miguel's shallow art world. But all his attempts fell flat. I was trying to breathe and shoo away the black birds of paranoia circling me. We tired from our walk and hailed a short cab ride home.

We slid into the back seat, and I gave the driver directions. I turned to David.

"Tell me more about your experimentation with Sergi."

He was instantly defensive. "Why are you making such a big deal about him? Do you think I'm gay or something?"

"I don't know. What the hell did happen with those Swiss guys then?"

"I told you, nothing, we just did lines together. What's wrong with you, Anna?"

"I just want you to tell me more about how you and Sergi first fooled around with each other."

We got back to my apartment and opened another bottle. I listened. I had no choice. I tried to appear calm. He delivered his words casually, like canapés swallowed with champagne. My own sepia-coloured movie reel rolled in my head as he spoke.

David explained that he never believed he was a homosexual. He worshipped girls in his classes when he was young, but absolutely no one paid him or Sergi any mind. They were hideous then, he claimed, and foreigners in a xenophobic country to boot. They were simply desperately horny, pimply little bastards who only had each other for company. Sergi's mother, their father's first wife, had died during childbirth. So Sergi lived with an aunt in his early years. He became too much to handle as a pre-teen, and his aunt sent him back to live with his father, his father's new wife and his half-brother.

The first time Sergi and David touched each other, they'd been sitting in front of their television set in their small apartment in Paris. While David's mother smoked cigarettes in the courtyard and their father banged university students in exchange for discounted books in the back of his shop, the boys gave one another their first blow job.

The television had been turned to one of Europe's many soft-core porn channels, where shapely naked women lathered one another in the shower. The boys' virginal cocks pulsed and rose, begging to be set free from their pants. Through the zipper of his blue jeans, Sergi, the taller and more handsome one, released his cock and stroked it wildly to its fullness while he stared straight ahead at the telly. His bottom lip jutted out as he bit down and broke through the violet skin of chapped lips. A rebel strand of wheat-coloured hair escaped from a thick mass of an overgrown pageboy haircut and dipped in and out of the pock hole on his upper cheekbone, a mark left from a severe case of the measles. David's cock swelled in sync from the excitement of seeing dozens of hardened nipples. The sound of his mother's voice giggled in the distance while Sergi worked on himself with a passionate energy that David had never witnessed before in his brother. Tense and excited, David took his out too. The boys, both sixteen, sat alongside each other on a couch too small for their rapidly growing limbs. They looked over at one another, glassy-eyed and trembling, as they pulled at their reddened cocks together. Sergi, who always felt he could control David, asked him in a desperate and unequivocally commanding voice to "Kiss it, now." And

David, without hesitation, leaned over and took in the warmth and mixture of perspiration and detergent smell of his best friend and half-brother's manliness.

David propelled himself up and down on Sergi only a pair of times before David, overcome with emotion, ejaculated burning droplets of embarrassment at the newness of it all. Sergi pushed David off and finished himself off with his own hand, feeling overwhelmed with the sight of David's come and now his own all over his trousers.

With a hand over his mouth, David pointed and laughed at the mess and Sergi, registering what had happened, stayed perfectly still. He gave David a shove and told him to go and get something to clean it up before David's mother walked in. David brought back some napkins, they cleaned themselves up, and they switched the channel to some American gangster flick.

I realized then that Sergi hadn't blown David and that, in game theory, he owed him one. But I didn't want to know any more.

David left for Barcelona a day before New York had its first big snowfall. He had an important engagement to attend back home at the Círculo de Lectores. I assured him I would join him as soon as I could figure out what to do about work. My first days and nights alone again were spent obsessing over Sergi and David. I imagined the wild, sexual adventures that awaited them when they reunited in Spain again.

After the reality that David had left set in, I spiralled from ecstasy to a one-lane freeway towards depression. I had been on a four-month hiatus from its dark fog, and now I was back. I began seeing my shrink again. I told Laura about my feelings of jealousy about David's experimentations and his intimate relationship with Sergi.

Sitting in front of me, on her hunter-green chair, in a long, flowing khaki-coloured skirt and brown riding boots, Laura was serene. She joined in the Greek chorus of those around me who pooh-poohed my irrational fear of thinking David a closet homosexual.

"This is natural behaviour for men. They're just as capable of experimenting with the same sex as women are," she said. She paused and asked, "You've been with women, right?"

"Yeah."

"Why is it different or more acceptable that you did?"

"I don't know. It's just *different*."

"It's the same. Just be grateful that he told you," she said. "This proves a wonderful aspect of his open character. He's sharing himself, his past, who he is with you."

"I guess so."

"He's chosen *you*, Anna. Trust him, trust yourself. OK?"

"OK."

Time was up and having him so far away didn't help my overactive imagination when I *wasn't* seated in my shrink's chair.

My life in New York was no longer mine for the few months that followed. I lived in an altered state, a time-zoned paralysis as I imagined his fabulous Barcelona life six hours ahead of mine. Six hours ahead on working wonders on his novel, gallivanting with his arty friends, meeting other fascinating, brilliant women, other dashing men.

He'd send me horny one-liners in awkward email English. *I click on your clit with my dick.* I'd get them at work. He had his 3 p.m. siesta jerk-off while I was hitting my 9 a.m. caffeine-fuelled "what am I doing here?" hour.

One day I found myself completely unable to concentrate on the stories I had to edit. I *needed* to kill the throbbing between my legs. So I decided to masturbate in the office bathroom. I watched myself in the mirror of the handicap stall, the one with the extra-large sink. With my head thrown back and my mouth pleading to be filled, I let my raised nipples loose from my bra. I thought of his dick rubbing against me and touched myself, my clitoris expanding underneath my fingers. I imagined him and a strange man he'd met in a bar. I pictured him and Sergi in one of their threesomes he had told me about. I saw him and random sexy girls speaking in that castrating Spanish of theirs under the sheets.

As I looked at myself in the mirror, I didn't recognize the savage woman that looked back, the edges of her mouth sinking, her skirt hitched up under her. I was becoming like them: my lascivious parents.

High on recklessness, I resigned the next day. Without a hint of remorse I asked my publisher, Martin Powers, if he would still allow me to submit articles from Spain on the goings on in the European market. He said yes. I told Martin, who had become a father figure to me (even though at times he was overcome with visible thoughts of incest) that I was going to be working on my next novel in Barcelona.

That night I went home to buy a one-way ticket to Barcelona. I called David to tell him that I had decided to come try it for a while. I could feel his lust and longing through the receiver. He whined and told me to come right then, and I could practically come just hearing his voice, but for that we had to wait another two weeks.

Then the vibrato of that joyous conversation lulled when he told me that my arrival would coincide with Sergi's, who'd be visiting from Madrid. He was going to be there for two weeks doing a series of talks on his latest tome for Barcelona's big literary festival, Diada de Sant Jordi.

I pouted over the phone line and told him that I preferred for us to be alone, reminding him that I wasn't a quiet fuck. It didn't go down well with David at first. He insisted that he had a large flat and plenty of extra rooms and bathrooms. It took some convincing with old truisms like, three's a crowd and a woman needs her privacy.

It annoyed me that David didn't innately understand my argument of wanting alone time after such a long period of not seeing each other. He finally grunted an OK, muttering that he'd tell him to find another place to stay. He was obviously worried about Sergi's reaction. And I celebrated winning this small battle for now.

On that cold and rainy April night at JFK airport, I crossed myself. I made the four-pointed arm gestures of the crucifix slowly as I waited in line to check in. *In the name of the Father ... the Son ... the Holy Spirit ... Amen.* Like I had seen old wrinkled-up women do in the face of the unknown.

* * *

It was 10 a.m. Barcelona time, 4 a.m. mine, when my plane arrived. David was waiting for me at the airport. A lover of public transportation, he insisted we take the metro back to his apartment in the centre of the city.

He was all skin and bones, wearing red unisex espadrilles as he rolled my fifty-pound suitcase over the furrows and protrusions of Barcelona's cobblestone streets. He was wearing a cream linen shirt, open to the third button from the top, exposing that pile of chest hair I so adored burrowing my face into. His skinny legs were sheathed in some army green–coloured cargo pants with one leg rolled up.

Despite the tremendous weight he dragged behind him, he zigzagged like a Twyla Tharp dancer from one side of the pavement to the other, escaping la Rambla de Catalunya's undulating pedestrian traffic. Used to the daily inconveniences of living in one of the world's most enchanted cities, he parted the crowd of morning tourists with a gentle brush of his extended right hand. They obeyed like a herd of cows, letting us pass at his command.

"Almost there," he reassured me, looking back to see if I was still with him. Then he made a sudden right on to a street with an impressive Gothic church rounding its corner. Never taking my eyes off his regal back, I followed him from behind. It was impossible to walk at his side on Barcelona's truncated sidewalks with my huge suitcase in the way. I appreciated the moment alone, so I could prepare myself for reuniting with him at his apartment. "OK," I sang back. I stared like an awed little girl at the ancient stone buildings that led to David's building, their flowers cascading over verandas and dark-shuttered doors with the promise of spreading open to mysterious lives above.

There was a morning chill in the air. My nipples rose to their points under my white shirtdress. I looked up and noticed an old man was looking down into my open neckline. I smiled, and he gave me a salacious grimace in return.

Carrer de Carme, 24. That's where my David lived. It was a busy side street off la Rambla in the Arab-dominated ghetto of el Raval. The neighbourhood was a mix of strange Old-

World seedy and pop bohemian artsy. It was undergoing its predictable gentrification. David had taken the inheritance his father left him and bought himself the coveted top floor of an architecturally impressive, but structurally dilapidated building. "This is it." He grinned, breathing hard through his teeth.

The building was called La India, and it had gargoyles and faces of ominous indigenous women skimming its rooftop. We walked into the cool of the building's open marbled lobby, past two sets of pillared columns and into a small metallic elevator-made-for-two hidden behind an antique glass door.

We were finally alone, nose to nose in the tiny elevator that smelled of days of accumulated sweat. I just stood there staring at him, expressionless from nerves. David shoved his hands up my dress. He slipped his hand into my underwear and cupped my wet sex. He grazed my clitoris with his fingers. I thought he was going to take me right there. His hardness was pressing up against me. We kissed furiously as the mechanical gears roared and until the elevator car jumped, signifying that we had landed. David removed his fingers from my insides and licked them clean. "We're here."

We tumbled out of the elevator into a dark, windowless hallway with a floor of large black-and-white squares of ceramic. There were only two doors on each floor, and David's apartment was behind the big wooden one on our left with an old metallic lion's head knocker in its centre. Once he turned the thick golden key he took out of his pocket, I heard a click, and he pushed it open.

In an instant, all of Barcelona's splendid light poured on to us through the uncurtained windows with such grandeur it was like we had been doused with a bucket of golden honey. He rolled my suitcase to the side and welcomed me. "You're home."

In that light, I swear he freaking shimmered. His black waves of hair painted with rays of white light. He'd be beautiful, even old.

Light was important for David and his writing life, to psychically be away from the city's dark and noisy streets below. I squinted, feeling a headache coming on. I desired my sunglasses.

"Wow" was all I could say. Some sort of low-grade aphasia had hit me with the jetlag setting in. And there was so much to absorb about David's world without me.

He took my hand and walked me through the long hallway of his railroad apartment. The floors were a swirling mosaic of salmons, browns and greens. Their florid hues had faded and veiny cracks of time now intermixed with their patterns instead. We passed sparsely furnished parlour rooms with white-curtained French doors. There were one-person guest beds and wooden bookshelves along with antique desks with mismatched chairs scattered throughout.

In one of those rooms, a medium-sized suitcase and a pair of men's fancy dress shoes sat beside the bed. The shoes were a shiny dark-brown leather, Italian, too elegant to be David's. Feeling my stomach drop, I intuited they had to have been Sergi's. I chose to remain silent. I didn't want to ruin our first moments. I decided to pretend I didn't notice them.

He showed me to our bedroom and told me to settle in. It was a large white room, with a balcony facing an interior courtyard where neighbouring families hung out their underwear to dry. I stepped on to it and looked down. I noticed there was a black-haired Barbie doll, her stiff arms raised over her head, lying naked on the cement. A small child tiring of her must have tossed her out the window, wondering if she could fly.

I looked around his bedroom. His style was minimalist, mostly from lack of need. A queen-size bed, covered in white sheets and a down comforter contrasted a dark wood chest of drawers, and two matching night tables. He had a bottle of water propped up on his nightstand and book casually left open. Nothing was out of place, everything had a purpose. He must have thought my place was a tornado disaster area.

"You should eat something," he said, in a tone that seemed suddenly formal.

His words startled me. I realized I was standing there dissecting it all in silence.

"I'd rather eat you," I said playfully, turning to face him. I stepped over to him, grabbed his crotch, and kissed his neck, taking in his Mediterranean blend of olive soap and tobacco smell.

"Don't," he said, unhooking my hands and placing them at my sides. His eyes darted back and forth in thought. All the sexual energy from before had been drained from the room.

"Don't what?" I said.

"Later, Anna." He said it in the way a woman might if she had a headache.

"Fine," I said, audibly pissed.

"We have all the time in the world to make love."

He always said that. "*Hacer el amor*" instead of *follar*, fuck, which I liked to say now. Like in the Almodóvar movies. He liked to correct me on this, disapproving of my crude Spanish. "We don't *fuck* Anna, we make *love*," he'd say with a smile.

I always rolled my eyes at this. The thought of making love all the time killed the mood.

"Let's put some food into you, OK? I pre-prepared our lunch."

Though he was going through the good host's manual step by step, he was still acting a little weird. I started to suspect he had second thoughts about me coming.

"I'll freshen up then." My voice came out a note higher than usual.

I turned to fidget blindly with the zipper of my suitcase, his eyes still on me. And just as that feeling of exasperation of being in this unknown place was rising, the hot tears ready to roll, David came up behind me and hugged my bent body, clasping his hands over my uterus. "I'm so happy you're here," he whispered in my ear.

Once he left the room, I went into the bathroom and unpacked my toiletry bag. There was a stale smell of old plumbing that turned my stomach, and I breathed through my mouth instead. Confronting my appearance in the mirror, I got back what I expected to see. I was green from a week's worth of little sleep and anxiety.

After brushing my teeth with my Tom's of Maine mint

toothpaste (David teased me about it, calling me nature *chica*), I dabbed on some lipstick and debated which of David's fragrances to put on to liven me up. Lavendar, Vetiver, Musk, Figuer. The latter was a high-end French cologne that smelled of dirt and figs. I remember thinking this was funny. *Figa*, in Italian, is slang for pussy. I hadn't known him to be a perfume wearer in New York. I went for the Figuer, in tribute to its symbolism.

Finished with my mild grooming, I went back into the hallway and walked towards the sound of banging dishes in the kitchen. On the way, I saw what seemed to be his study. I decided to dip into it before re-encountering him so soon.

On an old rickety side table adjacent to a big beige comfy reading chair sat a pair of framed photographs, the only ones I had seen in the house so far. One was of a thin, bearded man in a dress shirt and high-waisted slacks. He was standing in front of a bookstore with a proud look on his face. It was almost a smirk. It had to be his father.

Then there was the other photo. Two twenty-something boys in matching white T-shirts and jeans laughed hysterically, tears running down their faces, with their arms tightly enwound around each other's waists. Sergi and David, long haired and tanned, posing with that barely perceptible femininity in their stance that only I could clearly see. Sergi towered over David, who was nestled into the crevice of his armpit. Physically, Sergi was way more striking than David had ever suggested in his descriptions. And it was obvious he held the reins.

From what I gathered, Sergi was David's ringleader, his pimp. David was always under his tutelage in writing and when it came to getting laid. Throughout their teens and twenties they'd date the same women, bed them together, and get off on the group sex. Watching the other pump. Lending a generous hand, patting each other's backsides in brotherly support. I never had the nerve to ask David if they'd engage each other during these threesomes.

An unwanted vision of David's thin lips around Sergi's cock appeared in my head. My hands clamped up around the edges of the cold wood frame, my heart beat faster in panic. I wanted to throw the photo against the wall and smash their big smiles to pieces. Why the hell was I jealous of a man? What did he have that I didn't? I thought I already knew the answer.

"Anna, come to the balcony," David called out from a distance. The balcony spread along the back end of his apartment so you could enter it from various parts of the house: from his bedroom, the study, or from the hallway. He had quite a spread of Spanish culinary clichés awaiting me: olives, *jamón serrano*, Manchego cheese, grilled squid, *tortilla española*.

"You doing OK?" he asked as I stepped out into the dry, yellow sun. A comic *vroom vroom* of a motor scooter from the side street below answered his question before I could.

"Sure. Just feeling a little woozy. Probably hunger."

It was somewhere in the early afternoon, and David was pouring us glasses of full-bodied Rioja. I could still feel his tension and I was grateful for the upcoming intoxication.

He dragged out a metal lawn chair for me to sit down in and slowly, as if with arthritis, eased himself into his seat. The sky was monochromatically blue and the sun's rays were penetrating my scalp. David had his sunglasses on so I couldn't see his eyes, but I could tell his wheels were turning; he was pushing out his mouth in thought.

It was the quiet before the storm.

"So we're not alone, huh?" I ventured first. His silence was irritating me.

He sighed a sigh that weighed half his entire body weight. "Yes, Anna. I wanted to tell you beforehand, but I didn't want you to rearrange your plans or decide not to come or something crazy."

"Sergi's here, I know," I said.

David reached for his glass and took a swig. I reached for one of his Lucky Strikes, focusing on the bomb target symbol on its packaging. Neither of us had touched the food.

"Listen, I want you to meet him. He's part of my past. Yes, he's been a pain in the ass all his life, but he's family and I can't shut my door on him. He's harmless. God, why do you hate him so much?" His voice was whinier than usual. He looked at me, his upper lip in a curl, his mouth slightly ajar. I had never seen him look so annoyed, so nervous.

Then he put his head down, resting his elbows on his splayed knees, staring at the ground. He looked defeated. I caught a whiff of the Manchego.

I have to confess that his weakness gave me a whole new sense of strength. Sergi was obviously a touchy topic, and David was beginning to seem half the man I fell for in New York.

"Listen David," I said calmly, using my best phone operator voice. I was good at concealing the pain when I had to. "I thought we had agreed that he was going to stay somewhere else while I was getting settled in here at least. You told me this."

He sat up in his seat, "His plans fell through with some other apartment, OK? And he has to be here for a few Diada de Sant Jordi book events. Lord knows I have enough extra space in this place. What's the big deal? What do you have against someone you've never even met?"

"I have absolutely *nothing* against him," I said. "*Really, I don't*," I said even slower, sounding like I was gurgling underwater. "I guess I just feel kind of uncomfortable, perhaps threatened is a better word . . . with all the women and all your sexual liaisons together." I took a long drag of my cigarette. "I'm not into being shared, you know. I just don't need that sort of juvenile shit in my life."

"He's not going to try anything, Anna. That was the past. We're adults now. Trust me. He knows that you're special, and that I'm in love with you. We're done with all that."

David was visibly trying to pull himself together. I wanted our beginning to go as smoothly as possible. I flashed him my big joker smile instead. I knew it looked natural, but it wasn't. He laughed with a gullible relief.

"You're so nutty, Anna. You're a real paranoid case." He caressed my cheek, then licked it, and with the other hand he took a piece of ham and placed it into my mouth. It was salty and warm from sitting in the sun. I think it was the best ham I've ever tasted.

"I'm taking you to a fancy party tonight."

"Really?" A shiver of excitement raced down my spine.

"It's *Libros* magazine's kick-off party for Diada de Sant Jordi at the Ritz. Everyone will be there, including our friend Sergi. He's giving a brief speech, which will probably be inappropriate and sarcastic. People love to hate him here."

"Including you?" I asked.

He thought for a moment. "Yes, sometimes, including me. Don't take this badly, but you remind me of each other. You both can be charmingly arrogant on the exterior, but viciously insecure inside. Watch, you guys are going to become wicked pals." He laughed, tears filling in his eyes.

I wanted to believe him. I wanted to believe we could all be friends.

Barcelona's springtime literary love fest, Diada de Sant Jordi, is Cataluña's take on St Valentine's Day. The holiday takes place on 23 April, the anniversary of Cervantes' and Shakespeare's deaths. It spotlights love's finer accompaniments: books, roses and playing hooky from work. I loved this take on the holiday; it was a welcome switch from America's garish pink Hallmark cards, helium balloons, or the obligatory heart-shaped boxes of chocolates perfunctorily sent to one's cubicle.

Way back in the dark Middle Ages, the legendary and valiant Saint George (Sant Jordi) was said to have rescued his Catalan city and his pouty princess from a fire-breathing dragon that plagued the people. He stabbed the beast in the heart with his long sword and killed it. Now in tribute to all that reptilian bloodshed, and the miraculous rosebush that blossomed from it, it is the custom that men give red roses to their ladies. In return, the ladies give books to their men.

Local booksellers and flower vendors cram the length of la Rambla and other streets, and everyone in Barcelona finds a good excuse not to do a stitch of work. Instead, people stroll the streets with their lovers, browse for books, crowd the plazas and eye the fashionable authors of the day.

It is also a big day for cultural critics and the literati to see who got invited that year to sign their books around town.

The high-society Svengalis behind the Sant Jordi events had chosen Sergi as one of the honorary invitees, while David with a new book out, had been slighted in his own hometown.

David acted like it didn't bother him. He pointed out that he and Sergi had been invited previous years during the height of *Crack*'s popularity. I knew some part of him felt hurt. Could he be so above this kind of sibling rivalry? Was he already content with his literary credibility? I didn't know whether I'd ever be.

Deep down I already knew I was a better literary critic than I was a writer. I had graduated with an MFA in creative writing from a top school only to see all my friends get offered immediate high-profile book deals with their theses. I reworked my thesis over and over until I killed it. When I finally published it with some trendy indie publisher based in Brooklyn, it was so overwrought, so self-conscious, that one critic labelled it "cold and overly stylized". Somehow, this kind of criticism had never touched Sergi's dense work. His new book on Hadrian, an impenetrable thicket of pompous jargon and historical assumptions, was oddly more popular than David's last heartbreaking novel about alienation.

After David had caught me up on all the literary gossip on the terrace, we scurried into the bedroom. Talking about the book fair was our post-fight, verbal foreplay right before we finally sprang into bed and spread each other's folds open – the tension had been so ripe. We then passed out in a sun-drenched, red wine stupor, our sweaty bodies laid out naked above the sheets after a much-needed fuck.

The balcony doors were open to their full glory and I awoke to the soothing feeling of sunlight warming my bush. The sensation made me want him again, but I didn't want to wake him.

I needed water. I grabbed David's Chinese robe and straightened myself up before exiting the bedroom, thinking, perhaps *hoping*, I'd run into Sergi on my way to the kitchen. This time the room with the shoes' door was practically closed. I assumed Sergi had been here while we were napping. I tapped softly on the door and called out hello. There was no answer, so I pushed the door open.

The shoes were gone. The suitcase was now an explosion of white dress shirts, sleek belts and identical pairs of dark denim jeans. Sergi was obviously in a rush to get in and get out fast. There were copies of his books strewn on the floor. I picked one up and stared at the black-and-white author photo. It was a more recent photo than the one I'd seen in David's study, and he was still just as stunning, having grown more distinguished with age. He had grown facial hair, and I immediately thought it was a vain attempt to look smart, less pretty boy.

White sheets of paper with elegant and scripted writing were scattered hastily over the unmade bed. They looked like drafts of his short speech for *Libros* magazine's Sant Jordi event that night. Maybe he wasn't as spontaneous as David had suggested.

While I showered before the party, I imagined what my first words to Sergi could be. I chose my outfit carefully. I didn't want to look like another literary social climber in a flowery minidress and pristine pumps. I decided to go for a black-fitted pants suit instead. I let my braless breasts hang free in their teardrop position, rounding out the edges of my jacket. Black pointed flats provided maximum comfort while walking Barcelona's dark streets with the boys later that night.

I lined my eyes with black eyeliner and smoked them up with grey shadow. I skipped the lipstick. I wanted to be all eyes that night.

Surrounded by the unnaturally attractive Spanish publishing world, I was glad that I had fixed myself up. In the packed ballroom, the Ritz's chandeliers cast a romantic light on the wiry women in dramatically draped scarves and the men impeccably dressed in dark jackets.

We were boxed into a room of wall-to-wall mirrors where violins played and enormous golden vases with long-stemmed roses for Diada de Sant Jordi lined the walls. A mighty mix of booze, nerves and jetlag kicked in as David and I made our first rounds. I felt like Rita Hayworth's character trapped in the Hall of Mirrors in *The Lady from Shanghai*, where everything looks warped through the lens of paranoia.

I tried to spot Sergi or anybody I knew in the mirrors' reflection, but a low-lying cloud of cigarette smoke hung over our heads like a rain cloud, fogging up my view. Suddenly, David was dragged off by a pack of faceless arms in one direction. I was pulled in the opposite direction, in the liver-spotted, red-nailed clench of Catalan literary agent Silvia Riera.

I'd gotten to know Silvia well over the years through my reporting on the Spanish literary circuit. She was a *been-here-done-that* kind of woman in her late fifties, who I suspected was still up to lots of *that*. She came from a good Catalan family and got into the literary business because she liked highbrow books, cocktail parties and sleeping with struggling writers. She was asking me why the hell had I left my high-profile editorial position to come to Barcelona when I finally spotted Sergi. He stood five heads away from us, laughing big and showing fangs. He turned his head towards me as I eyed him up and down. I told Silvia I'd just gotten sick of New York.

It was impossible not to notice him. He was taller and blonder than most in the room. He turned his entire body to face me, even as he was still chatting up an austere, balding man, probably another veteran of Spanish letters making nice to the new lion. Silvia moved on to a woman she knew standing next to us, and Sergi kept on looking. Noticing he had lost Sergi's attention, the gentleman of letters spotted me, gave me the once-over, and continued his monologue anyway.

Despite his refined looks, Sergi's smile was vulgar. He raked his eyes over me as if I were standing there naked. I blushed like a nun and soaked myself at the same time. It reminded me of why I knew I'd hate him. Did he know who I was? *How* did he know who I was? He mouthed a hello. I nodded in camaraderie and gave him a frigid politician's smile. Then he turned away to continue his conversation with the gentleman.

Silvia had seen our unspoken exchange. She turned back to me. "Oh darling, watch out for him. Don't tell me you two have already . . .?" She paused.

"Nooo," I said loudly. I made a hissing sound to punctuate my negation, for both of our ears. "I'm here with David Canetti, not Sergi Canetti."

"Uuff," she said. "A *little* better, but still, the Canettis are quite the dogs around town you know." She looked at me sympathetically, reading it all so clearly on my face. She continued. "But David has always struck me as the Abel to his Cain in that strange brotherhood. It seems they never get too far from each other, like Frack and Frick," she said in English, pumping extra gasoline into her *rrr*s.

"Yes, they're tight," I added with an upturn in my voice. I tried to steer the conversation away from the sewage she was ready to spill.

I scanned the room, desperately looking for David. I spotted him. He was talking with Sergi and a group of Spanish literati. He was doing a lot of double-cheeked air-kissing and man-to-man back-rubbing. I thought about how much more people touched in Europe.

Despite my distraction, Silvia pressed on. "Don't worry. They'll treat you well. You're with *Publisher's Forum*, and they're dying for some recognition in New York." She placed her hand on my shoulder in pity. Though I hated the gesture, I appreciated her brutal honesty, as always. In exchange, she tolerated my bad reviews of her navel-gazing authors.

I excused myself. I looked for David, who had managed to slip into the crowd again. I was hoping we could do a little public fondling. That's when I saw Sergi cutting through the crowd, quickly moving in my direction.

The bar was packed. I managed to hide myself in a group of huddled men, waiting for my chance to order a drink. Sergi slid between the men and grabbed the top of my arm. I wasn't going anywhere; his grip was too tight. He towered over me, and I was forced to look up at him.

"Anna, I'm Sergi, David's brother." He leaned in to kiss me twice, speaking to me in English, not in Spanish like everyone else did. His English was perfect, far better than David's. His voice was deep, a smoker's raspy.

"I know," I said coldly in Spanish, not wanting to look like a foreigner. As we brushed faces, I could smell the Figuer cologne on him. "When's your little talk?" I asked.

And he continued in English as if he hadn't heard my question. "What are you drinking? Let me get it for you."

He raised a long finger and one of his thick and wickedly arched brows and instantly got the busy barmen's attention. I assumed he was a man who never had to wait for much.

"*Quiero un whiskey*," I said, insisting on speaking in Spanish. Sergi faced the bar looking away from me, staring stone-faced into the mirror in front of us. In the mirror, I saw people around us recognize him, subtly pointing as they whispered to each other. They must have recognized him from all the pre-Sant Jordi media blitz he had done. He ran his hand through his long and wavy hair with hints of grey in it and looked down at the floor momentarily before turning back to me. He was a man used to having eyes on him. And I was stunned by how good it felt to be the woman standing next to him.

"You are an absolutely stunning creature when you're naked. Has any man ever told you that, Anna?" He was still speaking to me in English, our drinks in hand, when he turned to face me.

I felt my sex draw back into itself, tight and tense. I just stared at him.

"I watched you and David fucking this afternoon," he said. "I want you to know I really got off on it. I'm surprised you didn't sense me there on the balcony," he said, incredulously.

"No, I didn't," I said back in English, in an icy, even tone. "David didn't tell me his brother was a stalker." Sergi registered my comment by looking away. I tried to remain cool, wondering whether David had known he was watching. Our lovemaking was especially acrobatic, David taking me, turning me every which way he could on to him.

We were silent, as partygoers pushed and bumped up to us like small pesky waves out in deep water. We just stood there, feet anchored to the ground, enveloped in a sticky net of paralysing hate for each other.

Then a young woman with a dark tan and a tight white sleeveless dress stepped between us, leaning into Sergi seductively to say something in his ear. He said OK. It was time for his speech. Before I could say a word, she pulled him away from me.

Sergi's speech was predictably stagey.

I looked for David as Sergi started his talk, his devoted listeners hanging on every word. And no one was more attentive than David, his most loyal fan, who I found standing at the corner of the stage.

"Look sweetie, it's Sergi." He giggled like a proud mother at a first dance recital. He was so proud of his conceited brother that I decided not to tell him about our conversation. He did not see him as I did, he never would. David and I had exchanged fluids. As had they. But they were flesh and blood. This was a battle between Sergi and me.

So I just stood there, next to David, and imagined Sergi naked, jerking off, coming pathetically into his hand, watching us. I imagined me sucking his oversexed sanguine cock with bravado. I couldn't deny the fact I found him attractive. I imagined David walking in on us fucking secretly in the marbled men's toilet of the Ritz, staring at us with repugnance and utter joy.

When the open bar at the Ritz closed, the three of us left with a large pack of horny literary alcoholics trailing behind us. They were middle-aged and preppy, sputtering vulgarities at the end of every sentence.

On the way out, Sergi swiped two long-stemmed roses from the Ritz's vases and presented them to David and me. "To my favourite lovers on Sant Jordi," was all he said before doing a disappearing act into the crowd behind us. I caught his sleazy double meaning. We flooded the streets with a group of about fifteen, half of whom, it seemed, had slept with either David or Sergi (or both) at one point or another. The babbling women were eager to share their nights of asphyxiating surrender to the Canettis' charm with me. The men were more reserved, but they eyed me like a woman would her ex's new conquest.

Then, without warning, David let go of my hand and clasped his rose between his teeth to jump into a comical flamenco dance in the middle of the street. My pulse raced, and I dropped Sergi's rose to the ground, letting it slip naturally from my hands. Then I flicked my cigarette butt at it. Our group shouted *olés*, and some joined him, while Sergi and I stood back and watched. He looked on with feigned amusement. I knew that he had watched me drop the rose. I clapped harder, faster, as David stomped furiously for his finale. Sergi burned holes through my suit with his eyes all the while.

We moved our parade to the next place. We drank rounds of whiskey at tavern after tavern as we walked from the architecturally breathtaking streets of upper Gracia to the piss holes of lower Barrio Gótico. The night's path paralleled my degenerative transformation into a walking oral fixation. I chain-smoked, accepted drinks from strangers, chatted up the group, and made out with David wherever I could. I was mad with the new-found freedom of Barcelona's street life and being surrounded by people who didn't know me. I felt grotesquely alive.

Sergi never strayed too far away from David and me. But he avoided talking to me alone at the bars. He liked standing next to me silently, making me uneasy. I heard him breathing. I could smell his odour of perspiring figs as he'd rub his pelvis as close to my body as possible when we were standing together cramped in a group.

He also enjoyed interrupting me. I was commenting on how much I liked Spanish writer Javier Marias' long run-on sentences and closeted narrator to an editor couple in our group when Sergi cut me off in mid-sentence. He said that Americans couldn't possibly understand Marias' genius. He liked attacking Americans' ignorance of foreign literature, making it clear that when he said "Americans", he meant me. He carried on and on, in love with the sound of his voice. But I was a snake as slick as he. When he finished, I asked him if he had been able to find an American publisher yet to translate his books into English. He smiled, his eyes said touché. But I could tell he was annoyed. He said that he hadn't found a publisher. I gave him my sympathies, excusing myself to find David.

Around 3 a.m., I opened my eyes in the midst of a room-spinning kiss with David and saw Sergi standing behind him, looking me directly in the eye. We were at a dive bar called Kentucky, and the group was down to a total of five, including the Canettis and me. Testing how far Sergi would go to follow us, I dragged a very drunk David to a dark corner of the bar by the bathrooms.

I had never seen him so wasted. The night's tension of having me and Sergi in a room together had driven him to it. I had watched him drink whiskey after whiskey to keep up with Sergi. But his body weight could never match his brother's. So as David got sloppier and sloppier, Sergi appeared in complete and eerie control.

David had asked me repeatedly throughout the night if I was happy, if I liked Sergi, and if we could all be friends. I lied and said yes to all his questions, assuaging his doubts. Standing by the bathrooms, he swayed like a palm tree at the mercy of a Caribbean windstorm. I held him still.

"Let's go," I said. "Let's put you to bed."

"No, I'm fine. Just touch me."

I pressed my body against his; I wanted him to feel my breasts. I began chewing on his ear and rubbing his cock over his trousers. And just as I suspected he would, Sergi appeared and leaned himself up against the wall in front of us. He was our one-member audience, standing in between two doors with the male and female gender symbols on them.

David's eyes were shut tight in ecstasy. I elongated my tongue, showing Sergi how long I could stretch it out into David's ear. I was waiting for some kind of response from Sergi. He watched without expression. It drove me mad.

David opened his eyes slowly. He saw Sergi and calmly asked, "Hey, man, what's up?"

"I need another drink. Do you have any cash?" Sergi asked, balancing open a sheet of rolling paper and sprinkling in the loose tobacco.

"We'll be right there," David said, finding my hands so I'd continue.

Sergi licked the cigarette shut, exposing a long pink tongue. Then he nodded and took his time walking away. I punched David in the arm, disgusted by his passiveness.

"What?" he said.

"You're going to fucking just let him interrupt us?"

He looked at me with eyes as glazed as glass marbles and began rubbing my crotch. He pushed the side of his hand in the crease of my pussy, calming me in an instant.

"Do you like it when I do this to you?"

I pushed his hand away. "We gotta go, remember?" I said. "Sergi needs his bottle."

The bar was getting ready to shut down as we went out into the main room to look for Sergi. The other couple had gone home at this point, and we found Sergi standing outside talking to a sweet-looking woman with long black curls. We waited for him to finish and when he said goodbye to her, she looked very disappointed. I pitied her.

Sergi's hands were tucked into the pockets of his blazer, his hair pulled back now into a messy stump of a ponytail. With his head tilted to the side he looked directly at me, ignoring David. "Shall we continue this journey?"

My anger neutralized with the thought of another drink and I had liked the tone that Sergi had addressed me with. "Sure," I said nonchalantly, and we began to walk towards some underground after-hours bar that both he and David seemed to know.

It was just the three of us now. A trio, a tribe, a *tribu*. Primitive cultures knew that when there were more than two people to a group, a new set of laws had to be established to maintain order.

Nobody was walking a straight line any more. Neither was the rest of Barcelona at that time of night. David was sputtering nonsensicalities about the dragon and Sant Jordi that made us laugh. We were somehow bonding over David's amateurish inebriation and our love for him.

I kept David's step steady with my arm as Sergi led the way to the next whiskey bar. David belted out the lyrics to an old Joy Division song in his bad British English. And I joined in. We were happy as could be.

We turned on to a dingy street in el Raval lined with African prostitutes giving us some serious come-hither looks. Sergi knocked on a nondescript rounded wooden door and a man popped his head out. After Sergi gave him some mumbled password, we were let into a cavelike lair blasting eerie opera music below. We ordered some Scotch, smoked the hashish that was passed to us, and all fell mute.

Sergi eventually left us to go wander in the back room while David and I zoned out to the music and to rubbing the skin on each other's arms.

Time went by; I can't say how much but I had the urge to pee and excused myself. As I walked to the back, I remember noticing that I was the only woman in the place. I climbed some rickety spiral stairs to an upper room with a cheap exposed red light bulb hanging in its corridor. Before I opened the door where the toilet was, I saw two men embracing, deep in a hungry kiss, leaning against the communal sink. The men hadn't sensed me there. But from the blazer and small ponytail, dark designer blue jeans, fine shoes, I knew it was Sergi.

I studied them, entranced by the forcefulness of the kiss. The other man was Latino looking, black shiny straight hair, olive skin, a long mestizo nose that thickened at the base and led into full bitable lips that Sergi was devouring. The other man noticed me but didn't stop what he was doing; he couldn't. Sergi now had his hand on top of the man's head and right shoulder, lowering him down to exactly where he wanted him. I suddenly thought I could do better and was stunned to feel myself turned on. Sergi was in total control. I backed out of the hallway as fast as I could. Forewent the peeing.

I told David the bathroom was broken and that we had to go. He asked if I had seen Sergi, and I told him he'd probably gone home already. It was around 5 a.m. and the streets were still littered with drunken Euro hipsters. We found a dark alleyway to piss in by some old Gothic church. David took it out and aimed at the wall beside me as I squatted and pushed my crotch out towards the wall, spreading my legs so the urine wouldn't slide under my shoes.

"So I saw Sergi sucking face with some guy at the bar," I said from below, getting up to zip myself up. I was surprised by how upset I felt again. "Sergi's a full-fledged bisexual, huh? Just like Hadrian, the Roman emperor."

"No he just fucks around occasionally," David said.

"Then you could say he's gay then?"

"The man is not gay, Anna. He loves women. He just likes flesh. Flesh is flesh, right?"

"Maybe it's more like he'll fuck anything that moves, including his own brother," I shot back.

I wanted to hit him from frustration. I wanted to ask him if he fucked men on the side. But I refrained. Then he grabbed me by the hips and drew me closer.

"Stop it, Anna. Don't be mad at me, but he told me he wants to sleep with you."

I could tell David was turned on, his hands caressing my ass, his pupils huge in the night's fading moonlight.

"And what did you say?"

"I told him to go to hell and that I'd never let him. He found you fascinating. What did you think of him?"

"Honestly, I think he's an asshole."

"No, I think you like him," he drawled drunkenly, his hands had moved to the sides of my breasts.

"No I *don't*, David." But I wasn't so sure.

"Yes, you do, all the girls do. But he can't have you, you're mine." He licked my neck.

"And he can't have you, either, you bastard," I said, wanting to possess him, completely.

Then a German couple walked in on us and kindly asked for directions.

We walked home in silence, still floating on a cloud of hashish. We passed minivans stocked with hoards of red roses and empty tables waiting for the books that would be displayed and bought tomorrow by idealistic, unassuming women for their seemingly perfect, Spanish men.

Our bedroom was encased by the purple glow of dawn when I awoke. We had been asleep for a half-hour, maybe a deep ten minutes, when I heard Sergi's footsteps in the hallway coming in the front door. I couldn't tell if he was alone or if he had brought someone back. Aroused instantly by his presence, I sat up in bed, fully awake, and listened.

I imagined him smelling like the cheap cologne and soilings of that man from the bar. I lay back down, with a desire to touch myself as David snored peacefully beside me. I threw the white sheet off David and reached for his cock, trying to waken him with my touch. Now I really needed him to enter me, fuck me hard, fuck me loud. I wanted Sergi to hear it all.

David let out a cranky moan as I planted my face between his legs, lifted him up from his buttocks, like a mother lifting her child to change him. Trailing his hair-lined stretch from anus to testicles with my tongue, I took his flaccid cock in my mouth and it came to life, even before David fully came to.

"What are you doing?" he asked. Propping himself up on his elbows, blinking hard. He was startled, his heart beating fast. I didn't answer; enthralled on getting him off, I held on with my mouth, kissing, sucking as loudly as I could.

There was no sound coming from the hallway or from any part of the apartment any more. The house was frozen in screaming silence aside from my mouth's wet popping sounds and David's gentle moaning. He was lying down again, tossing his head from side to side.

"God, I love you," he said softly. And I loved him too. But maybe I hated him more right now for making me feel so vulnerable. I wanted to hurt him, to hit him. So I did. I sat on top of him and slapped his face. It was harder than I meant to. He shot up like an alarm clock had gone off under him.

I pushed him back down and laughed loudly. I splayed his arms out like Jesus on the Cross and bit his neck hard, wanting to leave my marks on him for everyone to see.

"Stop it" he said. "That hurts."

And he looked hurt. I didn't feel like comforting him. "Wake up and fuck me then," I said. I got on all fours and lifted my ass to him. He obeyed like I knew he would. He licked my ass and stuck his fingers in my swelling cunt.

"Fuck me, David," I demanded.

He placed his delicate hands on my hips and positioned himself to carefully enter. And he pumped slowly, softly, as if he were nodding off on a swinging hammock. I closed my eyes and moaned for him. It felt so sweet, like being rocked in a lullaby. Holding my breath, I felt the first tinglings of an orgasm.

Then I saw a pair of strong thick legs with light-brown hairs on the shapely calves and a fat, rose-coloured prick being stroked happily in my peripheral vision. I didn't hear him enter the room, but I knew he'd come. I felt it.

I refused to look up at his face and concentrated on David inside of me instead. I wanted him to defend me, to scream for him to get out. He didn't. Instead, Sergi sat on the edge of the bed and cupped my left breast, weighing it, massaging it, as if he were buying a cantaloupe from the Boqueria market. He was whetting his mouth, moaning, "Mmmm," at the premonition of sweetness to come.

While Sergi concentrated on my torso, David's pump had gotten increasingly faster and even deeper with Sergi in the room. I could feel him spasming, becoming more erratic in his thrusts. I had become disconnected from my body. I floated to the corner of the room, took a seat, and saw it all. Sergi's power, David's frailty, my complete submission. My heart pounded, so did my head, my throat and my dripping cunt. Sergi stuck his hand in my mouth and I obediently sucked on his fingers. Where had those long and dirty fingers been all night? I caught whiffs of cigarette, semen and garlic.

It was all beginning to hit me hard and my entire body hot-flashed. Sensing this, Sergi ran his fingers through my short hair and clenched the taut skin on the back of my neck. Like you would a cat. David pinched my nipples and slapped my buttocks. I tingled and shivered, growing weaker and weaker with overwhelming pleasure. "Do you like us touching you?" David's voice was close to cracking from the excitement.

I heard a yes hissing from my throat and I wasn't sure where it had come from.

I was one of them now. Before meeting them I was woman who demanded respect. Now I'm a woman who accepts humiliation. There is a beautiful kind of strength in this kind of shame.

Sergi shoved his penis into my face. He hit my forehead, my eyelids, the bridge of my nose, with his swollen sword. He was getting back at me for the entire night, for something. Something he probably couldn't understand himself. Then he took aim and shoved his cock to the back of my throat. I gagged and coughed, unable to lift a hand.

Still on my knees, Sergi got off the bed and went somewhere behind David who had resumed fucking me. I hadn't felt Sergi get on the bed with us so I figured he was standing somewhere in the room. But where?

David put his lips to my ear and whispered, "Please don't be mad at me."

Then, as if David had just been shot in the head, he collapsed his entire weight over the curve of my back. Straightening myself, tensing my muscles, I held him up with all my strength while Sergi let out a wail and David cursed the air. Sergi was hurting him, thrusting himself gratuitously, forcing himself into David's small channel. Our interconnected motions awkward, stunted; like being connected to a long, thick, knotted sailor's rope catching, bumping, and slithering up the edge of a boat.

I fought and contorted myself trying to keep David inside of me. Caught in between us, David was falling apart, on the verge of bursting. He was snorting like Quixote's Rocinante, shouting for God, sobbing quietly, for all of us. I joined in their guttural wails. It was the holiest and saddest of choruses. And then like a crescendoing car alarm screaming at the night, it was over.

Sergi pulled out and walked out. David fell into a ball of wasted flesh in coital position beside me. At that moment, I couldn't imagine a greater pain than loving a weak man. He couldn't look at me, at least not yet. Then I thought of my mother, thought of what she would think, if anything as terrible had ever happened to her in her life.

I craved solitude and began sliding my body off the edge of the bed. My knees cracked, my joints ached. I reached for my pants suit lying in two disjointed pieces on the floor. I grabbed my shoes, my bag, and walked barefoot out of the room, down the swirling corridor of mosaic tiles, past Sergi's room with its door closed, and out the front door, leaving them alone in their stifling silence. My heart pounded loudly in my ears.

As I stepped out of the elevator and on to the shaded entrance of La India's outer lobby, I remember thinking that I didn't feel a single emotion. Neither happy nor sad. But I must have been wearing some kind of face, because a straight line of cheery tourists slowed down to look at me as they passed. I rummaged through my bag and found a last bent cigarette. I gave it one puff, looked right back at their innocent sun-blotched faces and had the urge to vomit.

Turning the corner off Carrer de Carme, I let it all out. The entire night's bile released on to the grey, rounded-stone streets of this Iberian port city that had witnessed so many centuries of misery.

I hung my head down for a while and watched the last string of saliva detach itself from my mouth. Holding myself up with one hand on the stone wall before me, I found its coldness provided a sobering effect. I wiped my chin with my sleeve and slicked my hair back from my face. As I straightened myself up, an old and squat Catalan couple walked by me, cautiously observing me with two sets of beady brown eyes. There was a rose in her hand and a book tucked safely under his left arm.

It was Diada de Sant Jordi. The sun felt strong. It's nice to be warm when you're feeling cold. I decided I would walk to las Ramblas and browse all those books I had yet to read. Buy a book, maybe two, maybe three. It was the new beginning I had wanted, though it was a beginning to an end. But I was good at endings.

Then a song popped into my head. It was a song that used to make my mother cry whenever she heard it in passing. "Perfidia", Treachery, was its name. *La perfidia de tu amor.*

There was no turning back. Barcelona's morning sky was the steeliest of blues.

Author Biographies

Matthew Addison
Matthew Addison's stories have appeared in *Fishnet*, *The Best American Erotica*, and *X: The Erotic Treasury*. He lives in Northern California.

Jacqueline Applebee
Jacqueline Applebee breaks down barriers with smut. Jacqueline's stories have appeared in various anthologies, including *Swing!*, *Best Women's Erotica* and *Best Lesbian Erotica*. She has also written several novellas available online at Excessica and Shadowfire Press. To learn more, visit her at *www.writing-in-shadows.co.uk*

Cheyenne Blue
Cheyenne Blue combines her two passions in life and writes travel guides and erotica. Her erotica has appeared in many anthologies, including *Best Women's Erotica*, *Mammoth Best New Erotica*, *Best Lesbian Erotica*, *Best Lesbian Romance* and on many websites. You can read more of her erotica on her website *www.cheyenneblue.com*

Kris Cherita
Kris Cherita has written for an eclectic range of publications under a variety of noms de porn, and has never been the principal of a girls' school nor is ever likely to be. The characters and institutions in "Peace de Resistance" are fictitious, and any resemblance to any businesses currently

in operation are purely coincidental and would be a huge surprise to the author, who probably couldn't afford them anyway. Kris lives in Australia and enjoys travel, writing, movies and threesomes.

Andrea Dale

Andrea Dale's stories have appeared in *Do Not Disturb: Hotel Sex Stories*, *Afternoon Delight: Erotica for Couples*, *The Mammoth Book of the Kama Sutra* and *Dirty Girls*, among others. With co-authors, she has sold novels to Cheek Books (*A Little Night Music*, Sarah Dale) and Black Lace Books (*Cat Scratch Fever*, Sophie Mouette) and even more short stories. She freely confesses that she has a thing for rock stars. Her website is at *www.cyvarwydd.com*

Lewis DeSimone

Lewis DeSimone is the author of the novel *Chemistry* (Lethe Press). His work has also appeared in a number of journals and anthologies, including *Second Person Queer: Who You Are (So Far)* and *My Diva: 65 Men on the Women Who Shaped Their Lives*. His contribution to the latter was highlighted on Salon. Lewis blogs regularly at *SexandtheSissy.wordpress.com*. He currently lives in San Francisco, where he is working on a new novel. He can be reached through *www.lewisdesimone.com*

Kate Dominic

Kate Dominic is a former aerospace editor and technical writer who now writes about much more interesting ways to put Tab A into Slot B (or C or D or many multiples thereof). She is the author of over 300 short stories, which have been published under many names in three solo books, a wide variety of anthologies, magazines and websites, and in several languages. Kate is currently taking a break from short stories and finishing a series of novels. She can be reached at *KateDominicWriting@yahoo.com*

Dorianne

Dorianne is a queer, kinky northern gal who writes in many realms, both erotic and not. She has written and directed plays for the stage and indie film and occasionally she takes her urge to entertain onstage herself to dance burlesque. In all her endeavours, she hopes to make her audience do any or all of the following: laugh; think; squirm in their seats; get a little wet.

David Findlay

David Findlay is a Toronto-based pornographer who does not have a sister. His parents are alive and well and he doesn't know where Abercrombie is. David's fiction, non-fiction, photos and videos tend to dwell on people enjoying things they really oughtn't to. His work appears in the anthology *First Person Queer*, among other venues. He is currently working on a bluegrass porn opera and a smutty comic book while collecting improbable experiences on the road.

Shanna Germain

Shanna Germain has a poor memory; she thinks that's why she became a writer, but she can't recall for certain. Her writing has appeared in places like *Best American Erotica 2007*, *Best Bondage Erotica 2*, *Best Gay Romance 2008* and *2009*, *Best Lesbian Erotica 2008* and *2009*, *Best Lesbian Romance 2009*, *Dirty Girls*, *The Affair* and more. Visit her online at *www.shannagermain.com*

K.D. Grace

K.D. Grace lives in England. She loves gardening, extreme walking, anything to do with nature. She has stories published by Black Lace, Xcite, Cleis and Ravenous Romance among others.

Isabelle Gray

Isabelle Gray's writing can be found in many places including *Dirty Girls*, *Iridescence*, *Bedding Down*, *Best Date Ever: True Stories that Celebrate Lesbian Relationships* and *Best Women's Erotica 2008*.

Nalo Hopkinson

Nalo Hopkinson is a Caribbean-Canadian author born in Jamaica. Her books include the novels *Blackheart Man, In the New Moon's Arms, The Salt Roads, Midnight Robber* and *Brown Girl in the Ring,* and the short story collection *Skin Folk.* She has also edited or co-edited various anthologies, including *Mojo: Conjure Stories, So Long Been Dreaming: Post-Colonial Science Fiction Stories* and *Whispers from the Cotton Root Tree: Caribbean Fabulist Fiction.*

Maxim Jakubowski

Maxim Jakubowski has for fifteen years been editing *The Mammoth Book of Erotica* series and is also highly active in the crime and mystery field. He lives in London where he writes, edits, lectures and broadcasts.

Rachel Kramer Bussel

Rachel Kramer Bussel (*www.rachelkramerbussel.com*) is an author, editor, blogger and reading series host. She's edited over twenty anthologies, including *The Mile High Club, Do Not Disturb, Spanked, Tasting Him, Tasting Her, Dirty Girls, Crossdressing, Yes, Sir, Yes, Ma'am* and the nonfiction *Best Sex Writing 2008* and *2009.* She is currently Senior Editor at *Penthouse Variations* and writes the Dating Drama column for *TheFrisky.com.* Her writing has been published in *Best American Erotica 2004* and *2006,* as well as in *Cosmopolitan,* Huffington Post, Mediabistro, *Newsday, New York Post, Penthouse, Tango, Time Out New York,* the *Village Voice* and *Zink,* and has appeared on NY1 and *The Martha Stewart Show.* She blogs at *lustylady. blogspot.com* and *cupcakestakethecake.blogspot.com*

Marilyn Jaye Lewis

Marilyn Jaye Lewis is the author of *Neptune and Surf, When Hearts Collide* and *When the Night Stood Still,* among other books. She is also editor or co-editor of *The Mammoth Book of Erotic Photography* (Constable & Robinson), *Zowie! It's Yaoi! Western Girls Write Hot Stories of Boys' Love* (Thunder's Mouth Press), and *Stirring Up a Storm: Tales of the Sensual, the Sexual, and the Erotic* (Thunder's Mouth Press), among others. She was the founder of the Erotic Authors Association, the first American organization to honour literary excellence in the erotic genre, and was its Executive Director from 2001–6.

Olivia London

Olivia London is the pseudonym of a writer living in Seattle. She is currently working on a novel. Many of Ms London's stories have appeared in the online magazine *Ruthie's Club*.

Adriana V. López

Adriana V. López is the founding editor of *Criticas*, *Publishers Weekly*'s sister magazine devoted to the Spanish-language publishing world, and the co-editor of *Barcelona Noir*, a short story anthology for Akashic Books. López's work has appeared in the *New York Times*, the *Los Angeles Times* and the *Washington Post*, among other publications and book anthologies. At work on her first novel, she divides her time between New York and Madrid. *www.adrianavlopez.com*

Catherine Lundoff

Catherine Lundoff lives in Minneapolis with her wife. She is the award-winning author of *Night's Kiss: Lesbian Erotica* (Lethe Press, 2009) and *Crave: Tales of Lust, Love and Longing* (Lethe Press, 2007) as well as over seventy published stories. She is also the editor of *Haunted Hearths and Sapphic Shades: Lesbian Ghost Stories* (Lethe Press, 2008).

Nick Mamatas

Nick Mamatas is the author of two novels, *Under My Roof* and *Move Under Ground*, and over fifty short stories. His pornographic fiction has appeared in the anthology *Short and Sweet, Suicide Girls*, and *Fishnet*. His other fiction has appeared in literary publications such as *subTERRAIN* and *Mississippi Review*, and in science fiction/horror venues including *Weird Tales*, *ChiZine* and *Polyphony*. Much of his recent short fiction was collected in the book *You Might Sleep* . . .

Sommer Marsden

Sommer Marsden is the author of *Lucky 13*, *Double Booked*, *The Mighty Quinn* and *The Seekers* trilogy, among many others. Her work has appeared in dozens of anthologies including *Best Women's Erotica 2009* and *2010*, *Ultimate Lesbian Erotica 2008*, *Love at First Sting*, *Playing With Fire*, *Spank Me*, *Bottoms Up*, *Never Have the Same Sex Twice*, *Lust at First Bite*, *Seduction* and *Liaisons*. Sommer's work can be found all over the web, to follow her dirty antics visit her at *SmutGirl.blogspot.com*

Mary Anne Mohanraj

Mary Anne Mohanraj was born in Sri Lanka, and currently lives in Chicago. Her books include *Bodies in Motion*, *Kathryn in the City* and *Torn Shapes of Desire*. She has also edited various anthologies, including *Aqua Erotica* and *Wet*. She holds a PhD in English literature from the University of Utah. In addition to her own writing, she has founded two online magazines – *Clean Sheets* (erotica) and *Strange Horizons* (SF) – as well as two organizations – the Speculative Literature Foundation and DesLit.

Alana Noel Voth

Alana Noel Voth is a single mom who lives in Oregon with her son, one dog, two cats and several freshwater fish. Her fiction has appeared in *Best Gay Erotica 2004* and *2007*; *Best American Erotica 2005*; *Best Women's Erotica 2004*; and online at *Cleansheets*, the *Big Stupid Review* and *Literary Mama*.

Achy Obejas

Achy Obejas is the author of the novels *Ruins* (Akashic), *Days of Awe* (Ballantine) and *Memory Mambo* (Cleis), the story collection *We Came All the Way From Cuba So You Could Dress Like This?* (Cleis) and the poetry collection *This Is What Happened in Our Other Life* (A Midsummer Night's Press). She also edited and translated the anthology *Havana Noir* (Akashic). As a journalist, she worked at the *Chicago Tribune* for over a decade, and has also written for the *Los Angeles Times*, the *Village Voice*, *Vogue*, *Playboy*, *Ms.*, the *Nation*, the *Advocate*,

Nerve.com, etc. Born in Cuba, she is currently the Sor Juana Visiting Writer at DePaul University.

Elspeth Potter

Elspeth Potter/Victoria Janssen has sold more than thirty short stories and is currently writing erotic novels for Harlequin Spice, including *The Duchess, her Maid, the Groom and their Lover* and *Moonlight Mistress* (December 2009). Her website is *www.victoriajanssen.com*

Carol Queen

Carol Queen is a writer, speaker, educator and activist with a doctorate in sexology. She is the author of such erotic/sexuality classics as *The Leatherdaddy and the Femme, Real Live Nude Girl* and *Exhibitionism for the Shy*. She is also the editor or co-editor of *PoMoSexuals: Challenging Assumptions About Gender and Sexuality, Switch Hitters: Lesbians Write Gay Male Erotica and Gay Men Write Lesbian Erotica, Best Bisexual Erotica 1* and *2, Sex Spoken Here* and *Five Minute Erotica*. With her partner, Robert Morgan Lawrence, she runs the Center for Sex and Culture in San Francisco. See *www.carolqueen.com* for more info about her.

Susan St Aubin

Susan St Aubin has been writing erotica for over twenty years, sometimes as Jean Casse. Her work has been published in *Yellow Silk, Libido, Herotica, Best American Erotica, Best Women's Erotica, Best Lesbian Erotica* and many other journals and anthologies, as well as on-line at *Clean Sheets, Fishnet* and *For The Girls*. Her most recent stories are in *Best Lesbian Erotica 2009* and *Peepshow* (Rachel Kramer Brussel, ed.), published by Cleis Press in November 2009.

Lisabet Sarai

Lisabet Sarai has published five erotic novels and two short story collections and has contributed to dozens of anthologies. She also reviews erotica for Erotica Readers and Writers Association and Erotica Revealed. Visit Lisabet online at

Lisabet's Fantasy Factory (*www.lisabetsarai.com*) and Oh Get a Grip! (*http://ohgetagrip.blogspot.com*).

Lacey Savage

Lacey Savage spends her days writing corporate press releases, and her nights breathing life into her steamy fantasies. Can you guess which of the two she prefers? Lacey's work has been widely published, both in print and in electronic format. These days, it's a wonder Lacey manages to write at all, considering her fanatical addiction to World of Warcraft. She lives in Canada, where she heats up the frigid nights with her husband of ten years.

Lawrence Schimel

Lawrence Schimel writes in both Spanish and English, and has published over ninety books as author or anthologist, including: *The Mammoth Book of Gay Erotica* (Constable & Robinson/Carroll & Graf); *The Mammoth Book of New Gay Erotica* (Constable & Robinson/Carroll & Graf); *I Like it Like That: True Tales of Gay Desire* (Arsenal Pulp); *The Future is Queer* (Arsenal Pulp); *Two Boys in Love* (Seventh Window); *Switch Hitters: Lesbians Write Gay Male Erotica and Gay Men Write Lesbian Erotica* (Cleis); and *Fairy Tales for Writers* (A Midsummer Night's Press), among others. He has twice won the Lambda Literary Award, for *First Person Queer* (Arsenal Pulp) and *PoMoSexuals: Challenging Assumptions About Gender and Sexuality* (Cleis). He lives in Madrid, Spain, where, in addition to his own writing, he works as a Spanish–English translator.

Cecilia Tan

Cecilia Tan started Circlet Press, devoted to erotic science fiction, in 1992, with the publication of her own *Telepaths Don't Need Safewords*. Since then she has published *The Hot Streak* (Ravenous Romance, 2009), *Black Feathers* (HarperCollins, 1998), *The Velderet* (Circlet, 2001), *Edge Plays* (EAA E-book, 2006) and *White Flames* (Running Press, 2008), as well as the

Magic University series from Ravenous Romance. She has also edited numerous erotica anthologies including *Sex in the System* (Thunder's Mouth Press, 2006), *The MILF Anthology* (Blue Moon Books, 2005), *Cowboy Lover* (Thunder's Mouth Press, 2007), and many, many others, including over forty anthologies for Circlet Press. Her stories, essays and articles have appeared in dozens of magazines and anthologies including *Best American Erotica*, *Best Lesbian Erotica*, *Best Women's Erotica*, *Playboy Online*, *The Mammoth Book of New Erotica*, *On a Bed of Rice*, *Dark Angels*, *Penthouse*, *Ms.*, *Asimov's*, Nerve.com, Gothic.net, *Fenway Fiction*, *Periphery*, and many more. Find out more at www.ceciliatan.com

Saskia Walker
Saskia Walker is an award-winning British author of sensual and erotic fiction. Her short stories have been published in over fifty anthologies and her novel-length fiction spans contemporary erotic romance to exotic fantasy. Saskia lives in the north of England on the windswept Yorkshire moors, where she happily spends her days spinning yarns. *www. saskiawalker.com*

Kendra Wayne
Kendra Wayne is the pseudonym for a mysterious writer who, obviously, enjoys perverting fairy tales to her own devious ends. This is her first publication under this name, and if you can figure out who she really is, you just might win a prize.

Kristina Wright
Kristina Wright (*www.kristinawright.com*) is an award-winning author whose steamy erotica and erotic romance has appeared in over seventy-five anthologies, including the Black Lace anthologies *Seduction*, *Liaisons* and *Sexy Little Numbers*; *Bedding Down: A Collection of Winter Erotica* (Avon Red); and *Dirty Girls: Erotica for Women* (Seal Press). She is also the editor of *Fairy Tale Lust: Erotic Bedtime Stories for Women* (Cleis Press). She holds degrees in English and Humanities and spends a great deal of time writing in coffee shops.